Robert Jordan and
The Wheel of Time®

"His huge, ambitious Wheel of Time series helped redefine the genre."

—George R. R. Martin, internationally bestselling author of *A Game of Thrones*

"Anyone who's writing epic secondary world fantasy knows Robert Jordan isn't just a part of the landscape, he's a monolith within the landscape."

—Patrick Rothfuss, internationally bestselling author of The Kingkiller Chronicle

"*The Eye of the World* was a turning point in my life. I read, I enjoyed. (Then continued on to write my larger fantasy novels.)"

—Robin Hobb, *New York Times* bestselling author of The Farseer Trilogy

"Robert Jordan's work has been a formative influence and an inspiration for a generation of fantasy writers."

—Brent Weeks, *New York Times* bestselling author of *The Way of Shadows*

"Jordan has come to dominate the world Tolkien began to reveal." —*The New York Times*

"One of fantasy's most acclaimed series." —*USA Today*

"Robert Jordan was a giant of fiction whose words helped a whole generation of fantasy writers, including myself, find our true voices. I thanked him then, but I didn't thank him enough."

—Peter V. Brett, internationally bestselling
author of The Demon Cycle

"[Robert Jordan's] impact on the place of fantasy in the culture is colossal. . . . He brought innumerable readers to fantasy. He became the *New York Times* Best Seller List's face of fantasy."

—Guy Gavriel Kay, internationally
bestselling author of *Tigana*

"Jordan's writing is so amazing! The characterization, the attention to detail!"

—Clint McElroy, cocreator of the
#1 podcast *The Adventure Zone*

"The Wheel of Time [is] rapidly becoming the definitive American fantasy saga. It is a fantasy tale seldom equaled and still less often surpassed in English."

—*Chicago Sun-Times*

"Hard to put down for even a moment. A fittingly epic conclusion to a fantasy series that many consider one of the best of all time."

—*San Francisco Book Review* on
A Memory of Light

The Wheel of Time®

By Robert Jordan

New Spring: The Novel
The Eye of the World
The Great Hunt
The Dragon Reborn
The Shadow Rising
The Fires of Heaven
Lord of Chaos
A Crown of Swords
The Path of Daggers
Winter's Heart
Crossroads of Twilight
Knife of Dreams

By Robert Jordan and Brandon Sanderson

The Gathering Storm
Towers of Midnight
A Memory of Light

By Robert Jordan and Teresa Patterson

The World of Robert Jordan's The Wheel of Time

By Robert Jordan, Harriet McDougal, Alan Romanczuk, and Maria Simons

The Wheel of Time Companion

WINTER'S HEART

ROBERT JORDAN

A TOM DOHERTY ASSOCIATES BOOK
NEW YORK

This is a work of fiction. All of the characters, organizations, and events portrayed in this novel are either products of the author's imagination or are used fictitiously.

WINTER'S HEART

Copyright © 2000 by Bandersnatch Group, Inc.

Excerpt from *Crossroads of Twilight* copyright © 2003 by Bandersnatch Group, Inc.

The phrase "The Wheel of Time" and the snake-wheel symbol are trademarks of Bandersnatch Group, Inc.

All rights reserved.

Maps by Ellisa Mitchell
Interior art by Matthew C. Nielsen and Ellisa Mitchell

A Tor Book
Published by Tom Doherty Associates
120 Broadway
New York, NY 10271

www.tor-forge.com

Tor® is a registered trademark of Macmillan Publishing Group, LLC.

ISBN 978-1-250-25210-4

Our books may be purchased in bulk for promotional, educational, or business use. Please contact your local bookseller or the Macmillan Corporate and Premium Sales Department at 1-800-221-7945, extension 5442, or by e-mail at MacmillanSpecialMarkets@macmillan.com.

First Edition: November 2000
First Premium Mass Market Edition: March 2020

Printed in the United States of America

0 9 8 7 6 5

Always for Harriet.
Always.

CONTENTS

The seals that hold back night shall weaken,
and in the heart of winter shall winter's heart be born
amid the wailing of lamentations and the gnashing of teeth,
for winter's heart shall ride a black horse,
and the name of it is Death.

—from *The Karaethon Cycle:
The Prophecies of the Dragon*

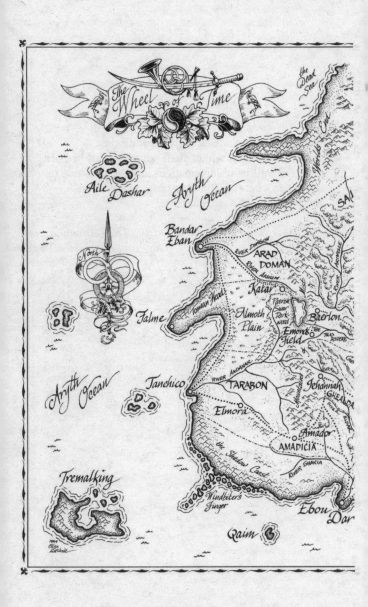

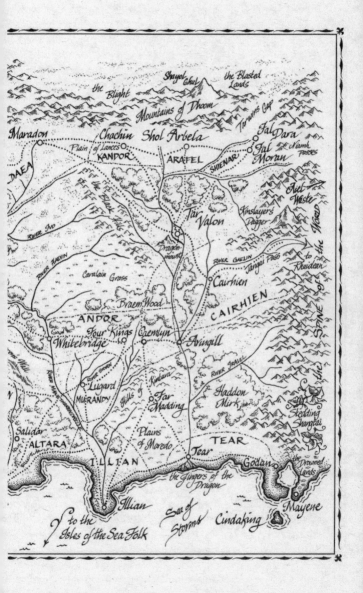

WINTER'S
HEART

PROLOGUE

Snow

Three lanterns cast a flickering light, more than enough to illuminate the small room with its stark white walls and ceiling, but Seaine kept her eyes fixed on the heavy wooden door. Illogical, she knew; foolish in a Sitter for the White. The weave of *saidar* she had pushed around the jamb brought her occasional whispers of distant footsteps in the warren of hallways outside, whispers that faded away almost as soon as heard. A simple thing learned from a friend in her long-ago novice days, but she would have warning long before anyone came near. Few people came down as deep as the second basement, anyway.

Her weave picked up the far-off chittering of rats. Light! How long since there had been rats in Tar Valon, in the Tower itself? Were any of them spies for the Dark One? She wet her lips uneasily. Logic counted for nothing in this. True. If illogical. She wanted to laugh. With an effort she crept back from the brink of hysteria. Think of something besides rats. Something besides . . . A muffled squeal rose in the room behind her, faltered into muted whimpering. She tried to stop up her ears. Concentrate!

In a way, she and her companions had been led to this room because the heads of the Ajahs seemed to be meeting in secret. She herself had glimpsed Ferane Neheran whispering in a secluded nook of the library with Jesse Bilal, who stood very high among the Browns if not at the very top. She thought she was on firmer ground concerning Suana Dragand, of the Yellows. She thought so. But why had Ferane gone walking with Suana in a secluded part of the Tower grounds, both swathed in plain cloaks? Sitters of different Ajahs still talked to one another openly, if coldly. The others had seen similar things; they would not give names from their own Ajahs, of course, but two had mentioned Ferane. A troubling puzzle. The Tower was a seething swamp these days, every Ajah at every other Ajah's throat, yet the heads met in corners. No one outside an Ajah knew for certain who within it led, but apparently the leaders knew each other. What *could* they be up to? What? It was unfortunate that she could not simply ask Ferane, but even had Ferane been tolerant of anyone's questions, she did not dare. Not now.

Concentrate as she would, Seaine could not keep her mind on the question. She knew she was staring at the door and worrying at puzzles she could not solve just to avoid looking over her shoulder. Toward the source of those stifled whimpers and snuffling groans.

As if thinking of the sounds compelled her, she looked back slowly to her companions, her breath growing more uneven as her head moved by inches. Snow was falling heavily on Tar Valon, far overhead, but the room seemed unaccountably hot. She made herself *see*!

Brown-fringed shawl looped on her elbows, Saerin stood with her feet planted apart, fingering the hilt of the curved Altaran dagger thrust behind her belt. Cold anger darkened her olive complexion enough to make the scar along her jaw stand out in a pale line. Pevara appeared calmer, at first glance, yet one hand gripped her red-embroidered skirts tightly and the other held the smooth white cylinder of the Oath Rod like a foot-long club she was ready to use. She might be ready; Pevara was far tougher than her plump exterior suggested, and determined enough to make Saerin seem a shirker.

On the other side of the Chair of Remorse, tiny Yukiri had her arms wrapped tightly around herself; the long silvery-gray fringe on her shawl trembled with her shivers. Licking her lips, Yukiri cast a worried glance at the woman standing beside her. Doesine, looking more like a pretty boy than a Yellow sister of considerable repute, displayed no reaction to what they were doing. She was the one actually manipulating the weaves that stretched into the Chair, and she stared at the *ter'angreal*, focusing so hard on her work that perspiration beaded on her pale forehead. They were all Sitters, including the tall woman writhing on the Chair.

Sweat drenched Talene, matting her golden hair, soaking her linen shift till it clung to her. The rest of her clothes made a jumbled pile in a corner. Her closed eyelids fluttered, and she let out a constant stream of strangled moans and mewling, half-uttered pleas. Seaine felt ill, but could not drag her eyes away. Talene was a friend. Had been a friend.

Despite its name, the *ter'angreal* looked nothing like a chair, just a large rectangular block of marbled gray. No one knew what it was made of, but the material was hard as steel everywhere except the slanted top. The statuesque Green sank a little into that, and somehow it molded itself to her no matter how she twisted. Doesine's weavings flowed into the only break anywhere on the Chair, a palm-sized rectangular hole in one side with tiny notches spaced unevenly around it. Criminals caught in Tar Valon were brought down here to experience the Chair of Remorse, to experience carefully selected consequences of their crimes. On release, they invariably fled the island. There was very little crime in Tar Valon. Queasily, Seaine wondered whether this was anything like the use the Chair had been put to in the Age of Legends.

"What is she . . . seeing?" Her question came out a whisper in spite of herself. Talene would be more than seeing; to her, it all would seem real. Thank the Light she had no Warder, almost unheard of for a Green. She had claimed a Sitter had no need for one. Different reasons came to mind, now.

"She is bloody being flogged by bloody Trollocs," Doesine said hoarsely. Touches of her native Cairhien had appeared in her voice, something that seldom happened except under stress. "When they are done. . . . She can see the Trollocs' cook kettle boiling over a fire, and a Myrddraal watching her. She must know it will be one or the other next. Burn me, if she doesn't break this time. . . ." Doesine brushed perspiration from her forehead irritably and drew a ragged breath. "Stop joggling my elbow. It has been a long while since I did this."

"Three times under," Yukiri muttered. "The toughest

strongarm is broken by his own guilt, if nothing else, after two! What if she's innocent? Light, this is like stealing sheep with the shepherd watching!" Even shaking, she managed to appear regal, but she always sounded like what she had been, a village woman. She glared around at the rest of them in a sickly fashion. "The law forbids using the Chair on initiates. We'll all be unchaired! And if being thrown out of the Hall isn't enough, we'll probably be exiled. And birched before we go, just to drop salt in our tea! Burn me, if we're wrong, we could all be stilled!"

Seaine shuddered. They would escape that last, if their suspicions proved right. No, not suspicions; certainties. They had to be right! But even if they were, Yukiri was correct about the rest. Tower law seldom allowed for necessity, or any supposed higher good. If they were right, though, the price was worth paying. Please, the Light send they were right!

"Are you blind and deaf?" Pevara snapped, shaking the Oath Rod at Yukiri. "She refused to reswear the Oath against speaking an untrue word, and it had to be more than stupid Green Ajah pride after we'd all done as much already. When I shielded her, she tried to *stab* me! Does *that* shout innocence? Does it? For all she knew, we just meant to talk at her until our tongues dried up! What reason would she have to expect more?"

"Thank you both," Saerin put in dryly, "for stating the obvious. It's too late to go back, Yukiri, so we might as well go forward. And if I were you, Pevara, I wouldn't be shouting at one of the four women in the whole Tower I knew I could trust."

Yukiri flushed and shifted her shawl, and Pevara looked a trifle abashed. A trifle. They might all be Sitters, but Saerin had most definitely taken charge. Seaine was unsure how she felt about that. A few hours ago, she and Pevara had been two old friends alone on a dangerous quest, equals reaching decisions together; now they had allies. She should be grateful for more companions. They were not in the Hall, though, and they could not claim Sitters' rights on this. Tower hierarchies had taken over, all the subtle and not-so-subtle distinctions as to who stood where with respect to whom. In truth, Saerin had been both novice and Accepted twice as long as most of them, but forty years as a Sitter, longer than anyone else in the Hall, counted for a great deal. Seaine would be lucky if Saerin asked her opinion, much less her advice, before deciding anything at all. Foolish, yet the knowledge pricked like a thorn in her foot.

"The Trollocs are dragging her toward the kettle," Doesine said suddenly, her voice grating. A thin keening escaped through Talene's clenched teeth; she shook so hard she seemed to vibrate. "I—I do not know if I can . . . can flaming make myself . . ."

"Bring her awake," Saerin commanded without so much as glancing at anyone else to see what they thought. "Stop sulking, Yukiri, and be ready."

The Gray gave her a proud, furious stare, but when Doesine let her weaves fade and Talene's blue eyes fluttered open, the glow of *saidar* surrounded Yukiri and she shielded the woman lying on the Chair without uttering a word. Saerin was in charge, and everyone knew it, and that was that. A very sharp thorn.

A shield hardly seemed necessary. Her face a mask of terror, Talene trembled and panted as though she had run ten miles at top speed. She still sank into the soft surface, but without Doesine channeling, it no longer formed itself to her. Talene stared at the ceiling with bulging eyes, then squeezed them shut, but they popped right open again. Whatever memories lay behind her eyelids were nothing she wanted to face.

Covering the two strides to the Chair, Pevara thrust the Oath Rod at the distraught woman. "Forswear all oaths that bind you and retake the Three Oaths, Talene," she said harshly. Talene recoiled from the Rod as from a poisonous serpent, then jerked the other way as Saerin bent over her.

"Next time, Talene, it's the cookpot for you. Or the Myrddraal's tender attentions." Saerin's face was implacable, but her tone made it seem soft by comparison. "No waking up before. And if that doesn't do, there'll be another time, and another, as many as it takes if we must stay down here until summer." Doesine opened her mouth in protest before giving over with a grimace. Only she among them knew how to operate the Chair, but in this group, she stood as low as Seaine.

Talene continued to stare up at Saerin. Tears filled her big eyes, and she began to weep, great shuddering, hopeless

sobs. Blindly, she reached out, groping until Pevara stuck
the Oath Rod into her hand. Embracing the Source, Pevara
channeled a thread of Spirit into the Rod. Talene gripped
the wrist-thick rod so hard that her knuckles turned white,
yet she just lay there sobbing.

Saerin straightened. "I fear it's time to put her back to
sleep, Doesine."

Talene's tears redoubled, but she mumbled through them.
"I—forswear—all oaths—that bind me." With the last word,
she began to howl.

Seaine jumped, then swallowed hard. She personally
knew the pain of removing a single oath and had speculated
on the agony of removing more than one at once, but now
the reality was in front of her. Talene screamed till there
was no breath left in her, then pulled in air only to scream
again, until Seaine half expected people to come running
down from the Tower itself. The tall Green convulsed,
flinging her arms and legs about, then suddenly arched up
till only her heels and head touched the gray surface, every
muscle clenched, her whole body spasming wildly.

As abruptly as the seizure had begun, Talene collapsed
bonelessly and lay there weeping like a lost child. The
Oath Rod rolled from her limp hand down the sloping gray
surface. Yukiri murmured something with the sound of a
fervent prayer. Doesine kept whispering, "Light!" over and
over in a shaken voice. "Light! Light!"

Pevara scooped up the Rod and closed Talene's fingers
around it again. There was no mercy in Seaine's friend, not
in this matter. "Now swear the Three Oaths," she spat.

For an instant, it seemed Talene might refuse, but slowly
she repeated the oaths that made them all Aes Sedai and
held them together. To speak no word that was not true.
Never to make a weapon for one man to kill another. Never
to use the One Power as a weapon except against Darkfriends or Shadowspawn, or in defense of her life, or that
of her Warder or of another sister. At the end, she began
weeping in silence, shaking without a sound. Perhaps it was
the oaths tightening down on her. They were uncomfortable
when fresh. Perhaps.

Then Pevara told the other oath they required of her.
Talene flinched, but muttered the words in tones of hope-
lessness. "I vow to obey all five of you absolutely." Other-

wise, she only stared straight ahead dully, tears trailing down her cheeks.

"Answer me truthfully," Saerin told her. "Are you of the Black Ajah?"

"I am." The words creaked, as if Talene's throat were rusty.

The simple words froze Seaine in a way she had never expected. She had set out to hunt the Black Ajah, after all, and believed in her quarry as many sisters did not. She had laid hands on another sister, on a Sitter, had helped bundle Talene along deserted basement hallways wrapped in flows of Air, broken a dozen Tower laws, committed serious crimes, all to hear an answer she had been nearly certain of before the question was asked. Now she had heard. The Black Ajah really did exist. She was staring at a Black sister, a Darkfriend who wore the shawl. And believing turned out to be a pale shadow of confronting. Only her jaw clenched near to cramping kept her teeth from chattering. She struggled to compose herself, to think rationally. But nightmares were awake and walking the Tower.

Someone exhaled heavily, and Seaine realized she was not the only one who found her world turned upside down. Yukiri gave herself a shake, then fixed her eyes on Talene as though determined to hold the shield on her by willpower if need be. Doesine was licking her lips, and smoothing her dark golden skirts uncertainly. Only Saerin and Pevara appeared at ease.

"So," Saerin said softly. Perhaps "faintly" was a better word. "So. Black Ajah." She drew a deep breath, and her tone became brisk. "There's no more need for that, Yukiri. Talene, you won't try to escape, or resist in any way. You won't so much as touch the Source without permission from one of us. Though I suppose someone else will take this forward once we hand you over. Yukiri?" The shield on Talene dissipated, but the glow remained around Yukiri, as if she did not trust the effect of the Rod on a Black sister.

Pevara frowned. "Before we give her to Elaida, Saerin, I want to dig out as much as we can. Names, places, anything. Everything she knows!" Darkfriends had killed Pevara's entire family, and Seaine was sure she would go into exile ready to hunt down every last Black sister personally.

Still huddled on the Chair, Talene made a sound half

bitter laugh, half weeping. "When you do that, we are all dead. Dead! Elaida is Black Ajah!"

"That's impossible!" Seaine burst out. "Elaida gave me the order herself."

"She must be," Doesine half whispered. "Talene's sworn the oaths again; she just named her!" Yukiri nodded vehemently.

"Use your heads," Pevara growled, shaking her own in disgust. "You know as well as I do if you believe a lie, you can say it for truth."

"And that *is* truth," Saerin said firmly. "What proof do you have, Talene? Have you seen Elaida at your . . . meetings?" She gripped her knife hilt so hard that her knuckles paled. Saerin had had to fight harder than most for the shawl, for the right to remain in the Tower at all. To her, the Tower was more than home, more important than her own life. If Talene gave the wrong answer, Elaida might not live to face trial.

"They don't have meetings," Talene muttered sullenly. "Except the Supreme Council, I suppose. But she must be. They know every report she receives, even the secret ones, every word spoken to her. They know every decision she makes before it's announced. Days before; sometimes weeks. How else, unless she tells them?" Sitting up with an effort, she tried to fix them each in turn with an intent stare. It only made her eyes seem to dart anxiously. "We have to run; we have to find a place to hide. I'll help you—tell you everything I know!—but they'll kill us unless we run."

Strange, Seaine thought, how quickly Talene had made her former cronies "they" and tried to identify herself with the rest of them. No. She was avoiding the real problem, and avoidance was witless. *Had* Elaida really set her to dig out the Black Ajah? She had never once actually mentioned the name. Could she have meant something else? Elaida had always jumped down the throat of anyone who even mentioned the Black. Nearly any sister would do the same, yet . . .

"Elaida's proven herself a fool," Saerin said, "and more than once I've regretted standing for her, but I'll not believe she's Black, not without more than that." Tight-lipped, Pevara jerked an agreeing nod. As a Red, she would want much more.

"That's as may be, Saerin," Yukiri said, "but we cannot hold Talene long before the Greens start asking where she is. Not to mention the . . . the Black. We'd better decide what to do fast, or we'll still be digging at the bottom of the well when the rains hit." Talene gave Saerin a feeble smile that was probably meant to be ingratiating. It faded under the Brown Sitter's frown.

"We don't dare tell Elaida anything until we can cripple the Black at one blow," Saerin said finally. "Don't argue, Pevara; it's sense." Pevara threw up her hands and put on a stubborn expression, but she closed her mouth. "If Talene is right," Saerin went on, "the Black knows about Seaine or soon will, so we must ensure her safety, as much as we can. That won't be easy, with only the five of us. We can't trust *anyone* until we are certain of them! At least we have Talene, and who knows what we'll learn before she's wrung out?" Talene attempted to look willing to be wrung out, but no one was paying her any mind. Seaine's throat had gone dry.

"We might not be entirely alone," Pevara said reluctantly. "Seaine, tell them your little scheme with Zerah and her friends."

"Scheme?" Saerin said. "Who's Zerah? Seaine? Seaine!"

Seaine gave a start. "What? Oh. Pevara and I uncovered a small nest of rebels here in the Tower," she began breathily. "Ten sisters sent to spread dissent." Saerin was going to make sure she was safe, was she? Without so much as asking. She was a Sitter herself; she had been Aes Sedai for almost a hundred and fifty years. What right had Saerin or anyone to . . . ? "Pevara and I have begun putting an end to that. We've already made one of them, Zerah Dacan, take the same extra oath Talene did, and told her to bring Bernaile Gelbarn to my rooms this afternoon without rousing her suspicions." Light, any sister outside this room might be Black. Any sister. "Then we will use those two to bring another, until they have all been made to swear obedience. Of course, we'll ask the same question we put to Zerah, the same we put to Talene." The Black Ajah might already have her name, already know she had been set hunting them. How could Saerin keep her safe? "Those who give the wrong answer can be questioned, and those who give the right can repay for a little of their treachery by hunting the Black under our direction." Light, how?

When she was done, the others discussed the matter at some length, which could only mean that Saerin was unsure what decision she would make. Yukiri insisted on giving Zerah and her confederates over to the law immediately—if it could be done without exposing their own situation with Talene. Pevara argued for using the rebels, though half-heartedly; the dissent they had been spreading centered around vile tales concerning the Red Ajah and false Dragons. Doesine seemed to be suggesting that they kidnap every sister in the Tower and force them all to take the added oath, but the other three paid little attention to her.

Seaine took no part in the discussion. Her reaction to their predicament was the only possible one, she thought. Tottering to the nearest corner, she vomited noisily.

Elayne tried not to grind her teeth. Outside, another blizzard pelted Caemlyn, darkening the midday sky enough that the lamps along the sitting room's paneled walls were all lit. Fierce gusts rattled the casements set into the tall arched windows. Flashes of lightning lit the clear glass panes, and thunder boomed hollowly overhead. Thunder snow, the worst kind of winter storm, the most violent. The room was not precisely cold, but . . . Spreading her fingers in front of the logs crackling in the broad marble fireplace, she could still feel a chill rising through the carpets layered over the floor tiles, and through her thickest velvet slippers, too. The wide black fox collar and cuffs on her red-and-white gown were pretty, but she was not sure they added any more to its warmth than the pearls on the sleeves. Refusing to let the cold touch her did not mean she was unaware.

Where *was* Nynaeve? And Vandene? Her thoughts snarled like the weather. *They should be here already! Light! I wish I could learn to go without sleep, and they take their sweet time!* No, that was unfair. Her formal claim for the Lion Throne was only a few days old, and for her, everything else had to take second place for the time being. Nynaeve and Vandene had other priorities; other responsibilities, as they saw them. Nynaeve was up to her neck planning with Reanne and the rest of the Knitting Circle how to spirit Kinswomen out of Seanchan-controlled lands before they were discovered and collared. The Kin were very good at staying low, but the Seanchan would not just pass them by for wilders the way Aes Sedai always had. Supposedly, Vandene was still shaken by her sister's murder, barely eating and hardly able to give advice of any sort. The barely eating part was true, but finding the killer consumed her. Supposedly walking the halls in grief at odd hours, she was secretly hunting the Darkfriend among them. Three days earlier, just the thought of that could make Elayne shiver; now, it was one danger among many. More intimate than most, true, but only most.

They were doing important tasks, approved and encouraged by Egwene, but she still wished they would hurry, selfish though it might be. Vandene had a wealth of good advice, the advantage of long experience and study, and Nynaeve's years dealing with the Village Council and the Women's Circle back in Emond's Field gave her a keen eye for practical politics, however much she denied it. *Burn me, I have a hundred problems, some right here in the Palace, and I need them!* If she had *her* way, Nynaeve al'Meara was going to be the Aes Sedai advisor to the next Queen of Andor. She needed all the help she could find—help she could trust.

Smoothing her face, she turned away from the blazing hearth. Thirteen tall armchairs, carved simply but with a fine hand, made a horseshoe arc in front of the fireplace. Paradoxically, the place of honor, where the Queen would sit if receiving here, stood farthest from the fire's heat. Such as it was. Her back began to warm immediately, and her front to cool. Outside, snow fell, thunder crashed and lightning flared. Inside her head, too. Calm. A ruler had as much need of calm as any Aes Sedai.

"It must be the mercenaries," she said, not quite managing to keep regret out of her voice. Armsmen from her estates surely would begin arriving inside a month—once they learned she was alive—but it might be spring before any significant numbers came, and the men Birgitte was recruiting would require half a year or more before they were fit to ride and handle a sword at the same time. "And Hunters for the Horn, if any will sign and swear." There were plenty of both trapped in Caemlyn by the weather. Too many of both, most people said, carousing, brawling, troubling women who wanted no part of their attentions. At least she would be putting them to good use, to stop trouble instead of beginning it. She wished she did not think she was still trying to convince herself of that. "Expensive, but the coffers will cover it." For a little while, they would. She had better start receiving revenues from her estates soon.

Wonder of wonders, the two women standing before her reacted in much the same fashion.

Dyelin gave an irritated grunt. A large, round silver pin worked with Taravin's Owl and Oak was fastened at the high neck of her dark green dress, her only jewelry. A show of pride in her House, perhaps too much pride; the High Seat of House Taravin was a proud woman altogether. Gray streaked her golden hair and fine lines webbed the corners of her eyes, yet her face was strong, her gaze level and sharp. Her mind was a razor. Or maybe a sword. A plainspoken woman, or so it seemed, who did not hide her opinions.

"Mercenaries know the work," she said dismissively, "but they are hard to control, Elayne. When you need a feather touch, they're liable to be a hammer, and when you need a hammer, they're liable to be elsewhere, and stealing to boot. They are loyal to gold, and only as long as the gold lasts. If they don't betray for more gold first. I'm sure this once Lady Birgitte will agree with me."

Arms folded tightly beneath her breasts and heeled boots planted wide, Birgitte grimaced, as always when anyone used her new title. Elayne had granted her an estate as soon as they reached Caemlyn, where it could be registered. In private, Birgitte grumbled incessantly over that, *and* the other change in her life. Her sky-blue trousers were cut the same as those she usually wore, billowing and gathered at the ankles, but her short red coat had a high white collar, and wide white cuffs banded with gold. She was the Lady Birgitte Trahelion *and* the Captain-General of the Queen's Guard, and she could mutter and whine all she wanted, so long as she kept it private.

"I do," she growled unwillingly, and gave Dyelin a not-quite-sidelong glare. The Warder bond carried what Elayne had been sensing all morning. Frustration, irritation, determination. Some of that might have been a reflection of herself, though. They mirrored each other in surprising ways since the bonding, emotionally and otherwise. Why, her courses had shifted by more than a week to match the other woman's!

Birgitte's reluctance to take the second-best argument was clearly almost as great as her reluctance to agree. "Hunters aren't much bloody better, Elayne," she muttered. "They took the Hunter's Oath to find adventure, and a place in the histories if they can. Not to settle down keeping the law. Half are supercilious prigs, looking down their flaming noses at everyone else; the rest don't just take necessary chances, they look for chances to take. And one whisper of a rumor of the Horn of Valere, and you'll be lucky if only two in three vanish overnight."

Dyelin smiled a thin smile, as though she had won a point. Oil and water were not in it compared to those two; each managed well enough with nearly anyone else, but for some reason they could argue over the color of charcoal. Could and would. "Besides, Hunters and mercenaries alike, nearly all are foreigners. That will sit poorly with high and low alike. Very poorly. The last thing you want is to start a rebellion." Lightning flared, briefly lighting the casements, and a particularly loud peal of thunder punctuated her words. In a thousand years, seven Queens of Andor had been toppled by open rebellion, and the two who survived probably wished they had not.

Elayne stifled a sigh. One of the small inlaid tables along the walls held a heavy silver ropework tray with cups and a tall pitcher of hot spiced wine. Lukewarm spiced wine, now. She channeled briefly, Fire, and a thin wisp of steam rose from the pitcher. Reheating gave the spices a slight bitterness, but the warmth of the worked-silver cup in her hands was worth it. With an effort she resisted the desire to heat the air in the room with the Power and released the Source; the warmth would not have lasted unless she maintained the weaves, anyway. She had conquered her unwillingness to let go every time she took in *saidar*—well, to some extent—yet of late, the desire to draw more grew every time. Every sister had to face that dangerous desire. A gesture brought the others to pour their own wine.

"You know the situation," she told them. "Only a fool could think it anything but dire, and you're neither of you fools." The Guards were a shell, a handful of acceptable men and a double handful of strongarms and toughs better suited to throwing drunks out of taverns, or being thrown out themselves. And with the Saldaeans gone and the Aiel leaving, crime was blooming like weeds in spring. She would have thought the snow would damp it down, but every day brought robbery, arson and worse. Every day, the situation *grew* worse. "At this rate, we'll see riots in a few weeks. Maybe sooner. If I can't keep order in Caemlyn itself, the people *will* turn against me." If she could not keep order in the capital, she might as well announce to the world that she was unfit to rule. "I don't like it, but it has to be done, so it will be." Both opened their mouths, ready to argue further, but she gave them no chance. She made her voice firm. "It will be done."

Birgitte's waist-long golden braid swung as she shook her head, yet grudging acceptance filtered through the bond. She took a decidedly odd view of their relationship as Aes Sedai and Warder, but she had learned to recognize when Elayne would not be pressed. After a fashion she had learned. There was the estate and title. And commanding the Guards. And a few other small matters.

Dyelin bent her neck a fraction, and perhaps her knees; it might have been a curtsy, yet her face was stone. It was well to remember that many who did not want Elayne Trakand on the Lion Throne wanted Dyelin Taravin instead. The woman had been nothing but helpful, but it was early days yet, and sometimes a niggling voice whispered in the back of Elayne's head. Was Dyelin simply waiting for her to bungle badly before stepping in to "save" Andor? Someone sufficiently prudent, sufficiently devious, might try that route, and might even succeed.

Elayne raised a hand to rub her temple but made it into adjusting her hair. So much suspicion, so little trust. The Game of Houses had infected Andor since she left for Tar Valon. She was grateful for her months among Aes Sedai for more than learning the Power. *Daes Dae'mar* was breath and bread, to most sisters. Grateful for Thom's teaching, too. Without both, she might not have survived her return as long as she had. The Light send Thom was safe, that he and Mat and the others had escaped the Seanchan and were on their way to Caemlyn. Every day since leaving Ebou Dar she prayed for their safety, but that brief prayer was all she had time for, now.

Taking the chair at the center of the arc, the Queen's chair, she tried to look like a queen, back straight, her free hand resting lightly on the carved chair arm. *Looking a queen is not enough,* her mother had told her often, *but a fine mind, a keen grasp of affairs, and a brave heart will go for nothing if people do not* see *you as a queen.* Birgitte was watching her closely, almost suspiciously. Sometimes the bond was decidedly inconvenient! Dyelin raised her winecup to her lips.

Elayne took a deep breath. She had harried this question from every direction she knew, and she could see no other way. "Birgitte, by spring, I want the Guards to be an army equal to anything *ten* Houses can put in the field." Impossible to achieve, likely, but just trying meant keeping the mercenaries who signed now and finding more, signing every man who showed the least inclination. Light, what a foul tangle!

Dyelin choked, her eyes bulging; dark wine sprayed from her mouth. Still spluttering, she plucked a lace-edged handkerchief from her sleeve and dabbed at her chin.

A wave of panic shot down the bond from Birgitte. "Oh, burn me, Elayne, you can't mean . . . ! I'm am archer, not a general! That's all I've ever been, don't you understand yet? I just did what I had to do, what circumstances forced on me! Anyway, I'm not her, anymore; I'm just me, and . . . !" She trailed off, realizing she might have said too much. Not for the first time. Her face went crimson as Dyelin eyed her curiously.

They had put it about that Birgitte was from Kandor, where country women wore something like her clothes, yet Dyelin clearly suspected the lie. And every time Birgitte let her tongue slip, she came closer to letting her secret slip, too. Elayne shot her a look that promised a talking-to, later.

She would not have thought Birgitte's cheeks could get any redder. Mortification drowned everything else in the bond, flooding through until Elayne felt her own face coloring. Quickly she put on a stern expression, hoping her crimson cheeks would pass for something other than an intense desire to squirm in her seat with *Birgitte's* humiliation. That mirroring effect could be *more* than merely inconvenient!

Dyelin wasted only a moment on Birgitte. Tucking her handkerchief back in its place, she carefully set her cup back on the tray, then planted her hands on her hips. Her face was a thunderhead, now. "The Guards have always been the *core* of Andor's army, Elayne, but this. . . . Light's mercy, this is madness! You could turn every hand against you from the River Erinin to the Mountains of Mist!"

Elayne focused on calm. If she was wrong, Andor would become another Cairhien, another blood-soaked land filled with chaos. And she would die, of course, a price not high enough to meet the cost. Not trying was unthinkable and in any case would have the same result for Andor as failure. Cool, composed, steely calm. A queen could not show herself afraid, even when she was. Especially when she was. Her mother had always said to explain decisions as seldom as possible; the more often you explained, the more explanations were necessary, until they were all you had time for. Gareth Bryne said to explain if you could; your people did better if they knew the why as well as the what. Today, she would follow Gareth Bryne. A good many victories had been won by following him.

"I have three declared challengers." And maybe one not declared. She made herself meet Dyelin's gaze. Not angrily; just eyes meeting eyes. Or maybe Dyelin did take it for anger, with her jaw tight and her face flushed. If so, so be it. "By herself, Arymilla is negligible, but Nasin has joined House Caeren to her, and whether or not he's sane, his support means she must be considered. Naean and Elenia are imprisoned; their armsmen are not. Naean's people may dither and argue until they find a leader, but Jarid is High Seat of Sarand, and he will take chances to feed his wife's ambition. House Baryn and House Anshar flirt with both; the *best* I can hope is that one goes with Sarand and one with Arawn. Nineteen Houses in Andor are strong enough that smaller Houses will follow where they lead. Six are arrayed against me, and I have two." Six so far, and the Light send she had two! She would not mention the three great Houses that had all but declared for Dyelin; at least Egwene had them tied down in Murandy for now.

She motioned to a chair near her, and Dyelin sat, carefully arranging her skirts. The storm clouds had left the older woman's face. She studied Elayne, giving no hint as to her questions or conclusions. "I know all that as well as you, Elayne, but Luan and Ellorien will bring their Houses to you, and Abelle will as well, I'm sure." A careful voice, too, but it gathered heat as she went on. "Other Houses will see reason, then. As long as you don't frighten them *out* of reason. Light, Elayne, this is not a Succession. Trakand succeeds Trakand, not another House. Even a Succession has seldom come to open fighting! Make the Guards into an army, and you risk everything."

Elayne threw her head back, but her laughter held no amusement. It fit right in with the peals of thunder. "I risked everything the day I came home, Dyelin. You say Norwelyn and Traemane will come to me, and Pendar? Fine; then I have five to face six. I don't think the other Houses will 'see reason,' as you put it. If any of them move before it's clear as good glass the Rose Crown is mine, it will be against me, not for." With luck, those lords and ladies would shy away from associating with cronies of Gaebril, but she did not like depending on luck. She was not Mat Cauthon. Light, most people were sure Rand had killed her mother, and few believed that "Lord Gaebril" had been one of the Forsaken. Mending the damage Rahvin had done in Andor might take her entire lifetime even if she managed to live as long as the Kinswomen! Some Houses would stand aside from supporting her because of the outrages Gaebril had perpetrated in Morgase's name, and others because Rand had said he intended to "give" her the throne. She loved the man to her toes, but *burn* him for giving voice to *that*! Even if it was what reined in Dyelin. The meanest crofter in Andor would shoulder his scythe to pull a puppet from the Lion Throne!

"I want to avoid Andoran killing Andoran if I can, Dyelin, but Succession or no Succession, Jarid is ready to fight, even with Elenia locked away. Naean is ready to fight." Best to bring both women to Caemlyn as soon as possible; too much chance of them slipping messages, and orders, out of Aringill. "*Arymilla* is ready, with Nasin's men behind her. To them, this *is* a Succession, and the only way to *stop* them from fighting is to be so strong they don't dare. If Birgitte can build the Guards into an army by spring, well and good, because if I don't have an army before then, I *will* have need of one. And if that isn't enough, remember the Seanchan. They won't be satisfied with Tanchico and Ebou Dar; they want everything. I won't let them have Andor, Dyelin, any more than I'll let Arymilla." Thunder roared overhead.

Twisting a little to look back at Birgitte, Dyelin moistened her lips. Her fingers plucked unconsciously at her skirts. Very little frightened her, but tales of the Seanchan had. What she murmured, though, as if to herself, was, "I had hoped to avoid outright civil war." And *that* might mean nothing, or a great deal! Perhaps a little probing might show which.

"Gawyn," Birgitte said suddenly. Her expression had lightened, and so had the emotions flowing though the bond. Relief stood out strong. "When he comes, he'll take command. He'll be your First Prince of the Sword."

"Mother's milk in a cup!" Elayne snapped, and lightning flared in the windows for emphasis. Why did the woman have to change the subject *now*? Dyelin gave a start, and heat flooded back into Elayne's face. By the older woman's gaping mouth, she knew exactly how coarse that curse was. Strangely embarrassing, that; it should not have counted for anything that Dyelin had been her mother's friend. Unthinking, she took a deep swallow of wine—and nearly gagged at the bitterness. Quickly she suppressed images of Lini threatening to wash out her mouth and reminded herself that she was a grown woman with a throne to win. She doubted her mother had ever found herself feeling foolish so often.

"Yes, he will, Birgitte," she went on, more calmly. "When he comes." Three couriers were on their way to Tar Valon. Even if none managed to get past Elaida, Gawyn would learn eventually that she had made her claim, and he would come. She needed him desperately. She had no illusions of herself as a general, and Birgitte was so fearful she could not live up to the legends about her that sometimes she seemed afraid to try. Face an army, yes; lead an army, never under the sun!

Birgitte was well aware of the tangle in her own mind. Right that moment her face was frozen, but her emotions were full of self-anger and embarrassment, with the first growing stronger by the moment. With a stab of irritation, Elayne opened her mouth to pursue Dyelin's mention of civil war before she began reflecting Birgitte's anger.

Before she could utter a word, though, the tall red doors opened. Her hopes for Nynaeve or Vandene were dashed by the entrance of two Sea Folk women, barefoot despite the weather.

A cloud of musky perfume wafted ahead of them, and by themselves they made up a procession in bright brocaded silk trousers and blouses, jeweled daggers and necklaces of gold and ivory. And other jewelry. Straight black hair with white at the temples nearly hid the ten small, fat golden rings in Renaile din Calon's ears, but the arrogance in her dark eyes was as plain as the medallion-laden golden chain that connected one earring to her nose ring. Her face was set, and despite a graceful sway to her walk, she appeared ready to stride through a wall. Nearly a hand shorter than her companion and darker than charcoal, Zaida din Parede wore half again as many golden medallions dangling on her left cheek and carried an air of command rather than arrogance, a sure certainty that she would be obeyed. Gray flecked her cap of tight black curls, yet she was stunning, one of those women who grew more and more beautiful as they aged.

Dyelin flinched at sight of them, and half raised a hand to her nose before she could stop herself. A common enough reaction in people unused to the Atha'an Miere. Elayne grimaced, and not for their nose rings. She even considered another curse, something still more . . . pungent. Excepting the Forsaken, she could not have named two people she wanted less to see right then. Reene was supposed to see this did not happen!

"Forgive me," she said, rising smoothly, "but I am very busy, now. Matters of state, you understand, or I would greet you as your stations deserve." The Sea Folk were sticklers for ceremony and propriety, at least on their own terms. Very likely they had gotten past the First Maid by simply not telling her they wanted to see Elayne, but they easily might take offense if she greeted them sitting before the crown was hers. And, the Light burn both of them, she could not afford to offend. Birgitte appeared at her side, bowing formally to take her cup; the Warder bond carried wariness. She was always ginger around the Sea Folk; she had let her tongue slip around them, too. "I will see you later in the day," Elayne finished, adding, "the Light willing." They also were great ones for ceremonial turns of phrase, and that one showed courtesy *and* gave a way out.

Renaile did not stop until she stood right in front of Elayne, and much too close. One tattooed hand gestured curt permission for her to sit. Permission! "You have been avoiding me." Her voice was deep for a woman, and as chill as the snow falling on the roof. "Remember that I am Windfinder to Nesta din Reas Two Moons, Mistress of the Ships to the Atha'an Miere. You still must fulfill the rest of the bargain you made for your White Tower." The Sea Folk knew of the division in the Tower—by this time, everyone and her sister knew—but Elayne had not seen fit to add to her difficulties by making public which side she was on. Not yet. Renaile finished on an imperious, commanding note. "You *will* deal with me, and *now*!" So much for ceremony and propriety.

"She has been avoiding me, I think, not you, Windfinder." In contrast to Renaile, Zaida sounded as though she were merely making conversation. Rather than rushing across the carpets, she moved idly about the room, pausing to touch a tall vase of thin green porcelain, then rising on her toes to peer through a four-barreled kaleidoscope atop a tall stand. When she glanced toward Elayne and Renaile, an amused glint twinkled in her black eyes. "After all, the bargain was with Nesta din Reas, speaking for the ships." In addition to Wavemistress of Clan Catelar, Zaida was an ambassador from the Mistress of the Ships. To Rand, not Andor, but her warrant gave the authority to speak and bind for Nesta herself. Changing one gold-chased barrel for another, she went on tiptoe to look through the eyepiece again. "You promised the Atha'an Miere twenty teachers, Elayne. So far, you have delivered one."

Their entrance had been so sudden, so dramatic, that Elayne was surprised to see Merilille turn from closing the doors. Shorter still than Zaida, the Gray sister was elegant in dark blue wool trimmed with silvery fur and sewn with small moonstones across the bodice, yet barely more than two weeks teaching the Windfinders had brought changes. Most were powerful women with a thirst for knowledge, more than ready to squeeze Merilille like a grape in the winepress, demanding the last drop of juice. Once, Elayne had thought her self-possessed beyond the ability to surprise, but now Merilille was constantly wide-eyed, her lips always a little parted, as though she had just been startled half out of her wits and expected to be startled again any moment. Folding her hands at her waist, she waited by the doorway, and appeared relieved to be out of the center of attention.

Harrumphing loudly, Dyelin got to her feet and scowled at Zaida and Renaile both. "Have a care how you speak," she growled. "You are in Andor, now, not on one of your ships, and Elayne Trakand will be Queen of Andor! Your *bargain* will be met in good time. For now, we have more important matters to contend with."

"Under the Light, there are none more important," Renaile rumbled in turn, rounding on her. "You say the bargain will be met? So you stand surety. Know there will be room to dangle you by your ankles in the rigging as well if—"

Zaida snapped her fingers. That was all, but a tremor passed though Renaile. Snatching the golden scent-box dangling from one of her necklaces, she pressed it to her nose and breathed deeply. Windfinder to the Mistress of the Ships she might be, a woman of great authority and power among the Atha'an Miere, but to Zaida, she was . . . a Windfinder. Which grated her pride excessively. Elayne was sure there must be a way to use that to keep them out of her hair, but she had not found it, yet. Oh, yes; for good or ill, *Daes Dae'mar* was in her bones, now.

She glided around a silently furious Renaile as if around a column, a part of the room, though not toward Zaida. If anyone had a right to be casual here, she did. She could not afford to give Zaida a hair of advantage, or the Wavemistress would shave her scalp for the wig-makers. At the fireplace, she spread her hands in front of the flames again.

"Nesta din Reas trusted we would fulfill the bargain, or she never would have agreed to it," she said calmly. "You have regained the Bowl of the Winds, but assembling nineteen more sisters to join you requires time. I know you worry about the ships that were at Ebou Dar when the Seanchan came. Have Renaile make a gateway to Tear. There are hundreds of Atha'an Miere vessels there." Every report said so. "You can learn what they know, and rejoin your people. They will have need of you, against the Seanchan." And she would be rid of them. "The other sisters will be sent to you as soon as can be arranged." Merilille did not move from

the doorway, but her face took on a green tinge of panic at
the possibility of being alone among the Sea Folk.

Zaida gave over looking through the kaleidoscope and
eyed Elayne sideways. A smile quirked her very full lips. "I
must remain here, at least until I speak with Rand al'Thor.
If he ever comes." That smile tightened for an instant before blooming once more; Rand would have a hard time
with her. "And I will keep Renaile and her companions, for
the time. A handful of Windfinders more or less will make
no great difference against these Seanchan, and here, the
Light willing, they may learn what will be useful." Renaile
snorted, just loudly enough to be heard. Zaida frowned
briefly and began fiddling with the eyepiece that stood level
with the top of her head. "There are five Aes Sedai here
in your palace, counting yourself," she murmured thoughtfully. "Perhaps some of you might teach." As though the
idea had just occurred to her. And if that were so, Elayne
could lift both Sea Folk women with one hand!

"Oh, yes, that would be wonderful," Merilille burst out,
taking a step forward. Then she glanced at Renaile and subsided, a blush suffusing her Cairhienin paleness. Folding
her hands at her waist once more, she snatched meekness
around herself like a second skin. Birgitte shook her head
in amazement. Dyelin stared as if she had never seen the
Aes Sedai before.

"Something may be worked out, if the Light pleases,"
Elayne said cautiously. Not rubbing at her temples took effort. She wished she could blame the ache inside her skull
on the incessant thunder. Nynaeve would erupt at the suggestion, and Vandene likely would ignore any such order,
but Careane and Sareitha might be possible. "For no more
than a few hours a day, you understand. When they have
time." She avoided looking at Merilille. Even Careane and
Sareitha might rebel at being tossed into that winepress.

Zaida touched the fingers of her right hand to her lips. "It
is agreed, under the Light."

Elayne blinked. That was ominous; in the Wavemistress's eyes, apparently, they had just made another bargain.
Her limited experience of dealing with the Atha'an Miere
was that you were lucky to walk away with your shift. Well,
this time things were going to be different. For instance,
what were the sisters to gain in it? There had to be two sides

to a bargain. Zaida smiled, as if she knew what Elayne was thinking and was amused. One of the doors opening again was almost a relief, giving her an excuse to turn away from the Sea Folk woman.

Reene Harfor slipped into the room with deference but without servility, and her curtsy was restrained, suitable for the High Seat of a powerful House to her Queen. But then, any High Seat worth a pinch of salt knew enough to offer respect to the First Maid. Her graying hair was arranged in a bun, like a crown atop her head, and she wore a scarlet tabard over her red-and-white dress, with the White Lion of Andor's head resting on her formidable bosom. Reene had no say in who would sit on the throne, but she had adopted full formal dress on the day of Elayne's arrival, as if the Queen already were in residence. Her round face hardened momentarily at the sight of the Atha'an Miere women who had bypassed her, but that was all the notice she gave them. For now. They would learn to their cost what incurring the animosity of the First Maid entailed.

"Mazrim Taim has come at last, my Lady." Reene managed to make that sound very like "my Queen." "Shall I tell him to wait?"

Not beforetime! Elayne muttered in her head. She had summoned the man two days ago! "Yes, Mistress Harfor. Give him wine. The third best, I think. Inform him that I will see him as soon as I—"

Taim strode into the room as though he owned the Palace. She did not need him named. Blue-and-gold Dragons wove round the sleeves of his black coat from elbows to cuffs, in imitation of the Dragons on Rand's arms. Though she suspected he would not appreciate the observation. He was tall, nearly as tall as Rand, with a hooked nose and dark eyes like augers, a physically powerful man who moved with something of a Warder's deadly grace, but shadows seemed to follow him, as if half the lamps in the room had gone out; not real shadows, but an air of imminent violence that seemed palpable enough to soak up light.

Two more black-coated men followed at his heels, a bald fellow with a long grizzled beard and leering blue eyes and a younger man, snake-slim and dark-haired, with the sneering arrogance young men often adopted before they learned better. Both wore the silver Sword and red-enameled Dragon on their tall collars. None of the three carried a sword on his hip, though; they did not need swords. Suddenly the sitting room felt smaller, and crowded.

Instinctively, Elayne embraced *saidar* and reached out to link. Merilille slipped into the circle easily; astoundingly, so did Renaile. A quick glance at the Windfinder lessened her surprise. Her face gray, Renaile was gripping the dagger thrust behind her sash so hard that Elayne could feel the pain in her knuckles through the link. She had been in Caemlyn long enough to be aware of what an Asha'man was.

The men knew someone had embraced *saidar*, of course, even if they could not see the glow surrounding the three women. The bald man stiffened; the slim young man clenched his fists. They stared with angry eyes. Surely they had seized *saidin*. Elayne began to regret giving in to reflex, but she was not going to let go of the Source, not now. Taim radiated danger the way a fire gave heat. She drew deeply through the link, to the point where the overwhelming sense of life became sharp, warning prickles. Even those felt . . . joyous. With that much of the Power in her, she could lay waste to the Palace, but she wondered whether it was enough to match Taim and the other two. She very much wished she had one of the three *angreal* they had found in Ebou Dar, now safely locked away with the rest of the things from the cache until she had time to study them again.

Taim shook his head contemptuously, a half-smile flickering across his lips. "Use your eyes." His voice was quiet, but hard and sneering. "There are two Aes Sedai here. Are you afraid of two Aes Sedai? Besides, you don't want to frighten the future Queen of Andor." His companions relaxed visibly, then began trying to emulate the unthinking dominance of his stance.

Reene knew nothing of *saidar* or *saidin*; she had rounded on the men, scowling, as soon as they entered. Asha'man or no Asha'man, she expected people to behave as they should. She muttered something almost under her breath. Not quite far enough under, though. The words "sneaking rats" were just audible.

The First Maid reddened when she realized everyone in the room had heard, and Elayne got a chance to see Reene

Harfor flustered. Which was to say that the woman drew herself up and said, with a grace and dignity any ruler might envy, "Forgive me, my Lady Elayne, but I've been told there are rats infesting the storerooms. Most unusual this time of year, and so many of them. If you will excuse me, I must make sure my orders for ratcatchers and poison baits are being carried out."

"Stay," Elayne told her coolly. Calmly. "Vermin can be dealt with in due time." Two Aes Sedai. He did not realize Renaile could channel, and he had *emphasized* two. Would just three women give some advantage? Or did it take more? Plainly the Asha'man knew of *some* advantage to women in numbers less than a circle of thirteen. Walk in on her without so much as a by-your-leave, would they? "You can show these goodmen out when I'm done with them." Taim's companions scowled at being called "goodmen," but the man himself merely flashed another of those almost-smiles. He was quick enough to know she had been thinking of him when she spoke of vermin. Light! Maybe Rand had needed this man once, but why would he keep him now, and in a position of such authority? Well, his authority counted for nothing here.

Unhurriedly, she took her chair again, and gave a moment to adjusting her skirts. The men would have to come around in front of her like supplicants, or else talk to the side of her head while she refused to look at them. For an instant she considered passing control of the small circle. The Asha'man would surely focus their attention on her. Renaile was still gray, though, anger and fear tumbling over one another inside her; she might strike out as soon as the link was hers. Merilille had some fear, just under control, mixed with a very great deal of a ... goosey ... feeling that matched her wide eyes and parted lips; the Light alone knew what *she* might do with the link.

Dyelin glided to the side of Elayne's chair, as if to shield her from the Asha'man. Whatever lay inside the High Seat of Taravin, her face was stern, unfrightened. The other women had wasted no time in preparing as best they could. Zaida stood very still beside the kaleidoscope, doing her best to look diminutive and harmless, but her hands were behind her back and the dagger was missing from behind her sash. Birgitte lounged beside the fireplace, left hand propped on the jamb, seemingly at her ease, but the sheath of her belt knife was empty, and from the way her other hand rested by her side, she was ready for an underhand throw. The bond carried . . . focus. Arrow nocked, drawn to cheek, ready to loose.

Elayne made no effort to look around Dyelin at the three men. "First you are too slow obeying my summons, Master Taim, and then too sudden." Light, *was* he holding *saidin*? There were methods of interfering with a man channeling short of shielding him, but it was a difficult skill, chancy, and she knew little more than the theory.

He did come in front of her, several paces off, but he did not look a supplicant. Mazrim Taim knew who he was and his own worth, though he plainly set it higher than the sky. Lightning flashing in the windows sent strange lights across his face. Many would feel overawed by him, even without his fancy coat or his infamous name. She did not. She *would* not!

Taim rubbed his chin thoughtfully. "I understand you've taken down the Dragon banners all over Caemlyn, Mistress Elayne." There was *amusement* in his deep voice, if none in his eyes! Dyelin hissed in fury at the slight to Elayne, but he ignored her. "The Saldaeans have withdrawn to the Legion of the Dragon's camp, I hear, and soon the last of the Aiel will be in camps outside the city, as well. What will he say when he learns?" There was no doubt who he meant. "And after he's sent you a gift, too. From the south. I'll have it delivered later."

"I will ally Andor with the Dragon Reborn in due course," she told him coldly, "but Andor is *not* a conquered province, not for *him* or anyone else." She made her hands stay relaxed on the arms of the chair. Light, talking the Aiel and Saldaeans into leaving had been her biggest achievement yet, and even with the flare-up in crime, it had been necessary! "In any case, Master Taim, it is not your place to call me to task. If Rand objects, I will deal with *him*!" Taim raised an eyebrow, and that odd quirk of his mouth lingered.

Burn me, she thought indignantly, *I shouldn't have used Rand's name!* The man clearly thought he knew *exactly* how she would deal with the anger of the bloody Dragon Reborn! The worst of it was, if she could trip Rand into a bed, she would. Not for this, not to *deal* with him, but because she wanted to. What sort of gift had he sent her?

Anger hardened her voice. Anger at Taim's tone, at Rand for staying away so long. At herself, for blushing and thinking of gifts. Gifts! "You've walled in four *miles* of Andor." Light, that was more than half as large as the Inner City! How many of these fellows could it hold? The thought made her skin crawl. "With whose permission, Master Taim? Don't tell me the Dragon Reborn. He has no right to give permission for *anything* in Andor." Dyelin shifted beside her. No right, but enough strength could make right. Elayne kept her attention on Taim. "You've refused the Queen's Guard entry to your . . . *compound*." Not that they had tried before she came home. "The law in Andor runs over *all* of Andor, Master Taim. Justice *will* be the same for lord or farmer—or Asha'man. I won't claim I can force my way in." He began to smile again, or nearly so. "I wouldn't demean myself. But unless the Queen's Guard is allowed in, I promise you not so much as a potato will go through your gates, either. I know you can Travel. Let your Asha'man spend their days Traveling to buy food." The almost-smile vanished in a faint grimace; his boots shifted slightly.

Annoyance lasted only an instant, though. "Food is a small problem," he said smoothly, spreading his hands. "As you say, my men can Travel. To anywhere I command. I doubt you could stop me buying whatever I want even ten miles from Caemlyn, but it wouldn't bother me if you could. Still, I am willing to allow visits whenever you ask. Controlled visits, with escorts at all times. The training is hard in the Black Tower. Men die almost every day. I would not want any accidents."

He was irritatingly accurate on how far from Caemlyn her writ ran. But no more than irritating. Were his remarks about Traveling anywhere he commanded and "accidents" meant to be veiled threats? Surely not. A wave of fury ran through her as she realized that she was certain he would not threaten her because of Rand. She would *not* hide behind Rand al'Thor. *Controlled* visits? When she *asked*? She ought to burn the man to a cinder where he stood!

Abruptly she became aware of what was coming through the bond from Birgitte, anger, a reflection of hers, joining with Birgitte's, reflecting from Birgitte to her, bouncing from her to Birgitte, feeding on itself, building. Birgitte's knife hand quivered with the desire to throw. And herself? Fury filled her! A whisker more, and she would lose *saidar*. Or lash out with it.

With an effort she forced rage down, into a semblance of calm. A rough, seething semblance. She swallowed, and struggled to keep her voice level. "The Guards will visit every day, Master Taim." And how she was to manage that in this weather, she did not know. "Perhaps I will come myself, with a few other sisters." If the thought of having Aes Sedai inside his Black Tower upset Taim, he did not show it. *Light*, she was trying to establish Andor's authority, not goad the man. Hurriedly she did a novice exercise—the river contained by the bank—seeking calm. It worked, a little. Now she merely wanted to throw all the winecups at him. "I will accede to your request for escorts, but nothing is to be hidden. I won't have crimes concealed by your secrets. Do we understand one another?"

Taim's bow was mocking—mocking!—but there was a tightness in his voice. "I understand you perfectly. Understand me, though. My men are not farmers knuckling their foreheads when you pass. Press an Asha'man too hard, and you may learn just how strong your law is."

Elayne opened her mouth to tell him exactly how strong the law was in Andor.

"It is time, Elayne Trakand," a woman's voice said from the doorway.

"Blood and ashes!" Dyelin muttered. "Is the whole *world* just going to walk in here?"

Elayne recognized the new voice. She had been expecting this summons, without knowing when it would come. Knowing that it must be obeyed, though, on the instant. She stood, wishing she could have a little longer to make matters clear to Taim. He frowned at the woman who had just entered, and at Elayne, clearly uncertain what to make of this. Good. Let him stew until she had time to set him straight on what special rights Asha'man had in Andor.

Nadere stood as tall as either of the two men by the door, a wide woman, as close to stout as any Aiel Elayne had seen. Her green eyes examined the pair for a moment before dismissing them as unimportant. Asha'man did not impress Wise Ones. Very little did. Adjusting her dark shawl on her shoulders in a clatter of bracelets, she walked over in front of Elayne, her back to Taim. Despite the cold, she wore only that shawl over her thin white blouse, though oddly, she carried a heavy wool cloak draped across one arm. "You must come now," she told Elayne, "without delay." Taim's eyebrows seemed to be climbing his forehead; no doubt he was unaccustomed to being so thoroughly ignored.

"Light of heaven!" Dyelin breathed, massaging her forehead. "I don't know what this is about, Nadere, but it will have to wait until—"

Elayne laid a hand on her arm. "You *don't* know, Dyelin, and it *can't* wait. I will send everyone away and come with you, Nadere."

The Wise One shook her head disapprovingly. "A child waiting to be born cannot take time to send people away." She shook out the thick cloak. "I brought this to shield your skin from the cold. Perhaps I should leave it, and tell Aviendha your modesty is greater than your desire for a sister." Dyelin gasped in sudden realization. The Warder bond quivered with Birgitte's outrage.

There was only one choice possible. No choice, really. Letting the link to the other two women dissolve, she released *saidar* herself. The glow remained around Renaile and Merilille, though. "Will you help me with my buttons, Dyelin?" Elayne was proud of how steady her voice was. She had expected this. *Just not with so many* witnesses! she thought faintly. Turning her back on Taim—at least she would not have to see him watching her!—she began with the tiny buttons on her sleeves. "Dyelin, if you please? Dyelin?" After a moment Dyelin moved as if sleepwalking and began fumbling with the buttons down Elayne's back, muttering to herself in shocked tones. One of the Asha'man by the doors snickered.

"About turn!" Taim snapped, and boots stamped by the doors.

Elayne did not know whether he had turned away as well—she was certain she could feel his eyes on her—but suddenly Birgitte was there, and Merilille and Reene, and Zaida, and even Renaile, crowding shoulder-to-shoulder, scowling as they formed a wall between her and the men. Not a very adequate wall. None were as tall as she, and neither Zaida nor Merilille stood higher than her shoulder.

Focus, she told herself. *I am composed. I am tranquil. I am. . . . I'm stripping naked in a room full of people is what I am!* She undressed as hurriedly as she could, letting her dress and shift fall to the floor, tossing her slippers and stockings on top of them. Her skin pebbled in the cool air; ignoring the chill just meant she was not shivering. And she rather thought the heat in her cheeks might have something to do with that.

"Madness!" Dyelin muttered in a low voice, snatching up the clothes. "Utter madness!"

"What is this about?" Birgitte whispered. "Should I come with you?"

"I must go alone," Elayne whispered back. "Don't argue!" Not that Birgitte gave any outward sign of it, but the bond carried volumes. Taking the golden hoops from her ears, she handed them to Birgitte, then hesitated before adding her Great Serpent ring. The Wise Ones had said she must come as a child came to birth. They had had a great many instructions, first among them to tell no one what was coming. For that matter, she wished *she* knew. A child came to birth without foreknowledge of what was to happen. Birgitte's muttering began to sound like Dyelin's.

Nadere came forward with the cloak, but simply held it out; Elayne had to take it and wrap it around herself hastily. She was still sure she could feel Taim's gaze. Holding the heavy wool close, her instinct was to hurry from the room, but instead she drew herself up and turned around slowly. She would not *scurry* out cloaked in shame.

The men who had come with Taim stood rigidly, facing the doors, and Taim himself was peering at the fireplace, arms folded across his chest. The feel of his eyes had been imagination, then. Excepting Nadere, the other women looked at her in variations of curiosity, consternation and shock. Nadere merely seemed impatient.

Elayne tried for her most queenly voice. "Mistress Harfor, you will offer Master Taim and his men wine, before they go." Well, at least it did not tremble. "Dyelin, please entertain the Wavemistress and the Windfinder, and see if you can allay their fears. Birgitte, I expect to hear your plan for recruiting tonight." The women she named blinked in startlement, nodded wordlessly.

Then she walked from the room, followed by Nadere, wishing she could have done better. The last thing she heard before the door closed behind her was Zaida's voice. "Strange customs, you shorebound have."

In the corridor she tried to move a little faster, though it was not easy while keeping the cloak from gaping. The red-and-white floor tiles were *much* colder than the carpets in the sitting room. A few servants, warmly bundled in good woolen livery, stared when they saw her, then hurried on about their tasks. The flames of the stand-lamps flickered; there were always drafts in the hallways. Occasionally the air stirred enough to make a wall hanging ripple lazily.

"That was on purpose, wasn't it?" she said to Nadere, not really asking a question. "Whenever you called me, you'd have made sure there were plenty of people to watch. To make sure adopting Aviendha was important enough to me." It had to be more important than *anything* else, they had been told. "What did you do to *her*?" Aviendha seemed to have very little modesty sometimes, often walking around her apartments unclothed and unconcerned, not even noticing when servants entered. Making *her* undress in a crowd would have proved nothing.

"That is for her to tell you if she wishes," Nadere said complacently. "You are sharp to see it; many do not." Her large bosom heaved in a grunt that might have been a laugh. "Those men, turning their backs, and those women, guarding you. I would have put a stop to it if the man in the embroidered coat had not kept looking over his shoulder to admire your hips. And if your blushes had not said you knew."

Elayne missed a step and stumbled. The cloak flared, losing the little body warmth it had trapped before she could snatch it closed again. "That filthy pig-kisser!" she growled. "I'll . . . ! I'll . . . !" Burn her, what *could* she do? Tell Rand? Let *him* deal with Taim? Never in life!

Nadere eyed her quizzically. "Most men enjoy looking at a woman's bottom. Stop thinking about men, and start thinking about the woman you want for a sister."

Flushing again, Elayne put her mind on Aviendha. It did nothing to settle her nerves. There were specific things she had been told to think on before the ceremony, and some made her uneasy.

Nadere kept her pace to Elayne's, and Elayne took great care not to let her legs flash through the cloak's opening—there were servants everywhere—so it took them some little time to reach the room where the Wise Ones were gathered, more than a dozen of them in their bulky skirts and white blouses and dark shawls, decked with necklaces and bracelets of gold and silver, gems and ivory, their long hair held back with folded scarves. All the furnishings and carpets had been cleared out, leaving bare white floor tiles, and there was no fire on the hearth. Here, deep in the Palace, with no windows, the crash of thunder was barely audible.

Elayne's eyes went straight to Aviendha, standing on the far side of the room. Naked. She smiled at Elayne nervously. Nervously! Aviendha! Hurriedly throwing off the cloak, Elayne smiled back. Nervously, she realized. Aviendha gave a soft laugh, and after a moment, Elayne did, too. Light, the air was *cold*! And the floor was colder!

She did not know most of the Wise Ones in the room, but one face jumped at her. Amys' prematurely white hair combined with features that appeared short of their middle years to give her something of the look of an Aes Sedai. She must have Traveled from Cairhien. Egwene had been teaching the dreamwalkers, to repay their teaching about *Tel'aran'rhiod*. And to meet a debt, she claimed, though she had never made clear what debt.

"I hoped Melaine would be here," Elayne said. She liked Bael's wife, a warm and generous woman. Not like two others in the room she recognized, bony Tamela with her angular face and Viendre, a beautiful, blue-eyed eagle. Both were stronger in the Power than she, stronger than any sister she had met save Nynaeve. That was not supposed to matter among Aiel, but she could think of no other reason why they always sneered and looked down their noses when they saw her.

She expected Amys to take charge—Amys always did, it seemed—but it was a short woman named Monaelle, her hair yellow with hints of red, who stepped forward. Not truly short, yet still the only woman in the room shorter than Elayne. And the weakest in the Power, too, barely strong enough, had she gone to Tar Valon, to have earned the shawl. Perhaps that really did not count with Aiel.

"Were Melaine here," Monaelle said, her tone brisk but not unfriendly, "the babes she carries would be part of the bond between you and Aviendha, if the weaves brushed them. If they survived, that is; the unborn are not strong enough for this. The question is, are the two of you?" She gestured with both hands, pointing to spots on the floor not far from her. "Come here to the middle of the chamber, both of you."

For the first time, Elayne realized that *saidar* was to be part of this. She had thought it would be just a ceremony, pledges exchanged, perhaps oaths given. What *was* going to happen? It did not matter, except . . . Her steps dragged as she moved toward Monaelle. "My Warder. . . . Our bond. . . . Will she be . . . affected . . . by this?" Aviendha, coming to face her, had frowned when Elayne hesitated, but at the question, she swung startled eyes to Monaelle. Clearly, it was something she had not thought of.

The short Wise One shook her head. "No one outside this chamber can be touched by the weaves. She may sense some part of what you share with each other, because of her bond with you, but only a very little." Aviendha heaved a sigh of relief that Elayne echoed.

"Now," Monaelle went on. "There are forms to be followed. Come. We are not clan chiefs discussing water-pledges over *oosquai*." Laughing, making what seemed to be jokes about clan chiefs and the strong Aiel liquor, the other women formed a circle around Aviendha and Elayne. Monaelle settled gracefully to the floor, sitting cross-legged two paces to one side of the bare women. Laughter ceased as her voice became formal. "We are gathered because two women wish to be first-sisters. We will see whether they are strong enough, and if they are, help them. Are their mothers present?"

Elayne gave a start, but the next moment Viendre was behind her. "I stand for Elayne Trakand's mother, who cannot be here." Hands on Elayne's shoulders, Viendre pushed her forward and pressed down until she was kneeling on the cold tiles in front of Aviendha, then knelt behind her. "I offer my daughter to her testing."

Tamela appeared behind Aviendha, pressing her down

with her knees almost touching Elayne's, kneeling at her
back. "I stand for Aviendha's mother, who cannot be here. I
offer my daughter to her testing."

Another time, Elayne might have giggled. Neither woman
looked more than a half-dozen years older than Aviendha or
her. Another time. Not now. The standing Wise Ones wore
solemn faces. They were studying her and Aviendha as if
weighing them, unsure they would measure up.

"Who will suffer the pangs of birth for them?" Monaelle
asked, and Amys stepped forward.

Two others came with her, a fiery redhead named Shyanda, whom Elayne had seen with Melaine, and a graying
woman she did not know. They helped Amys strip to her
skin. Proud in her nakedness, Amys faced Monaelle and
slapped her taut belly. "I have borne children. I have given
suck," she said, cupping breasts that looked as if she had
done nothing of the kind. "I offer myself."

At Monaelle's dignified nod of acceptance, Amys went to
her knees two paces on the other side of Elayne and Aviendha
and settled back on her heels. Shyanda and the graying
Wise One knelt flanking her, and suddenly the glow of the
Power surrounded every woman in the room except Elayne,
Aviendha and Amys.

Elayne took a deep breath, and saw Aviendha do the
same. Occasionally a bracelet clicked against another
among the Wise Ones, the only sound in the room beyond
breathing, and faint, distant thunder. It was almost a shock
when Monaelle spoke.

"You will both do as you are instructed. If you waver or
question, your dedication is not strong enough. I will send
you away, and that will be the end of it, forever. I will ask
questions, and you will answer truthfully. If you refuse to
answer, you will be sent away. If any here think you lie, you
will be sent away. You may leave at any time on your own,
of course. Which also will end this for all time. There are
no second chances here. Now. What is the best you know of
the woman you want for a first-sister?"

Elayne half-expected the question. This was one of the
things she had been told to think about. Choosing one virtue among many had not been easy, yet she had her answer
ready. When she spoke, flows of *saidar* suddenly wove together between her and Aviendha, and no sound came from

her tongue, or Aviendha's. Without thought, a part of her mind tucked away the weaves; even now, trying to learn was as much a part of her as the color of her eyes. The weaves vanished as her lips closed.

"Aviendha is so confident, so proud. She doesn't care what anyone thinks she should do, or be; she is who *she* wants to be," Elayne heard her own voice say, while Aviendha's words suddenly were audible at the same time. "Even when Elayne is so afraid that her mouth dries, her spirit will not bend. She is braver than anyone I have ever known."

Elayne stared at her friend. Aviendha thought she was *brave*? Light, she was no coward, but *brave*? Strangely, Aviendha was staring at *her* in disbelief.

"Courage is a well," Viendre said at Elayne's ear, "deep in some, shallow in others. Deep or shallow, wells go dry eventually, even if they fill again later. You will face what you cannot face. Your spine will turn to jelly, and your vaunted courage will leave you weeping in the dust. The day will come." She sounded as though she wanted to be there to see it come. Elayne gave a curt nod. She knew all about her spine turning to jelly; she fought it every day, it seemed.

Tamela was speaking to Aviendha, in a voice almost as satisfied as Viendre's. "*Ji'e'toh* binds you like bands of steel. For *ji*, you make yourself exactly what is expected of you, to the last hair. For *toh*, if necessary you will abase yourself and crawl on your belly. Because you care to your *bones* what *everyone* thinks of you."

Elayne nearly gasped. That was harsh, and unfair. She knew something of *ji'e'toh*, but Aviendha was not like that. Yet Aviendha was nodding, much as she herself had. An impatient acceptance of what she already knew.

"Fine traits to love in a first-sister," Monaelle said, lifting her shawl down to her elbows, "but what do you find worst in her?"

Elayne shifted on her chilling knees, licked her lips before speaking. She had dreaded this. It was not just Monaelle's warning. Aviendha had said they must speak the truth. *Must*, or what was sisterhood worth? Again the weaves held their words captive until they were done.

"Aviendha . . ." Elayne's voice said suddenly, hesitantly.

"She . . . she thinks violence is always the answer. At times, she won't think beyond her belt knife. At times, she's like a boy who won't grow up!"

"Elayne knows that . . ." Aviendha's voice began, then gulped and went on in a rush. "She knows she is beautiful, knows the power it gives her over men. She exposes half her bosom sometimes, in the open air, and she smiles to make men do what she wants."

Elayne gaped. Aviendha thought *that* of her? It made her sound a *lightskirt*! Aviendha frowned back and half-opened her mouth, but Tamela pressed her shoulders again and began to speak.

"You think men do not stare at your face in approval?" There was an edge in the Wise One's voice; strong was the best anyone would ever say of her face. "Do they not look at your breasts in the sweat tent? Admire your hips? You are beautiful, and you know it. Deny it, and deny yourself! You have taken pleasure in men's looks, and smiled at them. Will you never smile at a man to give your arguments more weight, or touch his arm to distract him from the weakness of your arguments? You will, and you will be no less for it."

Red flooded Aviendha's cheeks, but Elayne was having to listen to Viendre. And fight blushes of her own. "There is violence in you. Deny it, and deny yourself. Have you never raged and struck out? Have you never drawn blood? Have you never *wished* to? Without considering another way? Without any thought at all? While you breathe, that will be part of you." Elayne thought of Taim, and other times, and her face felt like a furnace.

This time, there was more than one response.

"Your arms will grow weak," Tamela was telling Aviendha. "Your legs will lose their swiftness. A youth will be able to take the knife from your hand. How will skill or ferocity avail you then? Heart and mind are the true weapons. But did you learn to use the spear in a day, when you were a Maiden? If you do not hone mind and heart now, you will grow old and children will befuddle your wits. Clan chiefs will sit you in a corner to play cat's cradle, and when you speak, all will hear only the wind. Take heed while you can."

"Beauty flees," Viendre went on, to Elayne. "Years will make your breasts sag, your flesh grow slack, your skin grow leathery. Men who smiled to see your face will speak to you as if you were just another man. Your husband may see you always as the first time his eyes caught you, but no other man will dream of you. Will you no longer be you? Your body is only clothing. Your flesh will wither, but you are your heart and mind, and they do not change except to grow stronger."

Elayne shook her head. Not in denial. Not really. She had never thought on aging, though. Especially not since going to the Tower. The years lay lightly even on very old Aes Sedai. But what if she lived as long as the Kinswomen? That would mean giving up being Aes Sedai, of course, but what if she did? The Kin took a very long time to grow wrinkles, but grow them they did. What was Aviendha thinking? She knelt there looking . . . sullen.

"What is the most childish thing you know of the woman you want for a first-sister?" Monaelle said.

This was easier, not so fraught. Elayne even smiled as she spoke. Aviendha grinned back, sullenness gone. Again the weaves took their words and released them together, voices with laughter in them.

"Aviendha won't let me teach her to swim. I've tried. She isn't afraid of anything, except getting into more water than a bathtub."

"Elayne gobbles sweets with both hands like a child who's escaped her mother's eye. If she keeps on, she will be fat as a pig before she grows old."

Elayne jerked. Gobbles? *Gobbles?* A taste, now and then, was all she took. Just now and then. *Fat?* Why was Aviendha glaring at *her?* Refusing to step into water more than knee-deep *was* childish.

Monaelle covered a slight cough with one hand, but Elayne thought she was hiding a smile. Some of the standing Wise Ones laughed outright. At Aviendha's silliness? Or her . . . *gobbling?*

Monaelle resumed dignity, adjusting her skirts spread out on the floor, but there was still a touch of mirth in her voice. "What is your greatest jealousy of the woman you want for a first-sister?"

Perhaps Elayne would have hedged her answer despite the requirement for truth. Truth had jumped up as soon as she was told to think on this, but she had found something

smaller, less embarrassing for them both, that would have
passed muster. Perhaps. But there was that about her smiling at men and exposing her bosom. Maybe she did smile,
but Aviendha walked in front of red-faced servingmen
without a *stitch* on and seemed not even to *see* them! So
she *gobbled* candy, did she? She was going to get fat? She
spoke the bitter truth while the weaves took her words and
Aviendha's mouth moved in grim silence, until at last what
they had said was loosed.

"Aviendha has lain in the arms of the man I love. I never
have; I may never, and I could weep over it!"

"Elayne has the love of Rand al'Th . . . of *Rand*. My
heart is dust for wanting him to love me, but I do not know
if he ever will."

Elayne peered into Aviendha's unreadable face. She was
jealous of her over *Rand*? When the man avoided Elayne
Trakand as if she had scabies? She had no time for more
thought.

"Strike her as hard as you can with your open hand,"
Tamela told Aviendha, removing her own hands from Aviendha's shoulders.

Viendre squeezed Elayne's lightly. "Do not defend yourself." They had not been told anything of this! Surely,
Aviendha would not—

Blinking, Elayne pushed herself up from the icy floor
tiles. Gingerly she felt her cheek, and winced. She was going to wear a palm print the rest of the day. The woman did
not have to hit her *that* hard.

Everyone waited until she was kneeling again, and then
Viendre leaned closer. "Strike her as hard as you can with
your open hand."

Well, *she* was not going to knock Aviendha on her ear.
She was not going to—Her full-armed slap sent Aviendha
sprawling, sliding on her chest across the tiles almost
to Monaelle. Elayne's palm stung almost as much as her
cheek.

Aviendha half pushed herself up, gave her head a shake,
then scrambled back to her position. And Tamela said,
"Strike her with the other hand."

This time, Elayne slid all the way to Amys' knees on the
frozen tiles, her head ringing, *both* cheeks burning. And
when she regained her own knees in front of Aviendha,

when Viendre told her to strike, she put her whole body into the slap, so much that she nearly fell over atop Aviendha as the other woman went down.

"You may go now," Monaelle said.

Elayne's eyes jerked toward the Wise One. Aviendha, halfway back to her knees, went stiff as stone.

"If you wish to," Monaelle continued. "Men usually do, at this point if not sooner. Many women do, too. But if you still love one another enough to go on, then embrace."

Elayne flung herself at Aviendha, and was met with a rush that nearly knocked her over backward. They clung together. Elayne felt tears trickling from her eyes, and realized Aviendha was crying as well. "I'm sorry," Elayne whispered fervently. "I'm sorry, Aviendha."

"Forgive me," Aviendha whispered back. "Forgive me.

Monaelle was standing over them, now. "You will know anger at one another again, you will speak harsh words, but you will always remember that you have already struck her. And for no better reason than you were told to. Let those blows pass for all you might wish to give. You have *toh* toward one another, *toh* you cannot repay and will not try to, for every woman is always in her first-sister's debt. You will be born again."

The feel of *saidar* in the room was changing, but Elayne had no chance to see how even had she thought of it. The light dwindled as if the lamps were being put out. The feel of Aviendha's hug dwindled. Sound dwindled. The last thing she heard was Monaelle's voice. "You will be born again." Everything faded. She faded. She ceased to exist.

Awareness, of a sort. She did not think of herself as she, she did not think at all, but she was aware. Of sound. A liquid swishing all around. Muted gurgles and rumbles. And a rhythmic thudding. That above all. *Thu-thud. Thu-thud.* She did not know contentment, but she was content. *Thu-thud.*

Time. She did not know time, yet Ages passed. There was a sound within her, a sound that *was* her. *Thu-thud.* The same sound, the same rhythm as the other. *Thu-thud.* And from another place, nearer. *Thu-thud.* Another. *Thu-thud.* The same sound, the same beat, as her own. Not another. They were the same; they were one. *Thu-thud.*

Forever went by to that pulse, all the time that had ever

been. She touched the other that was herself. She could feel. *Thu-thud*. She moved, she and the other that was herself, writhing against each other, limbs entangling, rolling away but always coming back to each other. *Thu-thud*. There was light sometimes, in the darkness; dim beyond seeing, but bright to one who had never known anything but darkness. *Thu-thud*. She opened her eyes, stared into the eyes of the other that was herself, and closed hers again, content. *Thu-thud*.

Change, sudden, shocking to one who had never known any change. Pressure. *Thu-thud-thu-thud*. That comforting beat was faster. Convulsive pressure. Again. Again. Getting stronger. *Thu-thud-thu-thud! Thu-thud-thu-thud!*

Suddenly, the other that was herself—was gone. She was alone. She did not know fear, but she was afraid, and alone. *Thu-thud-thu-thud!* Pressure! Greater than anything before! Squeezing her, crushing her. If she had known how to scream, if she had known what a scream was, she would have shrieked.

And then light, blinding, full of swirling patterns. She had weight; she had never felt weight before. A cutting pain at her middle. Something tickled her foot. Something tickled her back. At first she did not realize that wailing sound was coming from her. She kicked feebly, waved limbs that did not know how to move. She was lifted, laid on something soft but firmer than anything she had felt before, except for recollections of the other that was herself, the other that was gone. *Thu-thud. Thu-thud.* The sound. The same sound, the same beat. Loneliness reigned, unrecognized, but there was contentment, too.

Memory began to return, slowly. She lifted her head from a breast and looked up into Amys' face. Yes, Amys. Sweat-slick and weary-eyed, but smiling. And she was Elayne; yes, Elayne Trakand. But there was something more to her, now. Not like the Warder bond, but like it in a way. Fainter, but more magnificent. Slowly, on a neck that wobbled uncertainly, she turned her head to look at the other that was herself, lying on Amys' other breast. To look at Aviendha, her hair matted, her face and body shining with sweat. Smiling with joy. Laughing, weeping, they clutched each other and hung on as if they never intended to let go.

"This is my daughter Aviendha," Amys said, "and this is

my daughter Elayne, born on the same day, within the same hour. May they always guard one another, support one another, love one another." She laughed softly, tiredly, fondly. "And now will someone bring us garments before my new daughters and I all freeze to death?"

Elayne did not care at that moment if she did freeze to death. She clung to Aviendha in laughter and tears. She had found her sister. Light, she had found her sister!

Toveine Gazal woke to the sounds of quiet bustle, other women moving about, some talking softly. Lying on her hard narrow cot, she sighed with regret. Her hands around Elaida's throat had been just a pleasant dream. This tiny canvas-walled room was reality. She had slept poorly, and she felt thinned, drained. She had overslept, too; there would be no time for breakfast. Reluctantly she tossed off her blankets. The building had been a small warehouse of some sort, with thick walls and heavy rafters low overhead, but there was no heat. Her breath misted, and the crisp morning air pricked through her shift before her feet reached the rough floorboards. Even if she could have considered lying abed in this place, she had her orders. Logain's filthy bond made disobedience impossible, no matter how often she wished it.

She always tried to think of him as simply Ablar, or at worst Master Ablar, but it was always just Logain that came into her mind. The name he had made infamous. Logain, the false Dragon who had shattered the armies of his native Ghealdan. Logain, who had carved a path through the few Altarans and Murandians with nerve enough to try stopping him until he threatened Lugard itself. Logain, who had been gentled and somehow could channel again, who had dared to fix his cursed weave of *saidin* on Toveine Gazal. A pity for him he had not commanded her to stop thinking! She could *feel* the man, in the back of her head. He was always there.

For a moment, she squeezed her eyes shut. Light! Mistress Doweel's farm had seemed the Pit of Doom, years of exile and penance with no way out except the unthinkable, to become a hunted renegade. Barely half a week since her capture, she knew better. *This* was the Pit of Doom.

And there was no escape. Angrily, she shook her head, and scrubbed glistening dampness from her cheeks with her fingers. No! She would escape, somehow, if only for long enough to put her real hands on Elaida's throat. Somehow.

Aside from the cot, there were only three pieces of furniture, yet they left little space for her to move. She cracked the ice in the yellow-striped pitcher on the washstand with her belt knife, filled the chipped white basin, and channeled to heat the water till tendrils of steam rose. It was *allowed* to channel for that. That and no more. By rote she washed and scrubbed her teeth with salt and soda, then took a fresh shift and stockings from the small wooden chest at the foot of the cot. Her ring she left in the chest, tucked under everything else in a small velvet pouch. Another order. All of her things were here, except for her lapdesk. Luckily, that had been lost when she was taken. Her dresses hung on a cloakstand, the last of the room's furnishings. Choosing one without really looking, she put it on mechanically and used comb and brush on her hair.

The ivory-backed brush slowed as she really saw herself in the washstand's cheap, bubbled mirror. Breathing raggedly, she set the brush down beside the matching comb. The dress she had chosen was thick, finely woven wool of an unadorned red so dark it seemed nearly black. Black, like an Asha'man's coat. Her distorted image stared back at her, lips writhing. Changing would be a sort of surrender. Determinedly she snatched her marten-lined gray cloak from the stand.

When she pushed aside the canvas doorflap, twenty or so sisters already occupied the long central hallway lined with canvas rooms. Here and there a few were speaking in murmurs, but the rest avoided one another's eyes, even when they belonged to the same Ajah. Fear had its presence, but it was shame that coated most faces. Akoure, a stout Gray, was staring at the hand where she normally wore her ring. Desandre, a willowy Yellow, was hiding her right hand in her armpit.

The soft conversations trailed off when Toveine appeared. Several women glared at her openly. Including Jenare and Lemai, from her own Ajah! Desandre came to herself enough to turn her back stiffly. In the space of two days, fifty-one Aes Sedai had fallen captive to the black-coated monsters, and fifty of them blamed Toveine Gazal as though Elaida a'Roihan had no hand in the disaster at all. Except for Logain's intervention, they would have had their revenge their first night here. She did not love him for putting a stop to it and making Carniele Heal the welts left by belts, the bruises left by fists and feet. She would rather they had beaten her to death than she owe him.

Putting her cloak on her shoulders, she walked proudly down the corridor, out into pale morning sunshine that suited her washed-out mood. Behind her, someone shouted acid words before the closing door cut them off. Her hands trembled as she pulled up her hood, nestling the dark fur around her face. No one got away with pushing down Toveine Gazal. Even Mistress Doweel, who had crushed her into a semblance of submission over the years, learned that when her exile ended. She would show them. She would show them all!

The dormitory she shared with the others lay on the very edge of a large village, if a very strange one. A village of Asha'man. Elsewhere, so she had been told, ground was marked off for structures they claimed would dwarf the White Tower, but this was where most of them lived now. Five large, blocky stone barracks, spaced along streets as wide as anything in Tar Valon, could each hold a hundred Asha'man Soldiers. They were not full yet, the Light be thanked, but snow-covered scaffolding awaited the arrival of workmen around the thick walls of two more that were almost ready for roofing in thatch. Nearly a dozen smaller stone structures were made to hold ten Dedicated each, and another of those was under construction, too. Scattered around them stood nearly two hundred houses that might have been seen in any village, where some of the married men lived, and the families of others not far enough along in training.

Men who could channel did not frighten her. Once she had given in to panic for a moment, true, but that was beside the point. Five hundred men who could channel, however, were a scrap of bone wedged between two of her teeth where she could not free it. Five *hundred*! And they could Travel, some of them. A sharp scrap of bone. More, she had tramped the mile or more through the woods to the wall. *That* frightened her, what it signified.

Nowhere was the wall finished, nowhere more than twelve or fifteen feet high, none of the towers or bastions more than begun. In places, she could have clambered over the piles of black stone, except for her orders not to attempt escape. The thing ran for *eight* miles, though, and she believed Logain when he said it was begun less than three months ago. The man held her too tightly to bother with lying. He called the wall a waste of time and effort, and perhaps it was, but it made her teeth chatter. Just three months. Made using the Power. The male half of the Power. When she thought of that black wall, she saw an implacable force that could not be stopped, an avalanche of black stone sliding down to bury the White Tower. Impossible, of course. Impossible, but when she did not dream of strangling Elaida, she dreamed of that.

There had been snowfall in the night, and a heavy blanket of white covered every roof, but she did not have to pick her way along the broad streets. The hard-packed dirt had been cleared, a chore of men in training before the sun came up. They used the Power for everything from filling woodboxes to cleaning their clothes! Black-clad men hurried here and there in the streets, and more were gathering in rows in front of their barracks with others calling roll in loud voices. Women bundled up against the cold walked past them, placidly carrying baskets to the quartermaster's storehouse or water buckets to the nearest fountain, though how any woman could remain, knowing what her husband was, was beyond Toveine's comprehension. Even more bizarre, children ran up and down the street, around the squares of men who could channel, shouting and laughing, rolling hoops, tossing painted balls, playing with dolls or dogs. A drop of normality that heightened the evil stench of the rest.

Ahead of her, a mounted party was approaching up the street at a walk. In the short time she had been here—the endless time—she had not seen anyone ride in the village except workmen on carts or wagons. Nor any visitors, which some of these plainly must be. Five men in black were escorting a dozen in the red coats and cloaks of the Queen's Guards, with two yellow-haired women at the front, one in a red-and-white cloak lined with black fur and the other . . . Toveine's eyebrows climbed. The other wore green Kandori trousers and a coat made up as if it belonged to the Captain-

General of the Guard. Her red cloak even had golden knots of rank on the shoulder! Maybe she was mistaken about the men. That one would find short shift when she encountered real Guardsmen. In any case, it was strangely early for visitors.

Each time the odd party reached one of the formations, the man in front shouted, "Asha'man, attend front!" and boot heels stamped on the hardened earth as the others stiffened like pillars of stone.

Pulling her hood forward better to hide her face, Toveine moved to the side of the wide street, close beside the corner of one of the smaller stone barracks. A fork-bearded old man coming out, a silver sword pin on his high collar, glanced at her curiously without slowing his stride.

What she had done struck her like a bucket of cold water, and she nearly wept. None of those strangers would spot an Aes Sedai face, now, if they could recognize one. If either of those women could channel, unlikely though that was, she would not pass close enough to tell that Toveine could, too. She fretted and fumed over how to disobey Logain, and then did everything necessary to carry out his instructions without even thinking about it!

As an act of defiance, she stopped where she was, turning to watch the visitors. Automatically, her hands checked her hood before she could snatch them to her sides. It was pitiful, and ridiculous. She knew the Asha'man guiding the party, by sight at least, a bulky man in his middle years with oily black hair, an oily smile and eyes like augurs. None of the others, though. What could she hope to gain by this? How could she entrust a message to any of them? Even if the escort vanished, how could she get close enough to pass a message when she was forbidden to let any outsider discover the presence of Aes Sedai?

The augur-eyed fellow looked bored with his duty this morning, hardly bothering to hide his yawns behind a gloved hand. ". . . when we do finish here," he was saying as he rode past Toveine, "I will show you the Craft Town. Quite a bit bigger than this. We do have every kind of craftsfolk, from masons and carpenters to metalsmiths and tailors. We can make everything we need, Lady Elayne."

"Except turnips," one of the women said in a high voice, and the other laughed.

Toveine's head jerked. She watched the riders move on down the street accompanied by shouted orders and stamping boots. Lady Elayne? Elayne Trakand? The younger of the pair might match the description she had been given. Elaida did not reveal why she was so desperate to lay her hands on one runaway Accepted, even one who might become a queen, but she never let a sister leave the Tower without orders on what to do if she encountered the girl. *Be very careful, Elayne Trakand,* Toveine thought. *I would not like Elaida to have the satisfaction of laying hands on you.*

She wanted to think on this, on whether there was some way to use the girl's presence here, but abruptly she became aware of the sensations at the back of her head. A mild contentment and a growing purpose. Logain had finished his breakfast. He would be coming out, soon. He had told her to be there when he did.

Her feet were running before she thought. With the result that her skirts tangled in her legs, and she fell hard, knocking her breath out. Anger welled up, fury, but she scrambled to her feet and, without pausing to brush off the dust, gathered her skirts above her knees and began to run again, cloak billowing behind. Men's raucous shouts followed her down the street, and laughing children pointed as she ran past.

Suddenly a pack of dogs was around her, snarling, nipping at her heels. She leaped and spun and kicked, but they harried her. She wanted to shriek with frustration and fury. Dogs were always a bother, and she could not channel a feather to drive them off. A gray hound seized a mouthful of dangling skirt, pulling her sideways. Panic overwhelmed everything else. If she fell again, they would tear her to shreds.

A shouting woman in brown wool swung her heavy basket at the dog tugging Toveine's skirt, making it dodge away. A round woman's bucket caught a brindled cur in the ribs, and it ran yelping. Toveine gaped in astonishment, and for her inattention had to pull her left leg away from another dog at the cost of a piece of her stocking and a little skin. There were women all around her, flailing away at the animals with whatever they had to hand.

"Go on with you, Aes Sedai," a skinny, graying woman told her, slicing at a spotted dog with a switch. "They won't

bother you more. I'd like a nice cat, myself, but cats won't
abide the husband now. Go on."

Toveine did not wait to thank her rescuers. She ran, considering furiously. The women knew. If one did, they all did.
But they would carry no messages, give no help to an escape, not when they were willing to remain themselves. Not
if they understood what they were helping. There was that.

Just short of Logain's house, one of several down a narrower side street, she slowed and hastily let down her skirts.
Eight or nine men in black coats were waiting outside,
boys and oldsters and in between, but there was no sign of
Logain yet. She could still sense him, full of purpose but
concentrating. Reading, perhaps. She walked the rest of the
way at a dignified pace. Composed and every inch an Aes
Sedai, no matter the circumstances. She almost managed to
forget her frantic flight from the dogs.

The house surprised her every time she saw it. Others on
the street were as large and two larger. An ordinary wooden
house of two stories, though the red door, shutters and window frames looked odd. Plain curtains hid the interior,
but the glass in the windows was so poor she doubted she
could have seen anything clearly with the curtains drawn.
A house suitable for a not overly successful shopkeeper;
hardly the dwelling for one of the most notorious men alive.

Briefly she wondered what was keeping Gabrelle. The
other sister bonded to Logain had the same instruction she
did, and until now, she had always been here first. Gabrelle
was eager, studying the Asha'man as if she intended writing
a book on the subject. Perhaps she did; Browns would write
about anything. She put the other sister out of her mind.
Although, if Gabrelle did turn up late, she would have to
find out how the woman had managed it. For now, she had
her own studying.

The men outside the red door eyed her, but said nothing, even to one another. Still there was no animosity. They
were simply waiting. None had a cloak, though their breath
made pale feathers in front of their faces. All were Dedicated, with the silver sword pin on their collars.

It had been the same every morning she had *reported*
this way, though not always the same men. She knew some,
knew their names at least, and sometimes a few other gleaned
tidbits. Evin Vinchova, the pretty lad who had been there

when Logain captured her, leaning against the corner of the
house and toying with a bit of string. Donalo Sandomere, if
that was his real name, with his creased farmer's face and
sharply trimmed oiled beard, attempting the languid stance
he thought a nobleman would assume. The Taraboner Androl
Genhald, a square fellow with his heavy eyebrows drawn in
thought and his hands clasped behind his back; he wore a
gold signet ring, but she thought him an apprentice who had
shaved his mustaches and abandoned his veil. Mezar Kurin,
a Domani with gray at his temples, fingering the garnet in
his left ear; he very well might be a minor noble. She was
collecting a neat file of names and faces in her head. Sooner
or later they would be hunted down, and every piece of information that could help identify them would be useful.

The red door opened, and the men straightened, but it
was not Logain who came out.

Toveine blinked in surprise, then met Gabrelle's sooty
green eyes with a flat stare, making no effort to hide her
disgust. That accursed link with Logain had made clear
what he was up to the night before—she had been afraid
she would *never* fall asleep!—but not in her darkest imagin-
ings had she suspected Gabrelle! Some of the men seemed
as startled as she. Some attempted to hide smiles. Kurin
grinned openly and stroked his thin mustache with a thumb.

The dusky woman did not even have the grace to blush.
She lifted her upturned nose a trifle, then boldly adjusted
her dark blue dress over her hips as if to advertise that she
had just donned the garment. Sweeping her cloak around her
shoulders, she tied the ribbons as she glided toward Toveine,
as serene as if she were back in the Tower.

Toveine grabbed the taller woman's arm, pulling her a
little way from the men. "We may be captives, Gabrelle,"
she whispered harshly, "but that is no reason to surrender.
Especially to Ablar's vile lusts!" The other woman did not
so much as look abashed! A thought came. Of course. "Did
he . . . ? Did he *order* you?"

With something close to a sneer, Gabrelle pulled free.
"Toveine, it took me two days to decide I should 'surrender'
to his lusts, as you put it. I feel lucky it only required four
to convince him to let me. You Reds might not be aware,
but men love to talk and gossip. All you need do is listen, or
even pretend to, and a man will tell you his whole life." A

thoughtful frown creased her forehead, and the twist to her lips vanished. "I wonder whether it's like that for ordinary women."

"Whether what is like what?" Toveine demanded. Gabrelle was *spying* on him? Or just trying to get more material for her book? But *this* was unbelievable, even for a Brown! "What are you talking about?"

That musing expression never left the other's face. "I felt . . . helpless. Oh, he was gentle, but I never really thought before on how strong a man's arms are, and me unable to channel a whisker. He was . . . in charge, I suppose, though that isn't quite right. Just . . . stronger, and I knew it. It felt . . . strangely exhilarating."

Toveine shuddered. Gabrelle must be insane! She was about to tell her so when Logain himself appeared, closing the door behind him. He was tall, taller than any other man there, with dark hair that brushed wide shoulders and framed an arrogant face. His high collar carried both the silver sword and that ridiculous snake with legs. He flashed a smile at Gabrelle as the others gathered around him. The hussy smiled back, too. Toveine shuddered again. Exhilarating. The woman *was* insane!

As on previous mornings, the men began making reports. Most of the time, Toveine had not been able to make *up* from *down* with them, but she listened.

"I found two more who seem interested in that new kind of Healing this Nynaeve used on you, Logain," Genhald said, frowning, "but one can barely do the Healing we already know, and the other, he wants to know more than I could tell him."

"What you can tell him is all I know," Logain replied. "Mistress al'Meara didn't tell me much of what she was doing, and I could only learn bits and pieces listening to the other sisters talk. Just keep planting the seed and hope something grows. It's all you can do. Several other men nodded along with Genhald.

Toveine filed it away. Nynaeve al'Meara. She had heard that name often after returning to the Tower. Another runaway Accepted, another one Elaida wanted more than the normal desire to catch runaways seemed to account for. From the same village as al'Thor, too. And associated somehow with Logain. That might lead to something, eventually.

But a *new* kind of Healing? Used by an *Accepted*? That was unlikely bordering close on impossible, but she had seen the impossible happen before, so she tucked it away. Gabrelle was listening closely, too, she noticed. But watching her as well, out of the corner of her eye.

"There's a problem with some of those Two Rivers men, Logain," Vinchova said. An angry flush rose on his smooth face. "Men, I say, but these two are boys, fourteen at most! They won't say." He might have been a year or two older, with his beardless cheeks. "It was a crime, bringing them here."

Logain shook his head; whether it was in anger or regret was hard to say. "I've heard the White Tower takes girls as young as twelve. Look after the Two Rivers men where you can. No coddling, or the others will turn on them, but try to see they don't do anything stupid. The Lord Dragon might not like it if we kill too many from his district."

"He doesn't seem to be caring much at all as I can see," a sleek fellow muttered. The sound of Murandy was strong in his mouth, though his fiercely curled mustaches told where he was from plainly enough. He was rolling a silver coin across the backs of his fingers and seemed as intent on that as on Logain. "I was hearing it was the Lord Dragon himself told the M'Hael to pluck up anything male in this Two Rivers that could channel, down to the roosters. With the number he brought back, I'm just surprised he didn't bring the chicks and lambs, as well." Chuckles met his sally, but Logain's level tones cut them like a blade.

"Whatever the Lord Dragon ordered, I trust I've made my orders clear." Every head nodded this time, and some men murmured "Yes, Logain" and "As you say, Logain."

Toveine hastily smoothed the sneer from her lips. Ignorant louts. The Tower accepted girls under fifteen only if they had already begun channeling. The other was interesting, though. The Two Rivers again. Everyone said al'Thor had turned his back on his home, but she was not so certain. Why was Gabrelle watching her?

"Last night," Sandomere said after a moment, "I learned that Mishraile is having private lessons from the M'Hael." He stroked his pointed beard with satisfaction, as if he had produced a gem of great price.

Perhaps he had, but Toveine could not say what kind. Logain nodded slowly. The others exchanged silent looks with faces that might have been carved. She chewed frustration, watching. Too often it was like this, matters they saw no reason to comment on—or feared to?—and she did not understand. She always felt there *were* gems hidden there, beyond her reach.

A wide Cairhienin fellow, barely as tall as Logain's chest, opened his mouth, but whether he meant to speak of Mishraile, whoever he was, she never found out.

"Logain!" Welyn Kajima pounded down the street at a dead run, the bells at the ends of his black braids jangling. Another Dedicated, a man in his middle years who smiled too much, he had been there when Logain captured her, too. Kajima had bonded Jenare. He was almost out of breath when he pushed through the other men, and he was not smiling now.

"Logain," he panted, "the M'Hael's back from Cairhien, and he's posted new deserters on the board at the palace. You won't believe the names!" He spilled out his list in a breathless rush amid exclamations from the others that kept Toveine from hearing more than fragments.

"Dedicated have deserted before," the Cairhienin muttered when Kajima was done, "but *never* a full Asha'man. And now seven at once?"

"If you don't believe me," Kajima began, drawing himself up in a fussy manner. He had been a clerk, in Arafel.

"We believe you," Genhald said soothingly. "But Gedwyn and Torval, they are the M'Hael's men. Rochaid and Kisman, too. Why would they desert? He gave them anything a king could want."

Kajima shook his head irritably, making his bells chime. "You know the list never gives reasons. Just names."

"Good riddance," Kurin growled. "At least, it would be if we didn't have to hunt them down, now."

"It's the others I cannot understand," Sandomere put in. "I was at Dumai's Wells. I saw the Lord Dragon choose, after. Dashiva had his head in the clouds, like always. But Flinn, Hopwil, Narishma? You never saw men more pleased. They were like lambs let loose in the barley shed."

A sturdy fellow with gray in his hair spat. "Well, I wasn't

at the Wells, but I went south against the Seanchan." His
accents were Andoran. "Maybe the lambs didn't like the
butcher's yard as much as they did the barley shed."

Logain had been listening without taking part, arms
folded across his chest. His face was unreadable, a mask.
"Do you worry about the butcher's yard, Canler?" he said
now.

The Andoran grimaced, then shrugged. "I reckon we're
all headed there, soon or late, Logain. Don't see we have
much choice, but I don't have to grin about it."

"As long as you're there on the day," Logain said quietly.
He addressed the man called Canler, but several of the
others nodded.

Looking past the men, Logain considered Toveine and
Gabrelle. Toveine tried to look as if she had not been eavesdropping, and remembering names fiercely. "Go inside out
of the cold," he told them. "Have some tea to warm you. I'll
be back as soon as I can. Don't touch my papers." Gathering up the other men with a gesture, he led them off in the
direction Kajima had come from.

Toveine gritted her teeth in frustration. At least she would
not have to follow him to the training grounds, past the so-
called Traitor's Tree, where heads hung like diseased fruit
from the bare branches, and watch men studying how to destroy with the Power, but she had hoped for another day to
herself, free to wander about and see what she could learn.
She had heard men speak of Taim's "palace" before, and
today she had hoped to find it and perhaps catch a glimpse
of the man whose name was as black as Logain's. Instead,
she meekly followed the other woman through the red door.
There was no use in fighting it.

Inside, she looked around the front room while Gabrelle
hung her cloak on a peg. Despite the exterior, she had expected something grander for Logain. A low fire burned
in a rough stone fireplace. A long narrow table and ladder-
backed chairs stood on bare floorboards. A desk, only
slightly more elaborate than the other furnishings, caught
her eye. Stacks of lidded letterboxes littered the desktop,
and leather folders full of long sheets of paper. Her fingers
itched, but she knew that even if she sat at the desk, she
would not be able to lay a finger on anything more than the
pen or glass ink bottle.

With a sigh, she followed Gabrelle into the kitchen, where an iron stove gave too much heat and dirty breakfast dishes sat on a low cabinet beneath the window. Gabrelle filled a teakettle and put it on the stove, then took a green-glazed teapot and a wooden canister from another cabinet. Toveine draped her cloak over a chair and sat down at the square table. She did not want tea unless it came with the breakfast she had missed, but she knew she was going to drink it.

The silly Brown nattered on as she carried out her domestic tasks like a contented farmwife. "I've learned a good deal already. Logain is the only full Asha'man to live here in this village. The others all live in Taim's 'palace.' They have servants, but Logain hired the wife of a man in training to cook and clean for him. She'll be here soon, and she thinks he put the sun in the sky, so we best be done talking about anything important by then. He found your lapdesk."

Toveine felt as though an icy hand had seized her throat. She tried to hide it, but Gabrelle was looking straight at her.

"He burned it, Toveine. After reading the contents. He seemed to think he had done us a favor."

The hand eased, and Toveine could breathe again. "Elaida's order was among my papers." She cleared her throat to rid herself of hoarseness. Elaida's order to gentle every man found here and then hang them on the spot, without the trial in Tar Valon required by Tower law. "She imposed harsh conditions, and these men would have reacted harshly, if they knew." In spite of the heat from the stove, she shivered. That single paper could have gotten them all stilled and hanged. "Why would he do us favors?"

"I don't know why, Toveine. He isn't a villain, no more than most men. It could be as simple as that." Gabrelle set a plate of crusted rolls and another with white cheese on the table. "Or it could be that this bond is like the Warder bond in more ways than we know. Maybe he just did not want to experience the two of us being executed." Toveine's stomach rumbled, but she picked up a roll as if she did not care for more than a nibble.

"I suspect 'harsh' was a mild choice of words," Gabrelle went on, spooning tea into the teapot. "I saw you flinch. Of course, they went to a great deal of trouble to bring us here. Fifty-one sisters in their midst, and even with the bond, they must fear we'll find some way around their orders, some loophole they missed. The obvious answer is, if we were dead, the Tower would be roused to fury. With us alive and captive, even Elaida will move cautiously." She laughed, quietly amused. "Your face, Toveine. Did you think I've spent all my time thinking about tangling my fingers in Logain's hair?"

Toveine closed her mouth and put down the untouched roll. It was cold, anyway, and felt hard. Always a mistake to assume Browns were unworldly, absorbed in their books and studies to the exclusion of everything else. "What else have you seen?"

Still gripping the spoon, Gabrelle sat across the table from her and leaned forward intently. "Their wall may be strong when it's done, but this place is full of fractures. There is Mazrim Taim's faction, and Logain's faction, though I am uncertain either thinks of them so. Perhaps other factions, too, and certainly men who don't know there are factions. Fifty-one sisters should be able to make something of that, even with the bond. The second question is, what *do* we make of it?"

"The second question?" Toveine demanded, but the other woman merely waited. "If we manage to break those fissures open," she said finally, "we scatter ten or fifty or a hundred bands across the world, each more dangerous than any army ever seen. Catching them all might take a lifetime and rip the world apart like a new Breaking, and that with Tarmon Gai'don on its way. That is, if this fellow al'Thor really is the Dragon Reborn." Gabrelle opened her mouth, but Toveine waved away whatever she was going to say. That he was, very likely. It hardly mattered, here and now. "But if we don't . . . Put down the rebellion and gather those sisters back to the Tower, call back every retired sister, and I don't know whether all of us together could destroy this place. I suspect half the Tower would die in the attempt, either way. What is the first question?"

Gabrelle leaned back in her chair, her face suddenly weary. "Yes, not an easy decision. And they bring in more men every day. Fifteen or twenty since we've been here, I believe."

"I won't be trifled with, Gabrelle! What is the first question?" The Brown's gaze sharpened, stared at her for a long moment.

"Soon, the shock will wear off," she said finally. "What comes then? The authority Elaida gave you is finished; the expedition is finished. The first question is, are we fifty-one sisters united, or do we revert to being Browns and Reds, Yellows and Greens and Grays? And poor Ayako, who must be regretting that the Whites insisted on having a sister included. Lemai and Desandre stand highest among us." Gabrelle waved the spoon in admonishment. "The only chance we have of holding together is if you and I publicly submit to Desandre's authority. We must! That will start it, at any rate. I hope. If we can only bring a few others, to begin with, it will be a start."

Toveine drew a deep breath and pretended to stare at nothing, as if considering. Submitting to a sister who stood higher than she was no hardship, in itself. The Ajahs had always kept secrets, and sometimes schemed a little against one another, but the open dissension in the Tower now appalled her. Besides, she had learned how to be humble before Mistress Doweel. She wondered how the woman enjoyed poverty, and working on a farm for a taskmistress even harsher than herself.

"I can bring myself to it," she said finally. "We should have a plan of action to present to Desandre and Lemai, if we mean to convince them." She already had one partly formed, if not for presentation to anyone. "Oh, the water is boiling, Gabrelle."

Suddenly smiling, the foolish woman rose and hurried to the stove. Browns always were better reading books than people, come to think of it. Before Logain and Taim and the rest were destroyed, they would help Toveine Gazal bring down Elaida.

The great city of Cairhien was a hulking mass inside massive walls, crowding the River Alguenya. The sky was clear and cloudless, but a cold wind blew and the sun shone on roofs covered with snow, glinted on icicles that showed no sign of melting. The Alguenya was not frozen, but small, jagged ice floes from farther upriver spun in the currents, now and then banging against the hulls of ships waiting their turns at the docks. Trade slowed for winter and wars, and the Dragon Reborn, but it never really stopped, not until nations died. Despite the cold, wagons and carts and people flowed along streets that razored the terraced hills of the city. The City, it was called here.

In front of the square-towered Sun Palace, a crowd jammed together around the long entry ramp and stared up, merchants wrapped in fine woolens and nobles in velvets rubbing shoulders with grimy-faced laborers and dirtier refugees. No one cared who stood next to him, and even the cutpurses forgot to follow their trade. Men and women departed, often shaking their heads, but others took their places, sometimes hoisting a child to get a better view of the Palace's ruined wing, where workmen were clearing away the rubble of the third story. Throughout the rest of Cairhien, craftsmen's hammers and creaking axles filled the air, together with the cries of shopkeepers, the complaints of buyers, the murmurs of merchants. The crowd before the Sun Palace was silent.

A mile from the Palace, Rand stood at a window in the grandly named Academy of Cairhien, peering through the frosted panes at the stone-paved stableyard below. There had been schools called Academies in Artur Hawkwing's time and before, centers of learning filled with scholars from every corner of the known world. The conceit made no difference; they could have called it the Barn, so long as it did what he wanted. More important concerns filled his thoughts. Had he made a mistake, returning to Cairhien so soon? But he had been forced to flee too quickly, so it would be known in the right quarters that he actually had fled. Too quickly to prepare everything. There were questions he needed to ask, and tasks that could not be put off. And Min wanted more of Master Fel's books. He could hear her muttering to herself as she rummaged through the shelves where they had been stored after Fel's death. With the bounty for books and manuscripts it did not yet possess, the Academy's library was fast outgrowing the rooms that could be spared in Lord Barthanes' former palace. Alanna sat in the back of his head, sulking it seemed; she would know he was in the City. This near, she would be able to walk straight to him, but he would know if she tried. Blessedly, Lews Therin was silent for the moment. Of late, the man seemed madder than ever.

He rubbed a spot clear on a windowpane with his coatsleeve. Stout dark gray wool, good enough for a man with a little money and few airs, it was not a garment anyone would expect to see on the Dragon Reborn. The golden-maned Dragon's head on the back of his hand glittered metallically; it presented no danger here. His boot touched the leather scrip sitting below the window as he leaned forward to look out.

In the stableyard, the paving stones had been swept clear of snow, and a large wagon stood surrounded by buckets like mushrooms in a clearing. Half a dozen men in heavy coats and scarves and caps seemed to be working on the wagon's odd cargo, mechanical devices crowded around a fat metal cylinder that took up more than half the wagon bed. Even stranger, the wagon-shafts were missing. One of the men was moving split firewood from a large wheelbarrow into the side of a metal box fastened below one end of the big cylinder. The open door in the box glowed with the red of fire inside, and smoke rose from a tall, narrow chimney. Another fellow danced around the wagon, bearded, capless and bald-headed, gesturing and apparently shouting orders that did not seem to make the others move any faster. Their breath made faint white plumes. It was almost warm inside; the Academy had large furnaces in the cellars and an extensive system of vents. The half-healed, never healing wounds in his side were hot.

He could not make out Min's curses—he was sure they were curses—but her tone was enough to say they would not be leaving yet unless he dragged her away. There were one or two items he might ask about still. "What are people saying? About the Palace?"

"What you might expect," Lord Dobraine answered behind him with level patience, as he had answered all the other questions. Even when he admitted a lack of knowledge, his tone had not changed. "Some say the Forsaken attacked you, or that Aes Sedai did. Those who think you swore fealty to the Amyrlin Seat favor the Forsaken. Either way, there is considerable debate on whether you are dead or kidnapped or fled. Most believe you live, wherever you are, or say they do. Some, a good many I fear, think . . ." His voice faded to silence.

"That I've gone mad," Rand finished for him in the same level tone. Not a matter for concern, or anger. "That I destroyed part of the Palace myself?" He would not speak of the dead. Fewer than other times, other places, but enough, and some of their names appeared whenever he closed his eyes. One of the men below climbed down from the wagon, but the bald fellow caught his arm and dragged him back up, making him show what he had done. A man on the other side jumped to the pavement carelessly, skidding, and the capless man abandoned the first to chase around the wagon and make that one climb back up with him. What in the Light could they be doing? Rand glanced over his shoulder. "They're not far wrong."

Dobraine Taborwin, a short man with the front of his head shaved and formally powdered and the rest of his hair nearly all gray, looked back with dark impassive eyes. Not a handsome man, but steady. Blue-and-white stripes marched down the front of his dark velvet coat from his neck almost to his knees. His signet ring was a carved ruby, and he wore another at his collar, not much larger yet flamboyant for a Cairhienin. He was High Seat of his House, with more battles behind him than most, and not much frightened him. He had proved that at Dumai's Wells.

But then, the stocky, graying woman patiently waiting her turn at his shoulder appeared just as unafraid. In sharp contrast to Dobraine's noble elegance, Idrien Tarsin's sensible brown woolens were plain enough for a shopkeeper, yet she had her own well of authority and dignity. Idrien was Headmistress of the Academy, the title she had given herself since most of the scholars and mechanics called themselves master of this or mistress of that. She ran the school with a strong hand and believed in practical things, new methods of surfacing roads or making dyes, improvements to foundries and mills. She also believed in the Dragon Reborn. Whether or not that was practical, it was pragmatic, and he would settle for that.

He turned back to the window and cleared his patch on the glass again. Maybe it was for heating water—some of those buckets seemed to have water in them still; in Shienar, they used big boilers to heat water for the baths—but why on a wagon? "Has anyone left suddenly since I went? Or come unexpectedly?"

He did not expect that anyone had, anyone of importance to him. Between merchants' pigeons and White Tower eyes-and-ears—and Mazrim Taim; he must not forget Taim; Lews Therin snarled wordlessly at the name—with all those pigeons and spies and babbling tongues, in a few more days the whole world would be aware that he had vanished from Cairhien. All the world that mattered, here and now. Cairhien was no longer the ground where the battle would be fought. Dobraine's answer surprised him.

"No one, except . . . Ailil Riatin and some high Sea Folk official are both missing since the . . . attack." A bare pause, but a pause. Perhaps he was not so sure what had happened, either. Yet he would keep his word. He had proved that at Dumai's Wells, too. "No bodies were found, but they may have been killed. The Sea Folk Wavemistress refuses to countenance the possibility, though. She is raising a storm with demands that her woman be produced. In truth, Ailil may have fled to the countryside. Or gone to join her brother, despite her pledges to you. Your three Asha'man are still in the Sun Palace. Flinn, Narishma and Hopwil. They make people nervous. More so now than before." The Headmistress made a sound in her throat, and her shoes shifted audibly on the floorboards. They certainly made her nervous.

Rand dismissed the Asha'man. Unless much closer than the Palace, none was strong enough to have felt him open a gateway here. Those three had not been part of the attack on him, but a wise planner might have considered the chance of failure. Planned how to keep someone close to him if he survived. *You won't survive*, Lews Therin whispered. *None of us will survive.*

Go back to sleep, Rand thought irritably. He knew he was not going to survive. But he wanted to. A derisive laugh answered in his head, but the sound thinned and was gone. The bald man was letting the others climb down, now, and rubbing his hands together in a pleased fashion. Of all things, the fellow seemed to be giving a speech!

"Ailil and Shalon are alive, and they didn't flee," Rand said aloud. He had left them bound and gagged, stuffed under a bed, where they would have been found by servants in a few hours, though the shield he had woven on the Sea Folk Windfinder would have dissipated before that. The two women should have been able to free themselves then. "Look to Cadsuane. She'll have them in Lady Arilyn's palace."

"Cadsuane Sedai is in and out of the Sun Palace as if it were her own," Dobraine said judiciously, "but how could she have taken them out unseen? And why? Ailil is Toram's sister, yet his claim to the Sun Throne is dust now, if it was ever more. She is unimportant even as a counter, now. As for holding an Atha'an Miere of high rank . . . To what purpose?"

Rand made his voice light, uncaring. "Why is she keeping Lady Caraline and High Lord Darlin as 'guests,' Dobraine? Why do Aes Sedai do anything? You'll find them where I said. If she lets you in to look." Why was not a foolish question. He just did not have the answer. Of course, Caraline Damodred and Ailil Riatin did represent the last two Houses to hold the Sun Throne. And Darlin Sisnera led the nobles in Tear who wanted him thrown out of their precious Stone, out of Tear.

Rand frowned. He had been sure Cadsuane was focused on him despite her pretense otherwise, but what if it was not pretense? A relief, if so. Of course it was. The last thing he needed was an Aes Sedai who thought she could meddle in his affairs. The very last. Perhaps Cadsuane was directing her meddling elsewhere. Min had seen Sisnera wearing a strange crown; Rand had thought a great deal on that viewing of hers. He did not want to think of other things she had seen, concerning himself and the Green sister. Could it be as simple as Cadsuane thinking she could decide who would rule both Tear and Cairhien?

Simple? He almost laughed. But that was how Aes Sedai behaved. And Shalon, the Windfinder? Possessing her might give Cadsuane leverage with Harine, the Wavemistress, but he suspected she had just been scooped up with Ailil, to try hiding who took the noblewoman. Cadsuane would have to be disabused. Who would rule in Tear and Cairhien had already been decided. He would point that out to her. Later. It stood far down his list of priorities.

"Before I go, Dobraine, I need to give you—" Words froze on his tongue.

In the stableyard, the capless man had pulled a lever on the wagon, and one end of a long horizontal beam suddenly rose, then sank, driving a shorter beam down through a hole cut in the wagon bed. And, vibrating till it seemed ready to shake apart, trailing smoke from the chimney, the wagon lurched ahead, the beam rising and falling, slowly at first, then faster. It moved, without horses!

He did not realize he had spoken aloud until the Headmistress answered him.

"Oh, that! That's Mervin Poel's steamwagon, as he calls it, my Lord Dragon." Disapproval freighted her high, startlingly youthful voice. "Claims he can pull a hundred wagons with the contraption. Not unless he can make it go further than fifty paces without bits breaking or freezing up. It has only done that far once, that I know."

Indeed, the—steamwagon?—shuddered to a halt not twenty paces from where it first stood. Shuddered indeed; it seemed to be shaking harder by the heartbeat. Most of the men swarmed over it again, one of them frantically twisting at something with a cloth wrapped around his hand. Abruptly steam shot into the air from a pipe, and the shuddering slowed, stopped.

Rand shook his head. He remembered seeing this fellow Mervin, with a device that quivered on a tabletop and did nothing. And this marvel had come from that? He had thought it was meant to make music. That must be Mervin leaping about and shaking his fists at the others. What other odd things, what marvels, were people building here at the Academy?

When he asked, still watching the men in the courtyard work on the wagon, Idrien sniffed loudly. Respect for the Dragon Reborn held only a thin edge in her voice as she began, and quickly lost ground to disgust. "Bad enough I must give space to philosophers and historians and arithmetists and the like, but you said take in anyone who wanted to make anything new and let them stay if they showed progress. I suppose you hoped for weapons, but now I have dozens of dreamers and wastrels on my hands, every one with an old book or manuscript or six, *all* of which date back to the Compact of the Ten Nations, mind, if not the Age of Legends itself, or so they say, and they are all trying to make sense of drawings and sketches and descriptions of things they've never seen and maybe nobody ever did see. *I* have seen old manuscripts that talk about people with their eyes in their bellies, and animals ten feet tall with tusks longer than a man, and cities where—"

"But what are they making, Headmistress Tarsin?" Rand demanded. The men working on the thing below moved with an air of purpose, not as if they saw failure. And it had moved.

She sniffed louder this time. "Foolishness, my Lord Dragon, that is what they make. Kin Tovere constructed his big looking glass. You can see the moon through it plain as your hand, and what he claims are other worlds, but what is the good of that? He wants to build a bigger, now. Maryl Harke makes huge kites she calls gliders, and come spring, she will be throwing herself off hills again. Puts your heart in your mouth to see her sailing downhill on the things; she will break more than her arm next time one folds up on her, I warrant. Jander Parentakis believes he can move riverboats with waterwheels off a mill, or near enough, but when he put enough men into the boat to turn the cranks, there was no room for cargo, and any craft with sails could outrun it. Ryn Anhara traps lightning in big jars—I doubt even he knows why—and Niko Tokama is just as silly with her—"

Rand spun around so fast that she stepped back, and even Dobraine shifted on his feet, a swordsman's move. No, they were not sure of him at all. "He traps lightning?" he asked quietly.

Comprehension flooded her blunt face, and she waved her hands in front of her. "No, no! Not like . . . like that!" Not like you, she had almost said. "It is a thing of wires and wheels and big clay jars and the Light knows what. He calls it lightning, and I saw a rat jump down on one of the jars once, on the metal rods sticking out of the top. It certainly looked struck by lightning." A hopeful tone entered her voice. "I can make him stop, if you wish."

He tried to picture someone riding on a kite, but the image was ludicrous. Catching lightning in jars was beyond his ability to imagine. And yet . . . "Let them go on as before, Headmistress. Who knows? Maybe one of these inventions will turn out to be important. If any work as claimed, give the inventor a reward."

Dobraine's leathery, sun-darkened face looked dubious, though he almost managed to conceal it. Idrien bowed her head in sullen assent, and even curtsied, but plainly she thought he was asking to let pigs fly if they could.

Rand was not certain he disagreed. Then again, maybe one of the pigs *would* grow wings. The wagon *had* moved. He wanted very badly to leave something behind, something to help the world survive the new Breaking the Prophecies said he would bring. The trouble was, he had no idea what that might be, save for the schools themselves. Who knew what a marvel could do? Light, he wanted to build *something* that could last.

I thought I could build, Lews Therin murmured in his head. *I was wrong. We are not builders, not you, or I, or the other one. We are destroyers. Destroyers.*

Rand shivered, and scrubbed his hands through his hair. The other one? At times, the voice sounded sanest when it was the most mad. They were watching him, Dobraine very nearly hiding uncertainty, Idrien making no effort to. Straightening as if nothing was wrong, he drew two slim packets from inside his coat. Both carried the Dragon in a long lump of red wax on the outside. The belt buckle he was not wearing at the moment served for an impressive signet.

"The top one names you my steward in Cairhien," he said, handing the packets to Dobraine. A third still nestled next to his chest, for Gregorin den Lushenos, making him steward in Illian. "So there'll be no trouble with anyone questioning your authority while I'm gone." Dobraine could handle that sort of trouble with his armsmen, but best to make sure no one could claim ignorance or doubt. Maybe there would be no trouble to handle if everyone believed the Dragon Reborn would descend on transgressors. "There are orders about things I want done, but aside from those, use your own judgment. When the Lady Elayne lays claim to the Sun Throne, throw your full support behind her." Elayne. Oh, Light, Elayne, and Aviendha. At least they were safe. Min's voice sounded happier, now; she must have found Master Fel's books. He was going to let her follow him to her death because he was not strong enough to stop her. *Ilyena,* Lews Therin moaned. *Forgive me, Ilyena!* Rand's voice came out as cold as winter's heart. "You'll know when to deliver the other. Whether to deliver it. Pry him out if need be, and decide by what he says. If you decide no, or he refuses, I'll pick someone else. Not you."

Perhaps that was brusque, but Dobraine's expression hardly changed. His eyebrows rose slightly at the name written on the second packet; that was all. He made a smooth bow. Cairhienin usually were smooth. "It shall be as you say. Forgive me, but you sound as though you mean to be gone a long while."

Rand shrugged. He trusted the High Lord as far as he trusted anyone. Almost as far. "Who can say? The times are uncertain. Make sure Headmistress Tarsin has whatever coin she needs, and the men starting the school in Caemlyn. The school in Tear, as well, until matters change there."

"As you say," Dobraine repeated, tucking the packets into his coat. His face betrayed no emotion, now. An experienced player in the Game of Houses, was Dobraine.

For her part, the Headmistress managed to look pleased and disgruntled at the same time, and busied herself smoothing her dress unnecessarily the way women did when hard-pressed not to speak their minds. Complain how she would about dreamers and philosophers, she was jealous of the Academy's well-being. She would shed no tears if those other schools vanished and their scholars were forced to come to the Academy. Even the philosophers. What would she think of one particular order in Dobraine's packet?

"I've found everything I need," Min said, coming out from the shelves staggering slightly under the weight of the three bulging cloth scrips that hung from her. Her plain brown coat and breeches were very like what she had worn when he first saw her in Baerlon. For some reason, she had grumbled over them until anyone who knew her would have thought he was asking her to put on a dress. She smiled now, though, with delight and a hint of mischief. "I hope those packhorses are where we left them, or my Lord Dragon will have to be fitted for a packsaddle."

Idrien gasped, scandalized to hear him addressed so, but Dobraine merely smiled a little. He had seen Min around Rand before.

Rand got rid of them as quickly as possible then, since they had heard and seen as much as he wanted them to— sent them off with a final admonition that he had never been there at all. Dobraine nodded as if he had expected no less.

Idrien looked thoughtful as she left. If she let anything slip where a servant could hear, or a scholar, it would be all over the City in two days. There was not much time in any case. Perhaps no one who could tell had been close enough to feel him open a gateway here, but anyone looking for the signs would be sure by now there was a *ta'veren* in the city. It was not his plan to be found yet.

When the door closed behind them, he studied Min for a moment, then took one of the scrips and slung it from his shoulder.

"Only one?" she said. Setting the others on the floor, she planted her fists on her hips and scowled. "Sometimes you really are a sheepherder. These bags must be a hundred-weight each." But she sounded more amused than upset.

"You should have picked smaller books," he told her, pulling on riding gloves to hide the Dragons. "Or lighter." He turned toward the window, to fetch the leather scrip, and a wave of dizziness hit him. Knees turning to water, he stumbled. A shimmering face he could not make out flashed through his head. With an effort, he caught himself, forced his legs straight. And the whirling sensation vanished. Lews Therin panted hoarsely in the shadows. Could the face be his?

"If you think you'll make me carry them all that way, think again," Min grumbled. "I've seen better pretending from stablehands. You could try falling down."

"Not this time." He was ready for what happened when he channeled; he could control it to some extent. Usually. Most of the time. This dizziness without *saidin* was new. Maybe he had just turned too fast. And maybe pigs *did* fly. He settled the leather scrip's strap over his free shoulder. The men in the stableyard were still busy. Building. "Min—"

Her brows lowered immediately. She paused for an instant in drawing on her red gloves and began tapping her foot. A dangerous sign with any woman, especially one who carried knives. "We had this out, Rand bloody Dragon Reborn al'Thor! You are *not* leaving me behind!"

"The thought never crossed my mind," he lied. He was too weak; he could not make himself say the words, to make her stay. *Too weak,* he thought bitterly, *and she might well die for it, the Light burn me forever!*

It will, Lews Therin promised softly.

"I just thought you should know what we've been doing, and what we are going to do," Rand went on. "I haven't been very forthcoming, I suppose." Gathering himself, he seized *saidin.* The room seemed to whirl, and he rode the avalanche of fire and ice and filth with nausea seething in his belly. He was able to stand erect without swaying, though. Barely. And just able to weave the flows of a gateway that opened into a snowy clearing where two saddled horses were tethered to a low branch of an oak.

He was glad to see the animals still there. The clearing was well away from the nearest road, but there were still wanderers who had turned their backs on families and farms, trades and crafts, because the Dragon Reborn had broken all bonds. The Prophecies said so. On the other hand, a good many of those men and women, footsore and half-frozen now on top of it, were tired of searching without any notion what they were searching for. Even these nondescript mounts surely would have vanished with the first man to find them unattended. He had gold enough to buy others, but he did not think Min would have enjoyed the hour's walk to the village where they had left the packhorses.

Hurrying through into the clearing, pretending the change from floor to knee-deep snow caused his stumble, he only waited until she had snatched up her bags of books and staggered through after him before releasing the Power. They were five hundred miles from Cairhien, and nearer Tar Valon than anywhere else of note. Alanna had faded in his head when the gateway closed.

"Forthcoming?" Min said, sounding suspicious. Of his motives, he hoped, or anything but the truth. The dizziness and nausea faded slowly. "You have been as open as a mussel, Rand, but I am not blind. First we Traveled to Rhuidean, where you asked so many questions about this Shara place that anybody would think you meant to go there." Frowning faintly, she shook her head as she fastened one of her burdens to the saddle of her brown gelding. She grunted with the effort, but she was not about to set the other bag of books down in the snow. "I never thought the Aiel Waste was like that. That city is bigger than Tar Valon, even if it is half ruined. And all those fountains, and the lake. I couldn't even see the far side. I thought there wasn't any water in the Waste. And it was as cold as here; I thought the Waste was hot!"

"In summer, you fry during the day, but you still freeze at night." He felt recovered enough to begin shifting his own burdens to the gray's saddle. Almost enough. He did it anyway. "If you already know everything, what was I doing besides asking questions?"

"The same as in Tear last night. Making sure every cat and blackbird knew you were there. In Tear, it was Chachin you asked about. It's obvious. You are trying to confuse anyone who tries to find out where you are and where you're going next." The second bag of books balancing the first behind her saddle, she untied her reins and climbed into the saddle. "So, am I blind?"

"Your eyes belong on an eagle." He hoped his pursuers saw as clearly. Or that whoever directed them did. It would not do to have them haring off the Light knew where. "I need to lay some more false trails, I think."

"Why take the time? I know you have a plan, I know it concerns something in that leather scrip—a *sa'angreal*?— and I know it's important. Don't look so surprised. You barely let that bag out of your sight. Why not go ahead and do whatever it is you plan, *then* lay your false trails? And the real one, of course. You're going to turn on them when they least expect it, you said. You can hardly do that unless they follow where you want."

"I wish you'd never started reading Herid Fel's books," he muttered sourly, pulling himself into the gray's saddle. His head spun only a little. "You puzzle out too much. Can I keep any secrets at all from you, now?"

"You never could, woolhead," she laughed, and then, contradicting herself, "What *are* you planning? Aside from killing Dashiva and the rest, I mean. I have a right to know if I'm traveling with you." As if she had not insisted on traveling with him.

"I'm going to cleanse the male half of the Source," he said in a flat voice. A momentous announcement. A grand scheme, more than grand. Grandiose, most would say. He might have said he intended to take an afternoon stroll, for all of Min's reaction. She simply looked at him, hands folded on the pommel of her saddle, until he went on.

"I don't know how long it will take, and once I start, I think everyone within a thousand miles of me who can channel will know something is happening. I doubt I'll be able to just stop if Dashiva and the rest, or the Forsaken, suddenly appear to see what it is. The Forsaken, I can't do anything about, but with luck, I can finish the others." Maybe being *ta'veren* would give him the edge he needed so desperately.

"Depend on luck, and Corlan Dashiva or the Forsaken, either one, will have you for breakfast," she said, turning her horse out of the clearing. "Maybe I can think of a better way. Come on. There's a warm fire at that inn. I hope you're going to let us have a hot meal before we leave."

Rand stared after her incredulously. You would have thought five renegade Asha'man, not to mention the Forsaken, were less bother than a sore tooth. Booting the gray ahead in a spray of snow, he caught up to her and rode in silence. He still had a few secrets from her, this sickness that had begun affecting him when he channeled, for one. That was the real reason he had to deal with Dashiva and the others first. It gave him time to get over the sickness. If that was possible. If not, he was not sure the two *ter'angreal* riding behind his saddle were going to be any use at all.

CHAPTER
I

Leaving the Prophet

The Wheel of Time turns, and Ages come and pass, leaving memories that become legend. Legend fades to myth, and even myth is long forgotten when the Age that gave it birth comes again. In one Age, called the Third Age by some, an Age yet to come, an Age long past, a wind rose above the Aryth Ocean. The wind was not the beginning. There are neither beginnings nor endings to the turning of the Wheel of Time. But it was *a* beginning.

East the wind blew above the cold gray-green ocean swells, toward Tarabon, where ships already unloaded or waiting their turns to enter the harbor of Tanchico tossed at anchor for miles along the low coastline. More ships, great and small, filled the huge harbor, and barges ferrying people and cargo ashore, for there was no mooring empty at any of the city's docks. The inhabitants of Tanchico had been fearful when the city fell to its new masters, with their peculiar customs and strange creatures and women held on leashes who could channel, and fearful again when this fleet arrived, mind-numbing in its size, and began disgorging not only soldiers but sharp-eyed merchants, and craftsfolk with the tools of their trades, and even families with wagons full of farm implements and unknown plants. There was a new King and a new Panarch to order the laws, though, and if King and Panarch owed fealty to some far distant Empress, if Seanchan nobles occupied many of the palaces and demanded deeper obeisance than any Taraboner lord or lady, life was little changed for most people, except for the better. The Seanchan Blood had small contact with ordinary folk, and odd customs could be lived with. The anarchy that had ripped the country apart was just a memory, now, and hunger with it. The rebels and bandits and Dragonsworn who had plagued the land were dead or captured or driven north onto Almoth Plain, those who had not yielded, and trade moved once more. The hordes of starving refugees that had clogged the city streets were back in their villages, back on their farms. And no more of the newest arrivals remained in Tanchico than the city could support easily. Despite the snows, soldiers and merchants, craftsfolk and farmers fanned out inland in their thousands and tens of thousands, but the icy wind lashed a Tanchico at peace and, after its harsh troubles, for the most part content with its lot.

East the wind blew for leagues, gusting and fading, dividing but never dying, east and veering to the south, across forests and plains wrapped in winter, bare-branched and brown-grassed, at last crossing what had once been the border between Tarabon and Amadicia. A border still, but only in name, the customs posts dismantled, the guards gone. East and south, around the southern reaches of the Mountains of Mist, swirling across high-walled Amador. Conquered Amador. The banner atop the massive Fortress of the Light snapped in the wind, the golden hawk it bore truly seeming to fly with lightning bolts clutched in its talons. Few natives left their homes except at need, and those few hurried along the frozen streets, cloaks clutched around them and eyes down. Eyes down not just to mind footing on slick paving stones but to avoid looking at the occasional Seanchan riding by on a beast like a bronze-scaled cat the size of a horse, or steel-veiled Taraboners guarding groups of onetime Children of the Light, now chained and laboring like animals to haul refuse wagons out of the city. A bare month and a half in the Seanchan fold, the people of Amadicia's capital city felt the bitter wind like a scourge, and those who did not curse their fate meditated on what sins had brought them to this.

East the wind howled over a desolated land where as many villages lay burned and farms ruined as held people. Snow blanketed charred timbers and abandoned barns alike, softening the view even as it added freezing to starvation as a way of dying. Sword and axe and spear had been there already, and remained to kill again. East, until the wind moaned a dirge over unwalled Abila. No banners flew above the town's watchtowers, for the Prophet of the Lord Dragon was there, and the Prophet needed no banner save his name. In Abila, people shivered harder at the name of the Prophet than they did for the wind. People elsewhere shivered at that name, too.

Striding out of the tall merchant's house where Masema lived, Perrin let the wind whip his fur-lined cloak as he pulled on his gloves. The midday sun gave no warmth, and the air bit deep. He kept his face smooth, but he was too angry to feel the cold. Keeping his hands from the axe at his belt was an effort. Masema—he would not call the man Prophet, not in his own head he would not!—Masema was very likely a fool, and very certainly insane. A powerful fool, more powerful than most kings, and mad with it.

Masema's guards filled the street from side to side and stretched around the corners of the next streets, bony fellows in stolen silks, beardless apprentices in torn coats, once-plump merchants in the remains of fine woolens. Their breath was white mist, and some shivered without a cloak, but every man clutched a spear, or a crossbow with the bolt in place. Still, none looked outwardly hostile. They knew he claimed acquaintance with the Prophet, and they gaped as if expecting him to leap into the air and fly. Or at least turn somersaults. He filtered out the smell of woodsmoke from the town's chimneys. The lot of them stank of old sweat and unwashed bodies, of eagerness and fear. And of a strange fever he had not recognized before, a reflection of the madness in Masema. Hostile or not, they would kill him, or anyone, at Masema's word. They would butcher nations at Masema's word. Smelling them, he felt a coldness deeper than any winter wind. He was gladder than ever that he had refused to let Faile come with him.

The men he had left with the mounts were playing at dice alongside the animals, or going though the motions of it, on a space of paving stones scraped mostly clear of snowy slush. He did not trust Masema as far as he could throw his bay, and nor did they. They were paying more mind to the house, and the guards, than to their game. The three Warders sprang to their feet as soon as he appeared, their eyes going to his companions coming out behind him. They knew what their Aes Sedai had felt inside there. Neald was slower, pausing to scoop up the dice and coins. The Asha'man was a popinjay, always stroking his curled mustaches, strutting and smirking at women, but he stood on the balls of his feet now, wary as a cat.

"I thought we'd have to fight our way out of there for a time," Elyas murmured at Perrin's shoulder. His golden eyes were calm, though. A lanky old man in a broad-brimmed hat, with graying hair that hung down his back to his waist and a long beard fanning across his chest. A long knife at his belt, not a sword. But he had been a Warder. He still was, in a way.

"That's the only thing that went right," Perrin told him, taking Stayer's reins from Neald. The Asha'man quirked an eyebrow questioningly, but Perrin shook his head, not caring what the question was, and Neald, with a twist to his mouth, handed Elyas the reins of his mouse-colored gelding before climbing onto his own dapple.

Perrin had no time for the Murandian's sulks. Rand had sent him to bring back Masema, and Masema was coming. As always of late when he thought of Rand, colors swirled in his head, and as always, he ignored them. Masema was too great a problem for Perrin to waste thought fretting over colors. The bloody man thought it blasphemy for anyone but Rand to touch the One Power. Rand, it seemed, was not really mortal; he was the Light made flesh! So there would be no Traveling, no quick leap to Cairhien through a gateway made by one of the Asha'man, no matter how Perrin had tried to bring Masema around. They would have to ride the whole four hundred leagues or more, through the Light alone knew what. And keep it secret who they were, and Masema as well. Those had been Rand's orders.

"There's only one way I can see to do it, boy," Elyas said as if he had spoken aloud. "A slim chance. We might have had better odds knocking the fellow on the head and fighting clear anyway."

"I know," Perrin growled. He had thought of it more than once during the hours of argument. With Asha'man and Aes Sedai and Wise Ones all channeling, it might have been possible. But he had seen a battle fought with the One Power, men ripped to blood-soaked shreds in the blink of an eye, the earth itself blooming in fire. Abila would have been a butcher's yard before they were done. He would never look on the like again, if he had his way.

"What do you think this Prophet will make of it?" Elyas asked.

Perrin had to clear his mind of Dumai's Wells, and Abila looking like the field at Dumai's Wells, before he could think of what Elyas was talking about. Oh. How he was going to do the impossible. "I don't care what he makes of it." The man would make trouble, that was for certain sure.

Irritably, he rubbed at his beard. He needed to trim it. To have it trimmed, rather. If he picked up the scissors, Faile would take them away and give them to Lamgwin. It still seemed impossible that that hulking shoulderthumper with his scarred face and sunken knuckles should know the skills of a bodyservant. Light! A bodyservant. He was finding his footing with Faile and her strange Saldaean ways, but the better his footing, the more she managed to run things to suit herself. Women always did that anyway, of course, but sometimes he thought he had exchanged one sort of whirl-wind for another. Maybe he could try some of this master-ful shouting she seemed to like so much. A man ought to be able to put scissors to his own beard if he wanted. He doubted he would, though. Shouting at her was hard enough when she began shouting first. Fool thing to be thinking about now, anyway.

He studied the others making their way to the horses as he would have studied tools he needed for a hard job of work. He was afraid Masema would make this journey as bad a job as he had ever taken on, and his tools were full of cracks.

Seonid and Masuri paused beside him, the hoods of their cloaks pulled well forward, putting their faces in shadow. A razor-sharp quivering laced the faint scent of their per-fumes, fear under control. Masema would have killed them on the spot if he had had his way. The guards still might, if any recognized an Aes Sedai face. Among this many, there had to be some who could. Masuri was the taller by almost a hand, but Perrin still looked down on the tops of their heads. Ignoring Elyas, the sisters exchanged glances sheltered within their cowls; then Seonid spoke quietly.

"Do you see now why he must be killed? The man is . . . rabid." Well, the Green was seldom one to mince words. Luckily, none of the guards was close enough to overhear.

"You could choose a better place to say that," he said. He did not want to hear the arguments again, now or later, but especially not now. And it seemed he did not have to.

Edarra and Carelle loomed behind the Aes Sedai, dark shawls already wrapped around their heads. The bits that hung down across chest and back hardly seemed any protection from the cold, but then, snow bothered the Wise Ones more, just the existence of such a thing. Their sundark faces might have been carved for all they revealed, yet the scent of them was a steel spike, Edarra's blue eyes, usually so composed that they seemed odd set in her youthful features, were as hard as that spike. Of course, her composure masked steel. Sharp steel.

"This is no place for talking," Carelle told the Aes Sedai mildly, tucking a strand of fiery red hair beneath her shawl. As tall as many men, she was always mild. For a Wise One. Which only meant she did not bite your nose off without giving warning first. "Get to your horses."

And the shorter women curtsied to her briefly and hurried to their saddles as if they were not Aes Sedai at all. They were not, to the Wise Ones. Perrin thought he would never grow accustomed to that. Even if Masuri and Seonid seemed to have done so.

With a sigh, he swung up onto Stayer as the Wise Ones followed their Aes Sedai apprentices. The stallion frisked a few steps after his rest, but Perrin brought him under control with the pressure of his knees and steady hands on the reins. The Aiel women mounted awkwardly even after all the practice they had had these past weeks, their heavy skirts pushed up to bare wool-stockinged legs above the knee. They agreed with the two sisters about Masema, and so did the other Wise Ones back at his camp. A fine boiling stew for anyone to carry to Cairhien without being scalded.

Grady and Aram were already mounted, and he could not make out their scents among all the others. There was little need. He had always thought Grady looked a farmer despite his black coat and the silver sword on his collar, but not now. Statue-still in his saddle, the stocky Asha'man surveyed the guards with the grim eyes of a man deciding where to make the first cut. And the second, and third, and however many were needed. Aram, bilious green Tinker's cloak flailing the wind as he handled his reins, the hilt of his sword rising above his shoulder—Aram's face was a map of excitement that made Perrin's heart sink. In Masema, Aram had met a man who had given his life and heart and soul to the Dragon Reborn. In Aram's view, the Dragon Reborn ranked close behind Perrin and Faile.

You did the boy no favor, Elyas had told Perrin. *You helped him let go of what he believed, and now all he has to believe in is you and that sword. It's not enough, not for any man.* Elyas had known Aram when Aram was still a Tinker, before he picked up the sword.

A stew that might have poison in it, for some.

The guards might gaze at Perrin in wonder, but they did not move to clear a passage until someone shouted from a window of the house. Then they edged aside enough for the riders to leave single file. Reaching the Prophet was not easy, without his permission. Without his permission, leaving him was impossible.

Once away from Masema and his guards, Perrin set as fair a pace as he could through the crowded streets. Abila had been a large, prosperous town not so long ago, with its stone marketplaces, and slate-roofed buildings as tall as four stories. It was still large, but mounds of rubble marked where houses and inns had been torn down. Not an inn remained standing in Abila, or a house where someone had been slow to proclaim the glory of the Lord Dragon Reborn. Masema's disapproval was never subtle.

The throng held few who looked as if they lived in the town, drab folk in drab clothes for the most part scuttling fearfully along the sides of the street, and no children. No dogs, either; hunger was a likely problem in this place, now. Everywhere groups of armed men straggled through the ankle-deep muck that had been snow last night, twenty here, fifty there, knocking down people too slow to get out of their path, even making the ox-carts wend around them. There were always hundreds in sight. There had to be thousands in the town. Masema's army was a rabble, but their numbers had made up for other lacks so far. Thank the Light the man had agreed to bring along only a hundred. It had taken an hour's argument, but he had agreed. In the end, Masema's desire to reach Rand quickly, even if he would not Travel, had won the point. Few of his followers had horses, and the more that came afoot, the slower they would go. At least he would arrive at Perrin's camp by nightfall.

Perrin saw no one mounted except his own party, and they drew stares from the armed men, stony stares, fevered stares. Finely dressed folk came to the Prophet often enough, nobles and merchants hoping a submission in person would gain more blessings and fewer penalties, but they usually departed afoot. Their way was unimpeded, however, aside from the necessity of riding around the clumps of Masema's followers. If they left mounted, it must be by Masema's will. Even so, Perrin had no need to tell anyone to stay close. There was a feel of waiting in Abila, and no one with half a brain would want to be near when the waiting ended.

It was a relief when Balwer kneed his hammer-nosed gelding out of a side street just short of the low wooden bridge that led out of town, almost as great as the relief he felt when they had crossed the bridge and passed the last guards. The pinch-faced little man, all knobby joints and with his plain brown coat more hanging on him than worn, could look after himself in spite of appearances, but Faile was setting up a proper household for a noblewoman, and she would be more than displeased if Perrin let any harm come to her secretary. Hers, and Perrin's. Perrin was not sure how he felt about having a secretary, yet the fellow possessed skills beyond writing a fine hand. Which he demonstrated as soon as they were clear of the town, with low, forested hills all around. Most of the branches were stark and bare, and those that retained leaf or needle splashed a vivid green against the white. They had the road to themselves, but snow frozen in ruts kept their riding slow.

"Forgive me, my Lord Perrin," Balwer murmured, leaning in his saddle to peer past Elyas, "but I happened to overhear something back there you might find of interest." He coughed discreetly into his glove, then hurriedly recaptured his cloak and pulled it close.

Elyas and Aram hardly needed Perrin's gesture to fall

back with the others. Everyone was accustomed to the dry little man's desire for privacy. Why he wanted to pretend that no one else knew he ferreted out information at every town or village they passed, Perrin could not begin to guess. He had to know that Perrin discussed what he learned with Faile, and Elyas. In any case, he was very good at ferreting.

Balwer tilted his head to one side to watch Perrin as they rode side by side. "I have two pieces of news, my Lord, one I believe important, and one urgent." Urgent or not, even the fellow's voice sounded dry, like dead leaves rustling.

"How urgent?" Perrin made a wager with himself over who the first piece of news would be about.

"Very, perhaps, my Lord. King Ailron has brought the Seanchan to battle near the town of Jeramel, approximately one hundred miles west of here. This was about ten days ago." Balwer's mouth pursed momentarily in irritation. He disliked imprecision; he disliked not knowing. "Reliable information is scarce, but without doubt, the Amadician army is dead, captive or scattered. I would be very surprised if more than a hundred remain together anywhere, and those will take to banditry soon enough. Ailron himself was taken, along with his entire court. Amadicia no longer has any nobility, not to amount to anything."

Mentally, Perrin marked the wager lost. Usually, Balwer began with news of the Whitecloaks. "A pity for Amadicia, I suppose. For the people captured, anyway." According to Balwer, the Seanchan had a harsh way with those captured under arms opposing them. So Amadicia had no army left, and no nobles to raise or lead another. Nothing to stop the Seanchan spreading as fast as they wished, though they seemed to spread very quickly even when there was opposition. Best if he rode east as soon as Masema reached the camp, and then moved as fast as he could for as long as the men and horses could sustain it.

He said as much, and Balwer nodded, with a thin smile of approval. The man appreciated it when Perrin saw the value of what he reported.

"One other point, my Lord," he went on. "The White-cloaks took part in the battle, but apparently Valda managed to get most of them off the field at the end. He has the Dark One's own luck. No one seems to know where they have gone. Or rather, every tongue gives a different direction. If I may say so, I favor east. Away from the Seanchan." And toward Abila, of course.

The wager was not a loss, then. Though the man had not begun with it. A draw, maybe. Far ahead, a hawk soared high in the cloudless sky, heading north. It would reach the camp long before he would. Perrin could recall a time when he had had as few concerns as that hawk. Compared to now, at least. It had been a very long time ago.

"I suspect the Whitecloaks are more interested in avoiding the Seanchan than in bothering us, Balwer. Anyway, I can't move any faster for them than for the Seanchan. Were they the second piece of news?"

"No, my Lord. Simply a point of interest." Balwer seemed to hate the Children of the Light, most especially Valda—a matter of rough treatment somewhere in his past, Perrin suspected—but like everything else about the man, it was a dry, cold hate. Passionless. "The second news is that the Seanchan have fought another battle, this in southern Altara. Against Aes Sedai, possibly, though some mentioned men channeling." Half turning in his saddle, Balwer looked back at Grady and Neald in their black coats. Grady was in conversation with Elyas, and Neald with Aram, but both Asha'man appeared to be keeping as close an eye on the forests as did the Warders bringing up the rear. The Aes Sedai and the Wise Ones were talking in low voices, too. "Whoever they fought, my Lord, it is clear that the Seanchan lost and were sent reeling back into Ebou Dar."

"Good news," Perrin said flatly. Dumai's Wells flashed into his head again, stronger than before. For a moment, he was back-to-back with Loial again, fighting desperately, sure that every breath would be his last. For the first time that day, he shivered. At least Rand knew about the Seanchan. At least he did not have to worry about that.

He became aware of Balwer eyeing him. Considering him, like a bird considering a strange insect. He had seen him shiver. The little man liked to know everything, but there were some secrets no one would ever know.

Perrin's eyes returned to the hawk, barely visible now even to him. It made him think of Faile, his fierce falcon of a wife. His beautiful falcon of a wife. He put Seanchan and

Whitecloaks and battle and even Masema out of his mind. For the time, at least.

"Let's pick up the pace a little," he called back to the others. The hawk might see Faile before he did, but unlike the bird, he would be seeing the love of his heart. And today, he would not shout at her no matter what she did.

CHAPTER
2

Taken

The hawk soon passed out of sight, and the road remained empty of other travelers, but press as Perrin
would, frozen ruts ready to break a horse's leg and
a rider's neck allowed no great speed. The wind carried
ice, and a promise of snow again tomorrow. It was midafternoon by the time he turned off through the trees into
white drifts that were knee-deep on the horses in places,
and covered the last mile to the forest camp where he had
left the Two Rivers men and the Aiel, the Mayeners and
Ghealdanin. And Faile. Nothing there was as he expected.

As always, there were four camps spaced out among the
trees, in truth, but the Winged Guards' smoking campfires
stood abandoned around Berelain's striped tents, amid
overturned kettles and bits of gear dropped on the snow,
and the same signs of haste dotted the trampled ground
where Alliandre's soldiers had been set up when he left
that morning. The only evidence of life in either place was
the horse handlers and farriers and cart drivers, bundled in
woolens and huddled in clumps around the horselines and
high-wheeled supply carts. They were all staring toward
what caught his eye and held it.

Five hundred paces from the rocky, flat-topped hill where
the Wise Ones had placed their low tents, the gray-coated
Mayeners were drawn up, all nine hundred or so of them,
horses stamping impatiently, red cloaks and the long red
streamers on their lances rippling in the cold breeze. Nearer
the hill and off to one side, just at the near bank of a frozen
stream, the Ghealdanin made a block of lances just as large,
these with green streamers. The mounted soldiers' green

coats and armor appeared drab compared with the Mayeners' red helmets and breastplates, but their officers sparkled in silvered armor and scarlet coats and cloaks, with reins and saddlecloths fringed in crimson. A brave show, for men on parade, but they were not parading. The Winged Guards faced toward the Ghealdanin, the Ghealdanin toward the hill. And the crest of the hill was ringed by Two Rivers men, longbows in hand. No one had drawn, yet, but every man had a shaft nocked and ready. It was madness.

Booting Stayer to as near a gallop as the bay could manage, Perrin plowed through the snow, followed by the others, until he reached the head of the Ghealdanin formation. Berelain was there, in a fur-trimmed red cloak, and Gallenne, the one-eyed Captain of her Winged Guards, and Annoura, her Aes Sedai advisor, all apparently arguing with Alliandre's First Captain, a short, hard-bitten fellow named Gerard Arganda, who was shaking his head so hard the fat white plumes quivered on his gleaming helmet. The First of Mayene looked ready to bite iron, vexation showed through Annoura's Aes Sedai calm, and Gallenne was fingering the red-plumed helmet hanging at his saddle as though deciding whether to don it. At the sight of Perrin, they broke off and turned their mounts toward him. Berelain sat her saddle erect, but her black hair was windblown, and her fine-ankled white mare was shivering, the lather of a hard run freezing on her flanks.

With so many people about, it was all but impossible to make out individual scents, but Perrin did not need his nose to recognize trouble hanging by a hair. Before he could demand to know what in the Light they thought they were doing, Berelain spoke with a porcelain-faced formality that made him blink at first.

"Lord Perrin, your Lady wife and I were hunting with Queen Alliandre when we were attacked by Aiel. I managed to escape. No one else in the party has returned, yet, though it may be the Aiel took prisoners. I have sent a squad of lancers to scout. We were about ten miles to the southeast, so they should return with news by nightfall."

"Faile was captured?" Perrin said thickly. Even before crossing into Amadicia from Ghealdan they had heard of Aiel burning and looting, but it had always been somewhere else, the next village over or the one beyond that, if not farther. Never close enough to worry about, or to be sure they were more than rumor. Not when he had Rand bloody al'Thor's orders to carry out! And look what it had cost.

"Why are you all still here?" he demanded aloud. "Why aren't you all searching for her?" He realized he was shouting. He wanted to howl, to savage them. "Burn you all, what are you waiting for?" The levelness of her reply, as if reporting how much fodder was left for the horses, pushed needles of rage into his head. The more so because she was right.

"We were ambushed by two or three hundred, Lord Perrin, but you know as well as I, from what we have heard there easily could be a dozen or more such bands roaming the countryside. If we pursue in force, we may find a battle that will cost us heavily, against Aiel, without even knowing whether they are the ones who hold your Lady wife. Or even if she still lives. We must know that first, Lord Perrin, or the rest is worse than useless."

If she still lived. He shivered; the cold was inside him, suddenly. In his bones. His heart. She had to be alive. She had to be. Oh, Light, he should have let her come to Abila with him. Annoura's wide-mouthed face was a mask of sympathy framed by thin Taraboner braids. Suddenly he became aware of pain in his hands, cramping on the reins. He forced them to loosen their grip, flexed his fingers inside his gauntlets.

"She's right," Elyas said quietly, moving his gelding closer. "Hold on to yourself. Blunder around with Aiel, and you're asking to die. Maybe take a lot of men with you to a bad end. Dying does no good if it leaves your wife a prisoner." He tried to make his voice lighter, but Perrin could smell the strain. "Anyway, we'll find her, boy. She could well have escaped them, a woman like that. Be trying to make her way back here afoot. Take time, that would, in a dress. The First's scouts will locate traces." Raking fingers through his long beard, Elyas gave a self-deprecating chuckle. "If I can't find more than the Mayeners, I'll eat bark. We'll get her back for you."

Perrin was not fooled. "Yes," he said harshly. Nobody could escape Aiel afoot. "Go now. Hurry." Not fooled at all. The man expected to find Faile's body. She had to be alive, and that meant captive, but better a prisoner than . . .

They could not talk between themselves as they did with wolves, but Elyas hesitated as if he understood Perrin's thoughts. He did not try to deny them, though. His gelding set off southeast at a walk, as quick as the snow would allow, and after a quick glance at Perrin, Aram followed, his face dark. The one-time Tinker did not like Elyas, but he near enough worshipped Faile, if only because she was Perrin's wife.

It would do no good to founder the animals, Perrin told himself, frowning at their retreating backs. He wanted them to run. He wanted to run with them. Fine cracks seemed to be spidering through him. If they returned with the wrong news, he would shatter. To his surprise, the three Warders trotted their mounts through the trees after Elyas and Aram in splashes of snow, plain woolen cloaks streaming behind, then matched speed when they caught up.

He managed to give Masuri and Seonid a grateful nod, and included Edarra and Carelle. Whoever had made the suggestion, there was no doubt who had granted permission. It was a measure of the control the Wise Ones had established that neither sister was trying to take charge. They very likely wanted to, but their gloved hands remained folded on the pommels of their saddles, and neither betrayed impatience by so much as the flicker of an eyelid.

Not everyone was watching the departing men. Annoura alternated between beaming sympathy at him and studying the Wise Ones out of the corner of her eye. Unlike the other two sisters, she had made no promises, but she was almost as circumspect with the Aielwomen as they. Gallenne's one eye was on Berelain, awaiting a sign he should draw the sword he was gripping, while she was intent on Perrin, her face still smooth and unreadable. Grady and Neald had their heads together, casting quick, grim glances in his direction. Balwer sat very still, like a sparrow perched on the saddle, trying to be invisible, listening intently.

Arganda pushed his tall roan gelding past Gallenne's heavy-chested black, ignoring the Mayener's one-eyed glare of outrage. The First Captain's mouth worked angrily behind the shining face-bars of his helmet, but Perrin heard nothing. Faile filled his head. Oh, Light, Faile! His chest felt bound with iron straps. He was near to panic, holding to the precipice with his fingernails.

Desperately he reached out with his mind, frantically searching for wolves. Elyas must have tried this already—Elyas would not have given way to panic at the news—but he had to try himself.

Searching, he found them, Three Toes' pack and Cold Water's, Twilight's and Springhorn's and others. Pain flowed out with his plea for help, but grew greater inside him rather than less. They had heard of Young Bull, and they commiserated over the loss of his she, but they kept clear of the two-legs, who frightened away all the game and were death for any wolf caught alone. There were so many packs of two-legs about, afoot and riding the hard-footed four-legs, that they could not say whether any they knew of were the one he sought. Two-legs were two-legs, to them, indistinguishable except for those who could channel, and the few who could speak with them. Mourn, they told him, and move on, and meet her again in the wolf dream.

One by one, the images that his mind turned to words faded away, until only one lingered. Mourn, and meet her again in the wolf dream. Then that also was gone.

"Are you listening?" Arganda demanded roughly. He was not a smooth-faced noble, and despite his silks and the gold-work atop the silver of his breastplate he looked like what he was, a graying soldier who had first hefted a lance as a boy and probably carried two dozen scars. His dark eyes were almost as fevered as those of Masema's men. He smelled of rage, and fear. "Those savages took Queen Alliandre, as well!"

"We will find your Queen when we find my wife," Perrin said, his voice as cold and hard as the edge of his axe. She had to be alive. "Suppose you tell me what all this is about, you drawn up ready to charge, it looks like. And facing my people, at that." He had other responsibilities, too. Acknowledging that was bitter as gall. Nothing else counted alongside Faile. Nothing! But the Two Rivers men *were* his people.

Arganda dashed his mount close and seized Perrin's sleeve in a gauntleted fist. "You listen to me! The First Lady Berelain says it was Aiel took Queen Alliandre, and there are Aiel sheltering behind those archers of yours. I have men who will be happy enough to put them to the question." His heated gaze swung back to Edarra and Carelle for a moment. Perhaps he was thinking that they were Aiel with no archers barring his path.

"The First Captain is . . . overwrought," Berelain murmured, laying a hand on Perrin's other arm. "I have explained to him that none of the Aiel here were involved. I'm sure that I can convince him—"

He shook her off, ripped his arm away from the Ghealdanin. "Alliandre swore fealty to me, Arganda. You swore fealty to her, and that makes me your lord. I said I'll find Alliandre when I find Faile." The edge of an axe. She *was* alive. "You question no one, *touch* no one, unless I say. What you will do is take your men back to your camp, *now,* and be ready to ride when I give the order. If you're not ready when I call, you will be left behind."

Arganda stared at him, breathing hard. His eyes strayed again, this time toward Grady and Neald, then jerked back to Perrin's face. "As you command, my Lord," he said stiffly. Wheeling his roan, he shouted orders to his officers and was already galloping away before they began issuing their own. The Ghealdanin began to peel away by columns, riding after their First Captain. Toward their camp, though whether Arganda intended to remain there was anyone's guess. And whether it might not be for the worse if he did.

"You handled that very well, Perrin," Berelain said. "A difficult situation, and a painful time for you." Not formal at all, now. Just a woman full of pity, her smile compassionate. Oh, she had a thousand guises, Berelain did.

She stretched out a red-gloved hand, and he backed Stayer away before she could touch him. "Give it over, burn you!" he snarled. "My wife has been taken! I've no patience for your childish games!"

She jerked as if he had struck her. Color bloomed in her cheeks, and she changed again, becoming supple and willowy in her saddle. "Not childish, Perrin," she murmured, her voice rich and amused. "Two women contesting over you, and you the prize? I would think you'd be flattered. Attend me, Lord Captain Gallenne. I suppose we, too, should be ready to ride at command."

The one-eyed man rode back toward the Winged Guards at her side, as close to a canter as the snow made possible. He was leaning toward her as if hearing instructions. Annoura paused where she was, gathering the reins of her brown mare. Her mouth was a razored line beneath her beak of a nose. "Sometimes you are a very large fool, Perrin Aybara. Quite often, in fact."

He did not know what she was talking about, and did not care. At times she seemed resigned to Berelain chasing after a married man, and other times amused by it, even helping out by arranging for Berelain to be alone with him. Right then, First and Aes Sedai both disgusted him. Heeling Stayer in the flanks, he trotted away from her without a word.

The men on the hilltop opened enough to let him through, muttering to one another and watching the lancers below ride toward their respective camps, parted again to let the Wise Ones and Aes Sedai and Asha'man pass. They did not break up and crowd around him, as he had expected, for which he was grateful. The whole hilltop smelled of wariness. Most of it did.

The snow atop the hill had been trampled until some patches were clear except for frozen clumps and others were sheets of ice. The four Wise Ones who had remained behind when he rode to Abila were standing in front of one of the low Aiel tents, tall unruffled women with dark woolen shawls around their shoulders, watching the two sisters dismount with Carelle and Edarra, and seemingly paying no mind to what was going on around them. The *gai'shain* who served them in place of servants were going about their normal tasks quietly, meekly, faces hidden in the deep cowls of their white robes. One fellow was even beating a carpet hung over a rope tied between two trees! The only sign among the Aiel that they might have been on the brink of a fight was Gaul and the Maidens. They had been squatting on their heels, *shoufa* around their heads and black veils hiding all but their eyes, short spears and bull-hide bucklers in hand. As Perrin jumped down from his saddle, they rose.

Dannil Lewin trotted up, chewing worriedly at the thick mustache that made his nose look even bigger than it was. He had his bow in one hand and was sliding an arrow back into the quiver at his belt. "I didn't know what else to do, Perrin," he said in a jerky voice. Dannil had been at Dumai's Wells, and faced Trollocs back home, but this was outside his view of the world. "By the time we found out what happened, those Ghealdanin fellows were already starting this way, so I sent off Jondyn Barran and a couple of others, Hu Marwin and Get Ayliah, told the Cairhienin and your servants to make a circle with the carts and stay inside it—had to just about tie up those folks who're always following the Lady Faile around; they wanted to go off after her, and not a one of them knows a footprint from an oak tree—then I brought everybody else here. I thought those Ghealdanin might charge us, until the First got there with her men. They must be crazy, thinking any of our Aiel would hurt the Lady Faile." Even when they Perrined him, Faile nearly always received the honorific from the Two Rivers men.

"You did right, Dannil," Perrin said, tossing him Stayer's reins. Hu and Get were good woodsmen, and Jondyn Barran could follow yesterday's wind. Gaul and the Maidens were starting to leave, in single file. They were still veiled. "Tell off one man in three to stay here," Perrin told Dannil hurriedly; just because he had faced Arganda down was no reason to believe the man had changed his mind, "and send the rest back to pack up. I want to ride as soon as there's word."

Without waiting on a reply, he hurried to put himself in front of Gaul and stopped the taller man with a hand to his chest. For some reason, Gaul's green eyes tightened above his veil. Sulin and the rest of the Maidens strung out behind him went up on the balls of their feet.

"Find her for me, Gaul," Perrin said. "All of you, please find who took her. If anyone can track Aiel, it's you."

The tightness in Gaul's eyes vanished as suddenly as it had come, and the Maidens relaxed, too. As much as Aiel ever could be said to relax. It was very strange. They could not think he blamed them in any way.

"We all wake from the dream one day," Gaul said gently, "but if she still dreams, we will find her. But if Aiel took her, we must go. They will move quickly. Even in . . . this." He put considerable disgust in the word, kicking at a clod of snow.

Perrin nodded and hastily stepped aside, letting the Aiel set out at a trot. He doubted they could maintain that for very long, but he was sure they would keep the pace longer than anyone else could have. As the Maidens passed him, each quickly pressed fingers to the veil over her lips, then touched his shoulder. Sulin, right behind Gaul, gave him a nod, but none said a word. Faile would have known what they meant with their finger kissing.

There was something else odd about their departure, he realized as the last Maiden went by. They were letting Gaul lead. Normally, any of them would have stuck a spear in him before allowing that. Why . . . ? Maybe . . . Chiad and Bain would have been with Faile. Gaul did not care one way or the other about Bain, but Chiad was a different matter. The Maidens certainly had not been encouraging Gaul's hope that Chiad would give up the spear to marry him—anything but!—yet maybe that was it.

Perrin grunted in disgust at himself. Chiad and Bain, and who else? Even blind with fear for Faile, he should have asked that much. If he was going to get her back, he needed to strangle fear and *see*. But it was like trying to strangle a tree.

The flat hilltop swarmed now. Someone had already led Stayer away, and Two Rivers men were leaving the ring around the crest, hurrying toward their camp in a scattered stream, shouting to one another about what they would have done had the lancers charged. Occasionally a man raised his voice asking about Faile, did anyone know if the Lady was safe, were they going to look for her, but others always shushed him hurriedly with worried glances at Perrin. The *gai'shain* went about their tasks placidly in the middle of all the rush. Unless commanded to stop, they would have done the same if a battle had swirled around them, not raising a hand to help or hinder. The Wise Ones had all gone into one of the tents with Seonid and Masuri, and the flaps were not only down, but tied. They did not want to be disturbed. They would be discussing Masema, no doubt. Possibly discussing how to kill the man without him or Rand learning they had done it.

He smacked a fist into his palm in irritation. He had actually forgotten Masema until now. The man was supposed to be following before nightfall, with that honor guard of a hundred men. With luck, the Mayener scouts would be back by then, and Elyas and the others soon after.

"My Lord Perrin?" Grady said behind him, and he turned. The two Asha'man stood in front of their horses, fiddling uncertainly with their reins. Grady drew breath and went on with Neald nodding agreement. "The pair of us could cover a lot of ground, Traveling. And if we find the lot who kidnapped her, well, I doubt even a few hundred Aiel could stop two Asha'man from taking her back."

Perrin opened his mouth to tell them to start immediately, then closed it again. Grady had been a farmer, true, but never a hunter or woodsman. Neald thought any place without a stone wall was a village. They might know a footprint from an oak tree, yet if they did find tracks, very likely neither would be able to say which direction they were headed. Of course, he could go with them. He was not as good as Jondyn, but . . . He could go, and leave Dannil to deal with Arganda. And with Masema. Not to mention the Wise Ones' schemes.

"Go get yourselves packed," he said quietly. Where was Balwer? Nowhere in sight. Not very likely that *he* had gone haring off to find Faile. "You may be needed here."

Grady blinked in surprise, and Neald's mouth dropped open.

Perrin gave them no chance to argue. He strode over to the low tent with the tied flaps. There was no way to undo the ties from the outside. When Wise Ones wanted to remain undisturbed, they wanted to remain undisturbed, by clan chiefs or anyone else. Including a wetlander lumbered with the title of Lord of the Two Rivers. He drew his belt knife, and bent to slice the ties, but before he could slide the blade through the tight crack between the entry flaps, they jerked as if someone was unfastening them from inside. He straightened and waited.

The tentflaps opened, and Nevarin slipped out. Her shawl was tied around her waist, but except for the mist of her breath, she gave no evidence of the icy air. Her green eyes took in the knife in his hand, and she planted her fists on her hips in a rattle of bracelets. She was near enough bone-thin, with long sandy yellow hair held back by a dark folded kerchief, and more than a hand taller than Nynaeve, but that was who she always made him think of. She stood blocking the entrance to the tent.

"You are impetuous, Perrin Aybara." Her light voice was level, but he had the impression that she was considering boxing his ears. Very much like Nynaeve. "Though that might be understandable, in the circumstances. What do you want?"

"How . . . ?" He had to stop to swallow. "How will they treat her?"

"I cannot say, Perrin Aybara." There was no sympathy on her face, no expression at all. Aiel could give Aes Sedai lessons in that. "Taking wetlanders captive is against custom, except for Treekillers, though that has changed. So is killing without need. But many have refused to accept the truths the *Car'a'carn* revealed. Some were taken by the Bleakness and threw down their spears, yet they may have taken them up again. Others simply left, to live as they believe we are meant to. I cannot say what customs might be kept or abandoned by those who have abandoned clan and sept." The only emotion she displayed was a hint of disgust at the end, for those who abandoned clan and sept.

"Light, woman, you must have some idea! Surely you can make a guess—"

"Do not become irrational," she broke in sharply. "Men often do in such situations, but we have need of you. I think it will do your standing with the other wetlanders no good if we must bind you until you calm down. Go to your tent. If you cannot control your thoughts, drink until you cannot think. And do not bother us when we are in council." She ducked back into the tent, and the flaps jerked closed and began to twitch as they were tied again.

Perrin considered the closed flaps, running his thumb over the blade of his knife, then shoved it into the sheath. They just might do as Nevarin had threatened if he barged in. And they could not tell him anything he wanted to know. He did not think she would keep secrets at a time like this. Not about Faile, anyway.

The hilltop had grown quieter, with most of the Two Rivers men gone. The remainder, still watchful of the Ghealdanin camp below, stamped their feet against the cold, but no one talked. The scurrying *gai'shain* hardly made a sound. Trees obscured parts of the Ghealdanin and Mayener camps, but Perrin could see carts being loaded in both. He decided to leave men on guard anyway. Arganda could be trying to lull him. A man who smelled like that could be . . . *Irrational,* he finished the thought dryly.

There was nothing left for him to do on the hill, so he set

out to walk the half mile to his tent. The tent he shared with Faile. He stumbled as much as walked, laboring when the snow rose around his legs. As much to stop it snapping in the wind as for warmth, he held his cloak tight around him. There was no warmth.

The Two Rivers camp was aswarm with activity when he arrived. The carts still made a big circle, with men and women from Dobraine's estates back in Cairhien loading them, and others readying horses for saddling. In this depth of snow, cartwheels might as well have tried to roll through mud, so they were all lashed to the sides of the carts, now, replaced by pairs of broad wooden sleds. Bundled against the weather till most seemed twice as wide as they really were, the Cairhienin hardly paused to glance at him, but every Two Rivers man who saw him stopped to stare until someone else prodded the fellow to get on with whatever he was about. Perrin was glad none gave words to the sympathy in those stares. He thought he might break down and cry if anyone did.

There seemed to be nothing for him to do here, either. His big tent—his and Faile's—was already down and on a cart, along with its contents. Basel Gill was walking along the carts with a long list in his hands. The stout man had taken to the job of *shambayan,* running Faile's household, Perrin's, like a squirrel to a corn crib. More used to cities than traveling outside their walls, though, he suffered from the cold, and wore not only a cloak but a thick scarf around his neck, a floppy-brimmed felt hat and heavy woolen gloves. For some reason, Gill flinched at the sight of him, and mumbled something about seeing to the carts before hurrying off as fast as he could. Odd.

Perrin did think of one thing then, and finding Dannil, he gave orders to relieve the men on the hill every hour and make sure everyone had a hot meal.

"Take care of the men and horses first," a thin but strong voice said. "But then you must take care of yourself. There's hot soup in the kettle, and bread of a sort, and I've put by some smoked ham. A full belly will make you look less like murder walking."

"Thank you, Lini," he said. Murder walking? Light, he felt like one of the dead, not a murderer. "I'll eat in a little while."

Faile's chief maid was a frail-appearing woman, with skin like parchment and white hair in a bun on top of her head, but her back was straight and her dark eyes were clear and sharp. Worry creased her forehead now, though, and her hands gripped her cloak too tightly, straining. She would be worried about Faile, certainly, but . . .

"Maighdin was with her," he said, and did not need her nod. Maighdin was always with Faile, it seemed. A treasure, Faile called her. And Lini seemed to consider the woman her daughter, though sometimes Maighdin did not appear to enjoy that as much as Lini did. "I'll get them back," he promised. "All of them." His voice almost broke on that. "Get on with your work," he went on roughly, hurriedly. "I'll eat in a bit. I have to see to . . . to . . ." He strode away without finishing.

There was nothing he had to see to. Nothing he could think of, except Faile. He hardly knew where he was heading until his steps took him outside the circle of carts.

A hundred paces beyond the horselines, a low, stony ridge thrust a black peak through the snow. From there, he would be able to see the tracks left by Elyas and the others. From there, he would see them returning.

His nose told him he was not alone well before he reached the narrow crest of the ridge, told him who was up there. The other man was not listening, because Perrin crunched his way to the top before he sprang up from where he had been crouching on his heels. Tallanvor's gauntleted hands kneaded his long sword hilt, and he peered at Perrin uncertainly. A tall man who had taken hard knocks in his life, he usually was very sure of himself. Perhaps he expected a tirade for not having been there when Faile was taken, though she had rejected the armsman as a bodyguard, rejected any bodyguard. Beyond Bain and Chiad, at least, who apparently did not count. Or maybe he just thought he would be sent away, back to the carts, so Perrin could be alone. Perrin tried to make his face look less like—what had Lini called it?—murder walking? Tallanvor was in love with Maighdin, and would be wed to her soon if Faile's suspicions were correct. The man had a right to keep watch.

They stood there on the ridge while twilight fell, and nothing moved in the snowy forest they watched. Darkness came without movement, and without Masema, but Perrin did not even think of Masema. The gibbous moon shone white on the snow, giving nearly as much light as a full moon, it seemed. Until scudding clouds began to hide it, and moonshadows raced across the snow, thicker and thicker. Snow began to fall with a dry rustling. Snow that would bury traces and tracks. Silent in the cold, the two men stood there, watching into the snowfall, waiting, hoping.

CHAPTER
3

Customs

From the first hour after being captured, laboring through the snowy woods, Faile worried about freezing. Breezes stirred and died, stirred and died. Few of the scattered trees still carried leaves, and most of those hung dead and brown. The breezes swirled through the forest unhindered, and small as the gusts were, they carried ice. Perrin hardly entered her thoughts, except for a hope that he somehow learned of Masema's secret dealings. And of the Shaido, of course. Even if that trull Berelain was the only one who could tell him, now. She hoped Berelain had escaped the ambush and told Perrin everything. And then fallen into a hole and broken her neck. But she had far more pressing concerns than her husband.

She had called this weather autumnal, yet people froze to death in a Saldaean autumn, and of her clothes she retained only her dark woolen stockings. One lashed her elbows tight behind her back, while the second had been tied around her neck for a leash. Brave words made scant covering for bare skin. She was too cold for sweat, yet her legs soon ached with the struggle to keep up with her captors. The Shaido column, veiled men and Maidens, slowed when the snow rose toward their knees but immediately resumed a steady trot when it sank toward their ankles, and they did not seem to tire. Horses could not have moved faster over the distance. Shivering, she labored on at the end of her leash, doing her best to gulp air through teeth gritted to stop their chattering.

The Shaido were fewer than she had estimated during the attack, no more than a hundred and fifty she thought, and nearly all carried spears or bows at the ready. Small chance anyone could surprise them. Always alert, they ghosted along in silence except for the faint crunch of the snow under their soft, knee-high boots. The greens and grays and browns of their clothing stood out against the white landscape, though. Green had been added to the *cadin'sor* since crossing the Dragonwall, so Bain and Chiad had told her, to aid concealment in a green land. Why had these people not added white, for the winter? As it was, they could be seen at some distance. She tried to notice everything, remember anything that might prove useful later, when it came time to escape. She hoped her fellow prisoners were doing as much. Perrin would be hunting for her, certainly, but the thought of rescue never entered her calculations. Wait for rescue, and you might wait forever. Besides, they needed to escape as quickly as possible, before their captors joined with the rest of the Shaido. She could not see how, yet, but there must be a way. The one bit of luck was that the main body of Shaido must be days distant. This part of Amadicia was chaos, but thousands of Shaido could not be too near without her having heard of them.

Once, early on, she tried to look back at the women who had been captured with her, but the only result was a stumbling fall into a snowbank. Half-buried in the white powder, she gasped from the icy shock, and gasped again when the great hulking Shaido who held her leash set her back on her feet. As wide as Perrin and a full head taller, Rolan simply hauled her upright by a fistful of her hair, set her moving again with a brisk slap on her bare bottom, and once more took up the long strides that forced her to step quickly. The slap might have been given to make a pony move. Despite her nakedness, there was nothing of a man looking at a woman in Rolan's blue eyes. Part of her was very grateful. Part her was vaguely . . . taken aback. She certainly did not want him gazing at her with lust or even interest, but those bland glances were almost insulting! After that she made sure not to fall, though as the hours passed without a pause in the march, simply staying upright became more and more of an effort.

In the beginning she worried over which bits of her would freeze first, but by the time morning had rolled into afternoon without a pause in the march, she was focused on her feet. Rolan and those ahead of him trampled a sort of path for her, yet enough snowcrust remained for sharp edges, and she began to leave red stains freezing in her footprints. Worse was the cold itself. She had seen frostbite. How long before her toes began to turn black? Staggering, she flexed each foot as she swung it forward, and worked her hands constantly. Fingers and toes were in the worst danger, but any exposed skin was at risk. About her face and the rest of her she could only hope. The flexing hurt, making the cuts on her feet burn, but any feeling was better than none. When sensation went, she would have very little time left. Flex and stride, flex and stride. That filled her thoughts. She kept moving on quivering legs, and kept her hands and feet from freezing. She kept moving.

Abruptly, she stumbled into Rolan and rebounded from his wide chest, panting. Half dazed, or maybe more than half, she had not realized that he had stopped. So had the others ahead, a few looking back, the rest facing outward and warily on guard, weapons up as though expecting attack. That was all she had time to see before Rolan seized a handful of her hair again and bent to lift one of her feet. Light, the man really was treating her like a pony!

Releasing her hair and her foot, he snaked an arm around her legs, and the next moment her vision whirled as she was heaved up onto his shoulder, head-down beside the horn bow cased on his back. Indignation welled up as he casually shifted her about to find the easiest position for carrying, but she tamped it down as fast as it rose. This was no place or time. Her feet were out of the snow; that was what mattered. And she could catch her breath, like this. He could have warned her, though.

With an effort, she arched her neck so she could see her companions, and felt relief to find them all still there. Naked prisoners, true, but she was sure only a corpse would have been left behind. The others who walked were leashed with stockings or strips of cloth cut from their lost garments, and most also had their arms tied behind. Alliandre was no longer trying to bend double in an attempt to shield herself. Other concerns had replaced modesty for the Queen of Ghealdan. Panting and trembling, she might have fallen if the squat Shaido examining her feet had not supported her by her bound elbows. Squat for an Aiel meant he could have

passed unremarked most places, except for shoulders nearly
as wide as Rolan's. The dark hair spilling down Alliandre's
back was windblown, her face haggard. Behind her, Maighdin appeared in almost as bad a state, gulping air, red-gold
hair in disarray and blue eyes staring, yet she managed to
stay erect on her own with a bone-lean Maiden lifting her
foot. Somehow, Faile's maid looked more a queen than
Alliandre did, if a very disheveled queen.

In comparison, Bain and Chiad seemed in no worse state
than did the Shaido, though Chiad's cheek was yellowing
and swollen from a blow when they were first taken, and
the black blood matting Bain's short fiery hair and spread
across her face seemed to have frozen. That was bad; that
could scar. The two Maidens were not breathing hard,
though, and even raised their own feet for examination.
Alone of the prisoners they were unbound—except by custom stronger than chains. They had calmly accepted their
fate, to serve a year and a day as *gai'shain*. Bain and Chiad
might be of some help in escaping—Faile was not sure how
far custom constrained them—but they themselves would
not try to get away.

The last prisoners, Lacile and Arrela, attempted to pattern themselves after the Maidens, of course, with indiffer-
ent success. A tall Aielman had simply tucked tiny Lacile
under his arm to look at her feet, and crimson mortification stained her pale cheeks. Arrela was tall, but the pair of
Maidens who had charge of her were taller than Faile herself, and they handled the Tairen woman with impersonal
ease. A scowl contorted her dark face at their prodding, and
maybe at the rapid handtalk they were exchanging. Faile
hoped she would not make trouble, not now. Everyone in
Cha Faile tried to be like the Aiel, to live as they thought
the Aiel did, but Arrela wanted to *be* a Maiden, and she
resented the fact that Sulin and the others would not teach
her handtalk. She would have been worse if she knew Bain
and Chiad had taught Faile a little. Not enough to make
out more than every other word the Maidens were saying
now, but some. As well Arrela could not understand. They
thought the wetlander had soft feet, that she was altogether
too pampered and soft, and that surely would have set the
woman off.

As it turned out, Faile need not have worried about

Arrela. The Tairen stiffened when one of the Maidens hefted her onto a shoulder—pretending to stagger, the burdened woman used her free hand to flicker a message that made the other Maiden bark a laugh behind her veil—but after a glance at Bain and Chiad, already meekly belly down on Aielmen's shoulders, Arrela sullenly let herself hang limp. Lacile squealed when the big man holding her abruptly spun her about to land in the same position, but she quieted after that, though her face was still bright scarlet. There were definite advantages to their emulation of Aiel.

Alliandre and Maighdin, however, the last women Faile would have expected to cause problems, were another matter entirely. When they realized what was happening, the pair of them fought wildly. It was not much of a fight, two naked and exhausted women with their elbows bound tight behind their backs, but they twisted and shouted and kicked at anyone who came within reach, and Maighdin even sank her teeth into the hand of a careless Aielman, hanging on like a boarhound.

"Stop it, you fools!" Faile called to them. "Alliandre! Maighdin! Let them carry you! Obey me!" Neither her maid nor her vassal paid the slightest heed. Maighdin growled like a lion around her mouthful of Aiel. Alliandre was wrestled down, still shouting and flailing with her feet. Faile opened her mouth for another command.

"The *gai'shain* will be quiet," Rolan grunted, spanking her hard.

She ground her teeth and muttered under her breath. Which earned *another* slap! The man had her knives tucked behind his belt. If she could lay hands on just one . . . ! No. What must be endured, could be endured. She intended to escape, not make useless gestures.

Maighdin's fight lasted a little longer than Alliandre's, until a pair of burly men could pry her jaws from the Shaido's hand. It required a pair. To Faile's surprise, instead of cuffing Maighdin, the bitten fellow shook blood off his hand and laughed! That did not save her, though. In a trice, Faile's maid was facedown in the snow alongside the Queen. They were given only a few moments to gasp and writhe in the added cold. Two Shaido, one a Maiden, appeared out of the surrounding trees, shaving the stubs from long switches with their heavy belt knives. A foot planted between each woman's shoulder blades, a fist on bound elbows to raise fluttering hands out of the way, and red welts began to bloom on white hips.

At first both women continued to fight, twisting about despite the way they were held. Their struggle was even more useless than when they were upright. Little moved above their waists beyond tossing heads and wildly waving hands. Alliandre kept shrilling that they could not do this to her, understandable coming from a queen, if foolish in the circumstances. Plainly they could, and they were. Surprisingly, Maighdin raised her voice in the same piercing denials. Anyone would have thought her royalty instead of a lady's maid. Faile knew for a fact that Lini had taken a switch to Maighdin without all these histrionics. In any case, denials did no good for either woman. The methodical thrashings continued until they both were kicking and howling wordlessly, and a little longer for good measure. When they were finally hoisted like the other prisoners, they hung weeping, all fight gone out of them.

Faile felt no sympathy. The fools had earned every stripe, in her opinion. Frostbite and cut feet aside, the longer they remained outside without clothes, the more chance that some of them might not survive to escape. The Shaido had to be taking them to some sort of shelter, and Alliandre and Maighdin had delayed reaching it. Maybe it was little more than a quarter hour's delay, but minutes could be the difference between the living and the dead. On top of which, even Aiel would surely let down their guard a little once they found shelter and made fires. And they could rest, being carried. They could be ready to take their chance when it came.

Carrying their prisoners, the Shaido set out again at that ground-covering pace. If anything, they seemed to move through the forest more quickly than before. The hard leather bow case bumped Faile's side as she swayed, and she began to feel dizzy. Rolan's every long stride sent a jolt through her middle. Surreptitiously, she tried to find some position where she would not be poked and thudded quite so vigorously.

"Be still, or you will fall," Rolan muttered, patting her hip as he might have patted a horse to soothe it.

Raising her head, Faile peered back at Alliandre, scowling.

There was not much to be seen of the Queen of Ghealdan, and that crisscrossed by scarlet welts from the tops of her hips almost to the backs of her knees. Come to think of it, a short delay and a few stripes might be a small price to pay for biting a chunk out of this oaf toting her like a sack of grain. Not his hand, though. His throat would be about right.

Bold thoughts, and worse than useless. Foolish. Even being carried, she knew she must fight the cold. In some ways, she began to realize, being carried was worse. Walking, at least she had had the struggle to stay erect and on her feet to keep her awake, but as evening came on and deepened to darkness, the swaying motion on Rolan's shoulder seemed to have a lulling effect. No. It was the cold that was numbing her mind. Making her blood sluggish. She had to fight it, or she would die.

Rhythmically she worked her hands and bound arms, tensed her legs and relaxed them, tensed and relaxed, forcing her muscles to work her blood. She thought of Perrin, solid planning thoughts of what he should do about Masema, and how she could convince him if he balked. She went over the argument they would have when he learned she been using *Cha Faile* as spies, planned how she would meet his anger and turn it. There was an art to guiding a husband's anger in the direction you wanted, and she had learned from an expert, her mother. It would be a splendid argument. And a splendid making-up, after.

Thinking about making up with him made her forget to work her muscles, so she tried to concentrate on the argument, on the planning. Cold dulled her thoughts, though. She began losing the thread, having to shake her head and start over. Rolan's growls at her to be still helped, a voice to focus on, to keep her awake. Even the accompanying slaps on her upturned bottom helped, as much as she hated to admit the fact, each one a shock that jolted her to wakefulness. After a while, she began shifting more, then struggling almost to the point of falling, courting the rude smacks. Anything to stay awake. She could not have said how much time passed, but her twists and wriggles began to weaken, until Rolan no longer growled, much less gave her a slap. Light, she wanted the man to play her like a drum!

Why in the Light would I want a thing like that? she

thought dully, and a dim corner of her mind realized the battle was lost. The night seemed darker than it should be. She could not even make out the glow of moonlight on the snow. She could feel herself sliding, though, sliding faster and faster toward a deeper dark. Wailing silently, she sank into a stupor.

Dreams came. She was sitting on Perrin's lap with his arms so tight around her she could barely move, before a great fire roaring in a broad stone fireplace. His curly beard scratched her cheeks as he nipped her ears almost painfully. Suddenly a huge wind howled through the room, snuffing the fire like a candle. And Perrin turned to smoke that vanished in the gale. Alone in bitter darkness, she fought the wind, but it tumbled her end over end until she was so dizzy she could not tell up from down. Alone and endlessly tumbling into icy dark, knowing she would never find him again.

She ran across a frozen land, floundering from snowdrift to snowdrift, falling, scrambling up to run on in panic, gulping air so cold it sliced her throat like shards of glass. Icicles sparkled on stark branches around her, and a frigid wind keened through the leafless forest. Perrin was very angry, and she had to get away. Somehow, she could not recall the specifics of the argument, just that somehow she had pushed her beautiful wolf to real anger, to the point of throwing things. Only, Perrin did not throw things. He was going to turn her over his knee, as he had done once, long ago. Why was she running from that, though? There would still be the making-up. And she would make him pay for the humiliation, of course. Anyway, she had drawn a little blood from him a time or two with a well-aimed bowl or pitcher, not really meaning to, and she knew he would never really hurt her. But she also knew that she had to run, to keep moving, or she would die.

If he catches me, she thought dryly, *at least part of me will be warm.* And she began to laugh at that, until the dead white land spun around her, and she knew that soon she would be dead, too.

The monstrous bonfire loomed over her, a towering pile of thick logs roaring with flame. She was naked. And cold, so cold. No matter how near the fire she edged, her bones felt frozen, her flesh ready to shatter at a blow. She moved closer, closer. The heat of the blaze grew till she flinched at it, but the bitter cold remained trapped inside her skin. Closer. Oh, Light, it was hot, too hot! And still cold within. Closer. She began to scream at the burning, the searing pain, but she was still ice inside. Closer. Closer. She was going to die. She shrieked, but there was only silence, and the cold.

It was daylight, but leaden clouds filled the sky. Snow fell in a steady shower, feathery flakes swirling in the wind through the trees. Not a fierce wind, but it licked with tongues of ice. Ridges of white built on branches until they were tall enough to collapse from their own weight and the wind, sending heavier showers to the ground below. Hunger gnawed her belly with dull teeth. A very tall, bony man with a white woolen cowl sheltering his face forced something into her mouth, the rim of a large clay mug. His eyes were a startling green, like emeralds, and surrounded by puckered scars. He was kneeling on a large brown woolen blanket with her, and another blanket, striped in gray, was draped around her nakedness. The taste of hot tea thick with honey exploded on her tongue, and she seized the man's sinewy wrist weakly with both hands in case he tried to take the mug away. Her teeth chattered against the mug, but she gulped the steaming syrupy liquid greedily.

"Not too fast; you must not spill any," the green-eyed man said meekly. Meekness sounded odd from that fierce face, and in a gravelly voice. "They offended your honor. But you are a wetlander, so maybe it does not count with you."

Slowly it dawned on her that this was no dream. Thought came in a trickle of shadows that melted if she tried to hold them too hard. The white-robed brute was *gai'shain*. Her leash and bonds were gone. He pulled his wrist away from her feeble grip, but only to pour a dark stream from a leather water bag hanging from his shoulder. Steam rose from the mug, and the aroma of tea.

Shivering so hard she almost fell over, she clutched the thick striped blanket around her. Fiery pain was blossoming in her feet. She could not have stood had she tried. Not that she wanted to. The blanket managed to cover everything but her feet so long as she remained in a crouch; standing would have bared her legs and maybe more. It was warmth

she thought of, not decency, though there was little of either
to be had. Hunger's teeth grew sharp, and she could not stop
shaking. She was frozen inside, the tea's heat already just
a memory. Her muscles were week-old congealed pudding.
She wanted to stare at the filling mug, coveting the contents, but she made herself look for her companions.

They were all there in a line with her, Maighdin and Alliandre and everyone, slumped on their knees atop blankets,
shivering inside blankets speckled with snow. In front of
each a *gai'shain* knelt with a bulging water bag and a mug
or cup, and even Bain and Chiad drank like women half-
dead of thirst. Someone had cleaned the blood from Bain's
face, but unlike the last time Faile had seen them, the two
Maidens were as drawn and unsteady as anyone else. From
Alliandre to Lacile, her companions looked—what was
Perrin's phrase?—as if they had been dragged through a
knothole backward. But everyone was still alive; that was
the important thing. Only the living could escape.

Rolan and the other *algai'd'siswai* who had had charge
of them made a cluster at the far end of the kneeling line.
Five men and three women, the snow on the ground nearly
knee-deep on the Maidens. Black veils hanging down their
chests, they watched their prisoners and the *gai'shain* impassively. For a moment, she frowned at them, trying to
grasp a slippery thought. Yes; of course. Where were the
others? Escape would be easier if the rest had gone for some
reason. There was something more, another misty question
she could not quite catch.

Suddenly what lay beyond the eight Aiel leaped out at
her, and question and answer came at the same time. Where
had the *gai'shain* come from? A hundred paces or so distant, veiled by the scattered trees and falling snow, a steady
stream of people and pack animals, wagons and carts, was
flowing by. Not a stream. A flood of Aiel on the move. Instead of a hundred and fifty Shaido, she had the whole clan
to contend with. It seemed impossible that so many people
could pass within a day or two of Abila without raising
some alarm, even with the countryside in anarchy, but the
proof was right in front of her eyes. Inside, she felt leaden.
Maybe escape would be no harder, but she did not believe it.

"How did they offend me?" she asked jerkily, then
clamped her mouth shut to stop chattering. And opened

it again as the *gai'shain* raised the mug to her once more. She gulped the precious heat, choking, and forced herself to swallow more slowly. The honey, so thick it would have been cloying any other time, dulled her hunger a little.

"You wetlanders know nothing," the scarred man said dismissively. "*Gai'shain* are not clothed in any way until they can be given proper robes. But they feared you would freeze to death, and all they had to wrap you was their coats. You were shamed, named as weak, if wetlanders have shame. Rolan and many of the others are *Mera'din*, yet Efalin and the rest should know better. Efalin should not have allowed it."

Shamed? Infuriated was more like it. Unwilling to turn her head from the blessed mug, she rolled her eyes toward the hulking giant who had carried her like a sack of grain *and* smacked her unmercifully. Vaguely she seemed to recall welcoming those spanks, but that was impossible. Of course it was impossible! Rolan did not look like a man who had half-trotted through most of a day and a night besides, carrying someone. His white-misted breath came easily. *Mera'din?* She thought that would mean Brotherless in the Old Tongue, which told her nothing, but there had been a note of scorn in the *gai'shain*'s voice. She would have to ask Bain and Chiad, and hope it was not one of those things Aiel would not talk about to wetlanders, not even wetlanders who were close friends. Any piece of knowledge might aid escape.

So they had wrapped their prisoners up against the cold, had they? Well, no one would have been in any danger of freezing except for Rolan and the others. Still, she might owe him a small favor. Very small, considering everything. Perhaps she would only slice off his ears. If she ever got the chance, surrounded by thousands of Shaido. Thousands? The Shaido numbered in the hundreds of thousands, and tens of thousands of those were *algai'd'siswai*. Furious with herself, she fought despair. She would escape; they would all escape, and she would take the man's ears with her!

"I *will* see Rolan's repaid as he deserves," she muttered when the *gai'shain* took the mug away for refilling again. He gave her a narrow-eyed suspicious stare, and she hurried. "As you say, I am a wetlander. Most of us are. We don't follow *ji'e'toh*. By your customs, we shouldn't be made *gai'shain* at all, is that not right?" The man's scarred face did not change, not by so much as the twitch of an eyelid. A dim thought said it was too soon, she did not know the ground yet, but thoughts gelid with cold could not catch her tongue. "What if the Shaido decide to break other customs? They might decide not to let you go when your time is done."

"The Shaido break many customs," he told her placidly, "but I do not. I have over half a year yet to wear white. Until then, I will serve as custom demands. If you can talk so much, maybe you have had enough tea?"

Faile clumsily snatched the mug from him. His eyebrows lifted, and she rearranged her draperies one-handed as quickly as she could manage, her cheeks heating. *He* certainly knew he was looking at a woman. Light, she was blundering about like a blind ox! She had to think, to concentrate. Her brain was the only weapon she had. And at the moment, it might as well have been frozen cheese. Drinking deep of the hot sweet tea, she set herself to thinking of some way that being surrounded by thousands of Shaido could be turned to advantage. Nothing came to her, though. Nothing at all.

CHAPTER
4

Offers

W hat have we here?" a woman's hard voice said.
Faile looked up, and stared, hot tea gone from
her thoughts for the moment.

Two Aiel women with a much shorter *gai'shain* woman
between them came out of the swirling snow, sinking halfway up their calves in the white carpet that covered the
ground but still managing powerful strides. The taller
women did, anyway; the *gai'shain* stumbled and floundered
trying to keep up, and one of the others had a hand on her
shoulder to make sure she did. All three were worth a stare.
The woman in white kept her head meekly down as much
as she could and her hands folded in her wide sleeves as a
gai'shain was supposed to, but her robes had the sheen of
heavy silk, of all things. *Gai'shain* were forbidden jewelry,
yet a wide, elaborate belt of gold and firedrops cinched her
waist and a matching collar was just visible inside her cowl,
nearly covering her neck. Very few besides royalty could
afford the like. Strange as the *gai'shain* was, however, it
was the others Faile studied. Something told her they were
Wise Ones. There was too much authority about them for
anything else; these were women used to giving orders and
being obeyed. Beyond that, though, their simple presence
caught the eye. The woman pushing the *gai'shain* along,
a stern blue-eyed eagle with a dark gray shawl wrapped
around her head, stood a good span in height, as much as
most Aielmen, while the other was at least half a hand taller
than Perrin! She was not bulky, though, except in one particular. Sandy yellow hair flowed to her waist, held back
from her face by a wide dark kerchief, and her brown shawl

lay across her shoulders, open enough to show an incredible amount of bosom thrusting half out of her pale blouse. How did she avoid freezing, exposing so much skin in this weather? All those heavy necklaces of ivory and gold must feel like bands of ice!

As they stopped in front of the kneeling prisoners, the eagle-faced woman frowned disapprovingly at the Shaido who had captured them, and made a curt gesture of dismissal with her free hand. For some reason, she continued to hold on to the *gai'shain*'s shoulder tightly. The three Maidens turned immediately, hurrying toward the passing throng of Shaido. One of the men did, as well, but Rolan and the rest exchanged flat-eyed looks before they followed. Perhaps it meant something, perhaps nothing. Faile suddenly knew how someone in a whirlpool felt, grabbing desperately at straws.

"What we have is more *gai'shain* for Sevanna," the incredibly tall woman said in amused tones. She had a strong face that some might call pretty, but alongside the other Wise One, she seemed soft. "Sevanna will not be satisfied until the entire world is *gai'shain,* Therava. Not that I would object to that myself," she finished with a laugh.

The eagle-eyed Wise One did not laugh. Her face was stone. Her voice was stone. "Sevanna has too many *gai'shain* already, Someryn. We have too many *gai'shain.* They slow us to a crawl when we should race." Her iron stare ran along the kneeling line.

Faile flinched when that gaze touched her, and hurriedly buried her face in the mug. She had never seen Therava before, but in that glance she knew the woman's sort, eager to crush any challenge utterly and capable of seeing challenge in a casual glance. Bad enough when it was only a fool noble at court, or someone encountered on the road, but escape could become more than difficult if this eagle took a personal interest. Just the same, she watched the woman from the corner of her eye. It felt like watching a banded adder, scales glittering in the sun, coiled a foot from her face.

Meek, she thought. *I am kneeling here meekly, with no thought in my head but drinking my tea. No need to look at me twice, you cold-eyed witch.* She hoped the others saw what she did.

Alliandre did not. She tried to rise to her swollen feet,

tottered, then sank back to her knees with a wince. Even so, she knelt upright in the falling snow, head high, a red-striped blanket held around her as if it were a fine silk shawl over a splendid gown. Bared legs and windblown hair spoiled the effect somewhat, yet she was still arrogance on a pedestal.

"I am Alliandre Maritha Kigarin, Queen of Ghealdan," she announced loudly, very much queen addressing ruffian vagabonds. "You would be wise to treat me and my companions well, and punish those who have handled us so crudely. You can gain a large ransom for us, larger than you can imagine, and pardon for your crimes. My liege lady and I will require suitable accommodation for ourselves until arrangements can be made, and for her maid. Lesser will do for the others, so long as they are not harmed. I will pay no ransom if you ill-treat the least of my liege lady's servants."

Faile could have groaned—did the idiot woman think these people were simple bandits?—only she had no time to.

"Is that true, Galina? Is she a wetlander queen?" Another woman rode out from behind the prisoners, her tall black gelding walking softly in the snow. Faile thought she must be Aiel, but she was unsure. It was difficult to say for certain with the other woman on horseback, but she seemed at least as tall as Faile herself, and few women were except among the Aiel, certainly not with those green eyes in a sun-dark face. And yet . . . That wide, dark skirt looked like the Aiel women's at a glance, but it was divided for riding and appeared to be silk, as was her creamy blouse, and the hem revealed red boots in her stirrups. The wide folded kerchief that held back her long golden hair was brocaded red silk, and a thumb-thick circlet of gold and firedrops nestled over it. In contrast to the Wise Ones' worked gold and carved ivory, her ropes of fat pearls and necklaces of emeralds and sapphires and rubies half hid nearly as much bosom as Someryn had on display. The bracelets climbing almost to her elbows differed from those worn by the two Wise Ones in the same way, and Aiel did not wear rings, but gems sparkled on every finger. Instead of a dark shawl, a bright crimson cloak, bordered with golden embroidery and lined with white fur, flared around her in the stiff breeze. She did sit her saddle with the awkwardness of Aiel on horseback, though. "And a queen's," her tongue tripped unfamiliarly, "liege lady? That means the Queen swore oath to her? A truly powerful woman, then. Answer me, Galina!"

The silk-clad *gai'shain* hunched her shoulders and favored the mounted woman with a groveling smile. "A truly powerful woman, to have a queen swear fealty, Sevanna," she said eagerly. "I've never heard of the like. Yet I think she is who she claims. I saw Alliandre once, years ago, and the girl I recall could well have grown into this woman. And she was crowned Queen of Ghealdan. What she is doing in Amadicia, I don't know. The Whitecloaks or Ailron either one would snap her up in an instant if they—"

"Enough, Lina," Therava said firmly. The hand on Galina's shoulder tightened visibly. "You know I hate it when you natter."

The *gai'shain* flinched as if struck, and her mouth snapped shut. Practically writhing, she smiled up at Therava, fawning even more wretchedly than she had for Sevanna. Gold flashed on one of her fingers as she wrung her hands. Fear flashed in her eyes, too. Dark eyes. Definitely not Aiel. Therava seemed oblivious to the woman's truckling; a dog had been called to heel and had obeyed. Her attention was all on Sevanna. Someryn eyed the *gai'shain* sideways, her lips twisting with contempt, but she folded her shawl across her bosom and looked to Sevanna as well. Aiel did not give away much on their faces, yet plainly she disliked Sevanna, and was wary of her at the same time.

Faile's eyes followed the mounted woman, too, over the edge of her mug. In a way, it was like seeing Logain, or Mazrim Taim. Sevanna also had painted her name across the sky in blood and fire. Cairhien would need years to recover from what she had wrought there, and the ripples had spread to Andor and Tear and beyond. Perrin laid the blame to a man called Couladin, but Faile had heard enough of this woman to have a shrewd idea whose hand had been behind it all. And no one disputed that the slaughter at Dumai's Wells was Sevanna's fault. Perrin had almost died there. She had a personal claim on Sevanna for that. She might be willing to let Rolan keep his ears if she could settle that claim.

The flamboyantly garbed woman walked her mount slowly along the line of kneeling women, her steady green eyes almost as cold as Therava's. The sound of snow crunching beneath the black's hooves suddenly seemed loud. "Which of you is the maid?" An odd question. Maighdin hesitated, tight-jawed, before raising a hand from beneath her blanket. Sevanna nodded thoughtfully. "And the . . . liege lady?"

Faile considered holding back, but one way or another, Sevanna would learn what she wanted to know. Reluctantly, she lifted her hand. And shivered from more than the cold. Therava was watching with those cruel eyes, paying close attention. To Sevanna, and to those she marked out.

How anyone could be unaware of that augering gaze, Faile did not understand, yet Sevanna seemed so as she turned her gelding down the back of the line. "They cannot walk on those feet," she said after a moment. "I do not see why they should ride with the children. Heal them, Galina."

Faile gave a start and almost dropped the clay mug. She pushed it toward the *gai'shain,* trying to make out that that was what she had been doing all along. It was empty anyway. The scarred fellow calmly began filling it up again from his water bag of tea. Heal? Surely she could not mean . . .

"Very well," Therava said, giving the *gai'shain* woman a shove that staggered her. "Do it quickly, little Lina. I know you do not want to disappoint me."

Galina caught herself from falling, but only to struggle on toward the prisoners. She sank above her knees in places, her robes dragging in the snow, but she was intent on reaching her goal. Wide-eyed fear and revulsion mingled on her round face with . . . could it be, eagerness? All in all, it was a sickening combination.

Sevanna completed her circuit, coming back to where Faile could see her clearly, and reined in facing the Wise Ones. The woman's full mouth was tight. The icy breeze rippled her cloak, but she seemed unaware of it, or of the snow falling on her head. "I have just received word, Therava." Her voice was calm, though lightning bolts should have been flashing from her eyes. "Tonight we camp with the Jonine."

"A fifth sept," Therava replied flatly. For her, also, wind and snow might as well not have existed. "Five, while seventy-eight remain scattered on the wind. Well that you remember your pledge to reunite the Shaido, Sevanna. We will not wait forever."

Not lightning bolts, now. Sevanna's eyes were green volcanoes erupting. "I always do what I say, Therava. Well that you remember that. And remember that you *advise* me. *I* speak for the clan chief."

Wheeling her gelding, she drummed her heels on the animal's ribs, trying to make him gallop back toward the river of people and wagons, though no horse could do so in that depth of snow. The black managed something faster than a walk, but not much. Their faces expressionless as masks, Therava and Someryn watched horse and rider fade into the falling white veil.

An important exchange, at least to Faile. She knew tension tight as a harpstring when she saw it, and mutual hatred. A weakness that might be exploited, if she could puzzle out how. And it seemed the Shaido were not all here after all. Though more than enough seemed to be, judging by the unending river of them passing by. Galina reached her then, and anything else fled from her mind.

Smoothing her face to a ragged semblance of composure, Galina clutched Faile's head in both hands without speaking a word. Faile might have gasped; she could not be sure. The world seemed to fly by as she jerked halfway to her feet. Hours streaked by, or heartbeats crawled. The white-clad woman stepped back, and Faile collapsed on her face atop the brown blanket to lie panting against the rough wool. Her feet no longer hurt, but Healing always brought its own hunger, and she had eaten nothing since yesterday's breakfast. She could have wolfed down *plates* of anything that even looked like food. She no longer felt tired, but her muscles were water instead of pudding. Pushing herself up with arms that wanted to fold under her weight, she unsteadily gathered the gray-striped blanket again. She felt stunned as much by what she had seen on Galina's hand just before Galina seized her as she did by the Healing. Gratefully she let the scarred man hold the steaming mug to her mouth. She was not sure her fingers could have held on to it.

Galina was wasting no time. A dazed Alliandre was just attempting to rise from flat on her face, her striped covering blanket sliding to the ground unnoticed. Her welts were gone, of course. Maighdin still lay sprawled between her two blankets, loose limbs poking out in every direction and twitching as she feebly tried to collect herself. Chiad, with Galina's hands on her head, lurched all the way to her feet, arms flung wide, breath leaving her in a loud rush.

The yellowed swelling on her face faded away even as Faile watched. The Maiden dropped as if poleaxed when Galina moved on to Bain, though she began stirring almost at once.

Faile attended to her tea, and furious thought. The gold on Galina's finger was a Great Serpent ring. She might have thought it a strange present from whoever gave the woman her other jewels if not for the Healing. Galina was Aes Sedai. She must be. But what was an Aes Sedai doing here, in *gai'shain* robes? Not to mention apparently ready to lick Sevanna's wrist and kiss Therava's feet! An Aes Sedai!

Standing over a limp Arrela, the last in the line, Galina panted slightly from the effort of Healing so many so quickly, and gazed at Therava as though hopeful for a word of praise. Without so much as a look at her, the two Wise Ones started toward the river of Shaido, their heads together, talking. After a moment, the Aes Sedai scowled and lifted her robes, hurrying after them as quickly as she could. She glanced back more than once, though. Faile had the feeling that she did so even after the falling snow put a curtain between them.

More *gai'shain* came the other way, a dozen men and women, and only one was Aiel, a lanky redhead with a thin white scar from hairline to jaw. Faile recognized short, pallid Cairhienin, and others she thought might be Amadician or Altaran, taller and darker, and even a bronze-skinned Domani. The Domani and one of the other women wore wide belts of shiny golden chain tight around their waists, and collars of the flat links around their necks. So did one of the men! In any case, jewelry on *gai'shain* seemed unimportant except as an oddity, especially alongside the food and clothing they brought.

Some of the newcomers carried baskets with loaves of bread and yellow cheese and dried beef, and the *gai'shain* already there with their water bags of tea provided drink to wash it down. Faile was not alone in stuffing her mouth with unseemly haste even while she dressed, clumsily and with more mind to speed than modesty. The hooded white robe and two thick under-robes seemed wondrously warm, just to keep the air off, and so were heavy woolen stockings and soft Aiel boots that laced to her knees—even the boots had been bleached white!—but they did not fill up the hole in her middle. The meat was tough as boot leather, the cheese nearly rock hard and the bread not much softer, yet they tasted like a feast! Her mouth watered for every bite.

Chewing a mouthful of cheese, she knotted the last bootlace and stood, smoothing down her robes. As she reached for some more bread, one of the women wearing gold, plump and plain and weary-eyed, took another belt of golden chain out of a cloth sack hanging from her shoulder. Hastily swallowing, Faile stepped back. "I would rather not have that, thank you." She had a sinking feeling she had been wrong to dismiss the adornments as unimportant.

"What you want does not matter," the plump woman replied tiredly. Her accent was Amadician, and cultured. "You serve the Lady Sevanna, now. You will wear what you are given and do as you are told, or you will be punished until you see the error of your ways."

A few paces away, Maighdin was fending off the Domani, resisting being fitted with a collar. Alliandre was backing away from the man who wore golden chains, her hands raised and a sickly expression on her face. He held out one of the belts toward her. Thankfully, they were both looking to Faile, though. Perhaps that switching in the forest had done some good.

Exhaling heavily, Faile nodded to them, then allowed the plump *gai'shain* to fasten the wide belt around her. With her example, the other two let their hands fall. It seemed one blow too many for Alliandre, who stood staring at nothing as she was belted and collared. Maighdin did her best to glare a hole through the slim Domani. Faile tried smiling encouragement, but smiling was difficult. To her, the collar's catch snapping shut sounded like a prison door being locked. Belt and collar could be removed as easily as they had been put on, but *gai'shain* serving "the Lady Sevanna" surely would be watched very closely. Disaster was piling on disaster. Things had to get better from here on. They had to.

Soon, Faile found herself tramping though the snow on wobbly legs with a stumbling, dull-eyed Alliandre and a scowling Maighdin, surrounded by *gai'shain* leading pack animals, carrying large covered baskets on their backs, dragging loaded barrows with the wheels lashed to wooden sleds. The carts and wagons had sleds or broad runners, too, with the wheels tied on top of the snow-shrouded cargo. Snow might be unfamiliar to the Shaido, but they had learned something of traveling in it. Neither Faile nor the other two bore any burdens, though the plump Amadician woman made clear that they would be expected to carry or haul tomorrow and from then on. However many Shaido were in the column, it seemed a great city on the move, if not a nation. Children up to twelve or thirteen rode on the carts and wagons, but everyone else walked. All of the men wore the *cadin'sor,* but most women wore skirts and blouses and shawls like the Wise Ones, and most of the men carried only a single spear or no weapon at all and looked softer than the others. Soft meaning that there were stones softer than granite.

By the time the Amadician left, without giving her name or saying much more than obey or be punished, Faile realized that she had lost sight of Bain and the rest somewhere in the falling snow. No one tried to make her keep a particular place, so she tramped wearily back and forth across the column, accompanied by Alliandre and Maighdin. Keeping her hands folded together in her sleeves made walking difficult, especially wading through snow, but it did keep them warm. Warmer than the alternative, at least. The wind made sure they kept their hoods well up. Despite the identifying golden belts, neither *gai'shain* nor Shaido looked at them twice. Despite crossing the column a dozen times or more, however, the search proved fruitless. There were people in white robes everywhere, more than without, and any of those deep cowls could have hidden her other companions.

"We will have to find them tonight," Maighdin said finally. She actually managed to stalk through the deep snow, if in an ungainly fashion. Her blue eyes were fierce inside the cavern of her hood, and she gripped the broad golden chain around her neck with one hand as if wanting to rip it off. "As it is, we're taking ten steps to one for everyone else. Twenty for one. It will do us little good to arrive at tonight's camp too exhausted to move."

On Faile's other side, Alliandre roused from her numbness enough to raise an eyebrow at the decisiveness in Maighdin's voice. Faile merely looked at her maid, but that was enough to set Maighdin blushing and stammering. What had gotten into the woman? Still, it might not be what she expected from a serving woman, but she could not fault Maighdin's spirit in a companion for escape. A pity the

woman could not channel more. Faile had had great hopes
of that once, until she learned that Maighdin possessed so
little ability it was useless.

"Tonight it must be, Maighdin," she agreed. Or however
many nights it took. She did not mention that. Hurriedly she
surveyed the people nearest them to make sure no one was
close enough to overhear. The Shaido, whether in *cadin'sor*
or not, moved through the falling snow purposefully, pressing forward toward an unseen goal. The *gai'shain*—the other
gai'shain—moved with a different purpose. Obey or be punished. "The way they ignore us," she went on, "it should be
possible to just fall by the wayside, so long as you don't try
under a Shaido's nose. If either of you finds a chance, take
it. These robes will help you hide in the snow, and once you
find a village, the gold they've so graciously given us will
see you back to my husband. He will be following." Not too
quickly, she hoped. Not too closely, at least. The Shaido had
an army here. A small army, perhaps, compared to some,
but larger than Perrin's.

Alliandre's face hardened in determination. "I will not
leave without you," she said softly. Softly, yet in firm tones.
"I will not take my oath of fealty lightly, my Lady. I will
escape with you, or not at all!"

"She speaks for both of us," Maighdin said. "I may be
only a simple maid," she wrung the word with scorn, "but I
won't leave anyone behind to these . . . these bandits!" Her
voice was not simply firm; it brooked no opposition. Really,
after this, Lini would have to have a very long talk with her
before she was fit to hold her position!

Faile opened her mouth to argue—no, to command; Alliandre was her sworn woman, and Maighdin her maid,
however fire-brained captivity had made her! They *would*
follow her orders!—but she let the words die on her tongue.

Dark shapes approaching through the tide of Shaido and
the falling snow resolved into a cluster of Aiel-women with
their shawls framing their faces. Therava led them. A murmured word from her, and the others slowed to keep pace
behind while Therava joined Faile and her companions.
That was to say, she walked alongside them. Her fierce eyes
seemed to chill even Maighdin's enthusiasm, not that she
gave them more than a glance. To her, they were not worth
looking at.

"You are thinking of escape," she began. No one else opened her mouth, but the Wise One added, "Do not try denying it!" in a scornful voice.

"We will try to serve as we should, Wise One," Faile said carefully. She kept her head down in her cowl and made sure not to meet the taller woman's eyes.

"You know something of our ways." Therava sounded surprised, but it vanished quickly. "Good. But you take me for a fool if you think I believe you will serve meekly. I see spirit in the three of you, for wetlanders. Some never try to escape, but only the dead succeed. The living are always brought back. Always."

"I will heed your words, Wise One," Faile said humbly. Always? Well, there had to be a first time. "We all will."

"Oh, *very* good," Therava murmured. "You might even convince someone as blind as Sevanna. Know this, however, *gai'shain*. Wetlanders are not as others who wear white. Rather than being released at the end of a year and a day, you will serve until you are too bent and withered to work. I am your only hope of avoiding that fate."

Faile stumbled in the snow, and if Alliandre and Maighdin had not caught her windmilling arms, she would have fallen. Therava gestured impatiently for them to keep moving. Faile felt sick. *Therava* would help them escape? Chiad and Bain claimed the Aiel knew nothing of the Game of Houses and scorned wetlanders for playing it, but Faile recognized the currents swirling around her now. Currents that would pull all of them under if she misstepped.

"I do not understand, Wise One." She wished her voice did not sound so hoarse, suddenly.

Perhaps that very hoarseness convinced Therava, though. People like her believed in fear as a motivation before any other. At any rate, she smiled. It was not a warm smile, just a curving of thin lips, and the only emotion it conveyed was satisfaction. "All three of you will watch and listen while you serve Sevanna. Each day a Wise One will question you, and you will repeat every word Sevanna said, and who she spoke to. If she talks in her sleep, you will repeat what she mumbles. Please me, and I will see that you are left behind."

Faile wanted no part of this, but refusal was out of the question. If she refused, none of them would survive the night. She was certain of that. Therava would take no chances. They might not even survive until nightfall; this snow would hide three white-clad corpses quickly, and she very much doubted that anyone within sight would so much as protest if Therava decided to slit a few throats then and there. Everyone was focused on moving forward through the snow in any case. They might not even see.

"If she learns of it. . . ." Faile swallowed. The woman was asking them to walk out on a crumbling cliff. No, she was ordering them to. Did the Aiel kill spies? She had never thought to ask Chiad or Bain that. "Will you protect us, Wise One?"

The hard-faced woman caught Faile's chin with steely fingers, pulling her to a halt, pulling her up on her toes. Therava's eyes caught hers just as tightly. Faile's mouth went dry. That stare promised pain. "If she learns of it, *gai'shain,* I will trice you up for cooking myself. So make sure she does not. Tonight you will serve in her tents. You and a hundred others, so you will not have many labors to distract you from what is important."

A moment's careful study of the three of them, and Therava gave a satisfied nod. She saw three soft wetlanders, too weak to do anything but obey. Without another word she released Faile and turned away, and in moments she and the other Wise Ones were swallowed by the snow.

For a time, the three women struggled on in silence. Faile did not bring up anyone escaping alone, much less give orders. She was certain that if she did, the others would balk again. Aside from anything else, complying now would make it seem Therava had changed their minds, that fear of her had. Faile knew enough of the other two women to be sure they would die before admitting that the woman frightened them. Therava certainly frightened her. *And I'd swallow my tongue before admitting it aloud,* she thought wryly.

"I wonder what she meant by . . . cooking," Alliandre said finally. "Whitecloak Questioners sometimes turn prisoners over a fire on a spit, I've heard." Maighdin wrapped her arms around herself, shuddering, and Alliandre freed a hand from her sleeves long enough to pat the other woman's shoulder. "Do not worry. If Sevanna has a hundred servants, we may never get close enough to hear anything. And

we can choose what we report, so it cannot be traced back
to us."

Maighdin laughed bitterly inside her white hood. "You
think we still have small choices. We have none. You need
to learn about having no choices. That woman didn't pick
us out because we have *spirit*." She almost spat the word.
"I'll wager every one of Sevanna's *other* servants has had
that lecture from Therava, too. If we miss a word we should
have heard, you can be sure she'll know of it."

"You may be right," Alliandre allowed after a moment.
"But you will not speak to me again in that fashion, Maighdin. Our circumstances are trying, to say the least, but you
will remember who I am."

"Until we escape," Maighdin replied, "you are Sevanna's
servant. If you don't think of yourself as a servant every minute, then you might as well climb onto that spit. And leave
room for the rest of us, because you will put us on it, as well."

Alliandre's cowl hid her face, but her back grew stiffer
with every word. She was intelligent, and knew how to do
what she must, but she had a queen's temper when she did
not control it.

Faile spoke before she could erupt. "Until we manage to
get away, we are *all* servants," she said firmly. Light, the
last thing she needed was the pair of them squabbling. "But
you will apologize, Maighdin. Now!" Head averted, her
serving woman mumbled something that might have been
an apology. She let it pass for one, in any case. "As for you,
Alliandre, I expect you to be a *good* servant." Alliandre
made a noise, a half-protest, that Faile ignored. "If we are
to have any chance of escape, we must do as we are told,
work hard, and attract as little attention as possible." As if
they had not already attracted what seemed all the attention
in the world. "And we will tell Therava every time Sevanna
sneezes. I don't know what Sevanna will do if she finds out,
but I think we all have a good idea of what Therava will do
if we displease her."

That was enough to settle them all back into muteness.
They did all have a good idea of what Therava would do,
and killing might not be the worst of it.

The snow faded away to a few scattered flakes by midday. Dark roiling clouds still hid the sun, but Faile decided
it must be near enough midday, because they were fed. No

one stopped moving, but hundreds of *gai'shain* made their way through the column with baskets and scrips full of bread and dried beef, and water bags that contained water this time, cold enough to make her teeth ache. Strangely, she felt no more hungry than hours of walking through snow would account for. Perrin had been Healed once, she knew, and he had been ravenous for two days. Perhaps it was because her injuries had been so much less than his. She noticed that Alliandre and Maighdin ate no more than she.

Healing made her think of Galina, all the same questions that boiled down to an incredulous *why*? Why would an Aes Sedai—she *must* be Aes Sedai—why would she toady for Sevanna and Therava? For anyone? An Aes Sedai might help them escape. Or she might not. She might betray them, if it suited her purposes. Aes Sedai did what they did, and you had no alternative but to accept that unless you were Rand al'Thor. But he was *ta'veren,* and the Dragon Reborn on top of it; she was a woman with very few resources at the moment, and a considerable danger hanging over her head. Not to mention the heads of those she was responsible for. Any help would be welcome, from anyone. The brisk breeze failed while she prodded at Galina from every angle she could think of, and the snow came again, growing heavier, until she could not see ten paces. She could not decide whether to trust the woman.

Abruptly she became aware of another white-robed woman watching her, almost hidden by the snow. Not enough snow to mask that wide, jeweled belt, though. Faile touched her companions on the arm and nodded toward Galina.

When Galina saw she had been seen, she came to trudge along between Faile and Alliandre. She still did not move with any grace in the snow, but she seemed more used to walking in it than they. There was nothing of fawning about her, now. Her round face was hard within her hood, her eyes sharp. But she did keep turning her head, darting wary glances to see who else was nearby. She looked like a housecat pretending to be a leopard. "You know ·who I am?" she demanded, but in a voice that would have been inaudible ten feet off. "What I am?"

"You seem to be Aes Sedai," Faile said carefully. "On the other hand, you have a very peculiar place here for an Aes

Sedai." Neither Alliandre nor Maighdin gave the slightest start of surprise. Plainly they had already seen the Great Serpent ring that Galina was thumbing nervously.

Color bloomed in Galina's cheeks, and she tried to make it out as anger. "What I do here is of great importance to the Tower, child," she said coldly. Her expression said she had reasons they could not begin to comprehend. Her eyes darted, trying to pierce the falling snow. "I must not fail. That is all you need to know."

"We need to know whether we can trust you," Alliandre said calmly. "You must have trained in the Tower or you would not know Healing, but women earn the ring without earning the shawl, and I cannot believe you are Aes Sedai." It seemed Faile had not been the only one puzzling over the woman.

Galina's plump mouth hardened, and she clenched a fist at Alliandre, to threaten or show her ring, or both. "You think they will treat you differently because you wear a crown? Because you used to wear one?" There was no doubt of her anger, now. She forgot to keep lookout for listeners, and her voice was acid. Spittle flew with the force of her tirade. "You will bring Sevanna wine and wash her back just like the rest. Her servants are all nobles, or rich merchants, or men and women who know how to serve nobles. Every day she has five of them strapped, to encourage the rest, so they all carry tales to her hoping to curry favor. The first time you try to escape, they will switch the soles of your feet until you cannot walk, and tie you twisted up like a blacksmith's puzzle to carry on a cart until you can. The second time will be worse, and the third worse again. There is a fellow here who used to be a Whitecloak. He tried to escape nine times. A hard man, but the last time they brought him back, he was begging and crying before they even began stripping him for punishment."

Alliandre did not take the harangue well. She puffed up indignantly, and Maighdin growled, "Was that what happened to you? Whether Aes Sedai or Accepted, you are a disgrace to the Tower!"

"Be silent when your betters speak, wilder!" Galina snapped.

Light, if this went any further, they would be screaming at one another next. "If you mean to help us escape, then say so," Faile told the silk-clad Aes Sedai. She did not really doubt that about the woman. Just everything else. "If not, what do you want with us?"

Ahead of them a wagon loomed out of the snow, leaning where one of the sleds had come loose. Directed by a Shaido with the arms and shoulders of a blacksmith, *gai'shain* were rigging a lever to hoist the wagon enough for the sled to be lashed back in place. Faile and the others kept silent as they passed.

"Is this really your liege lady, Alliandre?" Galina demanded once they were out of earshot of the men around the wagon. Her face was still flushed with anger, her tone slicing. "Who is she that you would swear to her?"

"You can ask me," Faile said coldly. Burn Aes Sedai and their bloody secrecy! Sometimes she thought an Aes Sedai would not tell you the sky was blue unless she saw advantage in it. "I am the Lady Faile t'Aybara, and that's as much as *you* need to know. Do you mean to help us?"

Galina stumbled to one knee, peering at Faile so hard that she began to wonder whether she had made a mistake. A moment later, she knew she had.

Regaining her feet, the Aes Sedai smiled unpleasantly. She no longer seemed angry. In fact, she looked as pleased as Therava had, and worse, in much the same way. "t'Aybara," she mused. "You are Saldaean. There is a young man, Perrin Aybara. Your husband? Yes, I see I've hit the target. That would explain Alliandre's oath, certainly. Sevanna has grandiose plans for a man whose name is linked to your husband. Rand al'Thor. If she knew she had you in her hands . . . Oh, never fear she will learn from me." Her gaze hardened, and suddenly she seemed a leopard in truth. A starving leopard. "Not if you all do as I tell you. I will even help you get away."

"What do you want of us?" Faile said, more insistently than she felt. Light, she had been angry at Alliandre for drawing attention to them by naming herself, and now she had done the same. Or worse. *And I thought I was concealing myself by hiding my father's name,* she thought bitterly.

"Nothing too trying," Galina replied. "You marked Therava, of course? Of course, you did. Everyone notices Therava. She keeps something in her tent, a smooth white rod about a foot long. It is in a red chest with brass banding that is never locked. Bring it to me, and I will take you with me when I go."

"A small thing to do, it seems," Alliandre said doubtfully. "But if so, why do you not take it yourself?"

"Because I have you to fetch it for me!" Realizing she had shouted, Galina huddled in on herself, and her cowl swung as she searched for eavesdroppers among the snow-veiled throng. No one seemed to be so much as glancing their way, but her voice dropped to a feral hiss. "If you do not, I will leave you here until you are gray and wrinkled. And Sevanna will hear of Perrin Aybara."

"It may take time," Faile said desperately. "We won't be free to just sneak into Therava's tent whenever we want." Light, the last thing in the world she wanted was to go anywhere near Therava's tent. But Galina had said she would help them. Vile she might be, but Aes Sedai could not lie.

"You have all the time you need," Galina replied. "The rest of your life, Lady Faile t'Aybara, if you are not careful. Do not fail me." She gave Faile a last hard stare, then turned to labor away into the snow, holding her arms as if trying to hide her jeweled belt behind her wide sleeves.

Faile struggled onward in silence. Neither of her companions had anything to say, either. There did not seem to be anything to say. Alliandre appeared sunk in thought, hands in her sleeves, peering straight ahead as if seeing something beyond the blizzard. Maighdin had gone back to gripping her golden collar in a tight fist. They were caught in three snares, not one, and any of the three might kill. Rescue suddenly seemed very attractive. Somehow, though, Faile intended to find her way out of this trap. Pulling her hand away from her own collar, she fought through the snowstorm, planning.

CHAPTER
5

Flags

*H*e ran across the snow-covered plain, nose into the wind, hunting for a scent, for that one precious scent. The falling snow no longer melted on his chilled fur, but cold could not deter him. The pads of his paws were numb, yet his burning legs worked furiously, carrying him on, faster and faster, till the land blurred in his eyes. He had to find her.

Suddenly a great grizzled gray wolf, ragged-eared and scarred from many fights, settled down out of the sky to race the sun beside him. Another great gray wolf, but not so large as himself. His teeth would tear the throats of those who had taken her. His jaws would crush their bones!

Your she *is not here,* Hopper sent to him, *but you are here too strongly, and too long from your body. You must go back, Young Bull, or you will die.*

I must find her. Even his thoughts seemed to pant. He did not think of himself as Perrin Aybara. He was Young Bull. Once, he had found the falcon here, and he could again. He had to find her. Beside that need, death was nothing.

In a flash of gray the other wolf lunged against his side, and though Young Bull was the larger, he was tired, and he fell heavily. Scrambling to his feet in the snow, he snarled and launched himself at Hopper's throat. Nothing mattered more than the falcon.

The scarred wolf flew into the air like a bird, and Young Bull went sprawling. Hopper lighted on the snow behind him.

Hear me, cub! Hopper thought at him fiercely. *Your mind is twisted with fear! She is not here, and you will die if you*

*remain longer. Find her in the waking world. You can only
find her there. Go back, and find her!*

Perrin's eyes snapped open. He was bone tired and his
middle felt hollow, but hunger was a shadow beside the hol-
lowness in his chest. He was all hollow, and distanced even
from himself, as if he were another person watching Perrin Aybara suffer. Above him, a blue-and-gold-striped tent
roof rippled in the wind. The interior of the tent was dim
and shadowed, but sunlight made the bright canvas glow
softly. And yesterday had not been a nightmare any more
than Hopper was. Light, he had tried to kill Hopper. In the
wolf dream, death was . . . final. The air was warm, but he
shivered. He was lying on a feather mattress, in a large bed
with heavy cornerposts thickly carved and gilded. Through
the scent of charcoal burning in the braziers he smelled
musky perfume, and the woman wearing it. No one else
was present.

Without raising his head from the pillow, he said, "Have
they found her yet, Berelain?" His head felt too heavy to
lift.

One of her camp chairs squeaked faintly as she shifted.
He had been here before often, with Faile, to discuss plans.
The tent was big enough to house a family, and Berelain's
elaborate furnishings would not have looked out of place in
a palace, all intricate carving and gilt, though everything,
tables and chairs and the bed itself, was held together with
pegs. They could be disassembled for storage on a cart, but
the pegs did not make for true sturdiness.

Under the perfume, Berelain smelled of surprise that he
knew she was there, yet her voice was composed. "No. Your
scouts haven't returned yet, and mine . . . When they didn't
return by nightfall, I sent a full company. They found my
men dead in an ambush, killed before they had gone more
than five or six miles. I ordered Lord Gallenne to keep a
tight watch around the camps. Arganda has a strong guard
mounted, too, but he sent patrols out. Against my advice.
The man's a fool. He thinks no one can find Alliandre but
him. I am not sure he believes anyone else is really trying.
Certainly not the Aiel."

Perrin's hands tightened on the soft wool blankets covering him. Gaul would not be caught by surprise, or Jondyn,
not even by Aiel. They were still hunting, and that meant

Faile was alive. They would have been back long since if they had found her body. He had to believe that. He lifted one of the blue blankets a trifle. Beneath them, he was bare. "Is there an explanation for this?"

Her voice did not change, but caution shimmered in her scent. "You and your armsman might have frozen to death if I hadn't gone looking for you when Nurelle returned with news of my scouts. No one else had the nerve to disturb you; apparently you snarled like a wolf at everyone who did. When I found you, you were so numb you couldn't hear anyone speak to you, and the other man was ready to fall on his face. Your woman Lini kept him—all he needed was hot soup and blankets—but I had you carried here. You might have lost some toes at best without Annoura. She . . . She seemed afraid you might die even after she Healed you. You slept like a man already dead. She said you almost felt like someone who had lost his soul, cold no matter how many blankets were piled on you. I felt it, as well, when I touched you."

Too much explanation, and not enough. Anger flared, a distant anger, but he hammered it down. Faile was always jealous when he raised his voice to Berelain. The woman would get no shouts from him. "Grady or Neald could have done whatever was necessary," he said in a flat voice. "Even Seonid and Masuri were closer."

"My own advisor came to mind first. I never thought of the others till I was almost back here. Anyway, does it matter who did the Healing?"

So plausible. And if he asked why the First of Mayene herself was watching over him in a half-dark tent instead of her serving women, or some of her soldiers, or even Annoura, she would have another plausible answer. He did not want to hear it.

"Where are my clothes?" he asked, propping himself up on his elbows. His voice still had no expression.

A single candle on a small table beside Berelain's chair gave the only real light in the tent, but it was more than enough for his eyes, even grainy with tiredness as they were. She was garbed demurely enough, in a dark green riding dress with a high neck that nestled her chin in a thick ruff of lace. Putting demure on Berelain was like putting a sheepskin on a ridgecat. Her face was faintly shadowed, beautiful and untrustworthy. She would do what she promised, but like an Aes Sedai, for her own reasons, and the things she had made no promises about could stab you in the back.

"On the chest over there," she said, gesturing with a graceful hand nearly hidden in pale lace. "I had Rosene and Nana clean them, but you need rest and food more than clothing. And before we get to food, and business, I want you to know that no one hopes Faile is alive more than I." Her expression was so open and honest, he could have believed her had she been anyone else. She even managed to smell honest!

"I need my clothes now." He twisted around to sit up on the side of the bed with the blankets pulled across his legs. The clothes he had been wearing lay neatly folded on a banded travel chest that was carved and gilded within an inch of its life. His fur-lined cloak was draped across one end of the chest, and his axe leaned next to his boots on the brightly flowered carpets layered for a floor. Light, he was tired. He did not know how long he had been in the wolf dream, but awake there was awake, as far as your body was concerned. His stomach rumbled loudly. "And food."

Berelain made an exasperated sound in her throat and rose, smoothing her skirts, her chin lifted high with disapproval. "Annoura will not be pleased with you when she comes back from talking with the Wise Ones," she said firmly. "You can't just ignore Aes Sedai. You are not Rand al'Thor, as they will prove to you sooner or later."

But she left the tent, letting in a swirl of cold air. In her displeasure, she did not even bother to take a cloak. Through the momentary gap in the entry flaps, he saw that it was still snowing. Not as hard as last night, but white flakes drizzled down steadily. Even Jondyn would have difficulty finding sign after last night. He tried not to think about that.

Four braziers warmed the air in the tent, but ice seeped into his feet as soon as they hit the carpets, and he hurried to his clothes. Tottered to them, really, though not dallying about it. He was so tired he could have lain down on the carpets and gone to sleep again. On top of that, he felt weak as a newborn lamb. Perhaps the wolf dream had something to do with that, too—going there as strongly as he had, abandoning his body—but Healing likely had exacerbated matters. With nothing to eat since yesterday's breakfast and a night spent standing in the snow, he had had no reserve to draw on. Now his hands fumbled with the simple task of putting on his smallclothes. Jondyn would find her. Or Gaul would. Find her alive. Nothing else in the world mattered. He felt numb.

He had not expected Berelain to return herself, but a gust of cold entered carrying her perfume while he was still drawing on his breeches. Her gaze on his back was like stroking fingers, but he made himself go on as if alone. She would not have the satisfaction of seeing him hurry because she was watching. He did not look at her.

"Rosene is bringing hot food," she said. "There is only mutton stew, I'm afraid, but I told her enough for three men." She hesitated, and he heard her slippers shift on the carpets. She sighed softly. "Perrin, I know you are hurting. There are things you might want to say that you can't to another man. I can't see you crying on Lini's shoulder, so I offer mine. We can call a truce until Faile is found."

"A truce?" he said, carefully bending to tug on a boot. Carefully so he did not fall over. Stout wool stockings and thick leather soles would have his feet warm soon enough. "Why do we need a truce?" She was silent while he donned the other boot and folded the turndowns below his knees, not speaking until he had done up the laces of his shirt and was stuffing it into his breeches.

"Very well, Perrin. If that is how you want it." Whatever that was supposed to mean, she sounded very determined. Suddenly he wondered whether his nose had failed him. Her scent was affronted, of all things! When he looked at her, though, she wore a faint smile. On the other hand, those big eyes held a glint of anger. "The Prophet's men began arriving before daylight," she said in a brisk voice, "but as I far as I know, he hasn't come himself, yet. Before you see him again—"

"*Began* arriving?" he broke in. "Masema agreed to bring only an honor guard, a hundred men."

"Whatever he agreed, there were three or four thousand the last I looked—an army of ruffians, every man within miles who could carry a spear, it seemed—and more coming from every direction."

Hurriedly, he shrugged into his coat and buckled his belt

over it, settling the weight of the axe at his hip. It always felt heavier than it should. "We will see about that! Burn me, I won't be lumbered with his murderous vermin!"

"His *vermin* are an annoyance compared to the man himself. The danger lies with Masema." Her voice was cool, but tightly leashed fear quivered in her scent. It always did when she spoke of Masema. "The sisters and the Wise Ones are right about that. If you need more proof of it than your own eyes, he has been meeting with the Seanchan."

That hit him like a hammer, especially after Balwer's news of the fighting in Altara. "How do you know?" he demanded. "Your thief-catchers?" She had a pair, brought from Mayene, and she sent them off to learn what they could at every town or village. Between them they never discovered half of what Balwer did. Not that she told him, anyway.

Berelain shook her head slightly, regretfully. "Faile's . . . retainers. Three of them found us just before the Aiel attacked. They had talked with men who saw a huge flying creature land." She shivered a little too ostentatiously, but by her smell, it was a true reaction. No surprise; he had seen some of the beasts once, and a Trolloc did not look more like Shadowspawn. "A creature carrying a passenger. They traced her to Abila, to Masema. I don't believe it was a first meeting. It had the sound of practice, to me."

Suddenly her lips curved in a smile, slightly mocking, flirtatious. This time, her scent matched her face. "It was not very nice of you to make me think that dried-up little secretary of yours was finding out more than my thief-catchers when you have two dozen eyes-and-ears masquerading as Faile's retainers. I must admit, you had me fooled. There are always new surprises to find in you. Why do you look so startled? Did you really think you could trust Masema after all we've seen and heard?"

Perrin's stare had little to do with Masema. That news could mean a great deal or nothing at all. Perhaps the man thought he could bring the Seanchan to the Lord Dragon, too. He was mad enough for it. But . . . Faile had those fools *spying?* Sneaking into Abila? And the Light knew where else. Of course, she always said spying was a wife's work, but listening to gossip around a palace was one thing;

this was altogether different. She could have told him, at least. Or had she kept quiet because her retainers were not the only ones poking their noses where they should not? It would be just like her. Faile truly did possess a falcon's spirit. She might think it fun to spy herself. No, he was not going to get angry with her, certainly not now. Light, she *would* think it was fun.

"I am glad to know you can be discreet," Berelain murmured. "I would not have thought it in your nature, but discretion can be a fine thing. Especially now. My men were not killed by Aiel, unless Aiel have taken to using crossbows and axes."

His head jerked up, and despite his best intentions, he glared at her. "You just slip that in? Is there anything else you've forgotten to tell me, anything that escaped your mind?"

"How can you ask?" she almost laughed. "I would have to strip myself naked to reveal more than I already have." Spreading her arms wide, she twisted slightly like a snake as if to demonstrate.

Perrin growled in disgust. Faile was missing, the Light only knew whether she was alive—Light, let her be alive!—and Berelain chose *now* to flaunt herself worse than she ever had before? But she was who she was. He should be grateful she had clung to decency long enough for him to dress.

Eyeing him thoughtfully, she ran a fingertip along her lower lip. "Despite what you may have heard, you will be only the third man to share my bed." Her eyes were . . . smoky . . . yet she might have been saying he was the third man she had spoken to that day. Her scent . . . The only thing that came to mind was a wolf eyeing a deer caught in brambles. "The other two were politics. You will be pleasure. In more ways than one," she finished with a surprising touch of bite.

Just then Rosene bustled into the tent in a billow of icy air, her blue cloak thrown back and carrying an oval silver tray covered with a white linen cloth. Perrin snapped his mouth shut, praying she had not overheard. Smiling, Berelain seemed not to care. Setting the tray on the largest table, the stout serving woman spread her blue-and-gold-striped skirts in a deep curtsy for Berelain and another, shorter, for him. Her dark eyes lingered on him a moment, and she smiled, as pleased as her mistress, before gathering her cloak together and hurrying out again at a quick gesture from Berelain. She had overheard, all right. The tray gave off the smells of mutton stew and spiced wine that made Perrin's belly rumble again, but he would not have stayed to eat if his legs had been broken.

Flinging his cloak around his shoulders, he stalked out into the soft snowfall, tugging on his gauntlets. Heavy clouds shrouded the sun, but dawn was a few hours past, by the light. Paths had been beaten through the snow on the ground, yet the white drifting out of the sky was piling up on bare branches and giving the evergreens new coats. This storm was far from finished. Light, how could the woman talk to him that way? Why would she talk that way, and now?

"Remember," Berelain called after him, making no effort to mute her voice. "Discretion." With a wince, he quickened his step.

A dozen paces from the great striped tent he realized he had forgotten to ask the location of Masema's men. All around him the Winged Guards were warming themselves at campfires, armored and cloaked and near to their saddled mounts on the horselines. Their lances stood close at hand in steel-tipped cones that trailed red streamers in the wind. Despite the trees, a straight line could have been drawn through any row of those fires, and they were even as near the same size as humanly possible. The supply carts they had acquired coming south were all loaded, the horses harnessed, and they were arrayed in rigid lines, too.

The trees did not hide the crest of the hill completely. Two Rivers men still stood guard up there, but the tents were down, and he could make out loaded packhorses. He thought he saw a black coat, too; one of the Asha'man, though he could not see which. Among the Ghealdanin, knots of men stood staring up the hill, yet all in all, they appeared as ready as the Mayeners. The two camps were even laid out alike. But nowhere was there any sign that thousands of men were gathering, no broad trampled paths in the snow to follow. For that matter, there were no footprints

between the three camps at all. If Annoura was with the
Wise Ones, she had been on the hill for some time. What
were they talking about? Probably how to kill Masema
without him finding out they were responsible. He glanced
at Berelain's tent, but the thought of going back in there
with her made his hackles rise.

One other tent remained up, not far away, the smaller
striped tent belonging to Berelain's two serving women.
Despite the drizzling snow, Rosene and Nana sat on camp
stools in front of the smaller tent, cloaked and hooded and
warming their hands over a small fire. Alike as two peas in
the pod, neither was pretty, but they had company, likely
the reason they were not huddled around a brazier inside.
Doubtless Berelain insisted on more propriety in her serving women than she managed for herself. Normally Berelain's thief-catchers seldom seemed to speak more than
three words together, at least in Perrin's hearing, but they
were animated and laughing with Rosene and Nana. Plainly
dressed, the pair was so nondescript you would not notice
one bumping into him on the street. Perrin was still not sure
which was Santes and which Gendar. A small kettle set off
to one side of the fire smelled of mutton stew; he tried to
ignore it, but his stomach growled anyway.

Talk stopped as he approached, and before he reached
the fire, Santes and Gendar glanced from him to Berelain's
tent, faces absolutely blank, then pulled their cloaks around
them and hurried away, avoiding his eyes. Rosene and Nana
looked from Perrin to the tent, and tittered behind cupped
hands. Perrin did not know whether to blush or howl.

"Would you by any chance know where the Prophet's
men are gathering?" he asked. Keeping his voice level was
hard with all their arched eyebrows and smirks. "Your mistress forgot to tell me exactly." The pair exchanged looks
hidden by their hoods and giggled behind their hands again.
He wondered whether they were brainless, but he doubted
Berelain would tolerate fluff-brains around her for long.

After a great deal of tittering interspersed with quick
glances at him, at each other, at Berelain's tent, Nana allowed as how she was not really sure but thought it was
that way, waving a hand vaguely toward the southwest.
Rosene was certain she had heard her mistress say it was no

more than two miles. Or maybe three. They were still giggling when he strode away. Maybe they really were goose-brained.

Wearily he tramped around the hill thinking about what he had to do. The depth of snow he had to wade through once he left the Mayener camp made his foul mood no better. Nor did the decisions he reached. It only got fouler after he arrived where his own people were camped.

Everything was as he had ordered. Cloaked Cairhienin sat on loaded carts with the reins looped around a wrist or tucked under a haunch, and other short figures moved along the lead lines of remounts, soothing the haltered horses. The Two Rivers men not on the hilltop squatted around dozens of small fires scattered through the trees, dressed to ride and holding their horses' reins. There was no order to them, not like the soldiers in the other camps, but they had faced Trollocs, and Aiel. Every man had his bow slung across his back and a full quiver on his hip, sometimes balanced by a sword or short-sword as well. For a wonder, Grady was at one of the fires. The two Asha'man usually kept a little apart from the other men, and the other way around as well. No one was talking, just concentrating on staying warm. The glum faces told Perrin that Jondyn had not returned yet, nor Gaul, nor Elyas or anybody else. There was still a chance they would bring her back. Or at least find where she was held. For a time, it seemed those were the last good thoughts he would have for the day. The Red Eagle of Manetheren and his own Wolfshead banner hung limp in the falling snow, on two staffs leaning against a cart.

He had planned to use those flags with Masema in the same way he had to come south, hiding in the open. If a man was mad enough to try reclaiming Manetheren's ancient glories, no one looked further, to any other reason for him marching with a small army, and so long as he did not linger, they were far too pleased to see the madman ride on to try stopping him. There were enough troubles in the land without calling more down on your head. Let someone else fight and bleed and lose men who would be needed come spring planting. Manetheren's borders had run almost to where Murandy now stood, and with luck, he could have been into Andor, where Rand had a firm grip, before having to give up the deception. That was changed, now, and he knew the price of changing. A very large price. He was prepared to pay, only it would not be he who paid. He would have nightmares about it, though.

CHAPTER 6

The Scent of Madness

S eeking through the falling snow for Dannil, Perrin found him at one of the fires and pushed between the horses. The other men straightened and backed away enough to give him room. Not knowing whether to offer sympathy, they barely looked at him, and jerked their eyes away when they did, hiding their faces in their cowls. "Do you know where Masema's people are?" he asked, then had to conceal a yawn behind his hand. His body wanted sleep, but there was no time.

"About three miles south and west," Dannil replied in a sour voice, and tugged irritably at his mustache. So the goose-brains had been right after all. "Flocking in like ducks into the Waterwood in autumn, and the lot of them look like they'd skin their own mothers." Horse-faced Lem al'Dai spat in disgust through the gap in his teeth he had gotten tussling with a wool merchant's guard long ago. Lem liked to fight with his fists; he looked eager to pick a scrap with some of Masema's followers.

"They would, if Masema said to," Perrin said quietly. "Best you make sure everybody remembers that. You've heard how Berelain's men died?" Dannil gave a sharp nod, and some of the others shifted their boots and muttered angrily under their breath. "Just so you know. There's no proof of anything, yet." Lem snorted, and the rest looked about as bleak as Dannil. They had seen the corpses Masema's followers left behind.

The snow was picking up, fat flakes that dotted the men's cloaks. The horses kept their tails tucked in against the cold. It would be a full blizzard again in a few hours, if not sooner. No weather to be leaving the fires' warmth. No weather to be on the move.

"Bring everybody off the hill and start toward where the ambush was," he ordered. That was one of the decisions he had made, walking back. He had delayed too long already, no matter who or what was out there. The renegade Aiel had too much lead as it was, and if they were headed in any direction but south or east, someone would have brought word by this time. By this time, they would expect him to be following. "We'll ride until I have a better idea where we're heading, then Grady or Neald will take us there through a gateway. Send men to Berelain and Arganda. I want the Mayeners and Ghealdanin moving, too. Put scouts out, and flankers, and tell them not to look for Aiel so hard they forget there are others who might want to kill us. I don't want to stumble into anything before I know it's there. And ask the Wise Ones to stay close to us." He would not put it past Arganda to try putting them to the question in spite of his orders. If the Wise Ones killed some of the Ghealdanin defending themselves, the fellow might strike out entirely on his own, fealty or no. He had the feeling he was going to need every fighting man he could find. "Be as firm as you dare."

Dannil took in the flood of orders calmly, but at the last his mouth twisted in a sickly grimace. Likely, he would as soon try to be firm with the Women's Circle back home. "As you say, Lord Perrin," he said stiffly, touching a knuckle to his forehead before he swung into his high-cantled saddle and began calling out orders.

Surrounded by men scrambling to mount, Perrin caught Kenly Maerin's sleeve while the young man still had one foot in his stirrup and asked him to have Stepper saddled and brought. With a wide grin, Kenly knuckled *his* forehead. "As you say, Lord Perrin. Right away."

Perrin growled inside his head as Kenly tramped toward the horselines pulling his brown gelding behind. The young whelp should not grow a beard if he was going to scratch at it all the time. The thing was straggly, anyway.

Waiting for his horse, he moved close to the blaze. Faile said he had to live with all the Lord Perrining and bowing and scraping, and most of the time he managed to ignore it, but today it was another drop of bile. He could feel a chasm growing wider between him and the other men from home, and he seemed to be the only one who wanted to bridge it. Gill found him muttering to himself as he held his hands out to the flames.

"Forgive me for bothering you, my Lord," Gill said, bowing and briefly snatching off his floppy hat to reveal a thinly thatched scalp. The hat went right back on his head again to keep off the snow. City bred, he felt the cold badly. The stout man was not obsequious—few Caemlyn innkeepers were—but he seemed to enjoy a certain amount of formality. He had certainly fitted into his new job well enough to please Faile. "It's young Tallanvor. At first light, he saddled his horse and went off. He said you gave him permission, if . . . if the search parties hadn't gotten back by then, but I wondered, since you wouldn't let anyone else go."

The fool. Everything about Tallanvor marked him an experienced soldier, though he had never been very clear about his background, but alone against Aiel, he was a hare chasing weasels. *Light, I want to be riding with him! I shouldn't have listened to Berelain about ambushes.* But there had been another ambush. Arganda's scouts might end the same way. But he had to move. He had to.

"Yes," he said aloud. "I told him he could." If he said otherwise, he might have to take notice later. Lords had to do that sort of thing. If he ever saw the man alive again. "You sound as though you want to go hunting yourself."

"I am . . . very fond of Maighdin, my Lord," Gill replied. Quiet dignity marked his voice, and a degree of stiffness, as though Perrin had said he was too old and fat for the task. He certainly smelled of vexation, all prickly and ginger, though his cold-reddened face was smooth. "Not like Tallanvor—nothing like that, of course—but very fond all the same. And of the Lady Faile, of course," he added hastily. "It's just that it seems I've known Maighdin my whole life. She deserves better."

Perrin's sigh misted in front of his mouth. "I understand, Master Gill." He did. He himself wanted to rescue everyone, but he knew if he had to choose, he would take Faile and let the others go. Everything could go, to save her. Horse-scent was heavy in the air, but he smelled someone else who was irritated, and looked over his shoulder.

Lini was glaring at him from the middle of the turmoil,

shifting her ground just enough to keep from being ridden down accidentally by men jostling to form ragged files. One bony hand gripped the edge of her cloak, and the other held a brass-studded cudgel, nearly as long as her arm. It was a wonder she had not gone with Tallanvor.

"You'll hear as soon as I do," he promised her. A rumbling in his middle reminded him suddenly and forcefully of that stew he had scorned. He could almost taste the mutton and lentils. Another yawn cracked his jaws. "Forgive me, Lini," he said when he could talk. "I didn't get much sleep last night. Or a bite to eat. Is there anything? Some bread, and whatever's to hand?"

"Everyone's eaten long since," she snapped. "The scraps are gone, and the kettles cleaned and stored away. Sup from too many dishes, and you deserve a bellyache that'll split you open. Especially when they're not your dishes." Trailing off into dissatisfied mutters, she scowled at him a moment longer before stalking away, glaring at the world.

"Too many dishes?" Perrin muttered. "I haven't had a one; that's my trouble, not a bellyache." Lini was making her way across the campground, threading her way between horses and carts. Three or four men spoke to her in passing, and she barked at every one, even shaking her cudgel if they failed to take the hint. The woman must be out of her mind over Maighdin. "Or was that one of her sayings? They usually make more sense than that."

"Ah . . . well, as to that, now. . . ." Gill snatched his hat off again and peered inside, then stuffed it back on. "I . . . ah . . . I have to see to the carts, my Lord. Need to make sure all's ready."

"A blind man could see the carts are ready," Perrin told him. "What is it?"

Gill's head swung wildly in search of another excuse. Finding none, he wilted. "I . . . I suppose you'll hear sooner or later," he mumbled. "You see, my Lord, Lini . . ." He drew a deep breath. "She walked over to the Mayener camp this morning, before sunrise, to see how you were and . . . ah . . . why you hadn't come back. The First's tent was dark, but one of her maids was awake, and she told Lini . . . She implied . . . I mean to say . . . Don't look at me that way, my Lord."

Perrin smoothed the snarl from his face. Tried to, at any

rate. It stayed in his voice. "Burn me, I *slept* in that tent, man. That is all I did! You tell her that!"

A violent coughing fit wracked the stout man. "Me?" Gill wheezed once he could talk. "You want *me* to tell her? She'll crack my pate if I *mention* a thing like that! I think the woman was born in Far Madding in a thunderstorm. She probably told the thunder to be quiet. It probably did."

"You're *shambayan*," Perrin told him. "It can't all be loading carts in the snow." He wanted to bite someone!

Gill seemed to sense it. Mumbling his courtesies, he made a jerky bow and scurried away clutching his cloak close. Not to find Lini, Perrin was sure. Gill ordered the household, such as it was, but never her. No one ordered Lini except Faile.

Glumly Perrin watched the scouts ride out through the falling snow, ten men already watching the trees around them before they were beyond sight of the carts. Light, women would believe anything about a man so long as it was bad. And the worse it was, the more they had to talk about it. He had thought Rosene and Nana were all he had to worry about. Likely Lini had told Breane, Faile's other maid, first thing on getting back, and by this time, Breane surely had told every woman in the camp. There were plenty among the horse handlers and cart drivers, and Cairhienin being Cairhienin, they probably had been eager to pass everything on to the men, too. That sort of thing was not seen with charity in the Two Rivers. Once you gained the reputation, losing it was not easy. Suddenly the men backing away to give him room took on a new light, and the uncertain way they had looked at him, and even Lem spitting. In memory, Kenly's grin became a smirk. The one bright spot was that Faile would not believe it. Of course she would not. Certainly not.

Kenly returned at a stumbling trot through the snow, drawing Stepper and his own rangy gelding behind. Both horses were miserable with the cold, their ears folded back and tails tight, and the dun stallion made no effort to bite at Kenly's mount, as he usually would have.

"Don't show your teeth all the time," Perrin snapped, snatching Stepper's reins. The boy eyed him doubtfully, then slunk away glancing back over his shoulder.

Growling under his breath, Perrin checked the stallion's

saddle girth. It was time to find Masema, but he did not mount. He told himself it was because he was tired and hungry, that he wanted just a bit of rest and something in his belly, if he could find anything. He told himself that, but he kept seeing burned farms and bodies hanging by the side of the road, men and women and even children. Even if Rand was still in Altara, it was a long way. A long way, and he had no choice. None he could make himself take.

He was standing with his forehead sunk against Stepper's saddle when a delegation of the young fools who had attached themselves to Faile sought him out, near a dozen of them. He straightened wearily, wishing the snow would bury them all.

Selande planted herself alongside Stepper's hindquarters, a short slender woman with green-gloved fists on her hips and an angry scowl creasing her forehead. She managed to swagger standing still. Despite the falling snow, one side of her cloak was thrown back to give easy access to her sword, exposing six bright slashes across the front of her dark blue coat. All the women wore men's clothing and swords, and usually they were twice as ready to use them as the men, which was saying quite a bit. Men and women alike, they were touchy with everyone, and would have been fighting duels every day had not Faile put a stop to it. Men and women alike, the lot with Selande smelled angry, sullen, sulky and petulant, all jumbled together, a scent that twitched uncomfortably in his nose.

"I see you, my Lord Perrin," Selande said formally in the crisp accents of Cairhien. "Preparations are being made to move out, but still we are refused our horses. Will you have this made right?" She made it sound a demand.

She saw him, did she? He wished he did not see her. "Aiel walk," he growled, and stifled a yawn, not caring a whit for the furious glares that earned him. He tried to put sleep out of his mind. "If you won't walk, ride on the carts."

"You cannot do that!" one of the Tairen women announced haughtily, one hand tight on the edge of her cloak, the other on her sword hilt. Medore was tall, with bright blue eyes in a dark face, and if she missed beautiful, it was not by much. The fat, red-striped sleeves of her coat looked decidedly odd with her full bosom. "Redwing is my favorite mount! I won't be denied her!"

"Third time," Selande said cryptically. "When we stop tonight, we will discuss your *toh,* Medore Damara."

Supposedly, Medore's father was an aging man who had retired to his country estates years ago, but Astoril was still a High Lord for all that. As those things were reckoned, that put his daughter well above Selande, only a minor noble in Cairhien. Yet Medore swallowed hard, and her eyes widened till she looked as though she expected to be skinned alive.

Abruptly Perrin had had all he could take of these idiots and their dog's dinner of Aiel bits and pieces and pure high-born jacfoolery. "When did you start spying for my wife?" he demanded. They could not have gone stiffer had their backbones frozen.

"We carry out such small tasks and errands as the Lady Faile might require of us from time to time," Selande said after a long moment, in very careful tones. Wariness was thick in her scent. The whole gaggle of them smelled like foxes wondering whether a badger had taken over their den.

"Did my wife really go hunting, Selande?" he growled heatedly. "She's never wanted to before." Anger roared in him, flames fanned by all the events of the day. He pushed Stepper away with one hand and stepped closer to the woman, looming over her. The stallion tossed his head, sensing Perrin's humor. His fist ached in his gauntlet from its grip on the reins. "Or did she ride out to meet some of you, fresh from Abila? Was she kidnapped because of your bloody spying?"

That made no sense, and he knew it as the words left his mouth. Faile could have talked with them anywhere. And she would never have arranged to meet her eyes-and-ears—Light, her *spies!*—in company with Berelain. It was always a mistake to speak without thinking. He knew about Masema and the Seanchan because of their spying. But he wanted to lash out, he needed to lash out, and the men he wanted to hammer into nothingness were miles away. With Faile.

Selande did not back away from his anger. Her eyes narrowed to slits. Her fingers opened and closed on the hilt of her sword, and she was not alone. "We would die for the Lady Faile!" she spat. "Nothing we have done has put her in danger! We are sworn to her by water oath!" To Faile and not to him, her tone added.

He should apologize. He knew he should. Instead, he said, "You can have your horses if you give me your word you'll do as I say and not try anything rash." "Rash" was not the word for this lot. They were capable of rushing off alone as soon as they learned where Faile was. They were capable of getting Faile killed. "When we find her, I will decide how to rescue her. If your water oath says different, tie a knot in it, or I'll tie you in knots."

Her jaw tightened and her scowl deepened, but finally she said "I agree!" as though the words were being pried out of her. One of the Tairens, a long-nosed fellow named Carlon, grunted in protest, but Selande raised one finger, and he shut his mouth. With that narrow chin, he probably regretted shaving off his beard. The little woman had the rest of these fools in the palm of her hand, which did not make her any less a fool herself. Water oath, indeed! She did not take her eyes from Perrin's. "We will obey you until the Lady Faile is returned. Then, we are hers again. And she can decide our *toh*." That last seemed more for the others than him.

"Good enough," he told her. He attempted to moderate his tone, but his voice was still rough. "I know you are loyal to her, all of you. I respect that." That was about all he did respect in them. As an apology it was not very much, and that was just how they took it. A grunt from Selande was the only reply he got, that and glowers from the rest as they stalked off. So be it. As long as they kept their word. The whole bunch had never done an honest day's work between them.

The camp was emptying out. The carts had begun moving south, sliding on their sleds behind the carthorses. The horses left deep tracks, but the sleds made only shallow ruts that the falling snow began to bury immediately. The last of the men from the hill were scrambling into their saddles and joining the others already riding with the carts. Just off to one side, the Wise Ones' party began to pass, even the *gai'shain* leading the pack animals themselves mounted. However firm Dannil had dared to be, or not as was more likely, apparently it had been enough. The Wise Ones looked particularly awkward on horseback compared to the grace of Seonid and Masuri, though not so bad as the *gai'shain*. The white-robed men and women had all been riding since the third day in snow, yet they crouched low over the tall pommels of their saddles and clung to neck or mane as if expecting to fall off at the next step. Getting them mounted in the first place had required direct commands from the Wise Ones, and some would still slide down and walk if they were not watched.

Perrin pulled himself up onto Stepper. He was not sure he might not fall off himself. It was time to make this ride he did not want to make, though. He would have killed for a piece of bread. Or some cheese. Or a nice rabbit.

"Aiel coming!" someone shouted from the head of the column, and everything came to a halt. More shouts rang out, passing the word as if everyone had not already heard, and men unlimbered bows from their backs. Cart drivers stood up on their seats, peering ahead, or leaped down to crouch beside the cart. Growling under his breath, Perrin heeled Stepper in the flanks.

At the front of the column, Dannil was still in his saddle, and the two men carrying those bloody banners, but a good thirty were on the ground, coverings stripped from their bowstrings and arrows nocked. The men holding the horses for the dismounted men jostled about, pointing and trying to get a clear view. Grady and Neald were there, as well, peering ahead with intent faces but sitting on their horses calmly. Everyone else reeked of agitation. The Asha'man only smelled . . . ready.

Perrin could make out what they were staring at through the trees a good deal more clearly than they. Ten veiled Aiel trotting toward them through the falling snow, one leading a tall white horse. A little behind them rode three men, cloaked and hooded. There seemed to be something odd in the way the Aiel moved. And there was a bundle tied to the white's saddle. A fist gripped Perrin's heart until he realized it was not nearly large enough to be a body.

"Put up your bows," he said. "That's Alliandre's gelding. It must be our people. Can't you see the Aiel are all Maidens?" Not a one was tall enough to be an Aielman.

"I can barely make out they're Aiel," Dannil muttered, giving him a sidelong look. They all took it for granted that his eyes were good, even took pride in it—or used to—but he tried to keep them from knowing how good. Right then, he did not care, though.

"They are ours," he told Dannil. "Everybody stay here."

Slowly he rode out to meet the returning party. The Maidens began unveiling as he approached. In one of the deep cowls on the mounted men, he made out Furen Alharra's black face. The three Warders, then; they would have come back together. Their horses looked as tired as he felt, near exhaustion. He wanted to force Stepper to run, to hear what they had to report. He dreaded hearing. Ravens would have been at the bodies, and foxes, badgers maybe, and the Light alone knew what besides. Maybe they thought they were sparing him by not bringing back what they had found. No! Faile had to be alive. He tried to fix that thought in his head, but it hurt like gripping a sharp blade barehanded.

Dismounting in front of them, he stumbled and had to hold on to the saddle to keep from falling. He felt numb around the bright pain of holding on to that one thought. She had to be alive. Little details loomed large, for some reason. Not one bundle fastened to the elaborately tooled saddle, but a number of small bundles that looked like gathered rags. The Maidens wore snowshoes, rough-made of vines and supple pine branches with the needles still on. That was why they seemed to be moving oddly. Jondyn must have shown them how to make them. He tried to focus. He thought his heart was going to pound through his ribs.

Gripping spears and buckler in her left hand, Sulin took one of the small bundles of cloth from the saddle before she came to him. The pink scar running down her leathery cheek twisted as she smiled. "Good news, Perrin Aybara," she said softly, handing him the dark blue cloth. "Your wife lives." Alharra exchanged glances with Seonid's other Warder, Teryl Wynter, who frowned. Masuri's man, Rovair Kirklin, stared straight ahead stonily. It was as plain as Wynter's curled mustaches that they were not sure it was good news. "The others press on to see what more they can find," she went on. "Though we already have found oddities enough."

Perrin let the bundle fall open in his hands. It was Faile's dress, sliced down the front and along the arms. He inhaled deeply, pulling Faile's scent into him, a faint trace of her flowery soap, a touch of her sweet perfume, but most of all, the smell that was her. And no hint of blood. The rest of the Maidens gathered around him, mostly older women with hard faces, though not as hard as Sulin's. The Warders climbed down, showing no sign that they had been all night in the saddle, but they held back behind the Maidens.

"All of the men were killed," the wiry woman said, "but by the garments we found, Alliandre Kigarin, Maighdin Dorlain, Lacile Aldorwin, Arrela Shiego, and two more also were made *gai'shain*." The other two must have been Bain and Chiad; mentioning them by name, that they had been taken, would have shamed them. He had learned a little about Aiel. "This goes against custom, but it protects them." Wynter frowned in doubt, then tried to hide it by adjusting his hood.

The neat cuts were like those made skinning an animal. It hit Perrin suddenly. Someone had cut Faile's clothes off! His voice shook. "They only took women?"

A round-faced young Maiden named Briain shook her head. "Three men would have been made *gai'shain,* I think, but they fought too hard and were killed with knife or spear. All the rest died by arrow."

"It is not like that, Perrin Aybara," Elienda said hurriedly, sounding shocked. A tall woman with wide shoulders, she managed to look almost motherly, though he had seen her knock a man down with her fist. "Harming a *gai'shain* is like harming a child, or a blacksmith. It was wrong to take wetlanders, but I cannot believe they will break custom *that* far. I am sure they will not even be punished, if they can be meek until they are recovered. There are others who will show them." Others; Bain and Chiad again.

"What direction did they go?" he asked. Could Faile be meek? He could not picture her that way. At least let her try, till he could find her.

"Almost south," Sulin replied. "Much nearer south than east. After the snow hid their tracks, Jondyn Barran saw other traces. What the others are following. I believe him. He sees as much as Elyas Machera. There is much to see." Thrusting her spears behind the bow case on her back, she hung her buckler from the hilt of her heavy belt knife. Her fingers flashed handtalk, and Elienda unfastened a second, larger bundle and handed it to her. "Many people are moving out there, Perrin Aybara, and strange things. This you must see first, I think." Sulin unfolded another cut dress, this one green. He thought he remembered it on Alliandre. "These, we recovered where your wife was taken." Inside, forty or fifty Aiel arrows shifted in a heap. There were dark stains on the shafts, and he caught the scent of dried blood.

"Taardad," Sulin said, picking out an arrow and immediately throwing it to the ground. "Miagoma." She tossed two more aside. "Goshien." Those brought a grimace to her face; she was Goshien. Clan by clan, she named them all except the Shaido, dropping arrows until just over half lay scattered around her. She held up the cut dress holding the remainder in both hands, then spilled them. "Shaido," she said significantly.

Clutching Faile's dress to his chest—her scent eased the pain in his heart, and made it worse at the same time—Perrin frowned at the arrows jumbled on the snow. Already, some were half buried in the fresh fall. "Too many Shaido," he said at last. They should all be bottled up in Kinslayer's Dagger, five hundred leagues distant. But if some of their Wise Ones had learned to Travel . . . Maybe even one of the Forsaken . . . Light, he was rambling like a fool—what would the Forsaken have to do with this?—rambling when he had to think. His brain felt as weary as the rest of him. "The others are men who wouldn't accept Rand as the *car'a'carn*." Those cursed colors flashed in his head. He had no time for anything but Faile. "They joined the Shaido." Some of the Maidens averted their eyes. Elienda glared at him. They knew that some had done what he said, but it was one of those things they did not like to hear said aloud. "How many altogether, do you reckon? Not the whole clan, surely?" If the Shaido were here in a body, there would be more than rumors of distant raids. Even among all the other troubles, all of Amadicia would know.

"Near enough to be going on with, I'm thinking," Wynter muttered under his breath. Perrin was not meant to hear.

Reaching in among the bundles tied to the ornate saddle, Sulin drew out a rag doll dressed in *cadin'sor*. "Elyas Machera found this just before we turned back, about forty miles from here." She shook her head, and for a moment her voice and scent became . . . startled. "He said he smelled it beneath the snow. He and Jondyn Barran found scrapes on the trees they said were caused by carts. Very many carts. If there are children . . . I think it may be a whole sept, Perrin Aybara. Perhaps more than one. Even a single sept will have at least a thousand spears, and more at need. Every man but the blacksmiths will pick up a spear at need. They are days south of us. Perhaps more days than I think, in this snow. But I believe those who took your wife are going to meet them."

"This blacksmith has picked up a spear," Perrin murmured. A thousand, maybe more. He had over two thousand, counting the Winged Guards and Arganda's men. Against Aiel, though, the numbers would favor the Shaido. He fingered the doll in Sulin's sinewy hand. Was a Shaido child weeping over the loss of her doll? "We go south."

He was turning to mount Stepper when Sulin touched his arm to stop him. "I told you we saw other things. Twice, Elyas Machera found horse droppings and campfires under the snow. Many horses, and many campfires."

"Thousands," Alharra put in; His black eyes met Perrin's levelly, and his voice was matter-of-fact. He was simply reporting what was. "Five, maybe ten or more; it's hard to tell. But soldiers' camps. The same men both places, I think. Machera and Barran agree. Whoever it is, they're heading near enough south, too. Maybe they have nothing to do with the Aiel, but they could be following."

Sulin gave the Warder an impatient frown and continued with barely a pause for his interruption. "Three times we saw flying creatures like those you say the Seanchan use, huge things with ribbed wings and people riding their backs. And twice we saw tracks like this." Bending, she picked up one of the arrows and drew a rounded shape a little like a large bear's paw in the snow, but with six toes longer than a man's fingers. "Sometimes it shows claws," she said, marking them, longer even than one of the big bears in the Mountains of Mist. "It has a long stride. I think it runs very fast. Do you know what it is?"

He did not—he had never heard of anything with six toes except the cats in the Two Rivers; he had been surprised to find cats elsewhere only had five—but he could make a safe guess. "Another Seanchan animal." So there were Seanchan to the south as well as Shaido, and—what?—Whitecloaks, or a Seanchan army. It could not be anyone else. He trusted Balwer's information. "We still go south." The Maidens stared at him as if he had told them it was snowing.

Pulling himself up into Stepper's saddle, he turned back toward the column. The Warders walked, leading their weary horses. The Maidens took Alliandre's gelding with them as they trotted to where the Wise Ones were standing. Masuri and Seonid were riding to meet their Warders. He wondered why they all had not come to stick their noses in. Perhaps it was as simple as letting him be alone with his grief if the news turned out bad. Perhaps. In his head, he tried to fit everything together. The Shaido, however many they were. The Seanchan. The mounted army, whether Whitecloak or Seanchan. It was like the puzzles Master Luhhan had taught him to make, intricate twists of metal that slid apart and slipped back together like a dream, if you knew the trick. Only, his head felt muddled, groping at pieces that would not slide anywhere.

The Two Rivers men were all mounted again when he reached them. Those who had been on the ground with their bows ready looked a little abashed. They all eyed him uneasily, tentatively.

"She's alive," he said, and it was as if every man of them started breathing again. They took the rest of his news with a strange impassiveness, some even nodding as though they had expected no less.

"Won't be the first time we've faced long odds," Dannil said. "What do we do, my Lord?"

Perrin grimaced. The man was still stiff as an oak. "For starters, we're Traveling forty miles due south. After that, I will see. Neald, you go ahead and find Elyas and the others. Tell them what I'm doing. They will be a good deal further on, by this time. And have a care. You can't fight ten or a dozen Wise Ones." A whole sept should have at least that many who could channel. And if it was more than one? A bog he had to cross when he came to it.

Neald nodded before turning his gelding back toward the camp, where he had already memorized the ground. There were only a few more orders to give. Riders had to be sent to find the Mayeners and Ghealdanin, who would be moving apart as they camped apart. Grady thought he could memorize the ground right there before they could join up, so there was no need to turn everything around and follow Neald back. And that left only one thing.

"I need to find Masema, Dannil," Perrin said. "Somebody who can give him a message, anyway. With luck, I won't be long."

"You go among that filth alone, my Lord, and you'll need luck," Dannil replied. "I heard some of them talking about you. Said you're Shadowspawn, because of your eyes." His gaze met Perrin's golden eyes and slid sideways. "Said you'd been tamed by the Dragon Reborn, but still Shadowspawn. You ought to take a few dozen men to watch your back."

Perrin hesitated, patting Stepper's neck. A few dozen men would not be enough if Masema's people really thought he was Shadowspawn and decided to take matters into their own hands. All the Two Rivers men together might not be enough. Maybe he did not need to tell Masema, just let him learn for himself.

His ears caught a bluetit's trill from the trees to the west, followed a moment later by a second that everyone could hear, and the decision was taken away from him. He was sure of it, and wondered whether this was part of being *ta'veren*. He reined Stepper around and waited.

The Two Rivers men knew what it meant, hearing that particular bird from back home. Men coming, more than a handful, and not necessarily peaceful. It would have been a crookbill trilling if they were friends, and a mocker's cry of alarm had they been clearly unfriendly. This time, they behaved better. Along the west side of the column, every second man as far as Perrin could see in the snow dismounted and handed his reins to the man next to him, then readied his bow.

The strangers appeared through the scattered trees spread out in a line as if to increase the impression of their numbers. They were perhaps a hundred, with two in advance, but their slow advance did seem ominous. Half carried lances, not couched but held as though ready be tucked under an arm. At a steady walk they came on. Some wore armor, a breastplate or a helmet but rarely both. Still, they were better armed than the general run of Masema's followers. One of the pair out front was Masema himself, his zealot's face staring out of his cloak's cowl like a rabid mountain cat staring out of a cave. How many of those lances had borne a red streamer yesterday morning?

Masema stopped his men with a raised hand only when he was just a few paces from Perrin. Pushing back his hood, he ran his gaze along the dismounted men with their bows. He seemed unaware of the snow hitting his bare scalp. His companion, a bigger man with a sword on his back and another at his saddlebow, kept his cowl up, but Perrin thought his head was shaved, too. That one managed to study the column and watch Masema with equal intensity. His dark eyes burned almost as much as Masema's. Perrin thought about telling them that at this range, a Two Rivers longbow would put a pile shaft right through a breastplate, and out the wearer's back besides. He considered mentioning Seanchan. Discretion, Berelain had counseled. Perhaps it was a fine thing, in the circumstances.

"You were coming to meet me?" Masema said abruptly. Even the man's voice seethed with intensity. Nothing was ever casual on his tongue. Anything he had to say was important. The pale triangular scar on his cheek pulled his sudden smile crooked. There was no warmth in it anyway. "No matter. I am here, now. As you no doubt know by now, those who follow the Lord Dragon Reborn—the Light illumine his name!—refuse to be left behind. I cannot demand it of them. They serve him as I do."

Perrin saw a tide of flame rolling across Amadicia into Altara and perhaps beyond, leaving death and devastation behind. He took a deep breath, sucking cold into his lungs. Faile was more important than anything. Anything! If he burned for it, then he burned. "Take your men east." He was shocked at how steady his voice was. "I will catch up when I can. My wife has been kidnapped by Aiel, and I'm heading south to get her back." For once, he saw Masema surprised.

"Aiel? So they are more than rumor?" He frowned at the Wise Ones on the far side of the column. "South, you say?" Folding his gloved hands on the pommel of his saddle, he turned his study to Perrin. Insanity filled the man's scent; Perrin could not find anything but madness in it. "I will come with you," Masema said at last, as if reaching a decision. Odd, he had been impatient to reach Rand without delay. So long as he did not have to be touched by the Power to do so, at least. "All those who follow the Lord Dragon Reborn—the Light illumine his name!—will come. Killing Aiel savages is doing the Light's work." His eyes flickered toward the Wise Ones, and his smile was even colder than before.

"I would appreciate the help," Perrin lied. That rabble would be useless against Aiel. Still, they numbered in the thousands. And they had held off armies, if not armies of Aiel. A piece of that puzzle in his head shifted. Ready to drop with fatigue, he could not make out exactly how, just that it had. In any case, it was not going to happen. "They have a long lead on me, though. I intend to Travel, to use the One Power, to catch up. I know how you feel about that."

Uneasy murmurs ran through the men behind Masema, and they eyed one another and shifted weapons. Perrin caught muttered curses and also "yellow eyes" and "Shadowspawn." The second shaven-headed man glared at Perrin as though he had blasphemed, but Masema just stared, trying to bore a hole into Perrin's head and see what lay inside.

"*He* would be grieved if harm came to your wife," the madman said at last. The emphasis named Rand as clearly as the name Masema did not allow to be spoken. "There will be a . . . dispensation, in this one instance. Only to find your wife, because you are his friend. Only this." He spoke calmly—calmly for him—but his deep-set eyes were dark fire, his face contorted with unknowing rage.

Perrin opened his mouth, then closed it without speaking. The sun might as well rise in the west as Masema say what he just had. Suddenly Perrin thought that Faile might be safer with the Shaido than he was here and now.

CHAPTER

7

The Streets of Caemlyn

Elayne's entourage attracted plenty of attention as it rode through Caemlyn, along streets that rose and fell with the hills of the city. The Golden Lily on the breast of her fur-lined crimson cloak was sufficient to identify her for citizens of the capital, but she kept her hood back, framing her face so the single golden rose on the coronet of the Daughter-Heir was clearly visible. Not just Elayne, High Seat of House Trakand, but Elayne the Daughter-Heir. Let everyone see, and know.

The domes of the New City glinted white and gold in the pale morning light, and icicles sparkled on the bare branches of the trees down the center of the main streets. Even nearing its zenith the sun lacked warmth, despite a blessedly cloudless sky. Luckily, there was no wind today. The air was cold enough to frost her breath, yet with the paving stones cleared of snow even on the narrower, twisting ways, the city was alive again, the streets full and bustling. Carters and wagon drivers, harnessed by their work as surely as the horses between the shafts, clutched their cloaks in resignation as they made slow passage through the throng. A huge water wagon rumbled by, empty by the sound, on its way to be refilled for fighting the too-frequent arsons. A few hawkers and street peddlers braved the chill to cry their wares, but most folk hurried about their tasks, eager to be indoors as soon as possible. Not that hurrying meant moving very fast. The city bulged, its population swollen beyond that of Tar Valon. In such a swarm, even the few who were mounted moved no faster than a man could walk. In the whole morning she had seen only two or three carriages inching along the streets. If their passengers were not invalids or facing miles ahead, they were fools.

Everyone who saw her and her party paused at the very least, some pointing her out to others, or hoisting a child for a better view so one day they could tell their own children they had seen her. Whether they said they had seen the future Queen or simply a woman who held the city for a time was the question. Most people simply stared, but now and then a handful of voices cried out "Trakand! Trakand!" or even "Elayne and Andor!" as she passed. Better if there had been more cheering, yet silence was preferable to jeers. Andorans were outspoken folk, none more so than Caemlyners. Rebellions had begun and queens lost their thrones because Caemlyners voiced their displeasure in the streets.

An icy thought made Elayne shiver. Who holds Caemlyn holds Andor, the ancient saying went; it was not exactly true, as Rand had demonstrated, yet Caemlyn was Andor's heart. She had laid claim to the city—the Lion Banner and Trakand's Silver Keystone shared pride of place on the towers of the outer wall—but she did not yet hold the heart of Caemlyn, and that was far more important than holding stone and mortar.

They will all cheer me, one day, she promised herself. *I will earn their acclaim.* Today, though, the crowded ways felt lonely between those few upraised voices. She wished Aviendha were there, just for her company, but Aviendha saw no reason to climb onto a horse simply to move about the city. Anyway, Elayne could feel her. It was different from the bond with Birgitte, yet she could feel her sister's presence in the city, like sensing an unseen person in the same room, and it was comforting.

Her companions drew their own share of attention. After barely three years as Aes Sedai, Sareitha's dark square face had not yet achieved agelessness, and she looked a prosperous merchant in her fine bronze-colored woolens with a large silver-and-sapphires brooch holding her cloak. Her Warder, Ned Yarman, rode at her heels, and he certainly caught eyes. A tall, broad-shouldered young man with bright blue eyes and corn-yellow hair curling to his shoulders, he wore a shimmering Warder's cloak that made him appear a disembodied head floating above a tall gray gelding that was not entirely there either, where the cloak draped its haunches. There was no mistaking what he was, or that his presence announced an Aes Sedai. The others, maintaining a circle around Elayne as they made a way through the crowd, attracted just as many eyes, though. Eight women in the red coats and burnished helmets and breastplates of the Queen's Guard were not something seen every day. Or ever before, come to that. She had chosen them out from the new recruits herself for that very reason.

Their under-lieutenant, Caseille Raskovni, lean and hard as any Aiel Maiden, was that rarity of rarities, a woman merchant's guard, nearly twenty years in the trade, as she put it. Silver bells in her stocky roan gelding's mane named her Arafellin, though she was vague about her past. The only Andoran among the eight was a graying, placid-faced woman with wide shoulders, Deni Colford, who had kept order in a wagon drivers' tavern in Low Caemlyn, outside the walls, another rough and singular job for a woman. Deni did not yet know how to use the sword at her hip, but Birgitte said she had very quick hands and quicker eyes, and she was quite adept with the pace-long cudgel that hung opposite her sword. The remainder were Hunters for the Horn, disparate women, tall and short, slender and wide, dewy-eyed and gray-haired, with backgrounds as varied, though some were as discreet as Caseille and others clearly inflated their former station in life. Neither attitude was uncommon among Hunters. They had leaped at the chance to be listed on the Guards' roll, though. More important, they had passed Birgitte's close inspection.

"These streets are not safe for you," Sareitha said suddenly, heeling her chestnut up beside Elayne's black gelding. Fireheart almost managed to nip the sleek mare before Elayne reined his head away. The street was narrow here, compressing the crowd and forcing the Guardswomen in closer around them. The Brown sister's face pictured Aes Sedai composure, but apparent concern sharpened her tone. "Anything might happen in a crush like this. Remember who is staying at the Silver Swan, less than two miles from this spot. Ten sisters at one inn are not simply seeking their own for company. Elaida might well have sent them."

"She might not have, too," Elayne replied calmly. More calmly than she felt. A great many sisters seemed to be waiting on the side until the struggle between Elaida and

Egwene was over. Two had departed the Silver Swan and three more come just since her arrival in Caemlyn. That did not sound like a party sent on a mission. And none were Red Ajah; surely Elaida would include Reds. Still, they were being watched as well as she could arrange, though she did not tell Sareitha that. Elaida very much wanted her, much more than she would want a runaway Accepted, or one connected to Egwene and those Elaida called rebels. Why, she could not quite understand. A queen who was Aes Sedai would be a great prize for the White Tower, but she would not become queen if she was snatched back to Tar Valon. For that matter, Elaida had issued the order to bring her back by any means necessary long before there seemed any possibility she would assume the throne for many years to come. It was a puzzle she had fretted over more than once since Ronde Macura slipped her that foul brew that dulled a woman's ability to channel. A very worrying puzzle, especially now she was announcing her location to the world.

Her eyes lingered a moment on a black-haired woman in a blue cloak with her hood thrown back. The woman barely glanced at her before turning into a candlemaker's shop. A weighted cloth bag hung from her shoulder. Not an Aes Sedai, Elayne decided. Merely another woman who aged well, like Zaida. "In any case," she went on firmly, "I won't be penned up by fear of Elaida." What *were* those sisters at the Silver Swan up to?

Sareitha snorted, and not very softly; she seemed about to roll her eyes, then thought better of it. Occasionally Elayne caught an odd look from one of the other sisters in the Palace, doubtless thinking of how she had been raised, yet on the surface, at least, they accepted her as Aes Sedai, acknowledged that she stood higher among them than any except Nynaeve. That was not enough to stop them speaking their minds, often more bluntly that they would have with a sister who stood where she did and had achieved the shawl in more usual fashion. "Forget Elaida, then," Sareitha said, "and remember who else would like to have you in hand. One well-aimed rock, and you are an unconscious bundle, easily carried away in the confusion."

Did Sareitha really have to tell her water was wet? Kidnapping other claimants to the throne was almost customary, after all. Every House that stood against her had supporters in Caemlyn watching for an opportunity, or she would have her slippers for her midday meal. Not that they could succeed, not so long as she could channel, but they would make the attempt given a chance. She had never thought that simply reaching Caemlyn provided safety.

"If I don't dare leave the Palace, Sareitha, I will never get the people behind me," she said quietly. "I must be seen, out and about and unafraid." That was why she had eight Guards instead of the fifty Birgitte had wanted. The woman refused to grasp the realities of politics. "Besides, they would need two well-aimed rocks with you here."

Sareitha snorted again, but Elayne did her best to ignore the other's obstinacy. She wished she could ignore the woman's presence, but that was impossible. She had more reason for this ride than being seen. Halwin Norry gave her facts and figures by the ream, though the First Clerk's droning voice almost put her to sleep, yet she wanted to see for herself. Norry could make a riot sound as lifeless as a report on the state of the city's cisterns or the expense of cleaning the sewers.

The crowds were thick with foreigners, Kandori with forked beards and Illianers with beards that left their upper lips bare and Arafellin with silver bells in their braids, copper-skinned Domani, olive-skinned Altarans and dark Tairens, Cairhienin who stood out for their short stature and pale skins. Some were merchants, caught by the sudden onset of winter or hoping to steal a jump on their competition, smooth-faced puffed-up folk who knew that trade was the life's blood of nations, and every one of them claiming to be a major artery even when betrayed by a poorly dyed coat or a brooch of brass and glass. Many of the people afoot had worn and ragged coats, breeches out at the knee, dresses with tattered hems, and threadbare cloaks or none at all. Those were refugees, either harried from their homes by war or sent wandering by the belief that the Dragon Reborn had broken every bond that held them. They hunched against the cold, faces haggard and defeated, and let themselves be buffeted by the flow of others around them.

Watching a dull-eyed woman stagger through the crowd clutching a small child on her shoulder, Elayne fumbled a coin from her purse and handed it to one of the Guards, an apple-cheeked woman with cold eyes. Tzigan claimed to be from Ghealdan, the daughter of a minor noble; well, she might be Ghealdanin, at least. When the Guardswoman leaned down to proffer the coin, the woman with her child staggered on by unheeding, unseeing. There were too many in the city like that. The Palace fed thousands every day, at kitchens set up throughout the city, but too many could not even summon the energy to collect their bread and soup. Elayne offered a prayer for mother and child as she dropped the coin back into her purse.

"You cannot feed everyone," Sareitha offered quietly.

"Children are not allowed to starve in Andor," Elayne said, as if issuing a decree. But she did not know how to stop it. Food was still plentiful in the city, but no command could force people to eat.

Some of the other foreigners had come to Caemlyn that way, too, men and women who no longer wore rags and haunted faces. Whatever had sent them flying from their homes, they had begun thinking that they had traveled far enough, thinking about the trades they had abandoned, often along with everything they possessed. In Caemlyn, though, anyone with skill in a craft and a little drive could always find a banker with ready coin. There were new trades being followed in the city these days. She had seen three clockmakers' shops already this morning! Within her sight were two shops selling blown glass, and nearly thirty manufactories had been built north of the city. From now on, Caemlyn would export glass, not import it, and crystal as well. The city had lacemakers, now, producing as fine as Lugard ever had, and no wonder since nearly all of them had come from there.

That brightened her mood a little—the taxes those new crafts paid would help, though it would take time before they paid much—yet it was still others in the crowds she noticed most. Foreign or Andoran, the mercenaries were easily picked out, hard-faced men wearing swords, swaggering even when slowed to a crawl by the press. Merchants' guards also went armed, rough fellows shouldering aside most men who got in their way, but they seemed subdued and sober compared to the sell-swords. And on the whole, they displayed fewer scars. Mercenaries dotted the crowd like raisins in a cake. With such a large pool to draw on, and with winter employment for their skills always in short supply, she did not think they would come too dear. Unless, as Dyelin feared, they cost her Andor. Somehow, she had to find enough men that foreigners were not a majority in the Guards. And the money to pay them.

Abruptly, she became aware of Birgitte. The other woman was angry—she often was, of late—and coming closer. Very angry, and coming very quickly. An ominous combination that set alarm gongs ringing in Elayne's head.

Immediately she ordered a return to the Palace by the most direct route—that would be how Birgitte was coming; the bond would lead her straight to Elayne—and they took the next turn south, onto Needle Street. It was actually a rather wide street, though it meandered like a river, down one hill and up the next, but generations ago it had been full of needlemakers. Now a few small inns and taverns were jammed among cutlers and tailors and every sort of shop except needlemakers.

Before they had even reached the Inner City, Birgitte found them climbing Pearman's Lane, where a handful of fruit-sellers still clung to shops handed down since the days of Ishara, though there was precious little to be seen in their windows this time of year. Despite the crowd Birgitte cantered into sight, red cloak flaring behind, scattering people before her left and right, and only slowed her rangy gray when she saw them ahead.

As if to make up for her hurry, she took a moment to study the Guardswomen and return Caseille's salute before turning her mount to walk beside Elayne's. Unlike them, she wore neither sword nor armor. The memories of her past lives were fading—she said she could remember nothing at all clearly before the founding of the White Tower, now, though fragments still floated up—but one thing she claimed to recall absolutely. Every time she had tried to use a sword, she had nearly gotten herself killed, and had even done so more than once. Her strung bow was in a leather saddle-case, though, with a bristling quiver of arrows on the other side. Anger boiled in her, and she wore a frown that only deepened as she spoke.

"A half-frozen pigeon flew into the Palace cote a little while ago with word from Aringill. The men escorting Naean and Elenia were ambushed and killed not five miles out of the town. Luckily, one of their horses came back with blood on the saddle, or we'd have known nothing for weeks yet. I doubt our luck extends to that pair being held for ransom by brigands."

Fireheart pranced a few steps, and Elayne reined him in sharply. Someone in the crowd shouted what might have been a cry for Trakand. Or not. Shopkeepers trying to attract custom raised enough din to muffle the words. "So we have a spy in the Palace," she said, then compressed her lips, wishing she had held her tongue in front of Sareitha.

Birgitte did not seem to care. "Unless there's a *ta'veren* trotting around we don't know about," she replied dryly. "Maybe now you'll let me assign a bodyguard. Just a few Guards, well chosen and—"

"No!" The Palace was her home. She would not be guarded there. Glancing at the Brown, she sighed. Sareitha was listening very attentively. There was no point in trying to hide things now. Not this. "You let the First Maid know?"

Birgitte gave her a sidelong look that, combined with a burst of mild outrage through their shared bond, told her to go teach her grandmother to knit. "She intends to question every servant who didn't serve your mother at least five years. I'm not sure she doesn't mean to put them to the question. The look on her face when I told her, I was glad to get out of her study with a whole skin. I'm looking at others, myself." She meant the Guards, but she would not say so in hearing of Caseille and the others. Elayne did not think it likely. All the recruiting gave anyone a perfect opportunity to slip in eyes-and-ears, yet without any assurance they would ever be where they could learn anything useful.

"If there are spies in the Palace," Sareitha said quietly, "there may be worse. Perhaps you should accept the Lady Birgitte's suggestion of a bodyguard. There is precedent." Birgitte showed the Brown sister her teeth; as a smile, it was a miserable failure. However much she disliked being addressed by her title, however, she turned hopeful eyes on Elayne.

"I said no, and I mean no!" Elayne snapped. A beggar, approaching the slow-moving circle of horses with a wide, gap-toothed grin and his cap in his hand, flinched and scurried away into the throng before she could even think of reaching for her purse. She was not sure how much of her anger was her own and how much Birgitte's, but it was appropriate.

"I should have gone to get them myself," she growled bitterly. Instead, she had woven a gateway for the messenger and spent the rest of the day meeting with merchants and bankers. "At the least, I should have stripped the garrison at Aringill for escort. Ten men dead because I blundered! Worse—the Light help me, it *is* worse!—I've lost Elenia and Naean because of it!"

Birgitte's thick golden braid, hanging outside her cloak, swung as she shook her head emphatically. "In the first place, queens don't go running off to do everything themselves. They're bloody queens!" Her anger was dying down, a little, but irritation flared on top of it, and her tone reflected both. She really wanted Elayne to have a bodyguard, very likely even in her bath. "Your adventuring days are done. The next thing, you'd be sneaking out of the Palace in disguise, maybe even wandering around after nightfall, when you might get your skull cracked open by some tough you never even saw."

Elayne sat up straight in her saddle. Birgitte knew, of course—she did not know any way to get around the bond, though she was sure there must be one—but the woman had no right to bring it up now. If Birgitte offered enough hints, she would have other sisters trying to follow her with their Warders and likely squads of Guardsmen as well. Everyone was so ridiculous about keeping her safe. You would think she had never been in Ebou Dar, much less Tanchico, or Falme. Besides, she had only done it once. So far. And Aviendha went with her.

"Cold dark streets don't compare to a warm fire and an interesting book," Sareitha put in idly, as if talking to herself. Studying the shops they were passing, she seemed intent on them. "I very much dislike walking on icy pavement, myself, especially in the dark, without so much as a candle. Young, pretty women often think plain clothes and a dirty face make them invisible." The shift was so sudden, with no change in tone, that at first Elayne did not realize what she was hearing. "Being knocked down and dragged into an alley by drunken rowdies is a hard way to learn differently. Of course, if you are lucky enough to have a friend with you who also can channel, if she's lucky enough that the tough fails to hit her as hard as he should . . . Well, you cannot be lucky every time. Wouldn't you agree, Lady Birgitte?"

Elayne closed her eyes for a moment. Aviendha had said someone was following them, but she had been sure it was only a footpad. Anyway, it had not been like that. Not exactly. Birgitte's glare promised a talking to, later. She *refused* to understand that a Warder just did *not* dress down her Aes Sedai.

"In the second place," Birgitte went on grimly, "ten men or nearly three hundred, the bloody outcome would have been the bloody same. Burn me, it was a good plan. A few men could have brought Naean and Elenia to Caemlyn unnoticed. Emptying out the garrison would have pulled every flaming eye in the east of Andor, and whoever took them would have brought enough armsmen to be sure. Very likely, they'd hold Aringill now on top of it. Small as the garrison is, Aringill keeps anybody who wants to move against you in the east off balance, and the more Guards who come out of Cairhien, the better that gets, since they're nearly all loyal to you." For someone who claimed to be a simple archer, she had a good grasp of the situation. The only thing she had left out was the loss of the customs duties from the river trade.

"Who did take them, Lady Birgitte?" Sareitha asked, leaning to look past Elayne. "Surely that is a very important question." Birgitte sighed loudly, almost a whimper.

"We will know soon enough, I fear," Elayne said. The Brown quirked a doubting eyebrow at her, and she tried not to grind her teeth. She seemed to be doing that quite a lot since coming home.

A Taraboner woman in a green silk cloak stepped out of the way of the horses and made a deep curtsy, her thin, beaded braids swinging out of her cowl. Her maid, a diminutive woman with her arms full of small packages, imitated her mistress awkwardly. The two wide men close behind, guards carrying brass-ferruled quarterstaffs, remained upright and alert. Their long heavy leather coats would turn all but the most determined thrust of a knife.

Elayne inclined her head as they rode by to acknowledge the Taraboner's courtesy. She had not received as much from any Andoran in the streets, so far. The handsome face behind the woman's sheer veil showed too much age to be Aes Sedai. Light, she had too much on her plate to be worrying about Elaida now!

"It is very simple, Sareitha," she said in a carefully controlled voice. "If Jarid Sarand took them, Elenia will give Naean a choice. Declare Arawn for Elenia, with some sweetening of estates for Naean in return, or else have her throat slit in a quiet cell somewhere and her corpse buried behind a barn. Naean won't give in easily, but her House is arguing over who is in charge until she returns, so they'll dither, Elenia will threaten torture and maybe use it, and eventually Arawn will stand behind Sarand for Elenia. Soon to be joined by Anshar and Baryn; they will go where they see strength. If Naean's people have them, she will offer the same choices to Elenia, but Jarid will go on a rampage against Arawn unless Elenia tells him not to, and she won't if she thinks he has any hope of rescuing her. So we must hope to hear in the next few weeks that Arawn estates are being burned." *If not,* she thought, *I have four houses united to face, and I* still *don't know whether I really have even two!*

"That is . . . very nicely reasoned out," Sareitha said, sounding faintly surprised.

"I'm sure you could have, too, with time," Elayne said, too sweetly, and felt a stab of pleasure when the other sister blinked. Light, her mother would have expected her to see that much when she was ten!

The rest of the ride back to the Palace passed in silence, and she barely noticed the bright mosaic towers and grand vistas of the Inner City. Instead, she thought about Aes Sedai in Caemlyn and spies in the Royal Palace, about who had Elenia and Naean and how much Birgitte could step up recruiting, about whether it was time to sell the Palace's plate and the rest of her gems. A gloomy list to consider, but she kept her face smooth and serenely acknowledged the scant cheers that followed her. A queen could not show herself afraid, especially when she was.

The Royal Palace was a pure white confection of intricately worked balconies and columned walks atop the highest hill of the Inner City, the highest in Caemlyn. Its slender spires and gilded domes loomed against the midday sky, visible for miles, proclaiming the power of Andor. Grand entrances and departures were made at the front,

at the Queen's Plaza, where in the past great crowds had
gathered to hear the proclamations of queens and shout
their acclaim for Andor's rulers. Elayne entered at the rear
of the Palace, Fireheart's steel-shod hooves ringing on
the paving stones as she trotted into the main stableyard.
It was a broad space fronted on two sides by the rows of
tall arched doors of the stables, overlooked by a single long
white stone balcony, plain and sturdy. Several of the high,
columned walks offered partial views from above, but this
was a working place. In front of the simple colonnade that
gave entry to the Palace itself a dozen Guardsmen preparing to replace those on duty in the Plaza stood rigidly beside their horses, being inspected by their under-lieutenant,
a grizzled fellow with a limp who had been a bannerman
under Gareth Bryne. Along the outer wall, thirty more were
mounting, ready to begin patrols of the Inner City in pairs.
In normal days, there would have been Guardsmen whose
main duty was policing the streets, but with numbers so
reduced, those who protected the Palace had to do that as
well. Careane Fransi was there, as well, a stocky woman in
an elegant green-striped riding dress and blue-green cloak,
sitting her gray gelding while one of her Warders, Venr Kosaan, climbed onto his bay. Dark, with touches of gray in
his tight-curled hair and beard, the blade-slim man wore a
plain brown cloak. Apparently they did not mean to advertise who they were.

    Elayne's arrival bought a flash of surprise to the stab-
leyard. Not to Careane or Kosaan, of course. The Green
sister merely looked thoughtful in the sheltering cowl of
her cloak, and Kosaan not even that. He simply nodded to
Birgitte and Yarman, Warder to Warder. Without another
glance they rode out as soon as the last of Elayne's escort
cleared the iron-strapped gates. But some of those mounting along the wall paused with one foot in a stirrup, staring, and heads whipped toward the new arrivals among the
men standing inspection. She had not been expected back
for another hour at least, and excepting a few who never
thought beyond what their hands were doing, everyone in
the Palace knew the situation was volatile. Rumors spread
among soldiers even faster than among other men, and the
Light knew, that was saying something, the way men gos-
siped. These had to know that Birgitte had departed in a

hurry, and now she returned with Elayne, ahead of time. Was one of the other Houses marching on Caemlyn? Ready to attack? Were they to be ordered to the walls that they could not man completely, even with what Dyelin had in the city? Moments of surprise and worry, then the leathery under-lieutenant barked a command, and eyes snapped straight ahead, arms swept across chests in salute. Only three besides the former bannerman had been on the rolls a few days gone, but there were no raw recruits here.

Grooms in red coats with the White Lion embroidered on one shoulder came rushing out from the stable, though in fact there was little for them to do. The Guardswomen quietly dismounted at Birgitte's order and began leading their horses through the tall doors. She herself leaped from her saddle and tossed her reins to one of the grooms, and she was no quicker than Yarman, who hurried to hold Sareitha's bridle while she climbed down. He was what some sisters called "fresh caught," bonded less than a year—the term dated from a time when Warders had not always been asked whether they wanted the bond—and he was very assiduous in his duties. Birgitte just stood scowling, fists on her hips, apparently watching the men who would patrol the Inner City for the next four hours ride out in a column of twos. Elayne would have been surprised if those men more than crossed Birgitte's mind, though.

In any event, she had her own worries. Trying not to be obvious about it, she studied the wiry woman who held Fireheart's bridle, and the stocky fellow who put down a leather-covered mounting stool and held her stirrup as she dismounted. He was unsmilingly stolid and deliberate, while she was wrapped up in stroking the gelding's nose and whispering to him. Neither really looked at Elayne beyond a respectful bow of the head; courtesies came second to making sure she was not tossed from the saddle by a horse made skittish by bobbing people. No matter that she had no need of their help. She was not in the country any longer, and there were forms to be followed. Even so, she tried not to frown. Leaving them as they led Fireheart away, she did not look back. But she wanted to.

The windowless entry hall beyond the colonnade seemed dim, though a few of the mirrored stand-lamps were lit. Plain lamps here, the iron worked into simple scrolls. Everything was utilitarian, the plastered cornices unadorned, the white stone walls bare and smooth. Word of their arrival had spread, and before they were well inside, half a dozen men and women appeared, bowing and curtsying, to take cloaks and gloves. Their livery differed from the stable-folk's in having white collars and cuffs, and the Lion of Andor on the left breast rather than shoulder. Elayne did not recognize anyone on duty today. Most servants in the Palace were new, and others had come out of retirement to take the places of those frightened off when Rand captured the city. A bald, bluff-faced fellow did not quite meet her eyes, but he might have feared it would be too forward. A slender young woman with a squint put too much enthusiasm into her curtsy, and her smile, but perhaps she simply wanted to show eagerness. Elayne walked away, followed by Birgitte, before she began glaring at them. Suspicion had a bitter taste.

Sareitha and her Warder left them after a few paces, the Brown murmuring an excuse about books she wanted to see in the library. The collection was not small, though nothing in comparison to the great libraries, and she spent hours there every day, frequently pulling up age-worn volumes she said were unknown elsewhere. Yarman heeled her as she glided off down a crossing hallway, a dark stocky swan drawing a strangely graceful stork in her wake. He still carried his disturbing cloak, carefully folded over one arm. Warders rarely let those out of their own hands for long. Kosaan's likely was in his saddlebags.

"Would you like a Warder's cloak, Birgitte?" Elayne asked, walking on. Not for the first time, she envied Birgitte her voluminous trousers. Even divided skirts made an effort of anything beyond a sedate pace. At least she had on riding boots instead of slippers. The bare red-and-white floor tiles would have been freezing in slippers. There were not enough carpets to layer in the halls as well as in the rooms; they would have been worn out in no time, anyway, just from the constant traffic of servants keeping up the Palace. "As soon as Egwene has the Tower, I will have one made for you. You should have one."

"I don't care about flaming cloaks," Birgitte replied grimly. A foreboding scowl set her mouth in a hard line. "It was over so fast, I thought you'd just bloody stumbled and hit your bloody head. Blood and ashes! Knocked down by street toughs! The Light only knows what might have happened!"

"There is no need to apologize, Birgitte." Outrage and indignation began flooding through the bond, but she meant to seize the advantage. Birgitte's chiding was bad enough in private; she was not about to put up with it in the halls, with servants all around, scurrying by on errands, polishing the carved wall panels, tending stand-lamps that were gilded here. They barely paused to offer silent courtesies to Birgitte and her, but doubtless every one was wondering why the Captain-General looked like a thunderhead and had their ears wide to catch whatever they could. "You were not there because I didn't want you there. I'll wager Sareitha didn't have Ned with her." It hardly seemed possible that Birgitte's face could darken more. Perhaps mentioning Sareitha was a mistake. Elayne changed the subject. "You really must do something about your language. You are beginning to sound like the worst sort of layabout."

"My . . . language," Birgitte murmured dangerously. Even her strides changed, to something like a pacing leopard. "*You* talk about *my* language? At least I always know what the words I use mean. At least I know what fits where, and what doesn't." Elayne colored, and her neck stiffened. She *did* know! Most of the time. Often enough, at least. "As for Yarman," Birgitte went on, her voice still soft, and still dangerous, "he's a good man, but he isn't over being goggle-eyed that he's a Warder yet. He probably jumps when Sareitha snaps her fingers. I was *never* goggle-eyed, and I don't jump. Is *that* why you saddled me with a title? Did you think it would rein me in? Wouldn't have been the first silly thought in that head of yours. For someone who thinks so clearly most of the time . . . Well. I have a writing desk buried in flaming reports I have to shovel through if you're going to get even half the Guards you want, but we'll have a good long talk tonight. My Lady," she added, much too firmly. Her bow was almost mockingly formal. She stalked away, and her long golden braid should have been bristling like an angry cat's tail.

Elayne stamped her foot in frustration. Birgitte's title was a well-earned reward, earned ten times over just since she bonded the woman! And ten thousand times over before that. Well, she had *thought* of the other, but not until afterwards.

Much good it had done, anyway. Whether from liege lady or Aes Sedai, Birgitte chose which commands she obeyed. Not when it was important—not when *she* thought it was important, anyway—but over anything else, especially what she called unnecessary risks, or improper behavior. As if Birgitte Silverbow could talk to anyone about taking risks! And as for proper behavior, Birgitte caroused in taverns! She drank and gambled, and ogled pretty men to boot! She enjoyed looking at the pretty ones even if she did prefer those who looked as if they had been beaten about the head often. Elayne did not want to change her—she admired the woman, liked her, counted her a friend—but she wished there were a little more of Warder to Aes Sedai in their relationship. And much less of knowing older sister to scampish younger.

Abruptly she realized that she was standing there scowling at nothing. Servants hesitated as they went by, and tucked their heads down as if afraid she might be glaring at them. Smoothing her face, she gestured to a gangling, pimply-faced boy coming down the hall. He bowed so awkwardly and so deeply that he staggered and almost fell over.

"Find Mistress Harfor and ask her to see me immediately in my apartments," she told him, then added in a not unkindly voice, "And you might remember, your superiors won't be pleased if they find you gawking at the Palace when you should be working." His mouth dropped open as though she had read his mind. Perhaps he thought she had. His wide eyes flashed to her Great Serpent ring, and he squeaked and made an even deeper bow before darting away at a dead run.

She smiled in spite of herself. It had been a wild stab, but he was too young to be anyone's spy, and too nervous not to be up to something he should not. On the other hand . . . Her smile faded. On the other hand, he was not that much younger than she.

CHAPTER
8

Sea Folk and Kin

I t was no surprise to Elayne when she encountered the First Maid before reaching her apartments. After all, they were both heading for the same place. Mistress Harfor made her curtsy and fell in with her, carrying an embossed leather folder beneath one arm. She had certainly been up as early as Elayne if not earlier, but her scarlet tabard appeared freshly ironed, the White Lion on her front as clean and pale as new-fallen snow. The servants scurried faster and polished harder when they saw her. Reene Harfor was not harsh, but she kept as tight a discipline over the Palace as Gareth Bryne ever had over the Guards.

"I fear I haven't caught any spies yet, my Lady," she said in response to Elayne's question, her voice pitched to reach Elayne's ears alone, "but I believe I uncovered a pair. A woman and a man, both taken in service during the last months of the late Queen your mother's reign. They left the Palace as soon as word spread that I was questioning every-one. Without waiting to gather a scrap of their belongings, not so much as a cloak. That's as good as an admission, I'd say. Unless they were afraid of being caught out in some other mischief," she added reluctantly. "There have been cases of pilfering, I'm afraid."

Elayne nodded thoughtfully. Naean and Elenia had been much in the Palace during the last months of her mother's reign. More than enough opportunity to settle eyes-and-ears in place. Those two had been in the Palace, and more who had opposed Morgase Trakand's claim to the throne, accepted her amnesty once she had it, then betrayed her. She would not make her mother's mistake. Oh, there must be amnesty wherever possible—anything else was planting the seeds for a civil war—but she planned to watch those who took her pardon very closely. Like a cat watching a rat that claimed to have given up interest in the grain barns. "They were spies," she said. "And there may well be others. Not just for Houses. The sisters at the Silver Swan may have bought eyes-and-ears in the Palace, too."

"I will continue to look, my Lady," Reene replied, inclining her head slightly. Her tone was perfectly respectful; she did not so much as raise an eyebrow, but once again Elayne found herself thinking of teaching her grandmother to knit. If only Birgitte could handle matters the way Mistress Harfor did.

"As well you returned early," the plump woman went on. "You have a busy afternoon, I fear. To begin, Master Norry wishes to speak with you. On an urgent matter, he says." Her mouth hardened for an instant. She always required to know why people wanted to approach Elayne, so she could winnow out the chaff rather than let Elayne be buried under it, but the First Clerk never saw fit to give her even a hint of his business. Any more than she told him hers. Both were jealous of their fiefs. With a shake of her head, she dismissed Halwin Norry. "After him, a delegation of tabac merchants has petitioned to see you, and another of weavers, both asking remission of taxes because times are hard. My Lady does not need my advice to tell them times are hard for everyone. A group of foreign merchants is waiting as well; rather a large group. Merely to wish you well in a way that doesn't encumber them, of course—they wish to be on your good side without antagonizing anyone else—but I suggest meeting them briefly." She laid plump fingers on the folder under her arm. "Also, the Palace accounts require your signature before they can go to Master Norry. They'll make him sigh, I fear. I hardly expected it in winter, but much of the flour is full of weevils and moths, and half the cured hams have turned, as well as most of the smoked fish." Quite respectful. And quite firm.

I rule Andor, Elayne's mother had told her once, in private, *but at times I think Reene Harfor rules me.* Her mother had been laughing, but she sounded as if she meant it, too. Come to think on it, Mistress Harfor as a Warder would be ten times worse than Birgitte.

Elayne did not want to meet with Halwin Norry or with merchants. She wanted to sit quietly and think about spies, and who had Naean and Elenia, and how she could counter them. Except . . . Master Norry had kept Caemlyn alive since her mother died. In truth, by what she could see in the old accounts, he had done so almost from the day she had fallen into Rahvin's clutches, though Norry was vague about that. He seemed offended by the events of those days, in a rather dusty way. She could not simply shuffle him off. Besides, he never expressed urgency over anything. And the goodwill of merchants was not to be sneered at, even foreign merchants. And the accounts did need to be signed. Weevils and moths? And hams spoiling? In winter? That was decidedly odd.

They had reached the tall, lion-carved doors of her apartments. Smaller lions than on the doors to those her mother had used, and smaller apartments, but she never considered using the Queen's chambers. That would have been as presumptuous as sitting on the Lion Throne before her right to the Rose Crown was acknowledged.

With a sigh, she reached for the folder.

Down the hallway she caught sight of Solain Morgeillin and Keraille Surtovni, hurrying along as quickly as they could without appearing to run. Flashes of silver showed at the neck of the sullen woman squeezed between them, though the Kinswomen had draped a long green scarf around her to hide the *a'dam's* leash. That *would* cause talk, and it would be seen sooner or later. Better if she and the others did not have to be moved, but there was no way to avoid it. Between Kinswomen and Sea Folk Windfinders, rooms in the servants' quarters had been needed to hold the overflow even with two and three to a bed, and the Palace had basements for storage, not dungeons. How did Rand *always* manage to do the wrong thing? Being male just was not excuse enough. Solain and Keraille vanished around a corner with their prisoner.

"Mistress Corly asked to see you this morning, my Lady." Reene's voice was carefully neutral. She had been watching the Kinswomen, too, and a trace of frown remained on her broad face. The Sea Folk were odd, yet she could fit a clan Wavemistress and her entourage into her view of the world even if she did not know precisely what a clan Wavemistress was. A high-ranking foreigner was a high-ranking foreigner, and foreigners were expected to be odd. But she could not understand why Elayne had given shelter to nearly a hundred and fifty merchants and crafts-women. Neither "the Kin" nor "the Knitting Circle" would have meant anything to her had she heard them, and she did not understand the peculiar tensions between those women and the Aes Sedai. Nor did she understand the women the Asha'man had brought, prisoners in truth if not confined in cells, kept secluded and never allowed to speak to anyone but the women who escorted them through the halls. The First Maid knew when not to ask questions, yet she disliked not understanding what was going on in the Palace. Her voice did not change by a hair. "She said she had good news for you. Of a sort, she said. She did not petition for an audience, though."

Good news of any sort was better than going over the accounts, and she had hopes of what this news might be. Relinquishing the folder in the First Maid's hands, she said, "Leave that on my writing table, please. And tell Master Norry that I will see him shortly."

Setting out in the direction the Kin had come from with their prisoner, she walked quickly in spite of her skirts. Good news or no good news, Norry and the merchants did have to be seen, and the merchants, not to mention the ac-counts gone over and signed. Ruling meant endless weeks of drudgery and rare hours of doing what you wanted. Very rare hours. Birgitte lay in the back of her head, a tight ball of the purest irritation and frustration. No doubt, she was digging through that table piled with papers. Well, her own relaxation this day would be whatever time was required to change out of riding clothes and snatch a hasty meal. So she walked very quickly, lost in thought and hardly seeing what was in front of her. What did Norry find urgent? Surely not street repairs. How many spies? Small chance Mistress Harfor would catch them all.

As she rounded a corner, only the sudden awareness of other women who could channel kept her from run-ning headlong into Vandene coming the other way. They recoiled from one another in startlement. Apparently the Green had been deep in thought, too. Her two companions raised Elayne's eyebrows.

Kirstian and Zarya wore plain white and stayed a careful pace behind Vandene, hands folded meekly at their waists. Their hair was bound back simply, and they wore no jewelry. Jewelry was strongly discouraged among novices. They had been Kinswomen—Kirstian had actually been in the Knitting Circle itself—but they were runaways from the Tower, and there were prescribed ways of dealing with those, set in Tower law, no matter how long they had been gone. Returned runaways were required to be absolutely perfect in everything they did, the very model of an initiate striving for the shawl, and small slips that might be overlooked in others were punished swiftly and strongly. They faced a much stronger punishment when they reached the Tower, in addition, a public birching, and even then they would be held to their straight and painful path for at least a year. A returned runaway was made to know in her heart that she never, ever wanted to run away again. Not ever! Half-trained women were just too dangerous to be left loose.

Elayne had tried to be lenient, the few times she was with them—the Kinswomen were not really half-trained; they had as much experience with the One Power as any Aes Sedai, if not the training—she had tried, only to discover that even most of the other Kinswomen disapproved. Given another chance to become Aes Sedai—those who could, at least—they embraced all of the Tower's laws and customs with shocking fervor. She was not surprised at the subdued eagerness in the two women's eyes or the way they seemed to radiate a promise of good behavior—they wanted that chance as badly as anyone—just that they were with Vandene at all. Until now, she had ignored the pair entirely.

"I was looking for you, Elayne," Vandene said without preamble. Her white hair, gathered at the nape of neck with a dark green ribbon, had always given her an air of age despite her smooth cheeks. Her sister's murder had added grimness, soaked it into the bone, so she seemed like an implacable judge. She had been slender; now she was bony, her cheeks hollow. "These children—" She cut off, a faint grimace thinning her mouth.

It was the proper way to refer to novices—the worst moment for a woman who went to the Tower was not when she discovered she would not be considered fully adult until she earned the shawl, but when she realized that so long as she wore novice white, she really was a child, one who might injure herself or others through ignorance and blundering—the proper way, yet even to Vandene it must have seemed strange here. Most novices came to the Tower at fifteen or sixteen, and until recently, none over eighteen, except for a handful who had managed to carry off a lie. Unlike Aes Sedai, the Kin used age to set their hierarchy, and Zarya—she had been calling herself Garenia Roso-inde, but Zarya Alkaese was the name in the novice book, and Zarya Alkaese she would answer to—Zarya, with her strong nose and wide mouth, was more than ninety years old, though she appeared well short of her middle years. Neither woman had the agelessness despite their years of using the Power, and pretty, black-eyed Kirstian looked a little older, perhaps thirty or so. She was over three hundred, older than Vandene herself, Elayne was sure. Kirstian had been gone from the Tower so long that she had felt safe using her true name again, or part of it. Not at all the usual run of novices.

"These *children*," Vandene went on more firmly, a deep frown creasing her forehead, "have been thinking over events in Harlon Bridge." That was where her sister had been murdered. And Ispan Shefar, but as far as Vandene was concerned, the death of a Black sister counted with the death of a rabid dog. "Unfortunately, rather than keeping silent about their conclusions, they came to me. At least they haven't blathered where anyone could hear."

Elayne frowned slightly. Everyone in the Palace knew of the murders by this time. "I don't understand," she said slowly. And carefully. She did not want to give the pair hints if they had not really dug up painstakingly hidden secrets. "Have they worked out that it was Darkfriends instead of robbery?" That was the tale they had put about, two women in an isolated house, killed for their jewelry. Only she, Vandene, Nynaeve and Lan knew any real measure of the truth. Until now anyway, it seemed. They must have gotten that far, or Vandene would have sent them away with a flea in their collective ear.

"Worse." Vandene looked around, then moved a few paces to the center of where the hallways crossed, forcing Elayne to follow. From that vantage, they could see anyone coming along either corridor. The novices attentively maintained their positions relative to the Green. Maybe they had already gotten that flea, for all their eagerness. There were plenty of servants in sight, but no one approaching, no one close enough to overhear. Vandene lowered her voice anyway. Quietness did nothing to mask her displeasure. "They reasoned out that the killer must be Merilille, Sareitha or Careane. Good thinking on their part, I suppose, but they shouldn't have been thinking about it in the first place. They should have been kept at their lessons so hard they had no time to think of anything else." Despite the scowl she directed at Kirstian and Zarya, the two overaged novices beamed with delight. There had been a compliment buried in the scolding, and Vandene was sparing of compliments.

Elayne did not point out that the pair might have been kept a little busier if Vandene had been willing to take part of their lessons. Elayne herself and Nynaeve had too many other duties, and since they had added daily lessons for the Windfinders—everyone but Nynaeve had, anyway—no one at all had the energy for much time with the two novices. Teaching the Atha'an Miere women was like being fed through a laundress's mangle! They had little respect for Aes Sedai. And even less for rank among "the shorebound."

"At least they didn't speak to anyone else," she murmured. A blessing, if small.

It had been obvious when they found Adeleas and Ispan that their killer must be an Aes Sedai. They had been paralyzed with crimsonthorn before they were killed, and it was all but impossible that the Windfinders knew of an herb only found far from the sea. And even Vandene was sure the Kin numbered no Darkfriends among them. Ispan had run away herself as a novice, and even gotten as far as Ebou Dar, but she had been retaken before the Kin revealed themselves to her, that they were more than a few women put out of the Tower who had decided on a whim to help her. Under questioning by Vandene and Adeleas, she had revealed a great deal. Somehow she had managed to resist saying anything about the Black Ajah itself except for exposing old schemes long carried out, but she had been eager to tell anything else once Vandene and her sister were done with her. They had not been gentle, and they had plumbed her depths, yet she knew no more of the Kin than any other Aes Sedai. If there were any Darkfriends among the Kin, the Black Ajah would have known everything. So as much as they could wish otherwise, the killer was one of three women they had all grown to like. A Black sister in their midst. Or more than one. They had all been frantic to keep that knowledge secret, at least until the murderer was uncovered. The news would throw the entire Palace into a panic, maybe the entire city. Light, who else had been thinking over events in Harlon Bridge? Would they have the sense to hold silence?

"Someone had to take them in hand," Vandene said firmly, "to keep them out of further mischief. They need regular lessons and hard work," The pair's beaming faces had taken on a hint of smugness, but it faded a little at that. Their lessons had been few, but *very* hard, the discipline *very* strict. "That means you, Elayne, or Nynaeve."

Elayne clicked her tongue in exasperation. "Vandene, I hardly have a moment for myself to think. I'm already straining to give them an hour now and then. It will have to be Nynaeve."

"What will have to be Nynaeve?" the woman herself demanded cheerfully, joining them. Somehow she had acquired a long, yellow-fringed shawl embroidered with leaves and bright flowers, but it lay looped over her elbows. Despite the temperatures she wore a blue gown with quite a low neckline for Andor, though the thick, dark braid pulled over her shoulder and nestled in her cleavage kept the exposure from being too great. The small red dot, the *ki'sain,* in the middle of her forehead did look quite strange. According to Malkieri custom, a red *ki'sain* marked a married woman, and she had insisted on wearing it as soon as she learned. Toying idly with the end of her braid, she looked . . . content . . . not an emotion anyone usually associated with Nynaeve al'Meara.

Elayne gave a start when she noticed Lan, a few paces off, strolling a circle around them and keeping watch down both hallways. As tall as an Aielman in his dark green coat, with shoulders belonging on a blacksmith, the hard-faced man still managed to move like a ghost. His sword was buckled at his waist even here in the Palace. He always made Elayne shiver. Death gazed from his cold blue eyes. Except when he looked at Nynaeve, anyway.

Contentment vanished from Nynaeve's face as soon as

she learned what would have to be her task. She stopped
fingering her braid, and seized it in a tight fist. "Now you
listen to me. Elayne might be able to loll around playing
politics, but I have my hands full. More than half the Kin
would have vanished by now if Alise wasn't holding them
by the scruff of the neck, and since she hasn't a hope of
reaching the shawl herself, I'm not sure how much longer
she'll hold anybody. The rest think they can argue with me!
Yesterday, Sumeko called me . . . *girl!*"

She bared her teeth, but it was all her own fault, one way
and another. After all, she was the one who had hammered
at the Kin that they ought to show some backbone instead
of groveling to Aes Sedai. Well, they certainly had stopped
groveling. Instead, they were all too likely to hold sisters up
to the standard of their Rule. And find the sister wanting!
It might not be Nynaeve's fault, exactly, that she appeared
to be little more than twenty—she had slowed early—but
age was important to the Kin, and she had chosen to spend
most of her time with them. She was not jerking her braid,
just pulling at it so steadily it must be ready to pull free of
her scalp.

"And those cursed Sea Folk! Wretched women! Wretched;
wretched; wretched! If it wasn't for that *bloody* bargain . . . !
The last thing I need on my hands is a couple of whining,
bleating novices!" Kirstian's lips thinned for an instant, and
Zarya's dark eyes flashed indignation before she managed to
assume meekness again. A semblance of it. They had sense
enough to know that novices did not open their mouths to
Aes Sedai, though.

Elayne shoved down the desire to smooth everything
over. She wanted to slap Kirstian and Zarya both. They
had complicated everything by not keeping their mouths
shut in the first place. She wanted to slap Nynaeve. So she
finally had been cornered by the Windfinders, had she?
That earned no sympathy. "I'm not *playing* at anything,
Nynaeve, and you well know it! I have asked your advice
often enough!" Drawing a deep breath, she tried to calm
herself. The servants she could see beyond Vandene and
the two novices had paused in their work to goggle at the
cluster of women. She doubted they more than noticed Lan,
impressive as he was. Arguing Aes Sedai were something
to watch, and stay clear of. "Someone has to take charge of

them," she said more quietly. "Or do you think you can just tell them to forget all this? Look at them, Nynaeve. Left to themselves, they will be trying to find out who it is in a heartbeat. They wouldn't have gone to Vandene unless they thought she would let them help." The pair became pictures of wide-eyed novice innocence, with just a hint of offense at an unjust accusation. Elayne did not believe it. They had had a lifetime to work on disguising themselves.

"And why not?" Nynaeve said after a moment, shifting her shawl. "Light, Elayne, you have to remember they aren't what we normally expect in novices." Elayne opened her mouth in protest—what we normally expect, indeed!—Nynaeve might never have been a novice, but she had been Accepted not all that long ago; a whining, bleating Accepted, often enough, too!—she opened her mouth, and Nynaeve went right on. "Vandene can make good use of them, I'm sure," she said. "And when she isn't, she can give them regular lessons. I remember someone telling me you've taught novices before, Vandene. There. It's settled."

The two novices smiled broad, eager smiles of anticipation—they all but rubbed their hands together in satisfaction—but Vandene scowled. "I do not need novices getting under my feet while I—"

"You're just as blind as Elayne," Nynaeve broke in. "They have experience making Aes Sedai take them for something other than what they are. They can work at your direction, and that will give you time to sleep and eat. I don't believe you're doing either." She drew herself up, draping her shawl across her shoulders and along her arms. It was quite a performance. Short as she was, no taller than Zarya and markedly shorter than Vandene or Kirstian, she managed to seem the tallest one there by inches. It was a skill Elayne wished she could master. Although she would not try in a dress cut that way. Nynaeve was in danger of coming right out. Still, that did not diminish her presence. She was the essence of command. "You will do it, Vandene," she said firmly.

Vandene's scowl faded slowly, but fade it did. Nynaeve stood higher in the Power than she, and even if she never consciously thought of the fact, deeply ingrained custom made her yield, however unwillingly. By the time she turned to the two women in white, her face was as near composed as it had been since Adeleas' murder. Which just meant that the judge might not order an execution right now. Later, perhaps. Her gaunt face was calm, and starkly grim.

"I did teach novices for a time," she said. "A short time. The Mistress of Novices thought I was too hard on my students." The pair's eagerness cooled a bit. "Her name was Sereille Bagand." Zarya's face went as pale as Kirstian's, and Kirstian swayed as if suddenly dizzy. As Mistress of Novices and later Amyrlin Seat, Sereille was a legend. The sort of legend that made you wake in the middle of the night sweating. "I do eat," Vandene said to Nynaeve. "But everything tastes like ashes." With a curt gesture at the two novices, she led them away past Lan. They were staggering slightly as they followed.

"Stubborn woman," Nynaeve grumbled, frowning at the retreating backs, but there was more than a hint of sympathy in her voice. "I know a dozen herbs that would help her sleep, but she won't touch them. I've half a mind to slip something into her evening wine."

A wise ruler, Elayne thought, *knows when to speak and when not*. Well, that was wisdom in anyone. She did not say that Nynaeve calling anyone stubborn was the rooster calling the pheasant proud. "Do you know what Reanne's news is?" she said instead. "Good news—'of a sort'—so I understand."

"I haven't seen her this morning," the other woman muttered, still peering after Vandene. "I haven't been out of my rooms." Abruptly she gave herself a shake, and for some reason frowned suspiciously at Elayne. And then at Lan, of all things. Unperturbed, he continued to stand guard.

Nynaeve claimed her marriage was glorious—she could be *shockingly* frank about it with other women—but Elayne thought she must be lying to cover up disappointment. Very likely Lan was ready for an attack, ready to fight, even when asleep. It would be like lying down beside a hungry lion. Besides, that stone face was enough to chill any marriage bed. Luckily, Nynaeve had no idea what she thought. The woman actually smiled. An amused smile, oddly. Amused, and . . . could it be condescending? Of course not. Imagination.

"I know where Reanne is," Nynaeve said, settling her shawl back down to her elbows. "Come with me. I'll take you to her."

Elayne knew exactly where Reanne would be, since she was not closeted with Nynaeve, but once again she schooled her tongue, and let Nynaeve lead her. A sort of penance for arguing earlier, when she should have tried to make peace. Lan followed, those cold eyes scanning the halls. The servants they passed flinched when Lan's gaze fell on them. A youngish, pale-haired woman actually gathered her skirts and ran, bumping into a stand-lamp and setting it rocking in her flight.

That reminded Elayne to tell Nynaeve about Elenia and Naean, and about the spies. Nynaeve took it quite calmly. She agreed with Elayne that they would know soon enough who had rescued the two women, with a dismissive sniff for Sareitha's doubts. For that matter, she expressed surprise that they had not been taken right from Aringill long since. "I couldn't believe they were still there when we arrived in Caemlyn. Any fool could see they would be brought here sooner or later. Much easier to get them out of a small town." A small town. Aringill would have seemed a great city to her, once. "As for spies . . ." She frowned at a lanky, gray-haired man filling a gold-worked stand-lamp with oil, and shook her head. "Of course there are spies. I knew there must be, right from the start. You just have to watch what you say, Elayne. Don't say anything to anyone you don't know well unless you don't mind everyone knowing."

When to speak and when not, Elayne thought, pursing her lips. Sometimes that could be a true penance, with Nynaeve.

Nynaeve had her own information to impart. Eighteen of the Kin who had accompanied them to Caemlyn were no longer in the Palace. They had not run away, though. Since none was strong enough to Travel, Nynaeve had woven the gateways herself, sending them deep into Altara and Amadicia and Tarabon, into the Seanchan-held lands where they would try to find any of the Kin who had not already fled and bring them back to Caemlyn.

It would have been nice if Nynaeve had thought to inform her yesterday, when they left, or better yet, when she and Reanne reached the decision to send them, but Elayne did not mention that. Instead, she said, "That's very brave of them. Avoiding capture won't be easy."

"Brave, yes," Nynaeve said, sounding irritated. Her hand crept up to her braid again. "But that isn't why we chose them. Alise thought they were the most likely to run if we didn't give them something to do." Glancing over her shoulder at Lan, she snatched her hand back down. "I don't see how Egwene means to do it," she sighed. "All very well to say every one of the Kin will be 'associated' with the Tower somehow, but how? Most aren't strong enough to earn the shawl. Many can't even reach Accepted. And they certainly won't stand for being novices or Accepted the rest of their lives."

This time Elayne said nothing because she did not know what to say. The promise had to be kept; she had made it herself. In Egwene's name, true, and at Egwene's order, but she had spoken the words herself, and she would not break her word. Only, she did not see how to keep it unless Egwene came up with something truly wonderful.

Reanne Corly was just where Elayne had known she would be, in a small room with two narrow windows looking down on a small, fountained courtyard deep in the Palace, though the fountain was dry, this time of year, and the glass casements made the room a little stuffy. The floor was plain dark tile with no carpet, and for furnishings there were only a narrow table and two chairs. There were two people with Reanne when Elayne entered. Alise Tenjile, in simple high-necked gray, looked up from where she stood at the end of the table. Seemingly in her middle years, she was a woman of pleasant, unremarkable appearance who was quite remarkable indeed once you came to know her and could be very unpleasant indeed when it was called for. A single glance, and she returned to her study of what was going on at the table. Aes Sedai, Warders and Daughter-Heirs did not impress Alise, not any longer. Reanne herself was sitting on one side of the table, her face creased and her hair more gray than not, in a green dress more elaborate than Alise's; she had been put out of the Tower after failing her test for Accepted, and offered a second chance, she had already adopted the colors of her preferred Ajah. Across from her sat a plump woman in plain brown wool, her face set in stubborn defiance and her dark eyes locked on Reanne, avoiding the silvery segmented *a'dam* lying like a snake between them on the table. Her hands stroked the edge of the tabletop, though, and Reanne wore a confident smile that deepened the fine lines at the corners of her eyes.

"Don't tell me you have made one of them see reason," Nynaeve said before Lan had even shut the door behind them. She scowled at the woman in brown as though she wanted to box her ears if not worse, then glanced at Alise. Elayne thought Nynaeve was a little in awe of Alise. The woman was far from strong in the Power—she would never attain the shawl—but she had a way of taking charge when she wanted to and making everyone around her accept it. Including Aes Sedai. Elayne thought she might be just a little in awe of Alise herself.

"They still deny they can channel," Alise muttered, folding her arms beneath her breasts, and frowned at the woman facing Reanne. "They can't, really, I suppose, but I can feel . . . something. Not quite the spark of a woman born to it, but almost. It's as if she were right at the brink of being able to channel, one foot poised to step over. I have never sensed anything like it before. Well. At least they don't try to attack us with their fists anymore. I think I put them straight on that, at least!" The woman in brown flashed a sullen, angry glare at her, but jerked her eyes away from Alise's firm gaze, her mouth twisting in a sickly grimace. When Alise set somebody straight, they were set very straight indeed. Her hands continued to shift along the tabletop; Elayne did not think she was aware of it.

"They still deny seeing the flows, too, but they're trying to convince themselves," Reanne said in her high, musical voice. She continued to meet the other's obstinate stare with a smile. Any sister might have envied Reanne's serenity and presence. She had been Eldest of the Knitting Circle, the highest authority among the Kin. According to their Rule, the Knitting Circle existed only in Ebou Dar, but she was still the oldest among those in Caemlyn, a hundred years older than any Aes Sedai in living memory, and she could match any sister with her air of calm command. "They claim we trick them with the Power, use it to make them believe the *a'dam* can hold them. Sooner or later, they will run out of lies." Drawing the *a'dam* to her, she opened the collar's catch with a deft motion. "Shall we try again, Marli?"

The woman in brown—Marli—still avoided looking at the length of silver metal in Reanne's hands, but she stiffened and her hands fluttered on the table's edge.

Elayne sighed. What a gift Rand had sent her. A gift! Twenty-nine Seanchan *sul'dam* neatly held by *a'dam*, and five *damane*—she hated that word; it meant Leashed One, or simply Leashed; but that was what they were—five *damane* who could not be uncollared for the simple reason that they would try to free the Seanchan women who had held them prisoner. Leopards tied with string would have been a better gift. At least leopards could not channel. They had been given into the Kin's keeping because no one else had the time.

Still, she had seen right away what to do with the *sul'dam*. Convince them that they could learn to channel, then send them back to the Seanchan. Apart from Nynaeve, only Egwene, Aviendha and a few of the Kin knew her plan. Nynaeve and Egwene were doubtful, but however hard the *sul'dam* tried to hide what they were once they were returned, eventually one would slip. If they did not just report everything right away. Seanchan were peculiar; even the Seanchan among the *damane* truly believed that any woman who could channel had to be collared for the safety of everyone else. *Sul'dam*, with their ability to control women wearing the *a'dam*, were highly respected among the Seanchan. The knowledge that *sul'dam* themselves were able to channel would shake the Seanchan to their core, maybe even break them apart. It had seemed so simple, in the beginning.

"Reanne, I understood that you had good news," she said. "If the *sul'dam* haven't started breaking down, what is it?" Alise frowned at Lan, who stood silent guard in front of the door—she disapproved of him knowing their plans—but she said nothing.

"A moment, if you please," Reanne murmured. It was not really a request. Nynaeve truly had done her job too well. "There is no need for her to listen." The glow of *saidar* suddenly shone around her. She moved her fingers as she channeled, as though guiding the flows of air that bound Marli to her chair, then tied them off and cupped her hands as though shaping in her sight the ward against sound that she wove around the woman. The gestures were no part of channeling, of course, but necessary to her, since she had learned the weaves that way. The *sul'dam*'s lips twisted slightly in contempt. The One Power did not frighten her at all.

"Take your time," Nynaeve put in acidly, planting her hands on her hips. "There's no hurry." Reanne did not intimidate her the way Alise did.

Then again, Nynaeve no longer intimidated Reanne, either. Reanne did take her time, studying her handiwork, then nodded with satisfaction before rising. The Kin had always tried to channel as little as was necessary, and she took great pleasure in the freedom to use *saidar* as often as she wished, as well as pride in weaving well.

"The good news," she said, standing and smoothing her skirts, "is that three of the *damane* seem ready to be let out of their collars. Perhaps."

Elayne's eyebrows rose, and she exchanged surprised looks with Nynaeve. Of the five *damane* Taim had handed over to them, one had been taken by the Seanchan on Toman Head and another in Tanchico. The others had come from Seanchan.

"Two of the Seanchan women, Marille and Jillari, still say they *deserve* to be collared, *need* to be collared." Reanne's mouth tightened with distaste, but she paused for only a moment. "They truly seem horrified at the prospect of freedom. Alivia has stopped that. Now she says it was only because she was afraid she would be retaken. She says she hates all the *sul'dam,* and she certainly makes a good show of it, snarling at them and cursing them, but . . ." She shook her head slowly in doubt. "She was collared at thirteen or fourteen, Elayne, she's not certain which, and she's been *damane* for *four hundred years!* And aside from that, she is . . . she's . . . Alivia is considerably stronger than Nynaeve," she finished in a rush. Age, the Kin might discuss openly, but they had all the Aes Sedai reticence about speaking of strength in the Power. "Do we dare let her free? A Seanchan wilder who could tear the entire Palace apart?" The Kin shared the Aes Sedai view of wilders, too. Most did.

Sisters who knew Nynaeve had learned to take care with that word around her. She could become quite snappish when it was used in a disparaging tone. Now, she just stared at Reanne. Perhaps she was trying to find the answer. Elayne knew what her own answer would be, but this had nothing to do with claiming the throne, or Andor. It was a decision for Aes Sedai, and here, that meant it was Nynaeve's to make.

"If you don't," Lan said quietly from the door, "then you might as well give her back to the Seanchan." He was not at all abashed by the dark looks given him by the four women who heard his deep voice toll those words like a funeral gong. "You will have to watch her closely, but keep her collared when she wants to be free, and you are no better than they are."

"That isn't for you to say, Warder," Alise said firmly. He met her stern stare with cool equanimity, and she gave a small disgusted grunt and threw up her hands. "You should give him a good talking-to when you get him alone, Nynaeve."

Nynaeve must have been feeling her awe of the women particularly strongly, because her cheeks colored. "Don't think that I will not," she said lightly. She did not look at Lan at all. Finally condescending to notice the chill, she pulled her shawl up onto her shoulders, and cleared her throat. "He is right, though. At least we don't have to worry about the other two. I'm just surprised it took them this long to stop imitating those fool Seanchan."

"I am not so sure," Reanne sighed. "Kara was a sort of wise woman on Toman Head, you know. Very influential in her village. A wilder, of course. You would think she'd hate the Seanchan, but she doesn't, not all of them. She is very fond of the *sul'dam* captured with her, and very anxious that we shouldn't hurt *any* of the *sul'dam*. Lemore is just nineteen, a pampered noblewoman with the extreme bad luck to have the spark manifest itself in her on the very day Tanchico fell. She says she hates the Seanchan and wants to make them pay for what they did to Tanchico, but she answers to Larie, her *damane* name, as readily as to Lemore, and she smiles at the *sul'dam* and lets them pet her. I don't mistrust them, not the way I do Alivia, but I doubt either one could stand up to a *sul'dam*. I think if a *sul'dam* ordered either to help her escape, she would, and I fear she might not fight too hard if the *sul'dam* tried to collar her again."

After she stopped speaking, the silence stretched.

Nynaeve seemed to look inward, struggling with herself. She gripped her braid, then let go and folded her arms tight across her chest, the fringe of her shawl swaying as she hugged herself. She glared at everyone except Lan. Him, she did not so much as glance at.

Finally she took a deep breath, and squared herself to face Reanne and Alise. "We must remove the *a'dam*. We will hold on to them until we can be sure—and Lemore after; she needs to be put in white!—and we will make sure they are never left alone, especially with the *sul'dam,* but the *a'dam* come off!" She spoke fiercely, as if expecting opposition, but a broad smile of approval spread across Elayne's face. The addition of three more women they could not be sure of hardly counted as good news, but there had been no other choice.

Reanne merely nodded acceptance—after a moment— but a smiling Alise came around the table to pat Nynaeve's shoulder, and Nynaeve actually blushed. She tried to hide it behind clearing her throat roughly and grimacing at the Seanchan woman in her cage of *saidar*, but her efforts were not very effectual, and Lan spoiled them in any case.

"*Tai'shar Manetheren,*" he said softly.

Nynaeve's mouth fell open, then curled into a tremulous smile. Sudden tears glistened in her eyes as she spun to face him, her face joyous. He smiled back at her, and there was nothing cold in his eyes.

Elayne struggled not to gape. Light! Maybe he did not chill their marriage bed after all. The thought made her cheeks warm. Trying not to look at them, her eyes fell on Marli, still fastened in her chair. The Seanchan woman was staring straight ahead, tears flowing down her plump cheeks. Straight ahead. At the weaves holding sound away from her. She could not deny seeing the weaves now. But when she said as much, Reanne shook her head.

"They all weep if they are made to look at weaves very long, Elayne," she said wearily. And a touch sadly. "But once the weaves are gone, they convince themselves we tricked them. They have to, you understand. Else they'd be *damane,* not *sul'dam.* No, it will take time to convince the Mistress of the Hounds that she is really a hound herself. I am afraid I really haven't given you any good news at all, have I?"

"Not very much," Elayne told her. None, really. Just another problem to stack up on all the rest. How much bad news could be stacked before the pile buried you? She had to get some good, soon.

CHAPTER

9

A Cup of Tea

Once in her dressing room, Elayne hurriedly changed
out of her riding clothes with the help of Essande,
the white-haired pensioner she had chosen for
her maid. The slender, dignified woman was a trifle slow-
moving, but she knew her job and did not waste time chattering. In fact, she seldom said a word beyond suggestions
on clothing, and the comment given every day, that Elayne
looked like her mother. Flames danced atop thick logs on
a wide marble hearth at one end of the room, but the fire
did little to take the chill off the air. Quickly she put on a
fine blue wool with patterns of seed pearls on the high neck
and down the sleeves, her silver-worked belt with a small
silver-sheathed dagger, and the silver-embroidered blue velvet slippers. There might be no time to change again before
seeing the merchants, and they must be impressed at the
sight of her. She would have to be sure Birgitte was there;
Birgitte was *most* impressive in her uniform. And Birgitte
would take even listening to merchants as a break. By the
heated knot of irritation resting in the back of Elayne's
head, the Captain-General of the Queen's Guard was finding those reports heavy going.

Fastening clusters of pearls in her ears, she dismissed
Essande to her own fire, in the pensioners' quarters. The
woman had denied it when offered Healing, but Elayne suspected her joints ached. In any case, she herself was ready.
She would not wear the coronet of the Daughter-Heir; it
could stay atop the small ivory jewelry chest on her dressing table. She did not have many gems; most had already
been put in pawn, and the rest might have to go when the

plate did. No point worrying about it now. A few moments to herself, and she would have to leap back to duty.

Her dark-paneled sitting room with its wide cornices of carved birds contained two tall fireplaces with elaborate mantels, one at either end, which did a better job of warming than the one in the dressing room, though here, too, the carpets layered on the white-tiled floor were necessary. To her surprise, the room also contained Halwin Norry. Duty had leaped at her, it seemed.

The First Clerk stretched up out of a low-backed chair as she entered, clutching a leather folder to his narrow chest, and lurched around the scroll-edged table in the middle of the room to make an awkward leg. Norry was tall and lean, with a long nose, his sparse fringe of hair rising behind his ears like sprays of white feathers. He often reminded her of a heron. Any number of clerks under him actually wielded the pens, yet a small inkstain marred one edge of his scarlet tabard. The stain looked old, though, and she wondered whether the folder hid others. He had only taken to holding it against his chest when he donned formal dress, two days after Mistress Harfor. Whether he had done so as an expression of loyalty, or simply because the First Maid had, was still in question.

"Forgive me for being precipitate, my Lady," he said, "but I do believe I have matters of some importance, if not actual haste, to lay before you." Important or not, his voice still droned.

"Of course, Master Norry. I would not want to press you to haste." He blinked at her, and she tried not to sigh. She thought he might be more than a little deaf, from the way he tilted his head this way and that as if to catch sound better. Maybe that was why his voice almost never changed pitch. She raised hers a little. He might just be a bore, after all. "Sit, and tell me these matters of importance."

She took one of the carved chairs away from the table and motioned him to another, but he remained standing. He always did. She settled back to listen, crossing her knees and adjusting her skirts.

He did not refer to his folder. Everything on the papers in it would be inside his head, the papers there only in case she required to see with her own eyes. "Most immediate, my Lady, and perhaps most important, large deposits of alum have been discovered on your estates at Danabar. The first quality of alum. I believe the bankers will be . . . umm . . . less hesitant regarding my inquiries on your behalf once they learn of this." He smiled briefly, a momentary curving of thin lips. For him, that was near to capering.

Elayne sat up straight as soon as he mentioned alum, and she smiled much more broadly. She felt a little like capering herself. Had her companion been anyone but Norry, she might have. Her elation was so strong that for a moment she felt Birgitte's irritability wane. Dyers and weavers devoured alum, and so did glassmakers and papermakers among others. The only source for first quality alum was Ghealdan—or had been till now—and just the taxes on the trade had been sufficient to support the throne of Ghealdan for generations. What came from Tear and Arafel was not nearly so fine, yet it put as much coin in those countries' coffers as olive oil or gems.

"That *is* important news, Master Norry. The best I've had today." The best since reaching Caemlyn, very likely, but *certainly* the best today. "How quickly can you overcome the bankers' 'hesitation'?" It had been more like slamming the door in her face, only not so rude. The bankers knew to a man how many swords stood behind her at the moment, and how many behind her opponents. Even so, she had no doubts the riches of alum would bring them around. Neither did Norry.

"Quite quickly, my Lady, and on very good terms, I believe. I shall tell them if their best offers are insufficient, I will approach Tear or Cairhien. They will not risk losing the custom, my Lady." All in that dry, flat voice, without a hint of the satisfaction any other man would have. "It will be loans against future income, of course, and there will be expenses. The mining itself. Transportation. Danabar is in mountainous country, and some distance from the Lugard Road. Still, there should be sufficient to meet your ambitions for the Guards, my Lady. And for your Academy."

"Sufficient is hardly the word, if you've given over trying to talk me out of my plans for the Academy, Master Norry," she said, nearly laughing. He was as jealous of Andor's treasury as a hen with one chick, and he had been adamantly opposed to her taking over the school Rand had ordered founded in Caemlyn, returning to his arguments time and again until his voice seemed a drill boring into her skull. So far the school consisted of only a few dozen scholars with their students, scattered about the New City in various inns, but even in winter more arrived every day, and they had begun to clamor for more space. She did not propose giving them a palace, certainly, yet they needed something. Norry was trying to husband Andor's gold, but she was looking to Andor's future. Tarmon Gai'don was coming, yet she had to believe there would be a future afterward, whether or not Rand broke the world again. Otherwise, there was no point in going on with anything, and she could not see just sitting down to wait. Even if she knew for a fact that the Last Battle would end everything, she did not think she could sit on her hands. Rand started schools in case he *did* end breaking the world, in the hope of saving something, but this school would be Andor's, not Rand al'Thor's. The Academy of the Rose, dedicated to the memory of Morgase Trakand. There *would* be a future, and the future would remember her mother. "Or have you decided the Cairhienin gold can be traced to the Dragon Reborn after all?"

"I still believe the risk to be very small, my Lady, but no longer worth taking in view of what I have just learned from Tar Valon." His tone did not alter, but clearly he was agitated. His fingers drummed the leather folder against his chest, spiders dancing, then still. "The . . . umm . . . White Tower has issued a proclamation acknowledging . . . umm . . . Lord Rand as the Dragon Reborn and offering him . . . umm . . . protection and guidance. It also pronounces anathema on anyone approaching him save through the Tower. It is wise to be wary of Tar Valon's anger, my Lady, as you yourself are aware." He looked significantly at the Great Serpent ring on her hand resting on the carved arm of the chair. He knew of the split in the Tower, of course—maybe a crofter in Seleisin did not; no one else could fail to, by now—but he had been too discreet to ask her allegiance. Though plainly he had been about to say "the Amyrlin Seat" instead of "the White Tower." And the Light alone knew what in place of "Lord Rand." She did not hold that against him. He was a cautious man, a quality needed in his post.

Elaida's proclamation stunned her, though. Frowning, she thumbed her ring thoughtfully. Elaida had worn that ring longer than she herself had lived. The woman was arrogant, wrong-headed, blind to any view except her own, but she was not stupid. Far from it. "Can she possibly think he will *accept* such an offer?" she mused, half to herself. "Protection and *guidance?* I can't imagine a better way to put his back up!" Guidance? No one could *guide* Rand with a barge pole!

"He may possibly have accepted already, my Lady, according to my correspondent in Cairhien." Norry would have shuddered at the suggestion he was in any way a spymaster. Well, he would have twisted his mouth in distaste, anyway. The First Clerk administered the treasury, controlled the clerks who ran the capital, and advised the throne on matters of state. He certainly had no network of eyes-and-ears, like the Ajahs and even some individual sisters did. But he did exchange regular letters with knowledgeable and often well-connected people in other capitals, so his advice could be current with events. "She sends a pigeon only once a week, and it seems that right after her last, someone attacked the Sun Palace using the One Power."

"The Power?" she exclaimed, jerking forward in shock.

Norry nodded once. He might have been reporting the current state of street repairs. "So my correspondent reports, my Lady. Aes Sedai, perhaps, or Asha'man, or even the Forsaken. She repeats gossip here, I fear. The wing housing the apartments of the Dragon Reborn was largely destroyed, and he himself has vanished. It is widely believed that he has gone to Tar Valon to kneel before the Amyrlin Seat. Some do believe him dead in the attack, but not a great many. I advise doing nothing until you have a clearer picture." He paused, head tilted in thought. "From what I saw of him, my Lady," he said slowly, "I myself would not believe him dead unless I sat three days with the corpse."

She almost stared. That was very nearly a joke. A rough witticism, at least. From Halwin Norry! She did not believe Rand was dead, either. She would not believe he was dead. As for kneeling to Elaida, the man was too stubborn to submit to anyone. A great many difficulties could be surmounted if only he could bring himself to kneel to Egwene, but he would not do it, and she was his childhood friend. Elaida stood as much chance as a goat at a court ball, particularly once he learned of her proclamation. Who

are all gone. He may be a problem in the future, if his plan succeeds—for one thing, he will want those northern lands back—but he presents no immediate problems for Andor."

Norry's eyes widened, and he tilted his head first to one side then other, studying her. He wet his lips before speaking. "That would explain much, my Lady. Yes. Yes, it would." His tongue touched his lips again. "There was one other point mentioned by my correspondent in Cairhien which I . . . umm . . . forgot to mention. As you may be aware, your intention to claim the Sun Throne is well known there, and has large support. It seems that many Cairhienin speak openly of coming to Andor, to aide you in gaining the Lion Throne so you can take the Sun Throne sooner. I think perhaps you do not need my advice concerning any such offers?"

She nodded, quite graciously in the circumstances, she thought. Aid from Cairhien would be worse than the mercenaries, for there had been too many wars between Andor and Cairhien. He had not forgotten. Halwin Norry never forgot anything. So why had he decided to tell her, rather than let her be caught by surprise, perhaps by the arrival of her Cairhien supporters? Had her display of knowledge impressed him? Or made him fearful she might learn he had held back? He waited on her patiently, a dried-up heron waiting . . . on a fish?

"Have a letter prepared for my signature and seal, Master Norry, to be sent to every major House in Cairhien. Begin with setting out my right to the Sun Throne as the daughter of Taringail Damodred, and say that I will come to put forward my claim when events in Andor are more settled. Say that I will bring no soldiers with me, as I know that Andoran soldiers on Cairhienin soil would incite all of Cairhien against me, and rightly so. Finish with my appreciation of the support offered to my cause by many Cairhienin, and my hope that any divisions within Cairhien can be healed peacefully." The intelligent would see the message behind the words, and with luck, explain it to any who were not bright enough.

"A deft response, my Lady," Norry said, hunching his shoulders in a semblance of a bow. "I shall make it so. If I may ask, my Lady, have you had time to sign the accounts? Ah. No matter. I will send someone for them later." Bowing properly, if no less awkwardly than before, he prepared to go, then paused. "Forgive me for being so bold, my Lady, but you remind me very much of the late Queen your mother."

Watching the door close behind him, she wondered whether she could count him in her camp. Administering Caemlyn without clerks, much less Andor, was impossible, and the First Clerk had the power to bring a queen to her knees if unchecked. A compliment was not the same as a declaration of fealty.

She did not have long to mull the question, for only moments after he departed, three liveried maids entered, bearing silver-domed trays that they placed in a row on the long side table standing against one wall.

"The First Maid said my Lady forgot to send for her midday meal," a round, gray-haired woman said, curtsying as she gestured for her younger companion to remove the tall domes, "so she sent a choice for my Lady."

A choice. Shaking her head at the display, Elayne was reminded how long it had been since breakfast, eaten with the rising sun. There was sliced saddle of mutton with mustard sauce, and capon roasted with dried figs, sweetbreads with pinenuts, and creamy leek and potato soup, cabbage rolls with raisins and peppers, and a squash pie, not to mention a small plate of apple tarts and another of tipsy cake topped with clotted cream. Mists of steam rose from two squat silver pitchers of wine, in case she preferred one sort of spicing over another. A third held hot tea. And pushed scornfully into a corner of one tray was the meal she always ordered in the middle of the day, clear broth and bread. Reene Harfor disapproved of that; she claimed Elayne was "thin as a rail."

The First Maid had spread her opinions. The gray-haired woman put on a reproachful face as she set the bread and broth and tea on the table in the middle of the room with a white linen napkin, a thin blue porcelain cup and saucer, and a silver pot of honey. And a few of the figs on a dish. A full stomach at midday made for a dull head in the afternoon, as Lini used to say. *Her* opinions were not shared, however. The maids were all comfortably padded women, and even the younger pair looked disappointed as they departed with the remainder of the food.

It was very good broth, hot and lightly spiced, and the tea was pleasantly minty, but she was not left alone with her meal, and her thoughts that perhaps she could have taken a *little* of the tipsy cake, for long. Before she had swallowed two mouthfuls, Dyelin stormed into the room like a whirlwind in a green riding dress, breathing hard. Setting down her spoon, Elayne offered tea before realizing there was only the one cup she was already using, but Dyelin waved the offer aside, her face set in a dire frown.

"There is an army in Braem Wood," she announced, "like nothing seen since the Aiel War. A merchant down from New Braem brought the news this morning. A solid, reliable man, Tormon; an Illianer; not given to flights of fancy or jumping at shadows. He said he saw Arafellin, Kandori, and Shienarans, in different places. Thousands of them, altogether. Tens of thousands." Collapsing into a chair, she fanned herself with one hand. Her face was touched with red, as if she had run with the news. "What in the Light are Borderlanders doing nearly on the border of Andor?"

"It's Rand, I'll wager," Elayne said. Stifling a yawn, she drank the rest of her tea and refilled the cup. Her morning had been tiring, but enough tea would perk her up.

Dyelin stopped fanning and sat up straight. "You don't think he sent them, do you? To . . . help you?"

That possibility had not occurred to Elayne. At times she regretted letting the older woman know her feelings for Rand. "I cannot think he was . . . I mean, would be . . . *that* foolish."

Light, she *was* tired! Sometimes Rand behaved as if he were the King of the World, but surely he would not . . . Would not . . . What it was he would not do seemed to slide away from her.

She covered another yawn, and suddenly her eyes widened above her hand, staring at her teacup. A cool, minty taste. Carefully, she put the cup down, or tried to. She nearly missed the saucer altogether, and the cup toppled over, spilling tea onto the tabletop. Tea laced with forkroot. Even knowing there was no use, she reached out to the Source, tried to fill herself with the life and joy of *saidar,* but she might as well have tried to catch the wind in a net. Birgitte's irritation, less hot than before, was still lodged in a corner of her mind. Frantically she tried to pull up fear, or panic. Her head seemed stuffed with wool, everything in it dulled. *Help me, Birgitte!* she thought. *Help me!*

"What is it?" Dyelin demanded, leaning forward sharply. "You've thought of something, and by your face, it is horrific."

Elayne blinked at her. She had forgotten the other woman was there. "Go!" she said thickly, then swallowed heavily to try clearing her throat. Her tongue still felt twice its size. "Get help! I've . . . been poisoned!" Explaining would take too much time. "Go!"

Dyelin gaped at her, frozen, then lurched to her feet gripping the hilt of her belt knife.

The door opened, and a servant hesitantly put his head in. Elayne felt a flood of relief. Dyelin would not stab her before a witness. The man wet his lips, eye darting between the two women. Then he came in. Drawing a long-bladed knife from his belt. Two more men in red-and-white livery followed, each unsheathing a long knife.

I will not die like a kitten in a sack, Elayne thought bitterly. With an effort, she pushed herself to her feet. Her knees wobbled, and she had to support herself on the table with one hand, but she used the other to draw her own dagger. The pattern-etched blade was barely as long as her hand, but it would suffice. It would have, had her fingers not felt wooden gripping the hilt. A child could take it away. *Not without fighting back*, she thought. It was like pushing through syrup, but determined even so. *Not without fighting!*

Strangely little time seemed to have passed. Dyelin was just turning to her henchmen, the last of them just closing the door behind him.

"Murder!" Dyelin howled. Picking up her chair, she hurled it at the men, "Guards! Murder! Guards!"

The three tried to dodge the chair, but one was too slow, and it caught him on the legs. With a yell, he fell into the man next to him, and they both went down. The other, a slender, towheaded young man with bright blue eyes, skipped by with his knife advanced.

Dyelin met him with her own, slashing, stabbing, but he moved like a ferret, avoiding her attack with ease. His own long blade slashed, and Dyelin stumbled back with a shriek, one hand clutching at her middle. He danced forward nimbly, stabbing, and she screamed and fell like a rag doll. He stepped over her, walking toward Elayne.

Nothing else existed for her except him, and the knife in his hand. He did not rush at her. Those big blue eyes studied her cautiously as he advanced at a steady pace. Of course. He knew she was Aes Sedai. He had to be wondering whether the potion had done its work. She tried to stand straight, to glare at him, to win a few moments by bluff, but he nodded to himself, hefting his knife. If she could have done anything, it would have happened by now. There was no pleasure on his face. He was just a man with a job to do.

Abruptly, he stopped, staring down at himself in astonishment. Elayne stared, too. At the foot of steel sticking out from his chest. Blood bubbled in his mouth as he toppled into the table, shoving it hard.

Staggering, Elayne fell to her knees, and barely caught the edge of the table again to stop herself falling further. Amazed, she stared at the man bleeding onto the carpets. There was a sword hilt sticking out of his back. Her leaden thoughts were wandering. Those carpets might never come clean, with all that blood. Slowly she raised her eyes, past the motionless form of Dyelin. She did not appear to be breathing. To the door. The open door. One of the remaining two assassins lay in front of it, his head at an odd angle, only half attached to his neck. The other was struggling with another red-coated man, the pair of them grunting and rolling on the floor, both striving for the same dagger. The would-be killer was trying to pry the other's fist from his throat with his free hand. The other. A man with a face like an axe. In the white-collared coat of a Guardsman.

Hurry, Birgitte, she thought dully. *Please hurry.*

Darkness consumed her.

CHAPTER
10

A Plan Succeeds

Elayne's eyes opened in darkness, staring at dim shadows dancing on misty paleness. Her face was cold, the rest of her hot and sweaty, and something confined her arms and legs. For an instant panic flared. Then she sensed Aviendha's presence in the room, a simple, comforting awareness, and Birgitte's, a fist of calm, controlled anger in her head. They soothed her by being there. She was in her own bedchamber, lying beneath blankets in her own bed and staring up at the taut linen canopy with hot-water bottles packed along her sides. The heavy winter bedcurtains were tied back against the carved posts, and the only light in the room came from tiny flickering flames in the fireplace, just enough to make shadows shift, not dispel them.

Without thought she reached out for the Source and found it. Touched *saidar*, wondrously, without drawing on it. The desire to draw deeply welled up strong in her, but reluctantly she retreated. Oh, so reluctantly, and not just because her wanting to be filled with the deeper life of *saidar* was often a bottomless need that must be controlled. Her greatest fear during those endless minutes of terror had not been death, but that she would never touch the Source again. Once, she would have thought that strange.

Abruptly, memory returned, and she sat up unsteadily, the blankets sliding to her waist. Immediately, she pulled them back up. The air was *cold* against her bare skin slick with sweat. They had not even left her a shift, and try as she would to copy Aviendha's ease about being unclothed in front of others, she could not manage it. "Dyelin," she said anxiously, twisting to drape the blankets around herself better. It was an awkward operation; she felt wrung out and more than a little wobbly. "And the Guardsman. Are they . . . ?"

"The man didn't suffer a scratch," Nynaeve said, stepping out of the shifting shadows, a shadow herself. She rested her hand on Elayne's forehead and grunted in satisfaction at finding it cool. "I Healed Dyelin. She will need time to recover her strength fully, though. She lost a great deal of blood. You are doing well, too. For a time, I thought you were taking a fever. That can come on suddenly when you're weakened."

"She gave you herbs instead of Healing," Birgitte said sourly from a chair at the foot of the bed. In the near darkness, she was just a squat, ominous shape.

"Nynaeve al'Meara is wise enough to know what she cannot do," Aviendha said in level tones. Only her white blouse and a flash of polished silver were really visible, low against the wall. As usual, she had chosen the floor over a chair. "She recognized the taste of this forkroot in the tea and did not know how to work her weaves against it, so she did not take foolish chances."

Nynaeve sniffed sharply. No doubt as much at Aviendha's defense of her as Birgitte's acidity. Perhaps more so. Nynaeve being Nynaeve, she probably would have preferred to let slide what she did not know and could not do. And she was more prickly than usual about Healing, of late. Ever since it became clear that several of the Kin were already outstripping her skill. "You should have recognized it yourself, Elayne," she said in a brusque voice. "At any rate, greenwort and goatstongue might make you sleep, but they're sovereign for stomach cramps. I thought you would prefer the sleep."

Fishing leather hot-water bottles from under the covers and dropping them onto the carpets so she did not start roasting again, Elayne shuddered. The days right after Ronde Macura dosed her and Nynaeve with forkroot had been a misery she had tried to forget. Whatever the herbs were that Nynaeve had given her, she felt no weaker than the forkroot would have made her. She thought she could walk, so long as she did not have to walk far or stand long. And she could think clearly. The casements showed only thin moonlight. How deeply into the night was it?

Embracing the Source again, she channeled four threads of Fire to light first one stand-lamp, then a second. The small, mirrored flames brightened the room greatly after the darkness, and Birgitte put a hand up to shield her eyes, at first. The Captain-General's coat truly did suit her; she would have impressed the merchants no end.

"You should not be channeling yet," Nynaeve fussed, squinting at the sudden light. She still wore the same low-cut blue dress Elayne had seen her in earlier, with her yellow-fringed shawl caught in her elbows. "A few days to regain strength would be best, with plenty of sleep." She frowned at the hot-water bottles tumbled on the floor. "And you need to be kept warm. Better to avoid a fever than need to Heal it."

"I think Dyelin proved her loyalty today," Elayne said, shifting her pillows so she could lean back against the headboard, and Nynaeve threw up her hands in disgust. A small silver tray on one of the side tables flanking the bed held a single silver cup filled with dark wine that Elayne gave a brief, mistrusting look. "A hard way to prove it. I think I have *toh* toward her, Aviendha."

Aviendha shrugged. On their arrival in Caemlyn she had returned to Aiel garments with almost laughable haste, forsaking silks for *algode* blouses and bulky woolen skirts as though suddenly afraid of wetlander luxury. With a dark shawl tied around her waist and a dark folded kerchief holding her long hair back, she was the image of a Wise One's apprentice, though her only jewelry was a complicated silver necklace of intricately worked discs, a gift from Egwene. Elayne still did not understand her hurry. Melaine and the others had seemed willing to let her go her own way so long as she wore wetlander clothes, but now they had her back in their grip as tightly as any novice in the hands of Aes Sedai. The only reason they allowed her to stay any time at all in the Palace—in the city, for that matter—was that she and Elayne were first-sisters.

"If you think you do, then you do." Her tones of pointing out the obvious slid into an affectionate chiding. "But a small *toh,* Elayne. You had reason to doubt. You cannot assume obligation for every thought, sister." She laughed as if suddenly seeing a wonderful joke. "That way lies too much pride, and I will have to be overproud with you, only the Wise Ones will not call to you to account for it."

Nynaeve rolled her eyes ostentatiously, but Aviendha simply shook her head, wearily patient with the other woman's ignorance. She had been studying more than the Power with the Wise Ones.

"Well, we wouldn't want the pair of you being too proud," Birgitte said with what sounded suspiciously like suppressed mirth. Her face was much too smooth, almost rigid with the effort of not laughing.

Aviendha eyed Birgitte with a wooden-faced wariness. Since she and Elayne had adopted one another, Birgitte had adopted her, too, in way. Not as a Warder, of course, but with the same elder-sister attitude she often displayed toward Elayne. Aviendha was not quite sure what to make of it, or how to respond. Joining the tiny circle who knew who Birgitte really was certainly had not helped. She bounced between fierce determination to show that Birgitte Silverbow did not overawe her and a startling meekness, with odd stops in between.

Birgitte smiled at her, an amused smile, but it faded as she picked up a narrow bundle from her lap and began unfolding the cloth with great care. By the time she revealed a dagger with a leather-wrapped hilt and a long blade, her expression was severe, and tight anger flowed through the bond. Elayne recognized the knife instantly; she had last seen its twin in the hand of a tow-headed assassin.

"They were not trying to kidnap you, sister," Aviendha said softly.

Birgitte's tone was grim. "After Mellar killed the first two—the second by spearing him with his sword across the width of the room like somebody in a bloody gleeman's tale," she held the dagger upright by the end of the hilt, "he took this from the last fellow and killed him with it. They had four near identical daggers between them. This one is poisoned."

"Those brown stains on the blade are gray fennel mixed with powdered peach pit," Nynaeve said, sitting down on the edge of the bed, and grimaced in disgust. "One look at his eyes and tongue, and I knew that was what killed the fellow, not the knife."

"Well," Elayne said quietly after a moment. Well, indeed. "Forkroot so I couldn't channel, or stand up, for that matter, and two men to hold me on my feet while the third put a poisoned dagger in me. A complicated plan."

"Wetlanders like complicated plans," Aviendha said. Glancing at Birgitte uneasily, she shifted against the wall and added, "Some do."

"Simple, in its way," Birgitte said, rewrapping the knife with as great a care as she had shown unwrapping. "You were easy to reach. Everyone knows you eat your midday meal alone." Her long braid swung as she shook her head. "A lucky thing the first man to reach you didn't have this; one stab, and you'd be dead. A lucky thing Mellar happened to be walking by and heard a man cursing in your rooms. Enough luck for a *ta'veren*."

Nynaeve snorted. "You might be dead from a deep enough cut on your *arm*. The pit is the most poisonous part of a peach. Dyelin wouldn't have had a chance if the other blades had been poisoned as well."

Elayne looked around at her friends' flat, expressionless faces and sighed. A *very* complicated plan. As if spies in the Palace were not bad enough. "A *small* bodyguard, Birgitte," she said finally. "Something . . . discreet." She should have known the woman would be prepared, Birgitte's face did not change in the slightest, but the tiniest burst of satisfaction flared through their shared bond.

"The women who guarded you today, for a start," she said, without so much as *pretending* to pause for thought, "and a few more that I'll pick. Maybe twenty or so, altogether. Too few can't protect you day and night, and you bloody well must be," she put in firmly, though Elayne had not offered any protest. "Women can guard you where men can't, and they'll be discreet just by being who they are. Most people will think they're ceremonial—your very own Maidens of the Spear—and we'll give them something, a sash maybe, to make them look more so." That earned her a very sharp look from Aviendha, which she affected not to notice. "The problem is who to command," she said, frowning in thought. "Two or three nobles, Hunters, are already arguing for rank 'sufficient to their station.' The bloody women know how to give orders, but I'm not sure they know the right bloody orders to give. I could promote Caseille to lieutenant, but she's more a bannerman at heart, I think." Birgitte shrugged. "Maybe one of the others will show promise, but I think they are better followers than leaders."

Oh, yes; all thought out. Twenty or so? She would have to keep a close eye on Birgitte to make sure the number did not climb to fifty. Or more. Able to guard her where men could not. Elayne winced. That probably meant guards watching her bathe at the very least. "Caseille will do, surely. A bannerman can handle twenty." She was certain she could talk Caseille into keeping it all unobtrusive. And keeping the guards outside while she took a bath. "The man who arrived just in the nick of time. Mellar? What do you know of him, Birgitte?"

"Doilin Mellar," Birgitte said slowly, her brows drawing down at a sharp angle. "A coldhearted fellow, though he smiles a lot. Mainly at women. He pinches serving girls, and he's tumbled three in four days that I know of—he likes to talk about his 'conquests'—but he hasn't pressed anyone who said no. He claims to have been a merchant's guard and then a mercenary, and now a Hunter for the Horn, and he certainly has the skills. Enough that I made him a lieutenant. He's Andoran, from somewhere out west, near Baerlon, and he says he fought for your mother during the Succession, though he couldn't have been much more than a boy at the time. Anyway, he knows the right answers—I checked—so maybe he was involved in it. Mercenaries lie about their pasts without thinking twice."

Folding her hands on her middle, Elayne considered Doilin Mellar. She remembered only the impression of a wiry man with a sharp face, choking one of her assailants while they struggled over the poisoned dagger. A man with enough of a soldier's skills that Birgitte had made him an officer. She was trying to make sure that as many as possible of the officers, at least, were Andoran. A rescue just in time, one man against three, and a sword hurled across the room like a spear; very much like a gleeman's tale. "He deserves a suitable reward. A promotion to captain and command of my bodyguard, Birgitte. Caseille can be his second."

"Are you mad?" Nynaeve burst out, but Elayne shushed her.

"I'll feel much safer knowing he's there, Nynaeve. He won't try pinching *me*, not with Caseille and twenty more like her around him. With his reputation, they'll watch him like hawks. You did say twenty, Birgitte? I will hold you to that."

"Twenty," Birgitte said absently. "Or so." There was nothing absent about the gaze she fixed on Elayne, though. She leaned forward intently, hands on her knees. "I suppose you know what you're doing." Good; she was going to behave like a Warder for once instead of arguing. "Guardsman-Lieutenant Mellar becomes Guardsman-Captain Mellar, for saving the life of the Daughter-Heir. That will add to his swagger. Unless you think it's better to keep the whole thing secret."

Elayne shook her head. "Oh, no; not at all. Let the whole city know. Someone tried to murder me, and Lieutenant—Captain—Mellar saved my life. We *will* keep the poison to ourselves, though. Just in case someone makes a slip of the tongue."

Nynaeve harrumphed and gave her a sidelong glare. "One day you will be too clever, Elayne. So sharp you cut yourself."

"She is clever, Nynaeve al'Meara." Rising smoothly to her feet, Aviendha settled her heavy skirts, then patted her horn-hilted belt knife. It was not so large as the blade she had worn as a Maiden, yet still a credible weapon. "And she has me to watch her back. I have permission to stay with her, now."

Nynaeve opened her mouth angrily. And for a wonder, closed it again, composing herself visibly, smoothing her skirts and her features. "What are you all staring at?" she muttered. "If Elayne wants this fellow close enough to pinch her whenever he feels like, who am I to argue?" Birgitte's mouth dropped open, and Elayne wondered whether Aviendha was going to choke. Her eyes were certainly popping.

The faint sound of the gong atop the Palace's tallest tower, tolling the hour, made her jerk. It was later than she had thought. "Nynaeve, Egwene might already be waiting for us." None of her clothes were anywhere to be seen.

"Where's my purse? My ring is in it." Her Great Serpent ring was on her finger, but that was not the one she meant.

"I will see Egwene alone," Nynaeve said firmly. "You are in no condition to enter *Tel'aran'rhiod*. In any case, you just slept the afternoon away. You won't go to sleep again soon, I'll wager. And I know you've had no luck putting yourself into a waking trance, so that is that." She smiled smugly, certain of her victory. *She* had gone cross-eyed and dizzy attempting to enter the waking trance Egwene had tried to teach them.

"You'll wager that, will you?" Elayne murmured. "What will you bet? Because I intend to drink that," she glanced at the silver cup on the sidetable, "and *I* wager I'll go right to sleep. Of course, if you *didn't* put something in it, if you didn't intend trying to trick me into drinking it . . . Well, of course, you wouldn't do that. So what shall we wager?"

That insufferable smile slid greasily off Nynaeve's face, replaced by bright spots of color in her cheeks.

"A fine thing," Birgitte said, standing. Fists on hips, she squared herself at the foot of the bed, her face and tone alike censuring. "The woman saves you a roiling belly, and you snip at her like Mistress Priss. Maybe if you drink that cup and go to sleep and forget about adventuring in the World of Dreams tonight, I'll decide you've grown up enough that I can trust fewer than a hundred guards to keep you alive. Or do I need to hold your nose to make you drink?" Well, Elayne had not expected her to keep holding back for long. Fewer than a hundred?

Aviendha spun to face Birgitte before she finished, and barely waited for the last word to leave the other woman's mouth. "You should not speak to her so, Birgitte Trahelion," she said, drawing herself to gain the full advantage of her greater height. Given the raised heels on Birgitte's boots, it was not that much, yet with her shawl drawn tightly over her breasts, she looked very much a Wise One rather than an apprentice. Some had faces not much older than hers. "You are her Warder. Ask Aan'allein how to behave. He is a great man, yet he obeys as Nynaeve tells him." Aan'allein was Lan, The Man Alone, his story well known and much admired among the Aiel.

Birgitte eyed her up and down as if measuring her, and adopted a lounging posture that all but lost the extra inches of her boot heels. With a mocking grin, she opened her mouth, plainly ready to prick Aviendha's bubble if she could. She usually could. Before she said a word, Nynaeve spoke quietly and quite firmly.

"Oh, for the love of the Light, give over, Birgitte. If Elayne says she's going, then she is going. Now, not another word out of you." She stabbed a finger at the other woman. "Or you and I will have words, later."

Birgitte stared at Nynaeve, her mouth working soundlessly, the Warder bond carrying an intense blend of irritation and frustration. At last, she flung herself back into her chair, legs sprawled and boots balanced on her lion-head spurs, and began a sullen muttering under her breath. If Elayne had not known her better, she would have sworn the woman was sulking. She wished she knew how Nynaeve did it. Once, Nynaeve had been as much in awe of Birgitte as Aviendha ever was, but that had changed. Completely. Now Nynaeve bullied Birgitte as readily as anyone else. And more successfully than with most. *She's a woman just like any other*, Nynaeve had said. *She told me so herself, and I realized she was right.* As if *that* explained anything. Birgitte was still Birgitte.

"My purse?" Elayne said, and of all people, Birgitte went to fetch the gold-embroidered red purse from the dressing room. Well, a Warder did do that sort of thing, but Birgitte always made some comment when she did. Though perhaps her return was meant for one. She presented the purse to Elayne with a flourishing bow. And a twist of her lips for Nynaeve and Aviendha. Elayne sighed. It was not that the other women disliked one another; they really got on very well, if you ignored their little foibles. They just rubbed against each other sometimes.

The oddly twisted stone ring, strung on a plain loop of leather, lay in the bottom of the purse underneath a mix of coins, next to the carefully folded silk handkerchief full of feathers she considered her greatest treasure. The *ter'angreal* appeared to be stone, anyway, all flecks and stripes of blue and red and brown, but it felt as hard and slick as steel, and too heavy even for that. Settling the leather cord around her neck, and the ring between her breasts, she pulled the drawstrings tight and set the purse on the side table, taking up the silver cup instead. The fragrance was simply that of good wine, but she raised an eyebrow anyway and smiled at Nynaeve.

"I will go to my own room," Nynaeve said stiffly. Rising from the mattress, she shared out a stern look between Birgitte and Aviendha. Somehow, the *ki'sain* on her forehead made it seem even more uncompromising. "The pair of you stay awake and keep your eyes open! Until you have those women around her, she is still in danger. And after, I hope I don't have to remind you."

"You think I do not know that?" Aviendha protested at the same time that Birgitte growled, "I'm not a fool, Nynaeve!"

"So you say," Nynaeve answered them both. "I hope so, for Elayne's sake. And for your own." Gathering her shawl, she glided from the room, as stately as any Aes Sedai could wish to be. She was getting very good at that.

"You'd think she was the bloody queen here," Birgitte muttered.

"She is the one who is overproud, Birgitte Trahelion," Aviendha grumbled. "As proud as a Shaido with one goat." They nodded at one another in perfect agreement.

But Elayne noticed that they had waited to speak until the door had shut behind Nynaeve. The woman who had denied so hard wanting to be Aes Sedai was becoming very much Aes Sedai. Perhaps Lan had something to do with that. Coaching her, from his experience. She still had to work at staying composed, sometimes, but it seemed to come more and more easily since her peculiar wedding.

The first sip of the wine had no taste other than wine, a very good wine, but Elayne frowned at the cup and hesitated. Until she realized what she was doing, and why. The memory of forkroot hidden in her tea was still strong. What had Nynaeve put in here? Not forkroot, of course, but what? Raising the cup to take a full swallow seemed very difficult. Defiantly, she drained the wine. *I was thirsty, that's all*, she thought, stretching to set the cup back on the silver tray. *I certainly wasn't trying to* prove *anything*.

The other two women had been watching her, but as she began settling herself in a more comfortable position for sleep, they turned to one another.

"I'll keep watch in the sitting room," Birgitte said. "I have my bow and quiver in there. You stay here in case she needs you for anything."

Rather than arguing, Aviendha drew her belt knife and knelt, ready to spring up again, off to one side, where she would see anyone coming through the door before they saw her. "Knock twice, then once, and name yourself before you enter," she said. "Otherwise, I will assume it is an enemy." And Birgitte nodded as if that were the most reasonable thing in the world.

"This is sil—" Elayne smothered a yawn behind her hand. "Silly," she finished when she could speak again. "No one is going to try to—" Another yawn, and she could have put her fist into her mouth! Light, what *had* Nynaeve put in that wine? "To kill me—tonight," she said drowsily, "and you—both know—" Her eyelids were leaden, sliding down despite every effort to keep them open. Unconsciously snuggling her face into her pillow, she tried to finish what she had been about to say, but . . .

She was in the Grand Hall, the throne room of the Palace. In the Grand Hall's reflection in *Tel'aran'rhiod*. Here, the twisted stone ring that felt too heavy for its size in the waking world seemed light enough to float up from between her breasts. There was light, of course, seeming to come from everywhere and nowhere. It was not like sunlight, or lamps, but even if it was night here, too, there was always enough of that odd light to see. As in a dream. The ever-present sensation of unseen eyes watching was not dreamlike—more like a nightmare—but she had grown accustomed to that.

Great audiences were held in the Grand Hall, foreign ambassadors formally received, important treaties and declarations of war announced to gathered dignitaries, and the long chamber suited its name and function. Empty of people save for her, it seemed cavernous. Two rows of thick gleaming white columns, ten spans high, marched the length of the room, and at one end, the Lion Throne stood atop a marble dais, with red carpeting climbing the white steps from the red-and-white floor tiles. The throne was sized for a woman, but still massive on its heavy lion-pawed legs, carved and gilded, with the White Lion picked out in moonstones on a field of rubies at the top of its high back, announcing that whoever sat there ruled a great nation. From large, colored windows set in the arched ceiling high overhead, the queens who had founded Andor stared down, their images alternating with the White Lion and scenes of the battles they had fought to build Andor from a single city in Artur Hawkwing's shattering empire into that nation. Many lands that had come out of the War of the Hundred Years no longer existed, yet Andor had survived the thousand years since and prospered. Sometimes Elayne felt those images judging her, weighing her worth to follow in their footsteps.

No sooner did she find herself in the Grand Hall than another woman appeared, sitting on the Lion Throne, a dark-haired young woman in flowing red silk embroidered in silver lions on the sleeves and hem, with a strand of firedrops as large as pigeon's eggs around her neck and the Rose Crown sitting on her head. One hand resting lightly on the lion-headed arm of the throne, she gazed regally about the Hall. Then her eyes fell on Elayne, and recognition dawned, along with confusion. Crown and firedrops and silks vanished, replaced by plain woolens and a long apron. An instant later, the young woman vanished, too.

Elayne smiled in amusement. Even scullions dreamed of sitting on the Lion Throne. She hoped the young woman had not been wakened in fright by the start she received, or at least that she had gone on to another pleasant dream. A safer dream than *Tel'aran'rhiod*.

Other things shifted in the throne room. The elaborately worked stand-lamps standing in rows down the chamber seemed to vibrate against the tall columns. The great arched doors stood now open, now closed, in the blink of an eye. Only things that had stood in one place for a goodly time had a truly permanent reflection in the World of Dreams.

Elayne imagined a stand-mirror, and it was before her, reflecting her image in high-necked green silk worked in silver across the bodice, with emeralds in her ears and smaller ones strung in her red-gold curls. She made the emeralds disappear from her hair, and nodded. Fit for the Daughter-Heir, but not too ostentatious. You had to be careful of how you imagined yourself, here, or else. . . . Her modest green silk gown became the snug, form-hugging folds of a

Taraboner gown, then flashed to dark, wide Sea Folk trousers and bare feet, complete with golden earrings and nose ring and chain full of medallions, and even dark tattoos on her hands. But without a blouse, the way the Atha'an Miere went at sea. Cheeks coloring, she hastily returned everything to how it had been, then changed the emerald earrings for plain silver hoops. The simpler you imagined your garb, the easier it was to maintain.

Letting the stand-mirror disappear—she just had to stop concentrating on it—she looked up at those stern faces overhead. "Women have taken the throne as young as I," she told them. Not very many, though; only seven who had managed to wear the Rose Crown for very long. "Women younger than I." Three. And one of those lasted barely a year. "I don't claim I will be as great as you, but I will not make you ashamed, either. I *will* be a good queen."

"Talking to *windows?*" Nynaeve said, making Elayne start in surprise. Using a copy of the ring Elayne wore next to her skin, she appeared misty, almost transparent. Frowning, she tried to stride toward Elayne and staggered, nearly tripped by the hobbling skirt of a deep blue Taraboner dress that was much tighter than the one Elayne had imagined on herself. Nynaeve gaped down at the thing, and abruptly it was an Andoran gown in the same colored silk, embroidered in gold on the sleeves and atop the bodice. She still went on about "good, stout Two Rivers wool" being good enough for her, but even here where she could appear in it if she wished, she almost never did.

"What *did* you put in that wine, Nynaeve?" Elayne asked. "I went out like a snuffed candle."

"Don't try to change the subject. If you are talking to windows, you should *really* be asleep instead of here. I've half a mind to order you—"

"Please don't. I'm not Vandene, Nynaeve. Light, I don't even *know* half the customs Vandene and the others take for granted. But I would rather not disobey you, so don't, please."

Nynaeve glowered at her, giving her braid one firm tug. Details of her dress changed, the skirts growing a trifle fuller, the embroidery's pattern altering, the high neck sinking, then rising again, sprouting lace. She was just not very good at the necessary concentration. The red dot on her forehead never wavered, though.

"Very well," she said calmly, the scowl vanishing. Her yellow-fringed shawl appeared on her shoulders, and her face took on something of the Aes Sedai agelessness. There were wings of white at her temples. Her words contrasted with her appearance and composed tone, though. "Let me do the talking when Egwene gets here. I mean about what happened today. You always end up chattering as if you're brushing each other's hair for bed. Light! I don't want her coming to the Amyrlin with *me*, and you know she will be all over both of us if she finds out."

"If I find out what?" Egwene said. Nynaeve's head whipped around, eyes panic-stricken, and for a moment her fringed shawl and silk gown were replaced by an Accepted's banded white. Even the *ki'sain* went. Just a moment, and she was back as she had been except for the white in her hair, yet that was enough to put a rueful expression on Egwene's face. She knew Nynaeve very well. "If I find out what, Nynaeve?" she asked firmly.

Elayne drew a deep breath. She had not intended to hold anything back, exactly. Not anything important to Egwene, anyway. But in her present mood, Nynaeve was likely to babble everything, or else grow stubborn and try insisting there was nothing to find out. Which would only make Egwene dig harder.

"Someone put forkroot in my midday tea," she said, and went on succinctly about the men with their daggers and Doilin Mellar's fortuitous appearance, and how Dyelin had proved herself. For good measure she added the news of Elenia and Naean, and the First Maid's search for spies in the Palace, and even Zarya and Kirstian being assigned to Vandene, and the attack on Rand and his disappearance. Egwene appeared to be unruffled by the recital—she even cut Elayne short about Rand, saying she already knew—but she gave a dismissive shake of her head at hearing that Vandene had made no progress in learning who the Black sister was, and that was of the gravest concern to her. "Oh, and I'm to have a bodyguard," Elayne finished. "Twenty women, commanded by Captain Mellar. I don't think Birgitte will find me any Maidens, but she will come close."

A backless armchair appeared behind Egwene, and she sat without looking for it. She was much more skilled here than Elayne or Nynaeve. She wore a dark green woolen riding dress, fine and well-cut but unadorned, likely what she had worn awake that day. And it remained a green woolen riding dress. "I would tell you to join me in Murandy tomorrow—tonight," she said, "if the arrival of the Kinswomen would not light a wildfire among the Sitters."

Nynaeve had recovered herself, though she gave her skirts an unneeded adjusting shake. The embroidery on her dress was silver, now. "I thought you had the Hall of the Tower under your thumb, now."

"That's very much like having a ferret under your thumb," Egwene said dryly. "It twists and writhes and wriggles around to nip at your wrist. Oh, they do just as I say when it concerns the war with Elaida—they can't get around that, however much they grumble over the expense of more soldiers!—but the agreement with the Kin is no part of the war, or letting the Kin learn the Tower had known about them all along. Or thought it did. The entire Hall would have apoplexy, just at finding out how much they didn't know. They are trying very hard to find a way to stop accepting new novices."

"They can't, can they?" Nynaeve demanded. She made a chair for herself, but it was a copy of Egwene's when she looked to make sure it was there, a three-legged stool as she began to sit, and a ladder-backed farm chair by the time she settled on it. Her dress had divided skirts, now. "You made a proclamation. Any woman of any age, if she tested true. All you have to do is make another, about the Kin." Elaine made her own seat a copy of one of the chairs in her sitting room. Much easier to hold onto.

"Oh, an Amyrlin's proclamation is as good as law," Egwene said. "Until the Hall sees a way around it. The newest complaint is that we only have sixteen Accepted. Though most sisters do treat Faolain and Theodrin as if they were still Accepted. But even eighteen isn't near sufficient to give the novice lessons that Accepted are supposed to handle. Sisters have to take them, instead. I think some were hoping the weather would hold the numbers down, but it hasn't." She smiled suddenly, a light of mischief in her dark eyes. "There's one new novice I'd like you to meet,

Nynaeve. Sharina Melloy. A grandmother. I think you'll agree she's a remarkable woman."

Nynaeve's chair disappeared completely, and she hit the floor with an audible smack. She hardly seemed to notice, sitting there and staring at Egwene in astonishment. "Sharina Melloy?" she said in a shaky voice. "She's a novice?" Her dress was a style Elayne had never seen before, with flowing sleeves and a deeply scooped neck worked with flowers in embroidery and seed pearls. Her hair flowed to her waist, held by a cap of moonstones and sapphires on golden wires no thicker than threads. And there was a plain golden band on her left forefinger. Only the *ki'sain* and her Great Serpent ring remained the same.

Egwene blinked. "You know the name?"

Getting to her feet, Nynaeve stared at her dress. She held up her left hand and touched the plain gold ring almost hesitantly. Strangely, she left everything as it was. "It might not be the same woman," she muttered. "It couldn't be!" Making another chair like Egwene's, she frowned at it as if commanding it to stay, but it still had a high back and carving by the time she sat. "There was a Sharina Melloy. . . . It was during my test for Accepted," she said in a rush, "I don't have to talk about that; it's the rule!"

"Of course you don't," Egwene said, though the look she gave Nynaeve was certainly as strange as Elayne knew her own must be. Still, there was nothing to be done; when Nynaeve wanted to be stubborn, she could teach mules.

"Since you brought up the Kin, Egwene," Elayne said, "have you thought further on the Oath Rod?"

Egwene raised one hand as if to stop her, but her reply was calm and level. "There's no need to think further, Elayne. The Three Oaths, sworn on the Oath Rod, are what make us Aes Sedai. I didn't see that, at first, but I do, now. The very first day we have the Tower, I will swear the Three Oaths, on the Oath Rod."

"That's madness!" Nynaeve burst out, leaning forward in her chair. Surprisingly, still the same chair. And still the same dress. Very surprising. Her hands were fists resting on her lap. "You know what it does; the Kin are proof! How many Aes Sedai live past three hundred? Or reach it? And don't tell me I shouldn't talk about age. That's a ridiculous custom, and you know it. Egwene, Reanne was called Eldest because she was the oldest Kinswoman in Ebou Dar. The oldest anywhere is a woman called Aloisia Nemosni, an oil merchant in Tear. Egwene, she's nearly six . . . hundred . . . years . . . old! When the Hall hears that, I wager they'll be ready to put the Oath Rod on a shelf."

"The Light knows three hundred years is a long time," Elayne put in, "but I can't say I'm happy myself at the prospect of perhaps cutting my life in half, Egwene. And what of the Oath Rod and your promise to the Kin? Reanne wants to be Aes Sedai, but what happens when she swears? What about Aloisia? Will she fall over dead? You can't ask them to swear, not knowing."

"I don't *ask* anything." Egwene's face was still smooth, but her back had straightened, her voice cooled. And hardened. Her eyes augered deep. "Any woman who wants to be a sister *will* swear. And *anyone* who refuses and still calls herself Aes Sedai *will* feel the full weight of Tower justice."

Elayne swallowed hard under that steady gaze. Nynaeve's face paled. There was no mistaking Egwene's meaning. They were not hearing a friend now, but the Amyrlin Seat, and the Amyrlin Seat had no friends when it came time to pronounce judgment.

Apparently satisfied with what she saw in them, Egwene relaxed. "I do know the problem," she said in a more normal tone. More normal, but still not inviting argument. "I expect any woman whose name is in the novice book to go as far as she can, to earn the shawl if she can, and serve as Aes Sedai, but I don't want anyone to die for it when they could live. Once the Hall learns about the Kin—once they're over pitching fits—I think I can get them to agree that a sister who wants to retire should be able to. With the Oaths removed." They had decided long ago that the Rod could be used to unbind as well as bind, else how could Black sisters lie?

"I suppose that would be all right," Nynaeve allowed judiciously. Elayne simply nodded; she was certain there was more.

"Retire into the Kin, Nynaeve," Egwene said gently. "That way, the Kin are bound to the Tower, too. The Kin will keep their own ways, of course, their Rule, but they will have to agree that their Knitting Circle is beneath the Amyrlin, if not the Hall, and that Kinswomen stand below sisters. I do mean them to be part of the Tower, not go their own way. But I think they will accept."

Nynaeve nodded again, happily, but her smile faded as the full import reached her. She spluttered indignantly. "But . . . ! Standing among the Kin is by age! You'll have sisters taking orders from women who couldn't even reach Accepted!"

"Former sisters, Nynaeve." Egwene fingered the Great Serpent ring on her right hand and sighed faintly. "Even Kinswomen who earned the ring don't wear it. So we will have to give it up, too. We will be Kinswomen, Nynaeve, not Aes Sedai any longer." She sounded as if she could already feel that distant day, that distant loss, but she took her hand from the ring and took a deep breath. "Now. Is there anything else? I have a long night ahead of me, and I would like to get a little real sleep before I have to face the Sitters again."

Frowning, Nynaeve had clenched her fist tight and laid her other hand over it to cover her rings, but she appeared ready to give up arguing over the Kin. For the time being. "Do your headaches still trouble you? I'd think if that woman's massages did any good, you'd stop having them."

"Halima's massages work wonders, Nynaeve. I couldn't sleep at all without her. Now, is there . . . ?" She trailed off, staring toward the doors at the entrance of the throne room, and Elayne turned to look.

A man was standing there watching, a man as tall as an Aielman, with dark red hair faintly streaked with white, but his high-collared blue coat would never be worn by an Aiel. He appeared muscular, and his hard face seemed somehow familiar. When he saw them looking, he turned and ran down the corridor out of sight.

For an instant, Elayne gaped. He had not just accidentally dreamed himself into *Tel'aran'rhiod*, or he would have vanished by now, but she could still hear his boots, loud on the floor tiles. Either he was a dream-walker—rare among men, so the Wise Ones said—or he had a *ter'angreal* of his own.

Leaping to her feet, she ran after him, but as fast as she was, Egwene was faster. One instant Egwene was behind, the next she was standing in the doorway, peering the way the man had gone. Elayne tried thinking of herself standing beside Egwene, and she was. The corridor was silent, now, and empty except for stand-lamps and chests and tapestries, all flickering and shifting.

"How did you do that?" Nynaeve demanded, running up with her skirts hoisted above her knees. Her stockings were silk, and red! Hastily letting her skirts fall when she realized Elayne had noticed her stockings, she peered down the hallway. "Where did he go? He could have heard everything! Did you recognize him? He reminded me of someone; I don't know who."

"Rand," Egwene said. "He could have been Rand's uncle."

Of course, Elayne thought. *If Rand had a mean uncle.*

A metallic click echoed from the far end of the throne room. The door into the dressing rooms behind the dais, closing. Doors were open or closed or sometimes in between in *Tel'aran'rhiod;* they did not swing shut.

"Light!" Nynaeve muttered. "How many people have been eavesdropping on us? Not to mention who, and why?"

"Whoever they are," Egwene replied calmly, "they apparently don't know *Tel'aran'rhiod* as well as we do. Not friends, safe to say, or they wouldn't be eavesdropping. And I think they may not be friends to one another, otherwise, why listen from opposite ends of the room? That man was wearing a Shienaran coat. There are Shienarans in my army, but you both know them all. None resemble Rand."

Nynaeve sniffed. "Well, whoever he is, there are too many people listening at corners. That's what I think. I want to be back in my own body, where all I have to worry about are spies and poisoned daggers."

Shienarans, Elayne thought. Borderlanders. How could *that* have slipped her mind? Well, there had been the little matter of forkroot. "There is one more thing," she said aloud, though in a careful voice she hoped would not carry, and related Dyelin's news of Borderlanders in Braem Wood. She added Master Norry's correspondence, too, all the while trying to watch both ways along the corridor and the throne room as well. She did not want to be caught napping by another spy. "I think those rulers are in Braem Wood," she finished, "all four of them."

"Rand," Egwene breathed, sounding irritated. "Even when he can't be found he complicates things. Do you have

any idea whether they came to offer him allegiance or try to
hand him over to Elaida? I can't think of any other reasons
for them to march a thousand leagues. They must be boiling
shoes for soup by now! Do you have any idea how hard it is
to keep an army supplied on the march?"

"I think I can find out," Elayne said. "Why, I mean. And
at the same time. . . . You gave me the idea, Egwene." She
could not help smiling. Something good *had* come of today.
"I think I might just be able to use them to secure the Lion
Throne."

Asne examined the tall embroidery frame in front of her
and gave a sigh that turned into a yawn. The flickering
lamps gave a poor light for this, but that was not the reason
her birds all seemed lopsided. She wanted to be in her bed,
and she despised embroidery. But she had to be awake, and
this was the only way to avoid conversation with Chesmal.
What Chesmal called conversation. The smugly arrogant
Yellow was intent on her own embroidery, on the other side
of the room, and she assumed that anyone who took up a
needle had her own keen interest in the work. On the other
hand, Asne knew, if she rose from her chair, Chesmal would
soon start regaling her with tales of her own importance.
In the months since Moghedien vanished, she had heard
Chesmal's part in putting Tamra Ospenya to the question
at least twenty times, and how Chesmal had induced the
Reds to murder Sierin Vayu before Sierin could order her
arrest perhaps fifty! To hear Chesmal tell it, she had saved
the Black Ajah single-handed, and she *would* tell it, given
half a chance. That sort of talk was not only boring, it was
dangerous. Even deadly, if the Supreme Council learned of
it. So Asne stifled another yawn, squinted at her work, and
pushed the needle through the tightly stretched linen. Perhaps if she made the redbird larger, she could even up the
wings.

The click of the doorlatch brought both women's heads
up. The two servants knew not to bother them, and in any
case, the woman and her husband should be fast asleep.
Asne embraced *saidar*, readying a weave that would sear
an intruder to the bone, and the glow surrounded Chesmal,

too. If the wrong person stepped through that door, they would regret it until they died.

It was Eldrith, gloves in hand, with her dark cloak still hanging down her back. The plump Brown's dress was dark, too, and unadorned. Asne hated wearing plain woolens, but they did need to avoid notice. The drab clothes suited Eldrith.

She stopped at the sight of them, blinking, a momentary look of confusion on her round face. "Oh, my," she said. "Who did you think I was?" Throwing her gloves onto the small table by the door, she suddenly became aware of her cloak and frowned as if just realizing she had worn it upstairs. Carefully unpinning the silver brooch at her neck, she tossed the cloak onto a chair in a tumbled heap.

The light of *saidar* winked out around Chesmal as she twisted her embroidery frame aside so she could stand. Her stern face made her seem taller than she was, and she was a tall woman. The brightly colored flowers she had embroidered might have been in a garden. "Where have you been?" she demanded. Eldrith stood highest among them, and Moghedien had left her in charge besides, but Chesmal had begun taking only cursory notice if that. "You were supposed to be back by afternoon, and the night is half gone!"

"I lost track of the hour, Chesmal," Eldrith replied absently, appearing lost in thought. "It has been a long time since I was last in Caemlyn. The Inner City is fascinating, and I had a delightful meal at an inn I remembered. Though I must say, there were fewer sisters about then. No one recognized me, however." She peered at her brooch as though wondering where it had come from, then tucked it into her belt pouch.

"You lost track," Chesmal said flatly, lacing her fingers together at her waist. Perhaps to keep them from Eldrith's throat. Her eyes glittered with anger. "You lost track."

Once more Eldrith blinked, as if startled to be addressed. "Oh. Were you afraid Kennit had found me again? I assure you, since Samara I have been quite careful at keeping the bond masked."

At times, Asne wondered how much of Eldrith's apparent vagueness was real. No one so unaware of the world around her could have survived this long. On the other hand, she had been unfocused enough to let the masking slip more than once before they reached Samara, enough for her Warder to track her. Obedient to Moghedien's orders to await her return, they had hidden through the riots after her departure, waited while the so-called Prophet's mobs swept south into Amadicia, stayed in that wretched, ruined town even after Asne became convinced that Moghedien had abandoned them. Her lip curled at the memory. What had sparked the decision to leave was the arrival of Eldrith's Kennit in the town, sure that she was a murderer, half convinced she was Black Ajah, and determined to kill her no matter the consequences to himself. Not surprisingly, she had been unwilling to face those consequences herself, and refused to let anyone kill the man. The only alternative was to flee. Then again, Eldrith was the one who had pointed out Caemlyn as their only hope.

"Did you learn anything, Eldrith?" Asne asked politely. Chesmal was a fool. However tattered the world seemed at the moment, affairs would right themselves. One way or another.

"What? Oh. Only that the pepper sauce wasn't as good as I remembered. Of course, that was fifty years ago."

Asne suppressed a sigh. Perhaps after all it was time for Eldrith to have an accident.

The door opened and Temaile slipped into the room so silently they were all caught by surprise. The diminutive fox-faced Gray had tossed a robe embroidered with lions over her shoulders, but it gaped down the front, exposing a cream-colored silk nightdress that molded itself to her indecently. Draped over one hand she carried a bracelet made of twisted glass rings. They looked and felt like glass, at least, but a hammer could not have chipped one.

"You've been to *Tel'aran'rhiod*," Eldrith said, frowning at the *ter'angreal*. She did not speak forcefully, though. They were all a little afraid of Temaile since Moghedien had made them observe the last of Liandrin being broken. Asne had lost track of how often she had killed or tortured in the hundred and thirty-odd years since she gained the shawl, but she had seldom seen anyone so . . . enthusiastic . . . as Temaile. Watching Temaile and trying to pretend not to, Chesmal seemed unaware that she was licking her lips nervously. Asne hurriedly put her own tongue back behind her teeth and hoped no one had noticed. Eldrith certainly had not. "We agreed not to use those," she said, not very far short of pleading. "I'm certain it was Nynaeve who wounded Moghedien, and if she can best one of the Chosen in *Tel'aran'rhiod*, what chance do we have?" Rounding on the others, she attempted a scolding tone. "Did you two know about this?" She had managed to sound peevish.

Chesmal met Eldrith's stare indignantly, while Asne gave her surprised innocence. They had known, but who was going to stand in Temaile's way? She doubted very much that Eldrith would have made more than a token protest had she been there.

Temaile knew exactly her effect on them. She should have hung her head at Eldrith's lecture, fainthearted as it was, and apologized for going against her wishes. Instead, she smiled. That smile never reached her eyes, though, large and dark and much too bright. "You were right, Eldrith. Right that Elayne would come here, and right that Nynaeve would come with her, it seems. They were together, and it is clear they are both in the Palace."

"Yes," Eldrith said, squirming slightly under Temaile's gaze. "Well." And she licked *her* lips, and shifted her feet, too. "Even so, until we can see how to get at them past all those wilders—"

"They *are* wilders, Eldrith." Temaile threw herself down in a chair, limbs sprawling carelessly, and her tone hardened. Not enough to seem commanding, but still more than merely firm. "There are only three sisters to trouble us, and we can dispose of them. We can take Nynaeve, and perhaps Elayne in the bargain." Abruptly she leaned forward, hands on the arms of the chair. Disarrayed clothing or not, there was no shred of indolence about her now. Eldrith stepped back as though pushed by Temaile's eyes. "Else why are we here, Eldrith? It is what we came for."

No one had anything to say to that. Behind them lay a string of failures—in Tear, in Tanchico—that might well cost them their lives when the Supreme Council laid hands on them. But not if they had one of the Chosen for a patron, and if Moghedien had wanted Nynaeve so badly, perhaps another of them would, too. The real difficulty would be finding one of the Chosen to present with their gift. No one but Asne seemed to have considered that part of it.

"There were others, there," Temaile went on, leaning back once more. She sounded almost bored. "Spying on our two Accepted. A man who let them see him, and someone else I could not see." She pouted irritably. At least, it would have been a pout except for her eyes. "I had to stay behind a column so the girls would not see me. That should please you, Eldrith. That they did not see me. Are you pleased?"

Eldrith almost stammered getting out how pleased she was.

Asne let herself feel her four Warders, coming ever closer. She had stopped masking herself when they left Samara. Only Powl was a Friend of the Dark, of course, yet the others would do whatever she said, believe whatever she told them. It would be necessary to keep them concealed from the others unless absolutely necessary, but she wanted armed men close at hand. Muscles and steel were very useful. And if worse came to worst, she could always reveal the long, fluted rod that Moghedien had not hidden so well as she thought she had.

The early morning light in the sitting room's windows was gray, an earlier hour than the Lady Shiaine usually rose, but this morning she had been dressed while it was still full dark. The Lady Shiaine was how she thought of herself, now. Mili Skane, the saddler's daughter, was almost completely forgotten. In every way that mattered, she really was the Lady Shiaine Avarhin, and had been for years. Lord Willim Avarhin had been impoverished, reduced to living in a ramshackle farmhouse and unable to keep even that in good repair. He and his only daughter, the last of a declining line, had stayed in the country, far from anywhere their penury might be exposed, and now they were only bones buried in the forest near that farmhouse, and *she* was the Lady Shiaine, and if this tall, well-appointed stone house was not a manor, it still had been the property of a well-to-do merchant. She was long dead, too, after signing over her gold to her "heir." The furnishings were well made, the carpets costly, the tapestries and even the seat cushions embroidered with thread-of-gold, and the fire roared in a wide blue-veined marble fireplace. She had had the once-plain lintel carved with Avarhin's Heart and Hand row on row.

"More wine, girl," she said curtly, and Falion scurried with the tall-necked silver pitcher to refill her goblet with steaming spiced wine. The livery of a maid, with the Red Heart and Golden Hand on her breast, suited Falion. Her long face was a stiff mask as she hurried to replace the pitcher on the drawered highchest and take up her place beside the door.

"You play a dangerous game," Marillin Gemalphin said, rolling her own goblet between her palms. A skinny woman with lifeless pale brown hair, the Brown sister did not look an Aes Sedai. Her narrow face and wide nose would have fitted better above Falion's livery than it did above her fine blue wool, and that was suitable only for a middling merchant. "She is shielded somehow, I know, but when she can channel again, she will make you howl for this." Her thin lips quirked in a humorless smile. "You may find yourself wishing you could howl."

"Moridin chose this for her," Shiaine replied. "She failed in Ebou Dar, and he ordered her punished. I don't know the details and don't want to, but if Moridin wants her nose ground in the mud, I'll push it so deep she is breathing mud a year from now. Or do you suggest I disobey one of the Chosen?" She barely suppressed a shudder at the very thought. Marillin tried to hide her expression in drinking, but her eyes tightened. "What about you, Falion?" Shiaine asked. "Would you like me to ask Moridin to take you away? He might find you something less onerous." Mules might sing like nightingales, too.

Falion did not even hesitate. She bobbed a maid's straight-backed curtsy, her face going even paler than it already was. "No, mistress," she said hastily. "I am content with my situation, mistress."

"You see?" Shiaine said to the other Aes Sedai. She doubted very much that Falion was anything approaching content, but the woman would accept whatever was handed out rather than face Moridin's displeasure directly. For the same reason, Shiaine would rule her with a very heavy hand. You never knew what one of the Chosen might learn of, and take amiss. She herself thought her own failure was buried deep, but she would take no chances. "When she can channel again, she won't have to be a maid all the time, Marillin." Anyway, Moridin had said Shiaine could kill her if she wished. There was always that, if her position began to chafe too much. He had said she could kill both sisters, if she wished.

"That's as may be," Marillin said darkly. She cast a side-long glance at Falion and grimaced. "Now, Moghedien instructed me to offer you what assistance I thought I could give, but I'll tell you right now, I won't enter the Royal Palace. The whole city has too many sisters in it for my taste, but the Palace is stuffed with wilders on top. I wouldn't get ten feet without someone knowing I was there."

Sighing, Shiaine leaned back and crossed her legs, idly kicking a slippered foot. Why did people always think you did not know as much as they? The world was full of fools! "Moghedien ordered you to obey me, Marillin. I know, because Moridin told me. He did not say so right out, but I think when he snaps his fingers, Moghedien jumps." Talking about the Chosen this way was dangerous, but she had to make matters clear. "Do you want to tell me again what you won't do?"

The narrow-faced Aes Sedai licked her lips, darting another glance at Falion. Did the woman fear *she* would end up that way? Truth to tell, Shiaine would have traded Falion for a proper lady's maid in a heartbeat. Well, as long as she could retain her other services. Very likely, they both would have to die when this was finished. Shiaine did not like leaving loose ends.

"I wasn't lying about that," Marillin said slowly. "I really wouldn't get ten feet. But there's a woman already in the Palace. She can do what you need. It may take time to make contact, though."

"Just make sure it's not too long a time, Marillin." So. One of the sisters in the Palace was Black Ajah, was she? She would have to be Aes Sedai, not just a Darkfriend, to do what Shiaine needed.

The door opened, and Murellin looked in questioningly, his heavily muscled bulk almost filling the doorway. Beyond him, she could make out another man. At her nod, Murellin stepped aside and motioned Daved Hanlon to enter, closing the door behind him. Hanlon was swathed in a dark cloak, but he snaked out one hand to cup Falion's bottom through her dress. She glared at him bitterly, but did not move away. Hanlon was part of her punishment. Still, Shiaine had no wish to watch him fondle the woman.

"Do that later," she ordered. "Did it go well?"

A broad smile split his axe-like face. "It went exactly as I planned it, of course." He threw one side of the dark cloak over his shoulder, revealing golden knots of rank on his red coat. "You are speaking to the Captain of the Queen's Bodyguard."

CHAPTER

11

Ideas of Importance

Without even taking a look, Rand stepped through the gateway into a large dark room. The strain of holding the weave, of fighting *saidin*, made him sway; he wanted to gag, to double over and spew up everything in him. Holding himself upright was an effort. A little light crept through cracks between the shutters on a few small windows set high in one wall, just enough to see by with the Power in him. Furniture and large cloth-covered shapes nearly filled the room, interspersed with wide barrels of the sort used to store crockery, chests of all shapes and sizes, boxes and crates and knickknacks. Little more than walkways a pace or two wide remained clear. He had been sure he would not find servants hunting for something, or cleaning up. The highest floor of the Royal Palace had several such storerooms, looking like the attics of huge farmhouses and just about forgotten. Besides, he was *ta'veren,* after all. A good thing no one had been there when the gateway opened. One edge of it had sliced the corner off an empty chest bound in cracked, rotting leather, and the other had taken a glass-smooth shaving down the length of a long, inlaid table stacked with vases and wooden boxes. Maybe some Queen of Andor had eaten at that table, a century or two gone.

A century or two, Lews Therin laughed thickly in his head. *A very long time. For the love of the Light, let go! This is the Pit of Doom!* The voice dwindled as the man fled into the recesses of Rand's mind.

For once, he had his own reasons to listen to Lews Therin's complaints. Hastily he motioned Min to follow him from the forest clearing on the other side of the gateway, and as soon as she did, he let it close behind her in a quick vertical slash of light by releasing *saidin*. Blessedly, the nausea went with it. His head still spun a little, but he did not feel as if he were going to vomit or fall over or both. The feel of filth remained, though, the Dark One's taint oozing into him from the weaves he had tied off around himself. Shifting the strap of his leather scrip from one shoulder to the other, he tried to use the motion to hide wiping sweat from his face with his sleeve. He did not have to worry about Min noticing after all, however.

Her blue, heeled boots stirred the dust on the floor at her first step, and her second made it rise. She pulled a lace-edged handkerchief from her coatsleeve just in time to catch a violent sneeze, followed by a second and third, each worse than the last. He wished she had been willing to stay in a dress. Embroidered white flowers decorated the sleeves and lapels of her blue coat, and paler blue breeches molded her legs snugly. With yellow-embroidered bright blue riding gloves tucked behind her belt, and a cloak edged with yellow scrollwork and held by a golden pin in the shape of a rose, she did look as if she had arrived by more normal means, but she would draw every eye. He was in coarse brown woolens any laborer might wear. Most places in the last few days, he had been blatant with his presence; this time he did not want just to be gone before anyone knew he had been here, he did not want anyone but a special few to ever know he had been.

"Why are you grinning at me and thumbing your ear like a loobie?" she demanded, stuffing the handkerchief back into her sleeve. Suspicion filled her big, dark eyes.

"I was just thinking how beautiful you are," he said quietly. She was. He could not look at her without thinking so. Or without regretting that he was too weak to send her away to safety.

She drew a deep breath, and sneezed before she could even clap a hand over her mouth, then glared at him as if it were somehow his fault. "I abandoned my horse for you, Rand al'Thor. I curled my hair for you. I gave up my *life* for you! I will *not* give up my coat and breeches! Besides, no one here has ever seen me in a dress for more time than it took me to change out of it. You know this won't work unless I'm recognized. You certainly can't pretend you wandered in off the street with that face."

Unthinking, he ran a hand across his jaw, feeling his own face, but that was not what Min saw. Anyone looking at him would see a man inches shorter and years older than Rand al'Thor, with lank black hair, dull brown eyes and a wart on his bulbous nose. Only someone who touched him could pierce the Mask of Mirrors. Even an Asha'man would not see it, with the weaves inverted. Though if there were Asha'man in the Palace, it might mean his plans had gone further awry than he believed. This visit could not, must not, come to killing. In any case, she was right; it was not a face that would have been allowed into the Royal Palace of Andor unescorted.

"As long as we can finish this and be gone quickly," he said. "Before anyone has time to think that if you're here, maybe I am, too."

"Rand," she said, her voice soft, and he eyed her warily. Resting a hand on his chest, she looked up at him with a serious expression. "Rand, you really need to see Elayne. And Aviendha, I suppose; you know she's probably here, too. If you—"

He shook his head, and wished he had not. The dizziness had still not gone completely. "No!" he said curtly. Light! No matter what Min said, he just could not believe that Elayne and Aviendha *both* loved him. Or that the fact they did, if it was a fact, did not upset her. Women were not *that* strange! Elayne and Aviendha had reason to hate him, not love him, and Elayne, at least, had made herself clear. Worse, he was in love with both of them, as well as with Min! He had to be as hard as steel, but he thought he might shatter if he had to face all three at once. "We find Nynaeve and Mat, and go, as fast as we can." She opened her mouth, but he gave her no chance to speak. "Don't argue with me, Min. This is no time for it!"

Tilting her head to one side, Min put on a small, amused smile. "When do I ever argue with you? Don't I always do exactly as you tell me?" If that lie were not bad enough, she added, "I was going to say, if you want to hurry, why are we standing in this dusty storeroom all day?" For punctuation, she sneezed again.

She was the least likely to cause comment, even dressed

as she was, so she put her head out of the room first. Apparently the storeroom was not entirely forgotten; the heavy door's hinges barely creaked. A quick look both ways, and she hurried out, gesturing him to follow. *Ta'veren* or no, he was relieved to find the long corridor empty. The most timid servant might have wondered at seeing them emerge from a storeroom in the upper reaches of the Palace. Still, they would encounter people soon enough. The Royal Palace did not run as heavily to servants as the Sun Palace or the Stone of Tear, but there were still hundreds of them in a place this size. Walking along beside Min, he tried to shamble and gawk at bright tapestries and carved wall panels and polished highchests. None were so fine this high as they would be lower down, but a common workman would gawk.

"We need to get down to a lower floor as fast as we can," he murmured. There was still no one in sight, but there might be ten people around the next corner. "Remember, just ask the first servant we see where to find Nynaeve and Mat. Don't elaborate unless you have to."

"Why, thank you for reminding me, Rand. I knew something had slipped my mind, and I just couldn't imagine what." Her brief smile was much too tight, and she muttered something under her breath.

Rand sighed. This was too important for her to play games, but she was going to, if he let her. Not that she saw it that way. Sometimes, though, her ideas of important differed widely from his. Very widely. He would have to keep a close eye on her.

"Why, Mistress Farshaw," a woman's voice said behind them. "It is Mistress Farshaw, isn't it?"

The scrip swung and thumped Rand's back heavily as he spun around. The plump graying woman staring at Min in astonishment was perhaps the last person he wanted to meet, besides Elayne or Aviendha. Wondering why she was wearing a red tabard with the White Lion large on the front, he slouched and avoided looking at her directly. Just a workman doing his job. No reason to glance at him twice.

"Mistress Harfor?" Min exclaimed, beaming delightedly. "Yes, it's me. And you are just the woman I was looking for. I'm afraid I am lost. Can you tell me where to find Nynaeve al'Meara? And Mat Cauthon? This fellow has something Nynaeve asked him to deliver."

The First Maid frowned slightly at Rand before returning her attention to Min. She raised an eyebrow at Min's garments, or maybe at the dust on them, but she mentioned neither. "Mat Cauthon? I don't believe I know him. Unless he's one of the new servants or Guardsmen?" she added doubtfully. "As for Nynaeve Sedai, she's very busy. I suppose it will be all right with her if I accept whatever it is and put it in her room."

Rand jerked upright. Nynaeve *Sedai?* Why would the others—the real Aes Sedai—let her play at that still? And Mat was not here? Had never been here, apparently. Colors whirled in his head, almost an image he could make out. In a heartbeat it vanished, but he staggered. Mistress Harfor frowned at him again, and sniffed. Likely she thought him drunk.

Min frowned, too, but in thought, tapping a finger on her chin, and that only lasted a moment. "I think Nynaeve . . . Sedai wants to see him." The hesitation was barely noticeable. "Could you have him shown to her rooms, Mistress Harfor? I have another errand before I go. You mind your manners, now, Nuli, and do as you're told. There's a good fellow."

Rand opened his mouth, but before he could get out a word she darted away down the corridor, almost running. Her cloak flared behind her, she was moving so quickly. Burn her, she was going to try finding Elayne! She could ruin everything!

Your plans fail because you want to live, madman. Lews Therin's voice was a rough, sweaty whisper. *Accept that you are dead. Accept it, and stop tormenting me, madman!* Rand suppressed the voice to a muted buzz, a biteme buzzing in the darkness of his head. Nuli? What kind of name was Nuli?

Mistress Harfor gaped after Min until she vanished around a corner, then gave her tabard an adjusting tug it did not need. She turned her disapproval on Rand. Even with the Mask of Mirrors she saw a man who towered over her, but Reene Harfor was not a woman to let a small thing like that put her off stride for an instant. "I mistrust the looks of you, Nuli," she said, her eyebrows drawn down sharply, "so you watch your step. You'll watch it very carefully, if you have any brain at all."

Holding the scrip's shoulder strap with one hand, he tugged his forelock with the other. "Yes, Mistress," he muttered gruffly. The First Maid might recognize his real voice. Min had been supposed to do all the talking until they found Nynaeve and Mat. What in the Light was he going to do if she did bring Elayne? And maybe Aviendha. She probably was here, too. Light! "Pardon, Mistress, but we ought to hurry. It's urgent I see Nynaeve as soon as possible." He hefted the scrip slightly. "She wanted this real important like." If he was done when Min returned, he might be able to get away with her before he had to face the other two.

"If Nynaeve *Sedai* thought it was urgent," the plump woman told him tartly, placing heavy emphasis on the honorific he had omitted, "she would have left word you were expected. Now, follow me, and keep your comments and opinions to yourself."

She started off without waiting for a reply, without looking back, gliding along with a stately grace. After all, what could he do except as he had been told? As he recalled, the First Maid was accustomed to everyone doing as they were told. Striding to catch up, he took only one step at her side before her startled look made him drop back, tugging his forelock and mumbling apologies. He was not used to having to walk behind anyone. It was not calculated to moderate his mood. The tag end of dizziness hung on, too, and the filth of the taint. He seemed to be in a foul mood more often than not of late, unless Min was with him.

Before they had gone very far, liveried servants began to appear in the hallway, polishing and dusting and carrying, scurrying every which way. Plainly the absence of people when he and Min left the storeroom was a rare occurrence. *Ta'veren* again. Down a flight of narrow service stairs built into the wall, and there were even more. And something else, a great many women who were not in livery. Copper-skinned Domani women, short pale Cairhienin, women with olive skins and dark eyes who were certainly not Andoran. They made him smile, a tight satisfied smile. None had what he could call an ageless face, and a number even bore lines and wrinkles that never decorated any Aes Sedai's face, but sometimes goose bumps danced on his skin when he came near one of them. They were channeling, or

least holding *saidar*. Mistress Harfor led him past closed
doors where that prickling raced, too. Behind those doors,
still other women had to be channeling.

"Pardon, Mistress," he said in the coarse voice he had
adopted for Nuli. "How many Aes Sedai are there in the
Palace?"

"That is no concern of yours," she snapped. Glancing
over one shoulder at him, though, she sighed and relented.
"I don't suppose there is any harm in you knowing. Five,
counting the Lady Elayne and Nynaeve Sedai." A touch of
pride entered her voice. "It has been a long time since that
many Aes Sedai claimed guestright here at one time."

Rand could have laughed, though without amusement.
Five? No, that included Nynaeve and Elayne. Three real
Aes Sedai. Three! Whoever the rest were did not really
matter. He had begun to believe that the rumors of hundreds of Aes Sedai moving toward Caemlyn with an army
meant there really might be that many ready to follow the
Dragon Reborn. Instead, even his original hope for a double
handful of them had been wildly optimistic. The rumors
were only rumors. Or else some scheme of Elaida's making. Light, where *was* Mat? Color flashed in his head—for
an instant he thought it was Mat's face—and he stumbled.

"If you came here drunk, Nuli," Mistress Harfor said
firmly, "you will leave regretting it bitterly. I will see to it
myself!"

"Yes, Mistress," Rand muttered, jerking at his forelock.
Inside his head, Lews Therin cackled in mad, weeping
laughter. He had had to come here—it was necessary—but
he was already beginning to regret it.

Surrounded by the light of *saidar*, Nynaeve and Talaan
faced one another at four paces in front of the fireplace,
where a brisk blaze had managed to take all chill out of the
air. Or maybe it was effort that had warmed her, Nynaeve
thought sourly. This lesson had lasted an hour already, by
the ornate clock on the carved mantel. An hour of channeling without rest would warm anyone. Sareitha was supposed to be here, not her, but the Brown had slipped out of
the Palace leaving a note about an urgent errand in the city.

Careane had refused to take two days in a row, and Vandene still refused to take any, on the ridiculous grounds that teaching Kirstian and Zarya left her no time.

"Like this," she said, whipping her flow of Spirit around the boy-slim Sea Folk apprentice's attempt at fending her off. Adding the force of her own flow, she pushed the girl's further away and at the same time channeled Air in three separate weaves. One tickled Talaan's ribs through her blue linen blouse. A simple ploy, but the girl gasped in surprise, and for an instant her embrace of the Source lessened just a hair, the faintest flicker in the Power filling her. In that heartbeat Nynaeve stopped the pushing she had just begun on the other's flow and snapped her own back to its original target. Forcing the shield onto Talaan still felt much like slapping a wall—except the sting was spread evenly across her skin rather than just in her palm, hardly an improvement—but the glow of *saidar* vanished just as the last two flows of Air trapped Talaan's arms at her sides and pulled her knees together in their wide, dark trousers.

Very neatly done, if Nynaeve did think so herself. The girl was very agile, very deft with her weaves. Besides, trying to shield someone who held the Power was chancy at best and futile at worst, unless you were *very* much stronger than they—sometimes if you were—and Talaan matched her as closely as made no difference. That helped keep a satisfied smile from her face. It seemed a very short time ago that sisters had been startled at her strength and believed that only some of the Forsaken possessed greater. Talaan had not slowed, yet; she was little more than a child. Fifteen? Maybe younger! The Light alone knew what her potential was. At least, none of the Windfinders had mentioned it, and Nynaeve was not about to ask. She had no interest in knowing how much stronger than she a Sea Folk girl was going to be. None at all.

Bare feet shuffling on the patterned green carpet, Talaan made one futile attempt to break the shield that Nynaeve held easily, then sighed in defeat and lowered her eyes. Even when she had succeeded in following Nynaeve's instruction, she behaved as if she had failed, and now she slumped so dejectedly you might have thought the weaves of Air were all that held her upright.

Letting her flows dissipate, Nynaeve adjusted her shawl

and opened her mouth to tell Talaan what she had done wrong. And to point out—once again—that it was useless to try breaking free unless you were *much* stronger than whoever had shielded you. The Sea Folk hardly seemed to believe anything she told them until she told them ten times and showed them twenty.

"She used your own force against you," Senine din Ryal said bluntly before Nynaeve could speak. "And distraction, again. It is like wrestling, girl. You know how to wrestle."

"Try again," Zaida commanded with a brisk gesture of one dark, tattooed hand.

All of the chairs in the room had been moved against the wall, though there was no real need for a clear space, and Zaida sat watching the lesson flanked by six Windfinders, a riot of reds and yellows and blues in brocaded silks and brightly dyed linens, a flinch-inducing display of earrings and nose rings and medallion-laden chains. That was always the way; one of the two apprentices was used for the actual lesson—or Merilille, Nynaeve had heard, actually forced to take the part of an apprentice unless she herself was teaching—while Zaida and one group or another of Windfinders watched. The Wavemistress could not channel, of course, though she was always present, and none of the Windfinders would actually stoop to participating personally. Oh, never that.

In Nynaeve's estimation, today's grouping was very odd, considering the Sea Folks' obsession with rank. Zaida's own Windfinder, Shielyn, sat on her right, a slender, coolly reserved woman almost as tall as Aviendha and towering over Zaida. That was proper, as far as Nynaeve understood, but at Zaida's left was Senine, and she served on a soarer, one of the Sea Folk's smaller vessels, and hers among the smallest of those. Of course, the weathered woman, with her creased face and hair thick with gray, had worn more than her present six earrings in the past, and more golden medallions on the chain across her dark left cheek. She had been Windfinder to the Mistress of the Ships before Nesta din Reas was elected to the post, but by their law, when the Mistress of the Ships or a Wavemistress died, her Windfinder had to begin again at the lowest level. There was more to it than respect for Senine's former position, though, Nynaeve was certain. Rainyn, an apple-cheeked young

woman who served on a darter, occupied the chair next to
Senine, and stone-faced, flat-eyed Kurin sat beside Shielyn
like a black carving. This relegated Caire and Tebreille to
the outermost chairs, and they were both Windfinders to
Wavemistresses themselves, with four fat earrings in each
ear and nearly as many medallions as Zaida herself. Perhaps
it was just to keep the haughty-eyed sisters apart, though.
They hated one another with a passion only blood kin could
achieve. Perhaps that was it. Understanding the Atha'an
Miere was worse than trying to understand men. A woman
could go mad trying.

Muttering to herself, Nynaeve gave her shawl a jerk and
prepared herself, readying her flows. The pure joy of holding
saidar could hardly compete with her vexation. Try again,
Nynaeve. One more time, Nynaeve. Do it now, Nynaeve. At
least Renaile was not there. Often they wanted her to teach
things she did not know as well as others—too often, things
she barely knew at all, she admitted reluctantly; she had
not really had much training in the Tower—and whenever
she fumbled in the slightest, Renaile positively delighted in
making her sweat. The others made her sweat, too, but they
did not seem to take so much pleasure in it. Anyway, after
a solid hour, she was tired. Drat Sareitha and her errand!

She struck out again, but this time Talaan's flow of Spirit
met hers much more lightly than she expected, and her
own flow swept the other further aside than she had meant.
Abruptly six weaves of Air shot out from the girl, darting
toward Nynaeve, and Nynaeve quickly sliced them with
Fire. The severed flows snapped back into Talaan, jolt-
ing her visibly, but before they had vanished properly, six
more appeared, faster than before. Nynaeve slashed. And
gaped as Talaan's weave of Spirit flickered around hers and
wrapped around her, cutting off *saidar*. She was shielded!
Talaan had shielded her! For the final indignity, flows of
Air pinioned her arms and legs tightly, crushing her skirts.
If she had not been so upset at Sareitha, it never would have
happened.

"The girl has her," Caire said, sounding surprised. No
one would think she was Talaan's mother by the cold look
she gave her. Indeed, Talaan seemed embarrassed by her
own success, releasing the flows immediately and dropping
her eyes to the floor.

"Very good, Talaan," Nynaeve said, since no one else was offering a word of praise or encouragement. Irritably she shook out her shawl behind her and settled it into the crooks of her elbows. No need to tell the girl she had been lucky. She was quick, true, but Nynaeve was not sure she herself could keep channeling much longer. She certainly was not at her best now. "I'm afraid that is all the time I have today, so—"

"Try again," Zaida commanded, leaning forward intently. "I want to see something." That was not an explanation, or anything near apology, simply a statement of fact. Zaida never explained or apologized. She just expected obedience.

Nynaeve considered telling the woman she could not see anything they were doing anyway, but she rejected the thought immediately. Not with six Windfinders in the room. Two days earlier she had voiced her opinions freely, and she certainly did not want a repeat of that. She had tried thinking of it as a penance, for speaking without thinking, but that did not help very much. She wished she had never taught them to link.

"One more time," she said tightly, turning back to Talaan, "and then I must go."

She was ready for the girl's trick this time. Channeling, she met Talaan's weave more dexterously, and without so much force. The girl smiled at her uncertainly. Thinking Nynaeve would not be distracted by extraneous flows of Air this time, was she? Talaan's weave began to curl around hers, and she nimbly spun her own to catch it. She would be ready when the woman produced her flows of Air. Or maybe not Air, this time. Nothing dangerous surely. This was practice. Only, Talaan's flow of Spirit did not complete that curl, and Nynaeve's swung wide while Talaan's struck straight at her and latched on. Once again, *saidar* winked out of her, and bonds of Air snapped her arms to her sides, fastened her knees.

Carefully, she drew breath. She would have to congratulate the young woman. There was no getting out of it. If she had had a hand free, she would have yanked her braid right out of her scalp.

"Hold!" Zaida commanded, rising to stride gracefully toward Nynaeve, her red silk trousers whisking softly above her bare feet, intricately knotted red sash swaying against her thigh. The Windfinders stood with her and followed, in order of rank. Caire and Tebreille icily ignored one another as they hurried to take places nearest the Wavemistress while Senine and Rainyn fell a pace to the rear.

Obediently, Talaan held the shield on Nynaeve, and the bonds, leaving her standing like a statue. And fuming like a kettle too long on the boil. She refused to shuffle about, a broken puppet, and that was all that was left to her except standing still. Caire and Tebreille studied her with icy disdain, Kurin with the hard contempt she had for all land dwellers. The stone-eyed woman did not sneer or grimace or wear any real expression at all, but you could not be with her long without becoming aware of her opinion. Only Rainyn displayed the smallest touch of sympathy, a slight rueful smile.

Zaida's eyes met Nynaeve's levelly. They were much the same height. "She is held as tightly as you can, apprentice?"

Talaan bowed deeply, parallel to the floor, touching her forehead, lips and heart. "As you commanded, Wavemistress," she all but whispered.

"What is the meaning of this?" Nynaeve demanded. "Let me go. You may get away with treating Merilille this way, but if you think for one minute—!"

"You say there is no way to break this shield unless you are much stronger," Zaida cut her off. Her tone was not harsh, but she meant to be heard, not to listen. "The Light willing, we will learn whether you told us correctly. It is well known how Aes Sedai make truth spin like a whirl-pool. Windfinders, you will form a circle. Kurin, you will lead. If she does break free, see that she causes no harm. For incentive . . . Apprentice, prepare to turn her upside down at my count of five. One."

The light of *saidar* enveloped the Windfinders, all of them together, as they linked. Kurin stood with her feet apart and her hands on her hips, as if balancing on the deck of a ship. Her very lack of expression seemed to convey that she was already convinced they would uncover prevarica-tion if not an outright lie. Talaan drew a deep breath, and for once stood very straight, not even blinking as she kept her anxious eyes on Zaida.

Nynaeve blinked. No! They could not do this to her! Not

again! "I am telling you," she said, much more calmly than she felt, "there is no way for me to break the shield. Talaan is too strong."

"Two," Zaida said, folding her arms beneath her breasts and staring at Nynaeve as though she really could see the weaves.

Nynaeve pushed tentatively at the shield. She might as well push at a stone wall for all the give in it. "Listen to me, Za . . . uh . . . Wavemistress." There was certainly no need to antagonize the woman further. They were sticklers for proper forms of address. Sticklers for all too many things. "I'm sure Merilille has told you something about shielding, at least. She swore the Three Oaths. She *can't* lie." Maybe Egwene was right about the Oath Rod.

Zaida's gaze never wavered, her expression never changed. "Three."

"Listen to me," Nynaeve said, not caring at all if she sounded a bit desperate. Maybe more than just a bit. She pushed against the shield harder, then as hard as she could. She might as well have beat her head against a boulder for all the effect it had. Instinctively, uselessly, she struggled in the bonds of Air holding her, the fringe and loose folds of her shawl dancing around her. She had as much chance of breaking free of those bonds as she did of breaking through the shield, but she could not stop herself. Not again! She could not face that! "You have to listen!"

"Four."

No! No! Not again! Frantically she scrabbled at the shield. It might be as hard as stone, but it felt more like glass, sleek and slippery. She could feel the Source beyond it, almost see the Source, like light and warmth just beyond the corner of vision. In desperation, panting, she felt her way across the smooth surface. It had an edge, like a circle at once small enough to hold in her hands and large enough to cover the world, but when she attempted to slip around that edge, she found herself right back in the center of the slick hard circle again. This was useless. She had learned all this long ago, tried it all long ago. Her heart pounded fit to burst out of her ribs. Struggling vainly for calm, she hurriedly felt her way back to the edge, felt along it without trying to go around. There was one place where it felt . . . softer. She had never noticed that before. The soft point—a slight lump?—seemed no different in any other way from the rest, and it was not much softer, but she hurled herself at it. And found herself back in the center. In a frenzy, she flung all of her strength at the soft spot, again and again, being hurled back to the center, not even pausing before launching herself at it again. Again. Oh, Light! Please! She had to, before . . . !

Abruptly she realized that Zaida still had not said five. Gulping air as if she had run ten miles, she stared. Sweat rolled down her face, her back. It trickled between her breasts, slid down her belly. Her legs wobbled. The Wavemistress looked straight into her eyes, thoughtfully tapping full lips with a slim finger. The glow still enveloped the circle of six, Kurin still could have been a scornfully stony statue, but Zaida had not said five.

"Did she truly try as hard as it seemed, Kurin," the Wavemistress asked finally, "or was all that thrashing about and whimpering just a show?" Nynaeve tried to summon an indignant glare. She had *not* whimpered! Had she? Her scowl, such as it was, made no more impression on Zaida than rain on a rock.

"With that much effort, Wavemistress," Kurin said reluctantly, "she could have carried a raker on her back." The flat black pebbles of her eyes still held contempt, though. Only those who lived at sea got any respect from her.

"Release her, Talaan," Zaida commanded, and shield and bonds vanished as she turned away, starting back toward the chairs without another glance at Nynaeve. "Windfinders, I will have words with you after she goes. I will see you at the same hour tomorrow, Nynaeve Sedai."

Smoothing her rumpled skirts and irritably shaking out her shawl again, Nynaeve attempted to regather a little dignity. It was not easy, sweat-slicked and trembling. She *certainly* had not whimpered! She tried not to look at the woman who had shielded her. Twice! Standing there meek as butter, with her eyes fixed on the carpet. Ha! Nynaeve jerked her shawl around her shoulders. "Sareitha Sedai will take her turn tomorrow, Wavemistress." At least her voice was steady. "I will be busy until—"

"Your instruction is more edifying than that of the others," Zaida said, still not bothering to look at her. "At the same

had learned from Moghedien for this woman. Including a few they had all agreed were too nasty to do to anyone. Except . . . She was fairly certain the other woman could overpower her easily, whatever she did. Keeping her feet from shifting under that intense stare was not easy. "Until— unless!—we decide differently, you won't let me see you without two or three Kinswomen again, if you know what's good for you."

"If you say so," Alivia said, not at all abashed. "What message do you want me to take back to Mistress Corly?"

"Tell Mistress Corly I have to decline her kind invitation. And remember what I told you!"

"I'll tell her," the Seanchan woman drawled, completely ignoring the admonition. "But I don't think it was exactly an invitation. An hour after first dark, she said. You might want to remember that." With a slight, knowing smile, she walked away, not hurrying at all to return where she belonged.

Nynaeve glared at the retreating woman's back, and not because of her lack of a curtsy. Well, not only that. A pity she had not hung on to a few of her simpers, for sisters, anyway. With a glance at the door that hid the Atha'an Miere, Nynaeve considered following Alivia to make sure she did as she had been told. Instead, she went in the opposite direction. She did not hurry. It would be unpleasant if the Sea Folk came out and decided she had been eavesdropping, but she definitely did not hurry. She merely wanted to walk briskly. That was all.

The Atha'an Miere were hardly the only ones in the Palace she wanted to avoid. Not exactly an invitation, was it? Sumeko Karistovan, Chilares Arman and Famelle Juarde had been in the Knitting Circle with Reanne Corly. Dinner was only an excuse. They would want to talk to her about the Windfinders. More specifically, about the relationship between the Aes Sedai in the Palace and the Sea Folk "wilders." They would not quite upbraid her for failing to maintain the dignity of the White Tower. They had not gone that far; not yet, though they seemed to be coming closer. But the whole dinner would be full of pointed questions and sharper comments. Nothing she could simply order them to stop. She doubted they would for less than a command. And they were quite capable of coming to find her if she did not go to them. Trying to teach them to show backbone had been a terrible mistake. At least she was not the only one who had to put up with it, though she thought Elayne had managed to avoid the worst. Oh, how she looked forward to seeing them back in novice white or Accepted's dresses. How she looked forward to seeing the last of the Atha'an Miere!

"Nynaeve!" came a strangely muted cry behind her. In Sea Folk accents. "Nynaeve!"

Forcing her hand away from her braid, Nynaeve spun on her heel, ready to deliver a tongue-lashing. She was not teaching now, they were not on a ship, and they could bloody well leave her alone!

Talaan skidded to a halt in front of her, bare feet sliding on the dark red floor tiles. Panting, the young woman swiveled her head as if afraid someone would sneak up on her. She flinched every time a liveried servant moved just on the edge of her sight, and only breathed again when she saw it was just a servant. "Can I go to the White Tower?" she asked breathlessly, wringing her hands and dancing from foot to foot. "I will never be chosen. A sacrifice, they call it, leaving the sea forever, but I dream of becoming a novice. I will miss my mother terribly, but . . . Please. You must take me to the Tower. You must!"

Nynaeve blinked at the onslaught. Many women dreamed of becoming Aes Sedai, but she had never before heard one say she dreamed of becoming a novice. Besides . . . The Atha'an Miere refused passage to Aes Sedai on any ship whose Windfinder could channel, but to keep sisters from trying to look deeper, every so often an apprentice was chosen to go to the White Tower. Egwene said there were only three sisters from among the Sea Folk at present, all weak in the Power. For three thousand years that had been enough to convince the Tower that the ability was rare and small with Atha'an Miere women, not worth investigating. Talaan was right; no one as strong as she would ever be allowed to go to the Tower, even now that their subterfuge was coming to an end. In fact, it was part of the bargain with them that Atha'an Miere sisters be allowed to give up being Aes Sedai and return to the ships. The Hall of the Tower would not *half* howl about that!

"Well, the training is very hard, Talaan," she said gently,

"and you must be at least fifteen. Besides . . ." Something else the young woman ad said struck her suddenly. "You will miss your mother?" she said incredulously, not caring how it sounded.

"I am nineteen!" Talaan replied indignantly. Looking at that boyish face and form, Nynaeve was not sure she believed. "And of course I will miss my mother. Do I look unnatural? Oh; I see. You do not understand. We are very affectionate in private, but she must avoid any sign of favor in public. That is a serious crime, with us. It could have mother stripped of her rank, and *both* of us hung upside down in the rigging to be flogged."

Nynaeve grimaced at the mention of upside down. "I certainly can see where you would want to avoid that," she said. "Even so—"

"Everyone tries to avoid even a hint of favor, but it is worse for me, Nynaeve!" Really, the girl—woman—young woman—would have to learn not to step on what a sister was saying if she did become a novice. Not that she could, of course. Nynaeve tried to regain the initiative, but words poured out of Talaan in a torrent. "My grandmother is Windfinder to the Wavemistress of Clan Rossaine, my great-grandmother is Windfinder to Clan Dacan, and her sister to Clan Takana. My family is honored that five of us have risen so high. And everyone watches for signs that Gelyn abuses its influence. Rightly so, I know—favor cannot be allowed—but my sister was kept an apprentice five years longer than normal, and my cousin six! Just so no one can claim they were favored. When I cast the stars and give our position correctly, I am punished for being slow even when I have the answer as fast as Windfinder Ehvon! When I taste the sea and name the coast we are approaching, I am punished because the taste I name is not quite what Windfinder Ehvon tastes! I shielded you twice, but tonight I will hang by my ankles for not doing so sooner! I am punished for flaws ignored in others, for flaws I never make, because I *might!* Was your novice training any harder than that, Nynaeve?"

"My novice training," Nynaeve said faintly. She wished the woman would not keep bringing up being hung by the ankles. "Yes. Well. You really don't want to hear about that." *Four* generations of women with the ability? Light!

Even daughter following mother was rare enough. The Tower really would want Talaan. That was not going to happen, though. "I suppose Caire and Tebreille really love one another, too?" she said, trying to change the subject.

Talaan sneered. "My aunt is sly and deceitful. She celebrates any humiliation she can cause my mother. But my mother will bring her low, as she deserves. One day, Tebreille will find herself serving on a soarer, beneath a Sailmistress with an iron hand and sore teeth!" She gave a grim, satisfied nod at the thought. And then jumped, wide-eyed as a fawn, when a serving man hurried by behind her. That recalled her to her purpose. She went back to trying to look every way at once as she spoke hastily. "You cannot speak out during the lessons, of course, but any other time will do. Announce that I am to go to the Tower, and they will not be able to deny you. You are Aes Sedai!"

Nynaeve goggled at the girl. And they would have forgotten all about it by the next time she gave a lesson? The fool had *seen* what they did to her! "I can see how much you want to go, Talaan," she said, "but—"

"Thank you," Talaan broke in, making a quick bow. "Thank you!" And she darted back the way she had come at a dead run.

"Wait!" Nynaeve shouted, taking a few steps after her. "Come back! I didn't promise anything!"

Servants turned to stare at her, and continued to shoot wondering glances in her direction even after returning to their tasks. She would have run after the idiot except that she was afraid she would have to follow her straight to Zaida and the others. And the fool would probably gush out that she was going to the Tower, that Nynaeve had promised. Light, she would probably tell them anyway!

"You look as if you just swallowed a rotten plum," Lan said, appearing at her side, tall and starkly handsome in his well-fitting green coat. She wondered how long he had been there. It did not seem possible that a man so large, so commanding in his presence, could stand still enough that you failed to notice him, even without a Warder's cloak.

"A basketful of them," she murmured, pressing her face against her husband's broad chest. It felt very good to lean against his strength, just for a moment, while he stroked her hair softly. Even if she did have to shift his sword hilt out of her ribs. And anyone who wanted to stare at such a public display of affection could go hang themselves. She could see disaster piling up on disaster. Even if she told Zaida and the others she had no intention of taking Talaan anywhere, they were going to *skin* her. There would be no hiding it from Lan this time. If she had managed to the first. Reanne and the others would learn of it. And Alise! They would start treating her the way they did Merilille, ignoring her orders, giving her about as much respect as the Windfinders did Talaan. Somehow she would be saddled with guarding Alivia, and some catastrophe would come of it, some utter humiliation. That was all she seemed fit to do, lately; find another way to be humiliated. And every fourth day, she would still have to face Zaida and the Windfinders.

"Do you remember how you kept me in our rooms yesterday morning?" she murmured, looking up in time to catch a grin replacing concern on his face. Of course he remembered. Her face grew hot. Talking to friends was one thing, but being forward with her own husband still seemed quite another. "Well, I want you to take me back there right now and keep me from putting on any clothes for about a year!" She had been quite furious about that, at first. But he had ways to make her forget to be furious.

He threw back his head and laughed, a great booming sound, and after a moment, she echoed him. She wanted to weep, though. She had not really been joking.

Having a husband meant that she did not have to share a bed with another woman, or two, and it gained her a sitting room. It was not large, but it always seemed snug, with a good fireplace and a small table with four chairs. Certainly as much as she and Lan needed. Her hopes for privacy were dashed as soon as they entered the sitting room, though. The First Maid was waiting in the middle of the flowered carpet, as stately as a queen, as neatly turned out as if she had just finished dressing, and not at all pleased. And in one corner of the room was a roughly dressed, lumpy fellow with a horrible wart on his nose and a scrip dangling heavily from his shoulder.

"This man claims he has something you want urgently," Mistress Harfor said once she had made brief courtesies. Very brief, if proper; she did not waste them on anyone except Elayne. She sounded equally disapproving of Nynaeve and the fellow with the wart. "I don't mind telling you, I do not like the looks of him."

Tired as Nynaeve was, embracing the Source was almost beyond her, but she managed it in a flash, spurred by thoughts of assassins and the Light knew what. Lan must have caught some change in her face, because he took a step toward the warty fellow; he did not touch his sword, but suddenly his whole stance seemed as if the blade were already drawn. How he sometimes managed to read her mind when another held his bond, she could not say, but she was pleased. She had managed to match Talaan—in strength, at least!—but she was not sure she could channel enough right then to knock over a chair. "I never," she began.

"Pardon, Mistress," the lumpy fellow muttered hurriedly, tugging his greasy forelock. "Mistress Thane said you wanted to see me right away. Women's Circle business, she said. Something about Cenn Buie."

Nynaeve gave herself a shake, and after a moment remembered to close her mouth. "Yes," she said slowly, staring at the fellow. Seeing anything but that awful wart was difficult, but she was certain she had never laid eyes on him before. Women's Circle business. No man would be allowed a sniff of that. It was secret. She held on to *saidar*, though. "I . . . remember, now. Thank you, Mistress Harfor. I'm sure you have all sorts of things to see to."

Rather than take the hint, the First Maid hesitated, frowning at her suspiciously. That frown slid around to the lumpy man, then settled on Lan and vanished. She nodded to herself, as if his presence somehow made the difference! "I will leave you, then. I'm sure Lord Lan can handle this fellow."

Stifling her indignation, Nynaeve barely waited for the door to close before rounding on the lumpy fellow and his wart. "Who are you?" she demanded. "How do you know those names? You're no Two Riv—"

The man . . . rippled. There was no other word for it. He rippled and stretched taller, and suddenly it was Rand, grimacing and swallowing, in rumpled woolens with those awful heads glittering red-and-gold on the backs of his hands and a leather scrip on his shoulder. Where had he learned that? Who had taught him? She resisted the idea of disguising herself, just for a moment, to show him she could do as much.

"None of that is important now," Rand said, turning to the scrip on the table. She did not know whether he meant his wounds or where Mat was. From the scrip he produced two statuettes a foot high, a wise-looking, bearded man and an equally wise and serene woman, each in flowing robes and holding aloft a clear crystal sphere. From the way he handled them, they were heavier than they appeared. "I want you to keep these hidden for me until I send for them, Nynaeve." One hand on the figure of the woman, he hesitated. "And for you. I'll need you when I use them. When we use them. After I take care of those men. That has to come first."

"Use them?" she said suspiciously. Why did killing anyone have to come first? That was hardly the important question, though. "For what? Are they *ter'angreal*?"

He nodded. "With this, you can touch the greatest *sa'angreal* ever made for a woman. It's buried on Tremalking, I understand, but that doesn't matter." His hand moved to the figure of the man. "With this one, I can touch its male twin. I was told by . . . someone . . . once, that a man and woman using those *sa'angreal* could challenge the Dark One. They might have to be used for that, one day, but in the meantime, I hope they're enough to cleanse the male half of the Source."

"If it could be done, wouldn't they have done it in the Age of Legends?" Lan said quietly. Quiet the way steel sliding from a scabbard was quiet. "You said once that I could get her hurt." It seemed impossible his voice could grow any harder, but it did. "You could kill her, sheepherder." And his tone made clear that he would not allow that.

Rand met Lan's cold blue stare with one just as cold. "I don't know why they didn't. I don't care why. It has to be tried."

Nynaeve bit her lower lip. She supposed Rand made this a public occasion—shifting from public to private, deciding which was which, made her dizzy sometimes—but she did not care that Lan had spoken out of turn. He was bad that way, in any case, but she liked an outspoken man. She needed to think. Not about her decision. She had made that. About how to implement it. Rand might not like it. Lan certainly would not. Well, men always wanted their own way. Sometimes you just had to teach them they could not always have it.

"I think it is a wonderful idea," she said. That was not exactly a lie. It *was* wonderful, compared to the alternatives. "But I don't see why I should sit here waiting for your summons like a serving maid. I'll do it, but we all go together."

She had been right. They did not like it one bit.

CHAPTER
12

A Lily in Winter

Another serving man nearly fell on his nose bowing, and Elayne sighed as she glided past along the Palace corridor. At least, she tried to glide. The Daughter-Heir of Andor, stately and serene. She wanted to run, though her dark blue skirts probably would have tripped her had she tried. She could almost feel the stout man's goggling eyes following her and her companions. A minor irritant, and one that would pass; a grain of sand in her slipper. *Rand bloody thinks-he-knows-best-for-everybody al'Thor is itchoak down my back!* she thought. If he managed to get away from her this time . . . !

"Just remember," she said firmly. "He hears nothing about spies, or forkroot, or any of that!" The very last thing she needed was him deciding to "rescue" her. Men did that sort of nonsense; Nynaeve called it "thinking with the hair on their chests." Light, he would probably try to move the Aiel and the Saldaeans back into the city! Into the Palace itself! Bitter as it was to admit, she could not stop him if he did, not short of open war, and even that might not be enough.

"I don't tell him things he doesn't need to know," Min said, frowning at a lanky, wide-eyed serving woman whose curtsy nearly collapsed into a sprawl on the red-brown floor tiles. Eyeing Min sideways, Elayne remembered her own time wearing breeches, and wondered whether she might not try again. They were certainly freer than skirts. Not the heeled boots, though, she decided judiciously. They made Min almost as tall as Aviendha, but even Birgitte swayed in those, and with Min's snug breeches and a coat that barely covered her hips, it looked positively scandalous.

"You lie to him?" Suspicion larded Aviendha's tone. Even the way she adjusted her dark shawl on her shoulders carried disapproval, and she glared past Elayne at Min.

"Of course not," Min replied sharply, glaring right back. "Not unless it's necessary." Aviendha chuckled, then looked startled that she had, and put on a stony face.

What was she to do about them? They *had* to like one another. They just *had* to. But the two women had been staring at each other like strange cats in a small room ever since they met. Oh, they had agreed to everything—there really had been no choice, not when none of them could guess when they would all have the man at hand again—but she hoped they did not show one another again how skillfully they handled their knives. Very casually, not actually implying any threat, but very open about it, too. On the other hand, Aviendha had been quite impressed with the number of knives Min carried about her person.

A gangly young serving man carrying a tray of tall mantles for the stand-lamps bowed as she swept by. Unfortunately, he was staring so hard that he forgot to pay attention to his burden. The crash of glass shattering on the floor tiles filled the corridor.

Elayne sighed again. She did hope everyone became used to the new order of things soon. She was not the object of all that gaping, of course, or Aviendha, or even Min, though she probably drew some. No, it was Caseille and Deni, following close behind, who were making eyes pop and servants stumble. She had eight bodyguards, now, and those two had been standing guard at her door when she woke.

Very likely some of the gaping was just that Elayne had Guardswomen trailing behind her at all, and almost certainly that they *were* women. No one was used to that, yet. But Birgitte had said she would make them appear ceremonial, and she had. She must have set every seamstress and milliner in the Palace working as soon as she left Elayne's rooms the night before. Each woman wore a bright red hat with a long white plume lying flat along the wide brim, and a wide red sash edged in snowy laee across her chest with rampant White Lions marching up it. Their white-collared crimson coats were silk, and the cut had been altered a little,

so they fit better and hung almost to the knee above scarlet breeches with a white stripe up the outsides of the legs.
Pale lace hung thickly at their wrists and necks, and their
black boots had been waxed till they shone. They looked
quite dashing, and even placid-eyed Deni swaggered just
a little. Elayne suspected they would be even prouder once
the sword belts and scabbards with gold tooling were ready,
and the lacquered helmets and breastplates. Birgitte was
having breastplates made to fit women, which Elayne suspected had *certainly* made the Palace armorer's eyes pop!

At the moment, Birgitte was busy interviewing women
to round out the twenty for the bodyguard. Elayne could
feel her concentrating, with no sign of physical activity, so it
must be that, unless she was reading, or playing stones, and
she seldom took a moment away from her duties for herself.
Elayne hoped she would keep it to just twenty. She hoped
Birgitte was busy enough that she did not notice until too
late when she masked the bond. To think that she had been
so worried about Birgitte sensing what she did not want her
to when the solution lay in a simple question to Vandene.
The answer had been a rueful reminder how little she actually knew about being Aes Sedai, especially the parts other
sisters took for granted. Apparently, every sister who had a
Warder knew how, even those who remained celibate.

It was odd how things came about, sometimes. If not for
the bodyguards, if not for wondering how she could manage
to elude them *and* Birgitte, she would never have thought to
ask, would never have learned the masking in time for this.
Not that she planned to elude her guards any time soon, but
it was best to be prepared in advance of need. Birgitte certainly was not going to allow her and Aviendha to wander
the city alone, day *or* night, not any longer.

Their arrival at Nynaeve's door put thoughts of Birgitte
completely out of her head. Except that she must not
mask the bond until the very last instant. Rand was on the
other side of that door. Rand who sometimes crowded her
thoughts until she wondered whether she was like some fool
woman in a story who threw her head over the wall because
of a man. She had always thought those stories must have
been written by men. Only, Rand sometimes did make her
feel witless. At least he did not realize it, thank the Light.

"Wait out here, and admit no one," she commanded the

Guardswomen. She could not afford interruptions or attention now. With luck, her bodyguard was new enough that no one would even recognize what their fine uniforms meant. "I will only be a few minutes."

They saluted briskly, an arm across the chest, and took positions on either side of the door, Caseille stonefaced with a hand on her sword hilt, Deni taking her long cudgel in both hands and smiling faintly. Elayne was sure the stocky woman thought Min had brought her here to meet a secret lover. She suspected Caseille might, as well. They had hardly been as discreet in front of the two women as they might have; no one had mentioned his name, but there had more than enough of "he this" and "he that." At least neither had tried making an excuse to leave so she could report to Birgitte. If they were her bodyguard, then they were *her* bodyguard, not Birgitte's. Except that they would not keep Birgitte out if she masked the bond too soon.

And she was dithering, she realized. The man she dreamed of every night was on the other side of that door, and she was standing there like a witling. She had waited so long, wanted so much, and now she was almost afraid. She would not let this go wrong. With an effort, she gathered herself.

"Are you ready?" Her voice was not as strong as she could have hoped, but at least it did not tremble. Butterflies the size of foxes fluttered in her stomach. That had not happened in a long time.

"Of course," Aviendha said, but she had to swallow first.

"I'm ready," Min said faintly.

They went in without knocking, hurriedly closing the door behind them.

Nynaeve jumped to her feet, wide-eyed, before they were well into the sitting room, but Elayne barely noticed her or Lan, though the sweet smell of the Warder's pipe filled the room. Rand really was there; it had been hard to believe he would be. That dreadful disguise Min had described was gone, except for the shabby clothing and rough gloves, and he was . . . beautiful.

He leaped from his chair at the sight of her, too, but before he was completely upright, he staggered and grabbed the table with both hands, gagging and heaving with dry retches. Elayne embraced the Source and took a step toward him, then stopped and made herself let go of the Power. Her ability with Healing was tiny, and anyway, Nynaeve had moved as quickly as she, the shine of *saidar* suddenly around her, hands raised toward Rand.

He recoiled, waving her away. "It's nothing you can Heal, Nynaeve," he said roughly. "In any case, it seems you win the argument." His face was a rigid mask hiding emotion, but his eyes seemed to Elayne to be drinking her in. And Aviendha as well. She was surprised to feel gladdened by that. She had hoped it would be that way, hoped she could manage for her sister's sake, and now it took no managing at all. Straightening up was a visible effort for him, and pulling his gaze away from her and Aviendha, though he tried to hide both. "It is past time to be gone, Min," he said.

Elayne's jaw dropped. "You think you can just go without even *speaking* to me, to us?" she managed.

"Men!" Min and Aviendha breathed at almost the same instant, and gave one another startled looks. Hastily they unfolded their arms. For an instant, despite the disparity in just about everything about them, they had been almost mirror images of womanly disgust.

"The men who tried to kill me in Cairhien would turn this palace into a slag heap if they knew I was here," Rand said quietly. "Maybe if they just suspected. I suppose Min told you it was Asha'man. Don't trust any of them. Except for three, maybe. Damer Flinn, Jahar Narishma and Eben Hopwil. You may be able to trust them. For the rest . . ." He clenched gauntleted fists at his sides, seemingly unaware. "Sometimes a sword turns in your hand, but I still need a sword. Just stay away from any man in a black coat. Look, there's no time for talking. It's best I go quickly." She had been wrong. He was not exactly as she had dreamed of him. There had been a boyishness about him sometimes, but it was gone as if burned away. She mourned that for him. She did not think he did, or could.

"He is right in one thing," Lan said around his pipestem with the same sort of quiet. Another man who seemed never to have been a boy. His eyes were blue ice beneath the braided leather cord that encircled his brows. "Anyone near him is in great danger. Anyone." For some reason, Nynaeve snorted. Then put her hand on a leather scrip with hard bulges lying on the table and smiled. Though after a moment her smile faltered.

"Do my first-sister and I fear danger?" Aviendha demanded, planting her fists on her hips. Her shawl slipped from her shoulders and fell to the floor, but she was so intent that she seemed unaware of the loss. "This man has *toh* to us, Aan'allein, and we to him. It must be worked out."

Min spread her hands. "I don't know what anybody's toes have to do with anything, or feet either, but I'm not going anywhere until you talk to them, Rand!" She affected not to notice Aviendha's outraged glare.

Sighing, Rand leaned against a corner of the table and raked gloved fingers through the dark, reddish curls that hung to his neck. He seemed to be arguing with himself under his breath.

"I'm sorry you ended up with the *sul'dam* and *damane*," he said finally. He did sound sorry, but not very; he might have been regretting the cold. "Taim was supposed to deliver them to the sisters I thought were with you. But I suppose anyone can make a mistake like that. Maybe he thought all those Wisdoms and Wise Women Nynaeve has gathered were Aes Sedai." His smile was quiet. It did not touch his eyes.

"Rand," Min said in a low, warning tone.

He had the nerve to look at her questioningly, as if he did not understand. And he went right on. "Anyway, you seem to have enough of them to hold on to a handful of women until you can turn them over to the . . . the other sisters, the ones with Egwene. Things never turn out quite the way you expect, do they? Who would have thought a few sisters running away from Elaida would grow into a rebellion against the White Tower? With Egwene as Amyrlin! And the Band of the Red Hand for her army. I suppose Mat can stay there awhile." For some reason he blinked and touched his forehead, then went on in that irritatingly casual tone. "Well. A strange turn of events all around. At this rate, I won't be surprised if my friends in the Tower work up enough courage to come out in the open."

Arching an eyebrow, Elayne glanced, at Nynaeve. Wisdoms and Wise Women? The Band was Egwene's army, and Mat was with it? Nynaeve's attempt at wide-eyed innocence made her look like guilt nailed to a door. Elayne supposed it did not matter. He would learn the truth soon enough, if he could be talked into going to Egwene. In any case, she had more important matters to take up with him. The man was babbling, however offhand he managed to sound, tossing out anything they might snap at in hopes of diverting them.

"It won't do, Rand." Elayne tightened her hands on her skirts to keep herself from shaking a finger at him. Or a fist; she was not sure which it would be. The *other* sisters? The *real* Aes Sedai, he had been about to say. How *dare* he? And his *friends* in the Tower! Could he still believe Alviarin's strange letter? Her voice was cool and firm and steady, brooking no nonsense. "None of that matters a hair, not now. You and Aviendha and Min and I are what we need to talk about. And we will. We *all* will, Rand al'Thor, and you are *not* leaving the Palace until we do!"

For the longest time, he simply looked at her, his expression never changing. Then he inhaled audibly, and his face turned to granite. "I love you, Elayne." Without a pause, he went on, words rushing out of him, water from a burst dam. And his face a stone wall. "I love you, Aviendha. I love you, Min. And not one a whisker more or less than the other two. I don't just want one of you, I want all three. So there you have it. I'm a lecher. Now you can walk away and not look back. It's madness, anyway. I can't afford to love anybody!"

"Rand al'Thor," Nynaeve shrieked, "that is the most outrageous thing I ever heard out of your mouth! The very idea of telling *three* women you love them! You're *worse* than a lecher! You apologize right now!" Lan had snatched his pipe from his mouth and was staring at Rand.

"I love you, Rand," Elayne said simply, "and although you haven't asked, I want to marry you." She blushed faintly, but she intended to be much more forward before very long, so she supposed this hardly counted. Nynaeve's mouth worked, but no sound came out.

"My heart is in your hands, Rand," Aviendha said, treating his name like something rare and precious. "If I can convince my first-sister, we will make a bridal wreath for you." And she blushed, too, trying to cover it in bending to take her shawl from the floor and arranging it on her arms. By Aiel customs, she should never had said any of that. Nynaeve finally got a sound out. A squeak.

"If you don't know by this time that I love you," Min
said, "then you're blind, deaf and dead!" She certainly did
not blush; there was a mischievous light in her dark eyes,
and she seemed ready to laugh. "And as for marriage, well,
we'll work that out between the three of us, so there!"
Nynaeve took a grip on her braid with both hands and gave
it a steady pull, breathing heavily through her nose. Lan had
begun an intense study of the contents of his pipe's bowl.

Rand examined the three of them as if he had never seen
a woman before and wondered what they were. "You're all
mad," he said finally. "I'd marry any of you—all of you, the
Light help me!—but it can't be, and you know it." Nynaeve
collapsed into a chair, shaking her head. She muttered to
herself, though all Elayne could understand was something
about the Women's Circle swallowing their tongues.

"There is something else we need to discuss," Elayne
said. Light, Min and Aviendha could have been looking
at a pastry! With an effort she managed to make her own
smile a little less . . . eager. "In my rooms, I think. There's
no need to bother Nynaeve and Lan." Or rather, she was
afraid that Nynaeve would try to stop them, if she heard.
The woman was very quick to use her authority when it
came to Aes Sedai matters.

"Yes," Rand said slowly. And then, strangely, added, "I
said you'd won, Nynaeve. I won't leave without seeing you
again."

"Oh!" Nynaeve gave a start. "Yes. Of course not. I watched
him grow up," she blathered, turning a sickly smile on
Elayne. "Almost from the start. Watched his first steps. He
can't go without a good long talk with me."

Elayne eyed her suspiciously. Light, she sounded for all
the world like an aged nurse. Though Lini had never babbled. She hoped Lini was alive and well, but she was very
much afraid that neither was true. Why was Nynaeve carrying on in this fashion? The woman was up to something,
and if she was not going to use her standing to carry it off,
it was something even she knew was wrong.

Suddenly, Rand seemed to waver, as though the air
around him were shimmering with heat, and everything
else flew out of Elayne's head. In an instant, he was . . .
someone else, shorter and thicker, coarse and brutish. And
so repulsive to look at that she did not even consider the fact

that he was using the male half of the Power. Greasy black hair hung down onto an unhealthily pale face dominated by hairy warts, including one on a bulbous nose above thick slack lips that appeared on the edge of drooling. He squeezed his eyes shut and swallowed, hands gripping the arms of his chair, as if he could not stand to see them look at him.

"You are still beautiful, Rand," she said gently.

"Ha!" Min said. "That face would make a goat faint!" Well, it would, but she should not have said so.

Aviendha laughed. "You have a sense of humor, Min Farshaw. That face would make a *herd* of goats faint." Oh, Light, it *would!* Elayne swallowed a giggle just in time.

"I am who I am," Rand said, pushing himself up out of the chair. "You just won't see it."

At Deni's first sight of Rand in his disguise, the smile slid crookedly off the stocky woman's face. Caseille's mouth dropped open. *So much for thoughts of secret lovers,* Elayne thought, laughing to herself in amusement. She was sure he drew as many stares as the Guardswomen, shambling along between them with a sullen scowl. Certainly no one could suspect who he was. The servants in the corridors probably thought he had been apprehended in some crime. He certainly had the look. Caseille and Deni kept a hard eye on him as if they thought so, too.

The Guardswomen came near to arguing when they realized she intended them to wait outside her apartments while the three of them took him inside. Suddenly, Rand's disguise did not seem amusing at all any longer. Caseille's mouth thinned, and Deni's wide face set in stubborn displeasure. Elayne almost had to wave her Great Serpent ring beneath their noses before they took positions beside her door, scowling. She shut the door softly, cutting off the sight of their frowns, but she wanted to slam it. Light, the man could have chosen something a *little* less unsavory for his disguise.

And as for *him,* he went straight to the inlaid table, leaning against it while the air around him shimmered and he became himself once more. The Dragon's heads on the backs of his hands glittered metallically, scarlet and gold. "I need a drink," he muttered thickly, catching sight of the tall-necked silver pitcher on the long side-table against the wall.

Still not looking at her or Min or Aviendha, he walked
over unsteadily and filled a silver winecup that he half-
drained in one long swallow. That sweet spicy wine had
been left when her breakfast was taken away. It must be
cold as ice by now. She had not been expected to return
to her rooms so soon, and the fire on the hearth had been
banked down beneath ashes. But he made no move she
could see to warm the wine by channeling. She would have
seen steam, at least. And why had he walked to the wine,
instead of channeling to bring it to him? That was the sort
of thing he always did, floating winecups and lamps about
on flows of Air.

"Are you well, Rand?" Elayne asked. "I mean, are you
sick?" Her stomach tightened at the thought of what sickness it might be, with him. "Nynaeve can—"

"I am as fine as I can be," he said flatly. *Still* with his
back to them. Emptying the cup, he began to fill it again.
"Now what is it you don't want Nynaeve to hear?"

Elayne's eyebrows shot up, and she exchanged looks with
Aviendha and Min. If *he* had seen through her subterfuge,
Nynaeve *certainly* had. Why had she let them go? And how
had he seen through it? Aviendha shook her head slightly in
wonder. Min shook hers, too, but with a grin that said you
just had to expect this sort of thing now and then. Elayne
felt the smallest stab of—not quite jealousy; jealousy was
out of the question, for them—just irritation that Min had
had so much time with him and she had not. Well, if he
wanted to play surprises . . .

"We want to bond you our Warder," she said, smoothing her dress under her as she took a chair. Min sat on the
edge of the table, legs dangling, and Aviendha settled onto
the carpet cross-legged, carefully spreading out her heavy
woolen skirts. "All three of us. It is customary to ask, first."

He spun around, wine sloshing out of his cup, more pouring from the pitcher before he could bring it upright. With a
muttered oath, he hastily stepped out of the spreading wetness on the carpet and put the pitcher back on the tray. A
large damp spot decorated the front of his rough coat, and
droplets of dark wine that he tried to brush away with his
free hand. Very satisfactory.

"You really are mad," he growled. "You know what's
ahead of me. You know what it means for anyone I'm

bonded to. Even if I don't go insane, she has to live through me dying! And what do you mean, all three of you? Min can't channel. Anyway, Alanna Mosvani got there ahead of you, and she didn't bother asking. She and Verin were taking some Two Rivers girls to the White Tower. I've been bonded to her for months, now."

"And you kept it from me, you woolheaded sheepherder?" Min demanded. "If I'd known—!" She deftly produced a slim knife from her sleeve, then glared at it and glumly put it back. That cure would have been as hard on Rand as on Alanna.

"This was against custom," Aviendha said, half questioning. She shifted on the carpet and fingered her belt knife.

"Very much so," Elayne replied grimly. That a sister would do that to *any* man was disgusting! That Alanna had done it to *Rand* . . . ! She remembered the dark, fiery Green with her quicksilver humor and her quicksilver temper. "Alanna has more *toh* to him than she could repay in a *lifetime!* And to us. Even if she doesn't, she will wish I had just *killed* her after I lay hands on her!"

"After *we* lay hands on her," Aviendha said, nodding for emphasis.

"So." Rand peered into his wine. "You can see there's no point in this. I . . . I think I'd better go back to Nynaeve, now. Are you coming, Min?" Despite what they had told him, he sounded as though he did not really believe, as if Min might abandon him now. He did not sound afraid of it, only resigned.

"There *is* a point," Elayne said insistently. She leaned toward him, trying by the force of her will to make him accept what she was saying. "One bond doesn't ward you against another. Sisters don't bond the same man because of *custom,* Rand, because they don't want to *share* him, not because it can't be done. And it isn't against Tower law, either." Of course, some customs were strong as law, at least in the eyes of the sisters. Nynaeve seemed to go on more every day about upholding Aes Sedai customs and dignity. When she learned of this, she would probably explode right through the roof. "Well, we *do* want to share you! We *will* share you, if you agree."

How easy it was to say that! She had been sure she could not, once. Until she came to realize that she loved Aviendha as much as she did him, just in a different way. And Min, too; another sister, even if they had not adopted one another. She would stripe Alanna from top to bottom for touching him, given the chance, but Aviendha and Min were different. They were part of her. In a way, they *were* her, and she them.

She softened her tone. "I am asking, Rand. *We* are asking. Please let us bond you."

"Min," he murmured, almost accusingly. His eyes on Min's face were filled with despair. "You knew, didn't you? You knew if I laid eyes on them . . ." He shook his head, unable or unwilling to go on.

"I didn't know about the bonding until they told me less than an hour ago," she said, meeting his gaze with the most gentle look Elayne had ever seen. "But I knew, I hoped, what would happen if you saw them again. Some things have to be, Rand. They have to be."

Rand stared into the winecup, moments seeming to stretch like hours, and at last set it back on the tray. "All right," he said quietly. "I can't say I do not want this, because I do. The Light burn me for it! But think of the cost. Think of the price you'll pay."

Elayne did not need to think of the price. She had known it from the beginning, had discussed it with Aviendha to make sure she understood, too. She had explained it to Min. Take what you want, and pay for it, the old saying went. None of them had to think about the price; they knew, and they were willing to pay. There was no time to waste, though. Even now, she did not put it past him to decide that price was too high. As if that were his decision to make!

Opening herself to *saidar,* she linked with Aviendha, sharing a smile with her. The increased awareness of one another, the more intimate sharing of emotions and physical feelings, was always a pleasure with her sister. It was very much like what they would soon share with Rand. She had worked this out carefully, studied it from every angle. What she had been able to learn of the Aiel adoption weaves had been a great help. That ceremony had been when the idea first came to her.

Carefully she wove Spirit, a flow of over a hundred threads, every thread placed just so, and laid the weave on Aviendha sitting on the floor, then did the same to Min on the table's edge. In a way, they were not two separate weaves at all. They glowed with a precise similarity, and it seemed that looking at one, she saw the other as well. These were not the weaves used in the adoption ceremony, but they used the same principles. They *included;* what happened to one meshed in that weave, happened to all in it. As soon as the weaves were in place, she passed the lead of the circle of two to Aviendha. The weaves already made remained, and Aviendha immediately wove identical weaves around Elayne, and around Min again, blending that one until it was indistinguishable from Elayne's before passing control back. They did that very easily now, after a great deal of practice. Four weaves, or rather, three now, yet they all seemed the same weave.

Everything was ready. Aviendha was a rock of confidence as strong as anything Elayne had ever felt from Birgitte. Min sat gripping the edge of the table, her ankles locked together; she could not see the flows, but she gave an assured grin that was only spoiled a little when she licked her lips. Elayne breathed deeply. To her eyes, they three were surrounded and connected by a tracery of Spirit that made the finest lace seem drab. Now if only it worked as she believed it would.

From each of them, she extended the weave in narrow lines toward Rand, twisting the three lines into one, changing it into the Warder bond. That, she laid on Rand as softly as if she were laying a blanket on a baby. The spiderweb of Spirit settled around him, settled into him. He did not even blink, but it was done. She let go of *saidar.* Done.

He stared at them, expressionless, and slowly put his fingers to his temples.

"Oh, Light, Rand, the pain," Min murmured in a hurt voice. "I never knew; I never imagined. How can you stand it? There are pains you don't even seem to know, as if you've lived with them so long they're part of you. Those herons on your hands; you can still feel the branding. Those things on your arms hurt! And your side. Oh, Light, your side! Why aren't you crying, Rand? Why aren't you crying?"

"He is the *Car'a'carn,*" Aviendha said, laughing, "as strong as the Three-fold Land itself!" Her face was proud—oh, so proud—but even as she laughed, tears streamed down her sun-dark cheeks. "The veins of gold. Oh, the veins of gold. You do love me, Rand."

Elayne simply stared at him, felt him in her head. The pain of wounds and hurts he really had forgotten. The tension and disbelief; the wonder. His emotions were too rigid, though, like a knot of hardened pine sap, almost stone. Yet laced through them, golden veins pulsed and glowed whenever he looked at Min, or Aviendha. Or her. He *did* love her. He loved all three of them. And that made her want to laugh with joy. Other women might find doubts, but she would always know the truth of his love.

"The Light send you know what you've done," he said in a low voice. "The Light send you aren't . . ." The pine sap grew a trifle harder. He was sure they would be hurt, and was already steeling himself. "I . . . I have to go, now. At least I'll know you are all well now; I won't have to worry about you." Suddenly he grinned; he might have looked almost boyish if it had reached his eyes. "Nynaeve will be frantic thinking I've slipped away without seeing her. Not that she doesn't deserve a little flustering."

"There is one more thing, Rand," Elayne said, and stopped to swallow. Light, she had thought *this* would be the easy part.

"I suppose Aviendha and I have to talk while we can," Min said hurriedly, springing off the table. "Somewhere we can be alone. If you'll excuse us?"

Aviendha rose from the carpet gracefully, smoothing her skirts. "Yes. Min Farshaw and I must learn about one another." She eyed Min doubtfully, adjusting her shawl, but they left arm in arm.

Rand watched them warily, as if he knew their leaving had been planned. A cornered wolf. But those veins of gold gleamed in her head.

"There is something they have had from you that I haven't," Elayne began, and choked, a flush scalding her face. Blood and ashes! How *did* other women go about this? Carefully she considered the bundle of sensations in her head that was him, and the bundle that was Birgitte. There was still no change in the second. She imagined wrapping it in a kerchief, knotting the kerchief snugly, and Birgitte was gone. There was only Rand. And those shining golden veins. Butterflies the size of *wolfhounds* drummed their wings in her middle. Swallowing hard, she took a long breath. "You will have to help me with my buttons," she said unsteadily. "I cannot take this dress off by myself."

The two Guardswomen stirred when Min came into the corridor with the Aiel woman, and jerked erect when they realized, as Min closed the door, that no one else was coming out.

"Her taste *can't* be *that* bad," the blocky, sleepy-eyed one muttered under her breath, hands tightening on her long cudgel. Min did not think anyone had been meant to hear.

"Too much courage, and too much innocence," the lean, mannish one growled. "The Captain-General warned us about that." She put a gauntleted hand on the lion-headed doorlatch.

"You go in there now, and she might skin you, too," Min said blithely. "Have you ever seen her in a temper? She could make a bear weep!"

Aviendha disengaged her arm from Min's and put a little distance between them. It was the Guardswomen who received her scowl, though. "You doubt my sister can handle a single man? She is Aes Sedai, and has the heart of a lion. And you are oath-sworn to follow her! You follow where she leads, not put your noses up her sleeve."

The Guardswomen exchanged a long look. The heavier woman shrugged. The wiry one grimaced, but she took her hand from the doorlatch. "I'm oath-sworn to keep that girl alive," she said in a hard voice, "and I mean to. Now you children go play with your dolls and let me do my job."

Min considered producing a knife and performing one of the flashy finger-rolls Thom Merrilin had taught her. Just to show them who was a child. The lean woman was not young, but there was no gray in her hair, and she looked quite strong. And quick. Min wanted to believe some of the other woman's bulk was fat, but she did not. She could not see any images or auras around either, but neither looked in the least afraid to do whatever she thought needed doing. Well, at least they were leaving Elayne and Rand alone. Maybe the knife was unnecessary.

From the corner of her eye she caught sight of the Aiel

reluctantly letting a hand fall from her belt knife. If the woman did not stop mirroring her this way, she was going to start thinking there was more to this jiggery-pokery with the Power than she had been told. Then again, it had begun before the jiggery-pokery. Maybe they just thought alike. A disturbing idea. Light, all this talk about him marrying all three of them was very well for talk, but which one was he *really* going to marry?

"Elayne *is* brave," she told the Guards, "as brave as anybody I've ever met. And she isn't stupid. If you start off thinking she is, you'll soon go wrong with her." They stared down at her from the vantage of an added fifteen or twenty years, solid, unperturbed and determined. In a moment they would tell her to run along, again. "Well, we can't stand around here if we're going to talk, can we, Aviendha?"

"No," the Aiel woman breathed in a tight voice, glaring at the Guardswomen. "We cannot stand here."

The Guardswomen took no notice of their going at all. They had a job to do, and it had nothing to with watching Elayne's friends. Min hoped they did their job well. *She isn't at* all *stupid,* she thought. *She just lets her courage lead the way, sometimes.* She hoped they would not let Elayne scramble into brambles she could not get out of.

Walking along the hallway, she eyed the Aiel woman sideways. Aviendha strode along as far from her as she could be and still remain in the same corridor. Not even glancing in Min's direction, she pulled a thickly carved ivory bracelet from her belt pouch and slipped it over her left wrist with a small, satisfied smile. She had had a fly on her nose from the first, and Min did not understand why. Aiel were supposed to be used to women sharing a man. A far cry more than she could say for herself. She just loved him so badly she was willing to share, and if she must, then there was no one in the world she would rather share with than Elayne. With her, it almost wasn't like sharing at all. This Aiel woman was a stranger, though. Elayne had said it was important they get to know one another, but how could they if the woman would not talk to her?

She did not spend much time worrying about Elayne, though, or Aviendha. What lay in her head was too wondrous. Rand. A little ball that told her everything about him. She had been sure the whole thing would fail, for her at least. What would making love with him be like after this, when she knew *everything!* Light! Of course, he would know everything about her, too. She was *definitely* uncertain how she felt about *that!*

Abruptly she realized that the bundle of emotions and sensations was no longer the same as at first. There was a . . . red roaring . . . to it, now, like wildfire raging through a tinder dry forest. What could . . . ? Light! She stumbled, and just caught her footing short of tumbling. If she had known this furnace, this fierce hunger, was inside him, she would have been afraid to let him touch her! On the other hand . . . It might be nice, knowing she had sparked such an inferno. She could not wait to see whether she produced the same effect as . . . She stumbled again, and this time had to catch herself on an ornately carved highchest. Oh, Light! Elayne! Her *face* felt like a furnace. This was like peeking through the bedcurtains!

Hurriedly she tried the trick Elayne had told her about, imaging that ball of emotions tied up in a kerchief. Nothing happened. Frantically she tried again, but the raging fire was still there! She had to stop looking at it, stop feeling it. Anything to get her attention anywhere but there! Anything! Maybe if she started talking.

"She should have drunk that heartleaf tea," she babbled. She never told what she saw except to those involved, and only then if they wanted to hear, but she had to say something. "She'll get with child from this. Two of them; a boy and a girl; both healthy and strong."

"She wants his babies," the Aiel woman mumbled. Her green eyes stared straight ahead; her jaw was tight, and sweat beaded on her forehead. "I will not drink the tea myself if I—" Giving herself a shake, she frowned across the width of the hall at Min. "My sister and the Wise Ones told me about you. You really see things about people that come true?"

"Sometimes I see things, and if I know what they mean, they happen," Min said. Their voices, raised to reach each other, carried along the corridor. Red-and-white-liveried servants turned to stare at them. Min moved to the center of the hallway. She would meet the other woman halfway, no more. After a moment, Aviendha joined her.

Min wondered whether to tell her what she had seen

while they were all together. Aviendha would have Rand's babies, too. Four of them at once! Something was odd about that, though. The babies would be healthy, but still something odd. And people often did not like hearing about their futures, even when they said they wanted to. She wished someone could tell her whether she *herself* would. . . .

Walking along in silence, Aviendha wiped sweat from her face with her fingers and swallowed hard. Min had to swallow, too. Everything Rand was feeling was in that ball. Everything!

"The kerchief trick didn't work for you, either?" she said hoarsely.

Aviendha blinked, and crimson darkened her face. A moment later, she said, "That is better. Thank you. I . . . With him in my head, I forgot." She frowned. "It did not work for you?"

Min shook her head miserably. This was indecent! "It helps if I talk, though." She had to make friends with this woman, somehow, if this whole peculiar business was to have a hope of working. "I'm sorry for what I said. About toes, I mean. I know a little of your customs. There's something about that man that just makes me cheeky. I can't control my tongue. But don't think I'm going to let you start hitting me or carving on me. Maybe I have *toh,* but we'll have to find some other way. I could always groom your horse, when we have time."

"You are as proud as my sister," Aviendha muttered, frowning. What did she mean by that? "You have a good sense of humor, too." She seemed to be talking to herself. "You did not make a fool of yourself about Rand and Elayne the way most wetlander women would. And you did remind me. . . ." With a sigh, she flipped her shawl up onto her shoulders. "I know where there is some *oosquai.* If you are too drunk to think, then—" Staring down the hallway, she stopped dead. "No!" she growled. "Not yet!"

Coming toward them was an apparition that made Min's jaw drop. Consternation pushed Rand beyond awareness. From comments she had known that the Captain-General of Elayne's Guards was a woman, and Elayne's Warder to boot, but nothing else. This woman had a thick, intricate golden braid pulled over one shoulder of her short, white-collared red coat, and her voluminous blue trousers were tucked into boots with heels as high as Min's. Auras danced around her and images flickered, more than Min had ever seen around anyone, thousands it seemed, cascading over one another. Elayne's Warder and Captain-General of the Queen's Guards . . . wobbled . . . a little, as though she had already been into the *oosquai*. Servants who caught sight of her decided they had work in another part of the Palace, leaving the three of them alone in the corridor. She did not seem to see Min and Aviendha until she almost walked into them.

"You bloody helped her in this, didn't you?" she growled, focusing glassy-looking blue eyes on Aviendha. "First, she flaming vanishes out of my head, and then . . . !" She trembled, and visibly controlled herself, but even then she was breathing hard. Her legs did not seem to want to hold her upright. Licking her lips, she swallowed and went on angrily. "Burn her, I can't concentrate enough to shake it off! You let me tell you, if she's doing what I think she's doing, I'll kick her tickle-heart around the bloody Palace, and then I'll flaming welt her till she can't sit for a *month*—and you alongside her!—if I have to find *forkroot* to do it!"

"My first-sister is a grown woman, Birgitte Trahelion," Aviendha said truculently. Despite her tone, her shoulders were hunched, and she did not quite meet the other woman's stare. "You must stop trying to treat us as children!"

"When she bloody well behaves like an adult, I bloody well treat her as one, but she has no right to do *this,* not in my flaming head, she doesn't! Not in my—!" Abruptly, Birgitte's glazed blue eyes bulged. The golden haired woman's mouth dropped open, and she would have fallen if Min and Aviendha had not each seized an arm.

Squeezing her eyes shut, she sobbed, just once, and whimpered, "*Two* months!" Shaking free of them, she straightened and fixed Aviendha with blue eyes clear as water and hard as ice. "Shield her for me, and I'll let you off your share." Aviendha's sullen, indignant glare just slid off her.

"You're Birgitte Silverbow!" Min breathed. She had been sure even before Aviendha said the name. No wonder the Aiel woman was behaving as if she feared those threats would be carried out right then and there. Birgitte Silverbow! "I saw you at Falme!"

Birgitte gave a start as if goosed, then looked around hurriedly. Once she realized they were alone, she relaxed. A little. She eyed Min up and down. "Whatever you saw, Silverbow is dead," she said bluntly. "I'm Birgitte Trahelion, now, and that's all." Her lips twisted wryly for a moment. "The flaming *Lady* Birgitte Trahelion, if you flaming please. Kiss a sheep on Mother's Day if I can do anything about that, I suppose. And who might you be when you're to home? Do you always show off your legs like a bloody feather dancer?"

"I am Min Farshaw," she replied curtly. *This* was Birgitte Silverbow, hero of a hundred legends? The woman was *foul*-mouthed! And what did she mean, Silverbow was dead? The woman was standing right in front of her! Besides, those multitudes of images and auras flashed by too quickly for her to make out any clearly, but she was certain they indicated more adventures than a woman could have in one lifetime. Strangely, some were connected to an ugly man who was older than she, and others to an ugly man who was much younger, yet somehow Min knew they were the same man. Legend or no legend, that superior air irritated her no end. "Elayne, Aviendha and I just bonded a Warder," she said without thinking. "And if Elayne is celebrating a little, well, you better think twice about storming in, or *you'll* be the one sitting tender."

That was enough to make her aware of Rand again. That raging furnace was still there, hardly lessened at all, but thank the Light, he was no longer . . . Blood rushed into her cheeks. He had lain often enough in her arms, catching his breath in the tangle of their bedding, but this really did seem like peeping!

"Him?" Birgitte said softly. "Mothers' milk in a cup! She could have fallen in love with a cutpurse or a horsethief, but she had to choose him, more fool her. By what I saw of him at that place you mentioned, the man's too pretty to be good for any woman. In any case, she has to stop."

"You have no right!" Aviendha insisted in a sulky voice, and Birgitte took on a look of patience. Stretched patience, but still patience.

"She might be proper as a Talmouri maiden except when it comes to putting her head on the chopping block, but I think she'll wind up her courage to put him through his paces again, and even if she does whatever it was she did, she'll forget and be back in my head. I won't bloody go through that again!" She squared herself, plainly ready to march off and confront Elayne.

"Think of it as a good joke," Aviendha said pleadingly. Pleadingly! "She has played a good joke on you, that is all." A curl of Birgitte's lip expressed what she thought of that.

"There's a trick Elayne told me," Min said hurriedly, catching hold of Birgitte's sleeve. "It didn't work for me, but maybe . . ." Unfortunately, once she had explained . . .

"She's still there," Birgitte said grimly after a moment. "Step out of my way, Min Farshaw," she said, pulling her arm free, "or—"

"*Oosquai!*" Aviendha voice rose desperately, and she was actually wringing her hands! "I know where there is *oosquai!* If you are drunk . . . ! Please, Birgitte! I . . . I will pledge myself to obey you, as apprentice to mistress, but please do not interrupt her! Do not shame her so!"

"*Oosquai?*" Birgitte mused, rubbing her jaw. "Is that anything like brandy? Hmm. I think the girl is blushing! She really is prim most of the time, you know. A joke, you said?" Suddenly she grinned, and spread her arms expansively. "Lead me to this *oosquai* of yours, Aviendha. I don't know about you two, but I intend to get drunk enough to . . . well . . . to take off my clothes and dance on the table. And not a hair drunker."

Min did not understand that at all, or why Aviendha stared at Birgitte and suddenly began laughing about it being "a wonderful joke," but she was sure she knew why Elayne was blushing, if she actually was. That hard ball of sensations in her head was a raging wildfire again.

"Could we go find that *oosquai,* now?" she said. "I want to get drunk as a drowned mouse, and fast!"

When Elayne woke the next morning, the bedchamber was icy, a light snow was falling on Caemlyn, and Rand was gone. Except inside her head. That would do. She smiled, a slow smile. For now, it would. Stretching languorously beneath the blankets, she remembered her abandon the night before—and most of the day as well! She could hardly believe it had been her!—and thought that she should be blushing like the *sun!* But she wanted to be abandoned with Rand, and she did not think she would ever blush again, not for anything connected to him.

Best of all, he had left her a present. On the pillow beside her when she woke lay a golden lily in full bloom, the dew fresh on the lush petals. Where he could have gotten such a thing in the middle of winter she could not begin to imagine. But she wove a Keeping around it, and set it on a side table where she would see it every morning when she woke. The weave was Moghedien's teaching, but it would hold the blossom fresh forever, the dewdrops never evaporating, a constant reminder of the man who had given her his heart.

Her morning was taken up with the news that Alivia had vanished during the night, a serious matter that put the Kin in a tumult. It was not until Zaida appeared in a taking because Nynaeve had not come for a lesson with the Atha'an Miere that Elayne learned that Nynaeve and Lan were both gone from the Palace, too, and no one knew when or how. Not until much later did she learn that the collection of *angreal* and *ter'angreal* they had carried out of Ebou Dar was missing the most powerful of the three *angreal,* and several other items besides. Some of those, she was sure, were intended for a woman who expected to be attacked at any moment with the One Power. Which made the hastily scribbled note Nynaeve had left hidden among the remainder all the more disturbing.

CHAPTER
13

Wonderful News

The Sun Palace's sunroom was cold despite fires roaring on hearths at either end of the room, thickly layered carpets, and a slanted glass roof that let in bright morning light where snow caught on the thin muntins did not shield it, but it was suitable for holding audiences. Cadsuane had thought it best not to appropriate the throne room. So far, Lord Dobraine had remained quiet about her holding Caraline Damodred and Darlin Sisnera—she saw no better way to keep them from going on with their mischief than keeping them in a firm grip—but Dobraine might begin to fuss over that if she pushed beyond what he considered proper. He was too close to the boy for her to want to force him, and faithful to his oaths. She could look back on her life and recall failures, some bitterly regretted, and mistakes that had cost lives, but she could not afford mistakes or failure here. Most definitely not failure. Light, she wanted to *bite* someone!

"I demand the return of my Windfinder, Aes Sedai!" Harine din Togara, all in green brocaded silk, sat rigidly in front of Cadsuane, her full mouth tight. Despite an unlined face, white streaked her straight black hair. Wavemistress of her clan for ten years, she had commanded a large vessel long before that. Her Sailmistress, Derah din Selaan, a younger woman all in blue, sat on a chair placed a careful foot farther back in accordance with their notions of propriety. The pair might have been dark carvings of outrage, and their outlandish jewelry somehow added to the effect. Neither so much as flickered an eye toward Eben when he bowed and offered silver goblets of hot spiced wine on a tray.

The boy did not seem to know what to do next when they took nothing. Frowning uncertainly, he remained bent until Daigian plucked at his red coat and led him away smiling, an amused pouter pigeon in dark blue slashed with white. A slender lad with a big nose and large ears, never to be called handsome much less pretty, but she was very possessive of him. They took seats close together on a padded bench in front of one of the fireplaces and began playing cat's cradle.

"Your sister is assisting us in learning what happened on the unfortunate day," Cadsuane said smoothly, and somewhat absently. Taking a swallow of her own spiced wine, she waited, uncaring whether they saw her impatience. No matter how Dobraine grumbled about how impossible it was to meet the terms of that incredible bargain Rafela and Merana had made on behalf of the al'Thor boy, he still might have handled the Sea Folk himself. She could hardly give them half of her mind. Probably that was just as well for them. If she focused on the Atha'an Miere, she would be hard-pressed not to swat them like bitemes, though they were not the real source of her exasperation.

Five sisters were arrayed around the fireplace at the other end of the sunroom from Daigian and Eben. Nesune had a large wood bound volume from the Palace library spread on a reading stand in front of her chair. Like the others, she wore a plain woolen dress more suited to a merchant than an Aes Sedai. If any regretted the lack of silks, or money for silks, they did not show it. Sarene, with her thin, beaded braids, stood working at a large embroidery frame, her needle making the tiny stitches of yet another flower in a field of blossoms. Erian and Beldeine were playing stones, watched by Elza, who waited her turn to take on the winner. By all appearances they were enjoying an idle morning, without a care in the world. Perhaps they knew they were here because she wanted to study them. Why had they sworn fealty to the al'Thor boy? At least Kiruna and the others had been in his presence when they decided to swear. She was willing to admit that no one could resist the influence of a *ta'veren* when it caught you. But these five had taken a harsh penance for kidnapping him and reached their decision to offer oath before they were brought near him. In the beginning she had been inclined to accept their various explanations, but over the last few days that inclination had taken hard knocks. Disturbingly hard knocks.

"My *Windfinder* is not subject to your authority, Aes Sedai," Harine said sharply, as if denying the blood connection. "Shalon must and will be returned to me at once." Derah nodded curt agreement. Cadsuane thought the Sailmistress might do the same if Harine ordered her to jump from a cliff. In the Atha'an Miere's hierarchy, Derah stood a long distance below Harine. And that was almost as much as Cadsuane knew of them. The Sea Folk might prove useful or might not, but she could find a way to get a grip on them in any case.

"This is an Aes Sedai inquiry," she replied blandly. "We must follow Tower law." Loosely interpreted, to be sure. She had always believed the spirit of the law was far more important than the letter.

Harine puffed up like an adder and began yet another harangue listing her rights and demands, but Cadsuane listened with half an ear.

She could almost understand Erian, a pale, black-haired Illianer, fiercely insisting that she must be at the boy's side when he fought the Last Battle. And Beldeine, so new to the shawl that she had not yet achieved agelessness, so determined to be everything that a Green should be. And Elza, a pleasant-faced Andoran whose eyes almost glowed when she spoke of making certain that he lived to face the Dark One. Another Green, and even more intense than most. Nesune, hunched forward to peer at her book, looked like a black-eyed bird examining a worm. A Brown, she would climb into a box with a scorpion if she wanted to study it. Sarene might be fool enough to be startled that anyone thought her pretty, much less stunning, but the White insisted on the cool precision of her logic; al'Thor was the Dragon Reborn, and logically, she must follow him. Tempestuous reasons, idiotic reasons, yet she could have accepted them, if not for the others.

The door to the hall opened to admit Verin and Sorilea. The leathery, white-haired Aiel woman handed something small to Verin that the Brown tucked into her belt pouch.

Verin was wearing a flowered brooch on her simple bronze-colored dress, the first jewelry Cadsuane had ever seen on her aside from her Great Serpent ring.

"That will help you sleep," Sorilea said, "but remember, just three drops in water or one in wine. A little more, and you might sleep a day or longer. Much more, and you will not wake. There is no taste to warn you, so you must be careful."

So Verin was having trouble sleeping, too. Cadsuane had not had a good night's rest since the boy fled the Sun Palace. If she did not find one soon, she thought she *might* bite someone. Nesune and the others were eyeing Sorilea uneasily. The boy had made them *apprentice* themselves to the Wise Ones, and they had learned that the Aiel women took that very seriously. One snap of Sorilea's bony fingers could end their idle morning.

Harine leaned forward out of her chair and gave Cadsuane's cheek a sharp tap with her fingers! "You are not listening to me," she said harshly. Her face was a thunderhead, and that of her Sailmistress scarcely less stormy. "You *will* listen!"

Cadsuane put her hands together and regarded the woman over her fingertips. No. She would not stand the Wavemistress on her head here and now. She would not send the woman back to her apartments weeping. She would be as diplomatic as Coiren could wish. Hastily she scanned through what she had heard. "You speak for the Mistress of the Ships to the Atha'an Miere, with all of her authority, which is more than I can imagine," she said mildly. "If your Windfinder is not returned to you within the hour, you will see that the Coramoor punishes me severely. You require an apology for your Windfinder's imprisonment. And you require me to make Lord Dobraine set aside the land promised by the Coramoor immediately. I believe that covers the essential points." Except for the one about having her flogged!

"Good," Harine said, leaning back comfortably, in command now. Her smile was sickeningly self-satisfied. "You will learn that—"

"I do not care a fig for your Coramoor," Cadsuane continued, her voice still mild. All the figs in the world for the Dragon Reborn, but not one for the Coramoor. She did not alter her tone by a hair. "If you ever touch me again without permission, I will have you stripped, striped, bound and carried back to your rooms in a sack." Well, diplomacy had never been her strongest point. "If you do not cease pestering me about your sister . . . Well, I might actually grow angry." Standing, she ignored the Sea Folk woman's indignant puffing and gaping and raised her voice to be heard at the end of the room. "Sarene!"

The slender Taraboner whirled from her embroidery, beaded braids clicking, and hurried to Cadsuane's side, barely hesitating before spreading her dark gray skirts in a curtsy. The Wise Ones had had to teach them to leap when a Wise One spoke, but more than custom made them leap for her. There truly were advantages to being a legend, especially an unpredictable legend.

"Escort these two to their rooms," Cadsuane commanded. "They wish to fast and meditate on civility. See that they do. And if they offer one uncivil word, spank them both. But be diplomatic about it."

Sarene gave a start, half opening her mouth as if to protest the illogic of that, but one glance at Cadsuane's face and she quickly turned to the Atha'an Miere women, gesturing for them to rise.

Harine sprang to her feet, her dark face hard and scowling. Before she could utter a word of her no doubt furious tirade, though, Derah touched her arm and leaned close to whisper into her ring-heavy ear behind a cupped hand covered with dark tattoos. Whatever the Sailmistress had to say, Harine closed her mouth. Her expression certainly did not soften, yet she eyed the sisters at the far end of the room and after a moment curtly motioned Sarene to lead the way. Harine might pretend that it was her decision to leave, but Derah followed so close on her heels she appeared to be herding her and shot an uneasy glance back over her shoulder before the door shut her from sight.

Cadsuane almost regretted giving that frivolous order. Sarene would do exactly as she had been told. The Sea Folk women were an irritant, and useless thus far, besides. The irritation must be removed so she could concentrate on what was important, and if she found a use for them, tools needed to be shaped one way or another. She was too angry with them to care how that was done, and it might as well begin now as later. No, she was angry with the boy, but she could not lay hands on him yet.

With a loud harrumph, Sorilea turned from watching Sarene and the Atha'an Miere go and directed her scowl at the sisters gathered at the end of the solar. Bracelets clattered on her wrists as she adjusted her shawl. Another woman not in her best temper. The Sea Folk had peculiar notions of "Aiel savages"—though in truth not that much stranger than some Cadsuane herself had believed before meeting Sorilea—and the Wise One did not like them a hair.

Cadsuane went to meet her with a smile. Sorilea was not a woman you made come to you. Everyone thought they were becoming friends—which they might yet, she realized in surprise—but no one knew of their alliance. Eben appeared with his tray, and appeared relieved when she set her half-empty goblet on it.

"Late last night," Sorilea said as the red-coated boy hurried back to Daigian, "Chisaine Nurbaya asked to serve the *Car'a'carn*." Disapproval lay heavy in her voice. "Before first light, Janine Pavlara asked, then Innina Darenhold, then Vayelle Kamsa. They had not been allowed to speak to one another. There could be no collusion. I accepted their pleas."

Cadsuane made a vexed sound. "I suppose you already have them serving penance," she murmured, thinking hard. Nineteen sisters had been prisoners in the Aiel camp, nineteen sisters sent by that fool Elaida to kidnap the boy, and now they *all* had sworn to follow him! These last were the worst. "What could make *Red* sisters swear fealty to a man who can channel?"

Verin began to make an observation, but fell silent for the Aiel woman. Strangely, Verin had taken to her own enforced apprenticeship like a heron to the marsh. She spent more time in the Aiel camp than out of it.

"Not penance, Cadsuane Melaidhrin." Sorilea made a dismissive gesture with one sinewy hand in another rattle of gold and ivory bracelets. "They are attempting to meet *toh* that cannot be met. As foolish in its way as our naming them *da'tsang* in the first place, but perhaps they are not beyond redemption if they are willing to try," she allowed grudgingly. Sorilea more than merely disliked those nineteen sisters. She gave a thin smile. "In any event, we will teach them much they need to learn." The woman seemed to believe all Aes Sedai could do with time apprenticing under the Wise Ones.

"I hope you will continue to watch them all closely," Cadsuane said. "Especially these last four." She was sure they would keep that ridiculous oath, if not always in ways the boy would like, but there was always the possibility that one or two might be Black Ajah. Once she had thought herself on the point of rooting out the Black only to watch her quarry slip through her fingers like smoke, her bitterest failure except possibly for failing to learn what Caraline Damodred's cousin had been up to in the Borderlands until the knowledge was years too late to do any good. Now, even the Black Ajah seemed a diversion from what was truly important.

"Apprentices are always watched closely," the weathered woman replied. "I think I must remind these others to be grateful for being allowed to loll about like clan chiefs."

The remaining four sisters in front of the fireplace rose with alacrity at her approach, made deep curtsies, and listened carefully to what she told them in a low voice with much finger shaking. Sorilea might think she had much to teach them, but they had already learned that an Aes Sedai shawl offered no protection to a Wise One's apprentice. *Toh* seemed a great deal like penance to Cadsuane.

"She is . . . formidable," Verin murmured. "I am very glad she is on our side. If she is."

Cadsuane gave her a sharp look. "You have the appearance of a woman with something to say that you don't want to. About Sorilea?" That alliance was very vaguely defined. Friendship or no friendship, she and the Wise One still might turn out to be aiming at different goals.

"Not that," the stout little woman sighed. Despite a square face, tilting her head to one side made her look like a very plump sparrow. "I know it was not my business, Cadsuane, but Bera and Kiruna were getting nowhere with our guests, so I had a little talk alone with Shalon. After a little *gentle* questioning, she spilled out the whole story, and Ailil confirmed everything once she realized I already knew. Soon after the Sea Folk first arrived here, Ailil approached Shalon hoping to learn what they wanted with young al'Thor.

For her part, Shalon wanted to learn whatever she could about him, and about the situation here. That led to meetings, which led to friendship, which led to them becoming pillow friends. As much from loneliness as anything else, I suspect. In any case, that was what they were hiding more than their mutual snooping."

"They put up with days under the question to hide *that?*" Cadsuane said incredulously. Bera and Kiruna had had the pair howling!

Verin's eyes twinkled with suppressed mirth. "Cairhienin are prim and prudish, Cadsuane, in public at least. They might carry on like rabbits when the curtains are drawn, but they wouldn't admit to touching their own husbands if anyone might overhear! And the Sea Folk are almost as straitlaced. At least, Shalon is married to a man with duties elsewhere, and breaking marriage vows is a very serious crime. A breach of proper discipline, it seems. If her sister found out, Shalon would be—'Windfinder on a rowboat,' I think her exact words were."

Cadsuane was aware of her hair ornaments swaying as she shook her head. When the two women had been discovered right after the attack on the Palace, bound and gagged and stuffed under Ailil's bed, she had suspected they knew more of the attack than they were admitting. Once they refused to say why they had been meeting in secret, she was sure. Perhaps even that they were involved in some way, though the attack apparently was the work of renegade Asha'man. Supposedly renegade, at least. All that time and effort wasted on nothing. Or perhaps not quite nothing, if they were so desperate to keep things hidden.

"Return the Lady Ailil to her apartments with apologies for her treatment, Verin. Give her very . . . tenuous . . . assurances that her confidences will be kept. Be sure she is aware just how tenuous. And suggest *strongly* that she might wish to keep me abreast of anything she hears concerning her brother." Blackmail was a tool she disliked using, but she had already used it on the three Asha'man, and Toram Riatin might still cause trouble even if his rebellion did seem to have evaporated. In truth, she cared little who sat on the Sun Throne, yet the plots and schemes of those who considered thrones important often had a way of interfering with more significant matters.

Verin smiled, her bun bobbing as she nodded. "Oh, yes, I think that will work very nicely. Especially since she dislikes her brother intensely. The same for Shalon, I suppose? Except that you will want to hear of events among the Atha'an Miere? I'm not certain how far she will betray Harine, no matter the consequences to herself."

"She will betray what I require her to betray," Cadsuane said grimly. "Keep her until tomorrow, late." Harine must not be allowed to think for a moment that her demands were being met. The Sea Folk were another tool to be used on the boy, no more. Everyone and everything had to be viewed in that light.

Beyond Verin, Corele slipped into the sunroom and shut the door carefully behind her as if hoping not to disturb anyone. That was not her way. Boyishly slim, with thick black eyebrows and a mass of glossy black hair flowing down her back that gave her a wild appearance no matter how neat her clothes were, the Yellow was much more likely to sweep into a room laughing. Rubbing the end of her upturned nose, she looked at Cadsuane hesitantly, with none of the usual sparkle in her blue eyes.

Cadsuane made a peremptory gesture at her, and Corele drew a breath and glided across the carpets gripping her yellow-slashed blue skirts with both hands. Eyeing the sisters clustered around Sorilea at the far end of the room, and Daigian playing cat's cradle with Eben at the other end, she spoke in a soft voice that carried the lilting accents of Murandy.

"I have the most wonderful news, Cadsuane." By the sound of her, she was not all certain how wonderful it was. "I know you said I should keep Damer busy here in the Palace, but he insisted on looking at the sisters still in the Aiel camp. Mild-tempered as he is, he's very insistent when he wants to be, and sure as the sun there's nothing can't be Healed. And, well, the fact of it is, he's gone and Healed Irgain. Cadsuane, it's as if she'd never been . . ." She trailed off, unable to say the word. It hung in the air even so. Stilled.

"Wonderful news," Cadsuane said flatly. It was. Every sister carried the fear somewhere deep inside that she might be cut off from the Power. And now a way to Heal what could not be Healed had been discovered. By a man. There would be tears and recriminations before *this* was done with. In any case, while every sister who heard would consider it a world-shaking discovery—in more ways than one; a man!—it was a storm in a teacup compared to Rand al'Thor. "I suppose she is offering herself up to be beaten like the others?"

"She won't need to," Verin said absently. She was frowning at an inkstain on her finger, but she seemed to be studying something beyond. "The Wise Ones apparently decided that Rand had punished Irgain and the other two sufficiently when he . . . did what he did. At the same time they were treating the others like worthless animals, they have been working to keep those three alive. I heard talk about finding Ronaille a husband."

"Irgain knows all about the oaths the others swore." Corele's voice took on tones of amazement. "She started weeping for the loss of her Warders almost as soon as Damer finished with her, but she's ready to swear, too. The thing of it is, Damer wants to try with Sashalle and Ronaille, too." Surprisingly, she drew herself up almost defiantly. She had always been as arrogant as any other Yellow, but she had always known where she stood with Cadsuane. "I can't see letting a sister remain in that condition if there's a way out, Cadsuane. I want to let Damer try his hand with them."

"Of course, Corele." It seemed some of Damer's insistence was rubbing off on her. Cadsuane was willing to let that go, so long as it did not go too far. She had begun gathering sisters she trusted, those here with her and others, the day she first heard of strange events in Shienar—her eyes and ears had kept watch on Siuan Sanche and Moiraine Damodred for years without learning anything useful until then—yet just because she trusted them did not mean she intended to let them start going their own way. Too much lay at stake. But in any case, she could not leave a sister like that, either.

The door banged open to admit Jahar at a run, the silver bells on the ends of his dark braids jangling. Heads turned to look at the youth in the well-fitted blue coat Merise had chosen for him—even Sorilea and Sarene stared—but the words that came out of him in a rush drove away thoughts of how pretty his sun-dark face was.

"Alanna's unconscious, Cadsuane. She just collapsed in

the hallway. Merise had her taken to a bedchamber and sent me for you."

Riding over exclamations of shock, Cadsuane gathered Corele and Sorilea—who could not be left behind in this—and ordered Jahar to lead the way. Verin came as well, and Cadsuane did not stop her. Verin had a way of noticing what others missed.

The black-liveried servants had no idea who or what Jahar was, but they stepped lively to get out of Cadsuane's way as she walked quickly along behind him. She would have told him to be quicker about it, but any faster, and she would have had to run. Before she had gone very far, a short man with the front of his head shaved, in a dark coat with horizontal stripes of color down the front, stepped into her path and bowed. She had to stop for him.

"Grace favor you, Cadsuane Sedai," he said smoothly, "Forgive me for bothering you when you are in such a hurry, but I thought I should tell you that the Lady Caraline and the High Lord Darlin are no longer in the Lady Arilyn's palace. They are on a rivership bound for Tear. Beyond your reach by this time, I fear."

"You might be surprised what is within my reach, Lord Dobraine," she said in a cold voice. She should have left at least one sister at Arilyn's palace, but she had been certain the pair was secure. "Was this wise?" She had no doubt it was his work, though she doubted he had the nerve to admit it. No wonder he had not pressed her over them.

Her tone made no impression on the fellow. And he surprised her. "The High Lord Darlin is to be the Lord Dragon's Steward of Tear, and it did seem wise to send the Lady Caraline out of the country. She has fore-sworn her rebellion and her claims to the Sun Throne, but others still might try to use her. Perhaps, Cadsuane Sedai, it was unwise to leave them in the charge of servants. Under the Light, you must not hold them at fault. They were able to hold two . . . guests . . . but not to stand up to my armsmen."

Jahar was all but dancing with anxiety to go on. Merise had a firm hand. Cadsuane herself was anxious to reach Alanna.

"I hope you have the same opinion in a year," she said. Dobraine merely bowed.

The bedchamber where Alanna had been taken was the

nearest that had been available, and it was not large, appearing smaller for the dark paneling that Cairhienin liked so much. It seemed quite crowded once everyone was inside. Merise snapped her fingers and pointed, and Jahar retreated to a corner, but that helped little.

Alanna was lying on the bed, her eyes closed, with her Warder, Ihvon, kneeling beside it chafing her wrist. "She seems afraid to wake," the tall, slender man said. "There's nothing wrong with her that I can tell, but she seems afraid."

Corele brushed him aside so she could cup Alanna's face in her hands. The glow of *saidar* surrounded the Yellow, and the weave of Healing settled on Alanna, but the slim Green did not even twitch. Corele drew back, shaking her head.

"My skill with Healing, it may not equal yours, Corele," Merise said dryly, "but I did try." The accents of Tarabon were still strong in her voice after all these years, but she wore her dark hair drawn back severely from her stern face. Cadsuane trusted her perhaps more than any of the others. "What do we do now, Cadsuane?"

Sorilea stared at the woman stretched out on the bed with no expression beyond a thinning of her lips. Cadsuane wondered whether she was reevaluating their alliance. Verin was staring at Alanna, too, and she looked absolutely terrified. Cadsuane had not thought anything could frighten Verin that far. But she felt a thrill of terror herself. If she lost this connection to the boy now . . .

"We sit down and wait for her to wake," she said in a calm voice. There was nothing else to do. Nothing.

"Where is he?" Demandred growled, clenching his fists behind his back. Standing with his feet apart, he was aware that he dominated the room. He always did. Even so, he wished Semirhage or Mesaana were present. Their alliance was delicate—a simple agreement that they would not turn on one another until the others had been eliminated—yet it had held all this time. Working together, they had unbalanced opponent after opponent, toppling many to their deaths or worse. But it was difficult for Semirhage to attend these meetings, and Mesaana had been shy, of late. If she was thinking of ending the alliance . . . "Al'Thor has been seen in five cities, including that cursed place in the Waste, and a dozen towns since those blind fools—those idiots!—failed in Cairhien. And that only includes the reports we have! The Great Lord only knows what else is crawling toward us by horse, or sheep, or whatever else these savages can find to carry a message."

Graendal had chosen the setting, since she had been first to arrive, and it irritated him. View-walls made the striped wooden floor appear to be surrounded by a forest full of brightly flowered vines and fluttering birds that were even more colorful. Sweet scents and soft birdcalls filled the air. Only the arch of the doorway spoiled the illusion. Why did she want a reminder of what was lost? They could as soon make shocklances or sho-wings as a view-wall outside of this place, close to Shayol Ghul. In any case, she despised anything to do with nature, as he recalled.

Osan'gar frowned at "idiots" and "blind fools," as well he might, but he quickly smoothed that plain, creased face, so unlike the one he had been born with. By whatever name he was called, he had always known who he dared challenge and who not. "A matter of chance," he said calmly, though he did begin dry-washing his hands. An old habit. He was garbed like some ruler of this Age, in a coat so heavy with golden embroidery that it almost hid the red of the cloth, and boots fringed with golden tassels. There was enough white lace at his neck and wrists to clothe a child. The man had never known the meaning of excess. If not for his particular skills, he never would have been Chosen. Realizing what his hands were doing, Osan'gar snatched the tall *cuendillar* wineglass from the round table beside his chair and inhaled the dark wine's aroma deeply. "Simply probabilities," he murmured, trying to sound offhand. "Next time, he will be killed or taken. Chance can't protect him forever."

"You are going to depend on chance?" Aran'gar was stretched out in a long, flowing chair as though it were a bedchair. Directing a smoky smile at Osan'gar, she arched one leg on bare toes so the slit in her bright red skirts exposed her to the hip. Every breath threatened to free her from the red satin that just contained her full breasts. All of her mannerisms had changed since she became a woman, but not the core of what had been placed into that female body. Demandred hardly scorned fleshly pleasures, but one day her cravings would be the death of her. As they already had been once. Not that he would mourn, of course, if the next time was final. "You were responsible for watching him, Osan'gar," she went on, her voice caressing every syllable. "You, and Demandred." Osan'gar flinched, flicking his tongue against his lips, and she laughed throatily. "My own charge is . . ." She pressed a thumb down on the edge of the chair as if pinning something and laughed again.

"I should think you would be more worried, Aran'gar," Graendal murmured over her wine. She concealed her contempt about as well as the almost transparent silvery mist of her streith gown concealed her ripe curves. "You, and Osan'gar, and Demandred. And Moridin, wherever he is. Perhaps you should fear al'Thor's success as much as his failure."

Laughing, Aran'gar caught the standing woman's hand in one of hers. Her green eyes sparkled. "And perhaps you could explain what you mean better if we were alone?"

Graendal's gown turned to stark black concealing smoke. Jerking her hand free with a coarse oath, she stalked away from the chair. Aran'gar . . . giggled.

"What do you mean?" Osan'gar said sharply, struggling out of his chair. Once on his feet, he struck a lecturer's pose, gripping his lapels, and his tone became pedantic. "In the first place, my dear Graendal, I doubt that even I could devise a method to remove the Great Lord's shadow from *saidin*. Al'Thor is a primitive. Anything he tries inevitably will prove insufficient, and I, for one, cannot believe he can even imagine how to begin. In any event, we will stop him trying because the Great Lord commands it. I can understand fear of the Great Lord's displeasure if we somehow failed, unlikely as that might be, but why should those of us you named have any special fear?"

"Blind as ever, and dry as ever," Graendal murmured. With the return of composure, her gown was clear mist again, though red. Perhaps she was not so calm as she pretended. Or perhaps she wanted them to believe she was controlling some agitation. Except for the streith, her adornments all came from this age, firedrops in her golden hair, a large ruby dangling between her breasts, ornate golden bracelets on both wrists. And something quite strange, that

Demandred wondered whether anyone else had noticed. A simple ring of gold on the little finger of her left hand. Simple was never associated with Graendal. "If the young man does somehow remove the shadow, well . . . You who channel *saidin* will no longer need the Great Lord's special protection. Will he trust your . . . loyalty . . . then?" Smiling, she sipped her wine.

Osan'gar did not smile. His face paled, and he scrubbed a hand across his mouth. Aran'gar sat up on the edge of her long chair, no longer trying to be sensuous. Her hands formed claws on her lap, and she glared at Graendal as if ready to go for her throat.

Demandred's fists unclenched. It was out in the open at last. He had hoped to have al'Thor dead—or failing that, captive—before this suspicion reared its head. During the War of Power, more than a dozen of the Chosen had died of the Great Lord's suspicion.

"The Great Lord is sure you are all faithful," Moridin announced, striding in as though he were the Great Lord of the Dark himself. He had often seemed to believe he was, and the boy's face he wore now had not changed that. In spite of his words, that face was grim, and his unrelieved black made his name, Death, fit. "You need not worry until he stops being sure." The girl, Cyndane, trotted at his heels like a bosomy little silver-haired pet in red-and-black. For some reason, Moridin had a rat riding his shoulder, pale nose sniffing the air, black eyes studying the room warily. Or for no reason, perhaps. A youthful face had not made him any saner, either.

"Why have you called us here?" Demandred demanded. "I have much to do, and no time for idle talk." Unconsciously he tried to stand taller, to match the other man.

"Mesaana is absent again?" Moridin said instead of answering. "A pity. She should hear what I have to say." Plucking the rat from his shoulder by its tail, he watched the animal wave its legs futilely. Nothing except the rat seemed to exist for him. "Small, apparently unimportant matters can become very important," he murmured. "This rat. Whether Isam succeeds in finding and killing that other vermin, Fain. A word whispered in the wrong ear, or not spoken to the right. A butterfly stirs its wings on a branch, and on the other side of the world a mountain collapses."

Suddenly the rat twisted, trying to sink its teeth into his wrist. Casually, he flung the creature away. In midair, there was a burst of flame, something hotter than flame, and the rat was gone. Moridin smiled.

Demandred flinched in spite of himself. That had been the True Power; he had felt nothing. A black speck floated across Moridin's blue eyes, then another, in a steady stream. The man must have been using the True Power exclusively since he last saw him to gain so many *saa* so quickly. He himself had never touched the True Power except at need. Great need. Of course, only Moridin had that privilege now, since his . . . anointing. The man truly was insane to use it so freely. It was a drug more addictive than *saidin,* more deadly than poison.

Crossing the striped floor, Moridin laid a hand on Osan'gar's shoulder, his smile made more ominous by the *saa.* The shorter man swallowed, and gave a wavering smile in return. "It is well you've never considered how to remove the Great Lord's shadow," Moridin said quietly. How long had he been outside? Osan'gar's smile grew even more sickly. "Al'Thor is not as wise as you. Tell them, Cyndane."

The little woman drew herself up. By face and form she was a luscious plum, ready for plucking, but her big blue eyes were glacial. A peach, perhaps. Peaches were poisonous, here and now. "You recall the Choedan Kal, I suppose." No amount of effort could make that low, breathy voice anything except sultry, but she managed to inject sarcasm. "Lews Therin has two of the access keys, one for each. And he knows a woman strong enough to use the female of the pair. He plans to use the Choedan Kal for his deed."

Nearly everyone began to talk at once.

"I thought the keys were all destroyed!" Aran'gar exclaimed, surging to her feet. Her eyes were wide with fear. "He could shatter the world just *trying* to use the Choedan Kal!"

"If you had ever read anything besides a history book, you would know they're almost impossible to destroy!" Osan'gar snarled at her. But he was tugging at his collar as if it were too tight, and his eyes seemed ready to fall out of his face. "How can this girl know he has them? How?"

Graendal's wineglass had dropped from her hand as soon as the words were out of Cyndane's mouth, bouncing end over end across the floor. Her gown turned as crimson as fresh blood, and her mouth twisted as if she were going to vomit. "And you've just been hoping to blunder into him!" she screamed at Demandred. "Hoping someone will find him for you! Fool! Fool!"

Demandred thought Graendal had been a touch flamboyant even for her. He would wager the announcement had been no surprise to her. It seemed she bore watching. He said nothing.

Putting a hand over his heart, for all the world like a lover, Moridin tilted up Cyndane's chin on his fingertips. Resentment burned in her eyes, but her face might have been a doll's unchanging face. She certainly accepted his attentions like a pliable doll. "Cyndane knows many things," Moridin said softly, "and she tells me everything she knows. Everything." The tiny woman's expression never altered, but she trembled visibly.

She was a puzzle to Demandred. At first he had thought she was Lanfear reincarnated. Bodies for transmigration supposedly were chosen by what was available, yet Osan'gar and Aran'gar were proof of the Great Lord's cruel sense of humor. He had been sure, until Mesaana told him the girl was weaker than Lanfear. Mesaana and the rest thought she was of this Age. Yet she spoke of al'Thor as Lews Therin, just as Lanfear had, and spoke of the Choedan Kal as one familiar with the terror they had inspired during the War of Power. Only balefire had been more feared, and only just. Or had Moridin taught her for purposes of his own? If he had any real purposes. There had always been times when the man's actions had been sheer madness.

"So it seems he must be killed after all," Demandred said. Hiding his satisfaction was not easy. Rand al'Thor or Lews Therin Telamon, he would rest easier when the fellow was dead. "Before he can destroy the world, and us. Which makes finding him all the more urgent."

"Killed?" Moridin moved his hands as though weighing something. "If it comes to that, yes," he said finally. "But finding him is no problem. When he touches the Choedan Kal, you will know where he is. And you will go there and take him. Or kill him, if necessary. The Nae'blis has spoken."

"As the Nae'blis commands," Cyndane said eagerly,

bowing her head, and echos of her ran around the room, though Aran'gar sounded sullen, Osan'gar desperate, and Graendal oddly thoughtful.

Bending his neck hurt Demandred as much as speaking those words. So *they* would take al'Thor—while he was trying to use the Choedan Kal, no less, he and some woman drinking enough of the One Power to melt continents!—but there had been no indication that Moridin would be with them. Or his twin pets, Moghedien and Cyndane. The man was Nae'blis for now, but perhaps matters could be arranged so he did not get another body the next time he died. Perhaps it could be arranged soon.

CHAPTER
14

What a Veil Hides

*T*he *Victory of Kidron* rolled on long sea swells, making the gilded lamps in the stern cabin swing on their gimbals, but Tuon sat calmly as the razor in Selucia's sure hand slid across her scalp. Through the tall stern windows she could see other greatships crashing through the gray-green swells in sprays of white, hundreds of them row on row, stretching to the horizon. Four times as many had been left at Tanchico. The *Rhyagelle,* Those Who Come Home. The *Corenne,* the Return, had begun.

A soaring albatross seemed to be following the *Kidron,* an omen of victory indeed, though the bird's long wings were black instead of white. It must still mean the same thing. Omens did not change according to location. An owl calling at dawn meant a death and rain without clouds an unexpected visitor whether in Imfaral or Noren M'Shar.

The morning ritual with her dresser's razor was soothing, and she needed that today. Last night, she had given a command in anger. No command should be issued in anger. She felt almost *sei'mosiev,* as if she had lost honor. Her balance was disturbed, and that boded as ill for the Return as a loss of *sei'taer,* albatross or no albatross.

Selucia wiped away the last of the lather with a warm damp cloth, then used a dry cloth, and finally powdered her smooth scalp lightly with a brush. When her dresser stepped back, Tuon rose and let her elaborately embroidered blue silk dressing gown slide to the gold-and-blue patterned carpet. Instantly the cool air pebbled her dark bare skin. Four of her ten maids rose gracefully from where they had been kneeling against the walls, clean-limbed and comely in their filmy white robes. All had been purchased for their appearance as much as their skills, and they were very skilled. They had become used to the motions of the ship during the long voyage from Seanchan, and they scurried to fetch the garments that had already been laid out atop the carved chests and bring them to Selucia. Selucia never allowed the *da'covale* to actually dress her, not so much as stockings or slippers.

When she settled a pleated gown the color of well-aged ivory over Tuon's head, the younger woman could not help comparing the two of them in the tall mirror fastened to the inner wall. Golden-haired Selucia possessed a stately, cream-skinned beauty and cool blue eyes. Anyone might have taken her for one of the Blood, and of high rank, rather than *so'jhin,* if the left side of her head had not been shaved. A notion that would have shocked the woman to the quick, expressed aloud. The very idea of any stepping above her appointed station horrified Selucia. Tuon knew she herself would never have such a commanding presence. Her eyes were too large, and a liquid brown. When she forgot to keep a stern mask, her heart-shaped face belonged on a mischievous child. The top of her head barely came to Selucia's eyes, and her dresser was not a tall woman. Tuon could ride with the best, she excelled at wrestling and the use of suitable weapons, but she had always had to exercise her mind to impress. She had trained that tool as hard as she had trained at every other talent combined. At least the wide, woven belt of gold emphasized her waist enough that she would not be taken for a boy in a dress. Men watched when Selucia passed by, and Tuon had overheard some murmur about her full breasts. Perhaps that had nothing to do with a commanding presence, but it would have been nice to possess a little more bosom.

"The Light be upon me," Selucia murmured, sounding amused, as the *da'covale* hurried back to kneel upright against the walls. "You've done that every morning since the first day your head was shaved. Do you still think after three years that I'll leave a patch of stubble?"

Tuon realized that she had rubbed a hand across her bare scalp. Searching for stubble, she admitted to herself ruefully. "If you did," she said with mock severity, "I would have you beaten. A repayment for all the times you used a switch on me."

Placing a rope of rubies around Tuon's neck, Selucia laughed. "If you pay me back for all that, I'll never be able to sit down again."

Tuon smiled. Selucia's mother had given her to Tuon for a cradle-gift, to be her nursemaid, and more important, her shadow, a bodyguard no one knew about. The first twenty-five years of Selucia's life had been training for those jobs, training in secret for the second. On Tuon's sixteenth naming day, when her head was first shaved, she had made the traditional gifts of her House to Selucia, a small estate for the care she had shown, a pardon for the chastisements she had given, a sack of one hundred golden thrones for each time she had needed to punish her charge. The Blood assembled to watch her presented as an adult for the first time had been impressed by all those sacks of coin, more than many of them could have laid hand on themselves. She had been . . . unruly . . . as a child, not to mention headstrong. And the last traditional gift: the offer for Selucia to choose where she would be appointed next. Tuon was not sure whether she or the watching crowd had been more astonished when the dignified woman turned her back on power and authority, and asked instead to be Tuon's dresser, her chief maid. And her shadow still, of course, though that was not made public. She herself had been delighted.

"Perhaps in small doses, spread over sixteen years," she said. Catching sight of herself in the mirror, she held her smile long enough to make sure there was no sting in her words, then replaced it with sternness. She certainly felt more affection for the woman who had raised her than for the mother she had seen only twice a year before becoming an adult, or the brothers and sisters she had been taught from her first steps to battle for their mother's favor. Two of them had died in those struggles, so far, and three had tried to kill her. A sister and a brother had been made *da'covale* and had their names stricken from the records as firmly as if it had been discovered they could channel. Her place was far from secure even now. A single misstep could see her dead, or worse, stripped and sold on the public block. Blessings of the Light, when she smiled, she still looked sixteen! At best!

Chuckling, Selucia turned to take the close-fitting cap of golden lace from its red-lacquered stand on the dressing table. The sparse lace would expose most of her shaven scalp, and mark her with the Raven-and-Roses. Perhaps she was not *sei'mosiev,* but for the sake of the *Corenne,* she had to restore her balance. She could ask Anath, her *Soe'feia,* to administer a penance, but it was less than two years since Neferi's unexpected death, and she still was not entirely comfortable with her replacement. Something told her she must do this on her own. Perhaps she had seen an omen she had not recognized consciously. Ants were not likely on a ship, but several sorts of beetle might be.

"No, Selucia," she said quietly. "A veil."

Selucia's mouth tightened in disapproval, but she replaced the cap on its stand silently. In private, as now, she had license to free her tongue, yet she knew what could be spoken and what not. Tuon had only ever had to have her punished twice, and Light's truth, she had regretted it as much as Selucia. Wordlessly, her dresser produced a long sheer veil, draping it over Tuon's head and securing it with a narrow band of golden braid set with rubies. Even more transparent than the *da'covale*'s robes, the veil did not hide her face at all. But it hid what was most important.

Laying a long, gold-embroidered blue cape on Tuon's shoulders, Selucia stepped back and bowed deeply, the end of her golden braid touching the carpet. The kneeling *da'covale* bowed their faces to the deck. Privacy was about to end. Tuon left the cabin alone.

In the second cabin stood six of her *sul'dam,* three to either side, with their charges kneeling in front of them on the wide, polished planks of the deck. The *sul'dam* straightened when they saw her, proud as the silver lightning in the red panels on their skirts. The gray-clad *damane* knelt erect, full of their own pride. Except for poor Lidya, who crouched over her knees and tried to press her tearstained face against the deck. Ianelle, holding the red-haired *damane*'s leash, scowled down at her.

Tuon sighed. Lidya had been responsible for her anger last night. No, she had caused it, but Tuon herself was responsible for her own emotions. She had commanded the *damane* to read her fortune, and she should not have ordered her caned because she disliked what she heard.

Bending, she cupped Lidya's chin, laying long red-enameled fingernails against the *damane*'s freckled cheek, and drew her up to sit on her heels. Which produced a wince and a fresh set of tears that Tuon carefully wiped away with her fingers as she pulled the *damane* upright on her knees. "Lidya is a good *damane,* Ianelle," she said. "Paint her welts with tincture of sorfa and give her lionheart for the pain until the welts are gone. And until they *are* gone, she is to have a sweet custard with every meal."

"As the High Lady commands," Ianelle replied formally, but she smiled slightly. All the *sul'dam* were fond of Lidya, and she had not liked punishing the *damane*. "If she gets fat, I will take her for runs, High Lady."

Lidya twisted her head around to kiss Tuon's palm and murmured, "Lidya's mistress is kind. Lidya will not get fat."

Making her way along the two lines, Tuon spoke a few words to each *sul'dam* and petted each of the *damane*. The six she had brought with her were her best, and they beamed at her with a fondness equal to hers for them. They had competed eagerly to be chosen. Plump, yellow-haired Dali and Dani, sisters who hardly needed a *sul'dam*'s direction. Charral, her hair as gray as her eyes, but still the most agile in her spinning. Sera, with red ribbons in her tightly curled black hair, the strongest, and proud as a *sul'dam*. Tiny Mylen, shorter even than Tuon herself. Mylen was Tuon's special pride among the six.

Many had thought it odd when Tuon tested for *sul'dam* on reaching adulthood, though none could gainsay her, then. Except her mother, who had allowed it by remaining silent. Actually becoming a *sul'dam* was unthinkable, of course, but she found as much enjoyment in training *damane* as in training horses, and she was as good at one as the other. Mylen was the proof of that. The pale little *damane* had been half-dead with shock and fear, refusing to eat or drink, when Tuon bought her on the docks at Shon Kifar. The *der'sul'dam* all had despaired, saying she would not live long, but now Mylen smiled up at Tuon and leaned forward to kiss her hand before she even reached to stroke the *damane*'s dark hair. Once skin and bones, she was becoming a trifle plump. Instead of rebuking her, Catrona, who held her leash, let a smile crease her usually stern black face and murmured that Mylen was a perfect *damane*. It was true, no one would believe now that once she had called herself Aes Sedai.

Before leaving, Tuon gave a few orders concerning the *damane*'s diet and exercise. The *sul'dam* knew what to do, just like the other twelve in Tuon's entourage, or they would not have been in her service, but she believed no one should be allowed to own *damane* unless they took an active interest. She knew the quirks of every one of hers as well as she knew her own face.

In the outer cabin, the Deathwatch Guards, lining the walls in armor lacquered blood red and nearly black green, stiffened at her entrance. That is, they stiffened if statues could be said to stiffen. Hard-faced men, they and five hundred more like them had been charged personally with Tuon's safety. Any or all would die to protect her. They would die if she did. Every man had volunteered, asked to be in her guard. Seeing the veil, grizzled Captain Musenge ordered only two to accompany her on deck, where two dozen Ogier Gardeners in the red-and-green made a line to either side of the doorway, great black-tasseled axes upright in front of them and grim eyes watching for any danger even here. They would not die if she did, but they also had asked to be in her guard, and she would rest her life in any of those huge hands without a qualm.

The ribbed sails on the *Kidron*'s three tall masts were taut with the cold wind that drove the vessel toward the land that lay ahead, a dark shore near enough that she could make out hills and headlands. Men and women filled the deck, all of the Blood on the vessel in their finest silks, ignoring the wind that whipped their cloaks as they ignored the barefoot men and women of the ship's crew who darted between them. Some of the nobles were much too ostentatious about ignoring the crew, as though they could run the ship while kneeling or bowing every two paces. Prepared for prostration, the Blood made slight bows instead, one equal to another, when they saw her veil. Yuril, the sharp-nosed man everyone thought was her secretary, went to one knee. He was her secretary, of course, but also her Hand, commanding her Seekers. The Macura woman flung herself down prostrate and kissed the deck before a few quiet words from Yuril made her get back to her feet blushing and smoothing her pleated red skirts. Tuon had been uncertain about tak-

ing her into service, back in Tanchico, but the woman had
pleaded like a *da'covale*. She hated Aes Sedai in her bones,
for some reason, and despite the rewards already given for
her extremely valuable information, she hoped to do them
more injury.

Bowing her head to the Blood, Tuon climbed to the
quarterdeck followed by the two Deathwatch Guards. The
wind made handling her cape difficult, and pressed her veil
against her face one moment, then flailed it over her head
the next. It did not matter; that she wore it was sufficient.
Her personal banner, two golden lions harnessed to an ancient war-cart, flew at the stern above the six helmsmen
struggling to control the long tiller. The Raven-and-Roses
would have been packed away as soon as the first crew-
man to see her veil could pass the word. *Kidron*'s captain,
a wide, weathered woman with white hair and the most incredible green eyes, bowed as Tuon's slipper touched the
quarterdeck then immediately returned her attention to her
ship.

Anath was standing by the railing, in unrelieved black
silk, outwardly undisturbed by the chill wind in spite of her
lack of a cloak or cape. A slender woman, she would have
been tall even for a man. Her charcoal-dark face was beautiful, but her large black eyes seemed to pierce like awls.
Tuon's *Soe'feia,* her Truthspeaker, named by the Empress,
might she live forever, when Neferi died. A surprise, with
Neferi's Left Hand trained and ready to replace her, but
when the Empress spoke from the Crystal Throne, her word
was law. You certainly were not supposed to be *afraid* of
your *Soe'feia,* yet Tuon was, a little. Joining the woman,
she gripped the railing, and had to loosen her hands before
she broke a lacquered nail. That would have meant very bad
luck.

"So," Anath said, the word like a nail driven into Tuon's
skull. The tall woman frowned down at her, and contempt
lay thick in her voice. "You hide your face—in a way—and
now you are just the High Lady Tuon. Except that everyone
still knows who you really are, even if they won't mention
it. How long do you intend carrying on this farce?" Anath's
full lips sneered, and she made a curt, dismissive gesture
with one slim hand. "I suppose this idiocy is over having
the *damane* caned. You are a fool to think your eyes are

downcast by a little thing like that. What did she say to make you angry? No one seems to know, except that you threw a tantrum I am sorry to have missed."

Tuon made her hands be still on the railing. They wanted to tremble. She forced her face to maintain a stern appearance. "I will wear the veil until an omen tells me the time has come to remove it, Anath," she said, schooling her voice to calm. Only luck had kept anyone from overhearing Lidya's cryptic words. Everyone knew that *damane* could foretell the future, and if any of the Blood had heard, they would all have been chattering behind their hands about her fate.

Anath laughed rudely and began telling her again what a fool she was, in greater detail this time. Much greater detail. She did not bother to lower her voice. Captain Tehan was staring straight ahead, but her eyes were almost falling out of her lined face. Tuon listened attentively, though her cheeks grew hotter and hotter, until she thought her veil might burst into flame.

Many of the Blood called their Voices *Soe'feia,* but Voices of the Blood were *so'jhin,* and knew they could be punished if their owners were displeased by what they said even if they were called *Soe'feia.* A Speaker of Truth could not be commanded or coerced or punished in any way. A Truthspeaker was *required* to tell the stark truth whether or not you wanted to hear it, and to make sure that you heard. Those Blood who called their Voices *Soe'feia* thought that Algwyn, the last man to sit on the Crystal Throne, almost a thousand years ago, had been insane because he let his *Soe'feia* live and continue in her post after she slapped his face before the entire court. They did not understand the traditions of her family any more than the goggle-eyed captain did. The Deathwatch Guards' expressions never altered behind the half-concealing cheek-pieces of their helmets. They understood.

"Thank you, but I do not need a penance," she said politely when Anath finally ceased her harangue.

Once, after she cursed Neferi for dying by something as stupid as a fall down stairs, she had asked her new *Soe'feia* to perform that service for her. Cursing the dead was enough to make you *sei'mosiev* for months. The woman

had been almost tender about it, in an odd fashion, though
she left her weeping for days, unable to don even a shift.
That was not why she refused the offer, though; a penance
must be severe or it was useless in redressing balance. No,
she would not take the easier way because she had made her
decision. And, she had to admit, because she wanted to resist her *Soe'feia's* advice. Wanted not to listen to her at all.
As Selucia said, she always had been headstrong. Refusing
to listen to your Truthspeaker was abominable. Perhaps she
should accept after all, to redress that balance. Three long
gray porpoises rose beside the ship and sounded. Three,
and they did not rise again. Hold to your chosen course.

"When we are ashore," she said, "the High Lady Suroth
must be commended." Hold to your chosen course. "And
her ambition must be looked into. She has done more with
the Forerunners than the Empress, may she live forever,
dreamed of, but success on such a scale often breeds ambitions to match."

Peeved at the change of subject, Anath drew herself up,
lips compressing. Her eyes glittered. "I am sure Suroth has
only the best interests of the Empire for ambition," she said
curtly.

Tuon nodded. She herself was not sure at all. That sort of
sureness could lead to the Tower of the Ravens even for her.
Perhaps especially for her. "I must find a way to make contact with the Dragon Reborn as soon as possible. He must
kneel before the Crystal Throne before Tarmon Gai'don, or
all is lost." The Prophecies of the Dragon said so, clearly.

Anath's mood changed in a flash. Smiling, she laid a
hand on Tuon's shoulder almost possessively. That was going too far, but she was *Soe'feia,* and the feel of ownership
might have been only in Tuon's mind. "You must be careful," Anath purred. "You must not let him learn how dangerous you are to him until it is too late for him to escape."

She had more advice, but Tuon let it wash over her. She
listened enough to hear, yet it was nothing she had not heard
a hundred times before. Ahead of the ship she could make
out the mouth of a great harbor. Ebou Dar, from where the
Corenne would spread, as it was spreading from Tanchico.
The thought gave her a thrill of pleasure, of accomplish-
ment. Behind her veil, she was merely the High Lady Tuon,

of no higher rank than many others of the Blood, but in her heart, always, she was Tuon Athaem Kore Paendrag, Daughter of the Nine Moons, and she had come to reclaim what had been stolen from her ancestor.

CHAPTER
15

In Need of a Bellfounder

The boxlike wagon reminded Mat of Tinker wagons he had seen, a little house on wheels, though this one, filled with cabinets and workbenches built into the walls, was not made for a dwelling. Wrinkling his nose at the odd, acrid smells that filled the interior, he shifted uncomfortably on his three-legged stool, the only place for anyone to sit. His broken leg and ribs were near enough healed, and the cuts that he had suffered when that whole bloody building fell on his head, but the injuries still pained him now and then. Besides, he was hoping for sympathy. Women loved to show sympathy, if you played it out right. He made himself stop twisting his long signet ring on his finger. Let a woman know you were nervous, and she put her own construction on it, and sympathy went right out the window.

"Listen, Aludra," he said, assuming his most winning smile, "by this time you must know the Seanchan won't look twice at fireworks. Those *damane* do something called Sky Lights that makes your best fireworks look like a few sparks flying up the chimney, so I hear. No offense meant."

"Me, I have not seen these so-called Sky Lights myself," she replied dismissively in her strong Taraboner accent. Her head was bent over a wooden mortar the size of a large keg on one of the workbenches, and despite a wide blue ribbon gathering her dark waist-length hair loosely at the nape of her neck, it fell forward to hide her face. The long white apron with its dark smudges did nothing to conceal how well her dark green dress fit over her hips, but he was more interested in what she was doing. Well, as interested.

She was grinding at a coarse black powder with a wooden pestle nearly as long as her arm. The powder looked a little like what he had seen inside fireworks he had cut open, but he still did not know what went into it. "In any event," she went on, unaware of his scrutiny, "I will not give you the Guild secrets. You must understand this, yes?"

Mat winced. He had been working on her for days to bring her to this point, ever since a chance visit to Valan Luca's traveling show revealed that she was here in Ebou Dar, and all the while he had dreaded that she would mention the Illuminators' Guild. "But you aren't an Illuminator anymore, remember? They kicked . . . ah . . . you said you left the Guild." Not for the first time he considered a small reminder that he had once saved her from four Guild members who wanted to cut her throat. That sort of thing was enough to make most women fall on your neck with kisses and offers of whatever you wanted. But there had been a notable lack of kisses when he actually saved her, so it was unlikely she would begin now. "Anyway," he went on airily, "you don't have to worry about the Guild. You've been making nightflowers for how long? And nobody has come around trying to stop you. Why, I'll wager you never see another Illuminator."

"What have you heard?" she asked quietly, her head still down. The pestle's rotation slowed almost to a stop. "Tell me."

The hair on his scalp nearly stood on end. How did women do that? Hide every clue, and they still went straight to what you wanted to conceal. "What do you mean? I hear the same gossip you do, I suppose. Mostly about the Seanchan."

She spun around so fast that her hair swung like a flail, and snatched the heavy pestle up in both hands, brandishing it overhead. Perhaps ten years or so older than he, she had large dark eyes and a small plump mouth that usually seemed ready to be kissed. He had thought about kissing her a time or two. Most women were more amenable after a few kisses. Now, her teeth were bared, and she looked ready to bite off his nose. "Tell me!" she commanded.

"I was playing at dice with some Seanchan down near the docks," he said reluctantly, keeping a careful eye on the upraised pestle. A man might bluff and bluster and walk away if the matter was not serious, but a woman could crack your skull on a whim. And his hip was aching and stiff from sitting too long. He was not sure how quickly he could move from the stool. "I didn't want to be the one to tell you, but . . . The Guild doesn't exist anymore, Aludra. The chapter house in Tanchico is gone." That had been the only real chapter house in the Guild. The one in Cairhien was long abandoned now, and for the rest, Illuminators only traveled to put on displays for rulers and nobles. "They refused to let Seanchan soldiers inside the compound, and fought, tried to, when they broke in anyway. I don't know what happened—maybe a soldier took a lantern where he shouldn't have—but half the compound exploded, as I understand it. Probably exaggeration. But the Seanchan believed one of the Illuminators used the One Power, and they . . ." He sighed, and tried to make his voice gentle. Blood and ashes, he did not want to tell her this! But she was glaring at him, that bloody club poised to split his scalp. "Aludra, the Seanchan gathered up everyone left alive at the chapter house, and some Illuminators that had gone to Amador, and everybody in between who even looked like an Illuminator, and they made them all *da'covale*. That means—"

"I know what it means!" she said fiercely. Swinging back to the big mortar, she began pounding away with the pestle so hard that he was afraid the thing might explode, if that powder really was what went inside fireworks. "Fools!" she muttered angrily, thumping the pestle loudly in the mortar. "Great blind fools! With the mighty, you must bend your neck a little and walk on, but they would not see it!" Sniffing, she scrubbed at her cheeks with the back of her hand. "You are wrong, my young friend. So long as one Illuminator lives, the Guild, it lives too, and me, I still live!" Still not looking at him, she wiped her cheeks with her hand again. "And what would you do if I gave you the fireworks? Hurl them at the Seanchan from the catapult, I suppose?" Her snort told what she thought of that.

"And what's wrong with the idea?" he asked defensively. A good field catapult, a scorpion, could throw a ten-pound stone five hundred paces, and ten pounds of fireworks would do more damage than any stone. "Anyway, I have a better idea. I saw those tubes you use to toss nightflowers into the sky. Three hundred paces or more, you said. Tip one on its side more or less, and I'll bet it could toss a night-flower a *thousand* paces."

Peering into the mortar, she muttered almost under her breath. "Me, I talk too much," he thought it was, and something about pretty eyes that made no sense. He hurried on to stop her from starting up about Guild secrets again. "Those tubes are a lot smaller than a catapult, Aludra. If they were well hidden, the Seanchan would never know where they came from. You could think of it as paying them back for the chapter house."

Turning her head, she gave him a look of respect. Mingled with surprise, but he managed to ignore that. Her eyes were red-rimmed, and there were tearstains on her cheeks. Maybe if he put an arm around her . . . Women usually appreciated a little comforting when they cried.

Before he could even shift his weight, she swung the pestle between them, pointing it at him like a sword with one hand. Those slender arms must be stronger than they looked; the wooden club never wavered. *Light,* he thought, *she* couldn't *have known what I was going to do!*

"This is not bad, for one who only saw the lofting tubes a few days ago," she said, "but me, I have thought about this long before you. I had reason." For a moment, her voice was bitter, but it smoothed out again, and became a little amused. "I will set you the puzzle, since you are so clever, no?" she said, arching an eyebrow. Oh, she definitely was amused by something! "You tell me what use I might have for a bellfounder, and I will tell you *all* of my secrets. Even the ones that will make you blush, yes?"

Now, that did sound interesting. But the fireworks were more important than an hour snuggling with her. What secrets did she have that could make him blush? He might surprise her, there. Not all of those other men's memories that had been stuffed into his head had to do with battles. "A bellmaker," he mused, without a notion of where to go from there. None of those old memories gave even a hint. "Well, I suppose . . . A bellmaker could . . . Maybe . . ."

"No," she said, suddenly brisk. "You will go, and return in two or three days. I have the work to do, and you are too distracting with all of your questions and wheedling. No; no arguments! You will go now."

Glowering, he rose and clapped his wide-brimmed black hat onto his head. Wheedling? Wheedling! Blood and bloody ashes! He had dropped his cloak in a heap by the door on entering, and he grunted softly, bending to pick it up. He had been sitting on that stool most of the day. But maybe he had made a little headway with her. If he could solve her puzzle, anyway. Alarm bells. Gongs to sound the hour. It made no sense.

"I might think of kissing such a smart young man as you if you did not belong to another," she murmured in decidedly warm tones. "You have such a pretty bottom."

He jerked erect, keeping his back to her. The heat in his face was pure outrage, but she was sure to say he was blushing. He could usually manage to forget what he was wearing unless someone brought it up. There had been an incident or three in taverns. While he was flat on his back with his leg in splints and his ribs strapped and bandages just about everywhere else, Tylin had hidden all of his clothes. He had not found where, yet, but surely they were hidden, not burned. After all, she could not mean to hold on to him forever. All that remained of his own were his hat and the black silk scarf tied around his neck. And the silvery foxhead medallion, of course, hanging on a leather cord under his shirt. And his knives; he really would have felt lost without those. When he finally managed to crawl out of that bloody bed, the bloody woman had had new clothes made for him, with her sitting there watching the bloody seamstresses measure and fit him! Snowy lace at his wrists almost hid his bloody hands unless he was careful, and more spilled from his neck almost to his flaming waist. Tylin liked lace on a man. His cloak was a brilliant scarlet, as red as his too-tight breeches, and edged with golden scrollwork and white roses, of all bloody things. Not to mention a white oval on his left shoulder with House Mitsobar's green Sword and Anchor. His coat was blue enough for a Tinker, worked in red and gold Tairen mazes across the chest and down the sleeves for good measure. He did not like recalling what he had been forced to go through to convince Tylin to leave off the pearls and sapphires and the Light alone knew what else she had wanted. And it was short, to boot. Indecently short! Tylin liked his bloody bottom, too, and she did not seem to mind who saw it!

Settling the cloak around his shoulders—it was some covering, at least—he grabbed his shoulder-high walking staff from where it was leaning beside the door. His hip and leg were going to ache until he could walk the pain away. "In two or three days, then," he said with as much dignity as he could muster.

Aludra laughed softly. Not softly enough that he could not hear, though. Light, but a woman could do more with a laugh than a dockside bullyboy with a string of curses! And just as deliberately.

Limping out of the wagon, he slammed the door behind him as soon as he was far enough down the wooden steps that were fastened to the wagon bed. The afternoon sky was just like the morning sky had been, gray and blustery, thatched with sullen clouds. A sharp wind gusted fitfully. Altara had no true winter, but what it did have was enough to be going on with. Rather than snow, there were icy rains and thunderstorms racing in off the sea, and in between it was damp enough to make the cold seem harder. The ground had a sodden feel under your boots even when it was dry. Scowling, he hobbled away from the wagon.

Women! Aludra was pretty, though. And she did know how to make fireworks. A bellfounder? Maybe he could make it a short two days. So long as Aludra did not start chasing *him*. A good many women seemed to be doing that, of late. Had Tylin changed something about him, to make women pursue him the way she herself did? No. That was ridiculous. The wind caught his cloak, flaring it behind him, but he was too absorbed to master it. A pair of slender women—acrobats, he thought—gave him sly smiles as they passed, and he smiled and made his best leg. Tylin had not changed him. He was still the same man he had always been.

Luca's show was fifty times as large as what Thom had told him about, maybe more, a sprawling hodgepodge of tents and wagons the size of a large village. Despite the weather, a number of performers were practicing where he could see them. A woman in a flowing white blouse and breeches as tight as his swung back and forth on a sagging rope slung between two tall poles, then threw herself off and somehow caught her feet in the rope just before she hurtled to the ground below. Then she twisted to catch the rope with her hands, pulled herself back to her seat and began the same thing again. Not far off, a fellow was *running* on top of an egg-shaped wheel that must have been a good twenty feet long, mounted on a platform that put him higher above the ground when he dashed across the narrow end than the woman who was going to break her fool neck soon. Mat eyed a bare-chested man who was rolling three shiny balls along his arms and across his shoulders without ever touching them with his hands. That was interesting. He might be able to manage that himself. At least those balls would not leave you bleeding and broken. He had had enough of that to suit him a lifetime.

What really caught his eyes, however, were the horselines. Long horselines, where two dozen men bundled against the cold were shoveling dung into barrows. Hundreds of horses. Supposedly, Luca had given shelter to some Seanchan animal trainer, and his reward had been a warrant, signed by the High Lady Suroth herself, allowing him to keep all of his animals. Mat's own Pips was secure, saved from the lottery ordered by Suroth because he was in the Tarasin Palace stables, but getting the gelding out of those stables was beyond him. Tylin as good as had a leash around his neck, and she did not intend to let him go any time soon.

Turning away, he considered having Vanin steal some of the show's horses if the talks with Luca went badly. From what Mat knew of Vanin, it would be an evening stroll for the unlikely man. Fat as he was, Vanin could steal, and ride, any horse ever foaled. Unfortunately, Mat doubted he himself could sit a saddle for more than a mile. Still, it was something to consider. He was growing desperate.

Limping along, idly eyeing tumblers and jugglers and acrobats at their practice, he wondered how matters had come to this pass. Blood and ashes! He was *ta'veren!* He was supposed to shape the world around him! But here he was, stuck in Ebou Dar, Tylin's pet and toy—the woman had not even let him heal completely before leaping on him again like a duck on a beetle!—while everyone else was having a fine time of it. With those Kinswomen fawning at her heels, likely Nynaeve was lording it over everyone in sight. Once Egwene realized those stark raving mad Aes Sedai who had named her Amyrlin did not really mean it, Talmanes and the Band of the Red Hand were ready to spirit her away.

Light, Elayne might be wearing the Rose Crown by now, if he knew her! Rand and Perrin probably were lolling in front of a fire in some palace, swilling wine and telling jokes.

He grimaced and rubbed at his forehead as a faint rush of colors seemed to swirl inside his head. That happened lately whenever he thought about either man. He did not know why, and he did not want to know. He just wanted it to stop. If only he could get away from Ebou Dar. And take the secret of fireworks with him, of course, but he would take escape over the secret any day.

Thom and Beslan were still where he had left them, drinking with Luca in front of Luca's elaborately decorated wagon, but he did not join them immediately. For some reason, Luca had taken an instant dislike to Mat Cauthon. Mat returned the favor, but with reason. Luca had a smug, self-satisfied face, and a way of smirking at any woman in sight. And he seemed to think every woman in the world enjoyed looking at him. Light, the man was married!

Sprawled in a gilded chair he must have stolen from a palace, Luca was laughing and making expansive, lordly gestures to Thom and Beslan, seated on benches to either side of him. Golden stars and comets covered Luca's brilliant red coat and cloak. A *Tinker* would have blushed! His wagon would have made a Tinker weep! Much larger than Aludra's work-wagon, the thing appeared to have been *lacquered!* The phases of the moon repeated themselves in silver all the way around the wagon, and golden stars and comets in every size covered the rest of the red-and-blue surface. In that setting, Beslan looked almost ordinary in a coat and cloak worked in swooping birds. Thom, knuckling wine from his long white mustaches, seemed positively drab in plain bronze-colored wool and a dark cloak.

One person who should have been there was not, but a quick glance around found a cluster of women at a nearby wagon. They were every age from his own up to graying hair, but every one of them was giggling at what they surrounded. Sighing, Mat made his way there.

"Oh, I just cannot decide," came a boy's piping voice from the center of the women. "When I look at you, Merici, your eyes are the prettiest I have ever seen. But when I look at you, Neilyn, yours are. Your lips are ripe cherries, Gillin, and yours make me want to kiss them, Adria. And your neck, Jameine, graceful as a swan's. . . ."

Swallowing an oath, Mat quickened his pace as much as he could and pushed through the women muttering apologies left and right. Olver was in the middle of them, a short, pale boy posturing and grinning at one woman then another. That toothy grin alone was enough that any of them might decide to slap his ears off in a moment.

"Please forgive him," Mat murmured, taking the boy's hand. "Come on, Olver; we have to get back to the city. Stop waving your cloak about. He doesn't know what he's saying, really. I don't know where he picks up that sort of thing."

Luckily, the women laughed and ruffled Olver's hair as Mat led him away. Some murmured that he was a sweet boy, of all things! One slipped her hand under Mat's cloak and pinched his bottom. Women!

Once clear, he scowled at the boy tripping along happily at his side. Olver had grown since Mat first met him, but he was still short for his years. And with that wide mouth and ears to match, he would never be handsome. "You could get yourself in deep trouble talking to women that way," Mat told him. "Women like a man to be quiet, and well-mannered. And reserved. Reserved, and maybe a little shy. Cultivate those qualities, and you'll do well."

Olver gave him a gaping, incredulous stare, and Mat sighed. The lad had a fistful of uncles looking after him, and every one except Mat himself was a bad influence.

Thom and Beslan were enough to restore Olver's grin. Pulling his hand free, he ran ahead to them laughing. Thom was teaching him how to juggle and play the harp and the flute, and Beslan was teaching him how to use a sword. His other "uncles" gave him other lessons, in a remarkably varied set of skills. Mat intended to start teaching him to use a quarterstaff, and the Two Rivers bow, once he had his strength back. What the boy was learning from Chel Vanin, or the Redarms, Mat did not want to know.

Luca rose from his fancy chair at Mat's approach, his fatuous smile fading to a sour grimace. Eyeing Mat up and down, he swept that ridiculous cloak around himself with a wide flourish and announced in a booming voice, "I am a busy man. I have much to do. It may be that I soon will have the honor of guesting the High Lady Suroth for a private showing." Without another word he strode away holding the ornate cloak with just one hand, so gusts rippled it behind him like a banner.

Mat gathered his own with both hands. A cloak was for warmth. He had seen Suroth in the Palace, though never closely. As closely as he wanted, though. He could not imagine her giving a moment to Valan Luca's Grand Traveling Show and Magnificent Display of Marvels and Wonders, as the streamer strung between two tall poles at the entrance to the show announced in red letters a pace high. If she did, likely she would eat the lions. Or frighten them to death.

"Has he agreed yet, Thom?" he asked quietly, frowning after Luca.

"We can travel with him when he leaves Ebou Dar," the weathered man replied. "For a price." He snorted, blowing out his mustaches, and irritably raked a hand through his white hair. "We should eat and sleep like kings for what he wants, but knowing him, I doubt we will. He doesn't think we are criminals, since we're still walking free, but he knows we're running from something, or we would travel some other way. Unfortunately, he does not intend to leave until spring at the earliest."

Mat considered several choice curses. Not until spring. The Light knew what Tylin would have done to him, would have him doing, by spring. Maybe Vanin stealing horses was not such a bad notion. "Gives me more time for dice," he said, as if it did not matter. "If he wants as much as you say, I need to fatten my purse. One thing you can say for the Seanchan, they don't seem to mind losing." He tried to be careful how long he let his luck run, and he had not faced any threats of having his throat slit for cheating, at least since he had been able to leave the Palace on his own feet. At first, he had believed it was his luck spreading, or perhaps being *ta'veren* finally coming in for something useful.

Beslan regarded him gravely. A dark slender man a little younger than Mat, he had been blithely rakish when Mat first met him, always ready for a round of the taverns, especially if it ended with women or a fight. Since the Seanchan came, he had grown more serious, though. To him, they were very serious business. "My mother won't be pleased if she learns I am helping her pretty leave Ebou Dar, Mat. She will marry me to someone with a squint and a mustache like a Taraboner foot soldier."

After all this time, Mat still winced. He could never get used to Tylin's son thinking what his mother was doing with Mat was all right. Well, Beslan did believe she had become a little too possessive—just a little, mind!—but that was the only reason he was willing to help. Beslan claimed Mat was what his mother needed to take her mind off the agreements she had been forced into by the Seanchan! Sometimes, Mat wished he was back in the Two Rivers, where at least you knew how other people thought. Sometimes he did.

"Can we return to the Palace now?" Olver said, more a demand than a question. "I have a reading lesson with the Lady Riselle. She lets me rest my head on her bosom while she reads to me."

"A notable achievement, Olver," Thom said, stroking his mustaches to hide a smile. Leaning closer to the other two men, he pitched his voice to escape the boy's ears. "The woman makes me play the harp for her before she lets me rest *my* head on that magnificent pillow."

"Riselle makes everyone entertain her first," Beslan chuckled in a knowing way, and Thom stared at him in astonishment.

Mat groaned. It was not his leg, this time, or the fact that every man in Ebou Dar seemed to be choosing the bosom they rested their heads on except for Mat Cauthon. Those bloody dice had just started tumbling in his head again. Something bad was coming his way. Something very bad.

CHAPTER
16

An Unexpected Encounter

The walk back to the city was better than two miles, across low hills that worked the ache out of Mat's leg and put it back again before they topped a rise and saw Ebou Dar ahead, behind its extravagantly thick, white-plastered wall that no siege catapult had ever been able to break down. The city within was white, too, though here and there pointed domes bore thin stripes of color. The white-plastered buildings, white spires and towers, white palaces, gleamed even on a gray winter day. Here and there a tower ended in a jagged top or a gap showed where a building had been destroyed, but in truth, the Seanchan conquest had occasioned little damage. They had been too fast, too strong, and in control of the city before more than scattered resistance could form.

Surprisingly, such trade as there was this time of year had hardly faltered with the city's fall. The Seanchan encouraged it, though merchants and ship captains and crews were required to take an oath to obey the Forerunners, await the Return, and serve Those Who Come Home. In practice, that meant largely going about your life as usual, so few objected. The broad harbor was more crowded with ships every time Mat looked at it. This afternoon, it seemed he could have walked from Ebou Dar proper across to the Rahad, a rough quarter he would just as soon never revisit. Often in the days after he first managed to walk again, he had gone down to the docks to stare. Not at the vessels with ribbed sails or the Sea Folk ships that the Seanchan were re-rigging and manning with their own crews, but at craft flying the Golden Bees of Illian, or the Sword and Hand of

Arad Doman, or the Crescents of Tear. He no longer did. Today, he barely glanced toward the harbor. Those dice spinning in his head seemed to roar like thunder. Whatever was going to happen, he very much doubted he would like it. He seldom did, when the dice gave warning.

Though a steady stream of traffic flowed out of the great arched gateway, and people afoot seemed to be squeezing through to get in, a thick column of wagons and ox-carts, stretching all the way back to the rise, was waiting to enter and hardly moving. Everyone departing on a horse was Sean-chan, whether with skin as dark as one of the Sea Folk or pale as a Cairhienin, and they stood out for more than being mounted. Some of the men wore voluminous trousers and odd, tight coats with high collars that fit their necks snugly right to the chin and rows of shiny metal buttons down the front, or flowing, elaborately embroidered coats almost as long as a woman's dress. They were of the Blood, as were the women in strangely cut riding dresses that seemed made of narrow pleats, with divided skirts cut to expose color-fully booted ankles and wide sleeves that hung to their feet in the stirrups. A few wore lace veils that hid all but their eyes, so their faces were not exposed to the lowborn. Most of the riders by far, however, wore brightly painted armor of overlapping plates. Some of the soldiers were women, too, though there was no way to tell which with those painted helmets like the heads of monstrous insects. At least none wore the black-and-red of the Deathwatch Guard. Even other Seanchan seemed nervous around them, and that was enough to warn Mat to walk wide around them.

In any case, none of the Seanchan spared so much as a glance for three men and a boy slowly walking toward the city along the column of waiting carts and wagons. Well, the men walked slowly. Olver skipped. Mat's leg was set-ting their pace, but he tried not to let the others see how much he was leaning on his staff. The dice usually an-nounced incidents he managed to survive by the skin of his teeth, battles, a building dropping on his head. Tylin. He dreaded what would happen when they stopped this time.

Nearly all of the wagons and carts leaving the city had Sean-chan driving or walking alongside, more plainly dressed than those on horses, hardly peculiar looking at all, but those in the waiting line were more likely to belong to Ebou Dari or folk from the surrounding area, men in long vests, women with their skirts sewn up on one side to expose a stockinged leg or colorful petticoats, their wagons as well as their carts pulled by oxen. Outlanders dotted the column, merchants with small trains of horse-drawn wagons. There was more trade in winter here in the south than farther north, where merchants had to contend with snow-covered roads, and they came from far, some of them. A stout Domani woman with a dark beauty patch on her copper cheek, riding the lead of four wagons, clutched her flowered cloak around her and scowled at a man five wagons ahead of her in the line, a greasy-looking fellow, hiding long thick mustaches behind a Taraboner veil, beside the wagon driver. A competitor, no doubt. A lean Kandori with a large pearl in her left ear and silver chains across her chest sat her saddle calmly, gloved hand folded on the pommel, maybe still unaware that her gray gelding and her wagon teams alike would be put into the lottery once she was into the city. One horse in five had been taken from locals, and so as not to discourage trade, one in ten from outlanders. Paid for, true, and a fair price in other days, but not nearly what the market would bear, given the demand. Mat always noticed horses, even if with only half his mind or less. A fat Cairhienin in a coat as drab as those of his wagon drivers was shouting angrily about the delay and letting his fine bay mare dance nervously. A very good conformation on that mare. She would go to an officer, most likely. What was going to happen when the dice stopped?

The wide arched gates into the city had their guards, though it was likely only the Seanchan recognized them as such. *Sul'dam* in their lightning-paneled blue dresses threaded back and forth through the streams of traffic with gray-clad *damane* on silvery *a'dam*. Just one of those pairs would have been sufficient to quell any disturbance short of a full-scale assault, and maybe even that, but that was not the real reason for their presence. In the first days after Ebou Dar's fall, while he was still confined to bed, they had harrowed the city searching for the women they called *Marath'damane,* and now they made sure none could enter. The *sul'dam* each carried an extra leash coiled on her shoulder just in case. Pairs patrolled the docks, too, meeting every arriving ship and boat.

Beside the wide arched gate into the city, a long platform displayed, on spikes twenty feet above the ground, the tarred but still recognizable heads of over a dozen men and two women who had fallen afoul of Seanchan justice. Above them hung the symbol for that justice, a headsman's slant-edged axe with the haft wrapped in an intricately knotted white cord. A placard below each head announced the crime that had placed it there, murder or rape, robbery with violence, assault on one of the Blood. Lesser offenses brought fines or flogging, or being made *da'covale*. The Seanchan were evenhanded about it. None of the Blood themselves were on display—one of those who earned execution would be sent back to Seanchan, or strangled with the white cord—but three of those heads had been attached to Seanchan, and the weight of their justice fell on high as well as low. Two placards marked REBELLION hung below the heads of the woman who had been Mistress of the Ships to the Atha'an Miere and her Master of the Blades.

Mat had been through that gate often enough that he barely noticed the display, now. Olver skipped along singing a rhyming song. Beslan and Thom walked with their heads together, and once Mat caught a soft "risky business" from Thom, but he did not care what they were talking about. Then they were into the long, dim tunnel that carried the road through the wall, and the rumble of wagons passing through would have made listening impossible even had he wanted to. Keeping close to the side, well away from the wagon wheels, Thom and Beslan forged ahead talking in low murmurs, Olver darting after them, but when Mat emerged into daylight again, he walked into Thom's back before he realized that all of them had stopped, hard beside the tunnel's mouth. On the point of making a caustic comment, he suddenly saw what they were staring at. People afoot pushing out of the tunnel behind him shoved them aside, but he just stared, too.

The streets of Ebou Dar were always full of people, but not like this, as though a dam had burst and sent a flood of humanity into the city. The throng packed the street in front of him from one side to the other, surrounding pools of livestock the like of which he had never seen before, spotted white cattle with long up-swept horns, pale brown goats covered in fine hair that hung to the paving stones, sheep with four horns. Every street he could see looked as jammed. Wagons and carts inched through the mass where they moved at all, the shouts and curses of the wagon drivers and carters all but drowned in the babble of voices and the noise of the animals. He could not make out words, but he could distinguish accents. Slow, drawling Seanchan accents. Some of them nudged a neighbor and pointed at him in his bright clothing. They were gaping and pointing at everything, as if they had never seen an inn or a cutler's shop before, but he still growled under his breath and jerked his hat brim low over his eyes.

"The Return," Thom muttered, and if Mat had not been right at his shoulder he would not have heard. "While we were taking our ease with Luca, the *Corenne* has arrived."

Mat had been thinking of this Return that the Seanchan kept going on about as an invasion, an army. One of the wagon drivers shouted and waved her long-handled whip at some boys who had crawled up on the side of the wagon box to poke at what appeared to be grapevines in wooden tubs of earth. Another wagon held a long printing press, and still another, just managing to turn into the tunnel, carried what looked like brewers' vats and a faint smell of hops. Crates of strangely colored chickens and ducks and geese decorated some of those wagons, not birds for sale, but a farmer's stock. It was an army all right, only not the sort he had imagined. This kind of army would be harder to fight than soldiers.

"Stab my eyes, we'll have to wade to get though this!" Beslan grumbled in disgust, rising on his toes to try peering farther ahead over the crowd. "How far before we find a clear street?"

Mat found himself remembering what he had not really seen when it was in front of his eyes, the harbor full of ships. *Full* of ships. Maybe two or three times the vessels that had been there when they left for Luca's camp at first light, quite a few of them still maneuvering under sail. Which meant there might be more still waiting to enter the harbor. Light! How many could have disgorged their cargo since morning? How many remained to be unloaded? Light, how many people could be carried on that number of ships? And why had they all come here instead of Tanchico? A shiver ran down his spine. Maybe this was not all of them.

"You had best try to find your way by back streets and alleys," he said, raising his voice so they could hear over the cacophony. "You won't reach the Palace before night, otherwise."

Beslan turned a frown on him. "You aren't returning with us? Mat, if you try to buy passage on a ship again . . . You know she won't go easy on you this time."

Mat matched the Queen's son scowl for scowl. "I just want to walk around a little," he lied. As soon as he returned to the Palace, Tylin would start cosseting and petting him. It would not have been that bad, really—not really—except that she did not care who saw her caress his cheeks and whisper endearments in his ear, even her son. Besides, what if the dice in his head stopped when he reached her? Possessive was hardly the word for Tylin these days. Blood and ashes, the woman might have decided to marry him! He did not want to marry, not yet, but he knew who he was going to marry, and it was not Tylin Quintara Mitsobar. Only, what could he do if she decided differently?

Suddenly he remembered Thom's murmur of "risky business." He knew Thom, and he knew Beslan. Olver was gaping at the Seanchan as hard as they themselves were at everything around them. He started to dart away for a closer look, and Mat seized his shoulder just in time and pushed him, protesting, into Thom's hands. "Take the boy back to the Palace and give him his lessons when Riselle is done with him. And forget whatever madness you have in mind. You could put your heads on display outside the gate, and Tylin's, too." And his own. Never let that be forgotten!

The two men stared back at him without any expression, as good as confirming his suspicions.

"Perhaps I should walk with you," Thom said at last. "We could talk. You're remarkably lucky, Mat, and you have a certain flair for, shall we say, the adventurous?" Beslan nodded. Olver squirmed in Thom's grip, trying to stare at all the strange people at once and unconcerned with what his elders were talking about.

Mat grunted sourly. Why did people always want him to be a hero? Sooner or later that sort of thing was going to get him killed. "I don't need to talk about anything. They are here, Beslan. If you couldn't stop them getting in, sure as morning, you won't be able to push them out. Rand will deal with them, if the rumors are anything to go by." Again, those whirling colors spun through his head, almost obliterating the sound of the dice for an instant. "You took that bloody oath to wait on the Return; we all did." Refusal had meant being put in chains and set to work on the docks, or clearing the canals in the Rahad. Which made it no oath at all, in his book. "Wait on Rand." The colors came once more and vanished. Blood and ashes! He just had to stop thinking about . . . About certain people. Again they swirled. "It might come out right yet, if you give it time."

"You don't understand, Mat," Beslan said fiercely. "Mother still sits on the throne, and Suroth says she will rule all of Altara, not just what we hold around Ebou Dar, and maybe more besides, but mother had to lie down on her *face* and swear *fealty* to some woman on the other side of the Aryth Ocean. Suroth says I should marry one of their Blood and shave the sides of my head, and mother is listening to her. Suroth might pretend they are equals, but she *has* to listen when Suroth speaks. No matter what Suroth says, Ebou Dar isn't really ours anymore, and the rest won't be either. Maybe we can't push them out by force of arms, but we can make the country too hot to hold them. The Whitecloaks found out. Ask them what they mean by 'the Altaran Noon.'"

Mat could guess without asking anyone. He bit his tongue to keep from pointing out that there were more Seanchan soldiers in Ebou Dar than there had been Whitecloaks in all of Altara during the Whitecloak War. A street full of Seanchan was no place for a flapping tongue, even if most did appear to be farmers and craftsfolk. "I understand you're hot to put your head on a spike," he said quietly. As quietly as he could and still be heard in that din of voices and cattle lowing and geese honking. "You know about their Listeners. That fellow over there who looks like a stableman could be one, or that skinny woman with the bundle on her back."

Beslan glowered so hard at the pair Mat had pointed out that if they really were Listeners, they might report him for that alone. "Maybe you'll sing a different song when they reach Andor," he growled, and pushed his way into the throng, shoving anyone who got in his way. Mat would have been unsurprised to see a fight break out. He suspected that was what the man was looking for.

Thom turned to follow with Olver, but Mat caught his sleeve. "Cool his temper if you can, Thom. And cool your own while you're about it. I would think by this time you'd have had enough of shaving blind."

"My head is cool and I'm trying to cool his," Thom said drily. "He can't just sit, though; it is his country." A faint smile crossed his leathery face. "You say you won't take risks, but you will. And when you do, you'll make anything Beslan and I might try look like an evening stroll in the garden. With you around, even the barber is blind. Come along, boy," he said, swinging Olver up onto his shoulders. "Riselle might not let you rest your head if you're late for your lesson."

Mat frowned after him as he strode away, making much better progress with Olver straddling his neck than Beslan had. What did Thom mean? He never took risks unless they were forced on him. Never. He glanced casually toward the skinny woman, and the fellow with dung on his boots. Light, they *could* be Listeners. Anybody could be. It was enough to set a prickle between his shoulders, as if he were being watched.

He inched a goodly distance along streets that actually grew thicker with people and animals and wagons the nearer he came to the docks. The stalls on the bridges over the canals had their shutters down, the street peddlers had picked up their blankets, and the tumblers and jugglers that usually entertained at every street crossing would have had no room to perform if they had not gone away, too. There were too many Seanchan, that was how many there were, and maybe one in five a soldier, plain enough by their hard eyes and the set of their shoulders, so different from farmer or craftsman, even when they were not wearing armor. Now and then a group *sul'dam* and *damane* moved along the street in a little eddy of clear space, more even than soldiers got. It was not given out of fear, at least not by the Seanchan. They bowed respectfully to the women with lightning-marked red panels on the blue dresses, and smiled with approval as the pairs passed by. Beslan was out of his mind. The Seanchan were not going to be driven

off by anyone except an army with Asha'man, like the one
rumor said had fought them to the east a week ago. Or one
armed with the Illuminator's secrets. What in the Light
could Aludra want with a bellfounder?

He took pains not to come in sight of the docks. He had
learned his lesson on that. What he really wanted was a
game of dice, one that would last well into the night. Pref-
erably late enough that Tylin would be asleep when he returned to the Palace. She had taken away his dice, claiming
she did not like him gambling, though she did it after he
talked her into wagering forfeits, while he was still confined to bed. Fortunately, dice could always be found, and
with his luck, it was always better to use the other men's
dice anyway. Unfortunately, once he discovered she was not
about to pay a forfeit of letting him go—the woman pretended not to know what he was talking about!—he had
used them to give her back a bit of her own medicine. A
grave mistake, however much fun it had been at the time.
Since the forfeits ran out, she had been twice as bad as
before.

The taverns and common rooms he entered were as
packed as the streets, though, with barely room to lift a
mug, much less toss dice, full of Seanchan laughing and
singing, and glum-faced Ebou Dari who eyed the Seanchan
in sullen silence. He still queried the innkeepers and tap-
sters on the chance they might have a cubby hole he could
rent, but one and all they shook their heads. He had not really expected anything else. There had been nothing available even before all the new arrivals. Still, he began to feel
as gloomy as the foreign merchants he saw peering into
their wine and wondering how they were to get their goods
out of the city with no horses. He had gold to pay whatever
Luca wanted, and more, but it was all in a chest in the Tarasin Palace, and he was not about to try taking enough out in
one go, not after Palace servants had *carried* him back from
the docks like a stag taken in hunt. All he had been doing then was talking to ship captains; if Tylin learned, and
she would, that he was trying to leave the Palace with more
gold than he needed for an evening of gambling . . . Oh, no!
He had to have a room, a garret in some inn's attic the size
of a wardrobe, anything, where he could hide away gold a
little at a time, or he had to have a chance with the dice, one

or the other. Luck or no luck, though, he eventually realized that he was going to find neither today. And those bloody dice were still tumbling in his head, tumbling.

He did not stay in any one place long, and not just for the lack of a game or a room. His colorful clothes, his shame-a-Tinker-for-brightness clothes, drew eyes. Some of the Seanchan thought he was there for entertainment, and tried to pay him to sing! He almost let them, once or twice, but once they heard him, they would have demanded the money back. Some of the Ebou Dari men, with long curved knives tucked behind their belts and a bellyful of anger they could not take out on the Seanchan, thought to take it out on the buffoon who lacked only a painted face to look like a noble's fool. Mat ducked back into the crowded street whenever he saw such fellows eyeing him. He had learned the hard way that he was in no condition for a fight yet, and his killer's head going up beside the city gate would do him no good at all.

Mat took rest where he could find it, on an empty barrel abandoned beside the mouth of an alleyway, on the rare bit of bench in front of a tavern that had room for one more, on a stone step until the building's owner came out and knocked his hat off with a swipe of her broom. His belly was kissing his backbone, he was beginning to feel that everyone was gaping at his garish clothes, the dank cold was seeping into his bones, and the only dice he was going to find were those still thundering away in his head like horse's hooves. He did not think they had ever been this loud before.

"Nothing for it but to go back and be the Queen's bloody pet!" he growled, using his staff to lever himself up off a cracked wooden crate lying at the side of the street. Several passersby looked at him as if his face were already painted. He ignored them. Beneath his notice, they were. He was not beating them over the head with his staff as they deserved, goggling at a man that way.

The streets really were as full as earlier, he realized, and it would be well after nightfall before he got back to the Palace if he tried to make his way through the crowds. Of course, Tylin might be asleep by then. Maybe. His stomach growled, almost loudly enough to drown out the dice. She might order the kitchens not to feed him, if he was too late.

Ten hard-won paces through the press, and he turned

down an alley, narrow and dark. There were no paving
stones. The white plaster on the windowless walls was
cracked and falling to expose the brick beneath, often as
not. The air was rank with the fetid stench of decay, and
he hoped that what squished under his boots was mud even
when it gave off a loathsome odor. There were no people,
either. He could step out with a good stride. Or what passed
for one, today. He could hardly wait for the day he could
walk a few miles again without panting and aching and
needing to lean on a stick. Twisting alleys, most so narrow his shoulders brushed both sides, crisscrossed the city
in a maze that was easy to get lost in if you did not know
your way. He never took a wrong turn, even when a narrow,
crooked passage suddenly forked into three or even four
that all seemed to meander in roughly the same direction.
There had been a good many times in Ebou Dar when he
needed to avoid eyes, and he knew these alleys like he knew
his own hand. Though, oddly enough, he still had the feeling he was being watched. He expected to feel that as long
as he had to wear those bloody clothes.

If he had to struggle through a mass of people and animals from one alley to another, and occasionally shove his
way across a bridge that seemed a solid wall of humanity,
he was still almost back to the Palace in the time it would
have taken him to go three streets otherwise. Hurrying into
the shadowed passage between a well-lit tavern and a shut-
tered lacquerware shop, he wondered what the kitchens
would have ready. More capacious than most, wide enough
for three if they were friendly, this alley let out onto the
Mol Hara Square almost in front of the Tarasin Palace.
Suroth was living there, and the cooks had been outdoing
themselves since she had had the lot of them flogged after
her first meal. There might be oysters with cream, and perhaps gilded fish, and squid with peppers. Ten strides into
the shadows, his foot came down on something that did not
squish, and he went down in the freezing mud with a grunt,
twisting at the last instant so he did not land on his bad leg.
Icy liquid immediately soaked through his coat. He hoped
it was water.

He grunted again when boots landed on his shoulder.
The fellow toppled off of him, cursing and skidding deeper
into the alley on the mud, and went to one knee, just man-

aging to catch himself against the side of the tavern short of falling flat himself. Mat's eyes were accustomed to the dim light, enough for him to make out a slender, nondescript man. A man with what appeared to be a large scar on his cheek. Not a man, though. A creature he had seen rip out his friend's throat with one bare hand and take a knife out of its own chest and throw it back at him. And the thing would have landed right in front of him, in easy reach, if he had not tripped. Maybe a little twist of *ta'veren* shaping had worked in his favor, thank the Light! All that flashed through his head in the time it took the *gholam* to catch itself against the wall and turn its head to glare at him.

With an oath, Mat snatched his fallen walking staff and awkwardly hurled it at the creature like a spear. At its legs, hoping to tangle them, gain a moment. The thing flowed aside like water, avoiding the staff, boots sliding a little in the mud, then threw itself toward Mat. The delay had been enough, though. As soon as the staff left his hand, Mat fumbled inside his shirt for the foxhead medallion, breaking the leather cord as he snatched the medallion out. The *gholam* threw itself at him, and he swung the medallion desperately. Silver that had lain cool on his chest brushed across an outstretched hand with a hiss like bacon frying and a smell of burning flesh. Fluid as quicksilver, snarling, the thing tried to dodge by the whirling medallion, to seize some part of Mat. Once it laid hands on him, he was as good as dead. It would not try to toy with him this time, as it had in the Rahad. Flailing continuously, he caught it with the foxhead on the other hand, across the face, each time with a hiss and stench of burning as if he had struck with a hot iron. Teeth bared, the *gholam* backed away, but in a crouch on the balls of its feet, hands clawed, ready to jump at the slightest weakness.

Not letting the spinning medallion slow, Mat pushed unsteadily to his feet, watching the thing that looked a like a man. *He wants you dead as much as he wants her,* it had told him in the Rahad, smiling. It was not talking or smiling now. He did not know who the "her" was, or the "he," but the rest was clear as good glass. And here he was, barely able to stay on his feet. His leg and hip ached like fire, and his ribs. Not to mention the shoulder the *gholam* had landed on. He had to get back to the street, back among people.

Maybe enough people would deter the thing. A small hope, but the only hope he could see. The street was not far. He could hear the babble of voices, hardly softened by distance at all.

He took a careful step backward. His boot slid in something that gave off a foul smell and threw him against the tavern's wall. Only frantic swings of the silver foxhead kept the *gholam* back. Those voices in the street were so tantalizingly close. They might as well have been in Barsine. Barsine was long dead, and he would be too, soon.

"He's down this alley!" a man shouted. "Follow me! Hurry! He'll get away!"

Mat kept his eyes on the *gholam*. Its gaze flickered beyond him, toward the street, and it hesitated. "I am ordered to avoid notice, save by those I harvest," it spat at him, "so you will live a little longer. A little longer."

Spinning, it ran down the alley, slipping a little in the mud, yet still seeming to flow as it dodged around behind the tavern.

Mat ran after it. He could not have said why, except that it had tried to kill him, would try again, and his hackles were stiff. So it was going to kill him at leisure, was it? If the medallion could hurt it, maybe the medallion could kill it.

Reaching the corner of the tavern, he saw the *gholam* at the same time that it glanced back and saw him. Again, the thing hesitated for an instant. The tavern's back door stood ajar, letting out the sounds of revelry. The creature stuck its hands into a hole left by a missing brick in the back wall of the building opposite the tavern, and Mat stiffened. It hardly seemed to need weapons, but if it had hidden one in there . . . He did not think he would survive facing that thing with any sort of weapon. Arms followed hands, and then the *gholam*'s head went into the hole. Mat's jaw dropped. The *gholam*'s chest slithered through, its legs, and it was gone. Through an opening maybe the size of Mat's two hands.

"I don't think I have ever seen the like," someone said quietly beside him, and Mat gave a start at realizing he was no longer alone. The speaker was a stoop-shouldered, white-haired old man with a large hooked nose planted in the middle of a sad face and a bundle slung on his back. He was sliding a very long dagger into a sheath beneath his coat.

"I have," Mat said hollowly. "In Shadar Logoth." Sometimes bits of his own memory he thought lost floated up out of nowhere, and that one had just surfaced, watching the *gholam*. It was one memory he wished had remained lost.

"Not many survive a visit there," the old man said, peering at him. His weathered face looked familiar, somehow, but Mat could not place him. "Whatever took you to Shadar Logoth?"

"Where are your friends?" Mat said. "The people you were shouting to?" The alleyway held only the two of them. The sounds from the street continued unabated, and undisturbed by any cries about anyone getting away if they did not hurry.

The old man shrugged. "I'm not certain anyone out there understood what I was shouting. It's hard enough understanding them. Anyway, I thought it might scare off the fellow. Seeing that, though . . ." Gesturing toward the hole in the wall, he laughed mirthlessly, showing gaps in his teeth. "I think maybe you and I both have the Dark One's own luck."

Mat grimaced. He had heard that too often about himself, and he did not like it. Mainly because he was not sure it was not true. "Maybe we do," he muttered. "Forgive me; I should introduce myself to the man who saved my neck. I'm Mat Cauthon. Are you new-come to Ebou Dar?" That bundle strapped to the fellow's back gave him the look of a man on the move. "You will have a hard time finding a place to sleep." He took care with the gnarled hand the other man put in his. It was all knobs, as if every bone had been broken at the same time and had healed badly. It had a strong grip, though.

"I am Noal Charin, Mat Cauthon. No, I have been here some time. But my pallet in the attic of The Golden Ducks is now occupied by a fat Illianer oil merchant who was rousted from his room this morning in favor of a Seanchan officer. I thought I'd find somewhere back in this alley for tonight." Rubbing the side of his big nose with a crooked, knobby finger, he chuckled as if sleeping in an alley were of no moment. "It will not be the first time I've slept rough, even in a city."

"I think I can do better for you than that," Mat told him, but the rest of what he had been going to say died on his tongue. The dice were still spinning in his head, he realized. He had managed to forget them with the *gholam* trying to kill him, but they were still bouncing, still waiting to land. If they were warning of something worse than the *gholam,* he did not want to know. Only, he would. There was no doubt of that. He would, when it was too late.

CHAPTER 17

Pink Ribbons

Cold winds gusted through the Mol Hara, lifting
Mat's cloak and threatening to freeze the mud cak-
ing his clothing as he and Noal hurried out of the
alley. The sun sat on the rooftops, half-hidden, and the
shadows stretched long. With one hand for his staff and
the other gripping the broken cord of the fox-head, stuffed
into a coat pocket where he could snatch it out if need be,
he had to let his cloak go where it would. He ached from
head to foot, the dice rattled warning inside his skull, and
he hardly noticed either thing. He was too busy trying to
watch every direction at once, and wondering just how
small a hole that thing could get through. He found himself
uneasily eyeing cracks between the square's paving stones.
Though it hardly seemed likely the thing would come at
him in the open.

A hum carried from surrounding streets, but here only a
slat-ribbed dog moved, running past the fountained statue
of long-dead Queen Nariene. Some said her uplifted hand
pointed to the ocean's bounty that had enriched Ebou Dar,
and some that it pointed in warning of dangers. Others said
her successor had wanted to draw attention to the fact that
only one of the statue's breasts was uncovered, proclaiming
that Nariene had only been of middling honesty.

In other days the Mol Hara would have been full of strolling lovers and lingering street vendors and hopeful beggars
at this hour even in winter, but beggars found themselves
snatched off the streets and put to work, since the Seanchan came, and the rest stayed away even in daylight. The
reason was the Tarasin Palace, that great mound of white

domes and marble spires and wrought-iron balconies, the residence of Tylin Quintara Mitsobar, by the Grace of the Light, Queen of Altara—or as much of Altara as lay within a few days' ride of Ebou Dar—Mistress of the Four Winds and Guardian of the Sea of Storms. And, perhaps more important, the residence of the High Lady Suroth Sabelle Meldarath, commanding the Forerunners for the Empress of the Seanchan, might she live forever. A position of much greater eminence in Ebou Dar, at the moment. Tylin's green-booted guards stood at every entrance in their baggy white trousers and gilded breastplates worn over green coats, and so did men and women in those insectile helmets with armor striped in blue-and-yellow or green-and-white or any other combination you might happen to think of. The Queen of Altara required security and silence for her rest. Or rather, Suroth said she did, and what Suroth said Tylin wanted, Tylin soon decided that she did indeed want.

After a moment's consideration, Mat led Noal to one of the stableyard gates. There was more chance of getting a stranger in there than if he used the grand marble stairs that led down into the square. Not to mention a much better chance of getting all the mud off him before he had to face Tylin. She had made her displeasure markedly known the last time he came back disheveled, after a tavern brawl.

A handful of Ebou Dari guards stood to one side of the open gates with halberds, and the same number of Seanchan on the other with tasseled spears, all as stiff as Nariene's statue.

"The Light's blessing on all here," Mat murmured politely to the Ebou Dari guards. It was always best to be polite to Ebou Dari until you were sure of them. Afterwards, too, for that matter. Even so, they were more . . . flexible . . . than the Seanchan.

"And on you, my Lord," their stocky officer replied, ambling forward, and Mat recognized him, Surlivan Sarat, a good fellow, always ready with a quip and possessing a fine eye for horses. Shaking his head, Surlivan tapped the side of his pointed helmet with the thin, gilded rod of his office. "Have you been in another fight, my Lord? She will go up like a waterspout, when she sees you."

Squaring his shoulders, and trying not to lean so obviously on his staff, Mat bristled. Ready with a quip? Come to think on it, the sun-dark man had a tongue like a rasp. And his eye for horses was not all that fine, either. "Will there be any questions if my friend here beds down with my men?" Mat asked roughly. "There shouldn't be. There's room for one more with my fellows." Room for more than one, truth be told. Eight men had died so far, for following him to Ebou Dar.

"None from me, my Lord," Surlivan said, though he eyed the scrawny man at Mat's side and pursed his lips judiciously. Noal's coat appeared of good quality, though, at least in the dim light, and he did have his lace, and in a better state than Mat's. Perhaps that tipped the balance. "And she doesn't need to know everything, so none from her, either."

Mat scowled, but before intemperate words could put himself and Noal in the soup kettle, three armored Seanchan galloped up to the gate, and Surlivan turned to face them.

"You and your lady wife live in the Queen's Palace?" Noal enquired, starting toward the gate.

Mat pulled him back. "Wait on them," he said, nodding toward the Seanchan. His lady wife? Bloody women! Bloody dice in his bloody head!

"I have dispatches for the High Lady Suroth," one of the Seanchan announced, slapping a leather satchel hanging from one armored shoulder. Her helmet bore a single thin plume, marking her a low-ranking officer, yet her horse was a tall dun gelding with a look of speed. The other two animals were sturdy enough, but there was nothing to be said for them beyond that.

"Enter with the blessings of the Light," Surlivan said, bowing slightly.

The Seanchan woman's bow from her saddle was a mirror of his. "The blessings of the Light be on you also," she drawled, and the three of them clattered into the stable-yard.

"It is very strange," Surlivan mused, peering after the three. "They always ask permission of us, not them." He flicked his rod toward the Seanchan guards on the other side of the gates. They had not stirred an inch from their rigid stance, or even glanced at the arrivals that Mat had noticed.

"And what would they do if you said they couldn't go in?" Noal asked quietly, easing the bundle on his back.

Surlivan spun on his heel. "It is enough that I have given oath to my Queen," he said in an expressionless voice, "and she has given hers . . . where she has given it. Give your friend a bed, my Lord. And warn him, there are things better left unsaid in Ebou Dar, questions better left unasked."

Noal looked befuddled and began protesting that he was simply curious, but Mat exchanged further benisons and courtesies with the Altaran officer—as quickly as he could, to be sure—and hustled his new-found acquaintance through the gates, explaining about Listeners in a low voice. The man might have saved his hide from the *gholam,* but that did not mean he would let the fellow hand it over to the Seanchan. They had people called Seekers, too, and from the little he had heard—even people who spoke freely about the Deathwatch Guard locked their teeth when it came to the Seekers—from the little he had heard, Seekers made Whitecloak Questioners look like boys tormenting flies, nasty but hardly anything to worry a man.

"I see," the old man said slowly. "I hadn't known that." He sounded irritated with himself. "You must spend a good deal of time with the Seanchan. Do you know the High Lady Suroth as well, then? I must say, I had no idea you had such high connections."

"I spend time with soldiers in taverns, when I can," Mat replied sourly. When Tylin let him. Light, he might as well be married! "Suroth doesn't know I'm alive." And he devoutly hoped it remained that way.

The three Seanchan were already out of sight, their horses being led into the stables, but several dozen *sul'dam* were giving *damane* their evening exercise, walking them in a big circle around the stone-paved yard. Nearly half the gray-clad *damane* were dark-skinned women, lacking the jewelry they had worn as Windfinders. There were more like them in the Palace and elsewhere; the Seanchan had had a rich harvest from Sea Folk vessels that had failed to escape. Most wore sullen resignation or stony faces, but seven or eight stared ahead of them, lost and confused, disbelieving still. Each of those had a Seanchan-born *damane* at her side, holding her hand or with an arm around her, smiling and whispering to her under the approving eyes of the women who wore the bracelets attached to their silvery collars. A few of those dazed women clutched the *damane* walking with them as if holding to lifelines. It would have been enough to make Mat shiver, if his damp clothes had not already been doing the job.

He tried to hurry Noal across the yard, but the circle brought a *damane* who was neither Seanchan nor Atha'an Miere near him, linked to a plump, graying *sul'dam,* an olive-skinned woman who might have passed for Altaran and someone's mother. A stern mother with a possibly fractious child, from the way she regarded her charge. Teslyn Baradon had fleshed out after a month and a half in Seanchan captivity, yet her ageless face still looked as if she ate briars three meals a day. On the other hand, she walked placidly on her leash and obeyed the *sul'dam*'s murmured directions without hesitation, pausing to bow very deeply to him and Noal. For an instant, though, her dark eyes flashed hatred at him before she and the *sul'dam* continued their circuit of the stableyard. Placidly, obediently. He had seen *damane* upended and switched till they howled in this same stableyard for making any sort of fuss, Teslyn among them. She had done him no good turns, and maybe a few bad, but he would not have wished this on her.

"Better than being dead, I suppose," he muttered, moving on. Teslyn was a hard woman, likely plotting every moment how to escape, yet hardness only took you so far. The Mistress of the Ships and her Master of the Blades had died on the stake without ever screaming, but it had not saved them.

"Do you believe that?" Noal asked absently, fumbling awkwardly with his bundle again. His broken hands had handled that knife well enough, but they seemed clumsy at everything else.

Mat frowned at him. No; he was not sure he believed it. Those silver *a'dam* seemed too much like the invisible collar Tylin had on him. Then again, Tylin could tickle him under the chin the rest of his life if it kept him off the stake. Light, he wished those bloody dice in his head would just stop and get it over with! No, that was a lie. Since he had finally realized what they meant, he had never wanted the dice to stop.

The room Chel Vanin and the surviving Redarms shared lay not far from the stables, a long white-plastered chamber

with a low ceiling and too many beds for those who re-
mained alive. Vanin, a balding suety heap, was lying on
one in his shirtsleeves, an open book propped on his chest.
Mat was surprised the man *could* read. Spitting through a
gap in his teeth, Vanin eyed Mat's mud-smeared clothes.
"You been fighting again?" he asked. "She won't like that,
I reckon." He did not rise. With a few startling exceptions,
Vanin considered himself as good as any lord or lady.

"Trouble, Lord Mat?" Harnan growled, leaping to his
feet. He was a solid man, physically and by temperament,
but his heavy jaw clenched, twisting the hawk crudely tattooed on his cheek. "Begging your pardon, but you're in no
condition for it. Tell us what he looks like, and we'll sort
him out for you."

The last three gathered behind him with eager expressions, two grabbing for their coats while still tucking in
shirttails. Metwyn, a boyish-appearing Cairhienin who was
ten years older than Mat, instead picked up his sword from
where it was propped at the foot of his bed and eased a
little of the blade out of the scabbard to check the edge.
He was the best of them with a sword, very good indeed,
though Gorderan came close for all he looked a blacksmith.
Gorderan was not nearly as slow as his thick shoulders
made him appear. A dozen Redarms had followed Mat
Cauthon to Ebou Dar, eight of those were dead, and the rest
were stuck here in the Palace where they could not pinch
the maids, get into a fight over dice, and drink till they fell
on their faces, as they could have staying at an inn and
knowing the innkeeper would see them carried up to their
beds, though maybe with their purses a little lighter than
they had been.

"Noal here can tell you what happened better than I can,"
Mat replied, pushing his hat back on his head. "He'll be
bedding in here with you. He saved my life tonight."

That brought exclamations of shock, and cries of appro-
bation for Noal, not to mention slaps on the back that almost toppled the old fellow. Vanin went so far as to mark
his place in the book with a fat finger and sit up on the side
of his thin mattress.

Setting his bundle down on a vacant bed, Noal told the
tale with elaborate gestures, playing down his own role and

even making himself a bit of a buffoon, slipping in the mud
and gaping at the *gholam* while Mat fought like a cham-
pion. The man was a natural storyteller, as good as a gleeman for making you see what he described. Harnan and
the Redarms laughed genially, knowing what he was about,
not stealing their captain's thunder, and approving of it, but
laughter died when he came to Mat's attacker slipping away
through a tiny hole in a wall. He made you see that, too.
Vanin put down his book and spat through his teeth again.
The *gholam* had left Vanin and Harnan half-dead in the
Rahad. Half-dead because it was after other prey.

"The thing wants me for some reason, it seems," Mat
said lightly when the old man finished and sank onto the
bed with his belongings, seemingly exhausted. "It probably
played at dice with me some time I don't recall. None of
you has to worry, as long as you don't get between it and
me." He grinned, trying to make it all a joke, but no one so
much as smiled. "In any case, I'll parcel out gold to you in
the morning. You'll book passage on the first ship leaving
for Illian, and take Olver with you. Thom and Juilin, too, if
they'll go." He imagined the thief-catcher would, anyway.
"And Nerim and Lopin, of course." He had gotten used to
having a pair of serving men look after him, but he hardly
needed them here. "Talmanes must be somewhere close to
Caemlyn by this time. You shouldn't have much trouble
finding him." When they were gone, he would be alone
with Tylin. Light, he would rather face the *gholam* again!

Harnan and the other three Redarms exchanged looks,
Fergin scratching his head as if he did not quite understand.
He might not. The bony man was a good soldier—not the
best, mind, but good enough—yet he was not very bright
when it came to other things.

"That wouldn't be right," Harnan allowed finally. "One
thing, Lord Talmanes'd have our hides if we came back
without you." The other three nodded. Fergin could understand that.

"And you, Vanin?" Mat asked.

The fat man shrugged. "I take that boy away from Riselle,
and he'll gut me like a trout the first time I go to sleep. I
would myself, in his boots. Anyway, I got time to read,
here. Don't get much chance for that working as a farrier."

That was one of the itinerant trades he claimed to follow. The other was stableman. In truth, he was a horsethief and poacher, the best in two countries and maybe more.

"You're all mad," Mat said with a frown. "Just because it wants me, doesn't mean it won't kill you if you get in the way. The offer stays open. Anyone who comes to his senses can go."

"I have seen your like before," Noal said suddenly. The stooped old man was the image of hard age and exhaustion, but his eyes were bright and sharp studying Mat. "Some men have an air about them that makes other men follow where they lead. Some lead to devastation, others to glory. I think your name may go into the history books."

Harnan looked as confused as Fergin. Vanin spat and lay back down, opening his book.

"If all my luck goes away, maybe," Mat muttered. He knew what it took to get into the histories. A man could get killed, doing that sort of thing.

"Better clean up before she sees you," Fergin piped up suddenly. "All that mud will put a burr under her saddle for sure."

Snatching his hat off angrily, Mat stalked out without a word. Well, he stalked as well as he could, hobbling on a walking staff. Before the door closed behind him, he heard Noal starting a story about one time he sailed on a Sea Folk ship and learned to bathe in cold salt water. At least, that was how it began.

He intended to get himself clean before Tylin saw him—he did—but as he limped through hallways hung with the flowered tapestries Ebou Dari called summer-hangings, for the season they evoked, four serving men in the Palace's green-and-white livery and no fewer than seven maids suggested he might want to bathe and change his clothes before the Queen saw him, offering to draw him a bath and fetch clean garments without her learning of it. They did not know everything about him and Tylin, thank the Light—no one but Tylin and himself knew the worst bits—but they knew too bloody much. Worse, they approved, every last flaming servant in the whole flaming Tarasin Palace. For one thing, Tylin was Queen and could do as she pleased, so far as they were concerned. For another, her temper had been on a razor's edge since the Seanchan captured the city, and if Mat Cauthon scrubbed and bright in lace kept her from snapping their noses off for trifles, then they would scrub behind his ears and wrap him in lace like a Sunday gift!

"Mud?" he said to a pretty, smiling maid spreading her skirts in a curtsy. There was a twinkle in her dark eyes, and the plunging neckline of her bodice displayed a fair amount of bosom to almost rival Riselle's. On another day he might have taken a little time to enjoy looking. "What mud? I don't see any mud!" Her mouth dropped open, and she forgot to straighten, staring at him with her knees bent as he hobbled away.

Juilin Sandar, rounding a corner quickly, nearly walked into him. The Tairen thief-catcher leaped back with a muffled oath, his swarthy face turning gray until he realized who had almost run him over. Then he muttered an apology and started to hurry on by.

"Has Thom got you mixed into his foolishness, Juilin?" Mat said. Juilin and Thom shared a room deep in the servants' quarters, and there was no excuse for him to be up here. In that dark Tairen coat, flaring over his boot tops, Juilin would stand out among the servants like a duck in a chicken coop. Suroth was strict about things like that, stricter than Tylin. The only reason for it Mat could see was whatever Thom and Beslan were meddling with. "No; don't bother telling me. I've made an offer to Harnan and the others, and it's open to you, too. If you want to leave, I'll give you the money for it."

Actually, Juilin did not look ready to tell him anything. The thief-catcher tucked his thumbs behind his belt and met Mat's gaze levelly. "What did Harnan and the others say? And what is Thom doing that you call foolish? This is one set of rooftops he knows his way around better than you or I."

"The *gholam* is still in Ebou Dar, Juilin." Thom knew that the Game of Houses was what *he* knew, and he loved sticking his nose into politics. "The thing tried to kill me, earlier this evening."

Juilin grunted as if he had been hit in the pit of his belly, and scrubbed a hand through his short black hair. "I have a reason to stay a while longer," he said, "even so." His air changed slightly, to something stubborn and defensive and tinged with guilt. He had never shown a roving eye that Mat had seen, but when a man looked like that, it could only mean one thing.

"Take her with you," Mat said. "And if she won't go, well, you'll not be in Tear an hour before you have a woman on each knee. That's the thing about women, Juilin. If one says no, there's always another will say yes."

A serving man hurrying by with an armload of linen towels stared at Mat's muddiness in amazement, but Juilin thought it was at him, and snatched his thumbs free of his belt and attempted to adopt a more humble stance. Without much success. Thom might sleep with the servants, yet from the beginning he had somehow made it seem to be his own choice, an eccentricity, and no one thought it odd to see him up here, perhaps slipping into Riselle's rooms that had once been Mat's. Juilin had gone on at length about being a thief-catcher—never a thief-*taker*—and stared so many prickly lordlings and complacent merchants in the eye to show he was as good as they that everyone in the Palace knew who and what he was. And where he was supposed to be, which was belowstairs.

"My Lord is wise," he said, too loudly, and making a stiff, jerky bow. "My Lord knows all about women. If my Lord will forgive a humble man, I must return to my place." Turning to go, he spoke over his shoulder, still in a carrying voice. "I heard today that if my Lord comes back one more time looking like he's been dragged in the street, the Queen intends taking a switch to my Lord's person."

And that was the stone that broke the wagon clean in two.

Flinging open the doors of Tylin's apartments, Mat strode in, sailed his hat across the width of the room . . . And stopped dead, his mouth hanging open and everything he had planned to say frozen on his tongue. His hat hit the carpets and rolled, he did not see where. A gust of wind rattled the tall triple-arched windows that let out onto a long, screened balcony overlooking the Mol Hara.

Tylin turned in a chair carved to look like gilded bamboo and stared at him over her golden winecup. Waves of glossy black hair touched with gray at the temples framed a beautiful face with the eyes of a bird of prey, and not one best pleased at the moment. Inconsequential things seemed to leap at him. She kicked her crossed leg slightly, rippling layered green and white petticoats. Pale green lace trimmed the oval opening in her gown that half exposed her full breasts, where the jeweled hilt of her marriage knife dangled. She was not alone. Suroth sat facing her, frowning into her winecup and tapping long fingernails on the arm of her chair, a pretty enough woman despite her hair being shaved to that long crest, except that she made Tylin seem a rabbit by comparison. Two of those fingernails on each hand were lacquered blue. Seated at her side was a little girl, of all things, also in an elaborately flowered robe over pleated white skirts, but with a sheer veil covering her entire head—it seemed to be shaved completely!—and wearing a fortune in rubies. Even in a state of shock, he noticed rubies and gold. A slender woman, nearly as dark as her stark black gown and tall even had she been Aiel, stood behind the girl's chair with her arms folded and ill-concealed impatience. Her wavy black hair was short, but not shaved at all, so she was neither of the Blood nor *so'jhin*. Imperiously beautiful, she put Tylin and Suroth both in the shade. He noticed beautiful women, too, even when he did feel hit in the head with a hammer.

It was not the presence of Suroth or the strangers that jerked him to a halt, though. The dice had stopped, landing with a thunder that made his skull ring. That had never happened before. He stood there waiting for one of the Forsaken to leap out of the flames in the marble fireplace, or the earth to swallow the Palace beneath him.

"You aren't listening to me, pigeon," Tylin cooed in dangerous tones. "I said, take yourself down to the kitchens and have a pastry until I have time for you. Have a bath while you're about it." Her dark eyes glittered. "We will discuss your mud later."

In a daze, he ran it through again in his head. He had walked into the room, the dice had stopped, and . . . Nothing had happened. Nothing!

"This man has been set upon," the tiny, veiled figure said, rising. Her tone turned cold as the wind outside. "You told me the streets were safe, Suroth! I am displeased."

Something *had* to happen! It already should have! Something always happened when the dice stopped.

"I assure you, Tuon, the streets of Ebou Dar are as safe as the streets of Seandar itself," Suroth replied, and that pulled

Mat out of his stupor. She sounded . . . anxious. Suroth made other people anxious.

A slender, graceful young man in the almost transparent robe of a *da'covale* appeared at her side with a tall blue porcelain pitcher, bowing his head and silently offering to replenish her wine. And giving Mat another start. He had not realized anyone else was present in the room. The yellow-haired man in his indecent garment was not the only one, either. A slim but nicely rounded red-haired woman wearing the same sheer robe was kneeling beside a table that held spice bottles and more fine Sea Folk porcelain wine pitchers and a small gilded brass brazier with the pokers needed for heating the wine, while a graying nervous-eyed serving woman wearing green-and-white House Mitsobar livery stood at the other end. And in one corner, so motionless that he still almost missed her, yet another Seanchan, a short woman with half her golden head shaved and a bosom that might outmatch Riselle's if her dress of red-and-yellow panels had not covered her neck to the chin. Not that he had any real desire to find out. Seanchan were very touchy about their *so'jhin*. Tylin was touchy about any woman. There had not been a serving woman younger than his grandmother in her apartments since he was able to get out of bed.

Suroth looked at the graceful man as though wondering what he was, then shook her head wordlessly and turned her attention back to the child, Tuon, who waved the fellow away. The liveried serving maid scurried forward to take the pitcher from him and try to refill Tylin's cup, but the Queen made a very small gesture that sent her back to the wall. Tylin was sitting very, very still. Little wonder that she wanted to avoid notice if this Tuon frightened Suroth, as she plainly did.

"I am displeased, Suroth," the girl said again, sternly frowning down at the other woman. Even standing, she did not have all that far down to stare at the seated High Lady. Mat supposed she must be a High Lady, too, only Higher than Suroth. "You have recovered much, and that will please the Empress, may she live forever, but your ill-considered attack eastward was a disaster that must not be repeated. And if the streets of this city are safe, how can he have been set upon?"

Suroth's knuckles were white from gripping the chair

arm, and her winecup. She glared at Tylin as though the lecture were her fault, and Tylin gave her an apologetic smile and bowed her head. Oh, blood and ashes, he was going to pay for that!

"I fell down, that's all." His voice might as well have been fireworks for the way heads whipped around. Suroth and Tuon looked shocked that he had spoken. Tylin looked like an eagle who wanted her rabbit fried. "My Ladies," he added, but that did not seem to improve anything.

The tall woman suddenly reached out and snatched the winecup from Tuon's hand, throwing it into the fireplace. Sparks showered up the chimney. The serving woman stirred as if to retrieve the cup before it could be damaged further, then subsided at a touch from the *so'jhin*.

"You are being foolish, Tuon," the tall woman said, and her voice made the girl's sternness seem laughter. The too-familiar Seanchan drawl seemed almost absent entirely. "Suroth has the situation here well in her control. What happened to the east can happen in any battle. You must stop wasting time on ridiculous trifles."

Suroth gaped at her in astonishment for an instant before she could assume a frozen mask. Mat did a little gaping on his own part. Use that tone of voice to one of the Blood, and you were lucky to escape with a trip to the flogging post!

Shockingly, Tuon inclined her head slightly. "You may be right, Anath," she said calmly, and even with a touch of deference. "Time and the omens will tell. But the young man plainly is lying. Perhaps he fears Tylin's anger. But his injuries clearly are more than he could sustain falling down unless there are cliffs in the city I have not seen."

So he feared Tylin's anger, did he? Well, come to that, he did, a little. Only a little, mind. But he did not like being reminded of it. Leaning on his shoulder-high staff, he tried to make himself comfortable. They could ask a man to sit, after all. "I was hurt the day your lads took the city," he said with his cheekiest grin. "Your lot were flinging around lightning and balls of fire something fierce. I'm just about healed, though, thank you for asking." Tylin buried her face in her winecup, and still managed to shoot him a look over the rim that promised retribution later.

Tuon's skirts rustled as she crossed the carpets to him. The dark face behind that sheer veil might have been pretty, without the expression of a judge passing sentence of death. And with a decent head of hair instead of a bald pate. Her eyes were large and liquid, but utterly impersonal. All of her long fingernails were lacquered, he noticed, a bright red. He wondered whether that signified anything. Light, a man could live in luxury for years on the price of those rubies.

She reached up with one hand, putting her fingertips under his chin, and he started to jerk back. Until Tylin glared at him over Tuon's head, promising retribution here and now, if he did any such thing. Glowering, he let the girl shift his head for her study.

"You fought us?" she demanded. "You have sworn the oaths?"

"I swore," he muttered. "For the other, I had no chance."

"So you would have," she murmured. Circling him slowly, she continued her study, fingering the lace at his wrist, touching the black silk scarf tied around his neck, lifting the edge of his cloak to examine the embroidery. He endured it, refusing to shift his stance, glowering fit to match Tylin. Light, he had bought horses without so thorough an examination! Next, she would want to look at his teeth!

"The boy told you how he was injured," Anath said in frosty tones of command. "If you want him, then buy him and be done. The day has been long, and you should be in your bed."

Tuon paused, examining the long signet ring on his finger. It had been carved as a try-piece, to show the carver's skills, a running fox and two ravens in flight, all surrounded by crescent moons, and he had bought it by chance, though he had come to like it. He wondered whether she wanted it. Straightening, she stared up at his face. "Good advice, Anath," she said. "How much for him, Tylin? If he is a favorite, name your price, and I will double it."

Tylin choked on her wine and began coughing. Mat almost fell off his staff. The girl wanted to *buy* him? Well, she might as well have been looking at a horse for all the expression on her face.

"He is a free man, High Lady," Tylin said unsteadily when she could speak. "I . . . I cannot sell him." Mat could have laughed, if Tylin did not sound as though she were

trying to keep her teeth from chattering, if bloody Tuon had
not just asked his price. A free man! Ha!

The girl turned away from him as though dismissing him
from her mind. "You are afraid, Tylin, and under the Light,
you should not be." Gliding to Tylin's chair, she lifted her
veil with both hands, baring the lower half of her face, and
bent to kiss Tylin lightly, once on each eye and once on the
lips. Tylin looked astounded. "You are a sister to me, and to
Suroth," Tuon said in a surprisingly gentle voice. "I myself
will write your name as one of the Blood. You will be the
High Lady Tylin as well as Queen of Altara, and more, as
was promised you."

Anath snorted, loudly.

"Yes, Anath, I know," the girl sighed, straightening and
lowering her veil. "The day has been long and arduous, and
I am weary. But I will show Tylin what lands are in mind
for her, so she will know and be easy in her mind. There are
maps in my chambers, Tylin. You will honor me by accompanying me, there? I have excellent masseuses."

"The honor is mine," Tylin said, sounding not all that
much steadier than before.

At a gesture from the *so'jhin,* the yellow-haired man went
running to open the door and kneel holding it open, but there
was still all the smoothing and adjusting of clothes that
women had to do before they would go anywhere, Seanchan
or Altaran or from anywhere else. Though, the red-haired
da'covale performed the function for Tuon and Suroth. Mat
took the opportunity to draw Tylin a little aside, far enough
that he would not be overheard. The *so'jhin's* blue eyes kept
coming back to him, he realized, but at least Tuon, accepting the attentions of the slender *da'covale* woman, seemed
to have forgotten he existed.

"I didn't just fall down," he told Tylin softly. "The *gholam*
tried to kill me not much more than an hour ago. It might
be best if I left. That thing wants me, and it'll kill anybody
near me, too." The plan had just occurred to him, but he
thought it had a good chance of success.

Tylin sniffed. "He—it—it cannot have you, piglet." She
directed a look at Tuon that might have made the girl forget
about Tylin being a sister had she seen. "And neither can
she." At least she had sense enough to whisper.

"Who is she?" he asked. Well, it had never been more than a chance.

"The High Lady Tuon, and you know as much as I," Tylin replied, just as quietly. "Suroth jumps when she speaks, and she jumps when Anath speaks, though I would almost swear that Anath is some sort of servant. They are a very peculiar people, sweetling." Suddenly she flaked some mud from his cheek with one finger. He had not realized he had mud on his face, too. Suddenly, the eagle was strong in her eyes. "Do you recall the pink ribbons, sweetling? When I come back, we'll see how you look in pink."

She swanned out of the room with Tuon and Suroth, trailed by Anath and the *so'jhin* and the *da'covale,* leaving Mat with the grandmotherly serving woman who began to clean up the wine table. He sank into one of the bamboo carved chairs and rested his head in his hands.

Any other time, those pink ribbons would have had him gibbering. He never should have tried to get his own back with her. Even the *gholam* did not occupy much of his thoughts. The dice had stopped and . . . What? He had come face-to-face, or near enough, with three people he had not met before, but that could not be it. Maybe it was something to do with Tylin becoming one of the Blood. But always before, when the dice stopped, something had happened to him, personally.

He sat there worrying over it while the serving woman called in others to carry everything away, sat there until Tylin returned. She had not forgotten about the pink ribbons, and that made him forget about anything else for quite a long time.

CHAPTER 18

An Offer

The days after the *gholam* tried to kill him settled into rhythms that irritated Mat no end. The gray sky never altered, except to give rain or not.

There was talk in the streets of a man being killed by a wolf not far outside the city, his throat ripped. No one was worried, just curious; wolves had not been seen close to Ebou Dar in years. Mat worried. City people might believe a wolf would come that close to city walls, but he knew better. The *gholam* had not gone away. Harnan and the other Redarms stubbornly refused to leave, claiming they could watch his back, and Vanin refused without reasons, unless a muttered comment that Mat had a good eye for fast horses was supposed to be one. He spat after he said it, though. Riselle, her olive face pretty enough to make a man swallow, her big dark eyes knowing enough to dry his tongue, inquired about Olver's age, and when he said close on ten, she looked surprised and tapped her full lips thoughtfully, but if she changed anything in the boy's lessons, he still came away from them bubbling equally over her bosom and the books she read him. Mat thought Olver would almost have given up his nightly games of Snakes and Foxes for Riselle and the books. And when the lad ran out of the rooms that once had been Mat's, Thom often slipped in with his harp under his arm. By itself that was enough to make Mat grind his teeth, only that was not the half.

Thom and Beslan frequently went out together, not inviting him, and were gone for half the day, or half the night. Neither would say a word more about their schemes, though

Thom had the grace to look embarrassed. Mat hoped they were not going to get people killed for nothing, but they showed little interest in his opinions. Beslan glared at the very sight of him. Juilin continued to slip abovestairs and was seen by Suroth, which earned him a strapping hung up by his wrists from a stallpost in the stables. Mat saw his welts tended by Vanin—the man claimed doctoring men was the same as doctoring horses—and warned him it could be worse next time, but the fool was back on the upper floors that very night, still wincing from the weight of his shirt on his back. It had to be a woman, though the thief-catcher refused to say. Mat suspected one of the Seanchan noblewomen. One of the Palace servants could have met him in his own room, with Thom out of it so much.

Not Suroth or Tuon, to be sure, but they were not the only Seanchan High Blood in the Palace. Most of the Seanchan nobles rented rooms, or more often whole houses, in the city, but several had come with Suroth and a handful with the girl, too. More than one of the women looked a pleasant armful in spite of their crested heads and their way of staring down their noses at everybody without shaved temples. If they noticed them more than they did the furniture, that was. If it seemed unlikely that one of those haughty women would look twice at a man who slept in the servant's quarters, well, the Light knew women had peculiar tastes in men. He had no choice but to leave Juilin alone. Whoever the woman was, she might get the thief-catcher beheaded yet, but that sort of fever had to burn itself out before a man could think straight. Women did strange things to a man's head.

The newly arrived ships disgorged people and animals and cargo for days on end, enough that the city's massive walls would have burst from the inside had they all stayed, but they flowed through the city and out into the countryside with their families and their crafts and their livestock, prepared to put down roots. Soldiers passed through in thousands, too, well-ordered infantry and cavalry with the flair of veterans, moving north in bright-colored armor, and east across the river. Mat gave up trying to count them. Sometimes he saw strange creatures, though most of those were unloaded above the city to avoid the streets. *Torm* like three-eyed bronze-scaled cats the size of horses, sending most real horses around them into a frenzy just by their presence, and *corlm,* like hairy wingless birds as tall as a man, tall ears twitching constantly and long beaks seeming to yearn for flesh to rend, and huge *s'redit* with their long noses and longer tusks. *Raken* and the larger *to'raken* flew from their landing site below the Rahad, huge lizards spreading wings like bats and carrying men on their backs. The names were easy enough to pick up; any Seanchan soldier was eager to discuss the necessity of scouts on *raken* and the abilities of *corlm* at tracking, whether *s'redit* were useful for more than moving heavy loads and *torm* too intelligent to trust. He learned a great deal of interest from men who wanted what most soldiers did, a drink and a woman and a bit of a gamble, not necessarily in any given order. Those soldiers were indeed veterans. Seanchan was an Empire larger than all the nations between the Aryth Ocean and the Spine of the World, all under one Empress, but with a history of almost constant rebellions and revolts that kept its soldiers' skills keen. The farmers would be harder to dig out.

Not all the soldiers left, of course. A strong garrison remained, not only Seanchan, but steel-veiled Taraboner lancers and Amadician pikemen with their breastplates painted to resemble Seanchan armor. And Altarans, too, besides Tylin's House armsmen. According to the Seanchan, the Altarans from inland, with red slashes crisscrossing their breastplates, were Tylin's as much as the fellows guarding the Tarasin Palace, which, strangely, did not seem to best please her. It did not please the fellows from inland very much, either. They and the men in Mitsobar's green-and-white eyed each other like strange tomcats in a small room. There was plenty of glaring going on, Taraboners at Amadicians, Amadicians at Altarans, and the other way round, well-aged, long-standing animosities bubbling to the surface, but no one went further than shaken fists and a few curses. Five hundred men of the Deathwatch Guards had come off the ships and remained in Ebou Dar for some reason. The ordinary sort of crime expected in any large city had fallen off dramatically under the Seanchan, but the Guards took to patrolling the streets as if they expected cutpurses, bullyboys and maybe fully armed bands of brigands to spring out of the pavement. The Altarans and the Amadicians and the Taraboners kept their tempers reined in.

No one but a fool argued with the Deathwatch Guards, not more than once. And another contingent of the Guards had taken up residence in the city, too, a hundred Ogier, of all things, in the red-and-black. Sometimes they patrolled with the others, and sometimes they wandered about with their long-handled axes on their shoulders. They were not at all like Mat's friend Loial. Oh, they had the same wide noses and tufted ears and long eyebrows that drooped to their cheeks beside eyes the size of teacups, but the Gardeners looked at a man as though wondering whether he needed pruning of a few limbs. Nobody at all was fool enough to argue even once with the Gardeners.

Seanchan flowed out from Ebou Dar, and news flowed in. Even when they had to sleep in the attic, merchants preened in the common rooms of inns, smoking their pipes and telling what they knew that no one else did. So long as the telling did not affect their profits. The merchants' guards cared little for profits they would not share and told everything, some of it true. Seamen spread tales for anyone who would buy a mug of ale, or better, hot spiced wine, and when they had drunk enough, they talked even more, of ports they had visited, and events they had witnessed, and likely dreams they had had after the last time their heads were full of fumes. Still, it was clear the world outside Ebou Dar was seething like the Sea of Storms. Tales of Aiel loot-ing and burning came from everywhere, and armies were on the move other than the Seanchan, armies in Tear and Murandy, in Arad Doman and Andor, in Amadicia, which was not yet entirely under Seanchan control, and dozens of armed gatherings too small to be called armies in the heartland of Altara itself. Except for the men in Altara and Amadicia, no one really seemed sure who intended to fight whom, and there was some doubt about Altara. Altarans had a way of taking advantage of troubles to try paying off grievances against their neighbors.

The news that shook the city most, though, was of Rand. Mat tried his best not to think of him, or Perrin, but avoid-ing those odd swirls of color in his head was difficult when the Dragon Reborn was on everyone's lips. The Dragon Reborn was dead, some claimed, murdered by Aes Sedai, by the whole White Tower descending on him at once in Cairhien, or maybe it was in Illian, or Tear. No, they had kidnapped him, and he was held prisoner in the White Tower. No, he had gone to the White Tower on his own and sworn fealty to the Amyrlin Seat. The last gained great credence because a number of men claimed to have seen a proclamation, signed by Elaida herself, that announced as much. Mat had his doubts, about Rand being dead or swearing fealty, at least. For some odd reason, he felt sure he would know if Rand died, and as for the other, he did not believe the man would put himself within a hundred miles of the White Tower voluntarily. Dragon Reborn or no Dragon Reborn, he had to have more sense than that.

That news—all the versions of it—stirred the Seanchan the way a stick stirs an antheap. High-ranking officers strode the halls of the Tarasin Palace at every hour of the day and night, their odd, plumed helmets beneath their arms, their boots ringing on the floor tiles, their faces set. Couriers raced away from Ebou Dar, on horses and on *to'raken*. *Sul'dam* and *damane* began patrolling the streets instead of just standing guard at the gates, once more hunting for women who could channel. Mat kept out of the officers' way and nodded politely to the *sul'dam* when he passed one in the streets. Whatever Rand's situation was, he could do nothing about it in Ebou Dar. First, he had to get out of the city.

The morning after the *gholam* tried to kill him, Mat burned every last one of the long pink ribbons, the whole great wad of them, in the fireplace as soon as Tylin left her apartments. He also burned a pink coat she had had made for him, two pairs of pink breeches and a pink cloak. A stench of burning wool and silk filled the rooms, and he opened some windows to let it out, but he did not really care. He felt a great relief dressing himself in bright blue breeches and embroidered green coat, and a blue cloak with painfully ornate working. Even all the lace did not bother him. At least none of it was pink. He never wanted to *see* anything that particular color ever again!

Clapping his hat on his head, he stumped out of the Tarasin Palace with a renewed determination to find that cubbyhole to store what he needed for his escape, if he had to visit every tavern, inn and sailors' dive in the city ten times over. Even those in the Rahad. A hundred times! Gray gulls and black-winged skimmers swirled in leaden

sky that promised more rain, and an icy wind carrying the
tang of salt whipped across the Mol Hara, flailing cloaks
about. He thumped the paving stones as though intending to
crack every one. Light, if need be, he would go with Luca in
what he wore. Maybe Luca would let him work his way as a
buffoon! The man would probably insist on it. At least that
would keep him close to Aludra and her secrets.

He stalked the whole width of the square before he realized that he was in front of a wide white building he knew
well. The sign over the arched door proclaimed The Wandering Woman. A tall fellow in red-and-black armor strode
out, three thin black plumes on the front of the helmet under his arm, and stood waiting for his horse to be brought
around. A bluff-faced man with gray at his temples, he did
not look at Mat, and Mat avoided looking at him. No matter how pleasant the man might appear on the surface, he
was a Deathwatch Guard, after all, and a banner-general to
boot. The Wandering Woman, so near the Palace, had every
room rented by high Seanchan officers, and for that reason
he had not been back since he was able to walk again. Ordinary Seanchan soldiers were not such bad fellows, ready
to gamble half the night and buy a round when it came their
turn, but high-ranking officers might as well be nobles.
Still, he had to start somewhere.

The common room was almost as he remembered,
high-ceilinged and well-lighted by lamps burning on all
the walls despite the early hour. Solid shutters covered the
tall arched windows now, for warmth, and fires crackled
in both long fireplaces. A faint haze of pipesmoke filled
the air, and the smell of good cooking from the kitchens.
Two women with flutes and a fellow with a drum between
his knees were playing a quick, shrill Ebou Dari tune that
he nodded in time to. Not so different from when he had
stayed there, so far as it went. But all of the chairs held
Seanchan, now, some in armor, others in long, embroidered
coats, drinking, talking, studying maps spread out on the
tables. A graying woman with the flame of a *der'sul'dam*
embroidered on her shoulder seemed to be making a report
at one table, and at another a skinny *sul'dam* with a round-
faced *damane* at her heels appeared to be getting orders.
A number of the Seanchan had the sides and backs of their
heads shaved so they seemed to be wearing bowls, with the

hair remaining at the back left long in a sort of wide tail that hung to the shoulders on men and often to the waist on women. Those were simple lords and ladies, not High anything, but that hardly mattered. A lord was a lord, and besides, the men and women going to fetch a serving maid for more drinks had the smooth-cheeked disdainful look of officers themselves, which meant the folk they were fetching for had rank to cause a man trouble. Several noticed him and frowned, and he almost left.

Then he saw the innkeeper coming down the railless stairs at the back of the room, a stately hazel-eyed woman with large golden hoops in her ears and a little gray in her hair. Setalle Anan was not Ebou Dari, or even Altaran he suspected, but she wore the marriage-knife, hanging hilt-down from a silver collar into a deep narrow neckline, and a long curved blade at her waist. She knew he was supposed to be a lord, but he was not sure how far she believed any longer or what good it would do if she still swallowed the whole faradiddle. In any case, she saw him at the same instant and smiled, a friendly, welcoming smile that made her face even prettier. There was nothing for it but to go and greet her and ask after her health, not too elaborately. Her muscular husband was a fishing-boat captain with more dueling scars than Mat wanted to think about. Straight off she wanted to know about Nynaeve and Elayne, and to his surprise, whether he knew anything about the Kin. He had had no idea she had even heard of them.

"They went with Nynaeve and Elayne," he whispered, cautiously keeping watch to make sure no Seanchan was paying them any mind. He did not intend to say too much, but talking about the Kin where Seanchan might hear made the back of his neck prickle. "So far as I know, they're all safe."

"Good. I would be pained had any of them been collared." The fool woman did not even lower her voice!

"Yes; that's good," he muttered, and hurriedly explained his needs before she could start shouting how happy she was that women who could channel had escaped the Seanchan. He was happy, too, just not happy enough to put himself in chains for joy.

Shaking her head, she seated herself on the steps and put her hands on her knees. Her dark green skirts, sewn up on the left side, showed red petticoats. Ebou Dari really did seem to knock Tinkers on their heels when it came to choosing colors. The buzz of Seanchan voices fought with the high-pitched music all around them, and she sat there looking at him sternly. "You don't know our ways, that is the trouble," she said. "Pretties are an old and honored custom in Altara. Many a young man or woman has a final fling as a pretty, pampered and showered with presents, before settling down. But you see, a pretty leaves when she chooses. Tylin shouldn't be treating you as I hear she is. Still," she added judiciously, "I must say she dresses you well." She made a circling motion with one hand. "Hold out your cloak and turn around so I can get a better look."

Mat drew a deep, calming breath. And then three more. The color flooding his face was sheer fury. He was not blushing. Certainly not! Light, did the whole city know? "Do you have a space I can use or don't you?" he demanded in a strangled voice.

It turned out that she did. He could use a shelf in her cellar, which she said stayed dry year round, and there was the small hollow under the kitchen's stone floor where he once had kept his chest of gold. It turned out the rental price was for him to hold out his cloak and turn around so she could get a better look. She grinned like a cat! One of the Seanchan, a buzzard-faced woman in red-and-blue armor, enjoyed the show so much that she tossed him a fat silver coin with strange markings, a forbidding woman's face on one side and some sort of heavy chair on the other.

Still, he had his place to store clothes and money, and once he returned to the Palace, to Tylin's apartments, he found out he had clothes to store in it.

"I fear my Lord's garments are in a terrible state," Nerim said lugubriously. The skinny, gray-haired Cairhienin would have been as dolorous announcing the gift of a sack of firedrops, though. His long face was perpetually in mourning. He did keep an eye on the door against Tylin's return, however. "Everything is quite filthy, and I am afraid mildew has ruined several of my Lord's best coats."

"They were all in a cupboard with Prince Beslan's childhood toys, my Lord," Lopin laughed, tugging at the lapels of a dark coat like Juilin's. The balding man was the reverse of Nerim, stout instead of bony, dark instead of pale, his round belly always shaking with laughter. For a time after Nalesean's death it had seemed he intended to compete with Nerim at sighing, the way they did over everything else, but the intervening weeks had recovered him to his normal self. As long as no one mentioned his former master, anyway. "They are dusty, though, my Lord. I doubt anyone has been in that cupboard since the Prince put his toy soldiers away."

Feeling that his luck was running strong at last, Mat told them to start taking his clothes across to The Wandering Woman a few pieces at a time, and a pocket full of gold each trip. His black-hafted spear, propped in a corner of Tylin's bedchamber with his unstrung Two Rivers bow, would have to wait for last. Getting that out might be as difficult as getting himself out. He could always make a new bow for himself, but he was not going to abandon the *ashandarei*.

I paid too high a price for the bloody thing to leave it, he thought, fingering the scar hidden beneath the scarf around his neck. One of the first, among too many. Light, it would be nice to think that he had more to look forward to than scars and battles he did not want. And a wife he did not want or even know. There had to be more than that. First came getting out of Ebou Dar with a whole hide, though. That above all else, first.

Lopin and Nerim bowed themselves out of his presence with the equivalent of two fat purses spread about their clothing, so as not to create any bulges, but no sooner had they gone than Tylin appeared, wanting to know why his bodyservants were running in the halls as though racing each other. If he had been feeling suicidal he could have told her they were racing to see who would be first to reach the inn with his gold, or maybe just the first to start cleaning his clothes. Instead he busied himself diverting her, and soon enough that chased any other thoughts out of his head, except for a glimmer that his luck had finally begun to pay off at something besides gambling. All it needed to put the cap on would be for Aludra to give him what he wanted before he left. Tylin put her mind to what she was doing, and for a time he forgot fireworks and Aludra and escaping. For a time.

After a little searching through the city, he finally located a bellfounder. There were a number of gong-makers in Ebou Dar, but only one bellmaker, with a foundry outside the western wall. The bellmaker, a cadaverous, impatient fellow, sweated in the heat of his huge iron furnace. The sweltering foundry's one long room might have been some sort of torture chamber. Hoisting chains dangled from the rafters, and sudden flames gouted from the furnace, throwing flickering shadows and leaving Mat half-blind. And no sooner would he blink away the afterimage of raging fire than another eruption would leave him squinting again. Workmen dripping with sweat poured molten bronze from the furnace's melting pot into a square mold, half again as tall as a man, that had been levered into position on rollers. Other great molds like it stood around the stone floor, amid a litter of smaller molds in various sizes.

"My Lord is pleased to jest." Master Sutoma forced a chuckle, but he did not look amused, with his damp black hair hanging down and clinging to his face. His chuckle sounded as hollow as his cheeks, and he kept shooting frowns at his workmen as though suspecting they would lie down and go to sleep if he did not maintain a close watch on them. A dead man could not have slept in that heat. Mat's shirt stuck to him damply, and he was beginning to sweat his coat through in patches. "I know nothing of Illuminators, my Lord, and I wish to know nothing. Useless fripperies, fireworks. Not like bells. If my Lord will excuse me? I am very busy. The High Lady Suroth has commissioned thirteen bells for a victory set, the largest bells ever cast anywhere. And Calwyn Sutoma will cast them!" That it was a victory over his own city did not seem to bother Sutoma in the least. The last was enough to make him grin and rub his bony hands together.

Mat attempted to make Aludra relent, but the woman might as well have been cast bronze herself. Well, she was considerably softer than bronze once she finally let him put an arm around her, yet kisses that left her trembling did nothing to slacken her resolve.

"Me, I do not believe in telling a man more than he needs to know," she said breathlessly, sitting beside him on a padded bench in her wagon. She allowed no more than kisses, but she was very enthusiastic about those. The thin beaded braids she had taken to wearing again were a tangle. "Men gossip, yes? Chatter, chatter, chatter, and you yourselves don't know what you will say next. Besides, maybe I have made you the puzzle just to make you return, yes?" And she set about further disarraying her hair, and his as well.

She put up no more nightflowers, though, not after he told her about the chapter house in Tanchico. He tried two more visits to Master Sutoma, but on the second, the bell-maker had the doors barred against him. He was casting the largest bells ever made, and no foolish foreigner with foolish questions would be allowed to interfere with that.

Tylin began lacquering the first two fingernails on each hand green, though she did not shave the sides of her head. She would, eventually, she told him, pulling her flowing hair back with her hands to study herself in the gilt-framed mirror on the bedchamber wall, but she wanted to become used to the idea first. She was making her accommodations with the Seanchan, and he could not fault her for it, no matter how many dark scowls Beslan gave his mother.

There was no way she could suspect anything about Aludra, but the day after he first kissed the Illuminator, the grandmotherly maids disappeared from her chambers, replaced by women white-haired and wizened. Tylin began sticking her curved belt knife into one of the bedposts at night, close to hand, and musing aloud in his hearing about how he would look in a *da'covale*'s sheer robes. In fact, night was not the only time she stuck her knife in the bedpost. Grinning serving women started delivering summonses to Tylin's rooms by simply telling him that she had stabbed the bedpost, and he started trying to avoid any woman in livery he saw with a smile on her face. It was not that he disliked being bedded by Tylin, aside from the fact she was a queen, as snooty as any other noblewoman. And the fact that she made him feel like a mouse that had been made a pet by a cat. But there were only so many hours of daylight, if more than he was used to back home in winter, and for a bit he had to wonder whether she meant to consume all of them.

Luckily, Tylin began spending more and more time with Suroth and Tuon. Her accommodations seemed to have embraced friendship, with Tuon at least. No one could be friends with Suroth. Tylin seemed to have adopted the girl, or the girl had adopted her. Tylin told him little of what they talked about except in the sketchiest outlines, and often not even that, but they closeted themselves alone for hours, and swept along the Palace corridors conversing quietly, or sometimes laughing. Frequently Anath or Selucia, Tuon's golden-haired *so'jhin,* trailed along behind, and now and then a pair of hard-eyed Deathwatch Guards.

He still could not figure out the relationship between Suroth, Tuon and Anath. On the surface, Suroth and Tuon behaved as equals, calling each other by name, laughing at one another's jests. Tuon certainly never gave Suroth any order, at least not in his hearing, but Suroth seemed to take Tuon's suggestions as orders. Anath, on the other hand, badgered the girl unmercifully with razor-sharp criticisms, calling her a fool and worse.

"This is the worst sort of stupidity, girl," he heard her say coldly one midday in the halls. Tylin had not sent her crude summons—yet—and he was trying to sneak out before she could, slipping along the walls and peeking around corners. He had a visit to Sutoma planned, and another to Aludra. The three Seanchan women—four, counting Selucia, but he did not think they saw it that way—were clustered just around the next turning. Trying to keep an eye out for serving women wearing a smile, he waited impatiently for them to move. Whatever they were talking about, they would not appreciate him blundering by in the middle of it. "A taste of the strap will set you right, and clear your head of nonsense," the tall woman went on in a voice like ice. "Ask for it and be done."

Mat worked a finger in his ear, and shook his head. He must have misheard. Selucia, standing placidly with her hands folded at her waist, certainly never turned a hair.

Suroth gasped, though. "Surely you will punish her for this!" she drawled angrily, glaring holes through Anath. Or trying to. Suroth might as well have been a chair for all the notice the tall woman gave her.

"You do not understand, Suroth." Tuon's sigh stirred the veil covering her face. Covering but not concealing. She looked . . . resigned. He had been shocked to learn she was only a few years younger than he. He would have said more like ten. Well, six or seven. "The omens say otherwise, Anath," the girl said calmly, and not at all in anger. She was simply stating facts. "Be assured, I will tell you if they change."

Someone tapped him on the shoulder, and he looked

back into the face of a serving woman wearing a broad grin. Well, he had not really been that anxious to go out right away.

Tuon troubled him. Oh, when they passed in the hallways, he made his best leg politely, and in return she ignored him as completely as Suroth or Anath did, but it began to seem to him that they passed in the hallways a little too often.

One afternoon, he walked into Tylin's apartments, having checked and found out that Tylin was shut up with Suroth on some business or other, and in the bedchamber, he found Tuon examining his *ashandarei*. He froze at the sight of her fingering the words in the Old Tongue carved into the black shaft. A raven in some still darker metal was inlaid at each end of the line of script, and a pair of them engraved on the slightly curved blade. Ravens were an Imperial sigil, to the Seanchan. Not breathing, he tried to move backwards without making a sound.

That veiled face swivelled toward him. A pretty face, really, it might even have been beautiful if she ever stopped looking as though she was about to bite off a mouthful of wood. He no longer thought she looked like a boy—those tight wide belts she always wore made sure you noticed what curves there were—but she was the next thing to it. He seldom saw a grown woman younger than his grandmother that he did not at least think idly of what it would be like dancing with her, maybe kissing her, even those snooty Seanchan Blood, but never a glimmer of that crossed his mind with Tuon. A woman had to have something to put an arm around, or what was the point?

"I don't see Tylin owning a thing like this," she drawled coolly, setting the long-bladed spear back next to his bow, "so it must be yours. What is it? How did you come to possess it?" Those cold demands for information set his jaw. The bloody woman could have been ordering a servant. Light, as far as he was aware, she did not even know his name! Tylin said she had never asked about him or mentioned him since the offer of purchase.

"It's called a spear, my Lady," he said, resisting the urge to lean against the doorframe and tuck his thumbs behind his belt. She was Seanchan Blood, after all. "I bought it."

"I will give you ten times the price you paid," she said. "Name it."

He almost laughed. He wanted to, and not for pleasure, that was certain sure. No *would you think of selling,* just *I will buy it and here is what I will pay.* "The price wasn't gold, my Lady." Involuntarily, his hand went to the black scarf to make sure it still hid the ridged scar that encircled his neck. "Only a fool would pay it one time, let alone ten."

She studied him for a moment, her expression unreadable no matter how sheer her veil. And then, he might as well have vanished. She glided past him as though he were no longer there and swept out of the apartments.

That was not the only time he encountered her alone. Of course, she was not always followed by Anath or Selucia, or guards, yet it seemed to him that rather too often he would decide to go back for something and turn to find her by herself, looking at him, or he might leave a room suddenly and find her outside the door. More than once he looked over his shoulder leaving the Palace and saw her veiled face peering out of a window. True, there was nothing of staring about it. She looked at him and glided away as though he had ceased to exist, peered from a window and turned back into the room as soon as he saw her. He was a stand-lamp in the corridor, a paving stone in the Mol Hara. It began to make him nervous, though. After all, the woman had offered to *buy* him. A thing like that had a tendency to make a man nervous by its own self.

Even Tuon could not truly upset his welling sense that things were finally coming right, though. The *gholam* did not return, and he began to think maybe it had gone on an easier "harvest." In any event, he was staying away from dark and lonely places where it might have a chance at him. His medallion was all very well for what it did, but a good crowd was better. On his latest visit to Aludra she had almost let something slip—he was certain of it—before coming to herself and hastily bundling him out of her wagon. There was nothing a woman would not tell you if you kissed her enough. He stayed away from The Wandering Woman, to avoid rousing Tylin's suspicions, but Nerim and Lopin stealthily transferred his real clothing to the inn's cellar. Bit by bit, half the contents of the iron-bound chest under Tylin's bed traveled across the Mol Hara to the hidden hollow beneath the inn's kitchen.

That hollow under the kitchen floor began to trouble him,

see him, frowning as soon as he approached her. Two men had died by his hand in the inn when he was staying there; thieves who were trying to split his skull, to be sure, but that sort of thing did not happen at The Wandering Woman. She had made it clear she was happy to see the back of him when he moved out.

Marah was hardly interested in what he wanted now, either, and he could not really explain. Only Mistress Anan knew what was hidden in the kitchen, so he devoutly hoped, and he certainly was not about to bleat out the information in the common room. So he made up a tale about missing the dishes the cook turned out, and eyeing that blatantly sewn skirt, he slipped in the implication that he had missed looking at her even more. He could not understand why exposing a little more petticoat was scandalous when every woman in Ebou Dar walked around showing half her bosom, but if Marah was feeling rakish, maybe a few blandishments might ease his path. He gave her his very best smile.

Giving him half an ear in return, Marah seized a passing serving maid, a smoky-eyed cat of a woman he knew well. "Air Captain Yulan's cup is almost empty, Caira," Marah said angrily. "You are supposed to keep it full! If you can't do your job, girl, there are plenty in Ebou Dar who will!" Caira, several years older than Marah, made her a mocking curtsy. And scowled at Mat. Before Caira could straighten her knees again, Marah turned to grab a boy who was walking by carefully balancing a tray piled with dirty dishes. "Stop lollygagging, Ross!" she snapped. "There is work to be done. Do it, or I'll take you out to the stables, and you will not like that, I tell you!"

Marah's youngest brother glared at her. "I can't wait till spring, when I can work on the boats again," he muttered sullenly. "You've been in a bad skin ever since Frielle got married, just because she's younger than you and you haven't been asked yet."

She directed a cuff at his head that he easily eluded, though the stacked cups and plates rattled and nearly fell. "Why not just pin up your petticoats at the fishing docks?" he shouted, darting off before she could slap at him again.

Mat sighed as she finally turned her full attention to him. Pinning up petticoats was a new one on him, but from

Marah's face, he could guess. Steam should have been jetting from her ears. "If you want to eat, you must come back later. Or you can wait, if you like. I don't know how long before you can be served."

Her smile was malicious. No one would choose to wait in that common room. Every seat was taken by a Seanchan, and there were more Seanchan standing, enough that the aproned maids were forced to weave their way carefully, holding trays of food and drink aloft. Caira was filling the dark little man's cup and offering him the sort of sultry smiles she had once offered Mat. He did not know why she had soured on him, but he had as many women in his life as he could handle at the moment. What was an Air Captain, anyway? He would have to find out. Later.

"I will wait in the kitchen," he told Marah. "I want to tell Enid how much I enjoyed her cooking."

She started to protest, but a Seanchan woman raised her voice demanding wine. Grim-eyed in blue-and-green armor, with a helmet carrying two plumes under her arm, she wanted her stirrup cup right then. All of the maids seemed occupied, so Marah grimaced at him one last time and went scurrying, trying to set her face in a pleasant smile. And not getting far with it. Holding his walking staff wide, Mat flourished a bow to her retreating back.

The good smells that had mingled with sweet pipesmoke in the common room permeated the kitchen, roasting fish, baking bread, meats sizzling on the spits. The room was hot from the iron stoves and the ovens and the fire in the long brick fireplace, and six sweating women and three potboys were dashing about under the orders of the chief cook. Wearing a snowy white apron as if it were a tabard of office and wielding a long-handled wooden spoon to reign over her domain, Enid was the roundest woman Mat had ever seen. He did not think he could have gotten his arms around her had he wanted to. She recognized him right away, and a sly grin split her wide olive face.

"So, you found out I was right," she said, pointing the spoon at him. "You squeezed the wrong melon, and it turned out the melon was a lionfish in disguise and you were just a plump grunter." Throwing back her head, she cackled with laughter.

Mat forced a grin. Blood and bloody ashes! Everybody

really did know! *I have to get out of this bloody city,* he thought grimly, *or I'll hear them bloody laughing at me the rest of my life!*

Suddenly his fears about the gold began to seem foolish. The gray floorstone in front of the stoves appeared firmly in place, no different from any other in the kitchen. You had to know the trick in order to lift it. Lopin and Nerim would have told him if so much as a single coin had vanished between their visits. Mistress Anan likely would have tracked down and skinned the culprit if anyone tried thieving in her inn. He might as well be on his way. Maybe Aludra's willpower would be weaker at this hour. Maybe she would give him breakfast. He had slipped out of the Palace without waiting to eat.

So as not to rouse curiosity about his visit, he did tell Enid how much he had enjoyed her gilded fish, how it was better than that served in the Tarasin Palace, without having to exaggerate even a whisker. Enid was a marvel. The woman positively beamed, and to his surprise, lifted one out of the oven onto a platter just for him. Somebody in the common room could just wait, she told him, setting the platter at the end of the kitchen's long work-table. A wave of her spoon brought a stout potboy with a stool.

Looking at the golden-crusted flatfish, he felt his mouth watering. Aludra likely would be no weaker now than any other time. And if she was upset over being disturbed so early, she might not give him breakfast. His stomach rumbled loudly. Hanging his cloak on a peg beside the door to the stableyard and propping his walking staff beneath, he tucked his hat under the stool and turned back his lace to keep it out of the platter.

By the time Mistress Anan came in through the door to the stableyard, swinging her cloak off and shaking rain onto the floor, little remained beyond a tangy taste on his tongue and fine white bones on the platter. He had learned to enjoy a number of odd things since coming to Ebou Dar, but he left the eyes staring up at him. The things were on the same side of the fish's head!

Another woman slipped in behind Mistress Anan as he dabbed his mouth with a linen napkin. She closed the door behind her quickly, and kept her damp cloak on with the hood pulled well up. Rising, he caught a glimpse of the face inside that hood and nearly knocked his stool over. He thought he covered well, though, making a leg to the women, but his head was spinning.

"It is well you are here, my Lord," Mistress Anan said briskly, handing her cloak to a potboy. "I would have sent for you, otherwise. Enid, clear the kitchen, please, and watch the door. I need to speak with the young lord alone."

The cook briskly herded the under-cooks and potboys out into the stableyard, and despite their muttered complaints about the rain and wails about the food burning, it was clear they were as accustomed to this as Enid. She herself did not even glance at Mistress Anan and her companion again before hurrying through the door into the common room with her long spoon held up like a sword.

"What a surprise," Joline Maza said, tossing her hood back. Her dark woolen dress, with a deep neckline in the local style, fit loosely and looked worn and frayed. You would never have thought it from her carefree attitude, though. "When Mistress Anan told me she knew a man who might take me with him when he left Ebou Dar, I never guessed it was you." Pretty and brown-eyed, she had a smile almost as warm as Caira's. And an ageless face that screamed Aes Sedai. With dozens of Seanchan just the other side of a door guarded by a cook with a spoon.

Removing her cloak, Joline turned to hang it on one of the pegs, and Mistress Anan made an irritated sound in her throat. "That isn't safe yet, Joline," she said, sounding more as if talking to one of her daughters than to an Aes Sedai. "Until I have you safely—"

Suddenly a commotion rose at the door to the common room, Enid protesting in a shout that no one could enter, and a voice almost as loud, in Seanchan accents, demanding that she move aside.

Ignoring the protests of his leg, Mat moved faster than he thought he ever had in his life, grabbing Joline by the waist and plunking himself down on the bench by the door to the stableyard with the Aes Sedai on his lap. Hugging her close, he pretended to be kissing her. It was a fool way to try hiding her face, but all he could think of short of throwing her cloak over her head. She gasped indignantly, but fear widened her eyes when she finally heard the Seanchan voice,

and she snaked her arms around him in a flash. Praying for
his luck to hold, he watched the door open.

Still protesting loudly, Enid backed into the kitchen
thumping away with her spoon at the *so'jhin* with a wet
cloak hanging down his back who was pushing her ahead
of him. A heavyset scowling man with a stub of a braid that
did not even come close to reaching his shoulder, he fended
off most of her blows with his free hand and seemed to ignore the few he could not. He was the first *so'jhin* Mat had
seen with a beard, and it gave him a lopsided look, running
down the right side of his chin and up the left to stop dead at
the middle of his ear. A tall woman with sharp blue eyes in
a pale stern face followed him, flinging back an elaborately
embroidered blue cloak, held at her throat by a large silver
pin shaped like a sword, to reveal a pleated dress of a paler
blue. Her short dark hair was cut in the bowl, the rest shaved
off all the way around above her ears. Still, she was better
than a *sul'dam* with a *damane*. A little better. Realizing the
battle was lost, Enid backed away from the man, but by the
way she gripped her spoon and glared, she was ready to leap
on him again in a heartbeat if Mistress Anan gave the word.

"A fellow out front did say he did see the innkeeper going
round the back," the *so'jhin* announced. He was looking at
Setalle, but eyeing Enid warily. "If you be Setalle Anan,
then know this do be Captain of the Green Lady Egeanin
Tamarath, and she do have an order for rooms signed by
the High Lady Suroth Sabelle Meldarath herself." His tone
altered, becoming less a pronouncement and more the voice
of a man wanting accommodations. "Your best rooms,
mind, with a good bed, a view of the square out there, and a
fireplace that no does smoke."

Mat gave a start when the man spoke, and Joline, perhaps thinking someone was coming toward them, moaned
against his mouth in fear. Her eyes shone with unshed tears,
and she trembled in his arms. The Lady Egeanin Tamarath
glanced at the bench when Joline moaned, then grimaced
in disgust and turned so she could avoid seeing the pair. It
was the man who intrigued Mat, though. How in the Light
did an Illianer come to be *so'jhin*? And the fellow looked
familiar, somehow. Likely another of those thousands of
long-dead faces he could not help recalling.

"I am Setalle Anan, and my best rooms are occupied by Captain of the Air Lord Abaldar Yulan," Mistress Anan said calmly, unintimidated by *so'jhin* or Blood. She folded her arms beneath her breasts. "My second-best rooms are occupied by Banner-General Furyk Karede. Of the Death-watch Guards. I don't know whether a Captain of the Green outranks them, but either way, you will have to sort out for yourselves who stays and who has to go elsewhere. I have a firm policy of not expelling any Seanchan guest. So long as he pays his rent."

Mat tensed, waiting for the explosion—Suroth would have her flogged for half that!—but Egeanin smiled. "It's a pleasure to deal with someone who has a little nerve," she drawled. "I think we'll get on just fine, Mistress Anan. So long as you don't take nerve too far. Captain gives the orders, and crew obeys, but I never made anyone crawl on my deck." Mat frowned. Deck. A ship's deck. Why did that tug at something in his head? Those old memories were a nuisance, sometimes.

Mistress Anan nodded, never taking her dark eyes from the Seanchan's blue. "As you say, my Lady. But I hope you will remember that The Wandering Woman is my ship." Luckily for her, the Seanchan woman had a sense of humor. She laughed.

"Then you be captain of your ship," she chuckled, "and I will be Captain of the Gold." Whatever that meant. With a sigh, Egeanin shook her head. "Light's truth, I don't out-rank many here, I suspect, but Suroth wants me close at hand, so some move down, and somebody moves out unless they want to double up." Suddenly she frowned, half glancing toward Mat and Joline, and her lip curled in distaste. "I trust you don't let that sort of thing go on everywhere, Mistress Anan?"

"I assure you, you will never see the like again under my roof," the innkeeper replied smoothly.

The *so'jhin* was frowning at Mat and the woman on his lap, too, and Egeanin had to tug at his coatsleeve before he gave a start and followed her back into the common room. Mat grunted contemptuously. The fellow could pretend to be outraged like his mistress all he wanted; Mat had heard about festivals in Illian, though, and they were almost as bad as festivals in Ebou Dar when it came to people running around half-clothed or less. No better than *da'covale,* or those shea dancers the soldiers went on about.

He tried to ease Joline from his lap when the door swung shut behind the pair, but she clung to him and buried her face on his shoulder, weeping softly. Enid heaved a great sigh and sagged against the worktable as though her bones had softened. Even Mistress Anan appeared shaken. She dropped onto the stool Mat had vacated and put her head in her hands. Only for a moment, though, and then she was back on her feet.

"Count to fifty and then get everyone in out of the rain, Enid," she said briskly. No one would have known that she had been trembling a moment earlier. Gathering Joline's cloak from its peg, she took a long splinter from a box on the mantelpiece and bent to light it in the fire beneath the spits. "I will be in the cellar if you need me, but if anyone asks, you don't know where I am. Until I say otherwise, no one but you or I goes down there." Enid nodded as though this was nothing out of the ordinary. "Bring her," the innkeeper told Mat, "and don't dawdle. Carry her if you must."

He did have to carry her. Still weeping almost soundlessly, Joline would not loosen her hold on him or even lift her head from his shoulder. She was not heavy, thank the Light, yet even so, a dull ache began in his leg as he followed Mistress Anan to the cellar door with his burden. He might have enjoyed it in spite of the throbbing, if Mistress Anan had not taken her time about everything.

As though there were no Seanchan within a hundred miles she lit a lamp on a shelf beside the heavy door and carefully blew out the splinter before replacing the tall glass mantle, then laid the smoking splinter on a small tin tray. Unhurriedly producing a long key from her belt pouch, she undid the iron lock and, finally, motioned him to go through. The stairs beyond were wide enough to bring up a barrel, yet steep, vanishing into darkness. He obeyed, but waited on the second step while she drew the door shut and re-locked it, waited for her to take the lead with the lamp held high. The last thing he needed was a tumble.

"Do you do this often?" he asked, shifting Joline. She had stopped her crying, but she still held tight to him, trembling. "I mean, hiding Aes Sedai?"

"I heard whispers there was a sister still in the city,"

Mistress Anan replied, "and I managed to find her before
the Seanchan did. I couldn't leave a sister to them." She
glared back over her shoulder, daring him to say different.
He wanted to, but he could not make the words come. He
supposed he would have helped anyone get away from the
Seanchan, if he could, and he owed a debt to Joline Maza.

The Wandering Woman was a well-stocked inn, and the
dark cellar was large. Aisles stretched between barrels of
wine and ale stacked on their sides, high, slatted bins of
potatoes and turnips that stood up off the stone floor, rows
of tall shelves holding sacks of dried beans and peas and
peppers, mounds of wooden crates holding the Light alone
knew what. There appeared to be little dust, but the air had
the dry smell common to sound storerooms.

He spotted his clothes, neatly folded on a cleared shelf—
unless someone else was storing garments down there—but
he had no chance to look at them. Mistress Anan led the
way to the far end of the cellar, where he set Joline down
on an upturned keg. He had to pry her arms free in order
to leave her huddled there. Sniveling, she pulled a handkerchief from her sleeve and dabbed at red-rimmed eyes. With
her face blotchy, she was hardly the image of an Aes Sedai,
never mind her worn dress.

"Her nerve is broken," Mistress Anan said, putting
the lamp on a barrel that also stood on end, the bung in
its end gone. Several other empty barrels stood about the
floor where others had been removed, awaiting return to
the brewer. It was as close to a clear space as he had seen
in the cellar. "She's been hiding ever since the Seanchan
came. The last few days, her Warders have had to move her
several times when Seanchan decided to search a building
instead of just the streets. Enough to break anyone's nerve, I
suppose. I doubt they will try to search here, though."

Thinking of all those officers upstairs, Mat had to con-
cede she was probably right. Still, he was glad it was not
him taking the risk. Squatting in front of Joline, he grunted
at a stab of pain up his leg. "I will help you if I can," he said.
How, he could not have said, but there was that debt. "Just
be glad you were lucky enough to dodge them all this time.
Teslyn wasn't so lucky."

Snatching the handkerchief from her eyes, Joline glared
at him. "Luck?" she spat angrily. It she had been other than

Aes Sedai, he would have said she was sullen, sticking her lower lip out that way. "I could have escaped! It was all confusion the first day, as I understand. But I was unconscious. Fen and Blaeric barely managed to carry me out of the Palace before the Seanchan swarmed over it, and two men carrying a limp woman attracted too much attention for them to get anywhere near the city gates before they were secured. I am glad Teslyn was caught! Glad! She gave me something; I am sure she did! That is why Fen and Blaeric couldn't wake me, why I have been sleeping in stables and hiding in alleys, afraid those monsters would find me. It serves her right!"

Mat blinked at the tirade. He doubted he had ever heard so much pure venom in a voice before, even in those old memories. Mistress Anan frowned at Joline, and her hand twitched.

"Anyway, I'll help you as much as I can," he said hurriedly, rising so he could move between the two women. He would not put it past Mistress Anan to slap Joline, Aes Sedai or no Aes Sedai, and Joline looked in no mood to consider the possibility of a *damane* being upstairs to feel whatever she did in retaliation. It was a simple truth; the Creator made women so men would not find life too easy. How in the Light was he to get an Aes Sedai out of Ebou Dar? "I'm in debt to you."

A tiny frown wrinkled Joline's brow. "In debt?"

"The note asking me to warn Nynaeve and Elayne," he said slowly. He licked his lips and added, "The one you left on my pillow."

She flicked a hand dismissively, but her eyes, focused on his face, never blinked. "All debts between us are settled the day you help me get outside the city walls, Master Cauthon," she said, in tones as regal as a queen on her throne.

Mat swallowed hard. The note had been stuck into his coat pocket somehow, not left on his pillow. And that meant he was mistaken about who he owed the debt to.

He made his leave without calling Joline on her lie—a lie even if only by letting his mistake pass—and he left without telling Mistress Anan, either. It was his problem. It made him feel sick. He wished he had never found out.

Back in the Tarasin Palace, he went straight to Tylin's apartments and spread his cloak over a chair to dry. A

pounding rain beat against the windows. Putting his hat
atop one of the carved and gilded wardrobes, he toweled his
face and hands dry and considered changing his coat. The
rain had soaked through his cloak in a few places. His coat
was damp here and there. Damp. Light!

Growling in disgust, he wadded up the striped towel
and threw it on the bed. He was delaying, even hoping—a
little—that Tylin might walk in and stab the bedpost, so he
could put off what he had to do. What he had to do. Joline
had left him with no choice.

The Palace was laid out simply, if you cared to look at
it that way. Servants lived on the lowest level, where the
kitchens were, and some in the cellars. The next floor up
contained the spacious public rooms and the cramped studies of the clerks, and the third apartments for less favored
guests, most occupied now by Seanchan Blood. The highest
floor held Tylin's apartments, and rooms for more favored
guests, like Suroth and Tuon and a few others. Except, even
palaces had attics, of a sort.

Pausing at the foot of a flight of stairs hidden around
an innocuous corner where they would not be noticed,
Mat drew a deep breath before going up slowly. The huge
windowless room at the top of the stairs, low-ceiling and
floored with rough planks, had been cleared of whatever it
held before the Seanchan, and the space filled with a grid
of tiny wooden rooms, each with its own closed door. Plain
iron stand-lamps lit the narrow halls between. The rain
beating down on the roof tiles was loud here, just overhead.
He paused again on the top step, and only breathed again
when he realized that he could hear no footsteps. A woman
was crying in one of the tiny rooms, but no *sul'dam* was going to appear and demand to know what he was doing there.
Likely they would learn he had been, but not until after he
found out what he needed, if he was quick.

He did not know which room was hers, was the trouble.
He walked to the first and opened the door long enough
to peek in. An Atha'an Miere woman in a gray dress was
sitting on the side of a narrow bed, hands folded in her
lap. The bed and a washstand with bowl and pitcher and a
tiny mirror took up most of the room. Several gray dresses
hung from pegs on the wall. The segmented silver leash of
an *a'dam* ran in an arc from the silver collar around her

neck to a silver bracelet looped over a hook set in the wall. She could reach any part of the tiny room. The small holes where her earrings and nose ring had been had not yet had time to heal. They looked like wounds. When the door opened, her head came up with a fearful expression that faded into speculation. And maybe hope.

He closed the door without saying a word. *I can't save all of them,* he thought harshly. *I can't!* Light, but he hated this.

The next doors revealed identical rooms and three more Sea Folk women, one of them weeping loudly on her bed, and then a sleeping yellow-haired woman, all with their *a'dam* loosely stretched to hooks. He eased that door shut as though he were trying to filch one of Mistress al'Vere's pies right under her nose. Maybe the yellow-haired woman was not Seanchan, but he was not about to take the chance. A dozen doors later, he exhaled heavily in relief and slipped inside, pulling the door shut behind him.

Teslyn Baradon lay on the bed, her face pillowed on her hands. Only her dark eyes moved, stabbing at him. She said nothing, just looked at him as though trying to bore holes in his skull.

"You put a note in my coat pocket," he said softly. The walls were thin; he could still hear the weeping woman. "Why?"

"Elaida does want those girls as much as she ever wanted the staff and stole," Teslyn said simply, without moving. Her voice still had a harshness to it, but less than he recalled. "Especially Elayne. I did wish to . . . inconvenience . . . Elaida, if I could. Let her whistle for them." She gave a soft laugh tinged with bitterness. "I did even dose Joline with forkroot, so she could no interfere with those girls. And look what it did get me. Joline did escape, and I . . ." Her eyes moved again, to the silver bracelet hanging on the hook.

Sighing, Mat leaned against the wall beside the dresses hanging on pegs. She knew what had been in the note, a warning for Elayne and Nynaeve. Light, but he had hoped she would not, that someone else had put the bloody thing in his pocket. It had not done any good, anyway. They both knew Elaida was after them. The note had changed nothing! The woman had not really been trying to help them, anyway, just to . . . inconvenience . . . Elaida. He could walk away with a clean conscience. Blood and ashes! He should never actually have spoken to her. Now that he had actually exchanged words with her . . .

"I'll try to help you escape, if I can," he said reluctantly.

She remained still on the bed. Neither her expression nor her tone of voice changed. She might have been explaining something simple and unimportant. "Even if you can remove the collar, I will no get very far, perhaps no even out of the Palace. And if I do, no woman who can channel can walk through the city gates unless she does wear an *a'dam*. I have stood guard there myself, and I do know."

"I'll figure out something," he muttered, raking his fingers through his hair. Figure out something? What? "Light, you don't even sound as if you want to escape."

"You do be serious," she whispered, so low he nearly did not hear. "I did think you only did come to taunt me." Slowly she sat, swinging her feet down to the floor. Her eyes latched on to his intently, and her voice took on a low urgency. "Do I *want* to escape? When I do something that does please them, the *sul'dam* do give me sweets. I do find myself *looking forward* to those rewards." Breathy horror crept into her voice. "Not for liking of sweets, but because I have pleased the *sul'dam*." A single tear trickled from her eye. She inhaled deeply. "If you do help me escape, I will do anything you ask of me that does not encompass treason to the White—" Her teeth snapped shut, and she sat up straight, staring right through him. Abruptly, she nodded to herself. "Help me escape, and I will do *anything* you ask of me," she said.

"I will do what I can," he told her. "I must think of a way."

She nodded as though he had promised an escape by nightfall. "There do be another sister held prisoner here in the Palace. Edesina Azzedin. She must come with us."

"One other?" Mat said. "I thought I'd seen three or four, counting you. Anyway, I'm not sure I can get you out, much less—"

"The others do be . . . changed." Teslyn's mouth tightened. "Guisin and Mylen—I did know her as Sheraine Caminelle, but she do answer only to Mylen, now—those two would betray us. Edesina do still be herself. I will no leave her behind, even if she do be a rebel."

"Now, look," Mat said with a smile, soothingly, "I said I

will try to get you out, but I can't see any way to get *two* of you—"

"It do be best if you go now," she broke in again. "Men are no allowed up here, and in any case, you will rouse suspicions if you do be found." Frowning at him, she sniffed. "It would help if you did not dress so flamboyantly. Ten drunken Tinkers could no attract as much attention as you do. Go, now. Quickly. Go!"

He went, muttering to himself. Just like an Aes Sedai. Offer to help her, and the next thing you knew, she had you scaling a sheer cliff in the middle of the night to break fifty people out of a dungeon by yourself. That had been another man, a long time dead, but he remembered it, and it fit. Blood and bloody ashes! He did not know how to rescue one Aes Sedai, and she had him trying to rescue two!

He stalked around the innocuous corner at the foot of the stairs and almost walked into Tuon.

"*Damane* kennels are forbidden to men," she said, peering up at him coldly through her veil. "You could be punished just for entering."

"I was looking for a Windfinder, High Lady," he said hastily, making a leg and thinking as fast as he ever had in his life. "She did me a favor once, and I thought she might like something from the kitchens. Some pastries, or the like. I didn't see her, though. I suppose she wasn't caught when . . ." He trailed off, staring. The stern judicial mask the girl always wore for a face had melted into a smile. She really was beautiful.

"That is very kind of you," she said. "It's good to know you are kind to *damane*. But you must be careful. There are men who actually take *damane* to their beds." Her full mouth twisted in disgust. "You would not want anyone to think you are perverted." That severe expression settled on her face again. All prisoners would be executed immediately.

"Thank you for the warning, High Lady," he said, a little unsteadily. What kind of man wanted to bed a woman who was on a leash?

He disappeared then, as far as she was concerned. She just glided away down the hall as if she saw no one. For once, though, the High Lady Tuon did not concern him at all. He had an Aes Sedai hiding in the cellar of The Wandering

Woman and two wearing *damane* leashes who all expected
Mat bloody Cauthon to save their necks. He was sure Teslyn would inform this Edesina all about it as soon as she
was able. Three women who might start getting impatient if
he failed to waft them to safety soon enough. Women liked
to talk, and when they talked enough, they let slip things
better left unspoken. Impatient women talked even more
than the rest. He could not feel the dice in his head, but
he could almost hear a clock ticking. And the hour might
be struck by a headsman's axe. Battles he could plan in
his sleep, but those old memories did not seem much help
here. He needed a schemer, someone used to plotting and
crooked ways of thinking. It was time to make Thom sit
down and talk. And Juilin.

Setting out in search of either, he unconsciously began
humming "I'm Down at the Bottom of the Well." Well, he
was, and night was falling and the rain well and truly coming down. As often happened, another name drifted up out
of those old memories, a song of the Court of Takedo, in
Farashelle, crushed a thousand years ago and more by Artur Hawkwing. The intervening years had made remarkably
little change in the tune itself, though. Then, it had been
called "The Last Stand at Mandenhar." Either way, it fit too
bloody well.

CHAPTER
20

Questions of Treason

C limbing to the cramped kennels at the very top
of the Tarasin Palace, Bethamin held her writing
board carefully. Sometimes the ink jar's cork came
loose, and ink spots were difficult to remove from clothing.
She kept herself as presentable at all times as if she had
been called to appear before one of the High Blood. She
did not talk to Renna, who had the inspection duty with her
today, as they walked up the stairs. They were supposed to
be doing an assigned task, not chattering idly. That was part
of her reason. Where others jockeyed to be complete with
their favorite *damane,* and goggled at the strange sights
of this land, and speculated on the rewards to be gained
here, she focused on her duties, asking for the most difficult *marath'damane* to tame to the *a'dam,* working twice as
hard and twice as long as anyone else.

The rain had stopped, finally, leaving the kennels in
silence. The *damane* would get some exercise at least,
today—most grew sulky if confined to the kennels too long,
and these makeshift kennels were decidedly confining—but
regrettably, she was not assigned to walking today. Renna
never was, though once she had been Suroth's best trainer,
and well respected. A little harsh, sometimes, but highly
skilled. Once, everyone had said she would soon be made
der'sul'dam in spite of her youth. Matters had changed.
There were always more *sul'dam* than *damane,* yet no one
could recall Renna being complete since Falme, her or Seta,
whom Suroth had taken into personal service after Falme.
Bethamin enjoyed gossiping over wine about the Blood
and those who served them as much as anyone else, yet she

never ventured any opinion when the talk turned to Renna and Seta. She thought of them often, though.

"You start on the other side, Renna," she ordered. "Well? Do you want to be reported to Essonde for laziness yet again?"

Before Falme, the shorter woman had been nearly over-powering in her self-assurance, but a muscle twitched in her pale cheek, and she gave Bethamin a sickly, obsequious smile before hurrying into the kennel's warren of narrow passages patting at her long hair as though afraid it might be disordered. Everyone except Renna's closest friends bul-lied her at least a little, repaying her former lofty pride. To do otherwise was to mark yourself out, something Betha-min avoided except in carefully chosen ways. Her own se-crets were buried as deeply as she could bury them, and she held silent about the secrets no one knew she was aware of, but she wanted to fix in everyone's mind that Bethamin Zeami was the image of the perfect *sul'dam*. Absolute per-fection was what she strove for, in herself and in the *damane* she trained.

She set about her inspection briskly and efficiently, checking that the *damane* had kept themselves and their individual kennels neat, making a short notation in her neat hand on the top page pinned to the writing board when one had failed to, and she did not dawdle, except to give out hard candies to a few who were doing particularly well in the training. Most of those she had been complete with greeted her entrance with smiles even as they knelt. Whether from the Empire or from this side of the ocean, they knew she was firm yet fair. Others did not smile. For the most part, the Atha'an Miere *damane* met her with stony faces as dark as her own, or sullen anger they seemed to believe they were concealing.

She did not mark their anger down for punishment, as some would have. They still thought they were resisting, but unseemly demands for the return of their garish jew-elry already were a thing of the past, and they knelt and spoke properly. A new name was a useful tool with the most difficult cases, creating a break with what was done and gone, and they answered to theirs, however reluctantly. Re-luctance would fade, along with scowls, and eventually they would hardly remember they ever had other names. It was

Finishing ahead of Renna, Bethamin waited at the foot of the stairs until the other *sul'dam* came down. "Take this to Essonde when you take yours," she said, thrusting her writing board at Renna before she cleared the final step. Unsurprisingly, Renna accepted the task as meekly as she had accepted the earlier order, and hurried away eyeing the extra writing board as though wondering whether the pages held a report on her. She was a very different woman than she had been before Falme.

Fetching her cloak and leaving the Palace, Bethamin intended to return to the inn where she was forced to share a bed with two other *sul'dam,* but only long enough to take some coin from her lockbox. The inspection had been her only duty today, and the rest of the hours were her own. For a change, instead of seeking extra assignments, she would spend them buying souvenirs. Perhaps one of those knives the local women wore at their necks, if she could find one without the gems they seemed to like on the hilt. And lacquerware, of course; that was as good here as any in the Empire, and the designs were so . . . foreign. It would be soothing to shop. She needed soothing.

The paving stones of the Mol Hara still glistened damply from the morning's rain, and a pleasant tang of salt filled the air, reminding her of the village on the Sea of L'Heye where she had been born, though the freezing cold made her clutch her cloak around herself. It had never been cold in Abunai, and she had never become accustomed to it no matter how far she had traveled. Thoughts of home were no comfort, now, though. As she made her way through the crowded streets, Renna and Seta filled her head to the extent that she bumped into people and once almost walked right in front of a merchant's train of wagons leaving the city. A shout from a wagon driver caught her attention, and she leaped back just in time. The wagon rumbled across the paving stones where she would have been standing, and the woman wielding the whip did not even glance at her. These foreigners had no idea of the respect due a *sul'dam*.

Renna and Seta. Everyone who had been at Falme had memories they wanted to forget, memories they would not talk about except when they drank too much. She did, too, only hers were not about the shock of battling half-recognized ghosts out of legend, or the horror of defeat, or

mad visions in the sky. How often had she wished she had
not gone upstairs that day? If only she had not wondered
how Tuli was doing, the *damane* who had the marvelous
skill with metals. But she had looked into Tuli's kennel.
And she had seen Renna and Seta frantically trying to remove *a'dam* from each other's necks, shrieking with the
pain, wavering on their knees from the nausea, and still
fumbling at the collars. Vomit stained the fronts of their
dresses. In their frenzy they had not noticed her backing
away, horror-stricken.

Not simply horror at seeing two *sul'dam* revealed as
marath'damane, but her own sudden personal terror. Often she thought she could almost see *damane*'s weaves,
and she could always sense a *damane*'s presence and know
how strong she was. Many *sul'dam* could; everyone knew
it came from long experience at handling the *a'dam.* Yet
the sight of that desperate pair roused unwanted thoughts,
putting a different and frightening complexion on what she
had always accepted. Did she *almost* see the weaves, or did
she really see? Sometimes she thought she *felt* the channeling, too. Even *sul'dam* had to undergo the yearly testing,
until their twenty-fifth naming day, and she had passed by
failing every time. Only . . . . There would be a new testing
after Renna and Seta were discovered, a new testing to find
the *marath'damane* who somehow had evaded the first. The
Empire itself might tremble before such a blow. And with
the image of Renna and Seta burned into her brain, she had
known with total certainty that after those tests, Bethamin
Zeami would no longer be a respected citizen. Instead, a
damane called Bethamin would serve the Empire.

The shame curdled in her still. She had placed personal
fears ahead of the needs of the Empire, ahead of everything
she knew to be right and true and good. Battle came to
Falme, and nightmare, but she had not rushed to complete
herself with a *damane* and join the battle line. Instead, she
had used the confusion to secure a horse and flee, to run as
hard and as far as she could.

She realized she had stopped, staring into a seamstress's shop window without really seeing what was on
display inside. Not that she wanted to see. The blue dress
with its lightning-marked red panels was the only one she
had thought of wearing in years. And she certainly would

not wear something that exposed her so indecently. Skirts swirling about her ankles, she walked on, but she could not shake Renna and Seta from her thoughts, or Suroth.

Obviously Alwhin had found the collared pair of *sul'dam* and reported them to Suroth. And Suroth had sheltered the Empire by protecting Renna and Seta, dangerous as that was. What if they suddenly began channeling? Better perhaps for the Empire if she had arranged their deaths, though killing a *sul'dam* was murder even for the High Blood. Two suspicious deaths among the *sul'dam* would certainly have brought in Seekers. So Renna and Seta were free, if it could be called that when they were never allowed to be complete. Alwhin had done her duty, and been honored by becoming Suroth's Voice. Suroth had done her duty as well, however distasteful. There was no new testing. Her own flight had been for nothing. And if she had remained, she would not have ended up in Tanchico, a nightmare she wanted to forget even more than she did Falme.

A squad of the Deathwatch Guards marched by, resplendent in their armor, and Bethamin paused to watch them pass. They left a wake through the crowd like a greatship under full sail. There would be joy in the city, in the land, when Tuon finally revealed herself, and celebrations as though she had just arrived. She felt a guilty pleasure at thinking of the Daughter of the Nine Moons so, as when she had done something forbidden as a child, though of course, until Tuon removed her veil, she was merely the High Lady Tuon, no higher than Suroth. The Deathwatch Guards tramped on, dedicated heart and soul to Empress and Empire, and Bethamin went in the opposite direction. Appropriately, since she was dedicated heart and soul to preserving her own freedom.

The Golden Swans of Heaven was a grand name for a tiny inn squeezed between a public stable and a lacquerware shop. The lacquerware shop was full of military officers buying everything the shop contained, the stable was full of horses purchased in the lottery and not yet assigned, and The Golden Swans was full of *sul'dam*. Packed with them, in fact, at least once night came. Bethamin was lucky to have only two bedmates. Ordered to accommodate as many as she could, the innkeeper pushed four and five into a bed when she thought they would fit. Still, the bedding was clean and the food quite good, if peculiar. And given that the alternative was likely a hayloft, she was glad to share.

At this hour, the round tables in the common room were empty. Some of the *sul'dam* living there surely had duties, and the rest simply wanted to avoid the innkeeper. Arms folded, frowning, Darnella Shoran was watching several serving women sweep the green-tiled floor industriously. A skinny woman with gray hair worn rolled on the nape of her neck and a long jaw that gave her a belligerent appearance, she might have been a *der'sul'dam* in spite of the ridiculous knife she wore, its hilt studded with cheap red and white gems. Supposedly the serving women were free, but they jumped like property whenever the innkeeper spoke.

Bethamin jumped slightly herself when the woman rounded on her. "You are aware of my rules concerning men, Mistress Zeami?" she demanded. After all this time, the slow way these people talked still sounded odd. "I've heard about your foreign ways, and if that is how you are, it is your business, but not under my roof. If you want to meet with men, you will do it elsewhere!"

"I assure you, I have not been meeting men here or anywhere else, Mistress Shoran."

The innkeeper frowned at her in suspicion. "Well, he came around asking for you by name. A pretty, yellow-haired man. Not a boy, but not very old, either. One of your lot, dragging his words out so you could hardly understand him."

Making her tone placating, Bethamin did her best to convince the woman that she did not know anyone who met that description, and that she had no time for men with her duties. Both were true, yet she would have lied if necessary. The Golden Swans had not been commandeered, and three in a bed was *much* preferable to a hayloft. She tried to find out whether the woman might like some small gift when she went shopping, but the woman actually seemed offended when she suggested a knife with more colorful gems. She had not meant anything expensive, nothing in the way of a bribe—not really—yet Mistress Shoran seemed to take it so, huffing and frowning indignantly. In any case, she was not sure she succeeded in changing the woman's mind by a hair. For some reason, the innkeeper seemed to believe they spent all their free hours engaged in debauchery. She was still frowning when Bethamin started up the railless stairs at the side of the common room pretending that she had not a thought in her mind beyond shopping.

The man's identity did concern her, though. She certainly did not recognize the description. In all likelihood, he had come about her inquiries, but if that was the case, if he had been able to trace her here, then she had been insufficiently discreet. Perhaps dangerously so. Still, she hoped he came back. She needed to know. She needed to!

Opening the door to her room, she froze. Impossibly, her iron lockbox sat on the bed with its lid thrown open. That was a very good lock, and the only key lay at the bottom of her belt pouch. The thief was still there, and oddly, he was thumbing through her diary! How in the Light had the man gotten past Mistress Shoran's surveillance?

Paralysis lasted only an instant. Snatching her belt knife from its sheath, she opened her mouth to scream for help.

The fellow's expression never changed, and he neither tried to run nor to attack her. He just took something small from his pouch and held it up where she could see it, and her breath turned to lead in her throat. Numbly she fumbled her knife back into its scabbard and held out her hands to show him she held no weapon and was not attempting to reach one. Between his fingers was a gold-edged ivory plaque, engraved with a raven and a tower. Suddenly she really saw the man, yellow-haired and in his middle years. Perhaps he was pretty, as Mistress Shoran had said, but only a madwoman would think of a Seeker for Truth in that fashion. Thank the Light she had not recorded anything dangerous in her diary. But he must know. He had asked for her by name. Oh, Light, he must know!

"Close the door," he said quietly, returning the plaque to his pouch, and she obeyed. She wanted to run. She wanted to plead for mercy. But he was a Seeker, so she stood there, trembling. To her surprise, he dropped her diary back into the lockbox and gestured to the room's single chair. "Sit. There is no need for you to be uncomfortable."

Slowly, she hung up her cloak and settled onto the chair, for once not caring how uncomfortable the strange ladder-like back was. She did not try to hide her shivers. Even one of the Blood, even one of the High Blood, might, quake at

being questioned by a Seeker. She had a small hope. He had
not simply ordered her to accompany him. Perhaps he did
not know after all.

"You have been asking questions about a ship captain
named Egeanin Sarna," he said. "Why?"

Hope faltered with a thud she could feel in her chest. "I
was looking for an old friend," she quavered. The best lies
always contained as much truth as possible. "We were at
Falme together. I don't know whether she survived." Lying
to a Seeker was treason, but she had committed her first
treason in deserting during the battle at Falme.

"She lives," he said curtly. He sat down on the end of
the bed without taking his eyes from her. They were blue,
and made her want her cloak back. "She is a hero, a Captain of the Green, and the Lady Egeanin Tamarath, now.
Her reward from the High Lady Suroth. She is also here in
Ebou Dar. You will renew your friendship with her. And
report to me who she sees, where she goes, what she says.
Everything."

Bethamin clamped her jaws to keep from laughing
hysterically. He was after Egeanin, not her. The Light be
praised! The Light be praised in all its infinite mercy! She
had only wanted to know if the woman still lived, if she
had to take precautions. Egeanin had freed her once, yet in
the ten years Bethamin had known her before that, she had
been a model of duty. It had always seemed possible she
would repent that one aberration no matter the cost to herself, but, wonder of wonders, she had not. And the Seeker
was after her, not . . . ! Possibilities reared up in front of
her, certainties, and she no longer wanted to laugh. Instead,
she licked her lips.

"How . . . ? How can I renew our friendship?" It had
never been friendship anyway, merely acquaintance, but it
was too late to say that now. "You tell me she's been raised
to the Blood. Any overture must come from her." Fear em-
boldened her. And panicked her as it had at Falme. "Why
do you need me to be your Listener? You can take her for
questioning any time you decide to." She bit the inside of
her cheek to still her tongue. Light, she wanted nothing less
than she wanted him to do that. Seekers were the secret
hand of the Empress, might she live forever; in the Empress's name, he could put even Suroth to the question, or

he would wake, and they are aided by a venomous worm of treachery boring from within. Suroth may not even be that worm's head. For the Empire's sake, I dare not take her until I can kill the whole worm. Egeanin is a thread I can follow to the worm, and you are a thread to Egeanin. So you will renew your friendship with her, whatever it takes. Do you understand me?"

"I understand, and I will obey." Her voice shook, but what else could she say? The Light save her, what else could she say?

CHAPTER
21

A Matter of Property

E geanin lay on her back on the bed with her hands raised, palms toward the ceiling and fingers spread. Her pale blue skirts made a fan across her legs, and she tried to lie very still so as not to wrinkle the narrow pleats too much. The way dresses confined movement, they must be an invention of the Dark Lord. Lying there, she studied fingernails too long for her to lay hands on a line without breaking at least half. Not that she had personally handled lines in quite a few years, but she had always been ready and able to, at need.

"... plain foolheadedness!" Bayle growled, poking at the blazing logs in the brick fireplace. "Fortune prick me, *Seahawk* could sail nearer the wind, and faster, than any Seanchan ship ever made. There did be squalls ahead, too, and . . ." She listened only enough to know he had stopped grumbling about the room and taken up the same old argument. The dark-paneled chamber was not the best at The Wandering Woman, or even close, yet it met his requirements excepting the view. The two windows looked out on the stableyard. A Captain of the Green ranked with a banner-general, but in this place, most of those she outranked were aides or secretaries to senior officers of the Ever Victorious Army. Among the army as at sea, being of the Blood added little unless it was the High Blood.

The sea-green lacquer on the nails of her little fingers sparkled. She had always hoped to rise, eventually perhaps to Captain of the Gold, commanding fleets, as her mother had. As a girl, she had even dreamed of being named the Hand of the Empress at Sea just like her mother, to stand at the left hand of the Crystal Throne, *so'jhin* to the Empress herself, might she live forever, allowed to speak directly to her. Young women had foolish dreams. And she had to admit that once chosen for the Forerunners, she considered the possibility of a new name. Not hoping for it, certainly— that would have been getting above herself—yet everyone had known the recovery of the stolen lands would mean new additions to the Blood. Now she was Captain of the Green, ten years before she should have had any hope of it, and stood on the slopes of that steep mountain that rose through the clouds to the sublime pinnacle of the Empress, might she live forever.

She doubted she would be given command of one greatship, however, much less a squadron. Suroth claimed to accept her story, but if so, why had she been left sitting at Cantorin? Why, when orders finally came, were they to report here and not to a ship? Of course, there were only so many commands available, even for a Captain of the Green. It might be that. She might have been chosen for a position near Suroth, though her orders said only that she was to travel to Ebou Dar by the first available means and await further instructions. Maybe. The High Blood might speak to the low without the intervention of a Voice, but it seemed to her that Suroth had forgotten her as soon as she was dismissed after receiving her rewards. Which also might mean Suroth was suspicious. Arguments that ran in circles. In any case, she could live on seawater if that Seeker had given over his suspicions. He had no more, or she would already be in a dungeon shrieking, yet if he was in the city, too, he would be watching her, waiting for one misstep. He could not shed so much as a single drop of her blood, now, but the Seekers were experienced at dealing with that minor difficulty. So long as he left it to watching, though, he could stare at her until his eyes shriveled. She had a stable deck under her feet, now, and from here on she would take great care how she stepped. Captain of the Gold might no longer be possible, yet retiring as Captain of the Green was honorable.

"Well?" Bayle demanded. "What about that?"

Wide and solid and strong, just the sort of man she had always favored, he was standing beside the bed in his shirtsleeves, a frown on his face and his fists on his hips. Not a pose a *so'jhin* should take with his mistress. With a sigh, she let her hands drop onto her stomach. Bayle just would not learn how a *so'jhin* was supposed to behave. He took it all as a joke, or play, as though none of it were real. Sometimes he even said he wanted to be her Voice, no matter how often she explained she was not of the High Blood. Once, she had had him beaten, and afterwards he had refused to sleep in the same bed with her until she apologized. Apologized!

Hastily, she ran through what she had half-heard of his growling. Yes; still the same arguments after all this time. Nothing new. Swinging her legs over the side of the bed, she sat up and ticked points off on her fingers. She had done it so often, she could deliver them by rote. "Had you tried to run, the *damane* on the other ship would have snapped your masts like twigs. It was not a chance stop, Bayle, and you know it; their first hail was a demand to know whether you were *Seahawk*. By bringing you into the wind and announcing we were on our way to Cantorin with a gift for the Empress, may she live forever, I allayed their suspicions. Anything else—anything!—and we would all have been chained in the hold and sold as soon as we reached Cantorin. I doubt we'd have been lucky enough to face the headsman instead." She held up her thumb. "And last, if you had kept calm as I told you to, you would not have gone to the block, either. You cost me a great deal!" Several other women in Cantorin apparently had her same taste in men. They had pushed the bidding up extravagantly.

Stubborn man that he was, he scowled and scrubbed at his short beard irritably. "I do still say we could have dropped it all over the side," he muttered. "That Seeker had no proof I did have it aboard."

"Seekers do no need proof," she said, mocking his accent. "Seekers do find proof, and the finding do be painful." If he was reduced to bringing up what even he had conceded long since, maybe she was finally nearing the end of the whole thing. "In any case, Bayle, you have already admitted there is no harm in Suroth having that collar and bracelets. They can't be put on him unless someone gets close enough, and I've heard nothing that suggests anyone has or will." She refrained from adding that it would not matter if someone did. Bayle was not really familiar with even the versions of the Prophecies they had on this side of the World Sea, but he was adamant that none mentioned the necessity of the Dragon Reborn kneeling to the Crystal Throne. It might prove necessary for him to be fitted with this male *a'dam*, but Bayle would never see it. "What is done is done, Bayle. If the Light shines on us, we will live long in the service of the Empire. Now, you know this city, so you say. What is there interesting to see or do?"

"There always do be festivals of some sort," he said slowly, grudgingly. He never liked giving up his argument, no matter how futile. "Some may be to your taste. Some not, I do think. You do be . . . picky." What did he mean by that? Suddenly he grinned. "We could find a Wise Woman. They do hear marriage vows, here." He ran his fingers across the shaven side of his scalp, rolling his eyes upward as though trying to see it. "Of course, if I do recall the lecture you did give me on the 'rights and privileges' of my position, *so'jhin* can only marry other *so'jhin*, so you do need to free me, first. Fortune prick me, you do no have a foot of those promised estates, yet. I can take up my old trade and give you an estate soon enough."

Her mouth fell open. This was not something old. This was very, very new. She had always prided herself on being level-headed. She had risen to command by skill and daring, a veteran of sea battles and storms and shipwreck. And right that moment she felt like a first-voyage fingerling looking down from the main peak, panicked and dizzy, with the whole world spinning around her and a seemingly inevitable fall to the sea filling her eyes.

"It is not so simple," she said, surging to her feet so he was forced to step back. Light's truth, she hated sounding breathless! "Manumission requires me to provide for your livelihood as a free man, to see you can support yourself." Light! Words flooding out in a rush were as bad as being breathless. She imagined herself on a deck. It helped, a little. "In your case, that means buying a ship, I suppose," she said, sounding unruffled, at least, "and as you reminded me, I have no estates yet. Besides, I could not allow you to return to smuggling, and you know it." That much was simple truth, and the rest not really a lie. Her years at sea had been profitable, and if the gold she could call on was small gleanings to one of the Blood, she could buy a ship, so long as he did not want a greatship, but she had not actually denied being able to afford one.

He spread his arms, another thing he was not supposed to do, and after a moment she laid her cheek against his broad shoulder and let him enfold her. "It will be well, lass," he murmured gently. "Somehow, it will be well."

"You must not call me 'lass,' Bayle," she chided, staring beyond his shoulder toward the fireplace. It would not seem to come into focus. Before leaving Tanchico she had decided to marry him, one of those lightning decisions that had made her reputation. Smuggler he might be, but she could have put a stop to that, and he was steadfast, strong and intelligent, a seafarer. That last had always been a necessity, to her. Only, she had not known his customs. Some places in the Empire, men did the asking, and were actually offended if a woman even suggested. She knew nothing of enticing a man, either. Her few lovers had all been men of equal rank, men she could approach openly and bid farewell when one or the other of them was ordered to another ship or promoted. And now he was *so'jhin*. There was nothing wrong with bedding your own *so'jhin*, of course, so long as you did not flaunt the fact. He would make up a pallet at the foot of the bed as usual, even if he never slept on it. But freeing a *so'jhin*, casting him off from the rights and privileges Bayle sneered at, was the height of cruelty. No, she was lying by avoidance again, and worse, lying to herself. She wanted wholeheartedly to marry the man Bayle Domon. She was bitterly unsure she could bring herself to marry manumitted property.

"As my Lady do command, so shall it be," he said in a blithe mockery of formality.

She punched him under the ribs. Not hard. Just enough to make him grunt. He had to learn! She did not want to see the sights of Ebou Dar any longer. She just wanted to stay where she was, wrapped in Bayle's arms, not needing to make decisions, stay right where they stood forever.

A sharp knock sounded at the door, and she pushed him away. At least he knew enough not to protest that. While he tugged on his coat, she shook out the pleats of her dress and attempted to smooth away the wrinkles from lying on the bed. There seemed to be a good many, despite how still she had been. This knock might be a summons from Suroth or a maid seeing whether she needed anything, but whoever it was, she was not going to let anyone see her looking as if she had been rolling about on the deck.

Giving up the useless attempt, she waited until Bayle had buttoned himself up and adopted the attitude he thought proper for a *so'jhin*—*Like a captain on his quarterdeck ready to shout orders,* she thought, sighing to herself—then barked, "Come!" The woman who opened the door was the last she expected to see.

Bethamin eyed her hesitantly before darting in and closing the door softly behind her. The *sul'dam* took a deep breath, then knelt, holding herself stiffly upright. Her dark blue dress with its lightning-worked red panels looked freshly cleaned and ironed. The sharp contrast to her own dishevelment irritated Egeanin. "My Lady," Bethamin began uncertainly, then swallowed. "My Lady, I beg a word with you." Glancing at Bayle, she licked her lips. "In private, if it pleases you, my Lady?"

The last time Egeanin had seen this woman was in a basement in Tanchico, when she removed an *a'dam* from Bethamin and told her to go. That would have been enough for blackmail if she were of the High Blood! Without doubt the charge would be the same as for freeing a *damane*. Treason. Except that Bethamin could not reveal it without condemning herself, too.

"He can hear anything you have to say, Bethamin," she said calmly. She was in shoal waters, and that was no place for anything except calm. "What do you want?"

Bethamin shifted on her knees and wasted more time with lip licking. Then, suddenly, words came out in a rush. "A Seeker came to me and ordered me to resume our . . . our acquaintance and report on you to him." As if to stop herself babbling, she caught her underlip in her teeth and stared at Egeanin. Her dark eyes were desperate and pleading, just as they had been in that Tanchico basement.

Egeanin met her gaze coolly. Shoal waters, and an unexpected gale. Her strange orders to Ebou Dar suddenly were explained. She did not need a description to know it must be the same man. Nor did she need to ask why Bethamin was committing treason by betraying the Seeker. If he decided his suspicions were strong enough to take her for questioning, eventually Egeanin would tell him everything

she knew, including about a certain basement, and Bethamin would soon find herself once more wearing an *a'dam*.
The woman's only hope was to help Egeanin evade him.

"Rise," she said. "Have a seat." Luckily, there were two
chairs, though neither appeared comfortable. "Bayle, I
think there is brandy in that flask on the drawered chest."

Bethamin was so shaky that Egeanin had to help her up
and guide her to a chair. Bayle brought worked silver cups
holding a little brandy and remembered to bow and present
Egeanin's first, but when he returned to the chest, she saw
he had poured for himself, as well. He stood there, cup in
hand, watching them as if it were the most natural thing in
the world. Bethamin stared at him pop-eyed.

"You think you are poised over the impaling stake,"
Egeanin said, and the *sul'dam* flinched, her frightened gaze
jerking back to Egeanin's face. "You are wrong, Bethamin.
The only real crime I have committed was freeing you."
Not precisely true, but in the end, after all, she had placed
the male *a'dam* in Suroth's hands herself. And talking with
Aes Sedai was not a crime. The Seeker might suspect—he
had tried to listen at a door in Tanchico—but she was not
a *sul'dam,* charged with catching *marath'damane*. At worst
that meant a reprimand. "So long as he doesn't learn about
that, he has no reason to arrest me. If he wants to know
what I say, or anything else about me, tell him. Just remember that if he does decide to arrest me, I will give him your
name." A reminder could only guard against Bethamin suddenly thinking she saw a safe way out, leaving her behind.
"He won't have to make me scream once."

To her surprise, the *sul'dam* began to laugh hysterically.
Until Egeanin leaned forward and slapped her, anyway.

Rubbing her cheek sullenly, Bethamin said, "He knows
near enough everything *except* the basement, my Lady."
And she began to describe a fantastical web of treason con-
necting Egeanin and Bayle and Suroth and maybe even
Tuon herself with Aes Sedai, and *marath'damane,* and *damane* who had been Aes Sedai.

Bethamin's voice began to grow panicky as she darted
from one incredible charge to another, and before long,
Egeanin began sipping brandy. Just sips. She was calm.
She was in command of herself. She was . . . This was be-

yond shoal waters. She was riding close on a lee shore, and Soulblinder himself rode that gale, coming to steal her eyes. After listening for a time with his own eyes growing wider and wider, Bayle drank down a brimful cup of the dark raw liquor in one go. She was relieved to see his shock, and guilty at feeling relieved. She would not believe him a murderer. Besides, he was very good using his hands but only fair at a sword; with weapons or bare-handed, the High Lord Turak would have gutted Bayle like a carp. Her only excuse for even considering it was that he had been with two Aes Sedai in Tanchico. The whole thing was nonsense. It had to be! Those two Aes Sedai had not been part of any plot, just a chance meeting. Light's truth, they had been little more than girls, and near innocents at that, too softhearted to accept her suggestion they cut the Seeker's throat when they had the chance. A pity, that. They had *handed* her the male *a'dam*. Ice crept down her spine. If the Seeker ever learned she had intended disposing of the *a'dam* the way those Aes Sedai suggested, if anyone learned, she would be judged as guilty of treason as if she had succeeded in dropping it into the ocean's depths. *Are you not?* she demanded of herself. The Dark One was coming to steal her eyes.

Tears streaming down her face, Bethamin clutched her cup to her breasts as though hugging herself. If she was trying to keep from shaking, she failed miserably. Trembling, she stared at Egeanin, or perhaps at something beyond her. Something horrifying. The fire had not warmed the room very far yet, but sweat was beaded on Bethamin's face. ". . . and if he learns about Renna and Seta," she babbled, "he will know for sure! He'll come after me, and the other *sul'dam!* You have to stop him! If he takes me, I'll give him your name! I will!" Abruptly she tilted lifted the cup to her mouth unsteadily and gulped the contents, choking and coughing, then thrust it out toward Bayle for more. He did not move. He looked poleaxed.

"Who are Renna and Seta?" Egeanin asked. She was as frightened as the *sul'dam,* but as always, she kept her fear hard-reefed. "What can the Seeker learn about them?" Bethamin's eyes slid away, refusing to meet hers, and abruptly she knew. "They are *sul'dam,* aren't they, Bethamin? And they were collared, too, just like you."

"They are in Suroth's service," the woman whimpered. "They are never allowed to be complete, though. Suroth knows."

Egeanin rubbed at her eyes wearily. Perhaps there was a conspiracy, after all. Or Suroth might be hiding what the pair were to protect the Empire. The Empire depended on *sul'dam;* its strength was built on them. The news that *sul'dam* were women who could learn to channel might shatter the Empire to its core. It had surely shaken her. Maybe shattered her. She herself had not freed Bethamin out of duty. So many things had changed in Tanchico. She no longer believed that any woman who could channel deserved to be collared. Criminals, certainly, and maybe those who refused oaths to the Crystal Throne, and . . . She did not know. Once, her life had been made up of rock-solid certainties, like guiding stars that never failed. She wanted her old life back. She wanted a few certainties.

"I thought," Bethamin began. She would have no lips left if she did not stop licking them. "My Lady, if the Seeker . . . suffers an accident . . . perhaps the danger would pass with him." Light, the woman *believed* in this intrigue against the Crystal Throne, and she was ready to let it pass to save her own skin!

Egeanin rose, and the *sul'dam* had no choice but to follow. "I will think on it, Bethamin. You will come to see me every day you are free. The Seeker will expect it. Until I make my decision, you will do nothing. Do you understand me? Nothing except your duties and what I tell you." Bethamin understood. She was so relieved that someone else was dealing with the danger that she knelt again and kissed Egeanin's hand.

All but bundling the woman out of the room, Egeanin closed the door, then hurled her cup at the fireplace. It hit the bricks and bounced off, rolling across the small rug on the floor. It was dented. Her father had given her that set of cups when she gained her first command. All the strength seemed to have leached out of her. The Seeker had knitted moonbeams and happenstance into a strangling cord for her neck. If she was not named property instead. She shuddered at the possibility. Whatever she did, the Seeker had her trapped.

"I can kill him." Bayle flexed his hands, broad like the

rest of him. "He be a skinny man, as I recall. Used to every-one obeying his word. He will no be expecting anyone to snap his neck."

"You'll never find him to kill, Bayle. He won't meet her in the same place twice, and even if you followed her day and night, he might well be in disguise. You cannot kill every man she speaks to."

Stiffening her spine, she marched to the table where her writing desk sat and flipped open the lid. The wave-carved writing desk, with its silver-mounted glass inkpot and silver sand jar, had been her mother's gift at that first command. The neatly stacked sheets of fine paper bore her newly granted sigil, a sword and a fouled anchor. "I will write out your manumission," she said, dipping the silver pen, "and give you enough coin to buy passage." The pen glided across the page. She had always had a good hand. Log entries had to be legible. "Not enough to buy a ship, I fear, but it must do. You will depart on the first available ship. Shave the rest of your head, and you should have no trouble. It's still a shock, seeing bald men not wearing wigs, but so far no one seems to—" She gasped as Bayle slid the page right out from under her pen.

"If you do free me, you can no give me orders," he said. "Besides, you must ensure I can support myself if you do free me." He stuck the page into the fire and watched while it blackened and curled. "A ship, you did say, and I will hold you to it."

"Listen well and hear," she said in her best quarterdeck voice, but it made no impression on him. It had to be the cursed dress.

"You do need a crew," he said right over her, "and I can find you one, even here."

"What good will a crew do me? I don't have a ship. If I did, where could I sail that the Seeker couldn't find me?"

Bayle shrugged as though that was not important. "A crew, first. I did recognize that young fellow in the kitchens, the one with the lass on his knee. Stop grimacing. There be no harm to a little kissing."

She drew herself up, prepared to set him firmly to rights. She was frowning, not grimacing, that pair had been grop-ing at one another in public like animals, and he was her property! He could not speak to her this way!

"His name be Mat Cauthon," Bayle went on even as she opened her mouth. "By his clothes, he has come up in the world, and far. The first time I did see him, he did be in a farmer's coat, escaping Trollocs in a place even Trollocs be afraid of. The last time, half the town of Whitebridge did be burning, close enough to, and a Myrddraal did be trying to kill him and his friends. I did no see for myself, but anything else be more than I can believe. Any man who can survive Trollocs and Myrddraal do be useful, I think. Especially now."

"Someday," she growled, "I am going to have to see some of these Trollocs and Myrddraal you go on about." The things could not be half as fearsome as he described.

He grinned and shook his head. He knew what she thought about these so-called Shadowspawn. "Better still, young Master Cauthon did have companions on my ship. Good men for this situation, too. One, you do know. Thom Merrilin."

Egeanin's breath caught. Merrilin was a clever old man. A dangerous old man. And he had been with those two Aes Sedai when she met Bayle. "Bayle, is there a conspiracy? Tell me. Please?" No one said please to property, not even to *so'jhin.* Not unless they wanted something badly, anyway.

Shaking his head again, he leaned a hand on the stone mantelpiece and frowned into the flames. "Aes Sedai do plot the way fish swim. They could scheme with Suroth, but the question do be, could she scheme with them? I did see her look at *damane,* like they did be mangy dogs with fleas and catching diseases. Could she even talk to an Aes Sedai?" He looked up, and his eyes were clear and open, hiding nothing. "I do tell this for true. On my grandmother's grave, I do know of no plot. But did I know of ten, I still will no let that Seeker or anyone else harm you, whatever it do take." It was the sort of thing any loyal *so'jhin* might say. Well, no *so'jhin* she had ever heard of would have been so straightforward, but the sentiments were the same. Only, she knew he did not mean it that way, could never mean it that way.

"Thank you, Bayle." A steady voice was a necessity for command, but she was proud that hers was steady now. "Find this Master Cauthon, and Thom Merrilin, if you can. Perhaps something can be done."

He failed to bow before leaving her presence, but she did not even consider upbraiding him. She did not intend to let the Seeker take her, either. Whatever it took to stop him. That was a decision she had reached before she freed Bethamin. She filled the dented cup to the brim with brandy, meaning to get so drunk she could not think, but instead she sat peering into the dark liquid without touching a drop. Whatever it took. Light, she was no better than Bethamin! But knowing it changed nothing. Whatever it took.

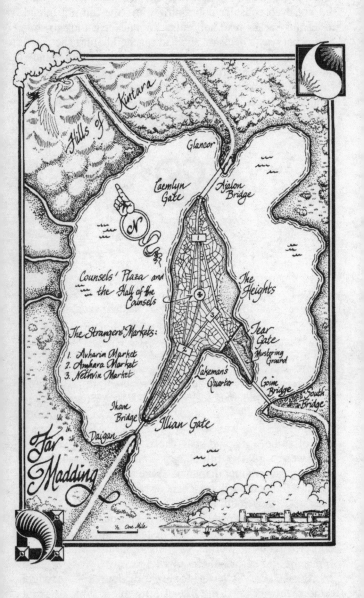

Hills of Kintara

Glancor

Laemlyn Gate

Ajalon Bridge

N

Counsels' Plaza and
the Hall of the
Counsels

The Heights

The Strangers' Markets:

1. Awharin Market
2. Amhara Market
3. Nethvin Market

Tear Gate

Mustering Ground

Lakeman's Quarter

Goim Bridge

South Bridge

Ikane Bridge

Illian Gate

Daigan

Far Madding

½   One Mile

CHAPTER

22

Out of Thin Air

The Amhara Market was one of three in Far Madding where foreigners were allowed to trade, but despite the name, the huge square had nothing of the look of a market, no market stalls or displays of merchandise. A few mounted riders, a handful of closed sedan chairs carried by brightly liveried bearers and the occasional coach with its window curtains drawn made their way though a sparse yet bustling crowd that might have been seen in any large city. Most were well wrapped in their cloaks against the morning winds blowing in off the lake that surrounded the city, and it was the cold that made them hurry more than any urgent business. Around the square, as at the city's other two Strangers' Markets, the tall stone houses of bankers rubbed shoulders with slate-roofed stone inns where the foreign merchants stayed and blocky windowless stone warehouses where their goods were stored, all jumbled in among stone stables and stone-walled wagon yards. Far Madding was a city of stone walls and slate roofs. This time of year, the inns were a quarter full at best, and the warehouses and wagon yards emptier than that. Come spring and the full revival of trade, though, merchants would pay triple for whatever space they could find.

A round marble pedestal in the center of the square held a statue of Savion Amhara, two spans tall and proud in fur-trimmed robes of marble, with elaborate marble chains of office around her neck. Her marble face was stern beneath the First Counsel's jeweled marble diadem, and her right hand firmly gripped the hilt of a marble sword, its point resting between her slippered feet, while her raised left hand aimed a warning marble finger toward the Tear Gate, some three-quarters of a mile away. Far Madding depended on merchants from Tear and Illian and Caemlyn, but the High Council was ever wary of foreigners and their corrupting outland ways. One of the steel-capped Street Guards, in a leather coat sewn with overlapping square metal plates and a Golden Hand on the left shoulder, stood below the statue using a long limber pole to frighten away black-winged gray pigeons. Savion Amhara was one of the three most revered women in Far Madding's history, though none was known very far beyond the lake's shores. Two men from the city were mentioned in every history of the world, though it had been called Aren Mador when one was born and Fel Moreina for the other, but Far Madding did its fervent best to forget Raolin Darksbane and Yurian Stonebow. In a real way, those two men were why Rand was in Far Madding.

A few people in the Amhara glanced at him as he passed, yet nobody glanced twice. That he was from off was plain enough, with his blue eyes and his hair cut at the shoulder. Men here wore it sometimes hanging all the way to the waist, either tied at the nape of the neck or held with a clip. His plain brown woolens were nondescript, though, no better than a moderately successful merchant might wear, and he was not the only one cloakless in spite of the lake winds. Most of the others were fork-bearded Kandori or Arafellin with belled braids, or hawk-nosed Saldaeans, men and women who found this weather mild compared to Borderland winter, but nothing about him said he was not a Borderlander, too. For his part, he simply refused to let the cold touch him, ignored it as he might have a fly buzzing. A cloak might get in his way, if he found his chance to act.

For once, even his height did not attract notice. There were a good many very tall men in Far Madding, few of them natives. Manel Rochaid himself was only a hand shorter than Rand, if that. Rand stayed well behind the man, letting people and sedan chairs sift between them and sometimes even hide his quarry. With his hair dyed black by herbs Nynaeve had provided, he doubted that the renegade Asha'man would notice him even if the man turned around. For his part, he was not worried about losing Rochaid. Most of the local men wore dull colors, with brighter embroidery about the chest and shoulders and perhaps a jeweled hair clip for the more prosperous, while the outland merchants favored sober unpretentious clothes, so as not to seem overly wealthy, and their guards and drivers bundled themselves in rough woolens. Rochaid's bright red silk coat stood out. He strode across the square like a king, one hand resting lightly on the hilt of his sword, a fur-edged cloak billowing behind him in the wind. He was a fool. That flapping cloak and the sword alike drew eyes. His waxed and curled mustaches named him a Murandian, who should be shivering like any normal human being, and that sword . . . A pure bull goose fool.

You *are the fool, coming to this place,* Lews Therin panted wildly inside his head. *Madness! Madness! We have to get out! We have to!*

Ignoring the voice, Rand pulled his snug gloves tighter and kept a steady pace after Rochaid. A number of the Street Guards in the square were watching the man. Foreigners were considered troublemakers and hotheads, and Murandians had a prickly reputation. A foreigner carrying a sword always attracted the Guards' attention. Rand was glad he had decided to leave his at the inn with Min. She nestled in the back of his head more strongly than Elayne or Aviendha, or Alanna. He was only vaguely aware of the others. Min seemed alive inside him.

As Rochaid left the Amhara, heading deeper into the city, flights of pigeons sprang up from the rooftops, but instead of making the unerring swoops that normally would have taken them into the sky, birds crashed into one another and some tumbled fluttering to the pavement. People gaped, including the Street Guards who had been watching Rochaid so intently a moment before. The man did not look back, but it would not have mattered had he seen. He knew Rand was in the city without seeing the effects of a *ta'veren,* or he would not have been there.

Following Rochaid onto the Street of Joy, really two broad straight streets separated by a measured row of leafless gray-barked trees, Rand smiled. Rochaid and his friends probably thought themselves very clever. Perhaps they had found the map of the northern Plains of Maredo replaced upside down in the racks in the Stone of Tear, or the book on cities of the south misshelved in the library of the Aesdaishar Palace in Chachin, or one of the other hints he had left behind. Small mistakes a man in a hurry might make, but any two or three together painted an arrow pointing to Far Madding. Rochaid and the others had been quick to see it, quicker than he had expected, or else they had had help to point it out. Either way, it did not matter.

He was not sure why the Murandian had come ahead of the others, but he knew they would come, Torval and Dashiva, Gedwyn and Kisman, to try finishing what they had bungled in Cairhien. A pity none of the Forsaken would be fool enough to come after him here. They would just send the others. He wanted to kill Rochaid before the rest arrived, if he could. Even here, where they were all on an equal footing, it would be best to cut down the odds. Two days Rochaid had been in Far Madding, openly asking questions about a tall red-haired man, swaggering about as if he had not a worry in the world. The man had seen any number who more or less met his description, but he still thought he was the hunter, not the hunted.

You've brought us here to die! Lews Therin moaned. Being *here is as bad as death!*

Rand shrugged uncomfortably. He agreed with the voice about that last. He would be as glad as Lews Therin to leave. But sometimes the only choice was between bad and worse. Rochaid was ahead of him, almost within reach. That was all that mattered now.

The gray stone shops and inns along the Street of Joy changed the farther Rand went from the Amhara Market. Silversmiths replaced cutlers, and then goldsmiths replaced silversmiths. Seamstresses and tailors displayed embroidered silks and brocades instead of woolens. The coaches that rumbled over the paving stones now had sigils lacquered on the doors and teams of four or six matched for size and color, and more riders were mounted on prime Tairen bloodstock or animals as good. Sedan chairs borne by trotting bearers became almost as common as people afoot, and, afoot, shopkeepers in coats or dresses heavily embroidered around the chest and shoulders were outnumbered by folk in livery as bright as that of the chair-bearers. Often as not, bits of colored glass now decorated men's hair clips, or occasionally pearls or richer gems, though few men walked whose wives could afford gems. Only the cold wind was the same, that and the Street Guards patrolling in threes, eyes alert for trouble. There were not so many as in the Strangers' Markets, yet as soon as one patrol strode out of sight another appeared, and wherever a street wider than an alleyway met the Street of Joy, a stone watchstand stood with two Guardsmen waiting at the foot in case the man atop spotted trouble. The peace was kept rigorously in Far Madding.

Rand frowned as Rochaid kept on along the street. Could he be headed for the Counsels' Plaza, in the middle of the island? There was nothing there but the Hall of the Counsels, monuments from more than five hundred years earlier, when Far Madding had been the capital of Maredo, and the countinghouses of the city's wealthiest women. In Far Madding, a wealthy man was one whose wife gave him a generous allowance or a widower who had been provided for. Maybe Rochaid was meeting Darkfriends. But if so, why had the man waited?

Suddenly a wave of dizziness hit him, a murky face filling his vision for an instant, and he staggered against a passerby. Taller than Rand himself, in bright green livery, the yellow-haired man shifted the large basket he was carrying and fended Rand off gently. A long, puckered scar ran down the side of his sun-dark face. Bowing his head, he murmured an apology and hurried on.

Righting himself, Rand growled a curse under his breath. *You destroyed them already,* Lews Therin whispered in his head. *Now you have someone else to destroy, and not beforetime. How many will we three kill before the end, I wonder.*

Shut up! Rand thought fiercely, but cackling, derisive laughter answered him. It was not the encounter with an Aielman that upset him. He had seen many since coming to Far Madding. For some reason, hundreds of the Aiel who fled after learning the truth of their history had ended up there, attempting to follow the Way of the Leaf when they had no more idea of what that entailed except that they were supposed to be lifelong *gai'shain.* He was not even worried about the dizziness, or whose face it was that he half saw when it struck. Ahead of him, a coach drawn by six grays clattered through the stream of sedan chairs and hurrying folk in livery, and men and women darting in and out of the

shops, but there was no sign of a red coat. He smacked a
gloved fist into his palm in irritation.

Going ahead blindly was idiotic. He might run right into
the man, or at least be seen. So far, Rochaid thought Rand
did not know he was in the city, an advantage too important
to squander. He knew where Rochaid had his rooms, one of
the inns that catered to foreign men. He could loiter outside
tomorrow and wait for another chance. The others might
arrive in the night, too. He thought he could kill any two
together, or maybe even all five, but it could not be done
quietly. He would take injuries against five, and at best, he
would have to abandon his sword, which he was reluctant to
do. It was a gift from Aviendha. At worst . . .

A flicker of fur-trimmed cloak caught his eye, fluttering
in the wind as it vanished around a corner ahead, and he ran
toward it. The Guardsmen at the watchstand there straightened, the man at the top taking his rattle from his belt. One
of those at the bottom of the stand hefted his long cudgel,
while the other lifted a catchpole from where it had leaned
against the watchstand's steps. The forked end was fash-
ioned to catch and hold an arm or a leg or a neck, and the
pole itself was belted with iron, proof against any sword or
axe. They watched him closely, with hard eyes.

He nodded to them and smiled, then ostentatiously
peered down the side street, searching the crowd there. Not
a running thief, just a man trying to catch up to someone.
The cudgel went back onto its belt hook, the catchpole returned to the steps. He did not look at the Guardsmen again.
Ahead, he got a glimpse of the cloak, and maybe a red coat,
as the wearer turned onto another street.

Raising his hand as if to hail somebody, Rand sped after the man, dodging between people and street peddlers'
barrows. Hawkers displaying pins or needles or combs on
their trays tried to catch his attention, or anyone's, with
their cries. Few people here wore embroidery, and a simple
cord tying a man's hair was much more common than even
the plainest clip. These streets were cramped at best, and
crooked, a haphazard maze where cheap inns and narrow
stone apartment buildings of three and four stories towered
over the shops of butchers and candlemakers and barbers,
tinsmiths and potters and coopers. Coaches would not have
fit along these streets, and there were no sedan chairs, either,

no riders, and only a handful of liveried servants, carrying baskets on errands but strolling and looking down their noses at everyone around them except the Street Guards. Their patrols and watchstands were present even here.

At last he got near enough for a clear view of the man he was following. Rochaid had finally shown enough sense to pull his cloak about him, hiding his red coat and his useless sword, but there was no doubt of who he was. In truth, he seemed to be trying to avoid notice altogether now, slinking along the side of the street with his shoulder brushing the shopfronts. Abruptly he looked around furtively, then darted into an alley between a tiny basketweaver's shop and an inn with a sign so dirty the name was completely obscured. Rand almost grinned, and wasted no time hurrying after him. There were no Street Guards or watchstands in Far Madding's alleyways.

Those alleys were even more crooked than the streets Rand had just left, making a warren of their own through the interior of every block of the city, and Rochaid was already out of sight, but Rand could hear his boots pounding on the damp stony dirt. The sound bounced and multiplied between the windowless stone walls until he could hardly tell where it was coming from, but he followed, running along passages barely wide enough for two men abreast. If they were friendly. Why had Rochaid come into this maze? Wherever he was going, he wanted to be there quickly. But he could not know how to use the alleys to get from one place to another.

Abruptly Rand realized the only boots he was hearing were his own and stopped dead. Silence. From where he stood, he could see three more narrow alleys splitting off from the one he stood in. Barely breathing, he strained his ears. Silence. Almost, he decided to turn back. And then he heard a distant clatter from the nearest alley mouth, as though someone had accidentally kicked a rock against a stone wall in passing. Best to kill the man and be done.

Rand turned the corner in to the alley, and found Rochaid waiting for him.

The Murandian had his cloak thrown back again, and both hands on his sword hilt. The Far Madding peace-bond wove hilt and scabbard inside a net of fine wire. He wore a small, knowing smile. "You were as easy to bait as a pigeon," he said, beginning to draw his sword. The wires had been cut, then fixed so they still appeared solid to a casual glance. "Run, if you want."

Rand did not run. Instead, he stepped forward, slamming his left hand down on the end of Rochaid's sword hilt, trapping the blade still half in its scabbard. Surprise widened the man's eyes, yet he still did not realize that pausing to gloat had already killed him. He moved back, trying to get room to complete his draw, but Rand followed smoothly, keeping the sword trapped, and pivoted from the hips, driving folded knuckles hard into Rochaid's throat. Cartilage cracked loudly, and the renegade forgot about trying to kill anyone. Staggering backwards, wide-eyed and staring, he clapped both hands to his throat and desperately tried to pull air through his ruined windpipe.

Rand was already beginning the killing stroke, beneath the breastbone, when a whisper of sound came to him from behind, and suddenly Rochaid's taunting took on new meaning. Backheeling Rochaid, Rand let himself fall to the ground atop the man. Hard-swung metal clanged against a stone wall, and a man cursed. Grabbing Rochaid's sword, Rand let the motion of falling turn into a roll, pulling the blade clear as he tumbled over his own shoulder. Rochaid gave a shrill, gurgling scream as Rand came up in a crouch facing back the way he had come.

Raefar Kisman stood gaping down at Rochaid, the blade he had meant to stab through Rand instead driven into Rochaid's chest. Blood bubbled on the Murandian's lips, and he dug his heels into the ground and bloodied his hands on the sharp steel as though he could push it out of him. Of only average height, and pale for a Tairen, Kisman wore clothes as plain as Rand's except for the sword belt. Hiding that beneath his cloak, he could have gone anywhere in Far Madding without being noticed.

His dismay lasted only an instant. As Rand rose, sword ready in both hands, Kisman jerked his own blade free and did not look at his thrashing accomplice again. He watched Rand, and his hands shifted nervously on the long hilt of his sword. No doubt he was one of those so proud of being able to use the Power as a weapon that he had disdained really learning the sword. Rand had not disdained. Rochaid gave a last twitch and was still, staring up at the sky.

"Time to die," Rand said quietly, but as he started forward, a rattle sounded somewhere behind the Tairen, an incessant chattering, and then another. The Street Guards.

"They'll take us both," Kisman breathed, sounding frantic. "If they find us standing over a corpse, they'll *hang* us both! You know they will!"

He was right, at least in part. If the Guards found them there, they would both be hauled off to the cells beneath the Hall of the Counsels. More rattles chattered, coming closer. The Guards must have noticed three men ducking one by one into the same alley. Perhaps they had even seen Kisman's sword. Reluctantly, Rand nodded.

The Tairen backed away cautiously, and when he saw Rand making no move to follow, he sheathed his blade and ran wildly, dark cloak flaring behind him.

Rand threw his borrowed sword down atop Rochaid's body and ran the other way. There were no rattles in that direction yet. With luck, he could be out into the streets, blending into the crowds, before he was seen. He had other fears than the noose. Stripping off his gloves, showing the Dragons that marked his arms, would be enough to prevent his hanging, he was sure. But the Counsels had proclaimed their acceptance of that odd decree Elaida had issued. Once he was in a cell, he would remain there until the White Tower sent for him. So he ran as hard as he could.

Melting into the crowd in the street, Kisman heaved a sigh of relief as three Street Guards ran into the alley he had just emerged from. Holding his cloak close to hide his scabbarded sword, he moved with the flow of traffic, no faster than anyone else and slower than some. Nothing to draw a Guardsman's eye. A pair of them passed with a trussed prisoner stuffed into a large sack slung from a quarterstaff carried on their shoulders. Only the man's head stuck out, his eyes wild and darting. Kisman shuddered. Burn his eyes, that could have been him! Him!

He had been a fool to let Rochaid talk him into this in the first place. They were supposed to wait until everyone had arrived, slipping into the city one by one to avoid notice. Rochaid had wanted the glory of being the one to kill al'Thor; the Murandian had burned with the desire to prove himself a better man than al'Thor. Now he was dead of it, and very nearly Raefar Kisman with him, and that made Kisman furious. He wanted power more than glory, perhaps to rule Tear from the Stone. Perhaps more. He wanted to live forever. Those things had been promised; they were his due. Part of his anger was because he was unsure they actually were supposed to kill al'Thor. The Great Lord knew he wanted to—he would not sleep soundly until the man was dead and buried!—and yet . . .

"Kill him," the M'Hael had ordered before sending them to Cairhien, but he had been as displeased that they were found out as that they had failed. Far Madding was to be their last chance; he had made that as plain as polished brass. Dashiva had simply vanished. Kisman did not know whether he had run or the M'Hael had killed him, and he did not care.

"Kill him," Demandred had commanded later, but he had added that it would be better they died than let themselves be discovered again. By anyone, even the M'Hael, as if he did not know of Taim's order.

And later still, Moridin had said, "Kill him if you must, but above all, bring everything in his possession to me. That will redeem your previous transgressions." The man said he was one of the Chosen, and no one was mad enough to make that claim unless it was true, yet he seemed to think al'Thor's belongings more important than his death, the killing incidental and not really necessary.

Those two were the only Chosen Kisman had met, but they made his head hurt. They were worse than Cairhienin. He suspected that what they left unsaid could kill a man quicker than a signed order from a High Lord. Well, once Torval and Gedwyn arrived, they could work out—

Abruptly something stung his right arm, and he stared down in consternation at the bloodstain spreading on his cloak. It did not feel like a deep cut, and no cutpurse would have slashed his forearm.

"He belongs to me," a man whispered behind him, but when he turned, there was only the crowd in the street, all going about their business. The few who noticed the dark stain on his cloak looked away quickly. In this place, no one wanted to be associated with even the smallest violence. They were good at ignoring what they did not want to see.

The wound throbbed, burning more than it had at first. Releasing his cloak to the wind, Kisman pressed his left hand over the bloody slash in his sleeve. His arm felt swollen to his touch, and hot. Suddenly he stared in horror at his right hand, stared as it turned as black and bloated as a week-old corpse.

Frantically he began to run, pushing people out of his way, knocking them down. He did not know what was happening to him, how it had been done, but he was sure of the result. Unless he could get out of the city, beyond the lake, up into the hills. He had a chance, then. A horse. He needed a horse! He had to have a chance. He had been promised he would live forever! All he could see were people afoot, and they were scattering before his charge. He thought he heard Guardsmen's rattles, but it might have been the blood pounding in his ears. Everything was going dark. His face hit something hard, and he knew he had fallen. His last thought was that one of the Chosen had decided to punish him, but for what, he could not have said.

Only a few men were sitting at the round tables in the common room of The Crown of Maredo when Rand walked in. Despite the grand name, it was a modest inn, with two dozen rooms on two floors above. The plastered walls of the common room were painted yellow, and the men serving table here wore long yellow aprons. A stone fireplace at either end of the room gave it a marked warmth after outside. The shutters were bolted, but lamps hung on the walls took the edge off the dimness. The smells drifting from the kitchens promised a tasty midday meal of fish from the lake. Rand would be sorry to miss that. The cooks at The Crown of Maredo were very good.

He saw Lan at a table by himself against the wall. The braided leather cord that held Lan's hair back drew sidelong glances from some of the other men, but he refused to give up wearing the *hadori* even for a little while. He met Rand's gaze, and when Rand nodded toward the stairs at the back of the room, he did not waste time with questioning looks; he just set down his winecup and rose, starting for the stairs. Even with just a small knife at his belt, he looked dangerous, but there was nothing to be done about that, either. Several men at the tables glanced Rand's way, but for some reason, they looked away hurriedly when he met their eyes.

Near the kitchen, at the door to the Women's Room, Rand stopped. Men were not allowed in there. Aside from a few flowers painted on the yellow walls, the Women's Room was not much fancier than the common room, though the stand-lamps were painted yellow, too, and the facings of the fireplace. The yellow aprons worn by the women who served table here were no different than those worn by the men in the common room. Mistress Nalhera, the slim, gray-haired innkeeper, was sitting at the same table as Min, Nynaeve and Alivia, all of them chatting and laughing over tea.

Rand's jaw tightened at the sight of the former *damane*. Nynaeve claimed the woman had insisted on coming along, but he did not believe anyone could "insist" on anything with Nynaeve. She wanted Alivia along for some secret reason. She had been behaving mysteriously, as though working as hard as she could at being Aes Sedai, ever since he went back for her after leaving Elayne. All three women had adopted high-necked Far Madding dresses, heavily embroidered with flowers and birds on the bodice and shoulders and right up to their chins, though sometimes Nynaeve grumbled over them. No doubt she would have preferred stout Two Rivers woolens to the finer material she found here. On the other hand, if the red dot of the *ki'sain* on her forehead were not enough to draw every eye, she had decked herself out in jewelry as though attending a royal audience, a slim golden belt and a long necklace and any number of bracelets, all but one set with bright blue sapphires and polished green stones he did not know, and every finger on her right hand had a ring to match. Her Great Serpent ring was tucked away somewhere, so as not to attract attention, but the rest drew ten times as much. Many people would not have known an Aes Sedai's ring at sight, but anyone could see money in those gems.

Rand cleared his throat and bent his head. "Wife, I need to speak with you upstairs," he said, remembering at the last moment to add, "if it pleases you." He could not make it more urgent than that, not and maintain the proprieties, but he hoped they did not linger. They might, if only to demonstrate for the innkeeper that they were not at his beck and call. For some reason, people in Far Madding actually seemed to believe that women from off jumped when men told them to!

Min twisted around in her chair to grin at him, the way she did every time he called her wife. The feel of her in his head was warmth and delight, suddenly sparkling with amusement. She found their situation in Far Madding very amusing. Leaning toward Mistress Nalhera without taking her eyes from him, she said something in a low voice that made the older woman cackle with laughter and gave Nynaeve a pained expression.

Alivia stood up, looking nothing like the subdued woman he vaguely remembered handing over to Taim. All those captured *sul'dam* and *damane* had been a burden he was glad to be free of, no more. There were threads of white in her golden hair and fine lines at the corners of her eyes, but those eyes were fierce now. "Well?" she drawled, staring down at Nynaeve, but somehow she made the word both a criticism and a command.

Nynaeve glared up at the woman and took her sweet time in standing and smoothing her skirts, but at least she stood.

Rand waited no longer before rushing upstairs. Lan was waiting at the head of the stairs, just out of sight of the common room below. Quietly, Rand gave a bare-bones account of what had happened. Lan's stony face never changed expression.

"At least one of them is done," he said, turning toward the room he shared with Nynaeve. "I'll get our things ready."

Rand was already in the room he and Min shared, hurriedly pulling their clothes out of the tall wardrobe and stuffing them any way they would go into one of the wicker pack hampers, when she finally entered the room. Followed by Nynaeve and Alivia.

"Light, you'll ruin our things that way," Min exclaimed, shouldering him away from the hamper. She began removing garments and folding them neatly on the bed beside his peace-bonded sword. "Why are we packing?" she asked, but gave him no chance to answer. "Mistress Nalhera says you wouldn't be so sulky if I switched you every morning," she laughed, shaking out one of the coats she did not wear here. He had told her he would buy her new, but she refused to leave the embroidered coats and breeches behind. "I told her I'd consider it. She likes Lan very much." Suddenly she pitched her voice high in imitation of the innkeeper. "A neat, mild-mannered man is much to be preferred over a pretty face, I always say."

Nynaeve snorted. "Who wants a man she can make jump through hoops whenever she likes?" Rand stared at her, and Min's mouth fell open. That was exactly what Nynaeve did to Lan, and how the man put up with it was more than Rand could understand.

"You think about men too much, Nynaeve," Alivia drawled. Nynaeve frowned but instead of saying anything, she just stood there fingering one of her bracelets, a peculiar piece with flat golden chains stretching down the back of her left hand to rings on all four fingers. The older woman shook her head as though disappointed at not getting a rise.

"I'm packing because we have to go, and be quick about it," Rand said hastily. Nynaeve might be quiet for the moment, odd as that was, but if her face got any darker she would be yanking her braid and shouting till no one could get a word in edgewise for hours.

Before he finished the same account he had given Lan, Min stopped folding things and started replacing her books in the second hamper, hurriedly enough that she did not pad them with cloaks the way she usually did. The other two women stood staring at him as though they had never seen him before. In case they were not being as quick to see as Min, he impatiently added, "Rochaid and Kisman ambushed me. They knew I was following. Kisman got away. If he knows this inn, he and Dashiva and Gedwyn and Torval might all turn up here, maybe in two or three days, or maybe in an hour or so."

"I am not blind," Nynaeve said, still staring at him. There was no heat in her voice; was she protesting just for the form of it? "If you want to hurry, help Min instead of standing around like a woolhead." She stared at him a moment longer, and shook her head before leaving.

Alivia paused in the act of following, and glared at Rand. No, there was nothing subdued about her any longer. "You could get yourself killed like that," she said disapprovingly. "You have too much to do to get killed yet. You must let us help."

He frowned at the door closing behind her. "Have you had any viewings about her, Min?"

"All the time, but not the kind you mean, nothing I understand." She wrinkled her nose at one of the books and set it aside. Small chance she would abandon a single volume of her not-so-small library. Undoubtedly she meant to carry that one, and read it at the first opportunity. She spent hours with her nose in those books. "Rand," she said slowly, "you did all that, killed one man and faced another, and . . . Rand, I didn't *feel* anything. In the bond, I mean. No fear, no anger. Not even *concern!* Nothing."

"I wasn't angry with him." Shaking his head, he began shoving clothes into the hamper again. "He just needed killing, that's all. And why would I be afraid?"

"Oh," she said in a small voice. "I see." She bent back to the books. The bond had gone very still, as if she were deep in thought, but there was a troubled thread worming though the stillness.

"Min, I promise I won't let anything happen to you." He did not know whether he could keep that promise, but he intended to try.

She smiled at him, almost laughing. Light, she was beautiful. "I know that, Rand. And I won't let anything happen to you." Love flowed along the bond like the blaze of a noonday sun. "Alivia's right, though. You do have to let us help somehow. If you describe these fellows well enough, maybe we can ask questions. You certainly can't search the whole city alone."

We are dead men, Lews Therin murmured. *Dead men should be quiet in their graves, but they never are.*

Rand barely heard the voice in his head. Suddenly he knew he did not have to describe Kisman and the others. He could draw them so well that anyone would recognize the faces. Except, he had never been able to draw in his life. Lews Therin could, though. That should have frightened him. It should have.

Isam paced the room, studying by the ever-present light of *Tel'aran'rhiod.* The bed linens shifted from rumpled to neatly made between one glance and the next. The coverlet changed from flowered to plain dark red to quilted. The ephemeral always changed here, and he barely noticed anymore. He could not use *Tel'aran'rhiod* the way the Chosen could, but here was where he felt most free. Here, he could be who he wanted to be. He chuckled at the thought.

Stopping beside the bed, he carefully unsheathed the two poisoned daggers and stepped out of the Unseen World into the waking. As he did, he became Luc. It seemed appropriate.

The room was dark in the waking world, but the single window let in sufficient moonlight for Luc to make out the mounded shapes of two people lying asleep beneath their blankets. Without hesitation he drove a blade into each. They woke with small cries, but he pulled the blades free and drove them in again and again. With the poison, it was unlikely either would have had the strength to shout loudly enough to be heard outside the room, but he wanted to make this kill his own in a way that poison could not grant. Soon they stopped twitching when he thrust a blade between ribs.

Wiping the daggers clean on the coverlet, he resheathed them with as much care as he had drawn them. He had been given many gifts, but immunity to poison, or any other weapon, was not among them. Then he took a short candle from his pocket and blew away enough ash from the banked coals in the fireplace to light the wick. He always liked to see the people he killed, after if he could not during. He had especially enjoyed those two Aes Sedai in the Stone of Tear. The incredulity on their faces when he appeared out of thin air, the horror when they realized he had not come to save them, were treasured memories. That had been Isam, not him, but the memories were none the less prized for that. Neither of them got to kill an Aes Sedai very often.

For a moment he studied the faces of the man and woman on the bed, then pinched out the candle's flame and returned the candle to his pocket before stepping back into *Tel'aran'rhiod*.

His patron of the moment was waiting for him. A man, he was sure of that much, but Luc could not look at him. It was not as it was with those slimy Gray Men, whom you just did not notice. He had killed one of them, once, in the White Tower itself. They felt cold and empty to the touch. It had been like killing a corpse. No, this man had done something with the Power so Luc's eyes slid away from him like water sliding down glass. Even seen at the corner of the eye, he was a blur.

"The pair sleeping in this room will sleep forever," Luc said, "but the man was bald, the woman gray."

"A pity," the man said, and the voice seemed to melt in Luc's ears. He would not be able to recognize it if he heard it without the disguise. The man had to be one of the Chosen. Few save the Chosen knew how to reach him, and none of the men among those few could channel, or would have dared trying to command him. His services were always begged, except by the Great Lord himself, and more recently by the Chosen, but none of the Chosen Luc had met had ever taken such precautions as this.

"Do you want me to try again?" Luc asked.

"Perhaps. When I tell you. Not before. Remember, not a word of this to anyone."

"As you command," Luc replied, bowing, but the man was already making a gateway, a hole that opened into a snowy forest glade. He was gone before Luc straightened.

It really was a pity. He had rather looked forward to killing his nephew and the wench. But if there was time to pass, hunting was always a pleasure. He became Isam. Isam liked killing wolves even more than Luc did.

CHAPTER

23

To Lose the Sun

Trying to hold the unfamiliar woolen cloak tightly around her with one hand, trying not to fall out of the even more unfamiliar saddle, Shalon awkwardly heeled her horse forward and followed Harine and her Swordmaster Moad through the hole in the air that led from a stableyard in the Sun Palace to . . . She was not sure where, except that it was a long open area—a clearing, was it called? she thought that was right—a clearing larger than a raker's deck, among stunted trees spaced out on hills. The pines, the only trees among them she recognized, were too small and twisted for any use but tar and turpentine. Most of the rest showed bare gray branches that made her think of bones. The morning sun sat just above the treetops, and if anything, the cold seemed more bitter here than it had in the city she had left behind. She hoped the horse did not misstep and tumble her down onto the rocks that stuck up wherever patches of snow did not cover the rotting leaves on the ground. She distrusted horses. Unlike ships, animals had minds of their own. They were treacherous things to climb on top of. And horses had teeth. Whenever her mount showed his, so near to her legs, she flinched and patted his neck and made soothing sounds. At least, she hoped the beast found them soothing.

Cadsuane herself, garbed in unrelieved dark green, sat easily on a tall horse with a black mane and tail, maintaining the weave that made the gateway. Horses did not bother her. Nothing bothered her. A sudden breeze stirred the dark gray cloak spread over the back end of her mount, but she gave no sign of feeling the cold at all. The golden hair ornaments dangling around her dark gray bun swung as she turned her head to watch Shalon and her companions. She was a handsome woman, but not one you would notice twice in a crowd except that her smooth face did not match her hair. Once you came to know her, it was too late.

Shalon would have given much to see how that weave was done, even if it had meant being near Cadsuane, but she had not been allowed into the stableyard until the gateway was complete, and seeing a sail spread on the yardarm did not teach you how to set a sail much less make one. All she knew was the name. Riding past, she avoided meeting the Aes Sedai's gaze, but she felt it. The woman's eyes made her toes curl, seeking a footing the stirrups could not give. She could see no way to escape, yet she hoped to find one through studying the Aes Sedai. That she knew very little about Aes Sedai, she was readily willing to admit—she had never met one before sailing to Cairhien, and thought about them only to praise the Light that she had not been chosen to become one—but there were currents among Cadsuane's companions, deep beneath the surface. Deep, strong currents could alter everything that seemed apparent on the surface.

The four Aes Sedai who had come through right after Cadsuane were waiting on their horses at one side of the . . . clearing . . . with three Warders. At least, Shalon was sure that Ihvon was the fiery Alanna's Warder, and Tomas was stout little Verin's, but she also was sure she had seen the very young man who stayed so close to plump Daigian's side wearing an Asha'man's black coat. Surely he could not be a Warder. Could he? Eben was just a boy. Yet when the woman gazed at him, her usual puffed-up pride seemed to swell further. Kumira, a pleasant-looking woman with blue eyes that could turn into knives when something interested her, sat her saddle a little to one side, studying young Eben so sharply it was a wonder he was not lying on the ground flensed.

"I will not put up with this much longer," Harine grumbled, thumping her mare with her bare heels to keep it moving. Her brocaded yellow silks did not help her keep a good seat in the saddle any more than did Shalon's blue. She swayed and slid with the animal's movements, on the point of toppling to the ground at every step. The breeze gusted again, flipping the dangling ends of her sash about, making her cloak billow, but she disdained to control the garment. Cloaks were not much used in the ships; they got in the way, and could tangle your arms and legs when you needed them for survival. Moad had refused one, trusting to the quilted blue coat he wore in the coldest seas. Nesune Bihara, all in bronze wool, rode through the gateway looking around as if trying to see everything at once, and then Elza Penfel, who wore a sullen expression for some reason and clutched her fur-lined green cloak tight. None of the other Aes Sedai seemed to bother much with sheltering themselves from the cold.

"I *may* be able to see the Coramoor, she says," Harine muttered, pulling at her reins until the mare turned toward the side of the clearing away from where the Aes Sedai were gathering. "May! And she offers this *chance* as though granting a privilege." Harine did not need to give a name; when Harine said "she" that way, like a jellyfish's sting, there could only be one woman she meant. "I have the right, bargained for and agreed! She denies me the agreed entourage! I must leave my Sailmistress behind, and my attendants!" Erian Boroleos appeared through the opening, as intent as if she expected to find a battle, followed by Beldeine Nyram, who did not even look like an Aes Sedai. Both wore green, Erian completely, Beldeine in slashes in her sleeves and skirts. Did that mean something? Likely not. "Am I to approach the Coramoor like a deckgirl touching my heart to a Sailmistress?" When several Aes Sedai were together, you could see the smooth-faced agelessness clearly, so you could not say whether any one was twenty or twice that even if her hair was white, and Beldeine simply looked a girl of twenty. And that told no more than did her skirts. "Am I to air my own bedding and wash my own linens? She turns protocol straight into the wind! I will not allow it! No more!" These were old complaints, voiced a dozen times since last night, when Cadsuane laid down her conditions if they were to accompany her. Those conditions had been strict, but Harine had had no choice save to accede, which only added to the bitterness.

Shalon listened with half an ear, nodding and murmuring the appropriate responses. Agreement, of course. Her sister expected agreement. Most of her attention was on the Aes Sedai. Surreptitiously. Moad did not pretend to listen, but then, he was Harine's Swordmaster. Harine might be tight as a wet knot with everyone else, yet she gave Moad so much leeway anyone might have thought the hard-eyed, gray-haired man was her lover, especially since both were widowed. At least, they might think it if they did not know Harine. Harine would never take a lover who stood lower than she, and now, of course, that meant she could take none. In any case, once they stopped their horses near the trees, Moad leaned an elbow on the tall pommel of his saddle, rested a hand on the long, carved ivory hilt of the sword thrust behind his green sash, and openly studied the Aes Sedai and the men with them. Where had he learned to ride a horse? He actually looked . . . comfortable. Anyone could tell his rank at a glance, from his eight earrings of the heaviest weight and the knotting of his sash, even if he was not wearing his sword and matching dagger. Did Aes Sedai have no way to do the same? Could they truly be so disorganized? Supposedly the White Tower was like some mechanical contrivance that ground up thrones and reshaped them to its will. Of course, the machinery did seem to be broken, now.

"I said, where has she brought us, Shalon?"

Harine's voice, like an icy razor, drained the blood from Shalon's face. Serving under a younger sibling was always difficult, but Harine made it more so. In private she was beyond cool, and in public she was capable of having a Sailmistress hung up by the ankles, not to mention a Windfinder. And since that young shorebound woman, Min, had told her she would be Mistress of the Ships one day, she had grown ever sharper. Staring hard-eyed at Shalon, she raised her golden scent-box as if to cover an unpleasant odor, though the cold killed all the perfume.

Hurriedly Shalon looked into the sky, trying to judge the sun. She wished her sextant were not locked away on *White Spray*—the shorebound were never allowed to see a sextant, much less see one being used—but she was uncertain it would have done her any good. These trees might be short, but she still could not make out a horizon. Close on to the north, the hills rose into mountains that slanted northeast to southwest. She could not say how high she was. There was far too much up and down about landside to suit her. Even so, any Windfinder knew how to make rough approximations. And when Harine demanded information, she expected to receive it.

"I can only guess, Wavemistress," she said. Harine's jaw tightened, but no Windfinder would present a guess as a firm position. "I believe we are three or four hundred leagues south of Cairhien. More, I cannot say." Any first-day apprentice using a string-stick who gave a fix that loose would have been bent over for the deckmaster's starter, but the words chilled Shalon's tongue as she heard what she was saying. A hundred leagues over the full turn of a day was good sailing for a raker. Moad pursed his lips thoughtfully.

Harine nodded slowly, looking right through Shalon as though she could see rakers under full sail gliding through holes woven in the air with the Power. The seas truly would be theirs, then. Giving herself a shake, she leaned toward Shalon, her eyes catching Shalon's like hooks. "You must learn this, whatever the cost. Tell her you will spy on me if she teaches you. If you convince her, she might, the Light willing. Or at least you may get close enough to one of the others to learn it."

Shalon licked her lips. She hoped Harine had not seen her jerk. "I refused her before, Wavemistress." She had needed some explanation of why the Aes Sedai had held her for a week, and a version of the truth had seemed safest. Harine knew everything. Except the secret Verin had winkled out. Except that Shalon had agreed to Cadsuane's demands in order to hide that secret. The Grace of the Light be upon her, she regretted Ailil, but she had been so lonely that she sailed too far before she knew it. With Harine, there were no evening talks over honeyed wine to soften the long months parted from her husband Mishael. At best, many more months would pass before she could lie in his arms. "With respect, why should she believe me now?"

"Because you want the learning." Harine chopped the air with one hand. "The shorebound always believe greed. You will have to tell some things, of course, to prove yourself. I will decide what each day. Perhaps I can steer her where I wish."

Hard fingers seemed to dig into Shalon's scalp. She had intended to tell Cadsuane as little as she could get by with, and as seldom, until she found a way free of her. If she had to talk with the Aes Sedai every day, and worse, lie to her outright, the woman would pry out more than Shalon wanted. More than Harine wanted. Much more. It was as certain as sunrise. "Forgive me, Wavemistress," she said with every ounce of deference she could find, "but if I may be allowed to say so—"

She cut off as Sarene Nemdahl rode up and reined to a halt before them. The last of the Aes Sedai and Warders had come through, and Cadsuane had let the gateway vanish. Corele, a thin woman if pretty, was laughing and tossing her mane of black hair as she spoke to Kumira. Merise, a tall woman with eyes bluer than Kumira's and a more than handsome face that was stern enough to give even Harine pause, was using sharp gestures to direct the four men leading packhorses. Everyone else was gathering reins. It seemed they were all getting ready to leave the clearing.

Sarene was lovely, though the absence of jewelry lessened her looks, of course, as did the plain white dress she wore. The shorebound seemed to have no joy of color at all. Even her dark cloak was lined with white fur. "Cadsuane, she has asked . . . instructed . . . me to be your attendant, Wavemistress," she said, inclining her head respectfully. "I will answer your questions, to the extent that I can, and help you with the customs, as well as I know them. I realize you might feel discomfort at being with me, but when Cadsuane commands, we must obey."

Shalon smiled. She doubted the Aes Sedai knew that in the ships, an attendant was what the shorebound would call a servant. Harine would probably laugh and demand to know whether the Aes Sedai could clean linens properly. It would be good to have her in a good mood.

Rather than laughing, though, Harine stiffened in her saddle as though her backbone had become a mainmast, and her eyes popped. "I feel no discomfort!" she snapped. "I simply prefer to . . . to put any questions to someone else . . . to Cadsuane. Yes. To Cadsuane. And *I* certainly do not have to obey her or anyone! Not anyone! Except the Mistress of the Ships!" Shalon frowned; it was unlike her sister to sound scatter-witted. Drawing a deep breath, Harine continued in a firmer tone, though in a way, just as oddly as before. "I speak for the Mistress of the Ships to the

Atha'an Miere, and I demand due respect! I demand it, do you hear me? Do you?"

"I can ask her to name someone else," Sarene said doubt-fully, as if she did not expect her asking would change any-thing. "You must understand that she gave me quite specific instructions that day. But I should not have lost my temper. That is a failing of mine. Temper destroys logic."

"I understand obeying orders," Harine growled, crouch-ing in the saddle. She looked ready to launch herself at Sarene's throat. "I *approve* of obeying orders!" she very nearly snarled. "However, orders that have been carried out can be forgotten. They no longer need be spoken of. Do you understand me?" Shalon stared sideways at her. What was she talking about? What orders had Sarene carried out, and why did Harine want them forgotten? Moad made no pretence of hiding his raised eyebrows. Harine was aware of his scrutiny, at least, and her face became a thunderhead.

Sarene seemed not to notice. "I do not see how one can deliberately forget," she said slowly, a small frown creas-ing her forehead, "but I suppose you mean that we should pretend to. Is that it?" The beaded braids dangling from her cowl clicked together as she shook her head at this foolish-ness. "Very well. I will answer your questions as well as I can. What do you wish to know?" Harine sighed loudly. Shalon might have taken it for impatience, but she thought it was relief. Relief!

Relieved or not, Harine became her normal self again, self-possessed and commanding, meeting the Aes Sedai's gaze as though trying to make her drop her eyes. "You can tell me where we are and where we are going," she de-manded.

"We are in the Hills of Kintara," Cadsuane said, appear-ing before them suddenly, her mount rearing and pawing the air, flinging snow, "and we are going to Far Madding." Not only did she stay in the saddle, she did not even seem to notice the animal's heaving!

"Is the Coramoor in this Far Madding?"

"Patience is a virtue, I am told, Wavemistress." Despite Cadsuane's use of Harine's proper title, there was no respect in her manner. Far from it. "You will ride with me. Keep up and try not to fall off. It would be unpleasant, if I had to have you carried like sacks of grain. Once we reach the city, keep silent unless I tell you to speak. I won't have you creating problems through ignorance. You will let Sarene guide you. She has her instructions."

Shalon expected an outburst of rage, but Harine held her tongue, though with obvious effort. Once Cadsuane turned away, Harine did mutter angrily under her breath, but she clamped her teeth tight when Sarene's horse moved. Plainly, her mutters were not to be overheard by Aes Sedai.

Riding with Cadsuane, it turned out, meant riding behind her, southward through the trees. Alanna and Verin actually rode beside the woman, but one look from her when Harine attempted to join them made clear that no one else was welcome. Once again the expected explosion did not come. Instead, Harine frowned at Sarene for some reason, then jerked her mount around to take position between Shalon and Moad. She did not bother asking any further questions of Sarene, on Shalon's other side, only glowered at the backs of the women ahead. If Shalon had not known Harine better, she would have said there was more sulk than anger in that glare.

For her part, Shalon was glad to ride in silence. Riding a horse was difficult enough without having to talk at the same time. Besides, she suddenly knew why Harine was behaving in such a peculiar fashion. Harine must be trying to smooth the waters with the Aes Sedai. It had to be that. Harine never controlled her temper without great need. The strain of controlling it now must have her boiling inside. And if her efforts did not end as she wanted, she would boil Shalon. Thinking about that made Shalon's head ache. The Light help and guide her, there had to be a way to avoid spying on her sister without finding her cheek-chain stripped of honors and herself assigned to a scow under a Sailmistress brooding over why she had never risen higher and ready to take out her grievances on everyone around her. Equally as bad, Mishael might declare their marriage vows broken. There just had to be a way.

Sometimes she twisted around in her saddle to look at the Aes Sedai riding behind her. There was nothing to learn from the women in front, certainly. Every so often Cadsuane and Verin exchanged words, but leaning close to one another and speaking too softly to be overheard. Alanna appeared intent on whatever lay ahead, her eyes always looking south. Two or three times she quickened her horse's pace for a few steps before Cadsuane brought her back with a quiet word that Alanna obeyed reluctantly, with hot-eyed stare or sullen grimace. Cadsuane and Verin appeared solicitous of the woman, Cadsuane patting her arm in almost the way Shalon patted her mount's neck and Verin beaming at her, as though Alanna were recovering from an illness. Which told Shalon nothing. So she thought about the others.

You did not rise in the ships just through your ability to Weave the Winds or predict the weather or fix a position. You needed to read the intent that lay between the words of your orders, to interpret small gestures and facial expressions; you had to notice who deferred to whom, even subtly, for courage and ability alone took you only so high.

Four of them, Nesune and Erian, Beldeine and Elza, rode in a cluster not far behind her, though they were not really together, only occupying the same space. They did not talk among themselves, or look at one another. They did not seem to like one another very much. In her mind, Shalon had them in the same boat with Sarene. The Aes Sedai pretended that they were all one under Cadsuane, yet that was plainly untrue. Merise, Corele, Kumira and Daigian crewed another boat, commanded by Cadsuane. Sometimes Alanna seemed in one boat, sometimes the other, while Verin appeared to be in some way of Cadsuane's boat but not in it. Swimming alongside, perhaps, with Cadsuane holding her hand. If that was not strange enough, there was the matter of deference.

Oddly, it seemed that Aes Sedai valued strength in the Power above experience or skill. They ranked themselves by strength, like deckmen squabbling in shoreside taverns. All deferred to Cadsuane, of course, yet there were oddities among the rest. By their own hierarchy, some in Nesune's boat were in a position to expect deference from some in Cadsuane's, but although those in Cadsuane's boat who should defer did so, they did so as though to a superior who had committed a grievous crime known to all. By that hierarchy, Nesune stood higher than any save Cadsuane and Merise, yet she faced Daigian, who stood at the very bottom, as if willfully defiant over committing that crime, and so did the others in her boat. It was all very discreet, a slightly lifted chin, a small arch of the eyebrow, a twist of the lips, but obvious to an eye trained climbing in the ships. Perhaps there was nothing in it that would help her, but if she had to pick oakum, the only way was to find a thread and pull.

The wind began to pick up; gusts flattened her cloak against her back and made it flap on either side ahead of her. She was hardly aware of it.

The Warders might be another thread. They were all at the very rear, hidden by the Aes Sedai riding behind Nesune and the other three. In truth, Shalon had expected that among twelve Aes Sedai, there would be more than seven Warders. Every Aes Sedai was supposed to have one, if not more. She shook her head irritably. Except the Red Ajah, of course. She was not *entirely* ignorant of Aes Sedai.

Anyway, the question was not how many Warders, but whether they all *were* Warders. She was certain she had seen grizzled old Damer and the so-pretty Jahar in black coats, too, before they suddenly took up with the Aes Sedai. At the time, she had been unwilling to look too closely at the blackcoats, and in truth, she had been half-blind with the dainty Ailil as well, but she *was* sure. And whatever the case with Eben, she was almost certain the other two were Warders, now. Almost. Jahar jumped as fast as Nethan or Bassane when Merise pointed, and from the way Corele smiled at Damer, he was either her Warder or her bedwarmer, and Shalon could not imagine a woman like Corele taking a nearly bald old man with a limp into her bed. She might know little about Aes Sedai, but she was sure bonding men who could channel was not an accepted practice. If she could prove they had done so, perhaps that was a knife sharp enough to cut herself free from Cadsuane.

"The men, they can no longer channel now," Sarene murmured.

Shalon straightened herself around in the saddle so quickly that she had to grab her horse's mane with both hands to keep from falling off. The wind blew her cloak over her head, and she had to fight that down before she could sit up. They were coming out of the trees above a wide road that curved southward out of the hills to a lake perhaps a mile off, on the edge of flat land covered with brown grass, a sea of brown stretching to the horizon. The lake, bordered along the west with a narrow wash of reeds, was a pitiful excuse for a body of water, no more than ten miles long at most and less than that wide. A fair-sized island crouched in the middle, surrounded by high, tower-studded walls as far as she could see, and covered by a city. She took all that in at a glance, her eyes fastening on Sarene. It was almost as if the woman had been reading her mind. "Why can they not channel?" she asked. "Did you . . . ? Have you . . . gentled . . . them?" She thought that was the right word, but that was supposed to kill the man. She had always supposed it was just an odd way to soften execution for some unknown reason.

Sarene blinked, and Shalon realized the Aes Sedai had been speaking to herself. For a moment she studied Shalon as they followed Cadsuane down the slope, then turned her gaze back to the city on the island. "You notice things, Shalon. It would be best if you keep what you have noticed about the men to yourself."

"Such as them being Warders?" Shalon said quietly. "Is that why you could bond them? Because you gentled them?" She hoped to jar some admission loose, but the Aes Sedai merely glanced at her. She did not speak again until they had reached the bottom of the hill and turned onto the road behind Cadsuane. The road was wide, the dirt packed hard by much traffic, but they had it to themselves.

"It is not exactly a secret," Sarene said at last, and not very willingly for something that was not a secret, "but neither is it well known. We do not speak of Far Madding often, except for sisters born there, and even they seldom visit. Still, you should know before you enter. The city possesses a *ter'angreal*. Or perhaps it is three *ter'angreal*. No one knows. They—or it—cannot be studied any more than they can be removed. They must have been made during the Breaking, when fear of madmen channeling the Power was the matter of every day. But to pay such a price for the safety." The beaded braids dangling onto her chest rattled together as she shook her head in disbelief. "These *ter'angreal,* they duplicate a *stedding*. In the important ways at least, I fear, though I suppose an Ogier would not think so." She gave a doleful sigh.

Shalon gaped at her, and exchanged confused looks with Harine and Moad. Why would fables frighten an Aes Sedai? Harine opened her mouth, then motioned for Shalon to ask

the obvious question. Perhaps she was to make friends with
Sarene to help smooth her course, too? Shalon's head really
did ache. But she was curious, too.

"What ways are those?" she asked carefully. Did the
woman really believe in people five spans tall who sang to
trees? There was something about axes, too. Here come the
Aelfinn to steal all your bread; here come the Ogier to chop
off your head. Light, she had not heard that since Harine
was still in leading strings. With their mother rising in the
ships, she had been charged with raising Harine along with
her own first child.

Sarene's eyes widened in surprise. "You truly do not
know?" Her gaze went back to the island city ahead. By
her expression, she was about to enter the bilges. "Inside
the *stedding,* you cannot channel. You cannot even feel the
True Source. No weave made outside can affect what is inside, not that that matters. In truth, here there are two *stedding,* one within the other. The larger affects men, but we
will enter the smaller before we reach the bridge."

"You will not be able to channel in there?" Harine said.
When the Aes Sedai nodded without looking away from
the city, a thin frosty smile touched Harine's lips. "Perhaps
after we find quarters, you and I can discuss instructions."

"You read the philosophy?" Sarene looked startled. "The
Theory of Instructions, it is not well thought of these days,
yet I have always believed there was much to learn there.
A discussion will be pleasant, to take my mind from other
matters. If Cadsuane allows us time."

Harine's mouth fell open. Gaping at the Aes Sedai, she
forgot to cling to her saddle, and only Moad seizing her arm
saved her from a fall.

Shalon had never heard Harine mention philosophy, but
she did not care what her sister was talking about. Staring
toward Far Madding, she swallowed hard. She had learned
to sheathe someone against using the Power, of course, and
been sheathed herself as part of her training, yet when you
were sheathed, you could still feel the Source. What would
it be like not to feel it, like the sun just out of sight beyond
the corner of your eye? What would it be like to lose the
sun?

As they rode nearer the lake, she felt more aware of the
Source than she had since her first joy at touching it. It was

all she could do not to drink of it, but the Aes Sedai would see the light and know, and likely know why. She would not shame herself or Harine in that manner. Small, beamy craft dotted the water, none more than six or seven spans in length, some hauling in nets, others creeping along on long sweeps. Judging by the windswept swells that rolled across the surface, sometimes crashing into one another in fountains of foam like surf, sails might have been as much hindrance as help. Still, the boats seemed almost a familiar thing, though nothing like the sleek fours or eights or twelves carried on the ships. A tiny comfort amid strangeness.

The road turned onto a spit of land jutting half a mile or more into the lake, and abruptly the Source vanished. Sarene sighed, but gave no other sign she had noticed. Shalon wet her lips. It was not so bad as she had feared. It made her feel . . . empty . . . but she could bear that. As long as she did not have to bear it too long. The wind, gusting and curling and trying to steal cloaks, suddenly felt much colder.

At the end of the spit, a village of gray stone houses with darker slate roofs stood between road and water on one side. Village women hurrying along with large baskets stopped at the sight of the mounted party. More than one felt at her own nose as she stared. Shalon had grown almost accustomed to those stares, in Cairhien. In any case, the fortification opposite the village drew her eyes, a mound of tight-fitted stone five spans high with soldiers watching through the barred faceguards of their helmets from atop towers at the corners. Some held drawn crossbows where she could see them. From a large iron-plated door at the end nearest the bridge, more helmeted soldiers spilled out into the road, men in square-scaled armor with a golden sword worked on the left shoulder. Some wore swords at their waists and others carried long spears or crossbows. Shalon wondered whether they expected the Aes Sedai to try fighting past. An officer with a yellow plume on his helmet motioned Cadsuane to a halt, then approached her and removed his helmet, freeing gray-streaked hair that spilled down his back to his waist. He had a hard, disgruntled face.

Cadsuane leaned low in her saddle to exchange a few quiet words with the man, then produced a fat purse from beneath her saddlebags. He took it and stepped back, motioning one of the soldiers forward, a tall bony man who was not wearing a helmet. He carried a writing board, and his hair, gathered at the back of his head like the officer's, also hung to his waist. He bent his neck respectfully before inquiring Alanna's name, and wrote it very carefully, with his tongue caught between his teeth, dipping his pen often. Helmet on his hip, the discontented officer stood studying the others behind Cadsuane with no expression. The purse hung from his hand as though forgotten. He seemed unaware he had been speaking with an Aes Sedai. Or maybe, he did not care. Here, an Aes Sedai was no different from any other woman. Shalon shuddered. Here, she was no different from any other woman, bereft of her gifts for the duration of her stay. Bereft.

"They take the names of all foreigners," Sarene said. "The Counsels, they like to know who is in the city."

"Perhaps they would admit a Wavemistress without bribes," Harine said drily. The bony soldier, turning away from Alanna, gave the usual shorebound start at Shalon and Harine's jewelry before coming toward them.

"Your name, Mistress, if it pleases you?" he said politely to Sarene, ducking his head again. She gave it without mentioning that she was Aes Sedai. Shalon gave hers as simply, but Harine offered the titles as well, Harine din Togara Two Winds, Wavemistress of Clan Shodein, Ambassador Extraordinary of the Mistress of the Ships to the Atha'an Miere. The fellow blinked, then bit his tongue and bent his neck over the writing board. Harine scowled. When she wanted to impress someone, she expected them to be impressed.

As the bony man was writing, a stocky, helmeted soldier with a leather scrip hanging from his shoulder pushed between Harine's horse and Moad's. Behind the bars of his faceguard, a puckered scar down his face pulled up one side of his mouth in a sneer, but he bowed his head to Harine respectfully enough. And then he tried to take Moad's sword.

"You must allow it or leave your blades here until you depart," Sarene said quickly when the Swordmaster twitched the scabbard out of the stocky man's hands. "This service, it is what Cadsuane was paying for, Wavemistress. In Far Madding, no man is allowed to carry more than the belt knife unless it is peace-bonded so it cannot be drawn. Even the Wall Guards like these men cannot take a sword away from their place of duty. Is that not so?" she asked the skinny soldier, and he replied that it was, and a good thing, too.

With a shrug, Moad lifted the sword from his sash, and when the fellow with the perpetual sneer demanded his ivory-hilted dagger as well, he handed that over. Tucking the long dagger behind his belt, the man produced a spool of fine wire from his scrip and deftly began wrapping the sword in a fine net. Every so often he paused to pluck a seal-press from his belt and fold a small lead disc around the wires, but he had quick, practiced hands.

"The list of names, it will be distributed to the other two bridges," Sarene went on, "and the men will have to show the wires unbroken or they will be held until a magistrate determines that no other crime has been committed. Even if none has, the penalty is both a very heavy fine and flogging. Most foreigners, they deposit their weapons before entering to save the coin, but that would mean we must leave by this bridge. The Light alone knows which direction we will want to go when we leave here." Looking toward Cadsuane, who appeared to be restraining Alanna from riding across the long bridge alone, Sarene added almost under her breath, "At least, I hope that is her reasoning."

Harine snorted. "This is ridiculous. How is he to defend himself?"

"No need for any man to defend himself in Far Madding, Mistress." The stocky man's voice was coarse, but he did not sound mocking. He was stating the obvious. "The Street Guards take care of that. Let any man as wants start carrying a sword, and soon we'd be as bad as everyplace else. I heard what they're like, Mistress, and we don't want that here." Bowing to Harine, he strode on down the column followed by the man with the writing board.

Moad briefly examined his sword and dagger, both neatly wrapped hilt and scabbard, then eased them back in place, taking care not to snag his sash on the seals. "Swords only become useful when wits fail," he said. Harine snorted again. Shalon wondered how that fellow had gained his scar if Far Madding was so safe.

Sounds of protest rose from the rear, where the other men were, but they were quickly silenced. By Merise, Shalon

TO LOSE THE SUN 431

would have wagered. At times, the woman made Cadsuane seem lax. Her Warders were like the trained guard dogs the Amayar used, ready to leap at a whistle, and she was not at all hesitant about calling down the other Aes Sedai's Warders. Soon enough all of the swords had been peace-bonded, and the packhorses searched for hidden weapons, and they rode out onto the bridge, hooves ringing on stone. Shalon tried to take in everything, not so much from interest as to take her mind off what was missing.

The bridge was flat and as wide as the road behind, with low stone copings on the side that would stop a wagon from plunging over but give no shelter to attackers, and it was long, too, perhaps as much as three-quarters of a mile, and straight as an arrow. Now and then one of the boats passed beneath, which they could not have done had they had masts. Tall towers flanked the city's iron-strapped gates—the Caemlyn Gate was the name Sarene gave—where guards with the golden sword on their shoulders bowed their heads to the women and cast suspicious eyes on the men. The street beyond. . . .

Trying to be observant was no use. The street was wide and straight, full of people and carts, lined with stone buildings two or three stories high, and it all seemed a blur. The Source was gone! She knew it would come back when she left this place, and, Light, she wanted to leave now. But how long before she could? The Coramoor might be in this city, and Harine meant to make herself fast to the Coramoor, perhaps because of who he was, perhaps because she thought he would help her rise to Mistress of the Ships. Until Harine left, until Cadsuane freed them from the agreement, Shalon was anchored here. Here, where there was no True Source.

Sarene talked incessantly, yet Shalon barely heard her. They crossed a large square with a huge statue of a woman in the center, but Shalon caught only her name, Einion Avharin, though she knew Sarene was telling her why the woman was famous in Far Madding and why her statue was pointing toward the Caemlyn Gate. A row of leafless trees divided the street beyond the square. Sedan chairs and coaches and men in square-scaled armor threaded though the crowds, but they registered only on her eyes. Trembling, she huddled in on herself. The city vanished. Time vanished. Everything

vanished except her fear that she would never feel the
Source again. She had never before realized what comfort
she had taken in its unseen presence. It had always been
there, promising joy beyond knowing, life so rich that colors paled when the Power was gone from her. And now the
Source itself was gone. Gone. That was all she was aware
of, all she could be aware of. It was gone.

CHAPTER
24

Among the Counsels

S omeone shook Shalon's arm. It was Sarene, and the
Aes Sedai was talking to her. "It is in there," Sarene
said, "in the Hall of the Counsels. Beneath the dome."
Withdrawing her hand, she took a deep breath and gathered her reins. "It is ridiculous to think that the effect is any
worse just because we are close," she muttered, "but it does
feel so."

Shalon roused herself with an effort. The emptiness
would not go away, but she forced herself to ignore it. Yet in
truth she felt cored like a piece of fruit.

They were in a huge—she supposed it was still called a
square, though this one was round—a huge square paved
with white stone. At the center stood a great palace, a round
structure all of white except for the tall blue dome on top,
like half of a ball. Massive fluted columns surrounded the
upper two levels below the dome, and a steady stream of
people flowed up and down the broad white stone stairs
leading up to the second level on either side. Except for
a pair of tall arched bronze gates standing open directly
ahead of them, the lowest level was all white stone carved
with diademed women more than twice life-size, and between them, white stone sheaves of grain and bolts of cloth
that seemed to have their free ends rippling in a wind, and
stacks of ingots that might have been meant for gold or silver or iron or perhaps all three, and sacks spilling out what
looked coins and gemstones. Beneath the women's feet,
much smaller white stone figures drove wagons and worked
forges and looms in a continuous band. These people had
made a monument proclaiming their success at trade. That

434   WINTER'S HEART

was foolish. When people decided you were better at trade
than they, they not only grew jealous, they became stubborn
and tried to demand ridiculous bargains. And sometimes
you had no alternative save to accept.

She realized that Harine was frowning at her, and straightened herself in the saddle. "Forgive me, Wavemistress," she
said. The Source was gone, but it would return—of course
it would!—and she had her duty. She was ashamed that she
had let herself give in to fear, yet the emptiness remained.
Oh, Light, the emptiness! "I am better, now. I will do better from here on." Harine merely nodded, still frowning,
and Shalon's scalp prickled. When Harine failed to deliver
an expected tongue-lashing, it was because she intended to
deliver worse.

Cadsuane rode straight across the square and through
the Hall of the Counsels' open gates into a large, high-
ceilinged room that appeared to be an indoor stableyard.
A dozen men in blue coats, squatting beside sedan chairs
with both a golden sword and a golden hand painted on the
doors, looked up in surprise when they rode in. So did the
men in blue vests who were unharnessing the team from a
coach with the sword-and-hand sigil, and those sweeping
the stone floor with large pushbrooms. Two more grooms
were leading horses down a wide corridor that gave off the
smell of hay and dung.

A plump, smooth-cheeked man in his middle years came
scurrying across the paving stones, bobbing his head in
small bows and dry-washing his hands. Where the other
men had their long hair tied at the nape of the neck, his was
caught with a small silver clip, and his blue coat appeared
of good quality wool, with the golden Sword-and-Hand
embroidered large on his left breast. "Forgive me," he said
with an unctuous smile, "I mean no offense, but I fear you
must have mistaken your direction. This is the Hall of the
Counsels, and—"

"Tell First Counsel Barsalla that Cadsuane Melaidhrin
is here to see her," Cadsuane broke in on him as she dismounted.

The man's smile slid off to one side, and his eyes widened. "Cadsuane Melaidhrin? I thought you were—!" He
cut himself short at her suddenly hard stare, then coughed
into his hand and reassumed his fulsome smile. "Forgive

me, Cadsuane Sedai. Will you allow me to show you and your companions to a waiting room where you can receive welcome while I send word to the First Counsel?" His eyes widened slightly as he took in those companions. Plainly he, too, could recognize Aes Sedai, at least in a group. Shalon and Harine made him blink, but he had self-control, for one of the shorebound. He did not gape.

"I'll allow you to run and tell Aleis I'm here as fast as your legs can carry you, boy," Cadsuane replied, unfastening her cloak and tossing it across her saddle. "Tell her I'll be in the dome, and tell her I don't have all day. Well? Hop!" This time the man's smile did not slide, it turned sickly, but he only hesitated a moment before setting off at a dead run while shouting for grooms to come take the horses.

Cadsuane had dismissed him from her attention as soon as she finished giving him his orders, however. "Verin, Kumira, you two will come with me," she announced briskly. "Merise, keep everyone together and ready until I—Alanna, come back and dismount. Alanna!" Reluctantly Alanna turned her mount away from the gates and climbed down with a sulky glower. Her slim Warder, Ihvon, watched her anxiously. Cadsuane sighed as though her patience was almost at an end. "Sit on her if you must to keep her here, Merise," she said, handing her reins to a small, wiry groom. "I want everyone ready to leave when I'm done with Aleis." Merise nodded, and Cadsuane turned to the groom. "A little water is all he needs," she said, giving her horse an affectionate pat. "I haven't exercised him much today."

Shalon was more than happy to turn her own horse over to a groom without instructions. She would not mind if he killed the creature. She did not know how far she had ridden in a daze, but she felt as though she had been in that saddle every mile of the however many hundred leagues to Cairhien. She felt rumpled in her flesh as well as her clothes. Abruptly, she realized that Jahar's pretty face was not with the other men. Verin's Tomas, a stocky gray-head as hard as any of the others, was leading the spotted gray pack animal that had been Jahar's. Where had the young man gotten to? Merise certainly did not appear concerned by his absence.

"This First Counsel," Harine growled, letting Moad help her down. She moved as stiffly as Shalon. He had simply leapt from his horse. "She is an important woman here, Sarene?"

"You might say she is the ruler of Far Madding, though the other Counsels, they call her first among equals, whatever that is supposed to mean." Handing over her own mount to a groom, Sarene looked quite unrumpled. Perhaps she had been upset before over this *ter'angreal* that stole the Source, but now she was all cool detachment, like carved ice. The groom stumbled over his own feet looking at her face. "Once, the First Counsel, she advised the queens of Maredo, but since Maredo's . . . dissolution . . . most First Counsels have considered themselves the natural heirs of Maredo's rulers."

Shalon knew that her knowledge of the shorebound's history was as uncertain as her knowledge of geography away from the shore, but she had never heard of any nation called Maredo. It was enough for Harine, though. If this First Counsel ruled here, the Wavemistress of Clan Shodein must meet her. Harine's dignity demanded no less. She hobbled determinedly across the stableyard to Cadsuane.

"Oh, yes," the insufferable Aes Sedai said before Harine could more than open her mouth. "You will come with me, as well. And your sister. I think not your Swordmaster, though. A man in the dome would be bad enough; but a man with a sword might make the Counsels fall over in fits. You have a question, Wavemistress?" Harine snapped her mouth shut with an audible click of teeth. "Good," Cadsuane murmured. Shalon groaned. This was not improving her sister's temper by a feather.

Cadsuane led them along broad, blue-tiled corridors hung with bright tapestries and lit by gilded stand lamps with glittering mirrors, where servants in blue first stared at them in surprise, then made hasty shorebound courtesies as they passed. She led them up long, swooping flights of white stone stairs that hung unsupported except where they touched a pale wall, which they did not always. Cadsuane glided like a swan, but at a speed that made the ache in Shalon's legs begin to burn. Harine's face set in a wooden mask, hiding the effort of trotting up stairs. Even Kumira seemed a trifle surprised, though Cadsuane's pace caused her no apparent exertion. Round little Verin churned away at Cadsuane's side, now and then smiling over her shoulder at Harine and Shalon. Sometimes Shalon thought she hated Verin, but there was no spite or amusement in those smiles, only encouragement.

Cadsuane took them up a final curling flight of stairs, enclosed by walls, and suddenly they were on a balcony with an intricate, gilded metal railing that ran all the way around. . . . For a moment, Shalon gaped. Above her rose an overarching blue dome a hundred feet or more high at its peak. Nothing held it up but itself. Her ignorance of the shorebound extended to architecture as well as geography and history—and Aes Sedai—in fact, her ignorance of the shorebound was almost complete, excepting only Cairhien. She knew how to draw the plans for a raker and see it built, but she could not begin to imagine how to construct this.

Arched doorways edged with white stone, like the one they had come through, marked stairs at three other places around the long balcony, but they were alone, and that seemed to please Cadsuane, though all she did was nod to herself. "Kumira, show the Wavemistress and her sister Far Madding's guardian." Her voice echoed faintly inside the vast dome. She drew Verin a little distance away, and the pair of them put their heads together. There was no echo of what they whispered.

"You must forgive them," Kumira told Harine and Shalon quietly. Even that produced a slight sound, if not quite an echo. "Peace, but this must be awkward, even for Cadsuane." She ran her fingers through her short brown hair and shook her head to settle it back in place. "The Counsels are seldom happy to see Aes Sedai, especially sisters born here. I think they would like to pretend the Power doesn't exist. Well, their history gives them reason, and for the last two thousand years they have had the means to support the pretense. In any event, Cadsuane is Cadsuane. She seldom sees a swelled head without deciding to deflate it, even when it happens to be wearing a crown. Or a Counsel's diadem. Her last visit was over twenty years ago, during the Aiel War, but I suspect some who remember it will want to hide under their beds when they learn she is back." Kumira gave a small, amused laugh. Shalon saw nothing to laugh at. Harine twisted her lips, but it made her look as though she suffered from a bad belly.

"You wish to see the . . . guardian?" Kumira went on.

"As good a name as any, I suppose. There isn't much to see." She stepped cautiously closer to the gilded railing and peered over as if fearing she might fall, but those blue eyes had sharpened again. "I would give anything to study it, but that is impossible, of course. Who knows what else it might be able to do beside what we already know?" Her tone held as much awe as regret.

Shalon had no fear of heights, and she pressed herself against the elaborately worked metal beside the Aes Sedai, wanting to see this thing that had taken the Source away. After a moment, Harine joined them. To Shalon's surprise, the drop that made Kumira uneasy was less than twenty feet, below, a smooth floor tiled in blue and white to make a convoluted maze centered on a double-pointed red oval rimmed with yellow. Beneath the balcony, three women in white sat on stools spaced equally around the edge of the floor, right against the dome's wall, and beside each woman, a disc a full span across that looked like clouded crystal had been set into the floor and inlaid with a long thin wedge of clear crystal that pointed toward the chamber's center. Metal collars surrounded the murky discs, marked off like a compass but with ever-smaller markings between the larger. Shalon could not be sure, but the collar nearest her appeared to be inscribed with numerals. That was all. No monstrous shapes. She had imagined something huge and black that sucked in the light. Her hands tightened on the rail to keep from trembling, and she locked her knees to hold herself still. Whatever was down there, it *had* stolen the Light.

A whisper of slippers announced new arrivals on the balcony by the same doorway they had used, about a dozen smiling women with their hair on top of their heads, in flowing blue silk robes worn over their dresses like sleeveless coats, richly embroidered in gold and trailing behind them on the floor. These people knew how to mark out rank. Each woman wore a large pendant in the shape of that gold-rimmed red oval suspended from a necklace of heavy golden links, and the same shape was repeated at the front of each narrow golden diadem. On one woman, the red ovals were made of rubies, not enamel, and sapphires and moonstones almost hid the golden circlet on her brows, and she wore a heavy golden signet ring on her right forefinger. She was tall and stately, her black hair drawn up in a large ball, heavily winged with white, though her face was unlined. The others were tall, short, stout, thin, pretty and plain, none young, and every one of them had an air of authority about her, but she stood out for more than her gems. Compassion and wisdom filled her large dark eyes, and it was command that she radiated, not simple authority. Shalon did not need to be told that this was the First Counsel, but the woman announced it anyway.

"I am Aleis Barsalla, First Counsel of Far Madding." Her mellifluous voice, deep for a woman, seemed to be making a proclamation, and expecting cheers. The sound of her voice bouncing inside the dome gave something like acclamation. "Far Madding gives welcome to Harine din Togara Two Winds, Wavemistress of Clan Shodein and Ambassador Extraordinary for the Mistress of the Ships to the Atha'an Miere. May the Light illumine you and see you prosper. Your coming gladdens every heart in Far Madding. I embrace the chance to learn more of the Atha'an Miere, but you must be weary from the rigors of your journey. I have arranged pleasant quarters for you in my palace. When you have rested and eaten, we can talk; to our mutual advantage, if it pleases the Light." The others spread the skirts of their robes and made half bows.

Harine inclined her head slightly, a hint of satisfaction in her smile. Here, at last, were those who showed her proper respect. And very likely it helped that they did not gape at her and Shalon's jewelry.

"The messengers from the gates are as quick as ever, it seems, Aleis," Cadsuane said. "Is there no welcome for me?" Aleis' smile thinned for a moment, and some of the other smiles faded altogether as Cadsuane moved to stand beside Harine. Those that remained were forced. A pretty woman with a serious cast to her face went so far as to scowl.

"We are grateful to you for bringing the Wavemistress here, Cadsuane Sedai." The First Counsel did not sound particularly grateful. She drew herself up to her full height and looked straight ahead, over Cadsuane's head rather than at her. "I am sure we can find some way to make the depth of our gratitude known before you leave."

She could not have made her dismissal plainer short of a

command, but the Aes Sedai smiled up at the taller woman. It was not an unpleasant smile, exactly, but neither was it in the least amused. "I may not be leaving for a while, Aleis. I thank you for the offer of accommodations, and accept. A palace on the Heights is always preferable to even the best inn." The First Counsel's eyes widened with startlement, then narrowed in determination.

"Cadsuane must stay with me," Harine said, managing to sound no more than half strangled, before Aleis could speak. "Where she is unwelcome, so am I." This had been part of the bargain forced on her, if they were to accompany Cadsuane. Among other things they must go when and where she said until they joined the Coramoor, and include her in any invitations they received. That last had seemed very small at the time, especially weighed against the rest, but plainly the woman had known exactly the reception she would receive.

"No need to be disheartened, Aleis." Cadsuane leaned toward the First Counsel confidingly, but she did not lower her voice. The reverberations in the dome magnified her words. "I'm sure you no longer have any bad habits for me to correct."

The First Counsel's face flooded with crimson, and behind her back, speculative frowns passed between the other Counsels. Some contemplated her as if with fresh eyes. How did they attain rank, and how lose it? Besides Aleis, they were twelve, surely a coincidence, but the First Twelve among a clan's Sailmistresses chose the Wavemistress, usually one of their own number, just as the First Twelve among the Wavemistresses chose the Mistress of the Ships. That was why Harine had accepted that strange girl's words, because she was of the First Twelve. That, and the fact that two Aes Sedai said the girl saw true visions. A Wavemistress or even the Mistress of the Ships could be deposed, though only for specified causes, such as gross incompetence or losing her wits, and the First Twelve had to speak with a unanimous voice. Things seemed to be done differently among the shorebound, and often sloppily. Aleis' eyes, fixed now on Cadsuane, were both hate-filled and hunted. Perhaps she could feel twelve sets of eyes on her back. The other Counsels had her on the scales. But if

Cadsuane had chosen to meddle in the politics of this place, why? And why so bluntly?

"A man just channeled," Verin said suddenly. She had not joined the rest and was peering over the rail, ten paces away. The dome made her voice carry. "Do you have many men channeling lately, First Counsel?"

Shalon looked down, and blinked. The formerly clear wedges were now black, and rather than pointing toward the chamber's heart, somehow they had turned in roughly the same direction. One of the women below was on her feet, bending over to study where along the marked collar the thin black wedge was pointing, and the other two women were already racing toward a round-topped doorway. Suddenly, Shalon knew. Triangulation was a simple matter to any Windfinder. Somewhere beyond that doorway was a chart, and soon the position where the man had channeled would be marked on it.

"It would be red for a woman, not black," Kumira said in almost a whisper. She still stood a little back from the rail, but she was gripping it with both hands and leaning forward to peer at the scene below. "It warns and locates and defends. And what else? The women who made it would have wanted more, perhaps needed more. Not knowing what else could be incredibly dangerous." She did not sound frightened, though. She sounded excited.

"An Asha'man, I expect," Aleis said calmly, pulling her gaze from Cadsuane. "They cannot trouble us. They are free to enter the city, so long as they obey the law." However calm she was, some of the women behind her tittered like new deckgirls their first time among the shorebound. "Forgive me, Aes Sedai. Far Madding gives you welcome. I am afraid I don't know your name, though."

Verin was still gazing down at the dome's floor. Shalon glanced over the rail again, and blinked as the thin black wedges . . . changed. One moment they were black and pointing north, the next clear and once again pointing to the center of the maze. They did not turn; they just were one thing, then the other.

"All of you may call me Eadwina," Verin said. Shalon barely suppressed a start. Kumira did not so much as blink. "Do you consider history, First Counsel?" Verin continued without looking up. "Guaire Amalasan's siege of Far Madding lasted just three weeks. A savage business, at the end."

"I doubt they want to hear about *him*," Cadsuane said sharply, and indeed, for some reason more than one of the Counsels looked uncomfortable. Who in the Light was this Guaire Amalasan? The name sounded vaguely familiar, but Shalon could not place it. Some shorebound conqueror, obviously.

Aleis glanced at Cadsuane, and her mouth tightened. "History records Guaire Amalasan as a remarkable general, Eadwina Sedai, perhaps second only to Artur Hawkwing himself. What brings him to mind?"

Shalon had never seen one of the Aes Sedai traveling with Cadsuane fail to heed her most casual warning as quickly as they obeyed her commands, but Verin paid no heed this time. She did not look up. "I was just thinking that he couldn't use the Power, yet he crushed Far Madding like an overripe plum." The stout little Aes Sedai paused as though something had just occurred to her. "You know, the Dragon Reborn has armies in Illian and Tear, in Andor and Cairhien. Not to mention many tens of thousands of Aiel. Very fierce, the Aiel. I wonder you can be so complacent about his Asha'man scouting you."

"I think you have frightened them quite enough," Cadsuane said firmly.

Verin finally turned from the gilded rail, her eyes open very wide, a round, startled shorebird. Her plump hands even fluttered like wings. "Oh. I didn't mean . . . Oh, no. I would think the Dragon Reborn would have moved against you already if he intended to. No, I suspect the Seanchan . . . You've heard of them? What we hear from Altara and farther west is really quite horrible. They seem to sweep everything before them. No, I suspect they're somewhat more important to his plans than capturing Far Madding. Unless you do something to anger him, of course, or upset his followers. But I am sure you are too intelligent to do that." She looked very innocent. There was a stir among the Counsels, the ripple that small fish made on the surface when a lionfish swam below.

Cadsuane sighed, her patience clearly at an end. "If you want to discuss the Dragon Reborn, Eadwina, you must do so without me. I want to wash my face and have some hot tea."

The First Counsel jerked as though she had forgotten Cadsuane's existence, incredible as that seemed. "Yes. Yes, of course. Cumere, Narvais, would you please escort the Wavemistress and Cadsuane Sedai to . . . to my palace and make them welcome?" That slight hitch was the only sign she gave of discomfort at having Cadsuane in her dwelling. "I wish to have some further talk with Eadwina Sedai, if it pleases her." Followed by most of the Counsels, Aleis glided away along the balcony. Verin looked suddenly alarmed and uncertain as they gathered her up and swept her along. Shalon did not believe the surprise or unease any more than she had the earlier innocence. She thought she knew now where Jahar was. She just did not know why.

The women Aleis had named, the pretty one who had scowled at Cadsuane, and a slim gray-haired woman, took the First Counsel's request as a command, which perhaps it was. They spread their robes and made those half bows, asking Harine whether she would be pleased to accompany them and announcing in flowery terms their pleasure at escorting her. Harine listened with a sour face. They could strew baskets of rose petals in her path if they wished, but the First Counsel had left her to underlings. Shalon wondered whether there was any way to avoid her sister until her temper cooled.

Cadsuane did not watch Verin leave with Aleis, not openly, but her mouth curved in a faint smile when they vanished through the next arched doorway along the balcony. "Cumere and Narvais," she said abruptly. "That would be Cumere Powys and Narvais Maslin? I have heard things about you." That jerked their attention away from Harine. "There are standards any Counsel should meet," Cadsuane went on in a firm tone, taking them each by a sleeve and turning them toward the stairs on either side of her. Exchanging worried glances, they let her, Harine apparently quite forgotten. At the doorway, Cadsuane paused to look back, but not at Harine or Shalon. "Kumira? Kumira!"

The other Aes Sedai gave a start, and with a last lingering look over the railing, pulled herself away to follow Cadsuane. Which left Harine and Shalon no option except to follow, too, or be left to try finding their own way out. Shalon darted after the others, and Harine was no less quick. Still gripping the Counsels to her sides, Cadsuane led the way

down the curling stairs, talking in a low voice. With Kumira between her and the three, Shalon could hear nothing.
Cumere and Narvais tried to speak, but Cadsuane allowed
neither more than a few words before she began again. She
seemed calm, matter-of-fact. The pair with her began to
look anxious. What in the Light was Cadsuane up to?

"This place troubles you?" Harine said suddenly.

"It is as if I have lost my eyes." Shalon shivered at the
truth of that. "I am afraid, Wavemistress, but the Light willing, I can control my fear." Light, she hoped she could. She
desperately needed to.

Harine nodded, frowning at the women ahead of them
down the stairs. "I do not know whether Aleis' palace has
a tub big enough for us to bathe together, and I doubt they
know honeyed wine, but we will find something." Glancing away from Cadsuane and the others, she touched Shalon's arm awkwardly. "I was afraid of the dark when I was a
child, and you never left me alone till the fear passed. I will
not leave you alone, either, Shalon."

Shalon missed a step and barely caught herself short of
tumbling down head over heels. Harine had not used her
name except in private since she was first made Sailmistress. She had not been this friendly in private since before
that. "Thank you," she said, and with an effort, added, "Harine." Her sister patted her arm again, and smiled. Harine
was unpracticed at smiling, but the awkward effort held
warmth.

There was no warmth in the look she directed toward the
women ahead, though. "Perhaps I truly can make a bargain
here. Cadsuane has already shifted their ballast so they
ride with a list. You must try to find out why, Shalon, when
you get close to her. I would like to put Aleis' eyeteeth on
a string—walking away from me without so much as a
word!—but not at the expense of letting Cadsuane mesh the
Coramoor in some trouble here. You must find out, Shalon."

"I think perhaps Cadsuane meddles the way anyone else
breathes," Shalon replied with a sigh, "but I will try, Harine. I will do my best."

"You always have, sister. You always will. I know that."

Shalon sighed again. It was much too soon to test the
depth of her sister's newfound warmth. Confession might

bring absolution or not, and she could not live with the loss of her marriage and her rank at one blow. But for the first time since Verin had bluntly laid out Cadsuane's terms for keeping her secret, Shalon began to consider confession.

CHAPTER
25

Bonds

I n his room at The Counsel's Head, Rand sat on the
bed with his legs folded and his back against the wall,
playing the silver-mounted flute Thom Merrilin had
given him so long ago. An Age ago. This room, with carved
wall panels and windows overlooking the Nethvin Market,
was better than that they had abandoned at The Crown of
Maredo. The pillows stacked beside him were goose down,
the bed had an embroidered canopy and curtains, and the
mirror above the washstand had not a single bubble. The
lintel above the stone fireplace even had a bit of simple
carving. It was a room for a well-to-do foreign merchant.
He was glad he had thought to bring enough gold when he
left Cairhien. He had lost the habit of carrying much. Everything had been provided for the Dragon Reborn. Still, he
could have earned a bed of some sort with the flute. The
tune was called "Lament for the Long Night," and he had
never heard it before in his life. Lews Therin had, though.
It was like the skill at drawing. Rand thought that should
frighten him, or make him angry, but he simply sat and
played while Lews Therin wept.

"Light, Rand," Min muttered, "are you just going to
sit there puffing on that thing?" Her skirts swirled as she
paced up and down the flowered carpet. The bond with
her and Elayne and Aviendha felt as though he had never
known anything else or wanted to. He breathed, and he was
bonded to them; one was as natural as the other. "If she
says one wrong word where it can be overheard, if she's
already said it . . . I am *not* letting anyone, haul you off to
a cell for Elaida!" Alanna's bond had never felt that way. It

had not changed, not in itself, yet increasingly since that day in Caemlyn, Alanna's bond seemed an intrusion, a stranger looking over his shoulder, a sandspur in his boot. "Do you *have* to play that? It makes me want to cry, and it makes my skin crawl at the same time. If she puts you in danger . . . !" Snatching one of her knives from its hiding place up a loose-fitting sleeve, she flourished it in her fist.

He took the flute away from his mouth and silently looked at her over it. Her face reddened, and with a sudden snarl, she hurled the blade to stick quivering in the door.

"She's there," he said, using the flute to point. Unconsciously, he shifted the instrument, following Alanna exactly. "She'll be here soon." She had been in Far Madding since the day before, and he did not understand why she had waited till now. Alanna was a tangle of emotions inside his skull, nervous and wary, worried and determined and above all, angry. In a barely restrained fury. "If you'd rather not be here, you can wait. . . ." Min shook her head fiercely. Right beside Alanna in his head lay the bundle that was her. She bubbled with worry and anger, too, but love shone through like a beacon whenever she looked at him and often when she did not. Fear shone through, as well, though she was trying to hide that.

He put the flute back to his lips and began "The Drunken Peddler." That was jolly enough to cheer the dead. Lews Therin snarled at him.

Min stood studying him, her arms folded, then abruptly gave her dress a twitch, settling it on her hips. With a sigh, he lowered the flute and waited. When a woman adjusted her clothes for no reason, it was like a man tightening the straps of his armor and checking his saddle girth; she meant to drive home a charge, and you would be cut down like a dog if you ran. Determination was as strong in Min now as it was in Alanna, twin suns flaring in the back of his brain.

"We will not talk about Alanna any more until she gets here," she said firmly, as though he had been the one insisting. Determination, and still the fear, stronger now than before, continually trampled down and continually springing back up.

"Why, of course, wife, if it pleases you," he replied, bending his neck in the approved Far Madding fashion. She sniffed loudly.

"Rand, I like Alivia. I do, even if she does make Nynaeve have kittens left and right." One fist planted on her hip, Min leaned forward and pointed a finger at his nose. "But she is going to kill you." She bit off every word.

"You said she was going to help me die," he said quietly. "Those were your words." How would he feel at dying? Sadness at leaving her, at leaving Elayne and Aviendha. Sadness for the pain he had brought them. He would like to see his father again before the end. Aside from those things, he almost thought death would be a relief.

Death is *a relief,* Lews Therin said fervently. *I want death. We deserve death!*

"Helping me die isn't the same as killing me," Rand went on. He was very good at ignoring the voice, now. "Unless you've changed your mind about what you saw."

Min flung up her hands in exasperation. "I saw what I saw and it's what I told you, but the Pit of Doom swallow me if I can see any difference. And I can't see why you think there is!"

"Sooner or later, I have to die, Min," he said patiently. He had been told by those he had to believe. To live, you must die. That still made no sense to him, but it left one cold hard fact. Just as the Prophecies of the Dragon seemed to say, he had to die. "Not soon, I hope. I plan not soon. I'm sorry, Min. I never should have let you bond me." But he had not been strong enough to refuse, any more than he had been strong enough to push her away. He was too weak for what had to be done. He needed to drink in winter, till he made winter's heart seem Sunday noon.

"If you hadn't, we'd have tied you up and done it anyway." Best not to ask how that would have differed from what Alanna had done, he decided. Certainly, she saw a difference. Climbing onto the bed on her knees, she cupped his face in her hands, "You listen to me, Rand al'Thor. I won't let you die. And if you manage it just to spite me, I'll follow you and bring you back." Suddenly a thick vein of amusement rippled through the seriousness he felt in his head. Her voice took on a mock sternness: "And then I'll bring you back here to live. I'll make you grow your hair below your waist and wear hair clips with moonstones."

He smiled at her. She could still make him smile. "I never heard of a fate worse than death, but I think that fits."

Someone knocked at the door, and Min froze. In a silent question, she mouthed Alanna's name. Rand nodded, and to his amazement, Min pushed him over onto the pillows and flung herself on his chest. Squirming around, she raised her head, and he realized she was trying to see herself in the washstand mirror. Finally she found a position she liked, lying half on top of him with one hand behind his neck and the other beside her face on his chest. "Come in," she called.

Cadsuane stepped into the room and stopped, frowning at the knife stuck in the door. In a dress of fine dark green wool and a fur-lined cloak held by a silver brooch at the neck, she might have passed for a successful merchant or a banker, though the golden birds and fish, stars and moons dangling from the iron-gray bun atop her head would have been ostentatious for either. She was not wearing her Great Serpent ring, so it seemed she was making some effort to avoid too much notice. "Have you children been arguing?" she asked mildly.

Rand could almost feel Lews Therin go still, like a ridge cat crouching in the shadows. Lews Therin was almost as wary of this woman as he was himself.

Red-faced, Min scrambled to her feet smoothing furiously at her dress. "You said it was her!" she said accusingly, just as Alanna entered. Cadsuane closed the door.

Alanna glanced once at Min and dismissed her, focusing on Rand. Without taking her dark eyes from him, she swept her cloak off and flung it over one of the room's two chairs. Her hands settled on her dark gray skirts, gripping them hard. She was not wearing her golden Aes Sedai ring, either. From the moment her eyes fell on him, joy bloomed along the bond. All the rest was still there, the nervousness, the fury, but he had never expected her to feel joy!

Not changing how he lay, he picked up the flute and toyed with it. "Should I be surprised to see you, Cadsuane? You pop up when I don't want to see you too often to suit. Who taught you to Travel?" It had to have been that. One moment Alanna had been a vague awareness on the edge of thought, and the next she sprang to life full strength in his head. At first, he had thought she herself had learned Traveling somehow, but seeing Cadsuane, he knew better.

Alanna's mouth tightened, and even Min looked disapproving. The emotions flowing along the Warder bond from one jumped and skittered; from the other, there was just anger mingled with delight, now. Why did Alanna feel *joy*?

"Still no more manners than a goat, I see," Cadsuane said dryly. "Boy, I hardly think I need your permission to visit my birthplace. As for Traveling, it is none of your business where or when I learned anything." Unpinning her cloak, she stuck the brooch on her belt, ready to hand, and folded the cloak over one arm as though making it neat were much more important than he was. Her voice took on an edge of irritation. "You've lumbered me with a lot of traveling companions, one way and another. Alanna was so frantic to see you again, only a heart of stone could have refused to bring her, and Sorilea said some of the others who pledged themselves to you would be good for nothing until they were allowed to go with Alanna, so I've ended up bringing Nesune, Sarene, Erian, Beldeine and Elza, too. Not to mention Harine, plus her sister and that Swordmaster of hers. She didn't know whether to faint, scream or bite someone when she found out Alanna was going off to find you. And then there are those three black-coated friends of yours. I don't know how eager they are to see you, but they're here, as well. Well, now that we've located you, I can send the Sea Folk and the sisters to you and let you deal with them."

Rand sprang to his feet with a muttered oath. "No! Keep them away from me!"

Cadsuane's dark eyes narrowed. "I've warned you before about your language; I will not warn you again." She frowned at him a moment longer, then nodded as though she thought he had taken the lesson to heart. "Now, what makes you think you can tell me what to do, boy?"

Rand struggled with himself. He could not issue orders here. He had never been able to order Cadsuane anywhere. Min said he needed the woman, that she would teach him something he needed to learn, but if anything, that only made him more uneasy about her. "I want to finish my business here and leave quietly," he said at last. "If you tell them, at least make sure they see I can't afford to have them come anywhere near me, not until I'm ready to leave." The woman raised an eyebrow at him, waiting, and he took a deep breath. Why did she always need to make everything difficult? "I would appreciate it very much if you didn't tell any of them where I am." Reluctantly, very reluctantly, he added, "Please." Min exhaled as though she had been holding her breath.

"Good," Cadsuane said after a moment. "You can show manners when you try, even if it does make you look as though your teeth ached. I suppose I can keep your secret for you, for the time being. Not all of them even know you are in the city. Oh, yes. I should tell you, Merise has bonded Narishma, Corele has Damer, and young Hopwil is Daigian's." She said that as though it were just a casual bit of information that might easily have slipped her mind.

He did not bother to mutter his oath this time, and Cadsuane's full-armed slap almost unhinged his jaw. Black spots shimmered in front of his eyes. One of the other women gasped.

"I did tell you," Cadsuane said placidly. "No more warnings."

Min took a step toward him, and he shook his head slightly. It helped to clear the spots. He wanted to rub his jaw, but he kept his hands at his sides. He had to make himself loosen his grip on the flute. For Cadsuane's part, the slap might never have occurred.

"Why would Flinn and the others accept being bonded?" he demanded.

"Ask them when you see them," she replied. "Min, I suspect Alanna wants to be alone with him awhile." Turning toward the door without waiting for Min's reply, she added, "Alanna, I will be waiting below, in the Women's Room. Don't be too long. I want to get back to the Heights. Min?"

Min glared at Alanna. She glared at Rand. Then she flung up her hands and stalked out after Cadsuane, muttering under her breath. She slammed the door behind her.

"I liked you better with your own hair." Alanna folded her arms beneath her breasts and studied him. Anger and joy warred with one another in the bond. "I had hoped that being close to you would be better, but you are still like a stone in my head. Even standing here, I can hardly tell whether you're upset or not. Even so, being here is better. I dislike being parted from a Warder so long."

Rand ignored her and the rippling joy that flowed along the bond. "She didn't ask why I came to Far Madding," Rand said quietly, staring at the door as if he could see Cadsuane through the wood. Surely, she had to wonder. "You told her I was here, Alanna. It had to be you. What happened to your oath?"

Alanna drew a deep breath, and a moment passed before she replied. "I am not sure Cadsuane cares two pins about you," she snapped. "I keep that oath as well as I can, but you do make keeping it hard." Her voice began to harden, and anger welled more strongly through the bond. "I owe fealty to a man who walks off and leaves me behind. Just how am I supposed to serve you? More importantly, what did you do?" Crossing the carpet, she stood staring up at him, fury burning in her eyes. He topped her by more than a foot, and she seemed not to notice. "You did something, I know. I was unconscious for three days! What did you do?"

"I decided if I was going to be bonded, it might as well be by someone I said could." He barely caught her hand before it landed on his face. "I've been slapped enough for one day."

She glared up at him, teeth bared as if ready to bite out his throat. The bond carried only fury and outrage, now, distilled to daggers. "You let someone else *bond* you?" she snarled. "How dare you! Whoever she is, I'll see her before a court! I'll see her *birched*! You are mine!"

"Because you *took* me, Alanna," he said coldly. "If more sisters knew, *you* would be the one birched." Min had told him once that he could trust Alanna, that she had seen the Green and four other sisters "in his hand." He did trust her, in an odd fashion, yet he was in Alanna's hand, too, and he did not want to be. "Release me, and I'll deny it ever happened." He had not even known that was possible until Lan told him about himself and Myrelle. "Release me, and I'll set you free of your oath."

The roiling anger flowing through the bond lessened without disappearing, but her face grew calm, and her voice was composed. "You are hurting my wrist."

He knew he was. He could feel the pain through the bond. He let go, and she massaged her wrist far more ostentatiously than required by the hurt he felt. Still rubbing her wrist, she sat on the second chair and crossed her legs. She seemed to be thinking.

"I've thought of being free of you," she said finally. "I have dreamed of it." She gave a small, rueful laugh. "I even asked Cadsuane to let me pass the bond to her. A sign of how desperate I was, to ask such a thing. But if anyone can handle you, Cadsuane can. Only, she refused. She was furious that I suggested it without asking you, outraged, but even if you agreed, she won't." She spread her hands. "So you are mine." Her face did not change, but as she said that, the joy flared anew. "However I acquired you, you are my Warder, and I have a responsibility. That is as strong in me as the oath I swore to obey you. Every bit as strong. So I will not release you to anyone unless I know she can handle you properly. Who bonded you? If she is capable, I will let her have you."

Just the possibility that Cadsuane might have received his bond sent icicles down Rand's spine. Alanna had never been able to control him with the bond, and he did not think any sister could, but he would never risk it with that one. Light!

"What makes you think she doesn't care about me?" he demanded instead of answering Alanna's question. Trust or no trust, no one would learn that answer if he could help it. What Elayne and Min and Aviendha had done might be allowed by Tower law, yet they had worse to fear than punishment from other Aes Sedai if it came out they were linked to him in this way. Sitting down on the edge of the bed, he turned the flute over in his hands. "Just because she refused my bond? Maybe she isn't as nonchalant about the consequences as you. She came to me in Cairhien, and stayed long after there could be any reason but me. Am I really supposed to believe she just decided to visit friends while I happen to be here? She brought you to Far Madding so she could find me."

"Rand, she wanted to know where you were every day," Alanna said dismissively, "but I doubt there's a shepherd in Seleisin who doesn't wonder where you are. The whole *world* wants to know that. I knew you were far to the south, that you hadn't moved for days. No more. When I found out she and Verin were coming here, I had to beg her—beg on my knees!—before she would let me come along. But I didn't know myself that you were here until I came out of the gateway in the hills above the city. Before that, I thought I might have to Travel halfway to Tear to find you. Cadsuane taught me that, when we came here, so don't think you can evade me so easily in the future."

Cadsuane had taught Alanna to Travel? That still did not say who had taught Cadsuane, though. Not that it mattered, he supposed. "And Damer and the other two allowed themselves to be bonded? Or did those sisters just take them the way you took me?"

A faint flush stained her cheeks, but her voice was steady. "I heard Merise ask Jahar. It took him two days to accept, and she never pressured him that I saw. I cannot speak for the others, but as Cadsuane said, you can always ask them. Rand, you must understand, those men were afraid to go back to this 'Black Tower' of yours." Her mouth twisted sourly around the name. "They were afraid they would be blamed in the attack on you. If they simply ran, they would be hunted down as deserters. I understand that is your standing order? Where else could they go, except to Aes Sedai? And a good thing they did, too." She smiled as though she had just seen something wonderful, and her voice became excited. "Rand, Damer has discovered a way to Heal being stilled! Light, I can say that word without freezing my tongue. He Healed Irgain and Ronaille and Sashalle. They've sworn fealty to you, too, just like all the others."

"What do you mean, all the others?"

"I mean all the sisters the Aiel were holding. Even the Reds." She sounded half disbelieving about that, as well she should, but disbelief melted into intensity as she put both feet on the floor and leaned toward him, her eyes fixed on his. "Every one of them has sworn and accepted the penance you put on Nesune and the others, the first five of them who swore. Cadsuane doesn't trust them. She wouldn't let them bring any of their Warders. I admit I was uncertain at first, but I believe you *can* trust them. They swore oath to you. You know what that means for a sister. We can't break an oath, Rand. It isn't possible."

Even the Reds. He had been surprised when those first five captives offered fealty. Elaida had sent them to kidnap him, and they had. He had been sure it was him being *ta'veren* that had done it, but that only altered chance, made what might happen one time in a million become a certainty. It was hard to believe that a Red would swear under any circumstances to a man who could channel.

"You need us, Rand." Rising, she shifted as if she wanted to pace, but instead she stood watching him, unblinking.

Her hands smoothed her skirts as if she was unaware of what they were doing. "You need the support of Aes Sedai. Without it, you will have to conquer every nation, and you haven't done very well at that thus far. The rebellion in Cairhien might seem finished to you, but not everyone likes Dobraine being named your Steward. A good many might go to Toram Riatin, if he reappears. The High Lord Darlin is snug in the Stone, so we hear, announced as your Steward in Tear, but the rebels there haven't come streaming out of Haddon Mirk to support him. As for Andor, Elayne Trakand might say she will support you once she has the throne, but she has maneuvered your soldiers out of Caemlyn, and I'll wear bells in the Blight if she lets them remain in Andor when she does succeed. Sisters can help you. Elayne will listen to us. The rebels in Cairhien and Tear will listen. The White Tower has stopped wars and ended rebellions for three thousand years. You may not like the treaty Rafela and Merana negotiated with Harine, but they got everything you asked for. Light, man, let us help you!"

Rand nodded slowly. It had seemed just a way to impress people with his power, that Aes Sedai gave him fealty. Fear that they might manipulate him to their own ends had blinded him to anything else. He did not like admitting that. He had been a fool.

A man who trusts everyone is a fool, Lews Therin said, *and a man who trusts no one is a fool. We are all fools, if we live long enough.* He almost sounded sane.

"Go back to Cairhien," he said. "Tell Rafela and Merana I want them to approach the rebels in Haddon Mirk. Tell them to take Bera and Faeldrin, too." Those were the four besides Alanna whom Min said he could trust. What had she said about the five others Cadsuane had brought with her? That each would serve him in her fashion. That was not strong enough, not yet. "I want Darlin Sisnera as my Steward and the laws I made left in place. They can negotiate away anything else as long as they end the rebellion. After that . . . What's the matter?"

Alanna's face had fallen, and she had sagged back in her chair. "It's just that I've come all this way, and you are sending me right off again. I suppose it is for the best, with that girl here," she sighed. "You have no idea what I went through in Cairhien, masking the bond just enough to keep what the two of you were doing from keeping me awake all night. That is much harder than simply masking it completely, but I dislike losing touch with my Warders completely. Only, going back to Cairhien will be almost as bad."

Rand cleared his throat. "That's what I want you to do." Women, he had learned, talked about some things much more openly than men, but it was still a shock when they did. He hoped Elayne and Aviendha masked the bond when he was making love with Min. When the two of them were together in bed, no one else existed except her, the same as it had been with Elayne. He certainly did not want to talk about it with Alanna. "I may be done here by the time you finish in Cairhien. If I haven't . . . If I haven't, you can return here. But you'll have to stay away from me until I say otherwise." Even with that restriction, the joy billowed up in her afresh.

"You aren't going to tell me who bonded you, are you?" He shook his head, and she sighed. "I had better go." Rising, she took up her cloak and draped it over her arm. "Cadsuane is impatient at best. Sorilea admonished her to look after us like a mother hen, and she does. After her fashion." At the door, she paused for one last question. "Why *are* you here, Rand? Cadsuane may not care, but I do. I'll keep it secret, if you wish. I have never been able to stay more than a few days in a *stedding*. Why would you be willing to stay here, where you can't even feel the Source?"

"Maybe it isn't that bad for me," he lied. He could tell her, he realized. He did trust her to keep it secret. But she did see him as her Warder, and she was a Green. No explanation could make her let him face it alone, but in Far Madding, she was no better able to defend herself than Min, maybe less. "Go on, Alanna. I've wasted enough time."

Once she was gone, he shifted himself to put his back against the wall again and sat fingering the flute. He thought instead of playing, though. Min said he needed Cadsuane, but Cadsuane was not interested in him except as a curiosity. A bad-mannered curiosity. Somehow, he had to make her interested. How in the Light was he going to do that?

With some difficulty Verin squeezed herself out of the sedan chair in the courtyard of Aleis' palace. She was simply not constructed to fit the things, but they were the fastest way to get about in Far Madding. Coaches always bogged down in the crowds sooner or later, and they could not go some places she wanted to. The damp winds off the lake were turning colder as evening deepened into twilight, but she let the wind whip her cloak about while she dug two silver pennies from her purse and gave them to the bearers. She was not supposed to, of course, since they were Aleis' boys, but Eadwina would not know that. They should not have accepted, but the silver vanished into their coats in a twinkling, and the younger of the pair, a handsome fellow in his middle years, even made her a flourishing bow before they picked up the chair and trotted off toward the stable, a low structure set in a corner against the front wall. Verin sighed. A boy in his middle years. It had not taken her long back in Far Madding to begin thinking as if she had never left. She had to be careful about that. It could be dangerous, not least if Aleis or the others discovered her deception. She suspected the warrants for Verin Mathwin's exile had never been suspended. Far Madding kept quiet when an Aes Sedai fell afoul of the law, but the Counsels had no reason to fear Aes Sedai, and for its own reasons, the Tower in turn kept quiet on those rare occasions when a sister found herself strung up for a judicial flogging. She had no intention of being the latest reason for the Tower to keep silence.

Aleis' palace was not a patch on the Sun Palace, of course, or the Royal Palace in Andor, or any of the palaces kings and queens ruled from. It was her own property, not attached to her position as First Counsel. Others, larger and smaller, marched away on either side, each surrounded by a high wall except on the end where the Heights, the only point approaching a hill on the entire island, fell away to the water in a sheer bluff. Still, it was not small, either. The Barsalla women had been dealing in trade and politics since the city was still called Fel Moreina. Tall-columned walks surrounded the Barsalla palace on both levels, and the white marble cube covered most of the walled grounds.

She found Cadsuane in a sitting room that would have offered a good view of the lake if the curtains had not been drawn to keep in the warmth of the blaze in the wide marble fireplace. Cadsuane sat, with her sewing basket on a small inlaid table beside her chair, calmly working with needle and embroidery hoop. She was not alone. Verin folded her cloak over the back of a padded chair and took another to wait.

Elza barely glanced at her. The usually pleasant-faced Green stood on the carpet in front of Cadsuane looking quite fierce, her face red and her eyes glaring. Elza was always very conscious of where she stood with respect to other sisters, perhaps too much so. For her to ignore Verin, much less confront Cadsuane, she must have been in a fine swivet. "How could you let her go?" she demanded of Cadsuane. "How are we to find him without her?" Ah, so that was it.

Cadsuane's head remained bent over her embroidery hoop, and her needle continued to make tiny stitches. "You can wait until she returns," she said calmly.

Elza's hands doubled into fists at her side. "How can you be so detached?" she demanded. "He is the Dragon Reborn! This place could be a death trap for him! You have to—!" Her teeth snapped shut as Cadsuane held up a finger. That was all Cadsuane did, but from her it was enough.

"I've put up with your tirade long enough, Elza. You may go. Now!"

Elza hesitated, but she really had no choice. Her face was still red as she bobbed a curtsy with her dark green skirts clutched in her fists, but if she stalked from the sitting room, she still left without further delay.

Cadsuane set the embroidery hoop on her lap and leaned back. "Will you make me some tea, Verin?"

In spite of herself, Verin gave a small start. The other sister had not looked in her direction once. "Of course, Cadsuane." A heavily worked silver teapot sat on a four-legged stand on one of the side tables, and was still hot, luckily. "Was it wise to let Alanna go?" she asked.

"I could hardly stop her without letting the boy know more than he should, now could I?" Cadsuane replied dryly.

Taking her time, Verin tipped the teapot to pour into a thin blue porcelain cup. Not Sea Folk porcelain, but very fine. "Do you have any idea why he came to Far Madding, of all places? I nearly swallowed my tongue when it came to me that the reason he had stopped leaping about might be because he was here. If it's something dangerous, perhaps we should try to stop him."

"Verin, he can do whatever his heart desires, anything at all, as long as he lives to reach Tarmon Gai'don. And as long as I can be at his side long enough to make him learn how to laugh again, and cry." Closing her eyes, she rubbed her temples with her fingertips and sighed. "He is turning into a stone, Verin, and if he doesn't relearn that he's human, winning the Last Battle may not be much better than losing. Young Min told him he needs me; I got that much out of her without rousing her suspicions. But I must wait for him to come to me. You see the way he runs roughshod over Alanna and the others. It will be hard enough teaching him, if he does ask. He fights guidance, he thinks he must do everything, learn everything, on his own, and if I do not make him work for it, he won't learn at all." Her hands dropped onto the embroidery hoop on her lap. "I seem to be in a confiding mood tonight. Unusual, for me. If you ever finish pouring that tea, I may confide some more."

"Oh, yes; of course." Hastily filling a second cup, Verin slipped the small vial back into her pouch unopened. It was good to be sure of Cadsuane at last. "Do you take honey?" she asked in her most muddled voice. "I never can remember."

CHAPTER
26

Expectation

Walking across the brown-grassed village green of Emond's Field with Egwene, Elayne felt saddened by the changes. Egwene seemed stunned by them. When she first appeared in *Tel'aran'rhiod,* a long braid had dangled down Egwene's back and she was in a plain woolen dress, of all things, with stout shoes peeking out beneath her skirts as she walked. Elayne supposed it was the sort of clothing she had worn when she lived in the Two Rivers. Now her dark hair hung about her shoulders, secured by a small cap of fine lace, and her garments were as fine as Elayne's, a rich blue embroidered with silver on the bodice and high neck as well as along the hem of her skirt and her cuffs. Silver-worked velvet slippers replaced the thick leather shoes. Elayne needed to maintain her focus to keep her own green silk riding dress from altering, perhaps in embarrassing fashion, but for her friend, without any doubt, the changes were deliberate.

She hoped Rand could still love Emond's Field, but it was no longer the village where he and Egwene had grown up. There were no people, here in the World of Dreams, yet clearly Emond's Field was a considerable town now, a prosperous town, with nearly one house in three made of well-dressed stone, some of three stories, and more roofed with tiles in every hue of the rainbow than with thatch. Some streets were paved with smooth well-fitted stone, new and unworn as yet, and there was even a thick stone wall going up around the town, with towers and iron-plated gates that would have suited a Borderland town. Outside the walls there were gristmills and sawmills, an iron foundry and large workshops for weavers of both woolens and carpets, and within were shops run by furniture makers, potters, seamstresses, cutlers, and gold- and silversmiths, many as fine as could be seen in Caemlyn, though some of the styles seemed to be from Arad Doman or Tarabon.

The air was cool but not cold, and there was not a sign of snow on the ground, at least for the moment. The sun stood straight overhead here, though Elayne hoped it was still night in the waking world. She wanted some real sleep before she had to face the morning. She was always tired, the last few days; there was just so much to be done, and so few hours. They had come here because it seemed unlikely any spy could find them here, but Egwene had lingered to stare at the changes in the place she was born. And Elayne had her own reasons, beyond Rand, for wanting to look over Emond's Field. The problem, one of the problems, was that one hour might pass in the waking world while you spent five or ten in the World of Dreams, but it could just as easily be the other way around. It might be morning already in Caemlyn.

Stopping at the edge of the green, Egwene gazed back at the wide stone bridge that arched over the rapidly widening stream running from a spring that gushed out of a stone outcrop strongly enough to knock a man down. A massive marble shaft carved all over with names stood in the middle of the green, and two tall flagpoles on stone bases. "A battle monument," she murmured. "Who could imagine such a thing in Emond's Field? Though Moiraine said that once a great battle was fought on this spot, in the Trolloc Wars, when Manetheren died."

"It was in the history I studied," Elayne said quietly, glancing at the bare flagpoles. Bare for the moment. She could not feel Rand, here. Oh, he was still in her head as much as Birgitte, a rocklike knot of emotions and physical sensations that was even more difficult to interpret now that he was far away, yet here in *Tel'aran'rhiod,* she could not know which direction he was. She missed that knowledge, small as it was. She missed him.

Banners appeared atop the flagpoles, remaining just long enough to ripple once lazily. Long enough to make out on one a red eagle flying across a field of blue. Not *a* red eagle; the Red Eagle. Once, visiting this place with Nynaeve in *Tel'aran'rhiod,* she had thought she glimpsed it, had decided she must be mistaken. Master Norry had begun setting her straight. She loved Rand, but if someone in the place he grew up was trying to raise Manetheren from its ancient grave, she would have to take cognizance, however much it pained him. That banner and that name still carried enough power to threaten Andor.

"I heard about changes from Bode Cauthon and the other novices from home," Egwene went on, frowning at the houses around the green, "but nothing like this." Most of those houses were stone. A tiny inn still stood beside the sprawling stone foundation of some much larger building, with a huge oak growing up through the middle of it, but what looked to be an inn many times bigger was almost finished on the other side of the foundation, with a large sign reading The Archers already hung above the door. "I wonder whether my father is still Mayor. Is my mother well? My sisters?"

"I know you are moving the army tomorrow," Elayne said, "if it isn't tomorrow already, but surely you could find a few hours to visit here once you reach Tar Valon." Traveling made such things easy. Perhaps she herself should send someone to Emond's Field. If she knew whom to trust for the mission. If she could spare anyone she did trust.

Egwene shook her head. "Elayne, I've had to order women I grew up with switched because they don't believe I am the Amyrlin Seat, or if they do, that they can break the rules because they knew me." Suddenly the seven-striped stole hung from her shoulders. Until she noticed it with a grimace, and it vanished again. "I don't think I can face confronting Emond's Field as Amyrlin," she said sadly. "Not yet." She gave herself a shake, and her voice firmed. "The Wheel turns, Elayne, and everything changes. I must get used to it. I *will* get used to it." She sounded a great deal like Siuan Sanche, as Siuan had sounded in Tar Valon before everything had changed. Stole or no stole, Egwene sounded like the Amyrlin Seat. "Are you certain I can't send you some of Gareth Bryne's soldiers? Enough to help secure Caemlyn, at least."

Abruptly, they were surrounded by glistening snow, standing knee-deep in it. Snow made gleaming white mounds on the rooftops as if from a heavy fall. This was not the first time such a thing had happened, and they simply refused to let the sudden cold touch them, rather than imagining cloaks and warmer clothes.

"No one is going to move against me before spring," Elayne said. Armies did not move in winter, at least, not unless they had the benefit of Traveling, like Egwene's army. Snow bogged everything down, and mud whenever the snow melted. Those Borderlanders probably had begun their march south thinking winter was never coming this year. "Besides, you will need every man when you reach Tar Valon."

Unsurprisingly, Egwene nodded acceptance without making the offer again. Even with this past month of hard recruiting behind her, Gareth Bryne still had no more than half the soldiers he had told her would be needed to take Tar Valon. According to Egwene, he was ready to begin with what he had, but clearly it troubled her. "I have hard decisions to make, Elayne. The Wheel weaves as the Wheel wills, but it is still me who has to decide."

Impulsively, Elayne waded through the snow and threw her arms around Egwene to hug her. At least, she started out wading. As she clasped the other woman to her, the snow vanished, leaving not so much as a damp spot on their dresses. The two of them staggered as if dancing with one another and almost fell.

"I know you will make the right decision," Elayne said, laughing in spite of herself. Egwene did not join her laughter.

"I hope so," she said gravely, "because whatever I decide, people are going to die for it." She patted Elayne's arm. "Well, you understand that sort of decision, don't you. We both need to be back in our beds." She hesitated before going on. "Elayne, if Rand comes to you again, you must let me know what he says, whether he gives you any clue what he means to do or where he means to go."

"I will tell you whatever I can, Egwene." Elayne felt a stab of guilt. She had told Egwene everything—almost everything—but not that she had bonded Rand with Min and Aviendha. Tower law did not prohibit what they had done. Very careful questioning of Vandene had made that much clear. But whether it would be permitted was not clear at all. Still, as she had heard an Arafellin mercenary

recruited by Birgitte say, "what was not forbidden was allowed." That sounded almost like one of Lini's old sayings,
though she doubted her nurse would ever have been so
permissive. "You're troubled by him, Egwene. More than
usual, I mean. I can tell. Why?"

"I have reason to be, Elayne. The eyes-and-ears report
very troubling rumors. Only rumors, I hope, but if they
aren't . . ." She was very much the Amyrlin Seat now, a
short slender young woman who seemed strong as steel and
tall as a mountain. Determination filled her dark eyes and
set her jaw. "I know you love him. I love him, too. But I am
not trying to Heal the White Tower just so he can chain Aes
Sedai like *damane*. Sleep well and have pleasant dreams,
Elayne. Pleasant dreams are more valuable than people realize." And with that, she was gone, back to the waking
world.

For a moment, Elayne stood staring at the spot where
Egwene had been. What had she been talking about? Rand
would never do that! If only for love of her, he would not!
She prodded that rock-hard knot in the back of her head.
With him so far away, the veins of gold shone only in memory. Surely he would not. Troubled in herself, she stepped
out of the dream, back to her sleeping body.

She needed sleep, but no sooner was she back in her
own body than sunlight fell on her eyelids. What hour *was*
it? She had appointments to keep, duties to carry out. She
wanted to sleep for months. She wrestled with duty, but
duty won. She had a busy day ahead. Every day was a busy
day. Her eyes popped open, feeling grainy, as if she had not
slept at all. By the slant of light through the windows, it was
well beyond sunrise. She could simply lie there. Duty. Aviendha shifted in her sleep, and Elayne poked her sharply
in the ribs. If she had to be awake, then Aviendha was not
going to loll about.

Aviendha woke with a start, stretching for her knife lying atop the small table on her side of the bed. Before her
hand touched the dark horn hilt, she let it fall. "Something
woke me," she muttered. "I thought a Shaido was—Look at
the sun! Why did you let me sleep so late?" she demanded,
scrambling from the bed. "Just because I'm allowed to stay
with you—" the words were muffled for an instant as she
jerked her sleep-wrinkled shift off over her head "—does

not mean Monaelle won't switch me if she thinks I am being lazy. Do you mean to lie there all day?"

With a groan, Elayne climbed out of the bed. Essande was already waiting at the door to the dressing room; she never waked Elayne unless Elayne remembered to order it. Elayne surrendered herself to the white-haired woman's almost silent ministrations while Aviendha dressed herself, but her sister made up for Essande's quiet with a laughing string of comments along the line of how having someone else put your clothes on you must feel like being a baby again and how Elayne might forget how to put on her own clothes and *need* somebody to dress her. She had done very much the same every morning since they had begun to share the same bed. Aviendha found it very funny. Elayne did not say a word, except to answer her tire-woman's suggestions on what she should wear, until the last mother-of-pearl button was done up and she stood examining herself in the stand-mirror.

"Essande," she said then, casually, "are Aviendha's clothes ready?" The fine blue wool with a little silver embroidery would do well enough for what she faced today.

Essande brightened. "All Lady Aviendha's pretty silks and laces, my Lady? Oh, yes. All brushed and cleaned and ironed and put away." She gestured to the wardrobes lining one wall.

Elayne smiled over her shoulder at her sister. Aviendha stared at the wardrobes as though they contained vipers, then gulped and hastily finished winding the dark folded kerchief around her head.

When Elayne had dismissed Essande, she said, "Just in case you need them."

"Very well," Aviendha muttered, putting on her silver necklace. "No more jokes about the woman dressing you."

"Good. Or I'll tell her to start dressing *you*. Now, that *would* be amusing."

Grumbling under her breath about people who could not take a joke, Aviendha plainly did not agree. Elayne half expected her to demand that all the clothes she had acquired be discarded. She was a little surprised Aviendha had not seen to it already.

For Aviendha, the breakfast laid out in the sitting room consisted of cured ham with raisins, eggs cooked with dried plums, dried fish prepared with pine nuts, fresh bread slathered with butter, and tea made syrupy with honey. Well, not actually syrupy, but it seemed so. Elayne got no butter on her bread, very little honey in her tea, and instead of the rest, a hot porridge of grains and herbs that was supposed to be especially healthy. She did not feel with child, no matter what Min had told Aviendha, but Min had told Birgitte, too, once the three of them began getting drunk. Between her Warder, Dyelin, and Reene Harfor, she now found herself limited to a diet "suitable for a woman in her condition." If she sent to the kitchens for a treat, somehow it never arrived, and if she slipped down there herself, the cooks gave her such glum disapproving stares that she slipped back out again with nothing.

She did not really mourn the spiced wine and sweets and the other things she was no longer allowed—not that much, anyway, except when Aviendha was gobbling tarts or puddings—but *everyone* in the Palace knew she was pregnant. And of course, that meant they knew how she had gotten that way, if not with whom. The men were not too bad, beyond the fact that they *knew,* and she *knew* they knew, but the women did not bother to hide knowing. Whether they accepted or deprecated the situation, half looked at her as though she were a hoyden and the other half with speculation. Forcing herself to swallow the porridge—it was not that bad, really, but she dearly would have loved some of the ham Aviendha was slicing, or a little of the egg with plums—spooning lumpy porridge into her mouth, she almost looked forward to the start of birthing sickness, so she could share the queasy belly with Birgitte.

The first visitor to enter her apartments that morning beside Essande was the leading candidate among the Palace women for the father of her barely quickened child.

"My Queen," Captain Mellar said, sweeping off his plumed hat in a flourishing bow. "The Chief Clerk awaits Your Majesty's pleasure." The captain's dark, unblinking eyes said he would never have dreams of the men he killed, and the lace-edged sash across his chest and the lace at his neck and wrists only made him look harder. Wiping grease from her chin with a linen napkin, Aviendha watched him with no expression on her face. The two Guardswomen standing one on either side of the doors grimaced faintly.

Mellar already had a reputation for pinching Guardswomen's bottoms, the prettier ones' at least, not to mention disparaging their abilities in the city's taverns. The second was far worse, in the Guardswomen's eyes.

"I am not a queen, yet, Captain," Elayne said briskly. She always tried to keep as much to the point as possible with the man. "How is recruiting for my bodyguard coming along?"

"Only thirty-two, so far, my Lady." Still holding his hat, the hatchet-faced man rested both hands on his sword hilt, his lounging posture hardly suitable for the presence of one he had called his queen. Nor was his grin. "Lady Birgitte has exacting standards. Not many women can match them. Give me ten days, and I can find a hundred men who'll better them and hold you as dear in their hearts as I do."

"I think not, Captain Mellar." It was an effort to keep a chill out of her voice. He had to have heard the rumors concerning himself and her. Could he think that just because she had not denied them, she might actually find him . . . attractive? Pushing away the half-empty porridge bowl, she suppressed a shudder. Thirty-two, so far? The numbers were growing quickly. Some of the Hunters for the Horn who had been demanding rank had decided that serving in Elayne's bodyguard carried a certain flair. She conceded that the women could not all be on duty day and night, but no matter what Birgitte said, the goal of a hundred seemed excessive. The woman dug in her heels now at any suggestion of fewer, though. "Please tell the Chief Clerk he can come in," she told him. He swept her another elaborate bow.

She rose to follow him, and as he pulled one of the lion-carved doors open, she laid a hand on his arm and smiled. "Thank you again for saving my life, Captain," she said, this time warm enough for a caress.

The fellow smirked at her! The Guardswomen stared straight ahead, frozen, those she could see out in the hall before the doors closed behind him as well as those inside, and when Elayne turned around, Aviendha was staring at her with little more expression than she had shown Mellar. That little was pure amazement, though. Elayne sighed.

Crossing the carpets, she bent to put an arm around her sister and spoke softly, for her ear alone. She trusted the women of her bodyguard with things she told very few others, but there were some matters she dared not trust to them. "I saw a maid passing, Aviendha. Maids gossip worse than men. The more who think this child is Doilin Mellar's, the safer it will be. If necessary, I'll let the man pinch my bottom."

"I see," Aviendha said slowly, and frowned into her plate as though seeing something other than the eggs and plums she began pushing around with her spoon.

Master Norry presented his usual blend of mundane maintenance of the Palace and the city, tidbits from his correspondents in foreign capitals, and information gleaned from merchants and bankers and others who had dealings beyond the borders, but his first piece of news was by far the most important to her, if not the most interesting.

"The two most prominent bankers in the city are ... amenable, my Lady," he said in that dry-as-dust voice of his. Clutching his leather folder to his narrow chest, he eyed Aviendha sideways. He was still not accustomed to her presence while he made his reports. Or the Guardswomen. Aviendha bared her teeth at him, and he blinked, then coughed into a bony hand. "Master Hoffley and Mistress Andscale were somewhat ... hesitant ... at first, but they know the market for alum as well as I. It would not be safe to say that their coffers are now yours, but I have arranged for twenty thousand gold crowns to be moved to the Palace strongroom, and more will come as needed."

"Inform the Lady Birgitte," Elayne told him, hiding her relief. Birgitte had not yet signed enough new Guards to hold a city as large as Caemlyn, much less do anything else, but Elayne could not expect to see revenue from her estates before spring, and the mercenaries *were* expensive. Now she would not lose them for lack of gold before Birgitte recruited men to replace them. "Next, Master Norry?"

"I fear the sewers must be given a high priority, my Lady. The rats are breeding in them as if it were spring, and ..."

He mingled it all together, according to what he felt was most pressing. Norry seemed to take it as a personal failure that he had not yet learned who had freed Elenia and Naean, though less than a week had passed since their rescue. The price of grain was climbing exorbitantly, along with that of every other sort of foodstuff, and it was already apparent that repairs to the Palace roof would take longer and cost more than the masons had first estimated, but food always grew more expensive as winter went on and masons always cost more than they first had said they would. Norry admitted that his last correspondence from New Braem was several days old, but the Borderlanders appeared content to remain where they were, which he could not understand. Any army, much less one as large as this was said to be, ought to be stripping the countryside around it bare by now. Elayne did not understand why either, but she was content that it was so. For the time being. Rumors in Cairhien of Aes Sedai swearing fealty to Rand at least gave a reason for Egwene's concern, though it hardly seemed likely any sister would actually do such a thing. That was the least important piece of news, in Norry's estimation, but not in hers. Rand could not afford to alienate the sisters with Egwene. He could not afford to alienate *any* Aes Sedai. But he did seem to find ways to do so.

Reene Harfor soon replaced Halwin Norry, nodding to the bodyguards at the door in passing and giving Aviendha an open smile. If the plump graying woman had ever been uncertain about Elayne calling Aviendha sister, she had never shown it, and now she genuinely appeared to approve. Smiles or no smiles, though, her report was much more grim than anything in the Chief Clerk's.

"Jon Skellit is in the pay of House Arawn, my Lady," Reene said, her round face stern enough to fit a hangman. "Twice now he has been seen accepting a purse from men known to favor Arawn. And there is no doubt that Ester Norham is in someone's pay. She isn't stealing, but she has over fifty crowns of gold hidden under a loose floorboard, and she added ten crowns last night."

"Do as with the others," Elayne said sadly. The First Maid had uncovered nine spies she was certain of, so far, four of them employed by people Reene had not yet been able to uncover. That Reene had found any at all was enough to anger Elayne, but the barber and the hairdresser were something more. Both had been in her mother's service. A pity they had not seen fit to transfer their loyalty to Morgase's daughter.

Aviendha grimaced as Mistress Harfor murmured that she would, but there was no point in discharging the spies, or killing them as Aviendha had suggested. They would just be replaced by spies she did not know. *A spy is your enemy's tool until you know her,* her mother had said, *but then she is your tool. When you find a spy,* Thom had told her, *wrap him in swaddling and feed him with a spoon.* The men and women who had betrayed their service would be "allowed" to discover what Elayne wanted them to know, not all true, such as the numbers Birgitte had recruited.

"And the other matter, Mistress Harfor?"

"Nothing yet, my Lady, but I have hopes," Reene said even more grimly than before. "I have hopes."

Following the First Maid's departure came two delegations of merchants, first a large group of Kandori with gem-studded earrings and silver guild-chains draped across their chests and then, right behind them, half a dozen Illianers with only a touch of embroidery on otherwise somber coats and dresses. She used one of the smaller reception rooms. The tapestries flanking the marble fireplace were of hunting scenes, not the White Lion, and the polished wooden wall panels were uncarved. They were merchants, not diplomats, though some seemed to feel slighted that she offered only wine and did not drink with them. Kandori or Illianers, they also looked askance at the two Guardswomen who followed her into the room and posted themselves beside the door, though if by this time they had not heard the tales of an attempt to kill her, they must be deaf. Six more of her bodyguard waited outside the door.

The Kandori studied Aviendha surreptitiously when not listening attentively to Elayne, and the Illianers avoided looking at her at all after the first widening of eyes in surprise. Doubtless they read significance into the presence of an Aiel, even if she only sat on the floor in a corner and said nothing, but whether Kandori or Illianers, the merchants wanted the same thing, reassurance that Elayne would not so anger the Dragon Reborn that he would interfere with trade by sending his armies and his Aiel to ravage Andor, though they did not come out and say so. Nor did they mention that Aiel and the Legion of the Dragon both had large encampments not many miles from Caemlyn. Their polite questions about her plans now that she had removed the Dragon banners and the Banners of Light from Caemlyn were sufficient. She told them what she told everyone, that Andor would ally itself to the Dragon Reborn but was not his conquest. In return, they offered vague wishes for her well-being, suggesting that they supported her claim to the Lion Throne wholeheartedly without actually saying any such thing. After all, if she failed, they would want to be welcome in Andor under whoever did gain the crown.

When the Illianers had made their bows and curtsies and departed, she closed her eyes for a moment and rubbed her temples. She still had a meeting with a delegation of glassmakers before the midday meal, and five more with merchants or craftsfolk later; a very busy day, full of mealy-mouthed platitudes and ambiguity. And with Nynaeve and Merilille gone, it was her turn to teach the Windfinders again tonight, at best a less pleasant experience than the worst meeting with merchants. Which might leave her a little time to study the *ter'angreal* they had brought out of Ebou Dar before she was so weary that she could no longer keep her eyes open. It was embarrassing when Aviendha had to half carry her to bed, but she could not stop. There was too much to be done and not enough time in a day.

There was almost an hour before the glassmakers, but Aviendha ruthlessly rode over her suggestion that she might take a peek at the things from Ebou Dar.

"Has Birgitte been talking to you?" Elayne demanded as her sister all but dragged her up a narrow flight of stone stairs. Four Guardswomen went ahead, and the others trailed behind, studiously ignoring what passed between her and Aviendha. Though she thought that Rasoria Domanche, a stocky Hunter for the Horn with the blue eyes and yellow hair occasionally found among Tairens, wore a tiny smile.

"Do I need her to tell me you spend too many hours inside and sleep too little?" Aviendha replied contemptuously. "You need fresh air."

The air in the high colonnade was certainly fresh. And crisp, though the sun stood high in a gray sky. A cold breeze blew around the smooth columns, so the Guardswomen standing ready to protect her from pigeons had to hang on to their plumed hats. Perversely, Elayne refused to ignore the chill.

"Dyelin talked to you," she grumbled, shivering. Dyelin claimed a woman with child needed long walks every day. She had been quick to remind Elayne that, Daughter-Heir or not, she was really only the High Seat of House Trakand for the moment, and if the High Seat of Trakand wanted to talk with the High Seat of Taravin, she could do it tramping up and down the Palace corridors or not at all.

"Monaelle has borne seven children," Aviendha replied. "She says I must see you get fresh air." Despite no more than her shawl pulled over her shoulders, she gave no sign of feeling the wind. But then, Aiel were as good as the sisters at ignoring the elements. Wrapping her arms around herself, Elayne scowled.

"Stop sulking, sister," Aviendha said. She pointed down to one of the stableyards, just visible over the white-tiled roofs. "Look, Reanne Corly is already checking to see if Merilille Ceandevin is returning." The familiar vertical slash of light appeared in the stableyard and rotated into a hole in the air ten feet tall and as wide.

Elayne scowled down at Reanne's head. She was *not* sulking. Perhaps she should not have taught Reanne to Travel, since the Kinswoman was not yet Aes Sedai, but none of the other sisters were strong enough to make the weave work, and if the Windfinders were allowed to learn, then the few Kinswomen who could should be allowed, too, in her book. Besides, she could not do everything herself. Light, had winter been this icy before she learned to stop heat and cold from touching her?

To her surprise, Merilille rode through the gateway shaking snow from her dark fur-lined cloak, followed by the helmeted Guardsmen who had been sent off with her seven days earlier. Zaida and the Windfinders had been most unpleasant over her disappearance, to put it mildly, but the Gray had leaped at a chance to escape them for however long. It had been necessary to check for her every day, opening a gateway to the same spot, yet Elayne had not expected her for a week yet at the very best. As the last of the ten red-cloaked Guards entered the stableyard, the slim little Gray sister climbed down from her saddle, handed her reins to a groom, and hurried into the Palace before the woman from the stables could more than get out of her way.

"I *am* enjoying the fresh air," Elayne said, just keeping her teeth from chattering, "but if Merilille is back, I must go down." Aviendha quirked an eyebrow as if she suspected the evasion, but she was the first to start for the stairs. Merilille's return was important, and by her haste, she brought either very good news or very bad.

By the time Elayne and her sister walked into her sitting room—followed by two of the Guardswomen, of course, who planted themselves beside the doors—Merilille was already there. Her damp-spotted cloak lay over the back of a chair, her pale gray riding gloves were tucked behind her belt, and her black hair could have used a brush. With purple crescents under her dark eyes, Merilille's pale face looked as weary as Elayne felt.

As quickly as she had come up from the stableyard, she was not alone. Birgitte, frowning pensively, stood with one hand on the carved mantel over the fireplace. The other gripped her long golden braid, almost like Nynaeve. Today, she wore voluminous dark green trousers with her short red coat, a combination to make the eye flinch. And Captain Mellar made Elayne an elaborate bow, waving his white-plumed hat about. He had no place here, but she let him stay, and even gave him a very warm smile. *Very* warm.

The plump young maid who had just placed a large silver tray on one of the sideboards blinked and looked wide-eyed at Mellar before remembering to make her curtsy on going. Elayne held her smile until the door closed. Whatever protected her baby, she was willing to do. There was hot spiced wine on the rope work tray for everyone else, and weak tea for her. Well, at least it was hot.

"I was quite lucky," Merilille sighed once she was seated, giving Mellar an uncertain glance over her winecup. She knew the tale of him saving Elayne's life, but she had left before the rumors began. "It turned out that Reanne had opened her gateway not five miles from the Borderlanders. They have not moved since arriving." Her nose wrinkled. "If not for the weather, the stench of latrines and horse dung would be overpowering. You were right, Elayne. All four rulers are there, in four camps a few miles apart. Each holds an army. I found the Shienarans the first day, and most of my time since has been spent talking with Easar of Shienar and the other three. We met in a different camp each day."

"You spent a little time looking too, I hope," Birgitte said respectfully from in front of the fireplace. She was respectful with every Aes Sedai except the one she was bonded to. "How many are they?"

"I don't suppose you got an accurate count," Mellar put in, sounding as though he expected anything but. For once, his narrow face was unsmiling. Peering into his wine, he shrugged. "Whatever you saw might have some value, though. If there are enough of them, they may starve themselves before they can threaten Caemlyn. The largest army in the world is just so many walking corpses without food and fodder." He laughed. Birgitte stared at his back darkly, but Elayne lifted a hand slightly at her side, motioning the other woman to keep silent.

"They are not in a good way for food, Captain," Merilille said coolly, sitting up straighter in spite of her obvious fatigue, "but neither are they starving quite yet. I should not count on starvation to defeat them, if it comes to that." After a little time away from the Sea Folk, her big eyes were no longer perpetually startled, and despite her smooth Aes Sedai composure, it was plain she had decided to dislike Doilin Mellar no matter whose life he had saved. "As for numbers, something over two hundred thousand, I should say, and I very much doubt anyone but their own officers could be more accurate than that. Even hungry, that is a great many swords," Mellar shrugged again, undisturbed by Aes Sedai stares.

The slim Gray sister neither looked at him again nor ignored him in any obvious way; he just seemed to become a piece of the furniture for her as she went on. "There are at least ten sisters with them, Elayne, though they made a great effort to hide the fact. Not adherents to Egwene, I should think, though they need not be Elaida's either. A good many sisters appear to be sitting to one side until the Tower's troubles are over, I fear." She sighed again, perhaps not from tiredness this time.

With a grimace, Elayne set her teacup aside. The kitchens had not sent up any honey, and she really did not like it bitter. "What do they want, Merilille? The rulers, not the sisters." Ten sisters made that army ten times as dangerous, especially to Rand. No, to anyone. "They haven't been sitting there in the snow all this time for the joy of it."

The Gray spread her slim hands slightly. "Over the long run, I can only make suppositions. Over the short, they want to meet you, and as soon as possible. They sent riders toward Caemlyn when they arrived at New Braem, but this time of year, it might take another week or more before they arrive here. Tenobia of Saldaea let slip, or pretended to let slip, that they know you have some connection to, or least a close acquaintance with, a certain person in whom they also apparently have an interest. Somehow, they know of your presence in Falme when certain events took place." Mellar frowned in confusion, but no one enlightened him. "I did not disclose Traveling, because of those sisters, but I did say I could return with a reply very soon."

Elayne exchanged a look with Birgitte, who also shrugged, though in her case neither from detachment nor from disdain. The largest hole in Elayne's hopes to use the Borderlanders to influence her opponents for the throne had been how to approach sitting rulers while she was merely the High Seat of Trakand and Daughter-Heir of a deceased queen. Birgitte's shrug said be thankful for the hole closing, but Elayne wondered how these people from the Borderlands had learned what very few others knew. And if they knew, how many more did, too? She *would* protect her unborn child.

"Would you be willing to go back right away, Merilille?" she asked. The other sister accepted with alacrity, and with a slight widening of her eyes that suggested she would put up with any amount of stench to avoid returning to the Windfinders a little longer. "Then we will go together. If they want to meet me soon, nothing can be sooner than today." They knew too much for delay. Nothing could be allowed to threaten her child. Nothing!

CHAPTER
27

To Surprise Queens and Kings

It was not quite so simple as just saying she would go, of course.

"This is unwise, sister," Aviendha said darkly as Merilille scurried off to freshen herself. Scurried in truth; the Gray seemed to be keeping a sharp eye out for Sea Folk before she reached the sitting room doors. When a sister of Elayne's standing said go, Merilille went. Arms folded and shawl wrapped around her so she looked very much the Wise One, Aviendha stood over Elayne at her writing table, "This is very unwise."

"Wise?" Birgitte growled, feet apart and fists planted on her hips. "Wise? The girl wouldn't know 'wise' if it bit her on the nose! Why this rush? Let Merilille do what Grays do, arrange a parley in a few days, or a week. Queens hate being surprised, and kings despise it. Believe me, I know it to my cost. They find ways to make you regret it." The Warder bond mirrored her anger and frustration.

"I *want* to catch them by surprise, Birgitte. It might help me to find out just how much they know about me." Grimacing, Elayne pushed away the blotted page and took another sheet from the inlaid rosewood paper-box. Her weariness had vanished with Merilille's news, but writing a steady, clean hand did seem difficult. The wording needed to be just right, too. This was not to be a letter from the Daughter-Heir of Andor, but from Elayne Trakand, Aes Sedai of the Green Ajah. They had to see what she wanted them to see.

"Try to talk some bloody sense into her, Aviendha," Birgitte muttered. "In case you can't, I had best see if I can scrape together a suitable flaming escort."

"No escort, Birgitte. Except for you. An Aes Sedai and her Warder. And Aviendha, of course." Elayne paused in writing to smile at her sister, who did not smile back.

"I know your courage, Elayne," Aviendha said. "I admire your courage. But even *Sha'mad Conde* know when to be cautious!" *She* spoke of caution? Aviendha would not know caution if . . . well . . . if it bit her on the nose!

"An Aes Sedai and her Warder?" Birgitte exclaimed. "I told you, you can't go running off trying to have adventures any more!"

"No escort," Elayne said firmly, dipping her pen for another try. "This isn't an adventure. It is just the way it must be done." Throwing up her hands, Birgitte growled several oaths, but nothing Elayne had not heard before.

To her surprise, Mellar made no objection to staying behind. A meeting with four rulers would hardly be as boring as meeting merchants, but he begged leave to be about his duties since she did not need him. That contented her. A Captain of the Royal Guards would make the Borderlanders think of her as Daughter-Heir sooner than she wanted. Not to mention that Mellar might decide to leer at her.

Captain Mellar's unconcern was not shared by the rest of her bodyguard, though. One of the Guardswomen apparently went running for Caseille, because the tall Arafellin woman came striding into the sitting room while Elayne was still writing, demanding to accompany Elayne with the entire bodyguard. Birgitte finally had to order her out to stop her protests.

For once, Birgitte appeared to recognize the fact that Elayne was not going to be budged, leaving with Caseille to change her clothes. Well, she stalked off grumbling oaths, slamming the door behind her with a crash, but at least she did go. You might have thought she would be happy for a chance to take off that Captain-General's coat, but the bond might as well have been an echo of her curses. Aviendha did not curse, but she kept up her admonitions. Everything had to be done in such a whirlwind, though, that Elayne had an excuse to ignore them.

Essande was summoned and began laying out suitable garments, while Elayne hastily ate her midday meal early. She had not sent for it; Aviendha had. Apparently, Monaelle said missing meals was as bad as eating too much. Mistress

Harfor, informed that she would have to handle the glass-makers, and the other delegations as well, grimaced faintly even as she inclined her head in acceptance. Before leaving, she announced that she had acquired goats for the Palace. Elayne needed to drink goat's milk, and lots of it. Careane groaned at hearing that she was to teach the Windfinders that night, but at least the woman made no comment on her diet. In truth, she hoped to be back in the Palace by nightfall, but she also expected to be as tired as if she had already taught that lesson. Vandene did not offer advice, either, not of that sort. Elayne had studied the nations of the Blightborder along with every other land as part of her education, and had discussed her intentions with the white-haired Green, who knew the Borderlands well, yet she would have dearly loved to take Vandene along. Someone who had actually lived in the Borderlands might see nuances that escaped her. But she did not dare do more than ask a few last hurried questions while Essande was dressing her, just to reassure herself on things Vandene had already told her. Not that she needed reassurance, she realized. She felt as focused as Birgitte drawing a bow.

Finally, Reanne had to be brought from where she was yet again trying to convince a former *sul'dam* that she, too, could channel. Reanne had been making that weave in the stableyard every day since she first wove it to send Merilille off; she could open it on the same spot in Braem Wood with no difficulty. There were no maps of that area in the Palace that were good enough for Merilille to mark the camp's positions very well, and if Elayne or Aviendha wove the gateway, it might open ten miles or more farther from the camps than the small clearing Reanne knew. The snow had stopped falling in Braem Wood before the Gray returned, yet even so, ten miles in fresh snow could mean another two hours at best. Elayne wanted this done quickly. Speed. Everyone had to move with speed.

The Sea Folk must have been aware of the bustle that enveloped the Palace, Guardswomen running through the hallways carrying messages and fetching this person or that, but Elayne made sure they were told nothing. Suppose Zaida decided to come along, she was capable of having one of the Windfinders make her own gateway if Elayne refused her, and the Wavemistress was a complication to be avoided. The woman already behaved as though she had as much right in the Palace as Elayne herself. Zaida trying to domineer could ruin everything as surely as Mellar leering at her.

Making haste seemed beyond Essande's ability, yet everyone else flew, and by the time the sun stood straight overhead, Elayne found herself riding Fireheart slowly through the snows of Braem Wood, near enough fifty leagues north of Caemlyn as the wild goose flew but only a step through the gateway into thick forest of tall pine and leatherleaf and oak mixed with gray-branched trees that had lost their leaves. Occasionally a broad meadow opened up, covered with snow like white carpets, unblemished save for the hoofprints of Merilille's running horse. Merilille had been sent ahead with the letter, and Elayne, Aviendha and Birgitte had followed after an hour, to give her time to reach the Borderlanders ahead of them. The road from Caemlyn to New Braem lay some miles to the west. Here, they could have been a thousand leagues from human habitation.

For Elayne, dressing had been as serious as choosing armor. Her cloak was lined with marten for added warmth, but the material was dark green wool, soft yet thick, and her riding dress was green silk, and unadorned. Even her snug riding gloves were plain dark green leather. Unless the swords had been drawn, that was the armor in which an Aes Sedai faced rulers. Her only visible jewelry was a small amber brooch in the shape of a turtle, and if anyone thought that odd, let them. An army of Borderlanders was beyond any trap one of her rivals could lay, or even Elaida, but those ten sisters—ten or more—might be Elaida's. She was not about to let herself be bundled off back to the White Tower.

"We can turn back from this without incurring *toh*, Elayne." Aviendha, scowling, still wore her Aiel garments, with her single silver necklace and heavy ivory bracelet. Her stocky bay was a hand shorter than Fireheart or Birgitte's lean gray, Arrow, and much gentler to handle, though she rode more easily than once she had. Dark-stockinged legs bared above the knee by straddling a saddle, she actually looked warm, except for the shawl wrapped around her head. Unlike Birgitte, she had not ceased her attempts to dissuade Elayne. "Surprise is all very well, but they will respect you more if they must meet you halfway."

"I can hardly abandon Merilille," Elayne said more patiently than she felt. Perhaps she was not weary any longer, but neither did she feel particularly fresh, not at all ready to put up with badgering. But she did not want to snap at Aviendha. "She might feel something of a fool, standing there with a letter announcing that I'm coming and I don't come. Worse, *I* would feel a fool."

"Better to feel a fool than be one," Birgitte muttered, half under her breath. Her dark cloak spread behind her saddle, and her intricate braid hung from the opening of her hood almost to her waist. Pulling that hood up just enough to frame her face was the one concession she had made to the cold and the gusting wind that sometimes lifted fresh-fallen snow like feathers. She did not want her vision obscured. The cover on her bow's saddle-case, meant to keep the bowstring dry, hung down so she could reach the bow quickly. The suggestion that she wear a sword had been quashed with as much indignation as if Elayne had asked Aviendha to wear one. Birgitte knew the bow, but she claimed she might stab herself trying to draw a sword. Still, her short green coat would have blended into woodlands at another time of the year, and for a wonder, her wide-legged trousers were the same color. She was a Warder now, not the Captain-General of the Queen's Guard, yet she was not so pleased by the title as might have been expected. The bond carried as much frustration as alertness.

Elayne sighed, her breath misting. "You two know what I hope to achieve here. You've known since I decided. Why are you suddenly treating me as if I'm made of blown glass?"

The pair exchanged looks past her, each waiting for the other to speak first, then silently turned to stare straight ahead, and suddenly she knew.

"When my child is born," she said dryly, "you can both apply to be her wet nurse." If her child was "her." If Min had said, it was lost in Aviendha and Birgitte's wine-hazed memories of that night. It might be better to have a son first, so he could begin his training before his sister came. Yet a daughter secured the succession, while a lone son would be pushed aside, and as much as she wanted more than one, nothing said she would have another child. The Light send her more of Rand's children, but she had to be practical. "I myself do not need a wet nurse."

Aviendha's sun-darkened cheeks turned darker with embarrassment. Birgitte's expression did not change, yet the same emotion oozed along the Warder bond.

They rode slowly, following Merilille's tracks for close on two hours, and Elayne was thinking that the nearest camp must be very close when Birgitte suddenly pointed ahead and said, "Shienarans," then eased her bow in its case. Alertness swallowed frustration and everything else in the bond. Aviendha touched the hilt of her belt knife as if making sure it was there.

Waiting beneath the trees, off to one side from Merilille's traces, men and horses alike were so still that Elayne almost took them for natural outcrops of some sort until she made out the strange swooping crests on their helmets. Their mounts were not armored, as Shienaran heavies' animals often were, but the men themselves wore plate-and-mail, with long-hilted swords on their backs, and swords and maces hung at their belts and from their saddles. Their dark eyes never blinked. One of the horses swished its tail, and the movement seemed startling.

A sharp-faced man with a harsh voice spoke as Elayne and the other two women drew rein in front of him. The crest atop his helmet looked like narrow wings. "King Easar sends his assurance of your safety, Elayne Sedai, and I add my own. I am Kayen Yokata, Lord of Fal Eisen, and may Peace abandon me and the Blight consume my soul if harm befalls you or anyone with you in our camp."

That was not so comforting as Elayne might have wished. All these guarantees of her safety only made clear that there had been some question of it, and might still be. "Does an Aes Sedai need assurances from Shienarans?" she said. She started to run through a novice exercise for calmness, and realized she did not need it. Very strange. "You may lead, Lord Kayen." He merely nodded and turned his horse.

Some of the Shienarans glanced at Aviendha without expression, recognizing an Aiel, but for the most part they simply fell in behind. Only the hooves crunching the harder snow beneath the fresh fall broke the silence of their short ride. She had been right. The Shienaran camp was very close. She began to see sentries, mounted and armored, just minutes later, and soon after that they rode into the Shienaran camp.

Sprawled among the trees, the encampment seemed larger than she had imagined. Whether she looked left, right or ahead, tents and cookfires, lines of tethered horses and rows of wagons stretched out of her sight. As she and her escort passed, soldiers looked up in curiosity, hard-faced men with their heads shaved except for a tuft on top that was sometimes long enough to reach the shoulders. Few wore any part of their armor, but armor and weapons always lay close to hand. The smell was not so bad as Merilille had described, though she could make out the faint odor of latrines and horse dung beneath the aroma of whatever was boiling in all these cookpots. No one appeared hungry, though many were lean. Not the leanness of starvation, though, just that of men who had never carried much fat on them. She did notice that there were no spits over any fire she could see. Meat would be harder to come by than grain, though grain itself was in short enough supply this late in winter. Barley soup did not strengthen a man the way meat did. They needed to move soon; nowhere could support four armies this size for long. She just had to make sure they moved in the right direction.

Not everyone she saw was a soldier with a shaven head, of course, though the men among them looked almost as hard. There were fletchers making arrows, wheelwrights working on wagons, farriers shoeing horses, laundresses stirring boiling kettles, women working with needles who might have been seamstresses or wives. Great numbers of people always followed an army, sometimes as many as the soldiers themselves. She did not see anyone who could have been Aes Sedai, though; sisters were unlikely to push up their sleeves and work wooden paddles in the laundry kettles, or don patched woolens and sit darning breeches. Why did they want to remain hidden? She resisted the desire to embrace the Source, to draw *saidar* through the turtle *angreal* pinned to her breast. One battle at a time, and first she must fight for Andor.

Before a much larger tent than any of the others she could see, pale canvas with a single long peak, Kayen dismounted and handed her down. He hesitated over whether to do the

same for Birgitte and Aviendha, but Birgitte solved his di-
lemma by stepping down smoothly and handing her reins
to a waiting soldier, Aviendha by half-falling out of the
saddle. She had improved her riding, but mounting and
dismounting still gave her difficulty. Glaring around her
to see whether anyone was laughing, she smoothed down
her bulky skirts, then unwrapped the shawl from around her
head and settled it on her shoulders. Birgitte watched her
horse being taken away as though she wished she had taken
her bow and quiver from the saddle. Kayen pulled open one
of the entry flaps and bowed.

Drawing a last deep calming breath, Elayne led the other
two women in. She could not allow them to see her as a supplicant. She was not here to beg, or to defend. *Sometimes,*
Gareth Bryne had told her when she was a child, *you find
yourself outnumbered, with no path to slip away. Always
do what your enemy least expects, Elayne. In that case, you
must attack.* From the start, she must attack.

Inside, Merilille glided to her across the layered carpets
laid down for a floor. The diminutive Gray's smile was not
precisely relieved, but clearly she was glad to see Elayne.
Aside from her, there were only five others present, two
women and three men, and one of the latter was a servant,
an old cavalryman by his bowed legs and scarred face, who
came to take cloaks and gloves—and blink at Aviendha—
before retreating to a plain wooden table that held a silver
tray with a tall-necked pitcher and an array of cups. The
other four ruled the nations of the Borderlands. A scattering of backless camp chairs and four large braziers holding
glowing coals completed the tent's furnishings. This was
not the sort of reception the Daughter-Heir of Andor might
have expected, with courtiers and many servants, and idle
conversation to be made before serious discussions could
begin, and men and women at those rulers' shoulders to advise them. What she found was what she had hoped for.

Healing had rid Merilille's eyes of their dark circles before she left the Palace, and she made Elayne's introduction
with simple dignity. "This is Elayne Trakand, of the Green
Ajah, as I told you." That, and nothing more. Elayne knew
enough from Vandene to pick out one from another of the
four rulers who faced her.

"I give you welcome, Elayne Sedai," Easar of Shienar

said. "Peace and the Light favor you." He was a short man, no taller than herself, slim in a bronze-colored coat, his face unwrinkled despite a long white topknot that hung over the side of his head. Looking at his sad eyes, she reminded herself that he was accounted a wise ruler and a skilled diplomat as well as a fine soldier. In appearance, he was none of those things. "May I offer you wine? The spices are not fresh, but they have gained extra sharpness with age."

"When Merilille told us you would come all the way from Caemlyn today, I confess I would have doubted her, were she not Aes Sedai." Ethenielle of Kandor, perhaps half a hand taller than Merilille, was plump, her black hair lightly dusted with gray, but there was nothing motherly about her despite her smile. Regal dignity clothed her as much as did her fine blue wool. Her eyes were blue, too, clear and level.

"We are pleased that you did come," Paitar of Arafel said in a surprisingly deep, rich voice that made Elayne feel warmed, somehow. "We have much to discuss with you." Vandene had said he was the most beautiful man in the Borderlands, and perhaps he had been long ago, but age had laid deep lines in his face, and only a fringe of short gray hair remained on his head. He was tall and broad-shouldered, though, in plain green, and he did look strong. And not a fool.

Where the others carried their years with grace, Tenobia of Saldaea flaunted youth if not beauty, with her eagle's beak of a nose and wide mouth. Her tilted, almost purple eyes, level with Elayne's, were her best feature. Perhaps her only one. Where the others dressed simply, even if they did rule nations, her pale blue dress was worked with pearls and sapphires and she wore more sapphires in her hair. Suitable for the court, but hardly for a camp. And where they were courteous . . . "Under the Light, Merilille Sedai," Tenobia said in a high voice, frowning, "I know you speak truth, but she looks more a child than an Aes Sedai. You did not mention she would be bringing a black-eyed Aiel."

Easar's face never changed, but Paitar's mouth tightened, and Ethenielle went so far as to cut her eyes briefly toward Tenobia in a glance that would have suited a mother. A very irritated and displeased mother.

"Black?" Aviendha muttered in confusion. "My eyes are

not black. I never saw black eyes except on a peddler until I crossed the Dragonwall."

"You know I can speak only the truth, Tenobia, and I assure you," Merilille began.

Elayne silenced her with a touch on the arm. "It is enough that you know I am Aes Sedai, Tenobia. This is my sister, Aviendha, of the Nine Valleys Sept of the Taardad Aiel." Aviendha smiled at them, or at least bared her teeth. "This is my Warder, Lady Birgitte Trahelion." Birgitte made a short bow, her golden braid swaying.

One announcement caused as many startled looks as the other—an Aiel woman was her *sister*? her Warder was a *woman*?—but Tenobia and the others ruled lands on the edge of the Blight, where nightmares truly might walk abroad in daylight and anyone who let themselves be startled too greatly was as good as dead. Elayne gave them no chance to recover fully, though. *Attack before they know what you are doing,* Gareth Bryne had said, *and keep attacking until you rout them or break through.*

"Shall we consider the niceties completed?" she said, taking a cup that gave off the aroma of spiced wine from the tray proffered by the old soldier. A surge of caution flowed along the Warder bond, and she saw Aviendha glance sideways at the cup, but she did not mean to drink. She was just glad neither actually spoke. "Only a fool would think you have come all this way to invade Andor," she said, walking to the chairs and sitting. Rulers or not, they had no choice but to follow or stare at her back. At Birgitte's back, since she stood behind her. As usual, Aviendha folded herself to the floor and arranged her skirts in a neat fan. They followed. "The Dragon Reborn brings you," Elayne went on. "You requested this audience with me because I was at Falme. The question is, why is that important to you? Do you think I can tell you more of what happened there than you already know? The Horn of Valere was sounded, dead heroes out of legend rode against Seanchan invaders, and the Dragon Reborn fought the Shadow in the sky for all to see. If you know that much, you know as much as I."

"Audience?" Tenobia said incredulously, pausing half-seated. The camp chair creaked as she let herself drop the rest of the way. "No one *requested* an *audience!* Even if you already held the throne of Andor—!"

"Let us stay to the point, Tenobia," Paitar broke in mildly. Rather than sitting, he stood, occasionally sipping at his wine. Elayne was glad she could see the wrinkles on his face. That voice could confuse a woman's thoughts, otherwise.

Ethenielle spared Tenobia another quick glance while seating herself, and murmured something under her breath. Elayne thought she heard the word "marriage," with a rueful sound, but that made no sense. In any case, she turned her attention to Elayne as soon as she was settled in her chair. "I might like your ferocity another time, Elayne Sedai, but there's little to enjoy falling into an ambush that one of your own allies has helped lay." Tenobia scowled, though Ethenielle did not even dart those sharp eyes in her direction. "What happened at Falme," the Queen of Kandor told Elayne, "is not so important as what came of it. No, Paitar; we must tell her what we must tell her. She already knows too much for anything else. We know that you were a companion to the Dragon Reborn at Falme, Elayne. A friend, perhaps. You are right; we have not come to invade. We have come to find the Dragon Reborn. And we have marched all this way only to find that no one knows where he is to be found. Do you know where he is?"

Elayne hid her relief at the blunt question. It would never have been asked if they thought she was more than a companion or friend. She could be just as blunt. Attack and keep attacking. "Why do you want to find him? Emissaries or messengers could take any word you wanted to send him." Which was as good as asking why they brought vast armies.

Easar had taken no wine, and he stood with his fists on his hips. "The war against the Shadow is fought along the Blight," he said grimly. "The Last Battle will be fought in the Blight, if not at Shayol Ghul itself. And he ignores the Borderlands and concerns himself with lands that have not seen a Myrddraal since the Trolloc Wars."

"The *Car'a'carn* decides where to dance the spears, wetlander," Aviendha sneered. "If you follow him, then you fight where he says." No one looked at her. They were all looking at Elayne. No one took the opening Aviendha had offered.

Elayne made herself breathe evenly and meet their gazes without blinking. A Borderland army was too great a trap for Elaida to lay in order to catch Elayne Trakand, but Rand al'Thor, the Dragon Reborn, might be another matter. Merilille shifted on her chair, but she had her instructions. No matter how many treaties the Gray sister had negotiated, once Elayne began, she was to keep silent. Confidence flowed along the bond with Birgitte. Rand was a stone, unreadable, and distant. "You know of the White Tower's proclamation regarding him?" she asked quietly. They must, by now.

"The Tower calls anathema on anyone who approaches the Dragon Reborn save through the offices of the Tower," Paitar said just as quietly. Taking a seat at last, he regarded her with serious eyes. "You are Aes Sedai. Surely that counts as the same thing."

"The Tower meddles everywhere," Tenobia muttered. "No, Ethenielle; I will say this! The whole world knows the Tower is divided. Do you follow Elaida or the rebels, Elayne?"

"The world seldom knows what it thinks it knows," Merilille said in a voice that seemed to lower the temperature in the tent. The tiny woman who ran when Elayne ordered her and squeaked when Windfinders looked at her sat up straight and faced Tenobia as an Aes Sedai, her smooth face as frosty as her tone. "The affairs of the Tower are for initiates to know, Tenobia. If you want to learn, ask to have your name written in the novice book, and in twenty years you might learn a little."

Her Illumined Majesty, Tenobia si Bashere Kazadi, Shield of the North and Sword of the Blightborder, High Seat of House Kazadi, Lady of Shahayni, Asnelle, Kunwar and Ganai, glared at Merilille with all the fury of a blizzard. And said nothing. Elayne's respect for her increased slightly.

Merilille's disobedience did not displease her. It saved her from trying to prevaricate while seeming to speak only the truth. Egwene said they must try to live as if they had already sworn the Three Oaths, and here and now, Elayne felt the weight of it. Here, she was not the Daughter-Heir of Andor struggling to claim her mother's throne, or not only that. She was an Aes Sedai of the Green Ajah, with more reason for taking care with her words than simply hiding what she wanted to remain hidden.

"I cannot tell you exactly where he is." Truth, because she could only have given them a vague direction, roughly toward Tear, and no telling how far; truth, because she did not trust them sufficiently for even that. She just had to be careful what she said, and how. "I do know that apparently he intends to remain where he is awhile." He had not moved for days, the first time since leaving her that he had remained in any one place longer than half a day. "I will tell you what I can, but only if you agree that you will march south within the week. You will run out of barley as well as meat if you remain here much longer, anyway. I promise, you will be marching toward the Dragon Reborn." To begin with they would be, at any rate.

Paitar shook his bald head. "You want us to enter Andor? Elayne Sedai—or should I call you Lady Elayne, now?—I wish you the Light's blessing in your quest for Andor's crown, but not enough to offer my men to fight for it."

"Elayne Sedai and Lady Elayne are one and the same," she told them. "I do not ask you to fight for me. In truth, I hope with all my heart that you cross Andor without so much as a skirmish." Raising her silver winecup, she wet her lips without drinking. A flash of caution surged through the Warder bond, and in spite of herself, Elayne laughed. Aviendha was watching her from the corner of her eye and frowning. Even now, they were going to look after the mother to be.

"I am glad someone finds this amusing," Ethenielle said wryly. "Try to think like a Southlander, Paitar. They play the Game of Houses here, and I think she is being very clever at it. She should be, I suppose; I've always heard that Aes Sedai created *Daes Dae'mar*."

"Think tactics, Paitar." Easar was studying Elayne, wearing a small smile. "We move toward Caemlyn as invaders, so any Andoran will see it. Winter may be mild here, but we'll still need weeks to ride that far. By the time we do, she will have rallied enough of the Andoran Houses against us, and to her, that she will have the Lion Throne, or near enough. At the least, enough strength will have been pledged to her that no one else will be able to stand long against her." Tenobia shifted on her chair, frowning and adjusting her skirts, but there was a respect in her eyes when she looked at Elayne that had not been there before.

"And when we reach Caemlyn, Elayne Sedai," Ethenielle said, "you will . . . negotiate . . . us into leaving Andor without a battle being fought." That came out as not quite a question, but almost. "Very clever indeed."

"If all works as she plans," Easar said, his smile fading. He put out a hand without looking, and the old soldier placed a winecup in it. "Battles seldom do; even this bloodless sort, I think."

"I very much want it all to be bloodless," Elayne said. Light, it had to be, or instead of saving her country from civil war, she had plunged it into worse. "I will work hard to see that it is. I expect you to do the same."

"Do you also happen to know where my Uncle Davram is, Elayne Sedai?" Tenobia said suddenly. "Davram Bashere? I would like to speak with him as much as with the Dragon Reborn."

"Lord Davram is not far from Caemlyn, Tenobia. I cannot promise he will still be there when you arrive, though. That is, if you agree?" Elayne made herself breathe, to hide her anxiety. She was beyond where she could turn back, now. They would move south now, she was certain, but without their agreement, there would be bloodshed.

For a long moment there was silence in the tent except for a coal cracking in one of the braziers. Ethenielle exchanged glances with the two men.

"So long as I get to see my uncle," Tenobia said heatedly, "I am agreed."

"On my honor, I am agreed," Easar said decisively, and almost atop him, if in a milder tone, Paitar said, "Under the Light, I am agreed."

"Then so are we all," Ethenielle breathed. "And now your part, Elayne Sedai. Where do we find the Dragon Reborn?"

A thrill shot through Elayne, and she could not say whether it was exhilaration, or fear. She had done what she had come for, risked the dangers for herself and for Andor, and only time would tell whether she had made the right decision. She answered without hesitation, "As I told you, I cannot say exactly where. A search in Murandy will be profitable, though." Truth, though the profit would be hers, not theirs, if any came. Egwene had moved from Murandy today, taking away the army that had held Arathelle Renshar and the other nobles in the south. Perhaps the Borderlanders moving south would force Arathelle and Luan and Pelivar to decide as Dyelin believed they would, to support her. The Light send it so.

Except for Tenobia, the Borderlanders did not seem at all exultant over learning where to find Rand. Ethenielle let out a long breath, almost a sigh, and Easar simply nodded and pursed his lips in thought. Paitar drank down half his wine, the first real drink he had taken. It very much seemed that however much they wanted to find the Dragon Reborn, they were not looking forward to meeting him. Tenobia, on the other hand, called for the old soldier to bring her wine and went on about how much she wanted to see her uncle. Elayne would not have thought the woman had so much family feeling.

Night came early that time of year, and only a few hours of daylight remained, as Easar pointed out, offering beds for the night. Ethenielle suggested that her own tent would be more comfortable, yet they gave no sign of disappointment when Elayne said she must leave immediately.

"Remarkable that you can cover such distance so quickly," Ethenielle murmured. "I have heard Aes Sedai speak of a thing called Traveling. A lost Talent?"

"Have you encountered many sisters on your journey?" Elayne asked.

"Some," Ethenielle replied. "There are Aes Sedai everywhere, it seems." Even Tenobia was suddenly expressionless.

Allowing Birgitte to lay the marten-lined cloak on her shoulders, Elayne nodded. "So there are. Would you have our horses brought?"

None of them spoke again until they were out of the camp, riding through the trees. The horse-smell and latrine-stink had seemed mild in the camp, but their absence here made the air seem very fresh, and the snow whiter, somehow.

"You were very quiet, Birgitte Trahelion," Aviendha said, thumping her bay's ribs with her heels. She always believed the animal would stop without reminders to keep going.

"A Warder doesn't speak for her Aes Sedai; she bloody listens and watches her back," Birgitte replied dryly. It was unlikely the forest contained anyone who might threaten them, this near the Shienaran camp, but her bow remained uncovered, and her eyes scanned the trees.

"A much hastier form of negotiation than I am used to, Elayne," Merilille said. "Normally, these matters require days or weeks of talking, if not months, before anything is agreed. You were lucky they are not Domani. Or Cairhienin," she admitted judiciously. "Borderlanders are refreshingly open and straightforward. Easy to deal with."

Open and straightforward? Elayne shook her head slightly. They wanted to find Rand, but concealed why. They concealed the presence of sisters, too. At least they would be moving away from him, once she had them on their way to Murandy. That would have to do, for now, but she had to warn him, once she could figure out how to do so without endangering him. *Take care of him, Min,* she thought. *Take care of him for us.*

A few miles from the camp, she reined in to study the forest as assiduously as Birgitte. Especially behind them. The sun sat low on the treetops. A trotting white fox appeared for an instant and was gone. Something flickered on a bare gray branch, a bird perhaps, or a squirrel. A dark hawk suddenly plummeted out of the sky, and a thin squeal broke the air and ended suddenly. They were not being followed. It was not the Shienarans she worried about, but those hidden sisters. The weariness that had vanished earlier, with Merilille's news, had returned with interest now that her meeting with the Borderlanders was done. She wanted nothing so much as to climb into her bed as soon as possible, but she did not want it enough to give the weave for Traveling to sisters she did not know.

She could have woven a gateway to the Palace stableyard, but only at the risk of killing someone who happened to be crossing where it opened, so instead she wove one for another place she knew just as well. She was so tired that it required effort to weave, so tired that she did not think of the *angreal* pinned to her dress until the silvery slash had appeared in the air and opened onto a field covered with brown grass beaten flat by earlier snowfalls, a field just south of Caemlyn where Gareth Bryne had often taken her to watch the Queen's Guards ride to command, breaking from columns to form a line four abreast at a shouted order.

"Are you just going to look at it?" Birgitte demanded.

Elayne blinked. Aviendha and Merilille were studying her with concern. Birgitte's face gave nothing away, but the bond carried worry, too.

"I was just thinking," Elayne said, and heeled Fireheart through the gateway. Bed would be wonderful.

From the old practice field to the tall arched gates set in the pale, fifty-foot-high city walls was a short ride. The long market buildings lining the approach to the gates were empty at this hour, but sharp-eyed Guardsmen still kept a watch. They watched her and the others ride in apparently without recognizing her. Mercenaries, very likely. They would not know her unless they saw her on the Lion Throne. With the help of the Light, and luck, they would see her there.

Twilight was fast approaching, the sky turning a deep gray and the shadows slanting long across the streets. Very few people were still out and about, a scattering of folk hurrying to finish their day's work before going home to dinner and a warm fire. A pair of bearers carrying a merchant's dark lacquered sedan-chair went trotting past along a street ahead, and a few moments later one of the big pump-wagons rumbled in the other direction behind eight running horses, its iron-shod wheels loud on the paving stones. Another fire, somewhere. They happened most often at night. A patrol of four Guardsman walked their horses toward her and on, without looking at her twice. They did not recognize her anymore than the men at the gates.

Swaying in her saddle, she rode wishing for her bed.

It was a shock to realize that she was being lifted down from her saddle. She opened eyes she did not remember closing and found herself being carried into the Palace in Birgitte's arms.

"Put me down," she said tiredly. "I can still walk."

"You can hardly stand up," Birgitte growled. "Be still."

"You cannot talk with her!" Aviendha said loudly.

"She really does need sleep, Master Norry," Merilille said in firm tones. "Tomorrow will have to do."

"Forgive me, but tomorrow will *not* do," Norry replied, for a wonder sounding very firm himself. "It is *urgent* I speak with her now!"

Elayne's head wanted to wobble as she lifted it. Halwin

Norry was clutching that leather folder to his skinny chest, as always, but the dry man who talked of crowned heads with the same dusty tone he used for speaking of the roof repairs was almost dancing on his toes in an effort to get by Aviendha and Merilille, who each had him by an arm, holding him back.

"Put me down, Birgitte," she said again, and for the second wonder in as many moments, Birgitte obeyed. She kept a supporting arm around Elayne, though, for which Elayne was grateful. She was not sure her legs would have supported her for very long. "What is it, Master Norry? Let the man go, Aviendha. Merilille?"

The First Clerk darted forward as soon they let go of him. "Word began arriving soon after you left, my Lady," he said, not sounding dusty at all. Worry pinched his brows. "There are four armies. . . . Small, I should say now, I suppose. Light, I recall when five thousand men *was* an army." He rubbed a hand over his bald head, leaving the white tufts rising behind his ears in ruffled disarray. "There are four small armies approaching Caemlyn, from the east," he went on in a more usual tone for him. Almost. "They will be here inside the week, I fear. Twenty thousand men. Perhaps thirty. I cannot be sure." He half extended the folder to her as if offering to show her the papers inside. He *was* agitated.

"Who?" she said. Elenia had estates, and forces, in the east, but so did Naean. But neither could raise twenty thousand men. And the snow and mud should have held them until spring. *"Should" and "would" build no bridges,* she seemed to hear Lini's thin voice say.

"I do not know, my Lady," Norry replied, "not yet."

It did not matter, Elayne supposed. Whoever it was, they were coming, and now. "At first light, Master Norry, I want you to begin buying all the foodstuffs you can find outside the walls and get it brought in. Birgitte, have the bannerman announcing the signing bounty add that mercenaries have four days to sign with the Guards or they must leave the city. And have announcements made to the people, too, Master Norry. Whoever wants to leave before the siege begins should go now. It will cut down the number of mouths we have to feed, and it might lead a few more men to enlist in the Guards." Pushing away from Birgitte's support,

she strode along the hallway, heading for her apartments.
The others were forced to follow. "Merilille, let the Kinswomen know, and the Atha'an Miere. They may want to
leave before it begins, too, Maps, Birgitte. Have the good
maps brought to my apartments. And another thing, Master
Norry . . ."

There was no time for sleep, no time for weariness. She
had a city to defend.

CHAPTER
28

News in a Cloth Sack

The morning after Mat promised to help Teslyn, if he could—and Joline, and this Edesina he had yet to lay eyes on!—Tylin announced that she was departing the city.

"Suroth is going to show me how much of Altara I control now, pigeon," she said. Her belt knife was stuck in the carved bedpost, and they were still lying on the rumpled linen sheets amid a tangle of bedding, him in only the silk scarf that hid the hanging scar around his neck, and her in her skin. A very fine skin it was, too, as smooth as he had ever touched. Idly she traced his other scars with a long, green-lacquered fingernail. One way and another, he had acquired quite a few, though not for want of trying to avoid them. His hide would not bring much at auction, that was for sure, but the scars fascinated her. "It wasn't her idea, actually. Tuon thinks it will . . . help me . . . if I see with my own eyes instead of just on a map, and what that girl suggests, Suroth does. She would like to see it done yesterday, though. We'll be going by *to'raken,* so to cover the ground quickly. As much as two hundred miles in a day, it seems. Oh, don't look sick, piglet. I won't make you climb on one of those things."

Mat heaved a sigh of relief. It had not been the prospect of flying that upset him. He thought he might actually like that. But if he was out of Ebou Dar for any length of time, the Light alone knew whether Teslyn or Joline or even this Edesina might grow impatient enough to do something stupid, or what idiocy Beslan might get up to. Beslan worried him almost as much as the women. Tylin, excited by her coming flight on one of the Seanchan beasts, looked more an eagle than ever.

"I'll be gone little more than a week, sweetling. Hmmm." That green fingernail traced the foot-long puckering that slanted across his ribs. "Shall I tie you to the bed so I'll know you will be safe till I return?"

Returning her wicked smile with his most winning grin took a bit of effort. He was fairly sure she was joking, but only fairly. The clothes she chose today put him all in red brilliant enough to hurt the eye; all red except for the flowers worked on the coat and the cloak, anyway, and his black hat and scarf. The white lace at his neck and wrists only made the rest look redder. Still, he scrambled into them, eager to get out of her apartments. With Tylin, a man was wise not to be too sure of anything. She might *not* be joking, too.

Tylin had not exaggerated Suroth's impatience, it appeared. In little more than two hours by the jeweled cylinder-clock in Tylin's sitting room, a gift from Suroth, he was accompanying the Queen to the docks. Well, Suroth and Tylin rode at the head of the twenty or so other Blood that were to accompany them, and their assorted *so'jhin,* men and women who bowed their half-shaved heads to the Blood and stared down their noses at everyone else, while he rode behind on Pips. An Altaran Queen's "pretty" could not ride with the Blood, which included Tylin herself now, of course. It was not as if he was a hereditary servant or anything of that level.

The Blood and most of the *so'jhin* were mounted on fine animals, sleek mares with arched necks and a delicate step, deep-chested geldings with fierce eyes and strong withers. His luck seemed to have no effect on horse racing, but he would have wagered on Pips against any of them. The blunt-nosed bay gelding was not showy, but Mat was sure he could outrun nearly all of those pretty animals in a sprint and all of them over a long haul. After so long in the stables, Pips wanted to frisk if he could not run, and it took all Mat's skill—well, all the skill that had somehow come with those other men's memories—to keep the animal in hand. Before they were halfway to the docks, though, his leg was aching to the hip. If he was to leave Ebou Dar any time soon, it would have to be by sea, or with Luca's show.

He had a good notion how to make the man leave before spring, if it came to that. A dangerous notion, maybe, but he did not see much choice. The alternative was riskier still.

He was not alone at the rear. More than fifty men and women, blessedly wearing thick white woolen robes over the sheer garments they usually went around in, marched behind him in two rows, some leading packhorses with large wicker hampers full of delicacies. The Blood could not do without their servants; in fact, they seemed to think they would be sleeping rough, with so few. The *da'covale* seldom raised their eyes from the paving stones, and their faces were meek as milk. He had seen a *da'covale* sent for a strapping once, a yellow-haired man about his age, and the fellow had raced to bring the instrument of his own punishment. He had not even tried to delay or hide, much less escape the strapping. Mat could not understand people like that.

Ahead of him rode six *sul'dam*, their short divided skirts showing their ankles. Very nice ankles on one or two, but the women sat their saddles as if they were of the Blood, too. The cowls of their lightning-paneled cloaks hung down their backs, and they let the cold gusts lift the cloaks as though the chill did not touch them, or would not dare. Two had leashed *damane* walking beside their horses.

Mat studied the women surreptitiously. One of the *damane,* a short woman with pale blue eyes, was linked by a silvery *a'dam* to the plump olive-skinned *sul'dam* he had seen walking Teslyn. The dark-haired *damane* answered to the name Pura. The Aes Sedai agelessness was clear on her smooth face. He had not really believed Teslyn when she said the woman had become a true *damane,* but the graying *sul'dam* leaned low in her saddle to say something to the woman who had been Ryma Galfrey, and whatever it was the *sul'dam* murmured, Pura laughed and clapped her hands in delight.

Mat shivered. She would bloody well shout for help if he tried to take the *a'dam* from her neck. Light, what was he thinking of! Bad enough that he was stuck with pulling three Aes Sedai's bacon off the fire for them—Burn him, but he did seem to get lumbered with doing that every time he bloody turned around!—bad enough that, without thinking about trying to get any more out of Ebou Dar.

Ebou Dar was a great seaport, with perhaps the largest harbor in the known world, and the docks were long gray fingers of stone thrusting out from the quay that ran the whole length of the city. Almost all the mooring spots were taken by Seanchan vessels of every size, the crews in the rigging and cheering vigorously as Suroth passed by, a thunder of voices calling her name. The men on other ships waved their arms and shouted as well, though many appeared confused as to who or what they were cheering. No doubt they thought it expected of them. On those vessels, the wind blowing across the harbor stirred the Golden Bees of Illian, and the Crescent Moons of Tear, and the Golden Hawk of Mayene. Apparently Rand had not ordered the merchants there to stop trading with Seanchan-held ports, or else the merchants were going behind his back. Colors flashed through Mat's skull, and he shook his head to clear it. Most merchants would trade with their mother's murderer if it brought profit.

The southernmost dock had been cleared of ships, and Seanchan officers with thin plumes on their lacquered helmets stood waiting to hand Suroth and Tylin down into one of the large rowboats that stood waiting, eight men on the long oars of each. After Tylin gave Mat a last kiss, anyway, almost yanking his hair out to pull his head down, and after she pinched his bottom as though no one was bloody watching! Suroth frowned impatiently until Tylin was settled in the long boat, and in truth, the Seanchan woman did not stop chafing even then, twitching her fingers at Alwhin, her *so'jhin,* so the sharp-faced woman was continually scrambling across the benches to fetch her one thing or another.

The rest of the Blood received deep bows from the officers, but had to climb down the ladders with their *so'jhin*'s aid. The *sul'dam* helped the *damane* into the boats, and no one at all helped the white-robed folk load the pack hampers and themselves. Soon enough, the boats were crossing the harbor toward where the *raken* and *to'raken* were kept south of the Rahad, spidering through the sprawling anchored fleet of Seanchan ships and the scores of captured Sea Folk vessels that dotted the harbor. The greater number of those appeared to have been rerigged with ribbed Seanchan sails and different lines. Their crews were Seanchan, too. Excepting the Windfinders he tried not to think about, and maybe some who had been sold, the surviving Atha'an Miere were all in the Rahad with the other *da'covale* clearing the silted-up canals. And there was nothing he could do about it. He did not owe them anything, he had more on his plate than he could handle already, and there was nothing he could do. That was all there was to it!

He wanted to ride away immediately, to leave the Sea Folk ships behind him. No one on the docks paid him the slightest heed. The officers had gone away as soon as the boats cast off. Someone, he did not know who, had taken the packhorses away. The seamen climbed out of the rigging and went back to their work, and the members of the cargo-loaders guild began pushing their low, heavy barrows stacked with bales and crates and barrels. But if he left too soon, Tylin might decide he was planning to keep riding right out of the city and send for him, so he sat Pips on the end of the dock and waved like a bull goose fool till she was far enough away that she could not see him without a looking glass.

Despite the throbbing leg, he rode slowly back up almost the whole length of the quay. He avoided looking at the harbor again. Soberly dressed merchants stood watching their cargo being loaded or unloaded, sometimes slipping a purse to a man or woman in a green leather vest to obtain gentler handling for their goods or more speed, not that it seemed possible the guildfolk could move any faster. Southerners always seemed to move at a half trot unless the sun was right overhead, when the heat here could roast a duck, and with a gray sky and a cutting wind off the sea, it would have been cold no matter where the sun stood.

By the time he was abreast of the Mol Hara, he had counted more than twenty *sul'dam* patrolling the docks with *damane,* poking their noses into boats leaving anchored ships that were not Seanchan, boarding any vessel newly arrived at the docks or, for that matter, ready to cast off lines. He had been quite sure they would be there. It was going to have to be Valan Luca. The only alternative was just too hazardous, except in an emergency. Luca was chancy, too, but the only real choice left.

Back at the Tarasin Palace, he climbed down off Pips with a wince and pulled his walking staff out from behind the saddle girth. Letting a groom take the bay, he limped inside, his left leg barely able to support his weight. Maybe a soak in a hot bath would take some of the pain. Maybe then he could think. Luca had to be caught by surprise, but before it came to Luca, there were a few other little problems to overcome.

"Ah, there you are," Noal said, popping up in front of him. Mat had caught only glimpses of the old man since getting him a bed, but he looked well-rested in his freshly brushed gray coat, considering that he vanished into the city every day and only returned to the Palace at night. Adjusting the bits of lace at his cuffs, he smiled confidingly, revealing the gaps in his teeth. "You are planning something, Lord Mat, and I would like to offer my services."

"I'm planning to take the weight off my leg," Mat said as casually as he could. Noal seemed harmless enough. According to Harnan, he told stories before going to sleep, stories that Harnan and the other Redarms seemed to swallow whole, even the one about some place called Shibouya, supposedly beyond the Aiel Waste, where women who could channel had tattooed faces, over three hundred crimes carried a penalty of death, and giants lived under the mountains, men taller than Ogier, with their faces on their bellies. He claimed to have been there. No one who made claims like that could be anything but harmless. On the other hand, the one time Mat had seen him handle those long daggers he carried under his coat, he had looked far from harmless. There was a way a man had of touching a weapon that said he was accustomed to using it. "If I decide to plan anything else, I'll keep you in mind."

Still smiling, Noal tapped one of those crooked fingers against the side of his beak of a nose. "You don't trust me, yet. That is understandable. Although, if I meant you any harm, all I had to do was stand back that night in the alley. You have the look in your eye. I've seen great men laying plans, and villains dark as the Pit of Doom, too. There is a look a man gets, laying dangerous plans he doesn't want known."

"My eyes are just tired," Mat laughed, leaning on his staff. Great men laying plans? The old fellow had probably seen them in Shibouya, with the giants. "I do thank you for that alley, you know. If there's ever anything more I can do for you, ask. But right now, I am going to find a hot bath."

"Does this *gholam* drink blood?" Noal asked catching Mat's arm as he started to hobble by.

Light, he wished he had not mentioned that name where the old man could hear. He wished Birgitte had never told him about the thing. "Why do you ask?" *Gholam* lived on blood. They ate nothing else.

"There was another man found with his throat torn out, last night, only there was almost no blood on him or his bedding. Did I mention? He was at an inn down near the Moldine Gate. If that thing did leave the city, it's back." Glancing beyond Mat, he made a low, elaborate bow to someone. "If you change your mind, I am always ready," he said in a lower voice when he straightened.

Mat looked over his shoulder as the old man hurried off. Tuon was standing beneath one of the gilded stand lamps, watching him through her veil. Looking at him, at least. Glancing? As always, the moment he saw her, she turned away and glided off down the hall, her pleated white skirts rustling faintly. There was no one with her, today.

For the second time that day, Mat shivered. A pity the girl had not gone with Suroth and Tylin. A man given a loaf should not complain that a few crumbs were missing, but Aes Sedai and Seanchan, *gholam* stalking him and old men poking their noses in and skinny girls staring at him was enough to give any man the golliwogs. Maybe he should forget about wasting time soaking his leg.

He felt better once he had sent Lopin to fetch the rest of his own clothes from Beslan's toy cupboard. And Nerim to find Juilin. His leg still hurt like fire and wobbled when he wanted to walk, but if he was not going to waste time, then he might as well get a move on about it. He wanted to be gone from Ebou Dar before Tylin came back, and that gave him ten days. Less, to be on the safe side.

When the thief-catcher stuck his head in at the bedroom door, Mat was studying himself in Tylin's tall stand-mirror. The red . . . garments . . . were tucked away in the wardrobe with the rest of the gauds she had given him. Maybe Tylin's next pretty could get some use of them. The coat he had put on was the plainest he owned, a fine-woven blue wool without a thread of embroidery. The sort of coat a man could be proud to wear, without having everybody stare at him. A decent coat.

"Maybe a little lace," he muttered, fingering the neck of his shirt. "Just a little." It really was a very plain coat, come to think. Almost sober.

"I don't know anything about lace," Juilin said. "Is that why you wanted me?"

"No, of course not. What are you grinning at?" The fellow was not just grinning; his smile nearly split his dark face in two.

"I am happy, that's all. Suroth is gone, and I am happy. If you don't want to ask me about lace, what do you want?"

Blood and bloody ashes! The woman he was interested in must be one of Suroth's *da'covale*! One she had left behind. He certainly had no other reason to care whether she was gone, much less be happy over it. And the man wanted to take one of her property! Well, maybe that was not so much, compared to taking a couple of *damane*.

Limping over to put an arm around Juilin's shoulders, Mat walked him out into the sitting room. "I need a *damane* dress to fit a woman about so high," he held up a hand just about his shoulder, "and slender." He gave the fellow his most sincere smile, but Juilin's own smile faded markedly. "I need three *sul'dam* dresses, too, and an *a'dam*. And it came to me that the man who knows best how to steal something without getting caught would be a thief-catcher."

"I am a thief-*catcher,*" the man growled, shaking off Mat's arm, "not a thief!"

Mat let his own grin vanish. "Juilin, you know the only way to take those sisters out of the city is if the guards think they're still *damane*. Teslyn and Edesina are wearing what they need, but we have to disguise Joline. Suroth will be back in ten days, Juilin. If we aren't gone by then, in all likelihood your pretty will still be her property when we go." He could not help feeling that if they were not gone by then, none of them would be going. Light, a man could shiver himself to death indoors in this city.

Stuffing his fists into the pockets of his dark Tairen coat, Juilin glared at him. Glared through him, really, at something the thief-catcher did not like. Finally he grimaced, and muttered, "It won't be easy."

The days that followed were anything but easy. The serving women clucked and laughed over his new clothes. His old clothes, that was. They grinned and made wagers where he could hear over how fast he could change back when Tylin returned—most seemed to think he would race through the halls ripping off whatever he was wearing as soon he heard she was on her way—but he paid them no mind. Except for the part about Tylin returning. The first time a serving woman mentioned it, he nearly jumped out of his skin thinking she actually had for some reason.

A number of the women and nearly all the men took his change of clothing to mean he was leaving. Running away, they called it disapprovingly, and did what they could to hamper him. In their eyes, he was the ointment to soothe Tylin's aching, tooth, and they did not want her to come back and bite them for losing it. If he had not made sure Lopin or Nerim was always in Tylin's apartments guarding his belongings, the clothes would have vanished again, and only Vanin and the Redarms kept Pips from disappearing out of the stables.

Mat tried to encourage the belief. When he went and two *damane* vanished at the same time, the events were sure to be linked, but with Tylin gone and his intention to run away plain before she returned, she would be safe from blame. Every day, even when it rained, he rode Pips in circles in the stable, for a longer time every day, as if trying to build up his stamina. Which he actually was, he realized after a while. His leg and hip still ached like fury, but he began to think he could manage as much as ten miles before needing to climb down. Eight miles, anyway.

Often, if the sky was clear, *sul'dam* were walking *damane* when he exercised. The Seanchan women were aware he was not Tylin's property, but on the other hand, he heard some call him her toy! Tylin's Toy, they said, as if that was his name! He was not important enough for them to learn if he had another. To them, someone was either *da'covale* or not, and this halfway business amused them no end. He rode to the sound of *sul'dam* laughing, and tried to tell himself it was all to the good. The more people who could tell that he worked to flee before Tylin returned, the better for her. It just was not very pleasant for him.

Now and then he saw Aes Sedai faces among the *damane* being walked, three besides Teslyn, but he had not a clue what Edesina looked like. She could have been the short pale woman who reminded him of Moiraine, or the tall one with silvery-golden hair, or the slender black-haired woman. Gilding along beside a *sul'dam,* any of them might have been taking a walk on her own, if not for the gleaming collar around her neck and the leash tying her to the *sul'dam*'s wrist. Teslyn herself looked increasingly grim every time he saw her, staring fixedly straight ahead. Every time, there seemed to be more determination on her face. And something that might have been panic, too. He began to worry about her, and her impatience.

He wanted to reassure Teslyn—he did not need those old memories to tell him that determination combined with panic could get people killed, but they confirmed it—he wanted to reassure her, only he dared not go near the kennels in the attic again. Tuon continued to be there when he turned around, looking at him or glancing or whatever she was doing, just too often for comfort. Not enough to make him think she was following him. Why would she do that? Just too often. Occasionally her *so'jhin* Selucia was with her, and now and then Anath, though the strange tall woman seemed to vanish from the Palace after a time, at least from the hallways. She was "on retreat," he heard, whatever that was supposed to mean, and he only wished she had taken Tuon with her. He doubted the girl would believe he was taking sweets to a Windfinder a second time. Maybe she still wanted to buy him? If that was the case, he still could not understand why. He had never been able to understand what attracted women to a man—they seemed to go pop-eyed over the most ordinary looking fellows—but he knew he was no beauty, no matter what Tylin said. Women lied to get a man into bed, and they lied worse once they had him there.

In any case, Tuon was a minor irritant. A fly on his ear. No more than that. It took more than chattering women or staring girls to make him sweat. Absent as she was, however, Tylin did. If she came back and caught him preparing to leave, she might change her mind about selling. She was a High Lady herself now, after all, and he was sure she would shave her hair to a crest before much longer. A proper Seanchan High Blood, and who knew what she would do then? Tylin caused a little sweat, but there was more than enough else to drench a man in it.

He continued to hear from Noal about the *gholam*'s murders, and sometimes from Thom. There was a fresh one every night, though no one but those two and him seemed to connect the killings. Mat kept to open places as much as he could, with people around as often as possible. He stopped sleeping in Tylin's bed, and never spent two nights running in the same place. If that meant a night in a stable loft, well, he had slept in haylofts before, although he did not recall hay sticking through his clothes quite that sharply. Still, better stuck by hay than having his throat torn out.

He had sought out Thom straight away after he decided to try freeing Teslyn, and had found him in the kitchens chatting with the cooks over a honey-glazed chicken. Thom got on as well with cooks as he did with farmers and merchants and nobles. He had a way of getting on with everyone, did Thom Merrilin, a way of hearing everyone's gossip and fitting it together to make a picture. He could look at things from a slant and see what others missed. As soon as he finished the chicken, Thom had come up with the only way to get the Aes Sedai past the guards. The whole thing had almost seemed easy, then. For a very short while. But other obstacles arose.

Juilin possessed the same sort of twisty way of looking at things, perhaps from his years as thief-catcher, and some nights Mat met with him and Thom in the tiny room the two men shared in the servants' quarters to try planning how to overcome those obstacles. Those were what really made Mat sweat.

At the first of those meetings, the night Tylin left, Beslan barged in looking for Thom, so he said. Unfortunately, he had listened at the door first, hearing enough that he could not be foisted off with a story. Very unfortunately, he wanted to take part. He even told them just how to do it.

"An uprising," he said, squatting on the three-legged stool between the two narrow beds. A washstand with a chipped white pitcher and bowl and no mirror finished crowding the room. Juilin sat on the edge of one bed in his shirtsleeves, his face unreadable, and Thom was stretched out on the other examining his knuckles with a frown. That left Mat to lean against the door to keep anyone else from barging in. He did not know whether to laugh or cry. Plainly Thom had known about this madness all along; this was what he had been trying to cool down. "The people will rise when I give the word," Beslan went on. "My friends and I have talked to men all over the city. They are ready to fight!"

Sighing, Mat eased his weight more onto his good leg. He suspected that when Beslan gave the word, he and his friends would rise alone. Most people were more willing to talk about fighting than to do it, especially against soldiers. "Beslan, in gleeman's tales, grooms with pitchforks and bakers with cobblestones defeat armies because they want to be free." Thom snorted so hard, his long white mustache stirred. Mat ignored him. "In real life, the grooms and the bakers get killed. I know good soldiers when I see them, and the Seanchan are very good."

"If we free the *damane* along with the Aes Sedai, they will fight beside us!" Beslan insisted.

"There must be two hundred or more *damane* up in the attic, Beslan, most of them Seanchan. Free them, and like as not, every last one will run to find a *sul'dam*. Light, we couldn't even trust all the women who aren't Seanchan!" Mat held up a hand to forestall Beslan's protest. "We have no way to find out which we can trust, and no time to. And if we did, we'd have to kill the rest. I'm not up to killing a woman whose only crime is that she's on a leash. Are you?" Beslan looked away, but his jaw was set. He was not giving up.

"Whether we free any *damane* or not," Mat went on, "if the people rise up, the Seanchan will turn Ebou Dar into a slaughter yard. They put down rebellions hard, Beslan. Very hard! We could kill every *damane* in the attic, and they would bring in more from the camps. Your mother will come back to find rubble inside the walls and your head stuck up outside them. Where hers will soon join it. You don't think they'll believe she did not know what her own son was planning, do you?" Light, *did* she? The woman was brave enough to try it. He did not think she was stupid enough, but . . .

"She says we are mice," Beslan said bitterly. "'When wolfhounds pass by, mice lie quiet or get eaten,'" he quoted. "I don't like being a mouse, Mat."

Mat breathed a little more easily. "Better a live mouse than a dead one, Beslan." Which might not have been the most diplomatic way to put it—Beslan grimaced at him—but it was true.

He encouraged Beslan to join the meetings, if just to keep a rein on him, but Beslan seldom came, and it fell to Thom to try to cool the man's ardor when and as he could. The most he could persuade Beslan to promise was that he could not call for the rising until the rest of them had been gone a month, to let them get clear. That was something settled, if not satisfactorily. Everything else seemed to be take two steps and hit a stone wall. Or a trip wire.

Juilin's lady love had quite a hold on him. For her, he seemed to not to mind doffing his Tairen clothes for a servant's green-and-white livery, or missing sleep to spend two nights sweeping the floor not far from the stairs that led up to the kennels. No one looked twice at a servant pushing a broom, not even the other servants. The Tarasin Palace had enough of those that they did not all know one another, and if they saw a man in livery with a broom, they assumed he was supposed to be using it. Juilin spent two whole days sweeping, too, and finally reported that *sul'dam* inspected the kennels first thing in the morning and just after dark, and might be in or out at any time of the day between, but at night the *damane* were left to themselves.

"I overheard a *sul'dam* say she was glad she wasn't out in the camps where . . ." Lying stretched out on his thin mattress, Juilin paused to yawn copiously behind his hand. Thom was sitting on the edge of his bed, which left the stool for Mat. It was better than standing, if not by much. Most people would be asleep at that hour. "Where she'd have to stand guard some nights," the thief-catcher continued when he could speak again. "Said she liked being able to let the *damane* sleep all night, too, so they were all fresh come sunrise."

"So we must move at night," Thom murmured, fingering his long white mustache. There was no need to add that anything moving at night drew eyes. Seanchan patrolled the streets at night, which the Civil Guard never had. The Guard had been amenable to bribes, too, until the Seanchan disbanded them. Now, at night, it was as likely to be the Deathwatch Guards in the street, and anyone who tried to bribe them might not live to face trial.

"Have you found an *a'dam* yet, Juilin?" Mat asked. "Or the dresses? Dresses can't be as difficult as an *a'dam*."

Juilin yawned into his hand again. "I'll get them when

I get them. They don't just leave either lying about, you know."

Thom discovered that simply walking *damane* through the gates was not possible. Or rather, as he freely admitted, Riselle had discovered it. It seemed that one of the high-ranking officers staying at The Wandering Woman had a singing voice she found most entertaining.

"One of the Blood can take *damane* out with no questions asked," Thom said at their next meeting. This time, he and Juilin both were sitting on their beds. Mat was beginning to hate that stool. "Or few enough, anyway. *Sul'dam,* though, need an order signed and sealed by one of the Blood, an officer who's captain or above, or a *der'sul'dam.* The guards at the gates and on the docks have lists of every seal in the city that qualifies, so I can't just make any sort of seal and think it will be accepted. I need a copy of the right sort of order with the right sort of seal. That leaves the question of who will be our three *sul'dam.*"

"Maybe Riselle will be one," Mat suggested. She did not know what they were doing, and telling her would be a risk. Thom had asked her all sorts of questions, as if he was trying to learn about life under the Seanchan, and she had been happy enough to ask her Seanchan friend, but she might not be happy enough to chance her pretty head going up on a spike. She could do worse than say no. "And what about your lady love, Juilin?" He had a thought on the third. He had asked Juilin to find a *sul'dam* dress that would fit Setalle Anan, though there had been no chance to actually put it to her, yet. He had only been back to The Wandering Woman once since Joline had walked into the kitchen, to make sure she understood he was doing all he could. She did not, but Mistress Anan had actually managed to smother the Aes Sedai's anger before she could begin shouting. She would make the perfect *sul'dam* for Joline.

Juilin shrugged uncomfortably. "I had a hard enough time convincing Thera to run away with me. She is . . . timid, now. I can help her overcome that, in time—I know I can—but I don't think she is up to anything like pretending to be a *sul'dam.*"

Thom tugged at his mustaches. "It's unlikely Riselle would leave under any circumstances. It seems she likes

Banner-General Lord Yamada's singing well enough that she has decided to marry him." He sighed regretfully. "There will be no more information from that well, I fear." And no more pillowing his head on her bosom, his expression said. "Well, both of you think on who we can ask. And see if you can lay hands on a copy of those orders."

Thom managed to find the proper inks and paper, and was ready to imitate anyone's hand and seal. He was contemptuous of seals; anyone with a turnip and a knife could copy those, he said. Writing another man's hand so the man himself would think he had written it was an art. But none of them were able to find a copy of orders with the necessary seal to copy. Like *a'dam,* the Seanchan did not leave orders lying about. Juilin seemed to making no progress with the *a'dam,* either. Two steps forward, and a stone wall. And six days were gone, just like that. Four left. To Mat, it felt as if six years had passed since Tylin's departure, and four hours remained till she came back.

On the seventh day, Thom stopped Mat in the hallway as soon as he came in from his ride. Smiling as though making idle conversation, the one-time gleeman pitched his voice low. The servants hurrying past could not have heard more than a murmur. "According to Noal, the *gholam* killed again last night. The Seekers have been ordered to find the killer if they have to stop eating or sleeping to do it, though I can't find out who gave the order. Even the fact that they have been ordered to do anything seems to be a secret. They are practically readying the rack and heating their irons already, though."

No matter that Thom's voice was low, Mat looked around to see whether anyone was listening. The only person in sight was a stout gray-haired man named Narvin, in livery but neither hurrying nor carrying anything. Servants as high as Narvin did not carry or hurry. He blinked at the sight of Mat trying to look every direction at once, and frowned. Mat wanted to snarl, but instead he grinned as disarmingly as he knew how, and Narvin went off scowling. Mat was sure the fellow had been responsible for the first attempt to remove Pips from the stable.

"Noal told you about the Seekers?" he whispered incredulously as soon as Narvin was far enough away.

Thom waved a lean hand dismissively. "Of course not. Just about the killing. Though he does seem to hear whispers, and know what they mean. A rare talent, that. I wonder whether he really has been to Shara," he mused. "He said he . . ." Thom cleared his throat under Mat's glare. "Well, later for that. I do have other resources than the much-lamented Riselle. Several of them are Listeners. Listeners really do seem to hear everything."

"You've been talking to Listeners?" Mat's voice squeaked like a rusty hinge. He thought his throat might have rusted solid!

"There's nothing to it, as long as they don't know you know," Thom chuckled. "Mat, with Seanchan you have to assume they are all Listeners. That way, you learn what you want to know without saying the wrong thing in the wrong ear." He coughed and knuckled his mustache, not quite hiding a smile so self-deprecating it all but invited praise. "I just happen to know two or three who really are. In any case, more information never hurts. You do want to be gone before Tylin returns, don't you? You seem to looking a little . . . forlorn . . . with her gone."

Mat could only groan.

That night, the *gholam* struck again. Lopin and Nerim were bubbling over with the news before Mat had finished his breakfast fish. The whole city was in an uproar, they claimed. The latest victim, a woman, had been discovered at the mouth of an alley, and suddenly people were talking, putting together one killing with another. There was a madman on the loose, and the people were demanding more Seanchan patrols on the streets at night. Mat pushed his plate away, all hunger gone. More patrols. And if that were not bad enough, Suroth might come back early if she learned of this, bringing Tylin with her. At best, he could only count on two more days. He thought he might lose what he'd already eaten.

He spent the rest of the morning pacing—well, limping—up and down the carpet in Tylin's bedchamber, ignoring the pain in his leg while he tried to think of something, anything, that would let him carry out the impossible in two days. The pain really was less. He had given up the walking stick, pushing himself to regain strength. He thought he might manage two or three miles on foot without needing to rest the leg. Without resting it very much, anyway.

At midday, Juilin brought him the only really good news he had heard in an Age. It was not news, exactly. It was a cloth sack containing two dresses wrapped around the silver length of an *a'dam*.

CHAPTER
29

Another Plan

The beam-ceilinged basement of The Wandering Woman was large, yet it seemed as cramped as the room Thom and Juilin shared, though it held only five people. The oil lamp set on an upended barrel cast flickering shadows. Farther away, the basement was all shadow. The aisle between the shelves and the rough stone walls was barely wider than a barrel was tall, but that was not what made it seem crowded.

"I asked for your help, not a noose around my neck," Joline said coldly. After near a week in Mistress Anan's care, eating Enid's cooking, the Aes Sedai no longer looked haggard. The frayed dress Mat had first seen on her was gone, replaced by high-necked fine blue wool with a touch of lace at her wrists and under her chin. In the wavering light, her face half shadowed, she looked furious, her eyes trying to bore holes through Mat's face. "If anything went awry—anything!—I'd be helpless!"

He was having none of it. Offer to help out of the goodness of your heart—well, sort of—and see what it got you. He practically shook the *a'dam* under her nose. It wiggled in his hand like a long silver snake, glinting in the dim lamplight, the collar and bracelet both scraping across the stone floor, and Joline gathered her dark skirts and stepped back to avoid being touched. It might have been a viper from the way her mouth twisted. He wondered whether it would fit her; the collar seemed larger than her slim neck. "Mistress Anan will take it off as soon as we get you outside the walls," he growled. "You trust her, don't you? She risked her head to hide you down here. I'm telling you, it is the only way!" Joline raised her chin stubbornly. Mistress Anan muttered angrily under her breath.

"She does not want to wear the thing," Fen said in a flat voice behind Mat.

"If she doesn't want to wear it, then she doesn't wear it," Blaeric said in an even flatter, at Fen's side.

Joline's dark-haired Warders were like peas in a pod for men so different. Fen, with his dark tilted eyes and a chin that could chip stone, was a touch shorter than Blaeric, and maybe a little heavier in the chest and shoulders, yet they could have worn each other's clothes without much difficulty. Where Fen's straight black hair hung almost to his shoulders, blue-eyed Blaeric's very short hair was slightly lighter in color. Blaeric was Shienaran, and he had shaved his topknot and was letting his hair grow in to avoid notice, but he did not like it. Fen, a Saldaean, seemed not to like much except for Joline. They both liked Joline a lot. The pair of them talked alike, thought alike, moved alike. They wore dingy shirts and workmen's plain woolen vests that hung down below their hips, yet anyone who took them for laborers, even in this poor light, was blind. By day, in the stables where Mistress Anan had them working . . . Light! They were looking at Mat as lions might look at a goat that had bared its teeth at them. He moved so he did not have to see the Warders even from the corner of his eye. The knives hidden about him in various places were small comfort, with them at his back.

"If you will not listen to him, Joline Maza, you will listen to me." Planting her hands on her hips, Setalle rounded on the slender Aes Sedai, her hazel eyes glaring. "I mean to see you back in the White Tower if I have to walk every step of the way pushing you! Perhaps along the way you will show me that you know what it means to be Aes Sedai. I'd settle for a glimpse of a grown woman. So far, all I have seen is a novice sniveling in her bed and throwing tantrums!"

Joline stared at her, those big brown eyes as wide as they would go, as if she could not believe her ears. Mat was not sure he believed his, either. Innkeepers did not leap down Aes Sedai's throats. Fen grunted, and Blaeric muttered something that sounded uncomplimentary.

"There's no need for you to go farther than beyond sight of the guards at the gates," Mat told Setalle hastily, hoping

to divert any explosion Joline might be considering. "Keep
the hood of your cloak pulled up . . ." Light, he had to get
her one of those fancy cloaks! Well, if Juilin could steal
an *a'dam,* he could steal a bloody cloak, too. ". . . and the
guards will just see another *sul'dam.* You can be back here
before daybreak, and no one the wiser. Unless you insist on
wearing your marriage knife." He laughed at his own joke,
but she did not.

"Do you think I could remain anywhere women are
turned into animals because they can channel?" she demanded, stalking across the floor till she stood toe-to-toe
with him. "Do you think I'd let my family stay?" If her eyes
had glared at Joline, they blazed up at him. Frankly, he had
never considered the question. Certainly he would like to
see the *damane* freed, but why should it matter this much
to her? Plainly, it did, though; her hand slid along the hilt
of the long curved dagger stuck behind her belt, caressing
it. Ebou Dari did not take kindly to insults, and she was
pure Ebou Dari to that extent. "I began negotiating the
sale of The Wandering Woman two days after the Seanchan arrived, when I could see what they are. I should have
handed everything over to Lydel Elonid days ago, but I've
been holding off because Lydel would not expect to find
an Aes Sedai in the basement. When you are ready to go,
I can hand over the keys and go with you. Lydel is growing impatient," she added significantly over her shoulder
to Joline.

And what about his gold? he wanted to ask indignantly.
Would Lydel have let him take that away, a windfall under her kitchen floor? Still, it was something else that made
him choke. Suddenly he could see himself saddled with
Mistress Anan's whole family, including the married sons
and daughters with their children, and maybe a few aunts
and uncles and cousins, as well. Dozens of them. Scores,
maybe. She might be from off, but her husband had rela-
tions all over the city. Blaeric slapped him on the back so
hard that he staggered.

He showed the fellow his teeth and hoped the Shienaran
would take it for a smile of thanks. Blaeric's expression
never altered. Bloody Warders! Bloody Aes Sedai! Bloody,
bloody innkeepers!

"Mistress Anan," he said carefully, "the way I mean to

get away from Ebou Dar, there's only room for so many."
He had not told her about Luca's show, yet. There was a
chance he could not convince the man, after all. And the
more people he had to convince Luca to take, the harder it
would be. "Come back here once we're outside the city. If
you have to leave, go on one your husband's fishing boats.
I suggest you wait a few days, though. Maybe a week or so.
Once the Seanchan discover two *damane* missing, they'll
be all over anything trying to leave."

"Two?" Joline put in sharply. "Teslyn and who?"

Mat winced. He had not meant to let that slip. He had
Joline pegged, and petulant, willful and spoiled were the
words that came most readily to mind. Anything at all
that made her think this more difficult, more likely to fail,
might just be enough to make her decide to try some crack-
brained scheme of her own. Something that would no doubt
ruin his own plans. She would be captured for sure if she
tried to run on her own, and she would fight. And once the
Seanchan learned there had been an Aes Sedai in the city,
right under their noses, they would intensify the searches
for *marath'damane* again, increase the street patrols more
than they already had for the "mad killer," and worst of all,
they might well make it even harder to pass the gates.

"Edesina Azzedin," he said reluctantly. "I don't know
anything more about her."

"Edesina," Joline said slowly. A tiny frown creased her
smooth forehead. "I heard that she had—" Whatever she
had heard, she snapped her teeth shut on it and fixed him a
fierce stare. "Are they holding any other sisters? If Teslyn is
getting free, I won't leave any other sister to them!"

It took an effort on Mat's part not to gape. Petulant and
spoiled? He was looking at a lioness to match Blaeric and
Fen. "Believe me, I won't leave an Aes Sedai in the kennels
unless she wants to stay," he said, making his voice as wry
as he could. The woman was still willful. She might insist
on trying to rescue the other two like Pura. Light, he should
never have let himself get tangled with Aes Sedai, and he
did not need any ancient memories to warn him! His own
would do very well, thank you.

Fen poked him on the back of his left shoulder with a
hard finger. "Don't be so light-tongued," the Warder said
warningly.

Blaeric poked him on the back of the other shoulder. "Remember who you are talking to!"

Joline sniffed at his tone, but she did not probe further.

Mat felt a knot loosen in the back of his neck, about where a headsman's axe would strike. Aes Sedai twisted words with other people; they did not expect others to use their own tricks on them.

He turned to Setalle. "Mistress Anan, you can see your husband's boats are much better—"

"It might be so," she broke in, "except that Jasfer sailed with all ten of his boats and all of our kin three days ago. I expect the guilds will want to talk to him if he ever returns. He isn't supposed to carry passengers. They are coasting to Illian, where they will wait for me. I don't really intend to go as far as Tar Valon, you see."

This time, Mat could not stop a wince. He had intended falling back on Jasfer Anan's fishing boats if he failed to persuade Luca. A dangerous option, true, more than dangerous. Mad, maybe. The *sul'dam* on the docks likely would have wanted to check any order that sent *damane* out on fishing boats, especially in the night. But the boats had always been in the back of his mind. Well, he was just going to have twist Luca's arm hard, just as hard as necessary.

"You let your kin go out in this season?" Disbelief and scorn mingled in Joline's voice. "When the worst storms are brewing?"

Her back to the Aes Sedai, Mistress Anan raised her head proudly, but it was not pride in herself. "I trust Jasfer to sail into the teeth of a cemaros, if need be. I trust him as much as you do your Warders, Green. More."

Frowning suddenly, Joline picked up the lamp by the iron base and moved it to cast light on the innkeeper's face. "Have we met somewhere before? Sometimes, when I cannot see your face, your voice sounds familiar."

Instead of answering, Setalle took the *a'dam* from Mat and fumbled at the flat segmented bracelet on one end of the round silver leash. The whole thing was made in segments, fitted together so cunningly you could not see how it had been done. "We might as well get the testing over with."

"Testing?" he said, and those hazel eyes gave him a withering look.

"Not every woman can be a *sul'dam*. You should know

that by now. I have hopes that I can, but better we find out before the last hour." Scowling at the stubbornly closed bracelet, she turned it in her hands. "Do you know how to open this thing? I cannot even find *where* it opens."

"Yes," he said faintly. The only times he had talked with Seanchan about *sul'dam* and *damane,* it had been cautious questions about how they were used in battle. He had never even thought about how *sul'dam* were chosen. He might have to fight them—those ancient memories hardly let him stop thinking about how to fight battles—but he had certainly never meant to recruit any. "Better to test it now." Instead of . . . Light!

The catches were a simple matter for him, the bracelet easiest. That was just a matter of squeezing the right spots, top and bottom, not quite opposite the leash. It could be done with one hand, and the bracelet popped open on one with a metallic click. The collar was a little trickier, and required both hands. Putting his fingers on the proper spots on either side of where the leash attached, he pressed, then twisted and pulled while holding the pressure. Nothing happened, that he could see, until he twisted the two sides the other way. Then they came apart right beside the leash, with a sharper click than the bracelet. Simple. Of course, figuring it out had taken him nearly an hour, back in the Palace, even with what Juilin had seen to help. Nobody here praised him, though. Nobody even looked as though he had done anything they could not!

Snapping the bracelet around her wrist, Setalle looped the leash in coils on her forearm, then held up the open collar. Joline stared it with loathing, her hands tightening into fists gripping her skirts.

"Do you want to escape?" the innkeeper asked quietly.

After a moment, Joline straightened and lifted her chin. Setalle closed the collar around the Aes Sedai's neck with the same crisp snap it had made opening. He must have been wrong about the size; it fit her quite snugly atop the high neck of her dress. Joline's mouth twitched, that was all, but Mat could almost feel Blaeric and Fen tensing behind him. He held his breath.

Side by side, the two women took a small step, brushing by Mat, and he began to breathe. Joline frowned uncertainly. Then they took a second step.

With a cry, the Aes Sedai fell to the floor, writhing in agony. She could not form words, only increasingly louder moans. She huddled in on herself, her arms and legs and even her fingers twitching and crooking at odd angles.

Setalle dropped to her knees as soon as Joline hit the floor, her hands going to the collar, but she was no quicker than Blaeric and Fen, though their actions did seem odd. Kneeling, Blaeric raised a wailing Joline and supported her against his chest while he began to massage her neck, of all things. Fen worked his fingers along her arms. The collar came loose, and Setalle fell back on her heels, but Joline continued to jerk and whimper, and her Warders continued to work over her as though trying to rub away cramps. They shot cold stares at Mat as though it were all his fault.

Looking down on all his fine plans lying in ruins, Mat barely saw the men. He did not know what to do next, where to begin. Tylin might be back in two more days, and he was sure he had to be gone before she returned.

Squeezing past Setalle, he patted her on the shoulder. "Tell her we'll try something else," he muttered. But what? Obviously it had to be a woman with a *sul'dam's* abilities to handle the *a'dam.*

The innkeeper caught him in the dark at the foot of the stairs leading up to the kitchen while he was gathering his hat and cloak. A stout, plain wool cloak with no embroidery. A man could do without embroidery. He certainly did not miss it. And all that lace! Certainly not!

"Do you have another plan ready?" she asked. He could not make out her face in the dark, but the silver length of the *a'dam* gleamed even so. She was groping at the bracelet on her wrist.

"I always have another plan," he lied, undoing the bracelet for her. "At least you can forget about risking your neck. As soon as I take Joline off your hands, you can go join your husband."

She just grunted. He suspected she knew he had no plan.

He wanted to avoid the common room full of Seanchan, so he went out through the kitchen into the stableyard and out through the gate into the Mol Hara. He was not afraid that any of them would mark him out or wonder why he was there. In his drab clothes, they seemed to take him for someone running an errand for the innkeeper when he came in. But there had been three *sul'dam* among the Seanchan, two with *damane*. He was beginning to be afraid he would have to leave Teslyn and Edesina collared, and he just did not want to look at *damane* right then. Blood and bloody ashes, he had only promised to try!

The weak sun still stood high in the sky, but the sea wind was picking up, full of salt and a cold promise of rain. Except for a squad of Deathwatch Guards marching across the square, humans rather than Ogier, everyone in the Mol Hara was hurrying to be done with whatever they were about before the rain came. As he reached the base of Queen Nariene's tall bare-breasted statue, a hand fell on his shoulder.

"I did no recognize you at first, without your fancy clothes, Mat Cauthon."

Mat turned to find himself facing the heavyset Illianer *so'jhin* he had seen the day Joline reappeared in his life. It was not a pleasant association. The round-faced fellow did look odd, between that beard and half the hair on his head missing, and he was shivering in his shirtsleeves, of all things.

"You know me?" Mat said cautiously.

The heavyset man beamed a wide smile at him. "Fortune prick me, I do. You did take a memorable voyage on my ship, once, with Trollocs and Shadar Logoth at one end and a Myrddraal and Whitebridge in flames at the other. Bayle Domon, Master Cauthon. Do you remember me now?"

"I remember." He did, after a fashion. Most of that voyage was vague in his head, tattered by the holes those other men's memories had filled. "We'll have to sit down over hot spiced wine some time and talk over old times." Which would never happen if he saw Domon first. What remained in his memory of that voyage was strangely unpleasant, like remembering a deathly illness. Of course, he had been ill, in a way. Another unpleasant memory.

"There be no time like now," Domon laughed, swinging a thick arm around Mat's shoulders and turning him back toward The Wandering Woman.

Short of fighting, there seemed to be no way to escape the man, so Mat went. A knock-down fight was no way to avoid being noticed. Anyway, he was not sure he would win. Domon looked fat, but the fat was layered over hard muscle. A drink would not go amiss in any case. Besides which, hadn't Domon been something of a smuggler? He might know paths in and out of Ebou Dar that others did not, and he might reveal them to a little judicious questioning. Especially over wine. A fat purse of gold lay in Mat's coat pocket, and he did not mind spending it all to get the man drunk as a fiddler at Sunday. Drunk men talked.

Domon hustled him through the common room, bowing left and right to Blood and officers who barely saw him if that, but he did not enter the kitchens, where Enid might have given them a bench in the corner. Instead, he took Mat up the railless stairs. Until he ushered Mat into a room at the back of the inn, Mat assumed Domon was going to fetch his coat and cloak. A good fire blazing on the hearth warmed the room, but Mat suddenly felt colder than he had outside.

Closing the door behind them, Domon planted himself in front of it with his arms folded across his chest. "You do be in the presence of Captain of the Green Lady Egeanin Tamarath," he intoned, then added in a more normal tone, "This be Mat Cauthon."

Mat looked from Domon to the tall woman seated stiffly on a ladder-backed chair. Her pleated dress was pale yellow today, and she wore a flower-embroidered robe over it, but he remembered her. Her pale face was hard, and her blue eyes were every bit as predatory as Tylin's. Only, he suspected Egeanin was not after kisses. Her hands were slender, but they had swordsman's calluses. He had no chance to ask what this was about, and no need.

"My *so'jhin* informs me you are not unfamiliar with danger, Master Cauthon," she said as soon as Domon finished speaking. Her slow Seanchan drawl still sounded peremptory and commanding, but then, she was of the Blood. "I need such men to crew a ship, and I will pay well, in gold not silver. If you know others like yourself, I will hire them. They must be able to hold their tongues, though. My business is my own. Bayle mentioned two other names. Thom Merrilin and Juilin Sandar. If either is here in Ebou Dar, I can use their skills, as well. They know me, and know they can trust me with their lives. So can you, Master Cauthon."

Mat sat down on the room's second chair and threw back his cloak. He was not supposed to sit even with one of the lesser Blood—as her dark bowl-cut hair and green-lacquered little fingernails proclaimed her to be—but he needed to think. "You have a ship?" he asked, in the main to gain time. She opened her mouth angrily. Asking questions of the Blood was supposed to be done delicately.

Domon grunted and shook his head, and for a moment she looked even angrier, but then her stern face smoothed. On the other hand, her eyes bored into Mat like augers, and she rose to stand with her feet apart and her hands on her hips, confronting him. "I will have a vessel by the end of spring at latest, as soon as my gold can be brought from Cantorin," she said in an icy voice.

Mat sighed. Well, there really had been no chance he could take Aes Sedai out on a ship owned by a Seanchan, not really. "How do you know Thom and Juilin?" Domon could have told her about Thom, certainly, but, Light, how could she know Juilin?

"You ask too many questions," she said firmly, turning away. "I fear I cannot use you after all. Bayle, put him out." The last was a peremptory command.

Domon did not move from the door. "Tell him," he urged her. "Soon or late, he must know everything or he will put you in greater danger than you face now. Tell him." Even for a *so'jhin,* he seemed to get away with a great deal. The Seanchan were great ones for property keeping its place. For everyone else keeping theirs, for that matter. Egeanin must not be a quarter as tough as she looked.

She looked very tough at the moment, kicking her skirts and striding back and forth, scowling at Domon, at Mat. Finally, she stopped. "I gave them some small aid in Tanchico," she said. After a moment she added, "And two women who were with them, Elayne Trakand and Nynaeve al'Meara." Her eyes focused on him intently, watching to see whether he knew the names.

Mat's chest felt tight. It was not a pain, but more like watching a horse he had bet on streak toward the finish line with others close behind and the question still in doubt. What in the Light had Nynaeve and Elayne been up to in Tanchico that they had needed a Seanchan's help, and had gotten it? Thom and Juilin had been closemouthed about the details. That was beside the point, anyway. Egeanin wanted men who could keep her secrets and did not mind danger. She herself was in danger. Very little was dangerous to one of the Blood, except for other Blood and . . . "The Seekers are after you," he said.

The way her head came up was confirmation enough, and her hand went to her side as though reaching for a sword. Domon shifted his feet and flexed his big hands, his eyes on Mat. Eyes suddenly harder than Egeanin's. The thick man no longer looked funny; he looked dangerous. Abruptly it came to Mat that he might not leave the room alive.

"If you need to get away from the Seekers, I can help you," he said quickly. "You'll have to go where the Seanchan aren't in control. Anywhere they are, the Seekers can find you. And it's best to go as soon as possible. You can always get more gold. If the Seekers don't take you first. Thom tells me they're getting very active about something. Heating the irons and getting the rack ready."

For a time Egeanin stood motionless, staring at him. At last, she exchanged a long look with Domon. "Perhaps it would be well to leave as soon as possible," she breathed. Her tone firmed immediately, though. If there had been worry on her face for a moment, it vanished. "The Seekers will not stop me leaving the city, I think, but they think they can follow me to something they want more than they want me. They will follow me, and until I leave the lands already held by the *Rhyagelle,* they can call on soldiers to arrest me, which they will as soon as they decide I *am* going to lands not yet gathered. That is when I will need the skills of your friend Thom Merrilin, Master Cauthon. Between here and there, I must vanish from the Seekers' sight. I may not have the gold from Cantorin, but I have enough to reward your help handsomely. You can rest assured of that."

"Call me Mat," he said, giving her his very best smile. Even hard-faced women softened for his best smile. Well, she did not soften visibly—if anything, she frowned slightly—but one thing he did know about women was the effect his smiles had. "I know how to make you vanish now. No use waiting, you know. The Seekers might decide to arrest you tomorrow." That hit home. She did not flinch—he suspected very little made her flinch—but she almost nodded. "There is just one thing, Egeanin." This still could blow up in his face like one of Aludra's fireworks, but he did not hesitate. Sometimes, you just had to toss the dice. "I don't need any gold, but I do have need of three *sul'dam* who will keep their mouths shut. Do you think you could supply those?"

After a moment that seemed to stretch hours, she nodded, and he smiled to himself. His horse had crossed first.

"Domon," Thom said in a flat voice around the pipestem clenched between his teeth. He was lying with a thin pillow doubled up beneath his head, and he seemed to be studying the faint blue haze that hung in the air of the windowless room. The single lamp gave a fitful light. "And Egeanin."

"And she is of the Blood, now." Sitting on the edge of his bed, Juilin peered into the charred bowl of his pipe. "I do not know as I like that."

"Are you saying we can't trust them?" Mat demanded, tamping down his tabac with a careless thumb. He snatched his thumb out with a mild oath and stuck it in his mouth to suck the burn away. Yet again he had the choice of the stool or standing, but for once he did not mind the stool. Dealing with Egeanin had taken little enough of the afternoon, but Thom had been out of the Palace until after dark, while Juilin had taken even longer to appear. Neither appeared nearly as pleased with Mat's news as he expected. Thom had just sighed that he had finally gotten a good look at one of the accepted seals, but Juilin glowered whenever he looked at the bundle lying in the corner of the room where he had hurled it. There was no bloody need for the man to carry on so just because they no longer needed the *sul'dam* dresses. "I tell you, they're both scared spitless over the Seekers," Mat went on when his thumb was cooled. Maybe not exactly spitless, but frightened nonetheless. "Egeanin may be Blood, but she never twitched an eyelid when I told her what I wanted *sul'dam* for. She just said she knew three who would do what we need, and she could have them ready tomorrow."

"An honorable woman, Egeanin," Thom mused. Every so often he paused to blow a smoke ring. "Odd, true, but then, she is Seanchan. I think even Nynaeve came to like her, and I know Elayne did. And she liked them. Even if they were Aes Sedai, as she believed. She was very useful in Tanchico. Very useful. More than merely competent. I truly would like to know how she came be raised to the Blood, but yes, I believe we can trust Egeanin. And Domon. An interesting man, Domon."

"A smuggler," Juilin muttered disparagingly. "And now he *belongs* to her. *So'jhin* are more than just property, you know. There are *so'jhin* who tell Blood what to do." Thom raised a shaggy eyebrow at him. Just that, but after a moment, the thief-catcher shrugged. "I suppose Domon is trustworthy," he said reluctantly. "For a smuggler."

Mat snorted. Maybe they were jealous. Well, he was *ta'veren,* and they had to live with it. "Then tomorrow night, we leave. The only change in the plan is that we have three real *sul'dam* and one of the Blood to get us through the gates."

"And these *sul'dam* are going to take three Aes Sedai out of the city, let them go, and never think of raising an alarm," Juilin muttered. "Once, while Rand al'Thor was in Tear, I saw a tossed coin land on its edge five times in a row. We finally walked away and left it standing there on the table. I suppose anything can happen."

"Either you trust them or you don't, Juilin," Mat growled. The thief-catcher glared at the bundled dresses in the corner, and Mat shook his head. "What did they do to help you in Tanchico, Thom? Blood and ashes, don't the two of you go all flat-eyed on me again! You know, and they know, and I might as well."

"Nynaeve said not to tell *anyone,*" Juilin said as if that really mattered. "Elayne said not to. We promised. You might say we swore an oath."

Thom shook his head on the pillow. "Circumstances alter cases, Juilin. And in any case, it wasn't an oath." He blew three perfect smoke rings, one inside the other. "They helped us acquire and dispose of a sort of male *a'dam,* Mat. The Black Ajah apparently wanted to use it on Rand. You can see why Nynaeve and Elayne wanted it kept quiet. If word spread that such a thing ever existed, the Light knows what kind of tales would spring up."

"Who cares what stories people tell?" A male *a'dam*? Light, if the Black Ajah had gotten that onto Rand's neck, or the Seanchan had . . . Those colors whirled through his head again, and he made himself stop thinking about Rand. "Gossip isn't going to hurt . . . anybody." No colors that time. He could avoid it as long as he did not think about . . .

The colors swirled again, and he ground his teeth on his pipestem.

"Not true, Mat. Stories have power. Gleemen's tales, and bards' epics, and rumors in the street alike. They stir passions, and change the way men see the world. Today, I heard a man say that Rand had sworn fealty to Elaida, that he was in the White Tower. The fellow believed it, Mat. What if, say, enough Tairens begin to believe? Tairens dislike Aes Sedai. Correct, Juilin?"

"Some do," Juilin allowed, then added as though Thom had dragged it from him, "Most do. But not many of us have met Aes Sedai, not to know it. They way the law was, forbidding channeling, few Aes Sedai came to Tear, and they very seldom advertised who they were."

"That's beside the point, my fine Aes Sedai-loving Tairen friend. And it gives weight to my argument in any event. Tear holds to Rand, the nobles do at least, because they're afraid if they do not, he'll come back, but if they believe the Tower holds him, then maybe he can't come back. If they believe he's a tool of the Tower, it is just one more reason for them to turn on him. Let enough Tairens believe those two things, and he might as well have left Tear as soon as he drew *Callandor*. That is just the one rumor, and just Tear, but it could do as much harm in Cairhien, or Illian, or anywhere. I don't know what sort of tales might spring from a male *a'dam*, in a world with the Dragon Reborn, and Asha'man, but I'm too old to want to find out."

Mat understood, in a manner of speaking. A man always tried to make whoever was commanding the troops against him believe that he was doing something other than what he was, that he was going where he had no intention of going, and the enemy tried to do the same to him, if the enemy was any good at the craft. Sometimes both sides could get so confused that very strange things happened. Tragedies, sometimes. Cities burned that no one had any interest in burning, except that the burners believed what was untrue, and thousands died. Crops destroyed for the same reason, and tens of thousands died in the famine that followed.

"So I won't crack my teeth about this *a'dam* for men," he said. "I suppose somebody has thought to tell . . . him?" Colors flashed. Maybe he could just ignore them, or grow used to them. They were gone as fast as they came, and they did not hurt. He just did not like things he could not understand. Especially when they might have to do with the Power in some way. The silver foxhead under his shirt might protect him against the Power, but that protection had as many holes as his own memories.

"We have not exactly been in regular communication," Thom said dryly, waggling his eyebrows. "I suppose Elayne and Nynaeve have found some way to let him know, if they think it important."

"Why should they?" Juilin said, bending to tug off a boot with a grunt. "The thing is at the bottom of the sea." Scowling, he hurled the boot at the bundled dresses in the corner. "Are you going to let us get any sleep tonight, Mat? I don't think we'll have any tomorrow night, and I like to sleep at least every other night."

That night, Mat chose to sleep in Tylin's bed. Not for old times' sake. That thought made him laugh, though his laughter had too much of the sound of a whimper to be very funny. It was just that a good feather mattress and goosedown pillows were preferable to a hayloft when a man did not know when his next decent night's sleep would come.

The trouble was that he could not sleep. He lay there in the dark with an arm behind his head and the medallion's leather cord looped through itself on his wrist, ready to hand in case the *gholam* slid through the crack under the door, but it was not the *gholam* that kept him awake. He could not stop going over the plan in his head. It was a good plan, and simple; as simple as it could be, in the circumstances. Only, no battle ever went according to plan, even the best. Great captains earned their reputation not just for laying brilliant plans, but for still being able to find victory after those plans began to fall apart. So when first light illumined the windows, he was still lying there, rolling the medallion across the back of his fingers and trying to think of what was going to go wrong.

CHAPTER

30

Cold, Fat Raindrops

The day dawned cold, with gray clouds that obscured the rising sun and winds off the Sea of Storms that rattled loose panes of glass in the window casements. In stories, not the sort of day for grand rescues and escapes. It was a day for murders. Not a pleasant thought when you were hoping to live past another dawn. But the plan *was* simple. Now that he had a Seanchan Blood to use, nothing could possibly go wrong. Mat tried very hard to convince himself of that.

Lopin brought him breakfast, bread and ham and some hard yellow cheese, while he dressed. Nerim was folding a few last pieces of clothing that were to go to the inn, including some of the shirts Tylin had had made. They were good shirts, after all, and Nerim claimed he could do something about the lace, though as usual he made it sound as if he was offering to sew a shroud. The lugubrious, gray-haired little fellow was handy with a needle, as Mat knew well. He had sewn up enough of Mat's wounds.

"Nerim and I will take Olver out by the refuse gate at the rear of the Palace," Lopin recited with exaggerated patience, his hands clasped at his waist. Servants in a palace seldom missed meals, and his dark Tairen coat fit more tightly than ever over his round belly. For that matter, the bottom of the coat did not appear to flare as much as it once had. "There is never anyone there except the guards until the refuse cart leaves in the afternoon, and they are accustomed to us taking my Lord's things out that way, so they won't remark us. At The Wandering Woman, we will secure my Lord's gold and the rest of my Lord's garments, and

Metwyn, Fergin and Gorderan will meet us with the horses. We and the Redarms will then take young Olver through the Dal Eira Gate at midafternoon. I have the lottery tokens for the horses, including both pack animals, in my pocket, my Lord. There is an abandoned stable on the Great North Road, about a mile north of the Circuit of Heaven, where we will wait until we see my Lord. I trust I have my Lord's instructions correctly?"

Mat swallowed the last of the cheese and dusted his hands. "You think I'm making you go over it too often?" he said, shrugging into his coat. A plain dark green coat. A man wanted to be plain while about business like today's. "I want to make sure you have it by heart. Remember, if you don't see me before sunrise tomorrow, you keep moving until you find Talmanes and the Band." The alarm would go up with the morning inspection of the kennels, and if he was not out of the city before that, he expected to learn whether his luck ran to stopping a headsman's axe. He had been told that he was fated to die and live again—a prophecy, or near enough one—but he was pretty sure that had already happened.

"Of course, my Lord," Lopin said blandly. "It will be as my Lord commands."

"Certainly, my Lord," Nerim murmured, funereal as ever. "My Lord commands, and we obey."

Mat suspected they were lying, but two or three days waiting would not hurt them, and by that time, they would have to see he was not coming. Metwyn and the other two soldiers would convince them, if need be. Those three might follow Mat Cauthon, but they were not fool enough to stretch their necks on the chopping block if his head had already fallen. For some reason, he was not as sure of Lopin and Nerim.

Olver was not as upset over leaving Riselle as Mat had feared he would be. He brought the subject up while he was helping the boy bundle his belongings to be carried over to the inn. All of Olver's things were laid out neatly on the narrow bed in what had been the sulking room, a small sitting room, when the apartments had been Mat's.

"She is getting married, Mat," Olver said patiently, as though explaining to someone who didn't see the obvious. Popping open a narrow little carved box Riselle had given him, just long enough to make sure his redhawk's feather was safe, he snapped it shut and tucked it into the leather scrip he would be carrying on his shoulder. He was as careful of the feather as he had been of the purse holding twenty gold crowns and a fistful of silver. "I don't think her husband would like her to keep teaching me to read. I would not, if I were her husband."

"Oh," Mat said. Riselle had worked quickly once she made her mind up. Her marriage to Banner-General Yamada had been announced publicly yesterday and was to take place tomorrow, though by custom there was usually a wait of months between. Yamada might be a good general—Mat did not know—but he had never stood a chance against Riselle and that marvelous bosom. Today they were looking at a vineyard in the Rhannon Hills that the groom was buying for her wedding gift. "I just thought you might want to—I don't know—take her with us, or something."

"I'm not a child, Mat," Olver said dryly. Folding the linen cloth back around his striped turtle shell, he added that to the scrip. "You *will* play Snakes and Foxes with me, won't you? Riselle enjoys playing, and you never have time any more." Despite the clothes Mat was bundling up in a cloak that would go into a pack hamper, the boy had a spare pair of breeches and some clean shirts and stockings in the scrip, too. And the game of Snakes and Foxes his dead father had made for him. You were less likely to lose what you kept on your person, and Olver had already lost more in his ten years than most people did in a lifetime. But he still believed you could win at Snakes and Foxes without breaking the rules, too.

"I will," Mat promised. He would if he managed to make it out of the city. He was certainly breaking enough rules to deserve to win. "You just take care of Wind till I get there." Olver ginned widely, and for him, that was very wide indeed. The boy loved that leggy gray gelding almost as much as he did Snakes and Foxes.

Unfortunately, Beslan was another who seemed to think you could win at Snakes and Foxes.

"Tonight," he growled, stalking up and down in front of the fireplace in Tylin's sitting room. The slender man's eyes were cold enough to take away the warmth of the blaze, and his hands were clasped behind his back as if to keep them from the hilt of his narrow-bladed sword. The jeweled cylinder-clock on the wave-carved marble mantel chimed four times for the second hour of the morning. "With a few days' warning, I could have laid on something magnificent!"

"I don't want anything magnificent," Mat told him. He did not want anything from the man, but by chance Beslan had seen Thom slipping into the stableyard of The Wandering Woman a little earlier. Thom had gone to keep Joline amused until Egeanin brought her *sul'dam* that evening, to settle her nerves and jolly her along with courtly manners, but there could have been any number of reasons for him to visit the inn. Well, maybe not that many, with it full of Seanchan, but several, surely. Only, Beslan had leaped to the reason like a duck leaping on a beetle, and he refused to be left out. "It will be enough if a few of your friends fire some of the stores the Seanchan have stockpiled on the Bay Road. After midnight, mind, as near as they can reckon it; better an hour later than any time before." With any luck, he would be out of the city before midnight. "That will draw their attention away south, and you know losing stores will hurt them."

"I said I would do it," Beslan said sourly, "but you can't say setting fires is exactly a grand gesture."

Sitting back, Mat rested his hands on the bamboo-carved arms of the chair and frowned. He wanted to rest his hands, anyway, but his signet ring made a metallic clicking on the gilded wood as he tapped his fingers. "Beslan, you will be seen at an inn when those fires are set, won't you?" The other man grimaced. "Beslan?"

Beslan flung up his hands. "I know; I know. I mustn't endanger Mother. I'll be seen. By midnight, I will be as drunk as an innkeeper's husband! You can wager I'll be seen! It just isn't very heroic, Mat. I'm at war with the Seanchan whether or not Mother is."

Mat tried not to sigh. He almost succeeded.

There was no way to hide the three Redarms moving horses out of the stables, of course. Twice that morning he noticed serving women handing coins to others, and both times the woman doing the handing over glared when she saw him. Even with Vanin and Harnan apparently still solidly ensconced in the long barracks room near the stables, the Palace knew that Mat Cauthon was leaving soon, and wagers were being paid already. He just had to make sure no one found out how soon before it was too late.

The wind picked up strength as the morning wore on, but he had Pips saddled and rode his endless circles in the Palace stableyard, huddling a little in his saddle and clutching his cloak close. He rode more slowly than usual, so Pips' steel shoes made a lazy, plodding sound on the paving stones. Now and then he grimaced at the darkening clouds in the sky and shook his head. No, Mat Cauthon did not like being out in this weather. Mat Cauthon would be staying somewhere warm and dry until the skies cleared, yes, he would.

The *sul'dam* walking *damane* in their own circle in the stableyard knew he was leaving soon, too. Maybe the serving women did not talk directly to the Seanchan women, but what one woman knew was always known to every woman inside a mile soon enough. Wildfire did not run through dry woods as fast as gossip ran through women. A tall yellow-haired *sul'dam* glanced in his direction and shook her head. A short stout *sul'dam* laughed out loud, splitting a face as dark as any of the Sea Folk. He was just Tylin's Toy.

The *sul'dam* did not concern him, but Teslyn did. For several days, until this morning, he had not seen her among the *damane* being exercised. Today the *sul'dam* let their cloaks fly with the wind, but the *damane* all held theirs tightly around them, except Teslyn's gray cloak flapped this way and that, forgotten, and she stumbled a little where the pavement was uneven. Her eyes were wide and worried in that Aes Sedai face. Occasionally she darted a glance at the buxom black-haired *sul'dam* wearing the other end of her silver leash, and when she did, she licked her lips uncertainly.

A tightness settled in Mat's belly. Where had the determination gone? If she was ready to knuckle under. . . .

"Everything all right?" Vanin said when Mat dismounted and gave him Pips' reins. Rain had begun to fall, cold fat drops, and the *sul'dam* were hurrying their charges inside, laughing and running to avoid getting wet. Some of the *damane* were laughing, too, a sound to chill Mat's blood. Vanin took no chances anyone might wonder why they were standing in the rain to talk. The fat man bent to lift

Pips' left foreleg and study the hoof. "You look a mite more peaked than usual."

"Everything is just fine," Mat told him. The ache in his leg and hip gnawed like a tooth, but he was barely aware of it or of the quickening rain. Light, if Teslyn was cracking now. . . . "Just remember. If you hear shouting inside the Palace tonight, or anything that sounds like trouble, you and Harnan don't wait. You ride out right then and go find Olver. He'll be—"

"I know where the little tyke'll be." Letting go of Pips' leg and straightening, Vanin spat through one of the gaps in his teeth. Raindrops ran down his face. "Harnan ain't too stupid to put his boots on alone, and I know what to do. You just take care of your piece of it and make sure your luck is working. Come on there, boy," he added much more warmly to Pips. "I got some good oats for you. And a fine hot fish stew for me."

Mat knew he should eat, too, but he felt as though he had swallowed a stone, and it did not leave room for food. Hobbling back up to Tylin's apartments, he threw his damp cloak over a chair, and for a time, stood staring at the corner where his black-hafted spear stood propped next to his un-strung bow. He planned to come back for the *ashandarei* at the last moment. The Blood should all be abed by the time he moved, and the servants, as well, with only the guards outside remaining awake, but he would not risk being seen with it before he had to. Even the Seanchan who called him Toy would take notice of him carrying a weapon through the halls in the middle of the night. He had meant to carry the bow, too. Good black yew was almost impossible to find outside the Two Rivers, and they cut it too short besides. Unstrung, a bow should be two hands taller than the man who would draw it. Maybe he should abandon it after all, though. He would need both hands to use the *ashandarei,* if it came to that, and the moment needed to drop the bow might be the moment that killed him.

"Everything will go according to plan," he said aloud. Blood and ashes, he sounded as wool-headed as Beslan! "I am not going to have fight my way out of the bloody Palace!" And almost as fool-witted. Luck was a very fine thing with the dice. Depending on luck other places could get a man dead.

Lying down on the bed, he propped one booted foot atop the other and lay studying the bow and the spear. With the door to the sitting room open, he could hear the cylinder-clock softly chime each hour away. Light, he needed his luck tonight.

The window light faded so slowly he almost got up to see whether the sun had stopped, but eventually gray light faded to purple twilight, then to full dark. The clock chimed twice, and then the only sounds were the drumming of the rain and the rush of the wind. Workmen who had been braving the weather would be downing tools to trudge home. No one came to light the lamps or tend the fires. No one expected him to be there, since he had slept in the bed the night before. The flames in the bedroom fireplace dwindled and died. Everything was in motion, now. Olver was snug in that old stable; it still had most of its roof. The clock sounded the first full hour of the night, and after no more than a week, four chimes for the second.

Rising from the bed, he felt his way into the pitch-dark sitting room and pulled open the hinged casement of one of the tall windows. The strong wind drove raindrops through the intricate white wrought-iron screen, quickly soaking his coat. The moon was hidden behind clouds, and the city was a mass of rain-shrouded darkness without even lightning to break it. All the streetlamps had apparently been extinguished by the rain and wind; the night would hide them when they left the Palace. And any patrol that saw them out in this weather would look twice. Shivering as the wind cut through his damp coat, he shut the casement.

Taking a seat on the edge of one of the bamboo-carved chairs, he propped his elbows on his knees and watched the clock above the dead fireplace. He could not see it in the darkness, but here, he could hear the steady tick. He remained motionless, though the single chime of another hour made him twitch. There was nothing now but to wait. In a little while, Egeanin would be introducing Joline to her *sul'dam*. If she really had been able to find three who would do as she claimed. If Joline did not panic when they first put the *a'dam* on her. Thom, Joline and the others from the inn would meet him just before he reached the Dal Eira. And if he did not reach it, Thom had gone ahead with carving his turnip; he was sure he could get them past the gates with his forged order. At least they had a chance, if it all fell apart. If. Too many ifs to think about, now. It was too late for that.

Ding, from the clock, like a piece of crystal tapped with a spoon. *Ding.* About now, Juilin would be making his way to his precious Thera, and with any luck Beslan was starting to drink hard at an inn somewhere. Drawing a deep breath, he stood in the blackness and checked his knives by feel, up his sleeves, beneath his coat, tucked into the turned-down tops of his boots, one hanging down inside the back of his collar. That done, he left the apartments. Too late for anything but beginning.

The empty hallways he walked along were only dimly lit. One stand lamp in three or four carried flames in front of the mirrors, little pools of light with pale shadows between that never quite reached darkness. His boots were loud on the floor tiles. They rang on the marble stairs. It was unlikely anyone at all would be awake this late, but if someone did see him, he must not look as if he were skulking. Tucking his thumbs behind his belt, he made himself saunter. It was no worse than stealing a pie from a kitchen window sill. Though, come to think of it, the spotty memories that remained of his boyhood seemed to contain getting half-skinned for that a time or two.

Stepping onto the columned walk that bordered the stableyard, he turned up his collar against the wind-driven rain flying between the fluted white columns. Bloody rain! A man could drown in it, even when he had not really been outside yet. The wall-mounted lamps had blown out, except for the pair flanking the open gates, the only glowing spots in the pouring rain. He could not make out the guards outside the gates. The Seanchan squad would be as motionless as if it were a pleasant afternoon. Very likely the Ebou Dari, too; they did not like being shown up in any way. After a moment he retreated to the anteroom door, to avoid getting completely drenched. Nothing moved in the stableyard. Where were they? Blood and bloody ashes, where . . . ?

Riders appeared in the gates, led by two men afoot carrying pole-lanterns. He could not count them in the rain, but they were too many. Would Seanchan messengers have lantern-bearers? Maybe, in this weather. Grimacing, he took another step back, into the anteroom. The thin light of a single stand-lamp behind him was enough to turn the night outside to a blanket of black, but he peered into it. In a few minutes, four heavily cloaked figures appeared, hurrying toward the door. If they were messengers, they would pass him by without a second glance.

"Your man Vanin is rude," Egeanin announced, throwing back her hood as soon she was beyond the fluted columns. In the darkness, her face was just a shadow, but the coldness of her voice was sufficient to tell him what he would see before she stepped into the anteroom, forcing him to move back. Her brows were drawn down sharply, and her blue eyes were icy augers. A grim-faced Domon followed her, shaking rain from his cloak, and then a pair of *sul'dam,* one pale and yellow-haired, the other with long brown hair. He could not see much more since they stood with their heads down, studying the floor tiles in front of their feet. "You didn't tell me she had two men with her," Egeanin went on, peeling her gloves off. Odd, how she could make that drawl sound brisk. She did not give a man room to squeeze in a word. "Or that Mistress Anan was coming. Luckily, I know how to adapt. Plans always need adapting, once the anchor is dry. Speaking of dry, have you been running around outside already? I trust you haven't gotten yourself noticed."

"What do you mean, you adapted, the plan?" Mat demanded, raking his hands through his hair. Light, it *was* wet! "I had everything laid out!" Why were those two *sul'dam* standing so still? If he had ever seen statues of reluctance, it was that pair. "Who are those others out there?"

"The people from the inn," Egeanin said impatiently. "For one thing, I need a proper entourage to look right for any street patrols. Those two—Warders?—are muscular fellows; they make excellent lantern-bearers. For another, I didn't want to risk missing them in this blow. Better that we are all together from the start." Her head turned, following his glances at the *sul'dam.* "These are Seta Zarbey and Renna Emain. I suspect they hope you'll forget those names after tonight."

The pale woman flinched at the name Seta, which made the other Renna. Neither raised her head. What hold did Egeanin have on them, anyway? Not that it mattered. All that mattered was that they were here and ready to do what was necessary.

"No point standing here," Mat said. "Let's get on with it."
He let her changes in the plan go without further comment.
After all, lying on that bed in Tylin's apartments, he had
decided to risk a change or two himself.

CHAPTER
31

What the Aelfinn Said

The Seanchan noblewoman expressed surprise, and no little irritation, when Mat accompanied her toward the kennels. Seta and Renna knew the way, of course, and he was supposed to be getting his cloak and whatever else he meant to carry. The two *sul'dam* followed them through the poorly lit halls, cloaks hanging down their backs and eyes on the floor. Domon brought up the rear as though shepherding the pair. The braid hanging down the side of his head swayed as his eyes darted down every crossing corridor, and sometimes he felt at his waist as though expecting to find a sword or a cudgel. Except for them, the tapestry-lined hallways were silent and still.

"I have a small errand up there," Mat told Egeanin, as casually as he knew how, and smiled for her. "No need to bother yourself. Won't take a minute." His very best smile seemed to make no more impression than it had yesterday in her room at the inn.

"If you wreck me now—" she growled in a threatening tone.

"Just remember who planned this," he muttered, and she grunted. Light, women always seemed to think they could just step in and take over, and do a better job than the man whose job it was!

At least she made no further complaint. They climbed quickly to the top floor of the Palace, then up the dark narrow stairs to the sprawling attic. Only a few of the lamps were lit, not even as many as in the hallways below, and the maze of narrow corridors between the tiny wooden rooms was a mass of pale shadows. Nothing moved, and Mat breathed a little more easily. He would have breathed easier still if Renna had not sighed with obvious relief.

She and Seta knew where the various *damane* were kenneled, and if they did not exactly hurry, they made no delay in heading deeper in the attic, perhaps because Domon still walked at their heels. It was not an image to inspire confidence. Well, if wishes were horses, beggars would ride. A man made do with what he had. Especially when he had no choice.

Egeanin gave him a last hard look and growled again, wordlessly this time, then strode off after the others, her cloak flaring behind her. He grimaced at her back. The way the woman walked, you could take her for a man if she was not wearing a dress.

He did have an errand, and maybe not so small. It was not something he wanted to do. Light, he had tried to talk himself out of it! It was something he bloody well had to do, though. As soon as Egeanin vanished around a corner after Domon and the others, he darted for the nearest room that he remembered containing one of the Sea Folk.

Easing open the plain wooden door soundlessly, he slipped into the pitch-black interior. The sleeping woman inside snored with a rasping sound. Slowly he felt his way forward until his knee bumped into the bed, then felt along the mound beneath the blankets more quickly, finding her head just in time to clamp his hand over her mouth as she jerked awake.

"I want you to answer a question," he whispered. Blood and ashes, what if he had mistaken the room? What if this was not a Windfinder at all, but one of the bloody Seanchan women? "What would you do if I took that collar off your neck?" Lifting his hand, he held his breath.

"I would free my sisters, if it pleases the Light that should happen." The Sea Folk accents in the darkness made him breathe again. "The Light be willing, we would cross the harbor, somehow, to where our people are held, and free as many as we were able." The unseen woman's voice remained low, but grew fiercer by the word. "The Light be willing, we would take back our ships, and fight our way to sea. Now! If this is a trick, punish me for it and be done, or kill me for it. I was on the brink of yielding, of giving up myself, and the shame of that will burn me forever, but you have reminded me who I am, and now I will never yield. Do you hear me? Never!"

"And if I asked you to wait for three hours?" he asked, still crouching over her. "I remember the Atha'an Miere judging the passage of an hour within minutes." That fellow had not been him, but the memory was his now, passage on an Atha'an Miere vessel from Allorallen to Barashta, and a bright-eyed Sea Folk woman who wept when she refused to follow him ashore.

"Who are you?" she whispered.

"I'm called Mat Cauthon, if it makes a difference."

"I am Nestelle din Sakura South Star, Mat Cauthon." He heard her spit, and knew what she was doing. He spat on his own palm, and their two hands found each other in the darkness. Hers was as callused as his, her grip strong. "I will wait," she said. "And I will remember you. You are a great and good man."

"I'm just a gambler," he told her. Her hand guided his to the segmented collar around her neck, and it came open for him with a metallic *snick*. She drew a very long breath.

He only had to put her fingers in the proper places and show her the trick once before she got it, but he made her close and open the collar three times before he was satisfied. If he was going to do this, he might as well make sure it was done right. "Three hours, as near as you can," he reminded her.

"As near as I can," she whispered.

She could ruin everything, but if he could not take a chance, then who could? He was the man with the luck, after all. Maybe it had not been all that much in evidence lately, but he had found Egeanin just when he needed her. Mat Cauthon still had the luck.

Slipping out of the room as quietly as he had entered, he closed the door. And almost choked on his tongue. He was staring at the back of a wide, gray-haired woman in a red-paneled dress. Beyond her stood Egeanin drawn up to her full height, and Teslyn, connected to Renna by the silver length of an *a'dam*. There was no sign of Domon or Seta or this Edesina he still had not seen to know her. Egeanin looked fierce as a lioness over her kill, but Teslyn was wide-eyed and trembling, terrified half out of her wits, and Renna's mouth had a twist that said she might sick up any moment now.

Not daring to breathe, he took a cautious step toward the gray-haired woman, stretching out his hands. If he over-powered her before she could cry out, they could hide her. . . . Where? Seta and Renna would want to kill her. No matter what hold Egeanin had on them, the woman could name them.

Egeanin's stern blue eyes caught his over the gray-haired *sul'dam's* shoulder for a brief instant before focusing on the other woman's face again. "No!" she said sharply. "There is no time to waste with changes to my plans, now. The High Lady Suroth said I could use any *damane* I wish, *Der'sul'dam.*"

"Of course, my Lady," the gray-haired woman replied, sounding confused. "I merely pointed out that Tessi is not really trained. I actually came up to look in on her. She *is* coming along very nicely, now, my Lady, but . . ."

Still not breathing, Mat backed away on tiptoe. He eased down the dark narrow stairs using his hands against the walls to support as much of his weight as possible. He did not remember any creaky steps coming up, but there were chances, and then there were chances. A man took those he had to, and did not press his luck otherwise. That was the way to a long life, something he wished for very much.

At the foot of the steps, he paused to suck in air until his heart stopped pounding. Until it slowed a little, anyway. It might not stop pounding till tomorrow. He was not sure he had drawn breath since seeing the gray-haired woman. Light! If Egeanin thought she had the matter in hand, well and bloody good, but just the same, Light! She must have nooses around the two *sul'dam's* necks! *Her* plan? Well, she had been right about no time to waste. He ran.

He ran until his hip gave a sharp twinge, and he stumbled into a turquoise-inlaid table. He caught a summer tapestry to keep from falling, and the bright-flowered length of silk tore free from the yellow marble cornice for half its length. The tall white porcelain vase sitting on the table toppled, shattering on the blue-and-red floor tiles with a crash that echoed along the hallway. After that, he hobbled. But he hobbled as fast as any man ever had. If anyone came to investigate the noise, they were not going to find Mat Cauthon standing over that mess, or within two corridors of it.

Limping the rest of the way to Tylin's apartments, he was across the sitting room and into the bedchamber before he realized that the lamps were all lit. The blaze in the bedroom fireplace had been renewed with split billets from the gilded wood-basket. Tylin, her arms doubled behind her to work at her buttons, looked up at his entrance and frowned. Her dark green riding dress was wrinkled. The fire crackled and spat a shower of sparks up the chimney.

"I didn't expect you back yet," he said, trying to think. Of everything he had considered going amiss tonight, Tylin returning early had never been in it. His brain seemed frozen.

"Suroth learned that an army had vanished in Murandy," Tylin replied slowly, straightening. She spoke absently, giving what she said a fraction of the attention she put into studying Mat Cauthon. "What army, or how any army can vanish, I don't know, but she decided her return was urgent. We left everyone behind, came as fast as one of the beasts could carry just the two of us and the woman who handled it, and commandeered two horses to ride up from the docks alone. She even went to that inn across the square where all their officers are instead of coming here. I don't think she intends to sleep tonight, or let any of them. . . ."

Letting her words trail off, Tylin glided to him across the carpets and fingered his plain green coat. "The trouble with having a pet fox," she murmured, "is that sooner or later it remembers it is a fox." Those big dark eyes peered up at him. Suddenly she seized two handfuls of his hair and pulled his head down for a kiss that curled his toes in his boots. "That," she said breathlessly when she finally let him go, "is to show you how much I will miss you." Without the slightest change of expression, she slapped him so hard that silver flecks floated in front of his eyes. "And that is for trying to sneak away while I was gone." Turning her back, she pulled her mane of raven hair over one shoulder. "Undo my buttons for me, my pretty little fox. We arrived so late I decided not to wake my maids, but these fingernails make buttons all but impossible. One last night together, and tomorrow I will send you on your way."

Mat rubbed his cheek. The woman could have broken a tooth for him! At least she had jarred his thoughts loose. If

Suroth was at The Wandering Woman, she was not in the Tarasin Palace to see what she should not. His luck was still good. He only had to worry about the woman in front of him. The only way was forward.

"I'm going tonight," he said, putting his hands on Tylin's shoulders. "And when I do, I'm taking a couple of Aes Sedai from the attic. Come with me. I'll send Thom and Juilin to find Beslan, and—"

"Go *with* you?" she said incredulously, moving away and turning to face him. Her proud face was scornful. "Pigeon, I don't fancy becoming *your* pretty, and I have no intention of becoming a refugee. Or of leaving Altara to whoever the Seanchan choose to replace me. I am the Queen of Altara, the Light help me, and I will not abandon my country now. You really mean to try freeing the Aes Sedai? I wish you well in it, if you must—I wish the sisters well—but it seems a good way to have your head stuck up on a spike, sweetling. It's too pretty a head to be cut off and covered with tar."

He tried to take her by the shoulders again, but she stepped back with a piercing look that made his hands fall. He put every scrap of urgency he could find into his voice. "Tylin, I made sure everybody knew I was leaving, and anxious to be gone before you returned, so the Seanchan would know you didn't have anything to do with it, but now—"

"I returned and surprised you," she broke in fiercely, "and you tied me up and left me under the bed. When I am discovered in the morning, I will be furious with you. Outraged!" She smiled, but her eyes glittered, not that far from outrage now, whatever she said about foxes and sending him on his way. "I will offer a bounty for you, and tell Tuon she can buy you when you're caught, if she still wants you. I will be the perfect High Blood in my anger. They'll believe me, duckling. I've already told Suroth I intend to shave my hair."

Mat grinned weakly. He certainly believed her. She really would sell him if he was caught. "Women are a maze through briars in the night," the old saying went, and even they do not know the way.

Tylin insisted on supervising her own binding. She seemed to take pride in it. She had to be bound with strips cut from her skirts, as if she had come on him by surprise and been overpowered. The knots had to be tight, so she could not escape however she struggled, and she did struggle against them once they were tied, thrashing about hard enough that it seemed she really was trying to get free. Maybe she was; her mouth twisted in a snarl when she failed. Her ankles and wrists had to be tied together in the small of her back, and a leash run from her neck to one leg of the bed, so she could not wriggle her way across the floor and out into the hall. And of course, she could not be able to shout for help, either. When he gently pushed one of her silk kerchiefs into her mouth and tied another to hold it in place, she smiled, but her eyes were fierce. A maze through briars in the night.

"I am going to miss you," he said quietly as he pushed her beneath the edge of the bed. To his surprise, he realized that he really would. Light! Hurriedly he gathered his cloak and gloves and spear, and snuffed the lamps on his way out. Women could tangle a man in that maze before he knew it.

The hallways remained empty, and silent save for the sound of his own limping bootsteps, but any relief he felt vanished when he reached the anteroom off the stableyard.

The single lit stand-lamp still cast a wavering light on those inevitable flowered tapestries, but Juilin and his woman were not there, and neither were Egeanin and the others. With the time he had taken up with Tylin, they all should have been waiting on him by now. Beyond the columned walk the rain was sheeting down in a solid black curtain that hid everything. Could they have gone on to the stables? That Egeanin seemed to change his plan whenever it suited her.

Grumbling under his breath, he hitched his cloak around him and prepared to make his way to the stables through the downpour. He had had just about all he could take of women tonight.

"So you *are* intending to leave. I cannot allow that, Toy."

With an oath, he spun on his heel and found himself facing Tuon, her dark face stern behind her long transparent veil. The narrow circlet holding the veil on her shaven head was a mass of firedrops and pearls, yet another fortune taken together with the wide jeweled belt that cinched her waist and the long necklace around her neck. A fine time it was to be noticing jewels, however rich. What in the Light was she doing awake? Blood and ashes, if she went running off, shouting for guards to stop him . . . !

Desperately he reached for the skinny girl, but she writhed away from his grip and sent the *ashandarei* flying with a sharp blow that half numbed his wrist. He expected her to flee, but instead she rained blows at him, punching with folded knuckles, chopping her hands like axe blades. He had quick hands, the quickest Thorn had ever seen according to the old gleeman, but it was all he could do to ward her off, forget about grabbing her. If he had not been trying so hard to keep her from breaking his nose—or something else, maybe; she hit very hard for such a tiny thing—except for that, he might have found the whole thing laughable. He towered over her, though he was not much above average height, yet she came at him in a concentrated fury, as though she were the taller and stronger and expected to overwhelm him. For some reason, after a few moments her full lips curved in a smile, and if he had not known better, he would have said those big liquid eyes took on a glow of delight. Burn him, thinking about how pretty a woman was at a time like this was as bad as trying to price her gems!

Abruptly, she flowed back from him, using both hands to readjust the circle of gems that secured her veil. There was certainly nothing like delight on her face now. Her expression was all concentration. Placing her feet carefully, never taking her eyes from his face, she began slowly gathering her white pleated skirts in her hands, inching them up above her knees in folds.

He could not understand why she was not already shouting for help, but he knew she was about to kick at him. Well, not if he had anything to say about it! He leaped for her, and everything happened at once. A stab of pain in his hip sent him to one knee. Tuon snatched her skirts almost to her own hips, and her slim, white-stockinged leg flashed out at him in a kick that passed over his head as she was suddenly hoisted into the air.

He thought he must be as surprised to see Noal with his arms wrapped around the girl as she was to have those arms there, but he reacted faster than she. As she opened her mouth to shout at last, Mat scrambled to his feet and began stuffing her veil between her teeth, tipping the jeweled circlet to the floor with a flip of his hand. She did not cooperate the way Tylin had, of course. A firm grip on her jaw was all that kept her from sinking her teeth into his fingers. Angry sounds came from her throat, and her eyes showed a fury they never had at the worst of her attack. She twisted in Noal's grip and flailed her legs, but the worn old man managed to shift his burden and himself to avoid every kick of her heels. Worn or not, he seemed to have no difficulty hanging on to her.

"Do you often have this sort of trouble with women?" he asked mildly around a gap-toothed smile. He was wearing his cloak, and his bundled belongings were tied over it across his back.

"Always," Mat replied sourly, and grunted when a knee caught his aching hip. Managing to untie his neck-scarf one-handed, he used it to secure the wadded veil in Tuon's mouth at the cost of a nipped thumb. Light, what was he going to *do* with her?

"I didn't know this was what you were planning," Noal said, not breathing hard in spite of the way the tiny woman thrashed herself about in his grip, "but as you can see, I'm leaving tonight, too. I thought that in a day or two, this might be an unpleasant place for someone you gave a bed to."

"A wise decision," Mat muttered. Light, he should have thought of warning Noal.

Lowering himself to his knees, he avoided Tuon's kicks—most of them, anyway—long enough to catch her legs. A knife plucked from his sleeve started a cut in the hem of her dress, and he tore away a long strip to tie her ankles. It was a good thing he had gotten all that practice with Tylin earlier. He was not accustomed to tying women up. Tearing off a second strip of cloth from the bottom of her skirt, he picked up the circle of gems from the floor, and stood with one grunt for the effort and a deeper one for a last, two-legged kick that set fire to his hip. When he set the circlet back on her head, Tuon stared him straight in the eye. She had stopped thrashing about uselessly, but she was not afraid. Light, in her place, he would have been soiling himself.

Juilin finally arrived, then, cloaked and fully accoutered, with his short sword and notched sword-breaker at his belt and his thin bamboo staff in one hand. A slender, dark-haired woman in the thick white robes worn by *da'covale* outside clung to his right arm. She was pretty, in a pouty way, with a rosebud mouth, but five or six years older than Mat had expected, and her large dark eyes darted timidly. At the sight of Tuon, she squeaked and let go of Juilin as though he were a hot stove, folding herself to the floor beside the door with her head on her knees.

"I had to talk Thera into running away all over again," the thief-catcher sighed, giving her a concerned look. That was all the explanation he made for his lateness, before turning his attention to Noal's burden. Pushing back the ridiculous conical red cap he wore, he scratched his head. "And what do we do with her?" he asked simply.

"Leave her in the stables," Mat replied. They would if Vanin had convinced the grooms to let him and Harnan tend to any messengers' horses that came in. Until now, that had seemed like only an added precaution, not really necessary. Until now. "In the hayloft. She shouldn't be found before morning, when they fork down fresh hay for the stalls."

"And I thought you were kidnaping her," Noal sighed, setting Tuon's bound feet back on the floor and shifting his hold on her to gripping her upper arms. Head high, the little woman disdained to struggle. Even with a gag in her mouth, scorn was clear on her face. She refused to fight, not because it was hopeless, but because she did not choose to fight.

Bootsteps echoed in the corridor leading to the anteroom, growing louder. It could be Egeanin at last. Or the way the night seemed to be turning, it might be Deathwatch Guards. The Ogier sort.

Hastily, Mat motioned the other toward corners out of sight of anyone coming through the door, then hobbled over to pick up his black spear. Juilin pulled Thera to her feet and drew her to his left, where she crouched in the corner while he stood in front of her with his staff held in both hands. It appeared a frail weapon, but the thief-catcher could use it to great effect. Noal dragged Tuon to the opposite corner of the room and released one of her arms to put a hand inside his coat, where he kept his long knives. Mat planted himself in the middle of the room with his back to the rain-soaked night, the *ashandarei* upright in front of him. No matter who came into the room, he was not going to be able to dance about, with his hip knotted in a fist from Tuon's kicks, but if worse came to worst, he could at least leave marks on a few people.

When Egeanin strode through that doorway, he sagged on the spear in relief. Two *sul'dam* entered after her, and Domon followed. Mat got his first look at Edesina to know who he was seeing, though he did recall her from one day when the *damane* were being exercised, a slender handsome woman in one of those plain gray dresses, with black hair spilling to her waist. Despite the *a'dam* leashing her to Seta's wrist, Edesina looked about her calmly. An Aes Sedai on a leash, perhaps, but an Aes Sedai confident that leash was coming off soon. Teslyn, on the other hand, was a quivering mass of eagerness, licking her lips and staring at the door to the stableyard. Renna and Seta hurried the two Aes Sedai along behind Egeanin without taking their eyes from the stableyard door.

"I had to soothe the *der'sul'dam*," Egeanin said, as soon as she was into the room. "They are very protective of their charges." Noticing Juilin and Thera, she scowled; there had not seemed any reason to tell her about Thera, not when she was willing to help *damane,* but clearly she did not like the surprise of woolen robes. "Her seeing Seta and Renna changes a few things, of course," she went on, "but—" Her words cut off as though sliced with a knife as her eyes fell on Tuon. Egeanin was a pale woman, but she went paler. Tuon glared back above her gag with the stern ferocity of a headsman. "Oh, Light!" Egeanin said hoarsely, sinking to her knees. "You madman! It's death by slow torture to lay hands on the Daughter of the Nine Moons!" The two *sul'dam* gasped, and knelt without hesitation, not only pulling the two Aes Sedai down with them but gripping the *a'dam* right at the collar to force their faces to the floor.

Mat grunted as though Tuon had just kicked him square in the belly. He felt as if she had. The Daughter of the Nine Moons. The Aelfinn had told him truth, much as he hated knowing. He would die and live again, if he had not already. He would give up half the light of the world to save the world, and he did not even want to think about what that meant. He would marry. . . . "She is my wife," he said softly. Somebody made a choking sound; he thought it was Domon.

"What?" Egeanin squeaked, her head whipping toward him so fast that her tail of hair swung around to slap her face. He would not have thought she *could* squeak. "You cannot say that! You *must* not say that!"

"Why not?" he demanded. The Aelfinn always gave true answers. Always. "She is my wife. Your bloody Daughter of the Nine Moons is my wife!"

They stared at him, except for Juilin, who took off his cap and stared into that. Domon shook his head, and Noal laughed softly. Egeanin's mouth hung open. The two *sul'dam* gaped as though at a madman, stark raving and loose. Tuon stared, but her expression was absolutely unreadable, hiding every thought behind those dark eyes. Oh, Light, what *was* he to do? For one thing, get a move on before . . .

Selucia scurried into the room, and Mat groaned. Was everybody in the whole bloody Palace going to walk in? Domon tried to grab her, but she eluded him, darting about. The buxom golden-haired *so'jhin* was not so stately as usual, wringing her hands and looking around in a hunted fashion. "Forgive me for speaking," she said in a fear-filled voice, "but what you do is foolish beyond madness." With a groan, she darted to half crouch between the kneeling *sul'dam* with one hand on the shoulder of each, as though seeking their protection. Her blue eyes never ceased flitting about the room. "Whatever the omens, this can still be rectified if you will only consent to draw back."

"Be easy, Selucia," Mat said in a soothing. She was not looking at him, but he made calming gestures anyway. In none of his memories could he find a way to deal with a hysterical woman. Except to hide. "No one is going to be hurt. No one! I promise you. You can be easy, now."

For some reason, consternation flashed across her face, but she settled to her knees and folded her hands in her lap. Suddenly, all her fear vanished, and she was as regal as ever she had been. "I will obey you, so long as you do not harm my mistress. If you do, I will kill you."

From Egeanin, that would have given him pause. Coming from this plump cream-cheeked woman, short even if she was taller than her mistress, he put it out of his mind. The Light knew women were dangerous, but he thought he could handle a lady's maid. At least she was no longer hysterical. Odd, how that came and went in women.

"I suppose you mean to leave them *both* in the hayloft?" Noal said.

"No," Mat replied, looking at Tuon. She stared right back, still with no expression he could read. A boy-slim little woman, when he liked women with flesh on their bones. Heir to the Seanchan throne, when noblewomen gave him goose bumps. A woman who had wanted to *buy* him, and now likely wanted to put a knife in his ribs. And she would be his wife. The Aelfinn always gave true answers. "We are taking them with us," he said.

At last, Tuon showed expression. She smiled, as if she suddenly knew a secret. She smiled, and he shivered. Oh, Light, how he shivered.

CHAPTER
32

A Portion of Wisdom

The Golden Wheel was a large inn, just off the Avharin Market, with a long, beam-ceilinged common room crowded with small square tables. Even at midday no more than one table in five had anyone sitting at it, though, usually an outland merchant facing a woman in sober colors with her hair worn on top of her head or gathered up at the nape of her neck. The women were merchants, too, or bankers; in Far Madding, banking and trade were forbidden to men. All the foreigners in the common room were male, since the women among them could be taken into the Women's Room. The smells of fish and mutton cooking in the kitchens filled the air, and occasionally a shout from one of the tables summoned one of the serving men who waited in a line at the back of the room. Otherwise, the merchants and bankers kept their voices low. The sound of the rain outside was louder.

"Are you certain?" Rand asked, taking the creased drawings back from a lantern-jawed serving man he had drawn off to one side of the room.

"I think it's him," the fellow said uncertainly, wiping his hands on a long apron embroidered with a yellow wagon wheel. "It looks like him. He should be back soon." His eyes darted beyond Rand, and he sighed. "You better buy a drink or go. Mistress Gallger doesn't like us talking when we should be working. And she wouldn't like me talking about her patrons any time."

Rand glanced over his shoulder. A lean woman with a tall ivory comb stuck in the dark bun on the back of her head was standing in the yellow-painted arch that led to the Women's Room. The way she looked over the common room—half queen surveying her domain, half farmer surveying her fields, and either way displeased with the sparsity of trade she saw—named her the innkeeper. When her gaze fell on Rand and the lantern-jawed fellow, she frowned.

"Mulled wine," Rand said, handing the man some coins, coppers for the wine and a silver mark for his information, uncertain as it was. More than a week had passed since he had killed Rochaid and Kisman had gotten away, and in all those days this was the first time he had gotten more than a shrug or a shake of the head when he showed the drawings.

There were a dozen empty tables right at hand, but he wanted to be in a corner at the front of the room, where he could see who came in without being seen himself, and as he edged his way between the tables, snatches of conversation caught his ear.

A tall pale woman in dark green silk shook her head at a stocky man in a tight-fitting black Tairen coat. An iron-gray bun made her look a little like Cadsuane from the side. He appeared to be made of stone blocks, but his dark square face was worried. "You can put your mind at ease about Andor, Master Admira," she said soothingly. "Believe me, the Andorans will shout and shake swords at one another, but they'll never let it come to actual fighting. It is in your best interests to stay with the present route for your goods. Cairhien would tax you a fifth more than Far Madding. Think of the added expense." The Tairen grimaced as if he were thinking of it. Or wondering whether his best interests really coincided with hers.

"I hear the body did be all black and swollen," a lean, white-bearded Illianer in a dark blue coat said at another table. "I hear the Counsels did order it burned." He raised his eyebrows significantly and tapped the side of a pointed nose that gave him the appearance of a weasel.

"If there was *plague* in the city, Master Azereos, the Counsels would have announced it," the slim woman sitting across from him said calmly. With two elaborate ivory combs in her rolled hair, she was pretty, in a fox-faced way, and cool as an Aes Sedai, though with faint lines at the corners of her brown eyes. "I really do suggest against moving *any* of your trade to Lugard. Murandy is *most* unsettled. The nobles will *never* stand for Roedran building an army. And there are *Aes Sedai* involved, as I'm sure you have heard. The Light alone knows what *they* will do." The Illianer shrugged uncomfortly. These days, no one was very certain what Aes Sedai would do, if they ever had been.

A Kandori with gray streaks in his forked beard and a large pearl in his left ear was leaning toward a stout woman in dark gray silk who wore her black hair in a tight roll along the top of her head. "I hear the Dragon Reborn has been crowned King of Illian, Mistress Shimel." A frown put more wrinkles in his forehead. "Given the White Tower's proclamation, I am considering sending my spring wagons to travel along the Erinin to Tear. The River Road may be a harder route, but Illian is not such a market for furs that I want to take too many risks."

The stout woman smiled, a very thin smile for such a round face. "I'm told the man has hardly been seen in Illian since he took the crown, Master Posavina. In any case, the Tower will deal with him, if it hasn't already, and this morning, I received word that the Stone of Tear is under siege. That is hardly a situation where you will find much market for furs, now is it? No, Tear is not a place to avoid risks." The wrinkles in Master Posavina's forehead deepened.

Reaching a small table in the corner, Rand tossed his cloak over the back of the chair and sat with his back to the wall, turning up his collar. The lantern-jawed fellow brought a steaming pewter cup of spiced wine, murmured a hurried thanks for the silver, and scurried off at a shout from another table. Two large fireplaces on either side of the room took the chill off the air, but if anyone noticed that Rand kept his gloves on, no one glanced at him twice. He pretended to stare into the winecup between his hands on the table while keeping an eye on the door to the street.

Most of what he had overheard did not interest him greatly. He had heard as much before, and sometimes knew more than the people he eavesdropped on. Elayne agreed with the pale woman, for example, and she had to know Andor better than any Far Madding merchant. The Stone under siege was new, though. Still, he need not trouble himself with it yet. The Stone had never fallen, except to him, and he knew Alanna was somewhere in Tear. He had felt her leap from just north of Far Madding to somewhere much farther north, then, a day later, to somewhere far to the south and east. She was distant enough that he could not say whether she was in Haddon Mirk or the city of Tear itself, yet he was confident she was one place or the other, with four other sisters he could trust. If Merana and Rafela could get what he wanted from the Sea Folk, they could from the Tairens, too. Rafela was Tairen, and that should help. No, the world could get along without him a little longer. It had to.

A tall man swathed in a long, damp cloak with the hood hiding his face came in from the street, and Rand's eyes followed him to the stairs at the back of the room. Starting up, the fellow threw back his cowl, revealing a fringe of gray hair and a pale pinched face. He could not be the one the serving man meant. No one with eyes would confuse him with Peral Torval.

Rand went back to studying the surface of his wine, his thoughts turning sour. Min and Nynaeve had refused to spend one more hour tramping the streets, as Min had put it, and he suspected Alivia was only going through the motions of showing the drawings. When she did even that. They were all three out of the city for the day, in the hills, he judged from what the bond told him of Min. She felt very excited about something. The three of them believed Kisman had fled after failing to kill Rand, and the other renegades had either gone with him or never come at all. They had all been trying to talk him into leaving for days, now. At least Lan had not given up.

Why can't the women be right? Lews Therin whispered fiercely in his head. *This city is worse than any prison. There is no* Source *here! Why would they stay? Why would any* sane *man stay? We could ride out, beyond the barrier, just for a day, a few hours. Light, just for a few hours!* The voice laughed uncontrollably, wildly. *Oh, Light, why do I have a madman in my head? Why? Why?*

Angrily, Rand forced Lews Therin to a muted hum, like a biteme buzzing nearby. He had thought about accompanying the women on their ride, just to feel the Source again, though only Min had shown much enthusiasm. Nynaeve and Alivia would not admit why they wanted to ride out when the morning sky had promised the rain that was pouring down outside now. This was not the first time they had gone. To feel the Source, he suspected. To drink in the One Power again, if only for a short time. Well, he could endure not being able to channel. He could endure the absence of the Source. He could! He had to, so he could kill the men who had tried to kill him.

That is not the reason! Lews Therin shouted, forcing past Rand's efforts to shut him up. *You are afraid! If the sickness takes you while you are trying to use the access* ter'angreal, *it could kill you, or worse! It could kill us all!* he moaned.

Wine slopped over Rand's wrist, soaking his coat-sleeve, and he loosened his grip on the winecup. The thing had not been in true round to begin with, and he did not think he had bent it enough to be noticed. He was *not* afraid! He refused to let fear touch him. Light, he had to die, eventually. He had accepted that.

They tried to kill me, and I want them dead for it, he thought. *If it takes a little time, well, maybe the sickness will pass by then. Burn you, I have to live until the Last Battle.* In his head, Lews Therin laughed more wildly than before.

Another tall man swaggered in, through the door to the stableyard, almost at the foot of the stairs in the back of the room. Shaking rain from his cloak, he tossed back his hood and strode to the doorway of the Women's Room. With his sneering mouth and sharp nose, and a gaze that swept contemptuously over the people at the tables, he did look something like Torval, but with twenty years' more wear on his face and thirty pounds of fat on his frame. Peering through the yellow arch, he called out in a high, prissy voice that was thick with the accents of Illian. "Mistress Gallger, I do be leaving in the morning. Early, so I do expect no charges for tomorrow, mind!" Torval was a Taraboner.

Gathering his cloak, Rand left his winecup on the table and did not look back.

The noon sky was gray and cold, and if the rain had slackened, it was not by much, and driven by blustery lake winds, it was enough to have driven almost everyone from the streets. He held the cloak around him one-handed, as much to shelter the drawings in his coat pocket as to keep the rest of him dry, and used the other to hold his hood against the gusts. The windblown raindrops hit his face like flecks of ice. A lone sedan chair passed him, the bearers' hair hanging sodden down their backs and their boots splashing in puddles on the paving stones. A few people trudged along the streets wrapped up in their cloaks. There were hours of daylight left, such as it was, but he walked by an inn called The Heart of the Plain without going in, and then by The Three Ladies of Maredo. He told himself it was the rain. This was no weather to be making his way from inn to inn. He knew he was lying, though.

A short stout woman coming down the street bundled in a dark cloak suddenly veered toward him. When she stopped in front of him and raised her head, he saw it was Verin.

"So you are here after all," she said. Raindrops fell on her upturned face, but she did not seem to notice. "Your innkeeper thought you intended to walk up to the Avharin, but she was not sure. I'm afraid Mistress Keene doesn't pay much attention to the comings and goings of men. And here I am with my shoes soaked through, and my stockings. I used to like walking in the rain when I was a girl, but it seems to have lost its charm somewhere along the way."

"Did Cadsuane send you?" he asked, trying to keep his voice from sounding hopeful. He had kept his room at The Counsel's Head after Alanna left so that Cadsuane could find him. He could hardly make her interested if she had to hunt for him inn by inn. Especially since she had shown no evidence that she would hunt.

"Oh, no; she would never do that." Verin sounded surprised at the thought. "I just thought you might want to hear the news. Cadsuane is out riding with the girls." She frowned thoughtfully, tilting her head. "Though I suppose I shouldn't call Alivia a girl. An intriguing woman. Much too old to become a novice, unfortunately; oh, yes, very unfortunate. She drinks in whatever she's taught. I believe she may know almost every way there is to destroy something with the Power, but she knows almost nothing else."

He drew her to the side of the street, where the deep overhanging eaves of a single-story stone house gave a little shelter from the rain, if not from the wind to any great extent. Cadsuane was with Min and the others? It might mean nothing. He had seen Aes Sedai fascinated with Nynaeve before, and according to Min, Alivia was even stronger. "What news, Verin?" he said quietly.

The round little Aes Sedai blinked as though she forgotten there was any news, then smiled suddenly. "Oh, yes. The Seanchan. They are in Illian. Not the city, not yet; no need to go pale. But they have crossed the border. They are building fortified camps along the coast and inland. I know little of military matters. I always skip over the battles when I read a history. But it does seem to me that whether they are in the city yet or not, that is where they are aiming. Your battles don't seem to have done much to slow them. That's why I don't read about the battles. They seldom seem to alter anything in the long run, only in the short. Are you well?"

He forced his eyes open. Verin peered up at him like a chubby sparrow. All that fighting, all those men dead, men he had killed, and it had changed nothing. Nothing!

She is wrong, Lews Therin murmured in his head. *Battles can alter history.* He did not sound pleased with it. *The trouble is, sometimes you cannot say how history will be changed until it is too late.*

"Verin, if I went to Cadsuane, would she talk with me? About something other than how my manners don't suit her? That's all she ever seems to care about."

"Oh, dear. I'm afraid Cadsuane is very much a traditionalist in some ways, Rand. I've never actually heard her call a man uppity, but . . ." She laid fingertips against her mouth in thought for a moment, then nodded, raindrops sliding down her face. "I believe she will listen to what you have to say, if you can manage to erase the bad impression you made on her. Or at least smudge it, as much as you can. Few sisters are impressed by titles or crowns, Rand, and Cadsuane less than any other I know. She cares much more about whether or not people are fools. If you can show her you aren't a fool, she will listen."

"Then tell her . . ." He drew a deep breath. Light, he wanted to strangle Kisman and Dashiva and all of them with his bare hands! "Tell her I'll be leaving Far Madding tomorrow, and I hope she will come with me, as my advisor." Lews Therin sighed with relief at the first part of that; if he had been more than a voice, Rand would have said he stiffened at the second part. "Tell her I accept her terms; I apologize for my behavior in Cairhien, and I will do my best to watch my manners in the future." Saying that hardly grated at all. Well, a little, but unless Min was wrong, he needed Cadsuane, and Min was never wrong with her viewings.

"So you found what you are after here?" He frowned at her, and she smiled back and patted his arm. "If you had come to Far Madding thinking you could conquer the city by announcing who you are, you would have left as soon as you realized you cannot channel here. That leaves wanting to find something, or someone."

"Maybe I found what I need," he said curtly. Just not what he wanted.

"Then come to the Barsalla palace, on the Heights, this evening, Rand. Anyone can tell you how to find it. I really am sure she will be willing to listen to you." Shifting her cloak, she seemed to notice the dampness of the wool for the first time. "Oh, my. I must go dry off. I suggest you do the same." Half turned to leave, she paused and looked back over her shoulder at him. Her dark eyes were unblinking. Suddenly she did not sound muddled at all. "You could do far worse than Cadsuane for an advisor, Rand, but I doubt you could do better. If she accepts, and you truly are not a fool, you will listen to her advice." She glided away through the rain looking nothing so much as a very stout swan.

Sometimes that woman frightens me, Lews Therin murmured, and Rand nodded. Cadsuane did not frighten him, but she made him wary. Any Aes Sedai who had not sworn to him made him wary, except for Nynaeve. And he was not always certain of her, either.

The rain died away while he was walking the two miles back to The Counsel's Head, but the wind picked up, and the sign over the door, painted with the stern visage of a woman wearing the jeweled coronet of a First Counsel, swung on creaking hinges. The common room was smaller than that of The Golden Wheel, but the wall panels were carved and polished, the tables beneath the red ceiling beams not so crowded together. The doorway to the Women's Room was red, too, and carved like intricate lace, as were the lintels of the pale marble fireplaces. At The Counsel's Head, the serving men secured their long hair with polished silver clips. Only two of them were to be seen, standing near the kitchen door, but there were just three men at the tables, foreign merchants sitting far apart, each engrossed in his own wine. Competitors, perhaps, since now and then one or another would shift on his chair and frown at the other two. One, a graying man, wore a dark gray silk coat, and a lean fellow with a hard face had a red stone the size of a pigeon's egg in his ear. The Counsel's Head catered to the wealthier outland merchants, and there were not many of those in Far Madding at present.

The clock on a mantel in the Women's Room—a clock with a silver case, so Min said—rang the hour with small bells as he came into the common room, and before he had finished shaking out his cloak, Lan entered. As soon as the Warder met Rand's eye, he shook his head. Well, Rand had not really expected to find them at this point. Even for a *ta'veren,* that might be pushing the impossible.

Once they both had steaming cups of wine and were settled on a long red bench in front of one of the fireplaces, he told Lan what he had decided, and why. Part of why. The important part. "If I had my hands on them right this minute, I'd kill them and take my chances escaping, but killing them changes nothing. It doesn't change enough, anyway," he corrected, frowning into the flames. "I can wait one more day, hoping to find them tomorrow, for weeks. Months. Only, the world won't wait for me. I thought I'd be done with them by now, but events are already marching ahead of what I expected. Just the events I know about. Light, what's happening that I don't know about because I haven't heard some merchant nattering about it over his wine?"

"You can never know everything," Lan said quietly, "and part of what you know is always wrong. Perhaps even the most important part. A portion of wisdom lies in knowing that. A portion of courage lies in going on anyway."

Rand stretched his boots toward the fire. "Did Nynaeve tell you she and the others have been keeping company with Cadsuane? They're on a ride with her right now." On the way back from it, rather. He could feel Min drawing closer. She would not be much longer. She was still excited about something, a feeling that surged and fell as if she were trying to hold it down.

Lan smiled, a rare event without Nynaeve present. It did not reach his icy eyes, though. "She forbade me to reveal it to you, but since you already know . . . She and Min convinced Alivia that if they could catch Cadsuane's interest themselves, they might be able to bring her closer to you. They found out where she is staying and asked her to teach them." The smile faded, leaving a face carved from stone. "My wife has made a sacrifice for you, sheepherder," he said quietly. "I hope you remember that. She will not say much, but I believe Cadsuane treats her as if she were still one of the Accepted, or maybe a novice. You know how hard that would be for Nynaeve to bear."

"Cadsuane treats everyone as if they were novices," Rand muttered. Uppity? Light, how was he to deal with the woman? And yet he had to find a way. They sat in silence, staring at the fire until steam began to rise from their out-thrust bootsoles.

The bond gave him warning, and he looked around just as Nynaeve appeared through the door to the stableyard, and then Min and Alivia, shaking the rain off their cloaks and adjusting their divided skirts and grimacing at damp spots as if they had expected to go riding in this weather without getting damp. As usual, Nynaeve was wearing her jeweled *ter'angreal,* belt and necklace, bracelets and rings, and the odd bracelet-and-rings *angreal.*

Still neatening herself, Min looked at Rand and smiled, not at all surprised to see him there, of course. Warmth flowed from her along the bond like a caress, though she was still trying to suppress her excitement. The other two women took longer to notice Lan and him, but when they did, they handed their cloaks to one of the serving men to be taken up to their rooms and joined the two men at the fireplace, holding out their hands to the warmth.

"Did you enjoy your ride in the rain with Cadsuane?" Rand asked, raising his cup to take a mouthful of the sweet wine. Min's head jerked toward him, and a flash of guilt stabbed along the bond, but the expression on her face was purest indignation. He almost choked in swallowing. How was her meeting Cadsuane behind his back *his* fault? "Stop glaring at Lan, Nynaeve," he said when he could talk. "Verin told me." Nynaeve shifted her dark glower to him, and he shook his head. He had heard women say that it, whatever "it" was, was always a man's fault, but sometimes women really seemed to believe it! "I apologize for whatever you've gone through with her on my behalf," he continued, "but you won't need to any longer. I asked her to be my advisor. Or rather, I asked Verin to tell her I want to ask. Tonight. With any luck, she will leave with us tomorrow." He expected exclamations of surprised relief, but that was not what he got.

"A remarkable woman, Cadsuane," Alivia said, patting her white-threaded golden hair into place. Her husky drawl sounded impressed. "A strict taskmistress, she can teach."

"Sometimes you can see the forest, woolhead, if you're led to it by the nose," Min said, folding her arms under her breasts. The bond carried approval, but he did not think it was for deciding to give up on finding the renegades. "Remember she wants an apology for Cairhien. Think of her as your aunt, the one who won't put up with any nonsense, and you will do all right with her."

"Cadsuane is not as bad as she seems." Nynaeve frowned at the other two women, and her hand twitched toward the braid drawn over her shoulder, though all they had done was look at her. "Well, she isn't! We will work out our . . . differences . . . in time. That's all it will take. A little time."

Rand exchanged glances with Lan, who shrugged slightly and took another drink. Rand exhaled slowly. Nynaeve had differences with Cadsuane she could work out with time, Min saw a strict aunt in the woman, and Alivia a strict teacher. The first would cause sparks to fly until it was worked out, if he knew Nynaeve, and the last two he did not want. But he was stuck with them. He took another swallow of wine himself.

The men at the tables were not near enough to overhear unless she spoke loudly, but Nynaeve lowered her voice and leaned toward Rand. "Cadsuane showed me what two of my *ter'angreal* do," she whispered, a glow of excitement in her eyes. "I'll wager those ornaments she wears are *ter'angreal*, too. She recognized mine as soon as she touched them." Smiling, Nynaeve thumbed one of the three rings on her right hand, the one with a pale green stone. "I knew this would detect someone channeling *saidar* as much as three miles away, if I set it, but she says it will detect *saidin,* too. She seemed to think it should tell me what direction they were, as well, but we could not see how."

Turning from the fireplace, Alivia sniffed loudly, but she also lowered her voice to say, "And you were satisfied when she could not. I saw it on your face. How can you be satisfied with not knowing, with ignorance?"

"Just with *her* not knowing everything," Nynaeve muttered, glowering over her shoulder at the taller woman, but an instant later her smile returned. "The most important thing, Rand, is this." Her hands settled on the slim jeweled belt around her waist. "She called it a 'Well.'" He gave a start as something brushed his face, and she giggled. Nynaeve actually giggled! "It *is* a well," she laughed behind fingers pressed over her mouth, "or a barrel, anyway. And full of *saidar*. Not very much, but all I have to do to refill it is embrace *saidar* through it as if it was an *angreal*. Isn't that wonderful?"

"Wonderful," he said without much enthusiasm. So Cadsuane was walking around with *ter'angreal* in her hair, was she, and very likely one of these "wells" among them, or she would not have recognized it. Light, he thought no one had *ever* found two *ter'angreal* that did the same thing. Meeting her tonight would have been bad enough without knowing she would be able to channel, even here.

He was about to ask Min to come with him, when Mistress Keene bustled up, the white bun on top of her head drawn so tight it seemed she was trying to pull the skin off of her face. She cast a suspicious, disapproving look over Rand and Lan and pursed her lips as if considering what they had done wrong. He had seen her give the same look to the merchants who stayed at the inn. The men, anyway. If the accommodations had not been so comfortable and the food so good, she might not have had any custom.

"This was delivered for your husband this morning, Mistress Farshaw," she said, handing Min a letter sealed with an untidy blob of red wax. The innkeeper's pointed chin rose. "And a woman was inquiring after him."

"Verin," Rand said quickly, to forestall questions and get rid of the woman. Who knew to send him a letter here? Cadsuane? One of the Asha'man with her? Maybe one of the other sisters? He frowned at the folded square of paper in Min's hand, impatient for the innkeeper to leave.

Min's lips twitched, and she avoided looking at him so hard that he knew he caused the smile. Her amusement trickled through the bond. "Thank you, Mistress Keene. Verin is a friend."

That sharp chin rose higher. "If you ask me, Mistress Farshaw, when you have a pretty husband, you need to watch your friends, too."

Watching the woman march back to the red arch, Min's eyes sparkled with the mirth that flowed along the bond, and her mouth struggled against laughing. Instead of handing the message to Rand, she broke the seal with her thumb and unfolded the letter herself, for all the world as if she were a native of this mad city.

She frowned slightly as she read, but a brief flare in the bond was the only warning he had. Crumpling the letter, she turned toward the fireplace; he bounded from the bench to snatch it from her hand just before she could toss it into the flames.

"Don't be a fool," she said, catching his wrist. She stared up at him, her large dark eyes deadly serious. All that came to him through the bond was a grim intensity. "Please don't be a fool."

"I promised Verin I'd try not," he said, but Min did not smile.

He smoothed out the page on his chest. The writing was in a spidery hand he did not recognize, and there was no signature.

I know who you are, and I wish you well, but I also wish you gone from Far Madding. The Dragon Reborn leaves death and destruction where he steps. I now know why you are here, too. You killed Rochaid, and Kisman also is dead. Torval and Gedwyn have taken the top floor above a bootmaker named Zeram on Blue Carp Street, just above the Illian Gate. Kill them and go, and leave Far Madding in peace.

The clock in the Women's Room rang the hour. Hours of daylight remained before he had to meet Cadsuane.

CHAPTER

33

Blue Carp Street

Min sat cross-legged on the bed, not as comfortable a position in a riding dress as it was in breeches, and rolled one of her knives across the backs of her fingers. It was an absolutely useless skill, Thom had told her, but sometimes it caught peoples' eyes and made them pay attention without need to do more. In the middle of their room Rand was holding his scabbarded sword up to study the cuts he had made in the peace-bond, and paid her no attention at all. The Dragon's heads on the backs of his hands glittered, metallic red and gold.

"You admit this has to be a trap," she growled at him. "Lan admits it. A half-blind goat in Seleisin has more brains than to walk into a trap! 'Only fools kiss hornets or bite fire!'" she quoted.

"A trap isn't really a trap if you know it's there," he said absently, bending the end of one of the severed wires a little to line up better with its mate. "If you know it's there, maybe you can see a way to walk in so it isn't a trap at all."

She threw the knife as hard as she could. It flew in front of his face to stick quivering in the door, and she gave a little jump recalling the last time she had done that. Well, she was not lying on top of him, now, and Cadsuane was not going to walk in, worse luck. Burn the man, that frozen knot of emotions in her head had not even quivered when the knife streaked by, not by so much as a flicker of surprise! "Even if you just see Gedwyn and Torval, you know the others will be there, hiding. Light, they could have fifty sell-swords waiting!"

"In Far Madding?" He stopped looking at the knife sticking in the door, but only to shake his head and go back to examining the peace-bond. "I doubt there are two mercenaries in the whole city, Min. Believe me, I don't intend to get myself killed here. Unless I can see how to spring the trap without getting caught, I won't go near it." There was no more fear in him than in a stone! And about as much sense! He did not intend to get killed, as if anyone ever *intended* to!

Scrambling off the bed, she opened the front of the bedside table long enough to take out the strap that Mistress Keene made sure was in every room, even if she did rent to outlanders. The thing was as long as her arm and as wide as her hand, with a wooden handle at one end and the other end split into three tails. "Maybe if I took this to you, it would clear your nose enough to smell what's in front of you!" she cried.

That was when Nynaeve and Lan and Alivia walked in. Nynaeve and Lan were cloaked, and Lan had his sword at his hip. Nynaeve had removed all of the jewelry except for one gemmed bracelet and the jeweled belt, the Well. Lan closed the door quietly. Nynaeve and Alivia stood staring at Min with the strap raised over her head.

Hastily she dropped the thing to the flowered carpet and kicked it underneath the bed with the side of her foot. "I don't understand why you're letting Lan do this, Nynaeve," she said as firmly as she could. At the moment, that was not particularly firm. Why did people *always* walk in at the worst time?

"A sister has to trust her Warder's judgment sometimes," Nynaeve said coolly, drawing on her gloves. Her face belonged on a porcelain doll for all the emotion it displayed. Oh, she was being Aes Sedai to her toenails.

He isn't your Warder, he's your husband, Min wanted to say, *and at least you can go along to look after him. I don't know if my Warder will* ever *marry me, and he threatened to tie me up if I* tried *to go with him!* Not that she had argued very hard on that point. If he was going to be a bullgoose fool, there were better ways to save him than trying to stick a knife in somebody.

"If we are going to do this, sheepherder," Lan said grimly, "best we be about it while there's still light to see." His blue eyes seemed colder than ever, and hard as polished stones. Nynaeve gave him a worried look that almost made Min feel sorry for her. Almost.

Rand belted his sword over his coat, then settled his cloak with the hood hanging down his back and turned toward her. His face was as hard as Lan's, his blue-gray eyes almost as cold, but in her head that frozen stone blazed with veins of fiery gold. She wanted to tangle her hands in the black-dyed hair that almost brushed his shoulders and kiss him no matter how many people were watching. Instead, she folded her arms across her chest and lifted her chin, making her disapproval clear. She did not intend for him to die here, either, and she was not about to let him start thinking she would give in just because he was stubborn.

He did not try to take her in his arms. Nodding as if he actually understood, he picked up his gloves from the small table by the door. "I'll be back as soon as I can, Min. Then we'll go to Cadsuane." Those golden veins continued to glow even after he left the room, followed by Lan.

Nynaeve paused, holding the door. "I will look after them both, Min. Alivia, please stay with her and see she doesn't do anything foolish." She was all cool, dignified Aes Sedai composure. Until she glanced into the hallway. "Burn them!" she yelped. "They're leaving!" And she ran, leaving the door standing half open.

Alivia closed it. "Shall we play games to pass the time, Min?" Crossing the carpet, she sat down on the stool in front of the fireplace and took a piece of string from her beltpouch. "Cat's cradle?"

"No, thank you, Alivia," Min said, almost shaking her head at the eagerness in the woman's voice. Rand might be complacent about what Alivia was going to do, but Min had set herself to get to know her, and what she had found was startling. On the surface, the former *damane* was a mature woman who appeared well into her middle years, stern and fierce and even intimidating. She certainly managed to intimidate Nynaeve. Nynaeve seldom said please to anyone except Alivia. But she had been made *damane* at fourteen, and her love of playing children's games was not the only oddity about her.

Min wished there was a clock in the room, though the only inn she could imagine with a clock in every room would be an inn for queens and kings. Pacing back and forth under Alivia's watchful gaze, she counted seconds in her head, trying to judge how long it would take Rand and the others to go beyond sight of the inn. When she decided enough time had passed, she took her cloak from the wardrobe.

Alivia darted to block the door, hands on her hips, and there was nothing childlike in her expression. "You aren't going after them," she drawled in a firm voice. "It would only cause trouble, now, and I can't allow that." With those blue eyes and that golden hair, her coloring was all wrong, but she reminded Min of her Aunt Rana, who always seemed to know when you had done something wrong and always saw to it that you did not want to do it again.

"Do you remember those talks we had about men, Alivia?" The other woman turned bright red, and Min hurriedly added, "I mean the one about how they don't always think with their brains." She had often heard women sneer that some other woman knew nothing about men, but she had never actually met one of those until she encountered Alivia. She really did know nothing! "Rand will get himself in more than enough trouble without me. *I* am going to find Cadsuane, and if you try to stop me . . ." She held up a clenched fist.

For a long moment, Alivia frowned at her. Finally she said, "Let me get my cloak, and I'll go with you."

There were no sedan chairs or liveried servants to be seen on Blue Carp Street, and carriages would never have fit along the narrow, twisting passage. Slate-roofed stone shops and houses lined the street, most of two stories, sometimes jammed one hard against the next and sometimes with a little alleyway between. The pavement was still slick from the rain, and the cold wind tried to carry Rand's cloak away, but people were back out and bustling about. Three Street Guards, one with a catchpole on his shoulder, paused to glance at Rand's sword, then went on their way. Not far along on the other side of the street, the building housing the shop of the bootmaker Zeram rose a full three stories, not counting the attic under the peaked roof.

A skinny man with very little chin dropped Rand's coin into his purse and used a thin strip of wood to lift a brown-crusted meatpie from the charcoal grill on his barrow. His face was lined, his dark coat shabby, and his long graying hair was tied with a leather cord. His eyes flickered to Rand's sword, and looked away quickly. "Why do you ask about the bootmaker? That's the best mutton, there." A toothy grin made his chin almost vanish, and his eyes suddenly looked very shifty. "First Counsel herself don't eat better."

There were meat pies called pasties when I was a boy, Lews Therin murmured. *We would buy them in the country and . . .*

Juggling the pie from hand to hand, the heat soaking through his gloves, Rand suppressed the voice. "I like to know what kind of man makes my boots. Is he suspicious of strangers, for instance? A man doesn't do his best work if he's suspicious of you."

"Yes, Mistress," the chinless fellow said, ducking his head to a stout gray-haired woman with a squint. Wrapping four meat pies in coarse paper, he handed her the package before taking her coins. "A pleasure, Mistress. The Light shine on you." She tottered away without a word, clutching the wrapped pies under her cloak, and he grimaced sourly at her back before returning his attention to Rand. "Zeram never had a suspicious bone, and if he did, Milsa wouldn't let him keep it. That's his wife. Since the last of the children married, Milsa's been renting out the top floor. Whenever she finds somebody don't mind being locked in at night, anyway," he laughed. "Milsa had stairs put in right up to the third floor, so it's private, but she wouldn't pay for having a new door cut as well, so the stairs come out in the shop, and she's not trusting enough to leave that unlocked at night. You going to eat that pie, or just look at it?"

Taking a quick bite, Rand wiped hot juice from his chin and walked over to shelter beneath the eaves of a small cutler's shop. Along the street others were snatching a quick meal from the food-peddlers, meat pies or fried fish or twisted paper cones heaped with roasted peas. Three or four men as tall as he, and two or three women as tall as most of the other men in the street, might have been Aiel. Maybe the chinless fellow was not as shifty as he seemed, or maybe it was just that Rand had eaten nothing since breakfast, but Rand found himself wanting to gobble the pie down and buy another. Instead, he made himself eat slowly. Zeram seemed to be doing a good business. A steady if not constant flow of men went into his shop, most carrying a pair of boots to be mended. Even if he let visitors go up without sending word ahead, he would be able to identify them later, and maybe so would two or three others.

If the renegades were renting the top floor from the boot-maker's wife, being locked in at night would not inconvenience them much. To the south, an alleyway separated the bootmaker's from a single-story house, a dangerous drop, but on the other side, a two-story building with a seamstress on the ground floor stood wall-to-wall with the bootmaker. Zeram's building had no windows except at the front—in back was another alley, for taking away rubbish; Rand had already checked—but there had to be a way onto the roof so the slates could be repaired when necessary. From there it would be a short drop to the seamstress's roof, with only three more to cross before another low building, a candle-maker's shop, and an easy jump to the street, or into the alley behind the buildings. There would not be a great deal of risk in it at night, or even in daylight, if you stayed back from the street and were careful about the Guard's patrols when you came down. The way Blue Carp Street bent, the nearest watchstands were out of sight.

Two men approaching the bootmaker's made him turn away and pretend to peer through the bubbled panes of the cutler's small shopwindow at a display of scissors and knives fastened to a board. One of the men was tall, though not as tall as the possible Aielmen. Their deep cowls hid their faces, but neither carried a pair of boots, and although they held their cloaks with both hands, the wind flipped the tails of them enough to show the bottoms of scabbarded swords. A gust pulled the shorter man's hood from his head, and he snatched it back again, but not before the damage was done. Charl Gedwyn had taken to wearing his hair caught at the nape of his neck in a silver clip set with a large red stone, but he was still a hard-faced man with a challenging look about him. And Gedwyn's presence made the other Torval. Rand was willing to wager on it. None of the others was as tall.

Waiting until the pair had gone into Zeram's shop, Rand licked a few greasy crumbs from his gloves and went in

search of Nynaeve and Lan. He found them before he was
far enough along the curve of the street to lose sight of the
bootmaker's. The candlemaker's he had marked as a way
down from the rooftops stood a little behind him, with an
alley at one side. Ahead, the narrow street twisted back the
other way. No more than fifty paces farther on was a watchstand with a Street Guard at the top, but another building
of three stories, a cabinetmaker's that shared the alleyway
with the candlemaker, blocked the rooftops beyond from
his view.

"Half a dozen people recognized Torval and Gedwyn,"
Lan said, "but none of the others." He kept his voice low,
though no one passing more than glanced at the three of
them. A glimpse of two men wearing swords beneath their
cloaks was enough to make everyone who noticed step a
little faster.

"A butcher down the street says those two buy from him,"
Nynaeve said, "but never more than enough for two." She
looked sideways at Lan as though hers was the real proof.

"I saw them," Rand said. "They're inside now. Nynaeve,
can you lift Lan and me to that rooftop from the alley behind the building?"

Nynaeve frowned at Zeram's building, rubbing the belt
around her waist with one hand. "One at a time, I could,"
she said finally. "But it would use more than half what the
Well holds. I wouldn't be able to lift you down again."

"Up is enough," Rand told her. "We will leave over the
rooftops, and climb down right over beside the candlemaker."

She protested, of course, as they walked back down the
street toward the bootmaker's shop. Nynaeve always fought
anything she had not thought of herself. "I am just supposed
to put you on the roof and wait?" she muttered, scowling
left and right so hard that as many people shied away from
her as from the men flanking her, swords or no swords. She
thrust her hand out from under her cloak to show the bracelet with its pale red stones. "This can cover me with armor
better than any steel. I'd hardly even feel a sword hitting
me. I *thought* I would be going inside with you."

"And do what?" Rand asked softly. "Hold them with the
Power for us to kill? Kill them yourself?" She frowned at
the paving stones in front of her feet.

Walking beyond Zeram's shop, Rand paused in front of the low house and looked around as casually as he could. There were no Street Guards in sight, but when he prodded Nynaeve into the narrow alley, he moved quickly. He had not seen any Guards before following Rochaid, either.

"You are very quiet," Lan said, following close behind.

She took three more quick steps before replying, without slowing or looking back. "I didn't think, before," she said quietly. "I was thinking of it as an adventure, confronting Darkfriends, renegade Asha'man, but you are going up there to execute them. You'll kill them before they know you're there if you can, won't you?"

Rand glanced over, his shoulder at Lan, but the older man only shook his head, as confused as he was. Of course they would kill them without warning if they could. This was not a duel; it was the execution she had named it. At least, Rand hoped very much it would be.

The alley that ran behind the buildings was a little wider than the one to the street, the rocky soil rutted with the tracks of the rubbish barrows that were pushed along it mornings. Blank stone walls rose around them. No one wanted a window to watch the rubbish carts.

Nynaeve stood peering up at the back of Zeram's building, then suddenly sighed. "Kill them in their sleep, if you can," she said, very quietly for such fierce words.

Something unseen wrapped snugly around Rand's chest beneath his arms, and slowly he rose into the air, floating higher until he drifted over the edge of the overhanging eave. The invisible harness vanished, and his boots dropped to the sloping roof, sliding a little on the damp gray slates. Crouching, he moved back on all fours. A few moments later, Lan floated up to land on the roof, too. The Warder crouched as well, and peered into the alley below.

"She is gone," Lan said finally. Twisting around to face Rand, he pointed. "There is our way in."

It was a trapdoor set among the slates high toward the peak, with metal flashing to keep water out of the attic that lifting it revealed. Rand lowered himself into a dusty space, dimly lit by the light through the trapdoor. For a moment, he hung by his hands, then let go, dropping the last few feet. Except for a chair with three legs and a chest with the lid thrown open, the long room was as empty as the chest. Apparently Zeram had stopped using the attic for storage when his wife began taking renters.

Stepping lightly, the two men searched the floorboards until they found another, larger trapdoor lying flat against the floor. Lan felt the brass hinges and whispered that they were dry but unrusted. Rand drew his sword and nodded, and Lan snatched the trapdoor open.

Rand was not sure what he would find when he sprang down through the opening, using a hand on the coping to control his fall. He landed lightly on the balls of his feet, in a room that seemed to have taken the attic's place from the wardrobes and cabinets shoved against the walls, the wooden chests piled on one another and tables with chairs standing atop them. The last thing he expected, though, was two dead men sprawled on the floor as if they had been dragged into the storage room and flung down. The black swollen faces were unrecognizable, but the shorter of the pair wore a silver hairclip set with a large red stone.

Dropping soundlessly from the attic, Lan looked at the corpses and raised an eyebrow. That was all. Nothing ever surprised him.

"Fain is here," Rand whispered. As if saying the name were a trigger, the twin wounds in his side began throbbing, the older like a disc of ice, the newer a bar of fire across it. "It was him sent the letter."

Lan gestured toward the trapdoor with his sword, but Rand shook his head. He had wanted to kill the renegades with his own hands, yet now that Torval and Gedwyn were dead—and almost certainly Kisman, too; there was that swollen corpse mentioned by the merchant at The Golden Wheel—now, he realized he did not care who killed them so long as they were dead. If a stranger finished Dashiva, it would not matter. Fain was another matter. Fain had harrowed the Two Rivers with Trollocs, and given him a second wound that would not heal. If Fain was within reach, Rand would not allow him to escape. He motioned for Lan to do as they had in the attic, and set himself in front of the door with his sword in both hands. When the other man pulled the door open, he darted into a large lamplit room with a posted bed against the far wall and a fire crackling in a small fireplace.

Only the speed of his movement saved him. A flicker of

movement caught the corner of his eye, something tugged at the cloak billowing behind him, and he spun awkwardly to fend off slashes of a curved dagger. Every movement was an effort of will. The wounds in his side no longer throbbed; they clawed at him, molten iron and the very soul of ice warring to rip him open. Lews Therin howled. It was all Rand could do to think, with the agony.

"I told you he's mine!" the bony man screamed, dancing away from Rand's cut. With his face contorted in fury, his big nose and ears that stuck out made him seem something contrived to frighten children, but his eyes held murder. Teeth bared in a snarl, he looked like a weasel wild with killing fury. A rabid weasel, ready to savage even a leopard. With that dagger, he could kill any number of leopards. "Mine!" Padan Fain shrieked, leaping back again as Lan rushed into the room. "Kill the ugly one!"

Only when Lan turned away from Fain did Rand realize someone else was in the room, a tall pale man who came almost eagerly to meet the Warder blade to blade. Toram Riatin's face was haggard, but he flowed into the dance of swords with the grace of the blademaster he was. Lan met him with an equal grace, a dance of steel and death.

Startled as Rand was to see the man who had tried to claim the throne of Cairhien in a worn coat in Far Madding, he kept his eyes on Fain and his sword toward the one time peddler. Darkfriend and worse, Moiraine had called him long ago. The blinding pain in Rand's side made him stumble as he advanced on Fain, ignoring the stamp of boots and the ring of steel on steel behind him as he ignored Lews Therin's groans in his head. Fain danced and darted, trying to get close enough to use the dagger that had made the never-healing slash in Rand's side, growling curses in a low voice as Rand's blade forced him back. Abruptly he turned and ran, toward the back of the building.

The torment tearing at Rand faded to mere throbbing as Fain vanished from the room, but he followed cautiously even so. At the doorway, though, he saw that Fain was not trying to hide. The man stood waiting for him at the head of stairs leading down, the curved dagger in one hand. The large ruby capping the hilt glittered, catching the light of the lamps set on tables about the windowless room. As soon as Rand stepped into the room, fire and ice raged in his side till he could feel his heart shuddering. Staying upright was an effort of iron will. Taking a step forward made that effort seem pale, but he took that step, and the next.

"I want him to know who is killing him," Fain whined petulantly. He was glaring straight at Rand, but he seemed to be talking to himself. "I want him to know! But if he's dead, then he will stop haunting my dreams. Yes. He will stop, then." With a smile, he raised his free hand.

Torval and Gedwyn came up the stairs with their cloaks over their arms.

"I say we aren't going near him until I know where the others are," Gedwyn growled. "The M'Hael will kill us if . . ."

Without thought, Rand twisted his wrists in Cutting the Wind and immediately followed with Unfolding the Fan.

The illusion of dead men come back to life vanished, and Fain leaped back with a shriek, blood streaming down the side of his face. Suddenly he tilted his head as though listening, and a moment later, aiming a scream of wordless fury at Rand, he fled down the stairs.

Wondering, Rand moved to follow the descending thumps of Fain's boots, but Lan caught his arm.

"The street out front is filling up with Guards, sheepherder." A dark wetness stained the left side of Lan's coat, but his sword was sheathed, proof of who had danced that dance the better. "Time we were on the roof, if we're going."

"A man can't even walk down an alley with a sword in this city," Rand muttered, sheathing his own blade. Lan did not laugh, but then, he seldom did except for Nynaeve. Shouts and screams rose up the stairwell from below. Maybe the Street Guards would capture Fain. Maybe he would hang for the corpses up here. It was not enough, but it would have to do. Rand was tired of what would have to do.

In the attic, Lan leapt to catch the coping of the trapdoor in the roof and pull himself up and out. Rand was not sure he could make that leap. The agony was gone with Fain, but his side felt as if it had been beaten with axehandles. As he was gathering himself to try, Lan put his head back through the trapdoor and extended a hand.

"They may not come up right away, sheepherder, but is there any point in waiting to see?"

Rand caught Lan's hand and let himself be drawn up to where he could catch the coping and pull himself out onto the roof. Crouching low, they moved along the damp slates to the back of the building, then began the short climb to the peak. There might be Guards in the street, but there was still a chance to get away unseen, especially if they could signal Nynaeve to make a distraction.

Rand reached for the roof peak, and behind him, Lan's boot slipped on the slates with a screech. Twisting around, Rand seized the other man's wrist, but Lan's weight pulled him down the slick gray slope. Vainly they scrabbled with their free hands for any hold, the edge of a slate, anything. Neither uttered a word. Lan's legs went over the edge, and then the rest of him. Rand's gloved fingers caught on something; he did not know what, and he did not care. His head and one shoulder stuck over the edge of the roof, and Lan was dangling from his grip above the ten-pace drop to the alley next to the low house.

"Let go," Lan said quietly. He looked up at Rand, his eyes cold and hard, no expression on his face. "Let go."

"When the sun turns green," Rand told him. If he could just pull the other man up a little, enough to catch the eave . . .

Whatever his fingers had caught broke with a sharp snap, and the alley rushed up to meet them.

CHAPTER
34

The Hummingbird's Secret

Trying not to be too obvious about watching the alley beside the candlemaker's, Nynaeve set the folded length of flat green braid back on the hawker's tray and slipped her hand inside her cloak to help hold it shut against the wind. It was a finer cloak than any on the people walking by, but plain enough that no one more than glanced at her in passing. They would if they saw her belt, though. Women who wore jewels did not frequent Blue Carp Street, or buy from street peddlers. After standing there for her to finger every last bit of braid on the tray, the lean woman grimaced, but Nynaeve had already bought three pieces of braid, two lengths of ribbon and a packet of pins from hawkers, just for a reason to loiter. Pins were always useful, but she did not know what she was going to do with the rest.

Suddenly she heard a commotion down the street, in the direction of the watchstand, the racket of Street Guards' rattles loud and growing louder. The Guardsman scrambled down from his perch. Passersby near the watchstand stared down the crossing street and further up Blue Carp Street, then hurriedly pressed themselves against the sides of the street as running Guardsmen appeared, swinging their wooden rattles overhead. Not a patrol of two or three, but a flood of armored men pounding down Blue Carp Street, and more joining the tide from the other street. People slow to get out of their way were shoved aside, and one man went down under their boots. They did not slow a step as they trampled him.

The braid-seller spilled half her tray scrambling to the side of the street, and Nynaeve was just as quick to squeeze herself against the stone housefront alongside the gaping woman. Filling the street, catchpoles and quarterstaffs jutting up like pikes, the mass of Guardsmen bumped her with shoulders, scraping her along the wall. The braid-seller yelled as her tray was ripped away and vanished, but the Guards were all staring ahead.

When the last man ran past, Nynaeve was a good ten paces farther down the street than she had been. The braid-seller shouted angrily and shook her fists at the men's backs. Indignantly pulling her twisted cloak into some proper order, Nynaeve was of a mind to do more than shout. She was half of a mind to . . .

Abruptly her breath froze in her throat. The Street Guards had stopped in a mass, perhaps a hundred men shouting to one another as if they suddenly were uncertain what to do next. They were stopped in front of the bootmaker's shop. Oh, Light, Lan. And Rand, too, always Rand, but first and foremost always the heart of her heart, Lan.

She made herself breathe. A hundred men. She touched the jeweled belt, the Well, around her waist. Less than half the *saidar* she had stored in it remained, but it might be enough. It would have to be enough, though she did not know for what exactly, yet. Tugging the cowl of her cloak up, she started toward the men in front of the bootmaker's. None was looking her way. She could . . .

Hands seized her, dragging her backward and spinning her around to face the other direction.

Cadsuane had one of her arms, she realized, and Alivia the other, the pair of them hurrying her along the street. Away from the bootmaker's. Walking beside Alivia, Min kept casting worried looks over her shoulder. Abruptly she flinched. "He . . . I think he fell," she whispered. "I think he's unconscious, but he's hurt, I don't know how badly."

"We will do him no good here, or ourselves," Cadsuane said calmly. The golden ornaments dangling from the front of her bun swung inside the hood of her cloak as she swivelled her head, her eyes searching through the people ahead of them. She held the deep cowl against the wind with her free hand, letting her cloak flap behind her. "I want to be away from here before one of those boys thinks of asking women to show their faces. Any Aes Sedai found near Blue Carp Street this afternoon will have questions to answer because of this child."

"Let me go!" Nynaeve snapped, pulling against them. Lan. If Rand had been knocked unconscious, what of Lan? "I have to go back and help them!" The two women dragged her along with hands like iron. Everyone they passed was peering toward the bootmaker's shop.

"You have done quite enough already, you fool girl." Cadsuane's voice was cold iron. "I *told* you about Far Madding's watchdogs. Phaw! You've put a panic in the Counsels with your channeling where *no* one can channel. If the Guards have them, it is because of you."

"I thought *saidar* wouldn't matter," Nynaeve said weakly. "It was only a little, and not for long. I . . . I thought maybe they wouldn't even notice."

Cadsuane gave her a disgusted glance. "This way, Alivia," she said, pulling Nynaeve around the corner by the abandoned watchstand. Small knots of excited people dotted the street, jabbering. A man gestured vigorously as if wielding a catchpole. A woman pointed to the empty watchstand, shaking her head in wonder.

"Say something, Min," Nynaeve pleaded. "We can't just leave them." She did not even think of addressing Alivia, who wore a face to make Cadsuane appear soft.

"Don't expect sympathy from me." Min's low voice was almost as chill as Cadsuane's. When she looked at Nynaeve, it was a sidelong glare before snapping her eyes back to the street ahead. "I begged you to help me stop them, but you had to be as wool-headed as they were. Now we have to depend on Cadsuane."

Nynaeve sniffed. "What can she do? Do I need to remind you that Lan and Rand are behind us, and getting farther behind by the minute?"

"The boy isn't the only one who needs lessons in manners," Cadsuane muttered. "He hasn't apologized to me, yet, but he told Verin he would, and I suppose I can accept that for the moment. Phaw! That boy puts me to more trouble than any ten I ever met before. I will do what I can, girl, which is a sight more than you could do trying to batter your way through the Street Guards. From here on, you will do exactly as I say, or I will have Alivia sit on you!" Alivia nodded. So did Min!

Nynaeve grimaced. The woman was *supposed* to defer to her! Still, a guest of the First Counsel *could* do more than plain Nynaeve al'Meara, even if she donned her Great Serpent ring. For Lan, she could put up with Cadsuane.

But when she asked what Cadsuane planned to do to free the men, the only answer the woman would give was "Much more than I want to, girl, if I can do anything at all. But I made the boy promises, and I keep my promises. I hope he remembers that." Delivered in a voice like ice, it was not a reply to inspire confidence.

Rand woke in darkness and pain, lying on his back. His gloves were gone, and he could feel a rough pallet beneath him. They had taken his boots, too. His gloves were gone. They knew who he was. Carefully, he sat up. His face felt bruised and every muscle in his body hurt as if he had been beaten, but nothing seemed to be broken.

Standing slowly, he felt his way along the stone wall beside the pallet, reaching a corner almost immediately, and then a door covered with rough iron straps. In the darkness his fingers traced a small flap, but he could not push it open. No hint of light seeped in around its edges. Inside his head, Lews Therin began to pant. Rand moved on, feeling his way, the floorstones cold beneath his bare feet. The next corner came almost immediately, and then a third, where his toes struck something that rattled on the stone floor. Keeping one hand on the wall, he bent and found a wooden bucket. He left it there and made himself complete the circuit, all the way back to the iron door. All the way. He was inside a black box three paces long and just over two paces wide. Raising one hand, he found the stone ceiling less than a foot above his head.

Closed in, Lews Therin panted hoarsely. *It's the box again. When those women put us in the box. We have to get out!* he howled. *We have to get out!*

Ignoring the screaming voice in his head, Rand backed away from the door until he thought he was in the center of the cell, then lowered himself to sit cross-legged on the floor. He was as far from the walls as he could put himself, and in the dark he tried to imagine them farther away, but it seemed that if he reached out, he would not have to straighten his arm fully to touch stone. He could feel himself trembling, as if it were someone else's body shaking uncontrollably. The walls seemed just beside him, the ceiling right over his head. He had to fight this, or he would be as mad as Lews Therin by the time anyone came to let him out. They would have to let him out eventually, if only to hand him over to whoever Elaida sent. How many months for a message to reach Tar Valon and Elaida's emissaries to return? If there were sisters loyal to Elaida closer than Tar Valon, it might happen sooner. Horror added to his shudders as he realized that he was hoping those sisters were closer, were in the city already, so they could take him out of this box.

"I will not surrender!" he shouted. "I will be as hard as I need to be!" In that confined space, his voice boomed like thunder.

Moiraine had died because he was not hard enough to do what had to be done. Her name always headed the list engraved on his brain, the women who had died because of him. Moiraine Damodred. Every name on that list brought anguish that made him forget the pains of his body, forget the stone walls just beyond his fingertips. Colavaere Saighan, who died because he had stripped her of everything she valued. Liah, Maiden of the Spear, of the Cosaida Chareen, who died at his own hands because she followed him to Shadar Logoth. Jendhilin, a Maiden of the Cold Peak Miagoma who died because she wanted the honor of guarding his door. He had to be hard! One by one he summoned up the names on that long list, patiently forging his soul in the fires of pain.

Preparation took longer than Cadsuane had hoped, largely because she had to impress on various people that a grand rescue in the best traditions of gleemen's tales was out of the question, so it was night before she found herself walking along the lamplit corridors of the Hall of the Counsels. Walking sedately, not hurrying. Hurry, and people assumed that you were anxious, that they had the upper hand. If ever in her life she had needed to keep the upper hand from the start, it was tonight.

The corridors should have been empty at this hour, but today's events had changed the normal course of things. Blue-coated clerks were scurrying everywhere, sometimes pausing to gape at her companions. Quite possibly, they had never seen four Aes Sedai at once—she was not willing to allow Nynaeve that title until she took the Three Oaths—and today's commotion would have added to their confusion at the sight. The three men bringing up the rear earned almost as many stares, though. The clerks might not know the meaning of their black coats or the pins on their high collars, but it was very unlikely any of those clerks had ever seen three men wearing swords in these hallways. In any case, with a little luck, no one would go running to inform Aleis who was coming to break in on the Counsels sitting in closed session. It was a pity she could not have brought the men by themselves, but even Daigian had displayed backbone at the suggestion. A great pity that all of her companions were not displaying the composure showed by Merise and the other two sisters.

"This will never work," Nynaeve grumbled, for perhaps the tenth time since leaving the Heights. "We should strike hard from the start!"

"We should have moved faster," Min muttered darkly. "I can feel him changing. If he was a stone before, he's iron, now! Light, what are they doing to him?" Along only because she was a link to the boy, she had been unceasing with her reports, each bleaker than the last. Cadsuane had not told her what the cells were like, not when the girl had broken down just telling her what the sisters who kidnapped the boy had done to him.

Cadsuane sighed. A ragtag army she had assembled, but even a makeshift army needed discipline. Especially with the battle just ahead. It would have been worse had she not forced the Sea Folk women to remain behind. "I can do this without either of you, if need be," she said firmly. "No; don't say anything, Nynaeve. Merise or Corele can wear that belt as well as you. So if you children do not stop whining, I will have Alivia take you back to the Heights and give you something to whine about." That was the only reason she had brought the strange wilder. Alivia had a tendency to become very mild-mannered around those she could not stare down, but she stared very fiercely at those two chattering magpies.

Their heads swiveled toward the golden-haired woman as one, and the magpies fell blessedly silent. Silent, yet hardly accepting. Min could grind her teeth all she wanted, but Nynaeve's sullen glower irritated Cadsuane. The girl had good material in her, but her training had been cut far too short. Her ability with Healing was little short of miraculous, her ability with almost anything else dismal. And she had not been put through the lessons that what must be endured, could be endured. In truth, Cadsuane sympathized with her. Somewhat. It was a lesson not everyone could learn in the Tower. She herself, full of pride in her new shawl and her own strength, had been taught by a near toothless wilder at a farm in the heart of the Black Hills. Oh, it was a very ragtag little army she had gathered to try standing Far Madding on its head.

Clerks and messengers half-filled the columned anteroom to the Counsels' Chamber, but they were, after all, only clerks and messengers. The clerks hesitated in officious puzzlement, each waiting for another to speak first, but the red-coated messengers, who knew it was not their place to say anything, backed across the blue floortiles to the sides of the room, and the clerks parted in front of her, none quite daring to be the first to open his mouth. Even so, she heard a collective gasp when she opened one of the tall doors carved with the Hand and Sword.

The Counsels' Chamber was not large. Four mirrored stand-lamps sufficed to light it, and a large Tairen carpet in red and blue and gold almost covered the floor tiles. A wide marble fireplace on one side of the room made a fair job of warming the air, though the glassed doors leading to the colonnade outside rattled in the night wind, loud enough to drown the ticking of the tall, gilded Illianer clock on the mantel. Thirteen carved and gilded chairs, very nearly thrones, made an arc facing the door, all occupied by worried-looking women.

Aleis, at the head of the arc, frowned when she saw Cadsuane lead her little parade into the chamber. "This session is closed, Aes Sedai," she said, at once formal and cold. "We may ask you to speak to us later, but—"

"You know who you have in the cells," Cadsuane cut in.

It was not a question, but Aleis tried to bluff her way past. "A number of men, I believe. Public drunkards, various foreigners arrested for fighting or stealing, a man from the Borderlands taken just today who may have murdered three men. I do not keep a personal record of arrests, Cadsuane Sedai." Nynaeve drew a deep breath at mention of a man taken for murder, and her eyes glittered dangerously, but at the least the child had sense enough to keep her mouth shut.

"So you will try to conceal that you hold the Dragon Reborn," Cadsuane said quietly. She had hoped—hoped fervently!—that Verin's spadework would make them back away from this. Perhaps it could still be done simply, though. "I can take him off your hands. I have faced more than twenty men who could channel, over the years. He holds no fears for me."

"We do thank you for the offer," Aleis replied smoothly, "but we prefer to communicate with Tar Valon, first." To negotiate his price, she meant. Well, what had to be, had to be. "Do you mind telling us how you learned—"

Cadsuane broke in again. "Perhaps I should have mentioned earlier, these men behind me are Asha'man."

The three stepped forward then, as they had been instructed, and she had to admit they gave a dangerous appearance. Grizzled Damer looked a graying bear with sore teeth, pretty Jahar seemed a dark, sleek leopard, and Eben's unblinking gaze was particularly ominous coming from that youthful face. They certainly had their effect on the Counsels. Some simply shifted in their chairs as if to draw back, but Cyprien let her mouth fall open, unfortunate with her protruding teeth. Sybaine, her hair as gray as Cadsuane's, sagged back in her chair and began fanning herself with a slender hand, while Cumere's mouth twisted as if she might vomit.

Aleis was made of sterner stuff, though she pressed both hands tight against her midriff. "I told you once that Asha'man were free to visit so long as they obeyed the law. We have no fear of Asha'man, Cadsuane, though I must say I am surprised to see you in their company. Particularly in view of the offer you have just made."

So, she was plain Cadsuane now, was she? Still, she regretted the necessity to break Aleis. She led Far Madding well, but she might never recover from tonight. "Are you forgetting what else happened today, Aleis? Someone channeled inside the city." Again Counsels shifted, and worried frowns creased more than one forehead.

"An aberration." The coolness was gone from Aleis'

voice, replaced by anger, and maybe a touch of fear. Her eyes shone darkly. "Perhaps the guardians were in error. No one who was questioned saw anything to suggest—"

"Even what we think is perfect can have flaws, Aleis." Cadsuane drew on her own Well, taking in *saidar* in a measured amount. She had practice; the little golden hummingbird could not hold near so much as Nynaeve's belt. "Flaws can pass unnoticed for centuries before they are found." The flow of Air she wove was just enough to lift the gem-encrusted coronet from Aleis' head and set it on the carpet in front of the woman's feet. "Once they are found, however, it seems that anyone who looks can find them."

Thirteen sets of shocked eyes stared at the coronet. One and all, the Counsels seemed frozen, barely breathing.

"Not so much a flaw as a barn door, seems to me," Damer announced. "I think it's prettier on your head."

The glow of the Power suddenly shone around Nynaeve, and the coronet flew toward Aleis, slowing at the last instant so that it settled above her bloodless face rather than cracking her head. The light of *saidar* did not vanish from the girl, though. Well, let her drain her Well.

"Will . . . ?" Aleis swallowed, but when she went on, her voice still cracked. "Will it be sufficient if we release him to you?" Whether she meant Cadsuane or the Asha'man was unclear, perhaps even to her.

"I think that it will," Cadsuane said calmly, and Aleis sagged like a stringless puppet. Shocked as they were by the display of channeling, questioning looks passed between the other Counsels. Eyes darted toward Aleis, faces firmed, nods were exchanged. Cadsuane drew a deep breath. She had promised the boy that whatever she did would be for his good, not the good of the Tower or anyone else's, and now she had broken a good woman for his good. "I am very sorry, Aleis," she said. *You are building up a large account already, boy,* she thought.

CHAPTER
35

With the Choedan Kal

Rand rode across the wide stone bridge leading north from the Caemlyn Gate without looking back. The sun was a pale golden ball just risen above the horizon in a cloudless sky, but the air was cold enough to mist his breath, and the lake winds made his cloak fly about. He did not feel the chill, though, except as something distant and not really connected to him. He was colder than any winter could be. The guards who had come to take him out of the cell the night before had been surprised to find him wearing a small smile. He wore it still, a slight curve of his mouth. Nynaeve had Healed his bruises using the last of the *saidar* in her belt, yet the helmeted officer who came into the road at the foot of the bridge, a stocky man with blunt features, gave a start at the sight of him, as though his face was still swollen and purple.

Cadsuane leaned from her saddle to speak a few quiet words and hand the officer a folded paper. He frowned at her and began to read, then jerked his head up to stare in amazement at the men and women waiting patiently on their horses behind her. Starting again at the top of the page, he read moving his lips silently, as if he wanted to be sure of every word, and small wonder. Signed and sealed by all thirteen Counsels, the order said that there was to be no checking of peace-bonds, no search of the packhorses. This party's names were to be blotted out completely in the record books, and the order itself burned. They had never come to Far Madding. No Aes Sedai, no Atha'an Miere, none of them.

"It's over, Rand," Min said gently, moving her sturdy

brown mare nearer to his gray gelding, though she already stayed as close to him as Nynaeve did to Lan. Lan's bruises, and a broken arm, had been Healed before she had attended to Rand. Min's face reflected the worry flowing through the bond. Letting her cloak go on the wind, she patted his arm. "You don't have to think about it anymore."

"I'm grateful to Far Madding, Min." His voice was emotionless, distant, as it had been when he seized *saidin* in the early days. He would have warmed it for her, but that seemed beyond him. "I really did find what I needed here." If a sword had memory, it might be grateful to the forge fire, but never fond of it. When they were waved through, he cantered the gray up the hard-packed dirt road and into the hills, and he did not so much as glance back until trees hid any sight of the city.

The road climbed and wound through forested winter hills, where only pine and leatherleaf showed green and most branches were stark and gray, and suddenly the Source was there again, seemingly just beyond the corner of his eye. It pulsed and beckoned and filled him with hunger like starvation. Without thought he reached out and filled the emptiness in himself with *saidin,* an avalanche of fire, a storm of ice, all larded with the filthy taint that made the larger wound in his side pulse. He swayed in the saddle as his head spun and his stomach clenched even as he fought to ride the avalanche that tried to sear his mind, to soar on the storm that tried to scour his soul. There was no forgiveness or pity in the male half of the Power. A man fought it, or died. He could feel the three Asha'man behind him filling themselves too, drinking at *saidin* like men just out of the Waste who had found water. In his head, Lews Therin sighed with relief.

Min reined her mount so close to him that their legs touched. "Are you all right?" she said worriedly. "You look ill."

"I'm as well as rainwater," he told her, and the lie was not just about his belly. He was steel, and to his surprise, still not hard enough. He had intended sending her to Caemlyn, with Alivia to protect her. If the golden-haired woman was going to help him die, he had to be able to trust her. He had planned his words, but looking into Min's dark eyes, he was not hard enough to make his tongue form them. Turning the gray in among the bare-branched trees, he spoke to Cadsuane over his shoulder. "This is the place."

She followed him, of course. They all did. Harine had barely let him out of her sight long enough to sleep a few hours last night. He would have left her behind, but on that subject, Cadsuane had given him her first advice. *You made a bargain with them, boy, the same as signing a treaty. Or giving your word. Keep it, or tell them it's broken. Otherwise, you are just a thief.* Blunt, to the point, and in tones that left no doubt as to her opinion of thieves. He had never promised to follow her counsel, but she was too reluctant about being his advisor at all for him to risk driving her away this soon, so the Wavemistress and the other two Sea Folk rode with Alivia, ahead of Verin and the other five Aes Sedai who had sworn to him, and the four who were Cadsuane's companions. She would as soon leave him as them, he was certain, maybe sooner.

To other eyes than his, nothing distinguished the place where he had dug before going into Far Madding. To his eyes, a thin shaft that shone like a lantern rose through the damp mulch on the forest floor. Even another man who could channel could have walked through that shaft without knowing it was there. He did not bother to dismount. Using flows of Air, he ripped aside the thick layer of rotting leaves and twigs and shoveled away damp earth until he uncovered a long, narrow bundle tied with leather cords. Clods of dirt clung to the wrapping-cloth as he floated *Callandor* to his hand. He had not dared carry that to Far Madding. Without a scabbard, he would have had to leave it at the bridge fortress, a dangerous flag waiting to announce his presence. It was unlikely there was another sword made of crystal to be found in the world, and too many people knew that the Dragon Reborn had one. And leaving it here, he had still ended up in a dark, cramped stone box under the . . . No. That was done and over. Over. Lews Therin panted in the shadows of his mind.

Thrusting *Callandor* under his saddle-girth, he reined the gray around to face the others. The horses held their tails tight against the wind, but now and then one stamped a hoof or tossed its head, impatient to be moving again after so long in the stable. The leather scrip that hung from Nynaeve's shoulder looked incongruous with all the begemmed *ter'angreal* she wore. Now that the time was near, she was stroking the bulging scrip, apparently without realizing what she was doing. She was trying to hide her fear, but her chin trembled. Cadsuane was looking at him impassively. Her cowl had fallen down her back, and sometimes a gust stronger than most swayed the golden fish and birds, stars and moons, dangling from her bun.

"I am going to remove the taint from the male half of the Source," he announced.

The three Asha'man, now in plain dark coats and cloaks like the other Warders, exchanged excited glances, but a ripple passed through the Aes Sedai. Nesune let out a gasp that seemed too large for the slender, bird-like sister.

Cadsuane's expression never altered. "With that?" she said, raising a skeptical eyebrow at the bundle beneath his leg.

"With the Choedan Kal," he replied. That name was another gift from Lews Therin, resting in Rand's head as if it had always been there. "You know them as immense statues, *sa'angreal,* one buried in Cairhien, the other on Tremalking." Harine's head jerked, making the golden medallions on her nose chain click together, at mention of the Sea Folk island. "They're too big to be moved with any ease, but I have a pair of *ter'angreal* called access keys. Using those, the Choedan Kal can be tapped from anywhere in the world."

Dangerous, Lews Therin moaned. *Madness.* Rand ignored him. For the moment, only Cadsuane mattered.

Her bay flicked one black ear, and at that he seemed more excitable than his rider. "One of those *sa'angreal* is made for a woman," she said coolly. "Who do you propose to use that? Or do these keys allow you to draw on both yourself?"

"Nynaeve will link with me." He trusted Nynaeve, to link with, but no one else. She was Aes Sedai, but she had been the Wisdom of Emond's Field; he had to trust her. She smiled at him and nodded firmly, her chin no longer trembling. "Don't try to stop me, Cadsuane." She said nothing, only studied him, dark eyes weighing and measuring.

"Forgive me, Cadsuane," Kumira broke into the silence, heeling her dapple forward. "Young man, have you considered the possibility of failure? Have you considered the *consequences* of failure?"

"I must ask the same question," Nesune said sharply. She sat very straight in her saddle, and her dark eyes met Rand's gaze levelly. "By everything I have read, the attempt to use those *sa'angreal* may result in disaster. Together, they might be strong enough to crack the world like an egg."

Like an egg! Lews Therin agreed. *They were never tested, never tried. This is insane!* he shrieked. *You are mad! Mad!*

"The last I heard," Rand told the sisters, "one Asha'man in fifty had gone mad and had to be put down like a rabid dog. More will have, by now. There is a risk to doing this, but it's all maybe and might. If I don't try, the certainty is that more and more men will go mad, maybe scores, maybe all of us, and sooner or later it will be too many to be killed easily. Will you enjoy waiting for the Last Battle with a hundred rabid Asha'man wandering about, or two hundred, or five? And maybe me one of them? How long will the world survive that?" He spoke to the two Browns, but it was Cadsuane who he watched. Her almost black eyes never left him. He needed to keep her with him, but if she tried to talk him out of it, he would reject her advice no matter the consequences. If she tried to stop him . . . ? *Saidin* raged inside him.

"Will you do the deed here?" she asked.

"In Shadar Logoth," he told her, and she nodded.

"A fitting place," she said, "if we are to risk destroying the world."

Lews Therin screamed, a dwindling howl that echoed inside Rand's skull as the voice fled into the dark depths. There was nowhere to hide, though. No safe place.

The gateway he wove did not open into the ruined city of Shadar Logoth itself, but to a thinly wooded, uneven hilltop a few miles to the north, where the horse hooves rang on sparse, stony soil that had stunted the leafless trees, and ragged patches of snow covered the ground. As Rand dismounted, his eye was caught by distant glimpses of the place once called Aridhol showing above the trees, towers that ended abruptly in jagged stone, and white onion-shaped domes that could have sheltered a village had they been whole. He did not look for long. Despite the clear morning sky, those pale domes failed to gleam as they should, as if something cast a shadow over the sprawling ruin. Even at this distance from the city, the second never-healing wound in his side had begun to throb faintly. The slash given by Padan Fain's dagger, the dagger that had come from Shadar Logoth, did not beat together with the pulsing of the larger wound it cut across, but rather against it, alternating.

Cadsuane took charge, issuing brisk commands, as might have been expected. One way or another, Aes Sedai always did, given half a chance, and Rand did not try to stop her. Lan and Nethan and Bassane rode down into the forest to scout, and the other Warders hurried to fasten the horses to low branches out of the way. Min stood up in her stirrups and pulled Rand's head to where she could kiss his eyes. Without speaking a word, she went to join the men with the horses. The bond surged with her love for him, with confidence and a trust so complete that he stared after her in amazement.

Eben came to take Rand's mount, grinning from ear to ear. Together with his nose, those ears still seemed to make up half his face, but he was a slender youth rather than gawky, now. "It will be wonderful, channeling without the taint, my Lord Dragon," he said excitedly. Rand thought Eben might be as much as seventeen, but he sounded younger. "That always makes me want to empty my belly, if I think on it." He trotted away with the gray, still grinning.

The Power roared in Rand, and the filth tarnishing the pure life of *saidin* seeped into him, rank runnels that would bring madness and death.

Cadsuane gathered the Aes Sedai around her, and Alivia and the Sea Folk Windfinder, too. Harine grumbled loudly about being excluded, until a finger pointed by Cadsuane sent her stalking across the hilltop. Moad, in his odd blue quilted coat, sat Harine down on an outcrop, and talked soothingly, though sometimes his eyes went to the surrounding trees, and then he slid a hand along the long ivory hilt of his sword. Jahar appeared from the direction of the horses, stripping the Cloth wrappings from *Callandor*. The crystal sword, with its long clear hilt and slightly curving blade, sparkled in the pale sunlight. At an imperious gesture from Merise, he quickened his step to join her. Damer was in that group, too, and Eben. Cadsuane had not asked to use *Callandor*. That could pass. For now, it could.

"That woman could try a stone's patience!" Nynaeve muttered, striding up to Rand. With one hand, she held the scrip's strap firmly on her shoulder, while the other was just as firmly around the thick braid hanging from her cowl. "To the Pit of Doom with her, that's what I say! Are you sure Min couldn't be wrong just this once? Well, I suppose not. But still . . . ! Will you stop smiling like that? You'd make a cat nervous!"

"We might as well begin," he told her, and she blinked.

"Shouldn't we wait on Cadsuane?" No one would suspect she had been complaining about the Aes Sedai a moment earlier. If anything, she sounded anxious not to upset her.

"She will do what she will do, Nynaeve. With your help, I will do what I must."

Still she hesitated, clutching the scrip to her chest and casting worried glances in the direction of the women gathered around Cadsuane. Alivia left that group and hurried toward them across the uneven ground holding her cloak closed with both hands.

"Cadsuane says I must have the *ter'angreal*, Nynaeve," she said in that soft Seanchan drawl. "Now don't argue; there isn't time. Besides, they are no good to you if you're going to be linked to him."

This time the look Nynaeve directed toward the women around Cadsuane was near murderous, but she stripped off rings and bracelets, muttering under her breath, and handed the jeweled belt and necklace to Alivia, as well. After a moment, she sighed and unfastened the peculiar bracelet connected to finger rings by flat chains. "You might as well take this, too. I don't suppose I need an *angreal* if I'm going to be using the most powerful *sa'angreal* ever made. But I want them all back, understand," she finished fiercely.

"I am not a thief," the hawk-eyed woman told her primly, slipping the four rings over the fingers of her left hand. Strangely, the *angreal* that fitted Nynaeve so well, fit on her longer hand just as easily. The two women both stared at the thing.

It came to him then that neither of them acknowledged any possibility that he might fail here. He wished he could be as certain. What had to be done, had to be done, though.

"Are you going to wait all day, Rand?" Nynaeve asked when Alivia set off back to Cadsuane, even more quickly than she had come. Smoothing her cloak under her, Nynaeve sat down on an upthrust gray stone the size of a small bench, pulled the scrip onto her lap, and flipped back the leather flap.

Rand folded himself to the ground cross-legged in front of her as she produced the two access keys, smooth white statues a foot tall, each holding a clear sphere in one upraised hand. The figure of a bearded man in robes, she handed to him. That of a robed woman, she set on the ground at her feet. The faces on those figures were serene and strong and wise with years.

"You must put yourself right on the edge of embracing the Source," she told him, smoothing skirts that did not need smoothing. "Then I can link with you."

With a sigh, Rand put down the bearded man and released *saidin*. Raging fire and cold vanished, and the grease-slick vileness of the taint, and with them, life seemed to dwindle, too, turning the world pale and drab. He placed his hands on the ground beside him against the sickness that would strike when he took hold of the Source again, but a different dizziness suddenly spun his head. For a heartbeat, a vague face filled his eyes, blotting out Nynaeve, a man's face, almost recognizable. Light, if that ever happened while he was actually grabbing hold of *saidin* . . . Nynaeve bent toward him, concern on her face.

"Now," he said, and reached for the Source through the bearded man. Reached, but did not seize it. He hung on the brink, wanting to howl with the agony as flickering flames seemed to broil him even while shrieking winds blasted particles of frozen sand across his skin. Watching Nynaeve take a quick breath, he knew it lasted only an instant, yet it seemed he endured for hours before . . .

Saidin flowed through him, all the molten fury and icy tumbling, all the foulness, and he could not control a hair-thin thread. He could see the flow from him into Nynaeve. To feel it seething through him, feel the treacherous tides and shifting ground that could destroy him in a heartbeat, to feel that without being able to fight or control was an agony in itself. He was aware of her, he realized suddenly, in much the same way he was aware of Min, but all he could think of was *saidin*, flooding through him uncontrolled.

She drew a shuddering breath. "How can you stand . . . *that*?" she said hoarsely. "All chaos and rage and death. Light! Now, you must try as hard as you can to control the flows while I—" Desperate to gain his balance in that never-ending war with *saidin,* he did as she said, and she yelped and jumped. "You were supposed to wait until I . . ." she began in angry tones, then went on in a merely irritated voice. "Well, at least I'm rid of it. What are you so wide-eyed about? I'm the one had her skin yanked off!"

"Saidar," he murmured in wonder. It was so . . . different.

Alongside the turmoil of *saidin, saidar* was a tranquil river flowing smoothly. He dipped into that river, and suddenly he was struggling against currents that tried to pull him further in, swirling whirlpools that tried to yank him under. The harder he struggled, the stronger the shifting fluxes grew. Only an instant since he had tried to control *saidar,* and already he felt as if he was drowning in it, being swept away into eternity. Nynaeve had warned him what he must do, but it seemed so foreign he had not truly believed until now. With an effort, he forced himself to stop fighting the currents, and as quickly as that the river was tranquil once more.

That was the first difficulty, to fight *saidin* while surrendering to *saidar.* The first difficulty, and the first key to what he had to do. The male and female halves of the True Source were alike and unalike, attracting and repelling, fighting against each other even as they worked together to drive the Wheel of Time. The taint on the male half had its opposite twin, too. The wound given him by Ishamael throbbed in time with the taint, while the other, from Fain's blade, beat counterpoint in time with the evil that had killed Aridhol.

Awkwardly, forcing himself to work gently, to use the unfamiliar *saidar*'s own immense strength to guide it as he wanted, he wove a conduit that touched the male half of the Source at one end and the distantly seen city at the other. The conduit had to be of untainted *saidar.* If this worked as he hoped, a tube of *saidin* might shatter when the taint began to leech out of it. He thought of it as a tube, at least, though it was not. The weave did not form at all as he expected it to. As if *saidar* had a mind of its own, the weave took on convolutions and spirals that made him think of a flower. There was nothing to see, no grand weaves sweeping down from the sky. The Source lay at the heart of creation. The Source was everywhere, even in Shadar Logoth.

The conduit covered distance beyond his imagining, and had no length at all. It had to be a conduit, no matter its appearance. If it was not . . .

Drawing on *saidin*, fighting it, mastering it in the deadly dance he knew so well, he forced it into the flowery weave of *saidar*. And it flowed through. *Saidin* and *saidar*, like and unlike, could not mix. The flow of *saidin* squeezed in on itself, away from the surrounding *saidar*, and the *saidar* pushed it from all sides, compressing it further, making it flow faster. Pure *saidin*, pure except for the taint, touched Shadar Logoth.

Rand frowned. Had he been wrong? Nothing was happening. Except . . . The wounds in his side seemed to be throbbing faster. Amid the firestorm and icy fury of *saidin*, it seemed that the foulness stirred and shifted. Just a slight movement that might have escaped notice had he not been straining to find anything. A slight stirring in the midst of chaos, but all in the same direction.

"Go on," Nynaeve urged. Her eyes were bright, as though just having *saidar* flow in her was enough for joy.

He drew more deeply on both halves of the source, strengthening the conduit as he forced more of *saidin* into it, drew on the Power until nothing he did would bring more. He wanted to shout at how much was flowing into him, so much that it seemed he did not exist any more, only the One Power. He heard Nynaeve groan, but the murderous struggle with *saidin* consumed him.

Fingering the Great Serpent ring on her left forefinger, Elza stared at the man she had sworn to serve. He sat on the ground, grim-faced, staring straight ahead as if he could not see the wilder Nynaeve sitting right in front of him, glowing like the sun. Perhaps he could not. She could feel *saidar* sweeping through Nynaeve in torrents undreamed of. All the sisters of the Tower combined could have wielded only a fraction of that ocean. She envied the wilder that, and at the same time she thought she might have gone mad from the sheer joy of it. Despite the cold, there were beads of sweat on Nynaeve's face. Her lips were parted, and her wide eyes stared rapturously beyond the Dragon Reborn.

"It will begin soon, I fear," Cadsuane announced. Turning

away from the seated pair, the gray-haired sister planted her hands on her hips and swept a piercing gaze across the hilltop. "They'll be feeling that in Tar Valon, and maybe on the other side of the world. Everyone to your places."

"Come, Elza," Merise said, the light of *saidar* suddenly around her.

Elza allowed herself to be drawn into a link with the stern-faced sister, but she flinched when Merise added her Asha'man Warder to the circle. He was darkly beautiful, but the crystal sword in his hands shone with a faint light, and she could feel the incredible seething tumult that must be *saidin*. Even though Merise was controlling the flows, the vileness of *saidin* turned Elza's stomach. It was a midden heap rotting in a sweltering summer. The other Green was a lovely woman in spite of her sternness, but her mouth thinned as if she, too, were struggling not to vomit.

All around the hilltop the circles were forming, Sarene and Corele linked with the old man, Flinn, and Nesune, Beldeine and Daigian with the boy Hopwil. Verin and Kumira even made a circle with the Sea Folk wilder; she was actually quite strong, and everyone had to be used. As soon as each of those circles formed, it moved off the hilltop, each vanishing among the trees in a different direction. Alivia, the very peculiar wilder who seemed to have no other name, strode off north, cloak flapping behind her, surrounded by the glow of the Power. A very *troubling* woman with those tiny lines around her eyes, and incredibly strong. Elza would have given a great deal to have her hands on those *ter'angreal* the woman wore.

Alivia and the three circles would provide an encircling defense, if it were needed, but the greatest need lay right there on the hilltop. The Dragon Reborn must be protected at all costs. That job Cadsuane had taken on herself, of course, but Merise's circle would remain there, too. Cadsuane must have had an *angreal* of her own, from the amount of *saidar* she was drawing, more than Elza and Merise combined, yet even that paled beside the Power that flowed though *Callandor*.

Elza glanced toward the Dragon Reborn and drew a deep breath. "Merise, I know I shouldn't ask, but may I meld the flows?"

She expected to have to plead, but the taller woman hesitated only a moment before nodding and passing control to her. Almost immediately Merise's mouth softened, though it could never be called soft. Fire and ice and filth welled up in Elza, and she shuddered. Whatever the cost, the Dragon Reborn had to reach the Last Battle. Whatever the cost.

Riding his cart down the snowy road to Tremonsien, Barmellin wondered whether old Maglin at The Nine Rings would pay what he wanted for the plum brandy in the cart behind him. He was not sanguine. She was tight with silver, Maglin was, the brandy was not very good, and this late in the winter, she might be willing to wait until spring to get better. Suddenly he realized that the day seemed very bright. Almost like summer noon instead of a winter morning. Strangest of all, the glow seemed to be coming from the huge pit beside the road where workmen from the City had been digging away until the previous year. There was supposed to be a monstrous statue down there, but he had never been interested enough to actually look for himself.

Now, almost against his will, he reined in his stout mare and climbed down into the snow to trudge to the brink of the pit. It was a hundred paces deep and ten times as far across, and he had to put his hands in front of his face against the blinding glare that came from the bottom. Squinting through his fingers, he could make out a glowing ball, like a second sun. Abruptly, it came to him that this must the One Power.

With a strangled yell he lumbered back through the snow to his cart and scrambled up, flailing Nisa with the reins to get her moving even as he was trying to jerk her head around to head back to his farm. He was going to stay in his own house and drink that brandy himself. All of it.

Strolling lost in thought, Timna barely saw the fallow fields that covered all the hillsides but one around her. Tremalking was a large island, and this far from the sea, the wind carried no hint of salt, yet it was the Atha'an Miere that troubled her. They refused the Water Way, yet Timna was one of the Guides chosen to protect them from themselves, if possible. That was very difficult now, with them all in an uproar over this Coramoor of theirs. Very few remained on the island. Even the Governors, always fretting at being away from the sea as the Atha'an Miere did, had set sail to search for him in any craft they could find.

Suddenly the one unplowed hill caught her eye. A great stone hand stuck out of the ground clasping a clear sphere as large as a house. And that sphere was shining like a glorious summer sun.

All thoughts of the Atha'an Miere gone, Timna gathered her cloak and sat down on the ground, smiling to think that she might see the fulfillment of prophecy and the end of Illusion.

"If you truly are one of the Chosen, I will serve you," the bearded man in front of Cyndane said doubtfully, but she did not hear what else he had to say.

She could feel it. That much of *saidar* being drawn to one spot was a beacon that any woman in the world who could channel would feel and locate. So he had found a woman to use the other access key. She would have faced the Great Lord—faced the Creator!—with him. She would have shared the power with him, let him rule the world at her side. And he had spurned her love, spurned her!

The fool babbling at her was an important man as such things were accounted here and now, but she did not have time to make certain of his trustworthiness, and without that, she could not leave him to babble, not when she could feel Moridin's hand caressing the *cour'souvra* that held her soul. A razor-thin flow of Air sliced the fellow's beard in two as it took off his head. Another flow shoved the body backward so the blood fountaining from the stub of his neck did not spot her dress. Before body or head hit the stone floor, she had spun her gateway. A beacon she could point to, beckoning her.

As she stepped into rolling forest where scattered carpets of snow littered the ground beneath stark branches bare save for the thick ropes of drooping brown vines, she wondered where the beacon had drawn her. It did not matter. South of her, that beacon shone, enough *saidar* to lay waste to a continent in one blow. He would be there, him and whoever the woman was he had betrayed her with. Carefully, she drew on the Power to spin a web for his death.

Lightnings such as Cadsuane had never seen streaked down from the cloudless sky, not jagged bolts but lances of silver-blue that struck at the hilltop where she stood, and struck instead the inverted shield she had woven, erupting with a deafening roar fifty feet above her head. Even within the shield the air crackled, and her hair stirred and lifted. Without the aid of the *angreal* that looked a little like a shrike dangling from her bun, she would not have been able to hold the shield up.

A second golden bird, a swallow, hung from her hand by its thin chain. "There," she said, pointing in the direction it seemed to be flying. A pity she could not say how far away the Power had been channeled, or whether by a man or a woman, but the direction would have to do. She hoped there would be no . . . mishaps. Her people were out there, too. If the warning came with an attack, though, there could not be much doubt.

As soon as the single word left her mouth, a fountain of flame erupted in the forest to the north, and then another and another, a staggered line racing northward. *Callandor* shone like a flame in young Jahar's hands. Surprisingly, from the intensity on Elza's face and the way she gripped her skirts in fists, she was the one directing those flows.

Merise took a fistful of the boy's black hair and gently shook his head. "Steady, my pretty," she murmured. "Oh, steady, my lovely strong one." He smiled at her, a ravishing smile.

Cadsuane shook her own head slightly. Understanding any sister's relationship with her Warder was difficult, especially among Greens, but she could not begin to fathom what passed between Merise and her boys.

Her real attention was on another boy, though. Nynaeve was swaying, groaning with the ecstasy of such an unbelievable mass of *saidar* flooding through her, but Rand sat like a stone, sweat rolling down his face. His eyes were blank, like polished sapphires. Was he even aware of what was happening around him?

The swallow turned on its chain beneath her hand.

"There," she said, pointing toward the ruins of Shadar Logoth.

Rand could not see Nynaeve any longer. He could not see anything, feel anything. He swam in surging seas of flame, scrambled across collapsing mountains of ice. The taint flowed like an ocean tide, trying to sweep him away. If he lost control for an instant, it would strip away everything that was him and carry that down the conduit, too. As bad, or maybe worse, despite the tide of filth flooding through that odd flower, the taint on the male half of the Source seemed no less. It was like oil floating on water in a coating so thin you would not notice till you touched the surface, yet covering the vastness of the male half, it was an ocean in itself. He had to hold on. He had to. But for how long? How long could he hold on?

If he could undo what al'Thor had done at the source, Demandred thought as he stepped through his gateway into Shadar Logoth, undo it sharply and suddenly, that might well kill the man, or at least sear the ability to channel out of him. He had reasoned out what al'Thor's plan had to be as soon as he realized where the access key was. A brilliant scheme, he did not mind admitting, however insanely dangerous. Lews Therin had always been a brilliant planner, too, if not so brilliant as everyone made out. Not nearly as brilliant as Demandred himself.

One look at the rubble-strewn street changed his mind about altering anything, though. Beside him rose half a pale dome, its shattered top two hundred feet or more above the street, and above it, the sky held the light of midmorning. From the broken rim of the ruin down to the street, though, the air was dark with shadows, as if night were already falling. The city . . . quivered. He could feel it through his boots.

Fire erupted in the forest, great explosions spun of *saidin* that hurled trees into the air on gouts of flame that sped toward him, but he was already weaving a gateway. Leaping through, he let it vanish and ran through the vine-draped trees as hard as he could, plowing through patches of snow, stumbling over rocks hidden in the mulch, but not slowing down, never that. The web had been reversed, for caution's sake, but so had the first, and he had been a soldier. Still running, he heard the explosions he expected, and knew they were racing toward where his gateway had been as surely as they had raced straight toward him among the ruins. They were far enough from him now to present no danger, though. Without slowing, he turned toward the access key. With the amount of *saidin* pouring through it, there might as well have been a fiery arrow in the sky pointing to al'Thor.

So. Unless someone in this accursed Age had discovered yet another unknown ability, al'Thor must have acquired a device, a *ter'angreal,* that could detect a man channeling. From what he knew of what people now called the Breaking, after he himself had been imprisoned at Shayol Ghul, any woman who knew how to make *ter'angreal* would have been trying to create one that would do that. In war, the other side always came up with something you did not expect, and you had to counter it. He had always been good at war. First, he needed to get closer.

Suddenly he saw people off to the right ahead of him through the trees, and sheltered behind a rough gray trunk. A bald-headed old man with a fringe of white hair was limping along between two women, one of them beautiful in a wild way, the other stunning. What were they doing in these woods? Who were they? Friends of al'Thor, or just people in the wrong place at the wrong time? He hesitated to kill them, whoever they were. Any use of the Power would warn al'Thor. He would have to wait until they passed. The old man's head was turning as if he were searching for something among the trees, but Demandred doubted a fellow that decrepit could see very far.

Abruptly the old man stopped and thrust out his hand straight toward Demandred, and Demandred found himself frantically fending off a net of *saidin* that struck his warding much harder than it should have, as hard as his own spinning would. That tottering old man was an Asha'man! And at least one of the women must be what passed for Aes Sedai in this time, and joined with the fellow in a ring.

He tried to launch his own attack and crush them, but the

old man flung web after web at him without pause, and it
was all he could do to fend them off. Those that struck trees
enveloped them in flame or blew the trunks apart in splin-
ters. He was a general, a great general, but generals did not
have to fight alongside the men they commanded! Snarling,
he began to retreat amid the crackle of burning trees and
the thunder of explosions. Away from the key. Sooner or
later the old man had to tire, and then he could take care of
killing al'Thor. If one of the others did not get there first.
He hoped fervently they did not.

Skirts hiked to her knees, cursing, Cyndane ran from her
third gateway as soon as she was through. She could hear
the explosions marching toward the site, but this time she
had realized why they came straight for her. Tripping on
vines hidden in the snow, bumping into tree trunks, she
ran. She hated forests! At least some of the others were
here—she had seen those fountaining fires speed elsewhere
than at her; she could feel *saidar* being spun at more than
one place, spun with fury—but she prayed to the Great
Lord that she would reach Lews Therin first. She wanted
to see him die, she realized, and for that, she would have to
get closer.

Crouching behind a fallen log, Osan'gar panted from the
exertion of running. Those months masquerading as Corlan Dashiva had not made him any fonder of exercise.
The explosions that had almost killed him died away, then
started up again somewhere in the distance, and he cautiously raised himself enough to peek over the log. Not that
he supposed a piece of wood was very much protection. He
had never been a soldier, not really. His talents, his genius,
lay elsewhere. The Trollocs were his making, and thus the
Myrddraal that had sprung from them, and many other
creatures that had rocked the world and made his name famous. The access key blazed with *saidin,* but he could feel
lesser amounts being wielded, too, in various directions.
    He had expected others of the Chosen to be here ahead
of him, had hoped they might have finished the task before
he arrived, but plainly they had not. Plainly al'Thor had

brought along some of those Asha'man, and by the amount of *saidin* that had gone into the eruptions that targeted him, *Callandor* as well. And maybe some of his tame, so-called Aes Sedai.

Crouching again, he bit his lip. This forest was a very dangerous place, more so than he had expected, and nowhere for a genius. But the fact remained that Moridin terrified him. The man had always terrified him, from the very beginning. He had been mad with power before they were sealed into the Bore, and since they had been freed, he seemed to think that *he* was the Great Lord. Moridin would find out somehow if he fled, and kill him. Worse, if al'Thor succeeded, the Great Lord might decide to kill both of them, and Osan'gar as well. He did not care whether they died, but he did very much about himself.

He was not good at judging time by the sun, but it was obviously still short of noon. Hauling himself from the ground, he dabbed at the dirt on his clothes, then gave up in disgust and began to skulk from tree to tree in what he imagined was a stealthy manner. It was toward the key that he skulked. Perhaps one of the others would finish the man before he got close to it, but if not, perhaps he would find the chance to be a hero. Carefully, of course.

Verin frowned at the apparition making its way through the trees off to her left. She could think of no other term for a woman walking through the forest in gems and a gown that shifted through every color from black to white and sometimes even turned transparent! She was not hurrying, but she was heading toward the hill where Rand was. And unless Verin was very much mistaken, she was one of the Forsaken.

"Are we just going to watch her?" Shalon whispered furiously. She had been upset that she was not the one to meld the flows, as if a wilder's strength counted with Aes Sedai, and hours tramping through the woods had not improved her temper.

"We must do *something*," Kumira said softly, and Verin nodded.

"I was just deciding what." A shield, she decided. A captive Forsaken might prove very useful.

Using the full strength of her circle, she wove her shield, and watched aghast as it rebounded. The woman was already embracing *saidar,* though no light shone around her, and she was immensely strong!

Then she had no time for thought of anything as the golden-haired woman spun around and began channeling. Verin could not see the weaves, but she knew when she was fighting off an attack on her life, and she had come too far to die here.

Eben hitched his cloak around himself and wished he were better at ignoring the cold. Simple cold, he could ignore, but not the wind that had sprung up since the sun passed its zenith. The three sisters linked to him simply let the wind take their cloaks as they tried to watch every direction at once. Daigian was leading the circle—because of him, he thought—but she was drawing so lightly that he felt barely a whisper of *saidin* passing through him. She would not want to face that until she had to. He lifted her cowl back into place on her head, and she smiled at him from its depths. The bond carried her affection to him, and his own back, he supposed. With time, he thought he might come to love this little Aes Sedai.

The torrent of *saidin* far behind him had a tendency to wash out his awareness of other channeling, but he could feel others wielding the Power. The battle had been joined, elsewhere, and so far all the four of them had done was walk. He did not mind that much, really. He had been at Dumai's Wells, and fought the Seanchan, and he had learned that battles were more fun in a book than in the flesh. What did irk him was that he had not been given control of the circle. Of course, Jahar had not, but he figured Merise amused herself by making Jahar balance a cookie on his nose. Damer had been given control of that circle, though. Just because the man had a few years on him—well, more than a few; he was older than Eben's da—was no reason for Cadsuane to look at him as if he were a—

"Can you help me? I seem to have lost my way, and my horse." The woman who stepped from behind a tree ahead of them did not even have a cloak. Instead, she wore a gown of deep green silk cut so low that half of her lush bosom was exposed. Waves of black hair surrounded a beautiful face, with green eyes that sparkled as she smiled.

"A strange place to be riding," Beldeine said suspiciously. The pretty Green had not been pleased when Cadsuane put Daigian in charge, and she had taken every opportunity to state her opinion of Daigian's decisions.

"I hadn't meant to ride so far," the woman said coming closer. "I see you're all Aes Sedai. With a . . . groom? Do you know what all the commotion is about?"

Suddenly, Eben felt the blood drain from his face. What he felt was impossible! The green-eyed woman frowned in surprise, and he did the only thing that he could.

"She's holding *saidin*!" he shouted, and threw himself at her as he felt Daigian draw deeply on the Power.

Cyndane slowed at the sight of the woman standing among the trees a hundred paces ahead of her, a tall yellow-haired woman who simply watched her come closer. The feel of battles being fought with the Power in other places made her wary at the same time it gave her hope. The woman was plainly dressed in wool, but incongruously decked with gems as if she were a great lady. With *saidar* in her, Cyndane could see the faint lines at the corners of the woman's eyes. Not one of those who called themselves Aes Sedai, then. But who? And why did she stand there as if she would bar Cyndane's way? It did not really matter. Channeling now would give her away, but she had time. The key still shone as a beacon of the Power. Lews Therin still lived. No matter how fierce the other woman's eyes, a knife would do for her, if she really thought she could be a bar. And just in case she proved to be what they called a wilder, Cyndane prepared a small present for her, a reversed web she would not even see until it was too late.

Abruptly the light of *saidar* appeared around the woman, but the ready ball of fire streaked from Cyndane's hand, small enough to escape detection she hoped, but enough to burn a hole through this woman who—

Just as it reached the woman, almost close enough to singe her garments, the web of Fire unraveled. The woman did not do anything; the net simply came apart! Cyndane had never heard of a *ter'angreal* that would break a web, but it must be that.

Then the woman struck back at her, and she suffered her second shock. She was stronger than Cyndane had been before the Aelfinn and the Eelfinn held her! That was impossible; no woman *could* be stronger. She must have an *angreal*, too. Shock lasted only the time it took her to slice the other woman's flows. She did not know how to reverse them. Maybe that would be enough advantage. She *would* see Lews Therin die! The taller woman jerked as her cut flows snapped back into her, but even as she shifted her feet with the blow, she channeled again. Snarling, Cyndane fought back, and the earth heaved beneath their feet. She *would* see him die! She *would*!

The high hilltop was not very near to the access key, but even so the key shone so brightly in Moghedien's head that she hungered for just a sip at that immense flow of *saidar*. To hold so much, the thousandth part of so much, would be ecstasy. She hungered, but this wooded vantage was as near as she intended going. Only the threat of Moridin's hands caressing her *cour'souvra* had driven her to Travel here at all, and she had delayed coming, prayed that it would be over before she was forced to. Always she had worked in secrecy, but she had had to flee an attack as soon as she arrived, and in widely separated places in the forest spread out before her, lightnings and fires woven of *saidar* and others that must have been *saidin* flashed and flared beneath the midafternoon sun. Black smoke rose in plumes from burning clumps of trees, and thunderous explosions rolled through the air.

Who fought, who lived, who died were all matters of indifference to her. Except that it would be pleasant if Cyndane or Graendal perished. Or both. Moghedien would not, not thrashing about in the middle of a battle. And if that were not bad enough, there was what stood beyond the shining key, an immense flattened dome of black in the forest, as though night had turned to stone. She flinched as a ripple passed across the dark surface and the dome heaved perceptibly higher. Madness to go any closer to that, whatever it was. Moridin would not know what she did here, or did not do.

Retreating to the back of the hilltop, away from the shining key and the strange dome, she sat down to do what she had done so often in the past. Watch from the shadows, and survive.

Inside his head, Rand was screaming. He was sure that he was screaming, that Lews Therin was screaming, but he could not hear either voice in the roar. The foul ocean of the taint was flooding through him, howling with its speed. Tidal waves of vileness crashed over him. Raging gales of filth ripped at him. The only reason he knew that he still held the Power was the taint. *Saidin* could be shifting, flaring, about to kill him, and he would never know. That putrid flood overwhelmed everything else, and he hung on by his fingernails to keep from being swept away on it. The taint was moving. That was all that counted, now. He had to hold on!

"What can you tell me, Min?" Cadsuane kept her feet despite her weariness. Holding that shield through most of a day was enough to tire anyone.

There had not been an attack on the hilltop for some time, and in fact, it seemed the only active channeling she could sense was what Nynaeve and the boy were doing. Elza was pacing an endless circle around the crest of the hill, still linked to Merise and Jahar, but there was nothing for her to do at the moment except scan the hills around them. Jahar was sitting on a stone with *Callandor* shining faintly in the crook of his arm. Merise sat on the ground beside him with her head on his knee, and he was stroking her hair.

"Well, Min?" Cadsuane demanded.

The girl looked up angrily from the depression in the stony ground where Tomas and Moad had bundled her and Harine. At least the men had sense enough to accept that they could not fight any part of this fight. Harine wore a sullen scowl, and more than once it had been necessary for one of the men to restrain Min from going to young al'Thor. They had actually had to take her knives away, after she tried to use the blades on them.

"I know he's alive," the girl muttered, "and I think he's hurting. Only, if I can feel enough to think he's hurting, then he's in agony. Let me go to him."

"You would only get in the way now."

Ignoring the girl's frustrated groan, Cadsuane walked across the uneven ground to where Rand and Nynaeve sat, but for a moment she did not look at them. Even at a distance of miles, the black dome looked immense, rearing a thousand feet at its height. And it was swelling. The surface looked like black steel, though it did not sparkle in the afternoon sun. If anything, the light seemed to dim around it.

Rand was sitting as he had since the beginning, an unmoving, unseeing statue with sweat rolling down his face. If he was in agony as Min said, he showed no sign of it. And if he was, Cadsuane did not know what she could do, what she dared to do. Disturbing him now in any way might have dire consequences. Glancing at that rising dead-black dome, Cadsuane grunted. Having let him begin in the first place might have dire consequences, too.

With a moan, Nynaeve slipped from her stone seat to the ground. Her dress was sodden with sweat, and strands of hair clung to her slick face. Her eyelids fluttered weakly, and her breasts heaved as she gulped air desperately. "No more," she whimpered. "I cannot stand anymore."

Cadsuane hesitated, something she was not accustomed to doing. The girl could not leave the circle until young al'Thor released her, but unless these Choedan Kal were flawed in the same way as *Callandor,* she would be buffered against taking in enough of the Power to damage her. Except that she was acting as a conduit for far more of *saidar* than the entire White Tower could have handled using every *angreal* and *sa'angreal* the Tower possessed. After having that flow through her for hours, simple physical exhaustion might be killing her.

Kneeling beside the girl, Cadsuane laid the swallow on the ground beside her, took the girl's head in her hands and lessened the amount of *saidar* she was putting into the shield. Her abilities with Healing were no more than average, but she could wash away some of the girl's exhaustion at least without falling over herself. She was very conscious of the weakened shield over them, though, and she wasted no time in forming the weaves.

* * *

Scrambling to the top of the hill, Osan'gar dropped to the ground on his belly and smiled as he crabbed sideways to shelter behind a tree. From here, with *saidin* in him, he could see the next crest clearly, and the people on it. Not as many as he had expected. One woman was making a slow circuit around the crest, peering into the trees, but everyone else was still, Narishma sitting with *Callandor* glowing in his hands and a woman's head on his knee. There were two other women that Osan'gar could see, one kneeling over the other, but they were obscured by a man's back. He did not need to see the man's face to know al'Thor. The key lying on the ground at his side named him. To Osan'gar's eyes, it shone brightly. In his head, it overwhelmed the sun, a thousand suns. What he could do with that! A pity it had to be destroyed along with al'Thor. But still, he could take *Callandor* after al'Thor was dead. No one else among the Chosen possessed so much as an *angreal*. Even Moridin would quail before him once he had that crystal sword. Nae'blis? Osan'gar would be named Nae'blis after he destroyed al'Thor and undid all that he had done here. Laughing softly, he wove balefire. Who would ever have thought that he would turn out to be the hero of the day?

Walking slowly, studying the forested hills around them, Elza suddenly stopped as a flicker of movement caught the corner of her eye. She turned her head slowly, and not as far as the hill where she had seen that flash. The day had been very difficult for her. In her captivity among the Aiel tents at Cairhien it had come to her that it was paramount for the Dragon Reborn to reach the Last Battle. It had suddenly become so blindingly obvious that it astounded her she had not seen it before. Now it was clear to her, as clear as *saidar* made the face of the man trying to hide on that hill while peeking around a tree trunk. Today, she had been forced to fight the Chosen. Surely the Great Lord would understand if she had actually killed any of them, but Corlan Dashiva was only one of those Asha'man. Dashiva raised his hand toward the hill where she stood, and she drew as hard as she could on *Callandor* in Jahar's hands. *Saidin* seemed well suited to destruction, to her. A huge ball of coruscating fire surrounded the other hilltop, red and gold and blue. When it was gone, that other hill ended in a smooth surface fifty feet lower than the old crest.

Moghedien was not sure why she had remained this long. There could not be more than two hours of daylight left, and the forest was quiet. Except for the key, she could not feel *saidar* being channeled anywhere. That was not to say that someone was not using small amounts somewhere, but nothing like the fury that had raged earlier. The battle was over, the other Chosen dead or flying in defeat. Plainly defeat, since the key still blazed in her head. Amazing that the Choedan Kal had survived continuous use for this long, at this level.

Lying on her belly atop her high vantage point with her chin in her hands, she was watching the great dome. Black no longer seemed to describe it. There was no term for it, now, but black was a pale color by comparison. It was half a ball, now, rearing like a mountain two miles or more into the sky. A thick layer of shadow lay around it, as though it were sucking the last light out of the air. She could not understand why she was not afraid. That thing might grow until it enveloped the entire world, or perhaps shatter the world, as Aran'gar had said it might. But if that happened, there was no safe place, no shadows for the Spider to hide in.

Suddenly something writhed up from that dark smooth surface, like a flame if flames were blacker than black, then another, another, until the dome boiled with stygian fire. The roar of ten thousand thunders made her clap her hands over her ears and shriek, soundlessly in that crash, and the dome collapsed in on itself in the space of a heartbeat, to a pinpoint, to nothing. It was wind that howled then, rushing toward the vanished dome, dragging her along the stony ground no matter how desperately she clawed for purchase, tumbling her against trees, lifting her into the air. Strangely, she still felt no fear. She thought if she survived this, she would never feel fear again.

* * *

Cadsuane let the thing that had been a *ter'angreal* drop to the ground. It could no longer be called a statue of a woman. The face was as wisely serene as ever, but the figure was broken in two and lumpy like bubbled wax where one side had melted, including the arm that had held the crystal sphere now lying in shattered fragments around the ruined thing. The male figure was whole, and already tucked away in her saddlebags. *Callandor* was secured, too. It was best not to leave temptation on the open hilltop. Where Shadar Logoth had been there was a now a huge opening in the forest, perfectly round and so wide that even with the sun low on the horizon she could see the far side sloping down into the earth.

Lan, leading his limping warhorse up the slope, dropped the black stallion's reins when he saw Nynaeve stretched out on the ground and covered to her chin with her cloak. Young al'Thor lay at her side also blanketed in his cloak, with Min curled up against him, her head on his chest. Her eyes were closed, but by her small smile, she was not asleep. Lan barely spared them a glance as he ran the last distance and fell on his knees to raise Nynaeve's head gently on his arm. She did not stir any more than the boy.

"They are just unconscious," Cadsuane told him. "Corele says it is better to let them recover on their own." And how long that might require, Corele had not been prepared to say. Nor had Damer. The wounds in the boy's side were unchanged, though Damer had expected they would be. It was all very disturbing.

A little farther up the hill, the bald Asha'man was bent over a groaning Beldeine, his fingers writhing just above her as he wove his strange Healing. He had been busy the last hour. Alivia could not stop staring in wonder and flexing the arm that had been broken as well as seared to the bone. Sarene walked unsteadily, but that was just tiredness. She had almost died out there in the forest, and her eyes were still wide with the experience. Whites were not used to that sort of thing.

Not everyone had been so lucky. Verin and the Sea Folk woman were sitting beside the cloak-covered form of Kumira, their lips moving silently in prayers for her soul, and Nesune was trying awkwardly to comfort a weeping Daigian, who cradled young Eben's corpse in her arms and rocked him like a baby. Greens were used to that sort of thing, but Cadsuane did not like losing two of her people in return for no more than a few singed Forsaken and one dead renegade.

"It's clean," Jahar said softly yet again. This time, Merise was the one sitting, with his head resting in her lap. Her blue eyes were as stern as ever, but she stroked his black hair gently. "It's clean."

Cadsuane exchanged looks with Merise over the boy's head. Damer and Jahar both said the same thing, the taint was gone, but how could they be sure some scrap did not remain? Merise had allowed her to link with the boy, and she could not feel anything like what the other Green had described, yet how could they be certain? *Saidin* was so alien that anything could be hidden in that mad chaos.

"I want to leave as soon as the rest of the Warders return," she announced. There were too many questions for which she had no answers to suit her, but she had young al'Thor now, and she did not intend to lose him.

Night fell. On the hilltop, the wind blew dust across the fragments of what had once been a *ter'angreal*. Below lay the tomb of Shadar Logoth, open to give the world hope. And on distant Tremalking, the word began to spread that the Time of Illusions was at an end.

The End

of the Ninth Book of

The Wheel of Time

GLOSSARY

A Note on Dates in This Glossary. The Toman Calendar (devised by Toma dur Ahmid) was adopted approximately two centuries after the death of the last male Aes Sedai, recording years After the Breaking of the World (AB). So many records were destroyed in the Trolloc Wars that at their end there was argument about the exact year under the old system. A new calendar, proposed by Tiam of Gazar, celebrated freedom from the Trolloc threat and recorded each year as a Free Year (FY). The Gazaran Calendar gained wide acceptance within twenty years after the Wars' end. Artur Hawkwing attempted to establish a new calendar based on the founding of his empire (FF, From the Founding), but only historians now refer to it. After the death and destruction of the War of the Hundred Years, a third calendar was devised by Uren din Jubai Soaring Gull, a scholar of the Sea Folk, and promulgated by the Panarch Farede of Tarabon. The Farede Calendar, dating from the arbitrarily decided end of the War of the Hundred Years and recording years of the New Era (NE), is currently in use.

armsmen: Soldiers who owe allegiance or fealty to a particular lord or lady.

Asha'man: (1) In the Old Tongue, "Guardian" or "Guardians," but always a guardian of justice and truth. (2) The name given, both collectively and as a rank, to the men who have come to the Black Tower, near Caemlyn in Andor, in order to learn to channel. Their training concentrates on the ways in which the One Power can be used as a weapon, and in another departure from the usages of the White Tower, once they learn to seize *saidin,* the male half of the Power, they are required to perform all chores and labors with the Power. When newly enrolled, a man is termed a Soldier; he wears a plain black coat with a high collar, in the Andoran fashion. Being raised to Dedicated brings the right to wear a silver pin, called the Sword, on the collar of his coat. Promotion to Asha'man brings the right to wear a Dragon pin, in gold and red enamel, on the collar opposite the Sword. Although many women, including wives, flee when they learn that their men actually can channel, a fair number of men at the Black Tower are married, and they use a version of the Warder bond to create a link with their wives. This same bond, altered to compel obedience, has recently been used to bond captured Aes Sedai as well.

Balwer, Sebban: Formerly Pedron Niall's secretary, in public, and secretly Niall's spymaster. He aided Morgase's escape from the Seanchan in Amador for his own reasons, and now is employed as secretary to Perrin t'Bashere Aybara and Faile ni Bashere t'Aybara.

Blood, the: Term used by the Seanchan to designate the nobility. One can be raised to the Blood as well as born to it.

Cha Faile: (1) In the Old Tongue, "the Falcon's Talon." (2) Name taken by the young Cairhienin and Tairens, attempted followers of *ji'e'toh,* who have sworn fealty to Faile ni Bashere t'Aybara. In secret, they act as her personal scouts and spies.

Companions, the: The elite military formation of Illian, currently commanded by First Captain Demetre Marcolin. The Companions provide a bodyguard for the King of Illian and guard key points around the nation. Additionally, the Companions have traditionally been used in battle to assault the enemy's strongest positions, to exploit weaknesses, and, if necessary, to cover the retreat of the King. Unlike most other such elite formations, foreigners (excepting Tairens, Altarans and Murandians) are not only welcome, they can rise even to the highest rank, as can commoners, which also is unusual. The uniform of the Companions consists of a green coat, a breastplate worked with the Nine Bees of Illian, and a conical helmet with a faceguard of steel bars. The First Captain wears four rings of golden braid on the cuffs of his coat, and three thin golden plumes on his helmet. The Second Captain wears three rings of golden braid on each cuff, and three golden plumes tipped with green. Lieutenants wear two yellow rings on their cuffs, and two thin green plumes, under-lieutenants one yellow ring and a single green plume. Bannermen are designated by two broken rings of yellow on the cuffs and a single yellow plume, squadmen by a single broken ring of yellow.

Consolidation, the: When the armies sent by Artur Hawkwing under his son Luthair landed in Seanchan, they discovered a shifting quilt of nations often at war with one another, where Aes Sedai often reigned. Without any equivalent of the White Tower, Aes Sedai worked for their own individual power, using the Power. Forming small groups, they schemed against one another constantly. In large part it was this constant scheming for personal advantage and the resulting wars among the myriad nations that allowed the armies from east of the Aryth Ocean to begin the conquest of an entire continent, and for their descendants to complete it. This conquest, during which the descendants of the original armies became Seanchan as much as they conquered Seanchan, took more than nine hundred years and is called the Consolidation.

*Corenne***:** In the Old Tongue, "the Return:" The name given by the Seanchan both to the fleet of thousands of ships and to the hundreds of thousands of soldiers, craftsmen and others carried by those ships, who will come behind the Forerunners to reclaim the lands stolen from Artur Hawkwing's descendants. *See also* Forerunners.

Daughters of Silence, the: During the history of the White Tower (over three thousand years), various women who have been put out have been unwilling to accept their fates and have tried to band together. Such groups— most of them by far, at least—have been dispersed by the White Tower as soon as found and punished severely and publicly to make sure that the lesson is carried to everyone. The last group to be dispersed called themselves the Daughters of Silence (794–798 NE). The Daughters

consisted of two Accepted who had been put out of the
Tower and twenty-three women they had gathered and
trained. All were carried back to Tar Valon and punished, and the twenty-three were enrolled in the novice
book. Only one of those managed to reach the shawl. *See
also* Kin, the.

da'covale: (1) In the Old Tongue, "one who is owned," or
"person who is property." (2) Among the Seanchan, the
term often used, along with property, for slaves. Slavery
has a long and unusual history among the Seanchan,
with slaves having the ability to rise to positions of great
power and open authority, including over those who are
free. *See also so'jhin.*

Deathwatch Guards, the: The elite military formation of
the Seanchan Empire, including both humans and Ogier.
The human members of the Deathwatch Guard are all
da'covale, born as property and chosen while young to
serve the Empress, whose personal property they are.
Fanatically loyal and fiercely proud, they often display
the ravens tattooed on their shoulders, the mark of a
da'covale of the Empress. The helmets and armor are
lacquered in dark green and blood-red, their shields are
lacquered black, and their spears and swords carry black
tassels. *See also da'covale.*

Defenders of the Stone, the: The elite military formation
of Tear. The current Captain of the Stone (commander
of the Defenders) is Rodrivar Tihera. Only Tairens are
accepted into the Defenders, and officers are usually of
noble birth, though often from minor Houses or minor
branches of strong Houses. The Defenders are tasked to
hold the great fortress called the Stone of Tear, in the city
of Tear, to defend the city, and to provide police services
in place of any City Watch or the like. Except in times
of war, their duties seldom take them far from the city.
Then, as with other elite formations, they are the core
around which the army is formed. The uniform of the
Defenders consists of a black coat with padded sleeves
striped black-and-gold with black cuffs, a burnished
breastplate, and a rimmed helmet with a faceguard of
steel bars. The Captain of the Stone wears three short
white plumes on his helmet, and on the cuffs of his coat
three intertwined golden braids on a white band. Cap-

tains wear two white plumes and a single line of golden braid on white cuffs, lieutenants one white plume and a single line of black braid on white cuffs and under-lieutenants one short black plume and plain white cuffs. Bannermen have gold-colored cuffs on their coats, and squadmen have cuffs striped black-and-gold.

Delving: (1) The ability to use the One Power to diagnose physical condition and illness. (2) The ability to find deposits of metal ores with the One Power. That this has long been a lost ability among Aes Sedai may account for the name becoming attached to another ability.

der'morat-: (1) In the Old Tongue, "master handler." (2) Among the Seanchan, the suffix applied to indicate a senior and highly skilled handler of one of the exotics, one who trains others, as in *der'morat'raken. Der'morat* can have a fairly high social status, the highest of all held by *der'sul'dam,* the trainers of *sul'dam,* who rank with fairly high military officers. *See also morat.*

Fain, Padan: Former Darkfriend, now more and worse than a Darkfriend, and an enemy of the Forsaken as much as he is of Rand al'Thor, whom he hates with a passion. Last seen using the name Jeraal Mordeth, advising Lord Toram Riatin in his rebellion against the Dragon Reborn in Cairhien.

Fists of Heaven, the: Lightly armed and lightly armored Seanchan infantry carried into battle on the backs of the flying creatures called *to'raken.* All are small men, or women, largely because of limits as to how much weight a *to'raken* can carry for any distance. Considered to be among the toughest soldiers, they are used primarily for raids, surprise assaults on positions at an enemy's rear, and where speed in getting soldiers into place is of the essence.

Forerunners, the: *See* Hailene.

Forsaken, the: The name given to thirteen powerful Aes Sedai, men and women both, who went over to the Shadow during the Age of Legends and were trapped in the sealing of the Bore into the Dark One's prison. While it has long been believed that they alone abandoned the Light during the War of the Shadow, in fact others did as well; these thirteen were only the highest ranking among them. The Forsaken (who call themselves the Chosen) are somewhat reduced in number since their awakening in the present day. The known survivors are Demandred, Semirhage, Graendal, Mesaana, Moghedien, and two who were reincarnated in new bodies and given new names, Osan'gar and Aran'gar. Recently, a man calling himself Moridin has appeared, and may be yet another of the dead Forsaken brought back from the grave by the Dark One. The same possibility may exist regarding the woman calling herself Cyndane, but since Aran'gar was a man brought back as a woman, speculation as to the identities of Moridin and Cyndane may prove futile until more is learned.

Hailene: In the Old Tongue, "Forerunners," or "Those Who Come Before." The term applied by the Seanchan to the massive expeditionary force sent across the Aryth Ocean to scout out the lands where Artur Hawkwing once ruled. Now under the command of the High Lady Suroth, its numbers swollen by recruits from conquered lands, the Hailene has gone far beyond its original goals.

Hanlon, Daved: A Darkfriend, formerly commander of the White Lions in service to the Forsaken Rahvin while he held Caemlyn using the name Lord Gaebril. From there, Hanlon took the White Lions to Cairhien under orders to further the rebellion against the Dragon Reborn. The White Lions were destroyed by a "bubble of evil," and Hanlon has been ordered back to Caemlyn for purposes as yet unknown.

Ishara: The first Queen of Andor (circa FY 994–1020). At the death of Artur Hawkwing, Ishara convinced her husband, one of Hawkwing's foremost generals, to raise the siege of Tar Valon and accompany her to Caemlyn with as many soldiers as he could break away from the army. Where others tried to seize the whole of Hawkwing's empire and failed, Ishara took a firm hold on a small part and succeeded. Today, nearly every noble House in Andor contains some of Ishara's blood, and the right to claim the Lion Throne depends both on direct descent from her and on the number of lines of connection to her that can be established.

Kin, the: Even during the Trolloc Wars, more than two thousand years ago (circa 1000–1350 AB), the White Tower continued to maintain its standards, putting out women who failed to measure up. One group of these women, fearing to return home in the midst of the wars, fled to Barashta (near the present-day site of Ebou Dar), as far from the fighting as was possible to go at that time. Calling themselves the Kin, and Kinswomen, they kept in hiding and offered a safe haven for others who had been put out. In time, their approaches to women told to leave the Tower led to contacts with runaways, and while the exact reasons may never be known, the Kin began to accept runaways, as well. They made great efforts to keep these girls from learning anything about the Kin until they were sure that Aes Sedai would not swoop down and retake them. After all, everyone knew that runaways were always caught sooner or later, and the Kin knew that unless they held themselves secret, they themselves would be punished severely.

Unknown to the Kin, Aes Sedai in the Tower were aware of their existence almost from the very first, but prosecution of the wars left no time for dealing with them. By the end of the wars, the Tower realized that it might not be in their best interests to snuff out the Kin. Prior to that time, a majority of runaways actually had managed to escape, whatever the Tower's propaganda, but once the Kin began helping them, the Tower knew exactly where any runaway was heading, and they began retaking nine out of ten. Since Kinswomen moved in and out of Barashta (and later Ebou Dar) in an effort to hide their existence and their numbers, never staying more than ten years lest someone notice that they did not age at a normal speed, the Tower believed they were few, and they certainly were keeping themselves low. In order to use the Kin as a trap for runaways, the Tower decided to leave them alone, unlike any other similar group in history, and to keep the very existence of the Kin a secret known only to full Aes Sedai.

The Kin do not have laws, but rather rules based in part on the rules for novices and Accepted in the White Tower, and in part on the necessity of maintaining secrecy. As might be expected given the origins of the Kin, they maintain their rules very firmly on all of their members.

Recent open contacts between Aes Sedai and Kinswomen, while known only to a handful of sisters, have produced a number of shocks, including the facts that there are twice as many Kinswomen as Aes Sedai and that some are more than a hundred years older than any Aes Sedai has lived since before the Trolloc Wars. The effect of these revelations, both on Aes Sedai and on Kinswomen, is as yet a matter for speculation. *See also* Daughters of Silence, the; Knitting Circle, the.

Knitting Circle, the: The leaders of the Kin. Since no member of the Kin has ever known how Aes Sedai arrange their own hierarchy—knowledge passed on only when an Accepted has passed her test for the shawl— they put no store in strength in the Power but give great weight to age, with the older woman always standing above the younger. The Knitting Circle (a title chosen, like the Kin, because it is innocuous) thus consists of the thirteen oldest Kinswomen resident in Ebou Dar, with the oldest given the title of Eldest. By the rules, all will have to step down when it is time for them to move on, but so long as they are resident in Ebou Dar, they have supreme authority over the Kin, to a degree that any Amyrlin Seat would envy. *See also* Kin, the.

Lance-Captain: In most lands, noblewomen do not personally lead their armsmen into battle under normal circumstances. Instead, they hire a professional soldier, almost always a commoner, who is responsible both for training and leading their armsmen. Depending on the land, this man can be called a Lance-Captain, Sword-Captain, Master of the Horse, or Master of the Lances. Rumors of closer relationships than Lady and servant often spring up, perhaps inevitably. Sometimes they are true.

Legion of the Dragon, the: A large military formation, all infantry, giving allegiance to the Dragon Reborn, trained by Davram Bashere along lines worked out by himself and Mat Cauthon, lines which depart sharply from the usual employment of foot. While many men simply walk in to volunteer, large numbers of the Legion are scooped up by recruiting parties from the Black Tower, who first gather all of the men in an area who were willing to follow the Dragon Reborn, and only after taking them through gateways to near Caemlyn winnow out those who can be taught to channel. The remainder, by far the greater number, are sent to Bashere's training camps.

marath'damane: In the Old Tongue, "those who must be leashed," and also "one who must be leashed." The term applied by the Seanchan to any woman capable of channeling who has not been collared as a *damane*.

Master of the Lances: *See* Lance-Captain.

Master of the Horse: *See* Lance-Captain.

Mera'din: In the Old Tongue, "the Brotherless." The name adopted, as a society, by those Aiel who abandoned clan and sept and went to the Shaido because they could not accept Rand al'Thor, a wetlander, as the *Car'a'carn,* or because they refused to accept his revelations concerning the history and origins of the Aiel. Deserting clan and sept for any reason is anathema among the Aiel, therefore their own warrior societies among the Shaido were unwilling to take them in, and they formed this society, the Brotherless.

morat-: In the Old Tongue, "handler." Among the Seanchan, it is used for those who handle exotics, such as *morat'raken,* a *raken* handler or rider, also informally called a flier. *See also der'morat-*.

Prophet, the: More formally, the Prophet of the Lord Dragon. Once known as Masema Dagar, a Shienaran soldier, he underwent a revelation and decided that he had been called to spread the word of the Dragon's Rebirth. He believes that nothing—nothing!—is more important than acknowledging the Dragon Reborn as the Light made flesh and being ready when the Dragon Reborn calls, and he and his followers will use any means to force others to sing the glories of the Dragon Reborn, Forsaking any name but "the Prophet," he has brought chaos to much of Ghealdan and Amadicia, large parts of which he controls.

Return, the: *See* Corenne.

Sea Folk hierarchy: The Atha'an Miere, the Sea Folk, are ruled by the Mistress of the Ships to the Atha'an Miere. She is assisted by the Windfinder to the Mistress of the Ships, and by the Master of the Blades. Below this come the clan Wavemistresses, each assisted by her Windfinder and her Swordmaster. Below her are the Sailmistresses (ship captains) of her clan, each assisted by her Windfinder and her Cargomaster. The Windfinder to the Mistress of the Ships has authority over all Windfinders to clan Wavemistresses, who in turn have authority over all the Windfinders of her clan. Likewise, the Master of the Blades has authority over all Swordmasters, and they in turn over the Cargomasters of their clans. Rank is not hereditary among the Sea Folk. The Mistress of the Ships is chosen, for life, by the First Twelve of the Atha'an Miere, the twelve most senior clan Wavemistresses. A clan Wavemistress is elected by the twelve seniormost Sailmistresses of her clan, called simply the First Twelve, a term which is also used to designate the senior Sailmistresses present anywhere. She can also be removed by a vote of those same First Twelve. In fact, anyone other than the Mistress of the Ships can be demoted, even all the way down to deckhand, for malfeasance, cowardice or other crimes. Also, the Windfinder to a Wavemistress or Mistress of the Ship who dies will, of necessity, have to serve a lower ranking woman, and her own rank thus decreases.

sei'mosiev: In the Old Tongue, "lowered eyes," or "downcast eyes." Among the Seanchan, to say that one has "become *sei'mosiev*" means that one has "lost face." *See also sei'taer.*

sei'taer: In the Old Tongue, "straight eyes," or "level eyes." Among the Seanchan, it refers to honor or face, to the ability to meet someone's eyes. It is possible to "be" or "have" *sei'taer,* meaning that one has honor and face, and also to "gain" or "lose" *sei'taer. See also sei'mosiev.*

Shen an Calhar: In the Old Tongue, "the Band of the Red Hand." (1) A legendary group of heroes who had many exploits, finally dying in the defense of Manetheren when that land was destroyed during the Trolloc Wars. (2) A military formation put together almost by accident by Mat Cauthon and organized along the lines of military forces during what is considered the height of the military arts, the days of Artur Hawkwing and the centuries immediately preceding.

so'jhin: The closest translation from the Old Tongue would be "a height among lowness," though some translate it as meaning "both sky and valley" among several other possibilities. *So'jhin* is the term applied by the Seanchan to hereditary upper servants. They are *da'covale*, property, yet occupy positions of considerable authority and often power. Even the Blood step carefully around *so'jhin* of the Imperial family, and speak to *so'jhin* of the Empress herself as to equals. *See also* Blood, the; *da'covale*.

Sword-Captain: *See* Lance-Captain.

Wise Woman: Honorific used in Ebou Dar for women famed for their incredible abilities at healing almost any injury. A Wise Woman is traditionally marked by a red belt. While some have noted that many, indeed most, Ebou Dari Wise Women were not even from Altara, much less Ebou Dar, what was not known until recently, and still is known only to a few, is that all Wise Women are in fact Kinswomen and use various versions of Healing, giving out herbs and poultices only as a cover. With the flight of the Kin from Ebou Dar after the Seanchan took the city, no Wise Women remain there. *See also* Kin, the.

PROLOGUE

A preview of
Crossroads of Twilight

Book Ten of
The Wheel of Time

Glimmers of the Pattern

R odel Ituralde hated waiting, though he well knew
it was the largest part of being a soldier. Waiting
for the next battle, for the enemy to move, to make
a mistake. He watched the winter forest and was as still
as the trees. The sun stood halfway to its peak, and gave
no warmth. His breath misted white in front of his face,
frosting his neatly trimmed mustache and the black fox
fur lining his hood. He was glad that his helmet hung at
his pommel. His breastplate held the cold and radiated it
through his coat and all the layers of wool, silk and linen
beneath. Even Dart's saddle felt cold, as though the white
gelding were made of frozen milk. The helmet would have
addled his brain.

Winter had come late to Arad Doman, very late, but with
a vengeance. From summer heat that lingered unnaturally
into fall, to winter's heart in less than a month. The leaves
that had survived the long summer's drought had been frozen before they could change color, and now they glistened
like strange, ice-covered emeralds in the morning sun. The
horses of the twenty-odd armsmen around him occasionally stamped a hoof in the knee-deep snow. It had been a
long ride this far, and they had farther to go whether this

day turned out good or ill. Dark clouds roiled the sky to northward. He did not need his weather-wise there to tell him the temperature would plummet before nightfall. They had to be under shelter by then.

"Not as rough as winter before last, is it, my Lord?" Jaalam said quietly. The tall young officer had a way of reading Ituralde's mind, and his voice was pitched for the others to hear. "Even so, I suppose some men would be dreaming of mulled wine about now. Not this lot, of course. Remarkably abstemious. They all drink tea, I believe. Cold tea. If they had a few birch switches, they'd be stripping down for snow baths."

"They'll have to keep their clothes on for the time being," Ituralde replied dryly, "but they might get some cold tea tonight, if they're lucky." That brought a few chuckles. Quiet chuckles. He had chosen these men with care, and they knew about noise at the wrong time.

He himself could have done with a steaming cup of spiced wine, or even tea. But it was a long time since merchants had brought tea to Arad Doman. A long time since any outland merchant had ventured farther than the border with Saldaea. By the time news of the outside world reached him, it was as stale as last month's bread, if it was more than rumor to begin. That hardly mattered, though. If the White Tower truly was divided against itself, or men who could channel really were being called to Caemlyn . . . well, the world would have to do without Rodel Ituralde until Arad Doman was whole again. For the moment, Arad Doman was more than enough for any sane man to go on with.

Once again he reviewed the orders he had sent, carried by the fastest riders he had, to every noble loyal to the King. Divided as they were by bad blood and old feuds, they still shared that much. They would gather their armies and ride when orders came from the Wolf; at least, so long as he held the King's favor. They would even hide in the mountains and wait, at his order. Oh, they would chafe, and some would curse his name, but they would obey. They knew the Wolf won battles. More, they knew he won wars. The Little Wolf, they called him when they thought he could not hear, but he did not care whether they drew attention to his stature—well, not much—so long as they rode when and where he said.

Very soon they would be riding hard, moving to set a trap that would not spring for months. It was a long chance he was taking. Complex plans had many ways to fall apart, and this plan had layers inside layers. Everything would be ruined before it began if he failed to provide the bait. Or if someone ignored his order to evade couriers from the King. They all knew his reasons, though, and even the most stiff-necked shared them, though few were willing to speak of the matter aloud. He himself had moved like a wraith racing on a storm since he received Alsalam's latest command. In his sleeve where the folded paper lay tucked above the pale lace that fell onto his steel-backed gauntlet. They had one last chance, one very small chance, to save Arad Doman. Perhaps even to save Alsalam from himself before the Council of Merchants decided to put another man on the throne in his place. He had been a good ruler, for over twenty years. The Light send that he could be again.

A loud crack to the south sent Ituralde's hand to the hilt of his longsword. There was a faint creak of leather and metal as others eased their weapons. For the rest, silence. The forest was as still as a frozen tomb. Only a limb breaking under the weight of snow. After a moment, he let himself relax—as much as he had relaxed since the tales came north of the Dragon Reborn appearing in the sky at Falme. Perhaps the man really was the Dragon Reborn, perhaps he really had appeared in the sky, but whatever the truth, those tales had set Arad Doman on fire.

Ituralde was sure he could have put out that fire, given a freer hand. It was not boasting to think so. He knew what he could do, with a battle, a campaign, or a war. But ever since the Council had decided the King would be safer smuggled out of Bandar Eban, Alsalam seemed to have taken into his head that he was the rebirth of Artur Hawkwing. His signature and seal had marked scores of battle orders since, flooding out from wherever the Council had him hidden. They would not say where that was, even to Ituralde himself. Every woman on the Council that he confronted went flat-eyed and evasive at any mention of the King. He could almost believe they did not know where Alsalam was. A ridiculous thought, of course. The Council kept an unblinking eye on the King. Ituralde had always believed the merchant Houses interfered too much, yet he wished they would interfere now. Why they remained silent was a mystery, for a king who damaged trade did not remain long on the throne.

He was loyal to his oaths, and Alsalam was a friend, besides, but the orders the King sent could not have been better written to achieve chaos. Nor could they be ignored. Alsalam was the King. But he had commanded Ituralde to march north with all possible speed against a great gathering of Dragonsworn that Alsalam supposedly knew of from secret spies, then ten days later, with no Dragonsworn yet in sight, an order came to move south again, with all possible speed, against another gathering that never materialized. He had been commanded to concentrate his forces to defend Bandar Eban when a three-pronged attack might have ended it all and to divide them when a hammer blow could have done the same, to harry ground he knew the Dragonsworn had abandoned, and to march away from where he knew they camped. Worse, Alsalam's orders often had gone directly to the powerful nobles who were supposed to be following Ituralde, sending Machir in this direction, Teacal in that, Rahman in a third. Four times, pitched battles had resulted from parts of the army blundering into one another in the night while moving to the King's express command and expecting none but enemies ahead. And all the while the Dragonsworn gained numbers, and confidence. Ituralde had had his triumphs—at Solanje and Maseen, at Lake Somal and Kandelmar—the Lords of Katar had learned not to sell the products of their mines and forges to the enemies of Arad Doman—but always, Alsalam's orders wasted his gains.

This last order was different, though. For one thing, a Gray Man had killed Lady Tuva trying to stop it from reaching him. Why the Shadow might fear this order more than any other was a mystery, yet it was all the more reason to move swiftly. Before Alsalam reached him with another. This order opened many possibilities, and he had considered every last one he could see. But the good ones all started here, today. When small chances of success were all that remained, you had to seize them.

A snowjay's strident cry rang out in the distance, then a second time, a third. Cupping his hands around his mouth, Ituralde repeated the three harsh calls. Moments later a shaggy, pale dapple gelding appeared out of the trees, his rider in a white cloak streaked with black. Man and horse alike would have been hard to see in the snowy forest had they been standing still. The rider pulled up beside Ituralde. A stocky man, he wore only a single sword, with a short blade, and there were a cased bow and a quiver fastened to his saddle.

"Looks like they all came, my Lord," he said in his permanently hoarse voice, pushing his cowl back from his head. Someone had tried to hang Donjel when he was young, though the reason was lost in the years. What remained of his short-cropped hair was iron-gray. The dark leather patch covering the socket of his right eye was a remnant of another youthful scrape. One eye or two, though, he was the best scout Ituralde had ever known. "Most, anyways," he went on. "They put two rings of sentries around the lodge, one inside the other. You can see them a mile off, but nobody will get close without them at the lodge hearing of it in time to get away. By the tracks, they didn't bring no more men than you said they could, not enough to count. Course," he added wryly, "that still leaves you outnumbered a fair bit."

Ituralde nodded. He had offered the White Ribbon, and the men he was to meet had accepted. Three days when men pledged under the Light, by their souls and hope of salvation, not to draw a weapon against another or shed blood. The White Ribbon had not been tested in this war, however, and these days some men had strange ideas of where salvation lay. Those who called themselves Dragonsworn, for instance. He had always been called a gambler, though he was not. The trick was in knowing what risks you could take. And sometimes, in knowing which ones you had to take.

Pulling a packet sewn into oiled silk from his boot top, he handed it to Donjel. "If I don't reach Coron Ford in two days, take this to my wife."

The scout tucked the packet somewhere beneath his cloak, touched his forehead, and turned his horse west. He had carried its like for Ituralde before, usually on the eve of battle. The Light send this was not the time Tamsin would have to open that packet. She would come after him—she had told him so—the first incident ever of the living haunting the dead.

"Jaalam," Ituralde said, "let us see what waits at Lady Osana's hunting lodge." As he heeled Dart forward, the others fell in behind him.

The sun rose to its height and began again to descend as they rode. The dark clouds in the north moved closer, and the chill bit deeper. There was no sound but the crunch of hooves breaking through the snow crust. The forest seemed empty save for themselves. He did not see any of the sentries Donjel had spoken of. The man's opinion of what could be seen from a mile differed from that of most. They would be expecting him, of course. And watching to make sure he was not followed by an army, White Ribbon or no White Ribbon. A good many of them likely had reasons they felt sufficient to feather Rodel Ituralde with arrows. A lord might pledge the White Ribbon for his men, but would all of those feel bound? Sometimes, there were chances you just had to take.

About midafternoon, Osana's so-called hunting lodge loomed suddenly out of the trees, a mass of pale towers and slender, pointed domes that would have fitted well among the palaces of Bandar Eban itself. Her hunting had always been for men or power, her trophies numerous and noteworthy despite her relative youth, and the "hunts" that had taken place here would have raised eyebrows even in the capital. The lodge lay desolate, now. Broken windows gaped like mouths with jagged teeth. None showed a glimmer of light or movement. The snow covering the cleared ground around the lodge had been well trampled by horses, however. The ornate brass-bound gates of the main courtyard stood open, and he rode through without slowing, followed by his men. The horses' hooves clattered on the paving stones, where the snow had been beaten to slush.

No servants came out to greet him, not that he had expected any. Osana had vanished early in the troubles that now shook Arad Doman like a dog shaking a rat, and her servants had drifted quickly to others of her house, taking whatever places they could find. These days, the masterless starved, or turned bandit. Or Dragonsworn. Dismounting in front of the broad marble stairway at the end of the courtyard, he handed Dart's reins to one of his armsmen, and Jaalam ordered the men to take shelter where they could find it for themselves and the animals. Eyeing the marble balconies and wide windows that surrounded the courtyard, they moved as if expecting a crossbow bolt between the shoulder blades. One set of stable doors stood slightly ajar, but in spite of the cold, they divided themselves between the corners of the courtyard, huddling with the horses where they could keep watch in every direction. If the worst came, perhaps a few might make it out.

Removing his gauntlets, he tucked them behind his belt and checked his lace as he climbed the stairs with Jaalam. Snow that had been trodden underfoot and frozen again crackled beneath his boots. He refrained from looking anywhere but straight ahead. He must appear supremely assured, as though there were no possibility events should go other than as he expected. Confidence was one key to victory. The other side believing you were confident was sometimes almost as good as actually being confident. At the head of the stairs, Jaalam pulled open one of the tall, carved doors by its gilded ring. Ituralde touched his beauty spot with a finger to make sure it was in place—his cheeks were too cold to feel the black velvet star clinging—before he stepped inside. As self-assured as he would have been at a ball.

The cavernous entry hall was as icy as the outside. Their breath made feathered mists. Unlit, the space seemed already wreathed in twilight. The floor was a colorful mosaic of hunters and animals, the tiles chipped in places, as though heavy weights had been dragged over them, or perhaps dropped. Aside from a single toppled plinth that might once have held a large vase or a small statue, the hall was bare. What the servants had not taken when they fled had long since been looted by bandits. A single man awaited them, white-haired and more gaunt than when Ituralde had last seen him. His breastplate was battered, and his earring was just a small gold hoop, but his lace was immaculate, and the sparkling red quarter moon beside his left eye would have gone well at court, in better times.

"By the Light, be welcome under the White Ribbon, Lord Ituralde," he said formally, with a slight bow.

"By the Light, I come under the White Ribbon, Lord Shimron," Ituralde replied, making his courtesy in return. Shimron had been one of Alsalam's most trusted advisors. Until he joined the Dragonsworn, at least. Now he stood high in their councils. "My armsman is Jaalam Nishur, honor bound to House Ituralde, as are all who came with me."

There had been no House Ituralde before Rodel, but Shimron answered Jaalam's bow, hand to heart. "Honor be to honor. Will you accompany me, Lord Ituralde?" he said as he straightened.

The great doors to the ballroom were gone from their hinges, though Ituralde could hardly imagine bandits looting those. They left a tall pointed arch wide enough for ten men to pass. Within the windowless oval room, half a hundred lanterns of every size and sort beat at shadows, though the light barely reached the domed ceiling. Separated by a wide expanse of floor, two groups of men stood against the painted walls, and if the White Ribbon had induced them to leave off helmets, all two hundred or more were armored otherwise, and certainly no one had put aside his swords. To one side were a few Domani lords as powerful as Shimron—Rajabi, Wakeda, Ankaer—each surrounded by his cluster of lesser lords and sworn commoners and smaller clusters, of few as two or three, many containing no nobles at all. The Dragonsworn had councils, but no one commander. Still, each of those men was a leader in his own right, some counting their followers in scores, a few in thousands. None appeared happy to be where he was, and one or two shot glares across the floor, to where fifty or sixty Taraboners stood in one solid mass and scowled back. Dragonsworn they might all be, yet there was little love lost between Domani and Taraboners. Ituralde almost smiled at the sight of the outlanders, though. He had not dared to count on half so many appearing today.

"Lord Rodel Ituralde comes under the White Ribbon." Shimron's voice rang through the lantern shadows. "Let whoever may think of violence search his heart, and consider his soul." And that was the end of formality.

"Why does Lord Ituralde offer the White Ribbon?" Wakeda demanded, one hand gripping the hilt of his longsword and the other in a fist at his side. He was not a tall man, though taller than Ituralde, but as haughty as if he held the throne himself. Women had called him beautiful, once. Now a slanting black scarf covered the socket of his missing right eye, and his beauty spot was a black arrowhead pointing at the thick scar running from his cheek up onto his forehead. "Does he intend to join us? Or ask us to surrender? All know the Wolf is bold as well as devious. Is he that bold?" A rumble rose among the men on his side of the room, part mirth, part anger.

Ituralde clasped his hands behind his back to keep from fingering the ruby in his left ear. That was widely known as a sign that he was angry, and sometimes he did it on purpose, but he needed to present a calm face, now. Even while the man spoke past his ear! No. Calm. Duels were entered into in anger, but he was here to fight a duel, and that required calm. Words could be deadlier weapons than swords.

"Every man here knows we have another enemy to the south," he said in a steady voice. "The Seanchan have swallowed Tarabon." He ran his gaze over the Taraboners, and met flat stares. He never had been able to read Taraboners' faces. Between those preposterous mustaches—like hairy tusks; worse than a Saldaean's!—and those ridiculous veils, they might as well wear masks, and the poor light from the lanterns did not help. But he had seen them veiled in mail, and he needed them. "They have flooded onto Almoth Plain, and moved ever north. Their intent is clear. They mean to have Arad Doman, too. They mean to have the whole world, I fear."

"Does Lord Ituralde want to know who we will support if these Seanchan invade us?" Wakeda demanded.

"I have true faith you will fight for Arad Doman, Lord Wakeda," Ituralde said mildly. Wakeda went purple at having the direct insult flung in his teeth, and his oath-men's hands went to hilts.

"Refugees have brought word that there are Aiel on the plain, now," Shimron put in quickly, as though he feared Wakeda might break the White Ribbon. None of Wakeda's oath-men would draw steel unless he did, or commanded them to. "They fight for the Dragon Reborn, so say the reports. He must have sent them, perhaps as an aid to us. No one has ever defeated an Aiel army, not even Artur Hawkwing. You recall the Blood Snow, Lord Ituralde, when we were younger? I believe you agree with me that we did not defeat them there, whatever the histories may say, and I cannot believe the Seanchan have the numbers we did then. I myself have heard of Seanchan moving south, away from the border. No, I suspect the next we hear will be of them *retreating* from the plain, not advancing on us." He was not a bad commander in the field, but he had always been pedantic.

Ituralde smiled. Word came more swiftly from the south than from anywhere else, but he had been afraid he would have to bring up the Aiel, and they might have thought he was trying to trick them. He could hardly believe it himself, Aiel on Almoth Plain. He did not point out that Aiel sent to help the Dragonsworn were more likely to have appeared in Arad Doman itself. "I've questioned refugees, too, and they speak of Aiel raids, not armies. Whatever the Aiel are doing on the plain may have slowed the Seanchan, but it hasn't turned them back. Their flying beasts have begun scouting on our side of the border. That does not smack of retreat."

Producing the paper from his sleeve with a flourish, he held it up so all could see the Sword and Hand impressed in green-and-blue wax. As always of late, he had used a hot blade to separate the Royal Seal on one side while leaving it whole, so he could show it unbroken to doubters. There had been plenty of those, when they heard some of Alsalam's orders. "I have orders from King Alsalam to gather as many men as I can, from wherever I can find them, and strike as hard as I can at the Seanchan." He took a deep breath. Here, he took another chance, and Alsalam might have his head on the block unless the dice fell the right way. "I offer a truce. I pledge in the King's name not to move against you in any way so long as the Seanchan remain a threat to Arad Doman, if you will all pledge the same and fight beside me against them until they are beaten back."

A stunned silence answered him. Bull-necked Rajabi appeared poleaxed. Wakeda chewed his lip like a startled girl.

Then Shimron muttered, "Can they *be* beaten back, Lord Ituralde? I faced their . . . their chained Aes Sedai on Almoth Plain, as did you." Boots scraped the floor as men shifted their feet, and faces darkened in bleak anger. No man liked to think he was helpless before an enemy, but enough had been there in the early days, with Ituralde and Shimron, for all to know what this enemy was like.

"They can be defeated, Lord Shimron," Ituralde replied, "even with their . . . little surprises." A strange thing to call the earth erupting under your feet, and scouts that rode what looked like Shadowspawn, but he had to sound assured as well as look it. Besides, when you knew what the enemy could do, you adapted. That had been one core of warfare long before the Seanchan appeared. Darkness cut the Seanchan advantages, and so did storms, and a weather-wise could always tell you when a storm was coming. "A wise man stops chewing when he reaches bone," he continued, "but so far, the Seanchan have had their meat sliced thin before they reached for it. I intend to give them a tough shank to gnaw. More, I have a plan to make them snap so fast they'll break their teeth on bone before they have a mouthful of meat. Now, I have pledged. Will you?"

It was hard not to hold his breath. Each man seemed to be looking inward. He could all but see them mulling it over. The Wolf had a plan. The Seanchan had chained Aes Sedai and flying beasts and the Light alone knew what else. But the Wolf had a plan. The Seanchan. The Wolf.

"If any man can defeat them," Shimron said finally, "you can, Lord Ituralde. I will so pledge."

"I *do* so pledge!" Rajabi shouted. "We'll chase them back across the ocean where they came from!" He had a bull's temperament as well as its neck.

Surprisingly, Wakeda thundered his agreement with equal enthusiasm, and then a storm of voices broke, calling that they would match the King's pledge, that they would smash the Seanchan, even some that they would follow the Wolf into the Pit of Doom. All very gratifying, but not all Ituralde had come for.

"If you ask *us* to fight for Arad Doman," one voice shouted above the rest, "then ask *us!*" The men who had been calling their pledges fell to angry mutters and half-heard curses.

Hiding his pleasure behind a bland expression, Ituralde turned to face the speaker, on the other side of the room. The Taraboner was a lean man, with a sharp nose that made a tent of his veil. His eyes were hard, though, and keen. Some of the other Taraboners frowned as if displeased he had spoken, so it appeared they had no one leader any more than the Domani, but he had spoken. Ituralde had hoped for the pledges he had received, but they were not necessary to his plan. The Taraboners were. At least, they would make it a hundred times more likely to work. He addressed the man courteously, with a bow.

"I offer you the chance to fight for Tarabon, my good

Lord. The Aiel are making some confusion on the plain; the refugees speak of it. Tell me, could a small company of your men—a hundred, perhaps two—cross the plain in that disorder and enter Tarabon, if their armor was marked with stripes, as those who ride for the Seanchan?"

It seemed impossible the Taraboner's face could grow any tighter, yet it did, and it was the turn of the men on his side of the room to mutter angrily and curse. Enough word had come north for them to know of a king and panarch put on their thrones by the Seanchan and swearing fealty to an empress on the other side of the Aryth Ocean. They could not like reminders of how many of their countrymen now rode for this empress. Most of the "Seanchan" on Almoth Plain were Taraboners.

"What good could one small company do?" the lean man growled, contemptuous.

"Little good," Ituralde replied. "But if there were fifty such companies? A hundred?" These Taraboners might have that many men behind them, all told. "If they all struck on the same day, all across Tarabon? I myself would ride with them, and as many of my men as can be outfitted in Taraboner armor. Just so you will know this is not simply a stratagem to get rid of you."

Behind him, the Domani began protesting loudly. Wakeda the loudest of all, if it could be believed! The Wolf's plan was all very well, but they wanted the Wolf himself at their head. Most of the Taraboners began arguing among themselves, over whether so many men could cross the plain without being discovered, even in such small bands, over what good if any they could do in Tarabon in small companies, over whether they were willing to wear armor marked with Seanchan stripes. Taraboners argued as easily as Saldaeans, and as hotly. Not the sharp-nosed man. He met Ituralde's gaze steadily. Then gave a slight nod. It was hard to tell, behind those thick mustaches, but Ituralde thought he smiled.

The last tension faded from Ituralde's shoulders. The fellow would not have agreed while the others argued if he were not more of a leader among them than he seemed. The others would come, too, he was certain. They would ride south with him into the heart of what the Seanchan considered their own, and slap them hard and full across the face.

The Taraboners would want to stay afterward, of course, and continue the fight in their own homeland. He could not expect anything more. Which would leave him and the few thousand men he could take with him to be hounded back north again, all the long way across Almoth Plain. If the Light shone on him, hounded with fury.

He returned the Taraboner's smile, if smile it was. With any luck, furious generals would not see where he was leading them until it was too late. And if they did . . . Well, he had a second plan.

About the Author

Robert Jordan was born in 1948 in Charleston, South Carolina. He taught himself to read when he was four with the incidental aid of a twelve-years-older brother, and was tackling Mark Twain and Jules Verne by five. He was a graduate of the Citadel, the Military College of South Carolina, with a degree in physics. He served two tours in Vietnam with the U.S. Army; among his decorations are the Distinguished Flying Cross with bronze oak leaf cluster, the Bronze Star with "V" and bronze oak leaf cluster, and two Vietnamese Gallantry Crosses with Palm. A history buff, he also wrote dance and theater criticism. He enjoyed the outdoor sports of hunting, fishing, and sailing, and the indoor sports of poker, chess, pool, and pipe collecting. He began writing in 1977 and continued until his death on September 16, 2007.